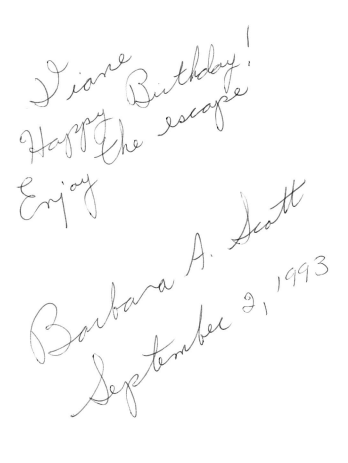

Diane
Happy Birthday!
Enjoy the escape

Barbara A. Scott
September 2, 1993

ALWAYS IN
A
FOREIGN LAND

By Barbara A. Scott

ZENAR BOOKS

Published by:

    ZENAR BOOKS
    P.O. Box 686
    Rancho Cordova, CA 95741-0860

Library of Congress Number 93-94049

ISBN 0-9637134-0-X

Manufactured in the United States of America

CHAPTER ONE

The cell door was open and the others had gone. Kon reached down to pick up Peterson's eyeglasses. He slipped them into his pocket, hoping to do this one small thing to make Peterson feel better about the team. Peterson had shown more fear of the team than of the guards they had overpowered to get him out.

Kon moved towards the door and stepped into the corridor. Suddenly he spotted a guard with his Tokarev aimed straight at him. Damn! Where the hell did he come from? There were supposed to be only four, Kon thought. He dove for the open door of the cell, but it was too late. He heard the blast and felt a searing stab in his left side. Letting out a loud cry, he staggered into the cell and fell to the floor. He lay on his back, listening to the echo of the guard's boots striking the stone floor. A moment later, the guard stepped though the door with his gun still drawn. Seeing Kon sprawled on the floor, he approached cautiously, and raised his foot to kick Kon in the ribs. Immediately Kon grabbed the guard's ankle and jerked it sharply across his body and upwards towards his head. The maneuver took the guard by surprise, and he fell over Kon, rolling onto his back by Kon's left. Instantly Kon sat up, lunged forward, and plunged the knife which was hidden in his right hand into the guard's chest. The guard drew in his breath, and seized Kon's arm. Kon struggled to hang on and twisted steadily downward on the knife. The guard made several horrible choking sounds, then quit struggling. Kon was still pushing the knife into the guard's chest when Paul appeared in the cell a moment later.

"What happened? Are you O.K.?" he asked, taking Kon by the arm and pulling him to his feet.

"I am well," Kon answered vaguely, and pulled his jacket closed.

Paul gave Kon a sharp look, but put his vacant expression off to the fact that he'd just killed a man. It never got easy, but doing it by hand at close range was especially bad.

"Let's get the hell away from this mess," Paul said, and pushed Kon through the cell door.

Kon ignored the pain in his side as they passed down the stone corridor and into the guard room. Four motionless bodies lay in various postures around the table. The drug had worked well. Those guards would cause no trouble for hours. Too bad about that other one, Kon thought, as he closed the knife he still held in his right hand.

Walking quickly, Kon and Paul reached the van and scrambled

in. Brad had the engine running, and just as they closed the door, the van shot forwards with a squeal of the tires. Kon noticed Peterson, who was sitting between Geilla and Jack, staring at him with a nearsighted squint. He reached into his pocket and produced Peterson's still unbroken eyeglasses.

"Here you are, friend. Take a good look at freedom," Kon said, offering Peterson his glasses.

Peterson blanched at the sight of Kon's bloody hand, but he took the glasses and pulled them onto his face. He peered around suspiciously.

"Sorry," Kon said, as he realized for the first time how bloody his arm was. Geilla threw Kon a towel and he wiped away the blood. He didn't discard the towel, but folded it carefully and put it aside.

"Where are you taking me?" Peterson stammered.

Brad turned his head to give the troubled man his answer. "We're headed for the train station south of Belgrade. We'll take the train to Bitola and cross the border there. If all goes well, you'll be back in the free world by morning."

"Who are you people anyway, and why should I trust you?" Peterson asked in alarm.

"We're working for an International Peace Foundation on special assignment," Brad continued. "I'm afraid you'll either have to trust us or find the way across the border yourself."

Geilla patted Peterson's trembling hand with her own petite one. "It's all right, Mr. Peterson," she said softly. "Dr. Cranston sent us to bring you back."

At the mention of Dr. Cranston, Peterson relaxed visibly. Only a few trusted colleagues even knew that he was working with Cranston. Anyway, he didn't seem to have much choice.

As the van sped along, the team members set about changing their appearances. Jack removed the uniform that he had worn into the jail to drug the guards, and switched into a casual shirt, slacks, and a heavy quilted jacket. Geilla slipped an ankle-length gathered skirt over her fitted leather pants and pulled a loose jacket over her leotard. With quick motions she removed the scarf from her closely cropped dark hair, and applied eye make-up. She looked back at Kon and smiled as she adorned herself with gold loop earrings. Kon forced a brief smile and nodded his head approvingly. Geilla rarely wore anything resembling a dress if she could help it. She preferred her form fitting black leotard, which showed off her lithe, graceful body to full advantage.

Geilla had been part of Kon's life for a long time. As they grew up in the theater together, he always thought of her as a delightful wisp of a girl, even as a younger sister. Later he had hoped to marry her, but she had betrayed him. Only after years of torment, had he succeeded in building a wall around himself, so that he could now relate to her with neither desire nor anger. However, even now when they were working close together and he caught a glimpse of her beautiful legs, or when her small breasts accidently brushed against him, something stirred inside him. Just for a fleeting moment he would imagine . . . but then he caught himself and raised the wall for protection. She was his friend, his nurse on occasion, and his trusted comrade in a dangerous business; but he never let her be anything more.

Kon carefully turned his back to the others as he took off his leather jacket. There was blood on his dark shirt, and not all of it was the guard's. He opened his bag and pulled out a neatly folded dress shirt. He put it on quickly and slipped into a sports jacket. As an extra precaution against a telltale stain, he pulled a trench coat over the jacket. Peterson was given a neat, but slightly worn suit and a clean overcoat. Jack handed him a small briefcase full of account ledgers and he clutched it with trembling hands. Paul removed his close fitting jacket and pulled on a light-weight nylon one.

When the van arrived at the railroad station, Brad parked well away from the platform. He switched his cheap jacket and cap for a well tailored three piece suit complete with tie and overcoat. It was hard for Brad to look common. His Eton and Oxford training gave him a distinguished air that was difficult to disguise. Although not much older than the others, Brad, short for Bradley, was the team leader. His cool British temperament was admired and respected by the others. They could count on him to formulate a logical plan, lay the groundwork in detail and keep their tempers in check if things went wrong.

Brad issued each member of the party a professionally forged passport and other papers. Brad was acting the part of a film producer who was planning to shoot some footage in Yugoslavia. Geilla was posing as the star of the film with Kon as her leading man, and Peterson was acting as Brad's business manager. Jack and Paul took roles as two restless Americans hiking across Europe.

Brad knew there would be passport checks at the boarding gate, because of the federal government's crackdown on the activities of the separatists; but there would be no reason for the authorities to connect the team with the trouble at the jail. The drugged guards had seen only Jack and the other one was permanently silenced. As they walked from the van to the platform, Brad stayed a few steps behind Peterson, who had agreed to say as little as possible. Peterson had a bookish air about him and looked convincing as an accountant. Brad hoped Peterson's hands would stop shaking long enough to show his passport.

The boarding check went without a hitch. Paul and Jack filed through followed by Peterson. Geilla went through next carrying a large picnic basket on her arm and beaming at everyone. Walking

3

slowly and looking grim, Kon followed Geilla through, and a smiling, confident Brad brought up the rear. Once aboard the train they filed down the narrow passageway, and as nonchalantly as possible, chose the same six-passenger cabin. Geilla took the rear window seat, Kon dropped down beside her, and Brad sat near the door.

Jack sat across from Brad, his long legs and massive shoulders magnified by the small cabin space. He leaned forward slightly, gazing from the window to the door ready to spring into action. Despite his tough, Marine trained exterior, Jack was still a Kansas farm boy at heart, unsophisticated, big, blunt, blond, and disarmingly shy.

Peterson occupied the middle position, his thin shoulders and neck dwarfed by Jack's sheer physical mass. He was the object and prize of this international rescue attempt. A nuclear scientist with a keen mind, but no political savvy, he had been lured into Yugoslavia to make some modifications on the country's first atomic power plant that had been opened the previous September. Once he arrived, he was been placed in a cell, and subjected to some very uncomfortable methods to persuade him to reveal the details of his yet unpublished work. His absolute shock at being treated so brutally had left him totally distrustful and thoroughly frightened. He sat bolt upright and kept his eyes on the door of the compartment.

By the window sat Paul. Paul wasn't his real name. He just started calling himself that back when he was a kid in Chicago. At age nine he got fed up with bashing kids who called him Chink, or Jap, or other insulting names instead of Pravat, his Thai name. Actually only Paul's mother was from Thailand, his father was an American. Paul had inherited his mother's beautiful almond-shaped eyes, graceful hands, and straight black hair. Paul had never bothered to make the name change legal. He didn't always bother about the niceties of the law. That occasionally came in handy on an assignment. Sometimes Kon wondered just where Paul drew the line between legal and not, but he knew he could depend on Paul – even for his life.

Shortly after the group had settled into their seats, and the train started moving south, Kon left the cabin. He made his way to the rest room. Locking the door of the tiny room, he took the folded towel from his pocket, and unbuttoned his overcoat. The lower half of his shirt was soaked with blood. Damn! he thought as he pulled it out from under his belt. The wound is still bleeding – not a gush, just a horrible steady ooze. With the aid of his knife Kon cut several strips from the towel and knotted them together into two long strands. He folded the remainder of the towel into a small wad, and pressed it into the wound. The room swayed several times as the train rocked around a bend. Only with difficulty was Kon able to wind the strands of towel around his ribs and secure the ends. He could not get much

4

pressure on the wound itself, but he hoped he could control and conceal the blood until it quit oozing. It's got to clot soon, he thought.

He tucked the lower end of the towel under his belt and buttoned his wet shirt over the crude bandage. Under the loose raincoat the bulge was hardly noticeable. The train swayed several times as Kon staggered back to the cabin, but he clung to the railing to keep from falling. Opening the cabin door, he lunged for the bench. The others were pretending to be asleep and didn't seem to notice his unsteady entrance.

Kon's side ached badly and every jolt of the train sent a stabbing pain between his ribs. He closed his eyes for a few moments, but his body would not relax. Shit! This is going to be a long night, he thought. Suddenly he remembered the picnic basket. Geilla had put some local food and wine in it as if she was bringing delicacies home with her. A bit of that wine might dull the growing pain, he reasoned. Leaning forward against the folded towel increased his discomfort, but he managed to reach the basket. His movements roused Geilla, who looked at him curiously. Feigning a joviality he did not feel he said, "We are supposed to be celebrating. Let's have some of that wine."

Geilla looked surprised, but spotting a guard coming down the passageway, she decided to play along with Kon. She brought out a bottle of wine and three glasses. She handed the bottle across Kon to Brad saying, "Won't you do the honors?"

Straightening in his seat, Brad eyed the guard, and put on his best public relations smile. "Let's have a toast," he said opening the bottle. Geilla passed glasses to Kon and Brad and held her own to be filled. Brad poured a measure for each with a quick flourish. "To the future Best Actress of the Year!" he said, raising his glass.

The guard paused as he passed and Geilla beamed at him. Kon forced a brief smile and gulped the wine. He emptied his glass quickly and held it out for a refill. Geilla turned her head briefly to watch the guard, and only Brad saw the glass shake in Kon's hand. He gave Kon a long look, but said nothing. Even the best men had a touch of nerves now and then.

Geilla took the glasses and returned them to the basket, but when Brad moved to hand her the half empty bottle, Kon stopped him. "I'll take that," he said quietly.

Brad stared at him, but handed him the bottle and sat back in his seat. What was Kon up to? he wondered. Kon was a heavy drinker, but he never drank on an assignment. Geilla was puzzled also, but she kept silent.

Geilla and Kon were friends, but often his behavior was a mystery to her. Kon had been merely fourteen when he came to work at the theater her father managed in Naples. She had been just

5

twelve, but it had not been love at first sight for them. In fact, she had thought the dark, lanky lad with the impossible name of Petros Kononellos was the most boorish lout she had ever met. She considered his face too thin and angular, and his eyes too deep set to match her movie idol image of handsome. He spoke only the rough Neapolitan dialect, and his clothes were ragged and badly in need of washing. She contemptuously shortened his name to Kon because it was easier to say, and because it fit the barbarian image she had of him. Kon accepted the name proudly for that very reason. He no longer wanted to be Petros, the fisherman's son.

Geilla's father, Zoel, hired Kon because he was quiet and did the dirtiest work without complaining. Kon had not come to the theater seeking glamour or excitement. He had come only to find a way to make some money and get enough to eat. Having arrived alone in Italy the year before, he had survived by doing odd jobs and stealing food. It had been hard for him to live in the streets, for unlike the hordes of homeless kids in Naples, he had too much pride to beg, and he had not been brought up to steal. Even when he stole food he was haunted by the idea that he was defiling his dead mother's memory. Shortly after he arrived, he had been beaten and stabbed by a gang of older boys. He would have died in the street, if the old woman who found him on her door step had not taken pity on him and nursed him back to life.

At first Kon was allowed only to sweep the theater, move furniture, and fetch food for the musicians. Then one night when one of the regular ushers did not arrive, Geilla's older brother Alonzo, cleaned Kon up, lent him a suit, and sent him to help seat the customers. Geilla, who was always working somewhere in the theater, could not help but notice how different Kon looked in stylish clothes. She smiled at him for the first time, but told him only that he looked better when he was not so dirty. Perhaps she would not have been so cruel if she had known that Kon lived in the alley behind the theater.

Kon's instant and complete hero worship of Geilla's older brother quickly won him a place in Alonzo's heart. Under his guidance, Kon learned to work the lights, arrange the sets, and control the sound system in the theater. In their spare time Alonzo taught Kon to play soccer, and the two would spend hours racing madly up and down the playing field or cheering wildly for their favorite team.

Everyone loved Alonzo. He was dashingly handsome, possessed a beautiful singing voice, and was as talented with the electronics in the theater as he was on the soccer field. He always wore the most fashionable clothes, and women found his charm irresistible. Alonzo sincerely liked Kon, and let Kon follow after him like a shadow. Despite the contrasts between the two, Kon treasured Alonzo's friendship. He prized even a single word of approval from Alonzo, and didn't mind that no one else paid the slightest attention to him.

The train swayed and so did Kon. He lurched sideways and the pain returned. He put the bottle to his lips and poured in another mouthful of wine. It felt like liquid fire when it hit his stomach, but he forced down as much as he could. He must take his mind off the pain. He thought back to the day before he left on this assignment. Had it been only two, no three days ago?

He had spent the day outside Paris with Alyce. As always the time he spent with Alyce was like a dream. She was refined, confident and beautiful, with ivory white skin and long dark hair. Her delicate, expressive hands were so full of life they seemed to float on the air when she moved them. Doubtless it was years of hard work in the ballet that gave them their elegance, but for Kon, just holding one of her fragile hands in his own broad, strong one brought him pleasure. Kon had seen Alyce dance at the ballet in Paris and had been completely mesmerized. Immediately after the performance he managed an introduction through some friends at the bank, and she had agreed to meet him the next afternoon.

For the past three years, their encounters had been infrequent, due to their full schedules, and Alyce never encouraged him to come more often. When she was alone with Kon, however, Alyce shed her cool, cultured exterior and let her passion come forward. She revelled in the pure carnal pleasure of submitting to him, but she could never match his fire. Afterwards she always felt ashamed of the depths of passion he aroused in her, and there was no lingering joy or fulfillment for her. Kon made her lose control and that frightened her. She always wanted to have the upper hand in her relationships, and she could not dominate Kon.

Alyce and Kon attended the theater, went to gallery openings, drank champagne, and danced with each other, but on some other level Kon could not explain, he always felt cheated. He never shared ideas with Alyce, and they made no plans for the future. Kon accepted the situation because of the nature of his business. He knew he could be called away on an assignment at any time and never was certain that he would return. He had, in fact, been seriously injured on occasion, but had never contacted Alyce until he was totally fit again. He knew instinctively that Alyce would not find a wounded leg, or a broken jaw attractive.

Only Brad and Geilla had met Alyce. Brad had received some helpful advice from her in his social dealing in Paris for his work in the Foreign Office. He admired her beauty, but thought her cold and aloof. Geilla had been awed by Alyce's beauty and elegance, but as she explained to Jack and Paul, "She is a shining jewel, but you can't spit in front of Alyce." Kon had laughed at her remark, but he knew the truth of it.

The train lurched again, and Kon opened his eyes. Suddenly

Paris was gone and he was back on the bench. He felt the warm, wet stickiness of blood on his thigh and tasted it in his mouth. He had been swallowing trickles of it for some time, but more kept coming. He closed his eyes and tried to think of Alyce, but he couldn't picture her clearly. Alyce had no part in this life where he hurt like hell, and blood was dripping down his side. Face it, Kon thought, this thing is still bleeding. I've got to get out of here. Even if I can make it to the rear platform, there will be a guard there. I can't even roll off this damn crate without help. God, I've made a mess of things. He swallowed another mouthful of blood and thought how much he hated the taste of it. He was tempted to just close his eyes, but he forced them open. If I wait we could all be killed, he thought. He put his hand on Brad's knee. "Brad, old friend, could you steer me to the toilet? This wine has gone to my head."

The team looked at him in surprise. This was not like Kon. None of them had ever been able to match his ability to drink voluminously with no ill effect.

"Sure, Kon," Brad answered coolly and stood up. Kon half rose and swayed, but Brad got an arm around him. "Come on," he said and pulled him up. With Brad's help Kon got down the passageway and into the bathroom. Brad closed the door and stood face to face with Kon.

"What the hell is the matter with you, Kon! The guard will be around any minute to check our tickets."

"I've got to get off this train before he comes by again," Kon gasped. He grabbed the empty towel rack to steady himself before he continued. "I caught a bullet back at the jail, and I can't stop the bleeding. If I'm discovered, the mission is over, Brad. You've got to help me get off this train."

Brad put his hand to his head and unconsciously pulled his hair. "Why didn't you say something before?"

"I didn't think it was this bad. It won't quit, Brad. You've got to help me get out of here."

Brad caught the desperation in Kon's voice. He sighed at this new complication. "Let's see it," he said at last.

Kon fumbled to unbutton the huge overcoat and Brad hastily pulled it open. "Oh bloody hell! Bloody hell!" he said when he saw what Kon meant.

"I'll be dripping on the floor soon, Brad. You've got to get me out of here before it's too late. Just help me roll off the rear platform. Distract . . ."

Brad grabbed Kon by the shoulders and looked him in the face. "Shut up, Kon," he said calmly, as if he was explaining something very simple. "Just shut up about getting off this train. I'm not letting you off this job until it's finished. We work as a team! Do you understand?"

8

The determination and authority in Brad's voice silenced Kon. Brad was in command as he always was and Kon accepted his order. He leaned against the wall and gave up the idea of rolling off the platform.

There was a knock at the door and they heard Paul's voice. He had finally guessed why Kon had looked so stunned when he found him in the cell. "I thought you might need this."

Brad unlatched the door and Paul slipped him his knapsack. "Hurry! The guard will be here any minute. Do you need my help?" Paul whispered. Brad shook his head and Paul quickly slipped back to the cabin and told the others to put on their best faces when the guard came by.

Brad secured the door again and rummaged in the sack. He pulled out two shirts, some twine and a cloth handkerchief. "Get that coat and shirt off," he said as he started to tear one shirt into pieces.

Kon was still struggling with his shirt when Brad turned back to him. "God, what a mess!" Brad said when he saw the blood soaked towel. "Give me your knife," he ordered, knowing full well Kon would have it on him. Kon silently produced the blade from his pocket. Immediately Brad cut away the bloody strands and removed the wad of towel. Throwing the towel into the sink, he pressed the dry handkerchief against the wound. Swiftly he wrapped the torn shirt around Kon's ribs and pulled. Kon drew in his breath and staggered. "Hold on to the towel rack with both hands," Brad ordered.

As Kon turned Brad wound more of the shirt around him and pulled. Kon hung on and gasped, "For God's sake, take it easy!"

"It's done," Brad answered. He helped Kon into a dry shirt and buttoned a few buttons near the neck. Kon clung to the towel rack while Brad rolled the bloody towel and shirt into a ball, forced open the window, and heaved them out.

Suddenly they heard the guard at the door, rattling the lock and calling to them. "Come out! Ticket check! Please come out now."

"Come on," Brad said and took Kon by the arm. Kon turned slowly, but even in the dim light from the single sooty bulb Brad could see the greenish color of his face.

"Don't give out on me now, friend," Brad said quietly. Quickly he shouted to the guard, "We're coming! We're coming!" Then, "Oh shit . . ." Just in time he pushed Kon's head over the toilet. Kon heaved and the wine came up mixed with blood. Brad quickly pressed the flush lever and opened the door just enough for the guard to hear the unmistakable sound as Kon heaved again.

Brad smiled knowingly at the guard, "Just a little too much wine for him," he said.

The guard opened the door a bit to satisfy himself that there was only one man inside the small room.

"Your ticket! Let's see your ticket," he snapped impatiently.

Brad took his ticket out of his pocket and handed it over.

"What about his?" The guard snarled, pointing to Kon.

Brad stepped back toward Kon. "Where's your ticket, Marcello?" he said addressing Kon by the forged name. Kon fumbled in his right pocket and handed his ticket to Brad.

"He is a fool to drink on an empty stomach," Brad said to the guard as he handed him the ticket. The guard started to step into the room, but he heard Kon heave again and stepped back.

"See that he doesn't make a mess in the cabin," he snapped and handed the ticket back to Brad.

"Yes, sir. Thank you sir. I'll take care of him."

"Peasants!" the guard spat as he turned away. "Pigs and peasants — that's all I ever get on this train."

Kon stood by the toilet and felt inclined to give in to the momentary weakness that follows vomiting. He was grateful when Brad turned him toward the sink and held the lever down so he could get his hands under the feeble squirt of water. He rinsed his mouth and cupped some water over his face.

"Damn, there never are any towels on these trains," Brad muttered under his breath. Reaching down he picked up the overcoat and wiped Kon's face with the lining. Then he drew the coat over Kon's arms and buttoned it again.

"God, I'm a pig to puke on a friend." Kon muttered.

"No extra charge," Brad answered wryly. "Besides you hit the toilet, remember?"

Brad kept his voice cheerful and calm as he steered Kon back to the cabin. It was part of the treatment to let the patient think everything was going to be O.K. He had been through it many times before. Cheerful and calm — even though they both knew that in a short while Kon would be out cold.

The others looked up anxiously when Kon and Brad came into the cabin. Paul had informed them that Kon had been hit, but they didn't know how badly. Brad was determined to keep his darkest fears for Kon from them for as long as possible.

Geilla took Kon's hand in both of hers as he sat down.

"Are you O.K.?" she asked.

"Sure, sure. I'll survive. Don't worry," he said weakly.

Geilla was not convinced, but she could control herself in front of Kon. She had been doing it for years. She was deeply in love with Kon, and would have given herself to him long ago if he had not walled her out. In the three years after Kon had come to the theater she had come to know him very well. He worked hard for her father by running the mechanics of the theater and keeping the accounts, for neither Zoel, nor Alonzo was particularly level headed about money. She followed Alonzo and Kon everywhere, and the three of them lived for the theater. They met performers from all over Europe and the size of the local orchestra grew. Kon learned to speak French and English, and Geilla learned to dance. It was a happy time for them until Alonzo was killed when his motorbike was struck by a car.

After the accident Zoel started drinking heavily, and he paid less and less attention to the theater. He would have lost many of the musicians if Kon had not talked them into staying. Geilla and Kon spent long hours trying to run the theater, but they were both so young, the performers from out of town would not take them seriously. They took turns breaking up fights between Zoel and the performers and carried Zoel to his bed after he had drunk himself into a stupor.

Early one evening Geilla and Kon were alone after they had arranged the various raised platforms for the orchestra on the stage. They had spent several hours setting the chairs and music stands in place in preparation for the evening's concert. It was to be the last event of the season and a well known pianist had arrived from Florence.

They were standing on the second level admiring their handiwork and looking forward with anticipation to the coming event, when almost without her knowing it, Kon had slipped his arm around her and kissed her on the neck. She had been surprised, but excited by this touch, and let him put his arms around her and kiss her on the lips. Their one youthful expression of feeling for each other was brutally interrupted when Zoel staggered in drunk and saw them together. Overcome with rage, Zoel rushed onto the stage, grabbed Kon by the arm, and struck him in the face with such furry that Kon lost his balance and fell backwards off the platform. He hit several chairs and heavy metal music stands in the violin section as he fell, and they crashed to the floor beneath him. Geilla, who had been speechless with surprise, suddenly began to scream and cry. Zoel called her a dirty name and cursed Kon, accusing him of defiling his daughter. Seconds later, Zoel leaped from the platform and flung his corpulent body on top of Kon. Taking Kon by the neck, he choked him and banged his head against one of the music stands.

Realizing he was fighting for his very life, Kon used his large hands and powerful wrists to keep Zoel's hands away from his throat. All the while Kon struggled, Zoel screamed curses in his face, telling him again and again that he would never be good enough for Geilla. Kon was unconscious by the time Geilla's cries and Zoel's shouting brought help. It had taken four men to subdue Zoel.

Geilla could still remember seeing her father on the floor. Some of the other performers had carried Kon away and a group of women were crowding around her. She was torn between her feeling for her father, and for Kon, and could not stop screaming. For hours she called alternately for Kon and for her father until at last she had fainted from exhaustion. When she awoke she learned that Kon was gone. Mario and some of the other musicians had left after the concert, taking Kon with them. They had had enough of Zoel and were on their way north to join another orchestra. Geilla did not see Kon again for a long time. He wrote to her once begging forgiveness from her and her father, but when she sent word asking him to visit her, he never answered. She had been just fifteen when he went away.

****

"We've got to stick to the plan," Brad was saying. "Geilla is the star, and her leading man here is just a little drunk. We've got to pretend we've all been drinking heavily to carry this off. Now hand me the wine, Geilla."

Brad poured a glass and handed it to Peterson, "Get the smell of this on your breath, but don't let it loosen your tongue," he warned. Peterson was not much of a drinker, but he sipped the wine and hoped it would calm his nerves. Brad gave the rest of the bottle to Jack, who took a gulp and passed the bottle to Paul.

Brad opened another bottle and carefully poured some wine down the front of Kon's overcoat. It made a dark stain, but he was careful not to get Kon's shirt wet. He took the bottle that Kon had emptied earlier and handed it to Jack. "Put some water in this, will you."

By the time the guard passed by again the occupants of the cabin appeared to be in the midst of a rowdy drinking binge. Jack was waving his cap and proposing toasts in a loud voice, and Geilla laughed and offered the guard a glass of wine. The guard gave the group a disgusted glance, but he seemed convinced that they were in truth drunken travellers.

Shortly after the guard passed Brad noticed that Kon was turning paler by the minute. He put his hand on Kon's shoulder. "Try to stay alert as long as you can," he said as calmly as he could.

"Don't get caught with a dead man, Brad," Kon whispered. "Put me off the train. Put me off now," he pleaded.

"You'll be all right, Kon. You'll be all right. I'll get you out," Brad promised.

Kon felt every movement of the train magnified a hundred fold. He tried to think of something to focus on, but he could no longer picture Alyce clearly. Although he was wearing an overcoat and the cabin was warm, he began to shiver uncontrollably. Geilla held his hand tightly, as if she would press life into him. She looked pale herself and she was trembling. She knew Kon was seriously ill for when he was well he rarely let her touch him. As he watched Geilla, Brad could not help wishing he had never let her join the team; but he knew she would continue to follow Kon no matter what it did to her.

"For Christ's sake, I can't sit here and watch you shake, Kon," Jack exploded. He stripped off his heavy jacket and laid it with surprising gentleness over Kon, tucking the sleeves behind his back. "Hang on, buddy, hang on," he urged. He held Kon by the shoulders for a moment to steady him. Kon tried to speak, but his teeth chattered so badly he had to clench his jaw.

Kon could not remember how long he had been shaking, but he felt very tired. He struggled to keep his eyes open, but he was losing the battle. He wanted only to rest. "Just for a moment," his body kept urging him. The others tried hard to keep him awake. He was vaguely aware of someone trying to pour something liquid down his throat. He was extremely thirsty, but he could taste only blood and would not drink. His breath was coming in short gasps.

Suddenly he felt very warm and couldn't remember where he was. He imagined it was some sort of interrogation session, because someone was slapping his face and shouting at him. He couldn't understand what they wanted from him, but he determined to tell them nothing – nothing at all. There was a terrible pain in his chest and it was hard to breathe. They must be trying to suffocate me, he thought and lurched violently to free himself. He heard a loud ringing in his ears and felt himself falling downwards into a deep, black, nothingness. He stopped struggling and was still. They moved Kon's limp body into the corner against the window, but did not lay him down for fear he would choke on his own blood.

There were two station stops before the border crossing, and Brad knew they would have to change their plans. He had hoped that Kon would not bleed so fast, but he had been wrong. Brad outlined his plan to the others and weighed their input. He knew there were only two guards assigned to each car. The one who came by after every station stop to check tickets carried a pistol, and the one who remained behind the doors that led into the next car was armed with an AK-47. There was a guarded check point at the exit of each station stop, which consisted of one guard with a weapon, but there would be a thorough check of their identification as they crossed the border. The chances of Kon's physical condition going undetected were pretty slim. They would have to get off the train before the border or face arrest.

Following Brad's directions Jack produced his tools from his pack. Since he was posing as a hiker he had felt free to carry some tools openly. Others he had hidden. Separating Jack from his tools would be like asking Kon to give up his knife. Carefully, Jack removed the cover from the overhead light in the cabin. He loosened the bulb in the socket and fashioned a noose around it with a very thin wire. He strung the wire across the overhead and down the wall behind one bench. It took a bit of skillful fussing, but once the cover was back in place, Jack could put out the cabin light by pulling on the wire.

After the train left the station and they heard the guard making his rounds, they feigned sleep. As the guard passed their cabin, Geilla opened the door and spoke to him. "Come quickly! I think something is wrong with my friend. The others are all drunk. Please help me!" she said anxiously and retreated into the cabin.

The guard followed her in, but as he bent over Kon, the cabin went dark. Paul was on the guard in a flash, catching him in a head lock. With the utmost skill, Paul applied pressure on the guard's carotid artery and the guard was unconscious in seconds. Paul let up. He didn't want to kill the man. Paul's mastery of martial arts was complete. He was lightening fast and totally controlled. Even Jack who was no slouch in a fight never sparred with Paul. "You could be looking straight at him and he'd sneak up behind you," Jack claimed.

"Get that jacket off him," Brad whispered. He tore off his own coat and trousers and slipped into the clothes that were handed to him in the dark. Quickly he stood and buttoned the coat over his shirt.

"Give me some light!" Brad called and at once the light came on. Brad opened the door of the cabin. The guard at the end of the car had seen the light go out and was coming down the passageway. Keeping his head down, Brad waved him back. "It's nothing," he said casually. "Everything's under control. Stay at your post."

Brad hoped his accent was good enough to fool the guard. Damn it! he thought, what a time for Kon to be out cold. In addition to having a natural ability with languages, Kon had spent years with tutors and tapes to perfect numerous accents. It was a game for him. Even Alyce who was highly critical of anything "common" considered Kon's French to be flawless. Before each assignment Kon painstakingly schooled the others in the local accent. Brad hoped he would remember enough of the phrases Kon had chosen to teach them for this assignment.

Boldly Brad stepped into the adjacent cabin and asked the passengers for their tickets. He noted that they did not act surprised to see a different guard. Moving slowly, he made the rounds of the other cabins, trying his best to keep his back toward the end of the car while he was in the passageway. According to the timetable, it would be thirty-five minutes before the next station stop.

As he moved from cabin to cabin, Brad picked up abandoned newspapers, blankets, and any other items he thought might come in handy. He rummaged in the pockets of the uniform he was wearing and found two cigarette lighters and a set of keys. When he passed by the cabin the team occupied, he handed the collection inside. On the seat where he had been sitting was the guard, now fully dressed in his suit. He was out for the moment, but Paul would have to give

14

him another "treatment" before long.

The train began to slow as it approached the next station. Just before it came to a full stop, Brad went to the door of the cabin where the team was waiting. As he opened the door, they started making a disturbance. Jack stepped half way into the passageway, grabbed Brad by the shoulder, and shouted, "I told you we don't want to get off here!" Brad struggled and stepped back, pulling Jack out of the cabin.

"Guard! Guard! Help!" Brad cried in alarm and motioned to the guard at the end of the car. Immediately Jack took hold of Brad's jacket and shook him. "We're not getting out!" he bellowed.

From the corner of his eye, Brad saw the guard open the door to the car and come rushing down the passageway. "Pull him off me! Pull him off me!" Brad yelled as the guard came up.

In his excitement the guard let go of his weapon and tried to grab Jack from behind. The guard had barely touched Jack, however, when Paul's powerful hand struck the guard across the back of the neck. The guard dropped to his knees without a sound, and Paul pulled him into the cabin. He took the guard's weapon and stripped the jacket and boots off his body.

"O.K. let's go!" Brad ordered. Together he and Paul lifted Kon's limp body and placed it over Jack's broad shoulders. Kon's light, lean, runner's body was no strain for Jack, but as he took hold and shifted Kon's weight, Kon moaned softly.

"Be careful with him!" Geilla cried and put her hand to her mouth.

Brad touched her shoulder gently, "It's a good sign, Geilla. It means Kon is still with us. Come on now. We've got to get him off the train. Just play your part a little while longer."

Geilla straightened herself and shook her head "yes". She stepped out of the cabin and Brad took her arm with authority. Peterson followed them carrying a half full wine bottle. He was still mistrustful, but since no one had hurt him so far, he kept his promise to remain silent and pretend to be drunk. Jack was about to take Kon out when Paul saw the blood on the back of Kon's overcoat.

"Hold it a minute, Jack," he said calmly, and gently laid a blanket over Kon's body, tucking one edge under him. Seeing the worried look on Jack's face, Paul touched his arm. "Hey . . . he'll be O.K. Kon won't admit it, but he's one hell of a tough Greek," Paul said with more confidence than he felt.

The team made their way to the end of the cabin and out the door. As they stepped off the train, Jack caught a glimpse of a jeep with a familiar insignia on the side door.

Walking quickly, Brad escorted Geilla to the check point where one guard was on duty. Brad stepped up to him and snapped, "Get these people out of here! They're drunken pigs and have been causing a disturbance all night."

Jack was right behind Brad. "Stop calling us pigs! We're just celebrating — that's all," he said, slurring his words to pretend he was drunk. "We're just having a little party here," Jack insisted again.

"Check them through," Brad ordered. The guard was about to ask for their papers when suddenly they heard Paul shout from the window of the train. "Fire! Fire on the train! Help! Help!"

Even as Paul yelled, a cloud of black smoke poured from the window, and they saw a flash of flame. A series of gun shots rang out, followed by the sound of people screaming hysterically.

"My God!" Brad exclaimed to the guard, "Go see what is happening! I'll watch the gate."

The guard was reluctant to leave his post, and watched in confusion as people fled screaming from the train. Suddenly they heard the sound of continuous gun fire.

"Go! Go!" Brad ordered again. "I'll watch the gate!"

The guard hesitated briefly, then ran towards the door of the train, fighting his way through the crowd of excited people who were clamoring and shrieking and rushing in all directions. Taking advantage of the total confusion, the team slipped quietly through the gate and into the darkness surrounding the station.

"Brad, some of those soldiers on the platform were General Jakupak's men. I saw the insignia on their jeep," Jack said.

Brad let his breath out slowly. "News of the trouble at the jail must be out," Brad answered. "I hope Paul got off O.K."

The town was asleep for the night and once they were away from the lights of the train station, they walked in almost total darkness. More by feel than by sight they made their way towards a group of buildings. Their doors were closed, but one had a sign advertising rooms to rent.

Brad had an idea, and briefed the others as they moved toward the back of the buildings away from the street. Jack set Kon down, carefully propping him against a wall. Brad wrapped the blanket around Kon and waited in the darkness with him and Peterson while Geilla and Jack went around to the front entrance.

Jack rapped firmly on the door. No one answered at first, but when he continued to knock and call out in English, an old man with sleep-tangled hair opened the door a crack. Jack knew that many people in Yugoslavia were multilingual, and that an innkeeper was sure to know a little English.

"What's going on? What do you want at this hour of the night?" the innkeeper snarled.

"I'm sorry," Jack apologized. "I'm sorry to bother you, but my wife . . ." He hesitated, and putting his arm around Geilla who was behind him, he pulled her forward. "My wife got sick on the train. There was no help and nowhere to go. Please, is there a doctor here?

16

I must get her to a doctor!"

The innkeeper only half listened to Jack's desperate pleas, but he gave Geilla a full appraisal as she stood in the dim light coming through the open door.

"Please sir," she pleaded meekly. "I must find a doctor."

"Oh, all right," the man said giving in to Geilla, who looked tired and pale. "We have only a small clinic here. You must go half a kilometer south, there at the corner. When you come to the fountain in the square, turn west and go six blocks. You will find a small building with a red cross in a circle over the door. I cannot promise that anyone will be there at this time of night. Now, please, let me sleep."

"Thank you, sir," Geilla said and smiled weakly. She turned to Jack. "Let us go quickly." They moved away and the man closed the door. After walking a few steps towards the corner indicated by the innkeeper, they stopped and waited to see if anyone was watching. Jack was on guard because while they were talking to the innkeeper, he had noticed a car drive up to the far curb about half a block away. The driver had dimmed the lights, but left the engine running. Jack could not see the vehicle clearly in the darkness, but it did not sound like a military jeep to him.

Jack decided it would be better for them to go away from the inn for a block before they doubled back to where Brad and the others were hiding. If there was trouble, he and Geilla could either make a run for it, or tough it out, but if either Kon or Peterson were discovered, the mission would be over. Cautiously they started walking toward the car, keeping to the opposite side of the street.

As they passed the vehicle, the door opened and a man stepped out. It was too dark to see if anyone else was in the car, but Jack reached for the guard's pistol that Brad had given him. He clicked off the safety. Keeping the gun hidden by his body, he glanced quickly down the street trying to spot an opening between the buildings they could duck into if the need arose. When he looked back, the man was gone.

Suddenly from close behind his head Jack heard, "Careful with that thing, Jack!" It was Paul. Jack snapped the safety on again, and Paul led the way to the car.

"Where did you find the car?" Jack asked as they got in.

"Well . . . there was this sort of used car lot next to the train station and I . . ." Paul started.

"Used car lot, my eye!" Jack laughed. "That was some commotion you stirred up at the station, Paul. What happened?"

"After you carried Kon out, I went to the opposite end of the car and fastened the door shut with a short piece of chain. Then I piled all the papers, blankets, and extra clothes on the cabin bench, broke open the two lighters, and started a fire. I set fire to the window shades and started calling out the window. When the bench started to smoke, I pulled the bodies of the two guards into the passageway. Then I ran up and down the passageway shouting 'Fire! Fire!' and doing my best to panic everyone. I guess the sight of two unconscious guards was very convincing, and a few women started screaming. When the people jammed the passageway, I went into the cabin and shot off a few rounds into the overhead with the guard's automatic. Then I slipped out with the crowd. After I got the vehicle, I went looking for you folks and spotted you at the inn. Where's Brad?"

"He's with Kon and Peterson behind the inn. We got directions to the clinic. We'd better get Kon there fast!"

CHAPTER TWO

Paul drove to the rear of the buildings, and helped Jack load Kon into the car. Since the vehicle was small, it was decided that Paul would drive Brad, Geilla, and Kon to the clinic, while Jack and Peterson went on foot. When the vehicle reached the clinic, Brad discovered that the door was unlocked, but he did not go straight in. Instead, Paul went around to the back, and made his way in through a window. The clinic consisted of only a few rooms, most of which were dark. Making his way toward the light, Paul came upon a man who had fallen asleep while working at a desk. Satisfied that there was no one else in the building, Paul passed down the hall and opened the street door. Brad carried Kon inside and laid him on one of the bare tables. Geilla stood close to Kon, clinging to his hand.

Brad shook the sleeping man who awoke with a start and seemed quite shaken to see Brad's uniform. "Doctor, we've got an injured man here who needs help," Brad said.

The man remained silent, but he stood up and looked quickly from Brad to Kon. It was obvious to Brad the man was trying to think fast and weigh every word.

"Please hurry," Brad said pushing the man toward the table.

Kon lay covered with the blanket, and as the man pulled it off Brad whispered to Paul, "Get Geilla out of here."

Paul nodded. "Geilla," he said calmly, "Let's go keep watch for the others."

"No, I want to stay here," she objected.

Paul looked at Brad for a clue. He didn't want to use force to get her out. Brad went to Geilla and gently took her hands from Kon. "He'll be all right, Geilla. I promise. Go see that Peterson stays calm. Please." Brad nodded to Paul who put his arm around Geilla and led her into the hall.

Once Geilla was gone Brad returned to the table. Hurriedly he unbuttoned Kon's overcoat. "Doctor, you've got to do something! He's been shot," he said and opened the coat. The man drew in his breath sharply. Brad's first reaction was to turn away, but he recovered quickly. Kon's shirt was soaked with blood as was the torn shirt bound around him.

The man's hands shook as he fingered the bloody shirt. "This is terrible," he said, "terrible."

"You've got to do something for him!" Brad shouted impatiently.

"I can do nothing," the man moaned. "I am only an orderly. The doctor has gone to the next town. We have only a small clinic here.

We are not equipped for anything like this!"

Brad felt a cold shiver down his back as the horrible truth sunk in.

"There is only the military hospital," the orderly continued. "They have taken all our equipment." Suddenly feeling the danger in his helplessness, the orderly moved toward the desk. "I will call the hospital authorities for you. They will send an ambulance." He picked up the phone, but Brad reached in front of him and pressed the receiver button down.

"There must be no calls to the authorities," he said quietly.

"But if I don't call for someone this man may die," the orderly insisted.

Brad surmised that the orderly did not want to be held responsible for the death of anyone connected with the government. He looked from the orderly to Kon and back. "If you don't call he may die, but if you call the authorities, he will die for sure."

The orderly looked Brad full in the face and studied him critically. At last he spoke. "I take it then you are not what you seem to be."

Brad shook his head. "You are right, my friend."

The orderly relaxed, then seemed to take on a new determination of purpose. "Then we have only one thing to do. We must get your friend to the hospital across the border."

The orderly took some gauze pads from a drawer and stepped back to the table. Moving swiftly now that he no longer feared being shot for botching a job, he cut away the torn shirt. "The bleeding has slowed, but it does not look good for him. When did this happen?"

"Shortly after 7:00 p.m.," Brad answered.

"No good, no good . . . it must be after midnight. You should have come sooner," the orderly declared. He pressed a large gauze pad over the wound. "Hold this in place while I bind it."

As they worked, the orderly described the route to the hospital for Brad. "We will leave his bloody shirt, but you must also put your jacket on him. It will go easier if he looks like a military man."

"No need for that," responded Jack, as he came into the room. "We have the jacket from the other guard." Jack stepped up to the table, "What's the story, doc? How is our friend here?"

The orderly dropped his gaze. "I am sorry," he said slowly. "I am not a doctor. I cannot help him."

Jack looked at Brad in disbelief. "What's he saying? He's got to do something for . . . Oh God," Jack said, suddenly seeing the bloody clothes. "I didn't know it was this bad. Is he going to make it?"

"It's not good, Jack," Brad confessed. "We've got to get him to the hospital across the border. Bring in that jacket, will you, and for God's sake tell Paul to keep Geilla out of here for a few minutes."

After the orderly finished bandaging Kon, Jack and Brad

struggled to put the guard's jacket on Kon and replaced his shoes with the guard's boots.

"Now you must hurry," said the orderly. "What transport do you have?"

"We have only a small car now. We will have to get another one," Brad answered.

The orderly gave Brad another long, hard look, then spoke quietly. "I am not a doctor, but in some matters I have much experience. There has been trouble at the train station, no?"

Brad nodded his head gravely, but said nothing.

The orderly thought again, then made his proposal. "You must all go in my truck. I have used it to take other . . . other equipment across the border. You will tell the border guards that there was trouble on the train, and that there are many wounded. It is a common thing lately to have explosions on the train. The military hospital is small, so some men must be taken across the border. You will wear these uniforms, and the woman must dress like a man. Give the name of General Smreck. He is the commandant here. If you are bold and act in his name, you will get across. The guards there are young and stupid. You must remind them they want a more glorious position in the government.

Once you are safely across you must go to the hospital in Florina. We will telegraph a message to Dr. Stamatis and he will be ready for you. You will then turn my truck over to my friend in Florina, and it will be returned to me." The orderly looked at Brad again. "Is it agreed?"

"Why are you willing to help us?" Brad asked.

"For one thing, I am no friend of this government," the orderly answered. "But to be practical, this friend of yours," he said gesturing toward Jack, "will take my truck whether I offer it or not. If you steal it and get caught, the truck will be traced to me, and I will have much trouble. So I must see that you do not get caught."

"What if we just make you come with us." Jack said menacingly, and took hold of the orderly's shirt.

The orderly looked at Brad for help.

"You must not do that," he pleaded. "If I go, my usefulness here will be finished."

"How do we know we can trust you?" Brad asked.

"There is no way," the orderly answered. "You must take my word. I have nothing to gain by betraying you."

It was now Brad's turn to study the orderly who returned his steady gaze.

"O.K." Brad said at length, "but you must come as far as the telegraph office with us."

"Agreed. Now we must hurry."

Jack released his grip on the orderly, and went with him to bring the truck near the back door. They piled several rough blankets on the floor and carried Kon out.

"You must keep his head up," the orderly cautioned, "and watch his breathing. Give him your own breath by mouth if you must. One more thing," the orderly said, "Where is the vehicle you came in?"

"It's out front," Brad said.

"I will have to see that no blood is found in it. Where did you put the wounded man?"

"In the back."

"Then we must search there for any stains." The orderly picked up a flashlight and motioned for Brad to follow him down the hall. He checked the street from the shelter of the half opened door. When he was convinced that no one was watching, he slipped out to the car. Brad followed and together they searched for telltale signs. There was one blood stain on the edge of the seat. The orderly took out his cigarette lighter and held it to the upholstery until it started to smolder. Moving the lighter around, he blackened the whole area. He then took a cigarette from his pocket and tore it in half. He lit one half and tossed it onto the back seat, where it burned a bit and charred another place on the seat.

"The people here are very poor," the orderly explained. "We must not waste a vehicle for a small stain. We could use a knife to complete the job."

Brad reached into his pocket and pulled out Kon's knife that he had retrieved from the discarded coat. He switched it open and slashed the seat in several places.

"Good," the orderly said, "the car will be reported only as stolen and vandalized."

The others were waiting in the truck when Brad and the orderly arrived. Brad got behind the wheel and drove in silence with the orderly sitting beside him as a guide.

"We must stop here and go on foot," the orderly directed after a short trip. "There will be only one man on duty and he is unarmed. I will leave it to you to gain entry, but do not be too rough as the man is old."

Brad got out and issued a few instructions to the others, before he approached the door on foot. There was a light on in the building, and one hung above the door. The door was locked when Brad tried it. He knocked loudly and called out. "Open up! Open up! I have an important message to be sent." After more loud knocking a thin old man opened the door part way.

"Who is there? What do you want?"

"I have come from the train," Brad declared boldly, "there has been trouble and I need to alert the next station." He took a step backwards so that he was in the shadow beyond the light, but the jacket of his uniform was clearly visible.

22

The man hesitated and Brad bristled with official indignation. "Hurry up old man! I must get back to the train."

The man opened the door and Brad quickly slipped inside, being careful not to latch the door. "Now quickly, get to your machine and I will write out the message."

Brad took up a pad of paper and pretended to write as the man sat down with his back to the door.

"Send this to . . ." Brad was saying as Paul passed like a shadow and grabbed the old man from behind. It took only a slight pressure on his neck to put him out. Paul lowered him to the floor. "I'll have to tie him. He won't be out for long."

Brad went to the door and signaled, and a moment later the orderly stepped out of the shadows and into the office.

"Good. Now you must send this message," the orderly said. He dictated what appeared to be a series of numbers to Brad, who quickly typed them into the machine along with the address of Dr. Stamatis.

"This code tells Stamatis that you are coming and gives him information concerning the condition of your friend. He will have everything ready when you arrive."

When Paul had finished tying the old man in his chair, they filed out of the building, leaving the light on.

"I have done all I can for you. Now you must let me leave," the orderly said to Brad as they approached the truck.

"I wish for many reasons that you were coming with us," Brad answered.

"I cannot, but please see that my truck is returned to me. Ask for this man at the address I have written," the orderly said, passing Brad a crumpled slip of paper.

"We will," Brad promised.

The orderly pulled Brad one step away from the truck and lowered his voice. "One word about Stamatis. He is not what you would call a city doctor. He has spent too much time in field hospitals and among the soldiers. He is gruff at best, but he can bring life to a stone. If anyone can help your friend, he can. Go now and good luck!" He held out his hand and Brad grasped it firmly.

"Thank you, my friend," Brad responded sincerely.

"I go now to establish my alibi," the orderly said. "On such a troubled night as this, it is not wise to sleep alone in one's office." He raised his hand to them and disappeared into the darkness.

Brad walked to the rear of the truck and pulled aside the canvas flap. "Geilla, it's 26 kilometers to the border and the road is in a deplorable state of repair. See how fast you can get us there without breaking an axle. Stop just short of the crossing so we can trade places."

Geilla nodded and slid out of the truck. She had discarded her

23

skirt and was wearing her leather pants and Kon's sports jacket which had a blood stain on the front. Even without makeup, however, Geilla did not look masculine. She would have to keep her face covered.

Brad knew he could depend on Geilla to give them a fast ride. Although it was Kon who owned the silver Ferrari, it was Geilla who reveled in driving it, fast and hard. She had occasionally given Brad a breathless ride to the airport in Rome. She maneuvered ruthlessly in the heavy traffic and could conquer the toughest cab driver with either her flashing smile, or a devastating reference to his mother's lack of morals.

"Jack, you ride shotgun for Geilla," Brad commanded. "Paul, I'll need you in the back with me." Paul nodded and silently moved to trade places with Jack who was supporting Kon.

"Let me have your flashlight, Jack," Brad said quietly as Jack scrambled out of the truck. "Right," Jack answered, and passed the light to Brad, who bounded in and sat on the other side of Kon. Brad switched the light on, and looked across at Peterson, who was cowering in the corner. "Just stay quiet and let us do the talking. We'll be across the border in no time," Brad said lightly. Peterson lurched as Geilla hit the gas and they were off. This had better work, Brad thought to himself. I promised Kon I'd get him across the border, but so far I haven't come through for him.

Geilla didn't let Brad down about keeping up the speed, and her keen eyesight kept them out of a ditch more than once. The trip was difficult for those in the back, however. The swaying and bumping were bad enough, but keeping Kon upright and listening to him gasp for breath was a nightmare.

Paul felt that Brad had been right to send Geilla up front. He knew quite well how deeply Geilla loved Kon and that she wanted to stay with him. She was a strong woman, but she might have gotten hysterical if she had been there when Kon stopped breathing. For a moment Paul was afraid that even Brad might go to pieces. Brad had knelt in front of Kon holding him by the shoulders and begging him to breathe. He recovered himself quickly, however, and together he and Paul took turns giving Kon mouth to mouth. Kon was a fighter and they knew he would try to keep going.

Paul worked hard to keep Kon's breath flowing. If Kon died, not only would he lose a true friend, he would never be able to face Geilla. Paul had met Geilla when she joined the team almost three years ago. Although Kon had objected violently to her presence and had threatened to quit, Brad had overruled him. Eventually Kon cooled down and was able to work with Geilla. Paul was well aware that Geilla loved Kon, and he could not understand why Kon never responded to her. She was beautiful and vibrant, and so like Kon in spirit. There were times when Geilla so longed for Kon physically, that she turned to Paul for satisfaction. He knew why she came, and

24

although Kon was his friend, he would not turn her away. He kissed her with exquisite tenderness, and lovingly soothed the fires of her passion. She marvelled that the same hands that could deliver a lethal blow could caress her so gently and melt away the tension desire created in her body. He sought not to inflame her desire, but to see that she felt fulfilled and satisfied. As in everything he did Paul was cool, and controlled, and very skillful.

Always waiting until she came to him, Paul never demanded anything of Geilla, never showed any jealously toward Kon and was totally discreet about their relationship. He was sure the others knew nothing of their meetings. Paul was truly fond of Geilla, but he had a deep wisdom and never let his passion interfere with his duty—to Kon, or to Geilla. None of the others had ever seen him show any sign of temper, and he kept his heart in check. There was only grief in loving a woman who loved someone else. He knew full well what frustrated love was doing to Geilla.

In less than a half hour the lurching stopped and Jack appeared at the back of the truck. He guessed immediately what Paul and Brad had been doing. "That bad, huh?"

"It's not good," Brad responded. "Take over, Jack. Remember to show the jacket when they open the back."

Brad got out and Jack moved in next to Kon. "Hang on buddy, we're almost there," Jack said, touching Kon on the shoulder. He shot a look at Paul and thought he looked worried. He had never seen Paul worry about anything and it unnerved him. Jack knelt beside Kon who gasped once and quit. "Damn it, Kon," Jack shouted, "don't quit on me. I'm not going to let you die in this stinking truck." He took over on the mouth to mouth with a vigor born of desperation.

By the time Brad reached the cab, Geilla had moved to the passenger side and was slumped against the door. She had turned the collar up on Kon's coat and retreated so deeply into it that her face was almost completely hidden.

"Is Kon going to make it?" she asked as Brad got in.

"Sure, sure . . . he's fine. We'll be at the hospital soon," Brad lied to reassure her. "Just stay quiet and keep your eyes open," he added slipping the truck into gear.

Brad brought the truck to a halt just behind the gate arm, but left the engine running. As the guard stepped up Brad took the initiative.

"We're from Bitola. There was trouble on the train and the military hospital is full. I have several wounded men who must go across to the hospital in Florina."

"Do you have orders?" the guard asked.

"I have Commandant Smreck's orders," Brad snapped back. "Didn't you get the message?"

The guard did not answer. He turned, walked to the back of the truck and opened the flap. Kon was propped upright between Paul and Jack.

"This man is from the train and is badly hurt. He must get to a hospital," Jack told the guard.

The guard noted the bloody uniform, but was suspicious of the others. He was about to ask more questions when Brad came up.

"This man works for General Jakupak. If he dies I will see that you answer for it," Brad threatened.

"But I have no orders," the guard protested. He looked worried and undecided, but stood his ground.

"Then we must call. Hurry, you fool! Get the military hospital on the phone."

The guard closed the canvas flap and moved toward the guard house. Brad was close on his heels as he entered.

The guard called to another soldier, "Ring up the military hospital. We will check this story."

Brad maintained a determined and confident appearance while he waited, but his mind was racing. Since both guards were inside the small building, he was tempted to signal Geilla to gun the truck and make a run through the gate. However, since there were two armed guards, he would never escape and the canvas flap would offer no protection to the others once the shooting started. Even if the truck got through, they would be caught and sent back for leaving without permission. They would have to wait and get the guard to open the gate.

After a long delay, the guard was put through to the military hospital. "Ask them if there was trouble on the train last night," Brad demanded, determined to dominate the conversation.

The guard asked the question and seemed satisfied by the answer.

"Ask if General Jakupak's men have arrived?"

Again the guard asked the question and was satisfied.

He was about to ask another question when Brad pressed the receiver button down with an impatient gesture. "Enough! Jakupak's man bleeds while you waste time. If he dies you will be standing sentry duty when your sons are old men!"

"All right," the guard acquiesced, "but you must sign the order book."

Brad looked him straight in the eye. "Bring it then," he shouted.

Brad signed with a forceful, but illegible mark. "Now open the gate!"

The guard hurried out and raised the arm. Striding to the truck, Brad saluted, climbed in and drove through. He had kept his promise to get Kon out. His only hope was that Kon was still alive to breathe the air of freedom.

Brad drove straight south, passing through the two small villages

26

the orderly had mentioned. About 16 kilometers farther on they came to Florina. They were almost through the town when they saw a two-story building with the cross and circle over the door. Someone had hung up a hand lettered sign that read "Hospital" in English. Brad decided that Kon was right in his assertion that a Greek had to be good at languages, because no one was going to bother to learn Greek.

No need to look for the emergency entrance in this place, Brad thought. He parked the truck by the door and went in to look for Dr. Stamatis. The orderly had been very specific in stating that he should ask for Stamatis and not settle for whoever was on duty when they arrived. Once inside, Brad saw a small desk in what be guessed was the patient reception area. An older woman was on duty. She looked up and scowled as Brad approached. Brad was surprised at her rudeness, until he remembered the uniform he was wearing.

"I am looking for Dr. Stamatis. He is expecting . . ." Brad began in English.

"Stamatis, eh," the woman grunted. She picked up the phone and said a few words in Greek to the other party. Then to Brad. "He comes."

Brad stared down the empty, poorly lit hall and serious doubts began to assail him. After the orderly's build up and the stop to send the telegram, he had hoped for a more efficient reception. As he gazed down the hall, Brad saw a short, stocky man with a very noticeable limp walking slowly towards him. Brad judged him to be in his mid-sixties. As he got closer Brad could see that he wore wire-rimmed glasses and was unshaven. He had on rumpled khaki slacks and a soiled shirt. He pushed a rolling stretcher straight up to Brad and without introduction asked almost rudely, "You have the man with the bad lung?"

"Bad lung? Well, I guess having a bullet hole in it makes it a bad lung!" Brad answered impatiently.

The man signaled Brad to keep his voice down.

"Look," Brad said more quietly, but with some agitation, "I sent a telegram for a Dr. Stamatis to meet us here. Everything is supposed to be ready. I have a badly injured man out . . ."

"Enough," the man said cutting Brad off. "I am Stamatis. We waste time. Let us bring him inside."

Brad stared at the man in disbelief. Oh God, what have I done! he almost groaned aloud. When Brad recovered from his shock, he noticed that another tall, thin man with a cart of equipment had arrived. He and Stamatis had passed Brad in the hall and were almost out the door. Brad felt as if he were moving through chest deep water as he walked towards the door. Before he got there, Jack and Paul had carried Kon to the stretcher and were holding him upright. Stamatis cut down the back of Kon's jacket and shirt in one quick movement. He pulled on the sleeves and slid them over Kon's arms exposing his chest and the now bloody bandage around his ribs. They laid him on his back.

"Yiosiph . . . the mask," Stamatis called to the thin man. "How is this one called?"

"Kon," Paul answered quickly.

"Just Kon?"

Paul nodded. Stamatis leaned over the stretcher, and quickly slid one of his huge arms beneath Kon's head. He took the mask from Yiosiph with his free hand and spoke firmly, but softly. "Now you must breathe for me, Kon," he said, bringing the mask up to Kon's face. Kon stiffened and tried to turn his head away as it touched him.

"Do not be frightened, Kon," Stamatis continued in a soothing voice. "It is only air." The air hissed close to Kon's face. "Think of the mountains. Breathe in, Kon, breathe in." Very slowly and gently he lowered the mask over Kon's face. "Breathe, Kon," he said louder and more firmly. "Breathe in deep, Kon! Breathe!" Stamatis pressed on Kon's abdomen away from the wound. "Exhale, Kon. Breathe out. That's it, now breathe in . . . Good . . . good, now again, breathe in."

Stamatis kept on firmly and softly. Kon's chest heaved with each command, but the breaths were uneven and seemed to cause him pain. He tried to draw back from the mask.

Stamatis looked at Geilla who stood pale and shaking by Kon's head. "He is Greek, no?" he asked her.

Geilla was silent for a long minute. She knew that if Kon was conscious he would almost choose to die rather than admit to being Greek. Finally she answered truthfully, "His father was Greek."

"Good enough . . . good enough."

Stamatis pressed the mask against Kon's face again and spoke to him in Greek. The others could not understand the words, but the tone seemed to alternate between coaxing and commanding. After a few minutes Kon gave in and breathed deeply though he quivered slightly at the end of each cycle.

Kon's mind was floating in and out of consciousness. He was partially aware of what was going on around him, but everything was distorted and had a dream-like quality. When Stamatis spoke to him in Greek, it brought back old memories. He was six years old and had been dragged off his father's fishing boat when he became tangled in the nets. The weight of the nets held him under the water and he could not breathe. He struggled, but he couldn't move. He was blue by the time his father had hauled him out. He imagined that he heard his father now, talking to him and telling him to breathe. He wanted to please his father, but it was so difficult to pull in the air and it hurt his chest. He listened to the voice. It was calm and soothing; not at all like his father's voice. He was confused, but he obeyed. Perhaps his father had forgiven him for whatever it was that he had done to make him angry. He never understood why, but his father had always been angry with him.

After a few moments Stamatis signaled to Yiosiph to take over holding the mask. Stamatis raised an arm on the stretcher and hung a plasma bottle from it. Attaching a large gauge needle and tubing to the bottle, he spoke softly to Kon, held his arm for a moment and slipped the needle into his vein. Kon twitched. Stamatis took a stethoscope from the cart and carefully listened on both sides of Kon's chest. He shook his head several times to indicate he didn't like what he heard.

"When did this happen?" he asked Paul.

"Just after 7 p.m."

"Why do you wait so long to bring him to me?" Stamatis said to no one in particular. "Does he tolerate penicillin?"

"No problem," Paul answered, "but go easy on the anesthetics. He doesn't handle them well."

"It is not so easy then to prevent the pain," Stamatis commented.

"I know, I know, but keep the dosage small, or he'll never wake up," Paul warned.

Stepping around to Kon's other arm, Stamatis drew a syringe full of blood and filled a test tube with it.

"Order blood, Yiosiph. Start with three units."

He carefully filled a small syringe only one third full from a bottle and slipped the needle into Kon's arm.

"Come now, Kon," he said in English, "Let us see what we can do about that lung."

Ignoring the team members, Stamatis pushed the stretcher down the hall and through the swinging doors at the end, all the while talking alternately to Kon and Yiosiph in Greek. As the stretcher disappeared, the team stood together looking after it in silence, each thinking their own dark thoughts. They were surprised, but grateful when a short time later a young boy appeared and asked them politely, in English, to follow him. They were led to a room with several wooden arm chairs, a table, and a cot with a blanket. There was a pot of tea and cups on the table along with bread and butter. "Be pleased to wait here," the boy said. "Stamatis said to tell it will be a long wait."

The waiting was not easy to take. The men thought that Geilla should rest on the cot, but she was too worried and upset. She paced nervously back and forth until Paul brought her to sit beside him. He put his arm around her and tried to comfort her with lies about Kon's chances for recovery. Kon was tough. Kon was indestructible. They had hauled him back broken and beaten from other assignments and he had always pulled through. But unspoken was Paul's thought that he had never seen a man bleed so badly and survive.

Brad was lost in his own fears that Stamatis was incompetent and that the facilities at the clinic were inadequate to handle such a serious case. He searched his mind for a thought as to what he could have done differently to save Kon. He could think of nothing, under the circumstances. At least when they had last seen Kon he was breathing again.

While the others sat or paced, Peterson threw himself on the cot in exhaustion. The night had been one of absolute terror for him. He understood that he was free, but he was haunted by the idea that a man might die because of him.

It was almost three and a half hours later when Stamatis came into the room looking tired and more disheveled than before. He pulled out a chair and sat facing the group. "I cut him here," he said gesturing across his left side below the ribs. "The bullet is out, but there is still some bleeding from the lung, and it does not work for now. He must have a tube in the chest to drain the fluid," Stamatis continued softly. He sighed and studied the tired, worried faces before him. It was a sad tale he had to tell, but they must know. "The wound opened the lung and there is now infection in one lung, and possibly in the lining of both lungs. Breathing is very difficult for him. I gave him penicillin, but your friend will have fever I fear." He paused and rubbed his head with his hand. "He is very weak, but he lives yet."

"What are his chances, doc?" Jack asked, voicing the question for all of them.

"I am a surgeon. I fix what I can. I am not the giver of life!" Stamatis answered impatiently.

"Can we see him, please?" Geilla begged.

"Yes, yes. He will need friends now to care for him. You must be with him day and night. Call to him, touch him, don't let him sink into the loneliness. I have seen loneliness and fear claim a man who had more life than this one. Come now."

Stamatis led them to a long ward on the second floor. Thin white curtains hanging from the high ceiling separated the rows of mostly empty beds. Their footsteps echoed on the bare marble floors as they walked to the end of the room.

Peterson followed the others when they left with Stamatis. He did not know this man they were so concerned about, but he had been impressed by how devotedly his friends had cared for him ever since he became ill on the train. They had taken care of him also, pushing and shoving him here and there to keep him safe. Peterson looked around with scientific curiosity as he walked. He noticed there were no modern hospital beds, no heart monitoring machines, and few nurses. He shuddered at the thought of lying ill in the midst of such bleak surroundings.

Kon lay on a narrow bed near the large window at the end of

the long ward. In place of his bloody clothes, Kon now wore a plain white gown which accented his distressing pallor. His left arm was folded across his chest, his right arm lay outstretched towards the edge of the bed. There was a large needle in it, connected to a unit of blood hanging from a fixture attached to the ceiling. Another tube ran from Kon's chest to a large glass bottle containing water which stood next to the bed. With each breath that Kon took, a thin stream of blood trickled slowly down to the bottle and mingled with the water. They could almost see life draining from him. A catheter tube ran to a bag which hung at the foot of the bed, and a cylinder of oxygen with a mask stood like a silent sentinel in the corner. Yiosiph stood by the bed, dutifully holding Kon's broad hand and talking softly to him.

"You must take over now," Stamatis said quietly and pushed Geilla forward. "And no tears," he warned.

Geilla glided slowly around the bed and took Kon's hand between her own. "Kon? . . . Kon? Can you hear me?" she asked softly. "It's going to be O.K. now. We're all here with you. We'll take good care of you."

Aside from the rising and falling of his chest with each labored breath, Kon lay absolutely still. Geilla held her lip between her teeth. It was going to be hard to obey the order for no tears.

"He is quiet now from the drug," Stamatis commented, "but we must watch later for the fever." He motioned to Brad to follow him as he left the curtained area. "Go now and make sleeping arrangements for yourself and the others. Rest while he is quiet and one can watch. It is the night when death and devils stalk the sick and the weak. Send for me if he is too much troubled from pain. And leave this foreigner's coat when you go out. There are many here who would be angry to see it." With these instructions, Stamatis left.

This Stamatis is a bit mad, but he's right about getting some rest, Brad thought as he watched Stamatis limp slowly down the ward. The town they had found themselves in was on the rail line, but it had little to offer visitors. Brad managed to find two adjoining rooms with a bath in a small hotel near the hospital. The rooms were shabby and the toilet leaked, but at least there was a shower. He was sorry the accommodations were so poor, but it was all part of the life they led. They didn't always work in the best places.

Brad went back to the hospital and worked out a schedule for staying with Kon. Although Geilla looked pale and tired, she would not leave, and it was finally decided that Paul would stay with her, and that Jack would relieve them in four hours. Brad sent Jack and Peterson to the hotel to get some sleep. It had been a long hard night for Brad and he felt tired, but he had to finish closing out the rescue mission before he could rest. He must also see about returning the truck to the orderly, getting Peterson returned to the States, and notifying Carl that the mission was complete though Kon was down.

Carl was group chief in London. It was Carl who originated the mission plans and provided tactical support. He worked through Brad and had never met the other team members. He wanted to keep it that way. He knew how hard Brad took it when any of his team were captured or hurt. However impersonal he kept the relationship, Carl supported the team, even to the point of jeopardizing his career, and his anonymity. Brad had to let Carl know their situation. The sudden change of plans had left them with no equipment, little money, and the wrong papers for who they were supposed to be. At the moment, Brad wasn't sure just who they were supposed to be.

CHAPTER THREE

Brad drove the truck to the address the orderly had given him. It was a warehouse near the edge of town. The six men who were hanging about in the small office became suspicious and agitated when Brad asked for Vidosevich by name. Brad was glad Stamatis had advised him to leave the guard's jacket behind. Peterson's worn suit coat didn't fit well, but it was far less conspicuous.

"What do you want with Vidosevich?" one of the surly men asked Brad.

"I come on business," Brad answered coldly.

"Vidosevich does no business with foreigners. Go away!" another man growled.

Brad stiffened. He was not as brawny as these men, but he was taller and emanated authority. "I have come to see Vidosevich and I will not leave until I see him," he answered firmly. When he heard a knife click open somewhere to his left, he reached calmly under his jacket and pulled out his gun. He turned it in his hand several times, and then looked from it to the group of men, as if selecting his first target. He was glad to have the weapon, but hoped the man with the knife was not as good with it as Kon was. Brad knew that Kon favored a knife for "close work" as he called it, but Kon also carried a gun for "group encounters."

There was some muttering in Greek as Brad produced the gun, but the men held their ground. They were staring at Brad when the door opened and another man rushed in shouting excitedly in Greek. Brad glanced quickly at the man, and guessed that he had told the others about the truck. Brad heard whispering in the back of the room, and suddenly the man with the knife came forward, demanding angrily, "Where did you get that truck?"

Brad remained unruffled. "I came to see Vidosevich and I will answer to no one else."

"I am Vidosevich. Speak!"

Brad quickly sized up Vidosevich. He was shorter than Brad, but heavily built. He had an unyielding look about him, and it was difficult to connect him with the orderly, who had been so calm and kind.

"Do you discuss all your business in public?" Brad asked, looking around at the group.

"There are no secrets here," Vidosevich answered. It suddenly occurred to Brad that there had been some type of conference in progress when he came in.

"Very well," Brad said more evenly, "I have come with a truck that I borrowed from an orderly in Bitola last night. He said you would see that it is returned to him."

"What was his name?" Vidosevich demanded.

"I do not know," Brad said calmly. "We did not exchange names. He was a help to my friends and me."

"So it was you!" Vidosevich shouted at Brad. "And you dare to come here?"

Something is wrong here, Brad thought quickly, wondering what he had walked into. "I came to return the truck as I promised," he declared.

"You do not know that Artukovich has been arrested?"

Brad controlled his expression and did not betray his shock. "How can that be, I saw him early this morning?" he replied evenly.

There was a tense silence in the room for a moment before Vidosevich said quietly, "We have much to discuss. Be pleased to put the gun away and sit down."

Brad slipped the gun back into his belt and took the chair Vidosevich offered.

"Bring us coffee!" Vidosevich called over his shoulder, and sat across from Brad.

****

Paul and Geilla were still keeping watch with Kon when Brad returned to the hospital.

"Any change?" Brad asked as he came in.

"He has hardly moved at all," Geilla answered sadly.

"You'll wear yourself out, Geilla," Brad remarked. "There's nothing you can do right now. Please, get some rest."

"He needs me. I won't leave him," Geilla insisted. She sat as she had since morning, holding Kon's hand and watching his face.

She is the most stubborn woman I've ever met, Brad thought, pulling up one of the chairs Yiosiph had brought for the group. He had come earlier to hang a fresh unit of blood for Kon. I wonder if Kon even knows we're here, Brad thought. On impulse he reached up and touched him on the shoulder. "Kon? Can you hear me?" he said softly. "Hold on, old friend. We're behind you all the way. You've fought your way through worse than this." Kon turned his head when Brad spoke to him. It was probably just a restless movement, Brad thought, but he was glad he had said something. "There's been a new development," Brad said at last to Paul and Geilla. "When I went to return the truck, I learned that the orderly who helped us last night has been arrested."

The others looked up in surprise. "What happened?" Paul asked.

"Apparently he went to visit two friends to establish an alibi, but when that car we used was reported stolen, some people became suspicious. The police came to take him in for questioning. He tried to make a run for it and was shot in the leg. He is being held at the military hospital. They've accumulated quite a file on him, and it doesn't look good. We were not the first people he has helped to cross the border, but our visit was unusually close to the last incident. It didn't help that the car we stole belonged to some minor official. Damn! I wish he had come with us last night."

"Shit! I should have been more careful about the car," Paul said.

"It's not your fault. How could you have known?" Brad said calmly.

"Does he have any contacts here?" Paul asked.

"I met the group he works with. They know a good deal about the commandant, and the layout of the hospital. Unfortunately, they are all known to the police, and don't dare attempt a rescue." Brad paused. He looked from Paul and Geilla to Kon and back again. "I told them we would try to get the orderly out."

Geilla looked distressed, "We can't leave Kon here alone, Brad. I refuse to go!"

"I'm not asking you to go, Geilla. Your job is here with Kon, but I can't abandon the orderly. Without his help, we would never have gotten Kon to the hospital in time."

"You're right," Paul agreed. "We have to try to help him. You know Kon would go with us if he could, Geilla. He always honors his obligations."

Geilla had no answer for Paul's argument. She knew Kon would take any risk to help a friend. He would not want the burden of knowing a man was in prison on his account.

When Jack and Peterson returned from the hotel, Brad took Jack aside and told him of his decision to go back for the orderly. Jack didn't need to hear all the details. He was ready to go. Since Paul's watch with Kon was over, he prevailed upon Geilla to go with him to eat. Brad decided to join them. He had too much to do to think of resting, but he thought some food might help him stay alert.

Jack and Peterson were on duty with Kon when Yiosiph came in and started a fresh unit of blood for him. The chest tube was still showing blood draining from the lining of the lung. Jack had been thinking about the new rescue mission, and he suddenly came up with some ideas. As Kon still showed no signs of waking, Jack asked Peterson to stay with Kon for a short time while he joined Brad and the others.

Following the example of the others, Peterson sat and dutifully held Kon's hand. He could think of little to say and kept repeating, "Don't worry. Everything will be O.K.," perhaps more to himself than to Kon. It had become important to him that Kon live. He remembered Kon's bloody hand as he gave him the glasses. Perhaps if Kon had not stayed behind to find them, he might not have been shot. It's not fair, Peterson thought. One little gesture of kindness should not cost a man his life. These people are involved in a terrible business!

Jack had been gone only a few minutes when Yiosiph came in and hastily terminated the blood transfusion. He pushed the drainage bottle under the bed and hung a sheet from the edge of the mattress to conceal it. He seemed agitated and said something to Peterson in Greek, but Peterson could not make it out. Yiosiph hurried out, and Stamatis appeared immediately. "You must leave now," he told Peterson.

Peterson looked at him in confusion. Stamatis was the one that had carried on about not leaving Kon alone. "I can't leave while the others are away," he told Stamatis.

"Go! Go!" Stamatis shouted at him. "Leave him to me." Stamatis twisted the valves on the oxygen tank in the corner and set the mask over Kon's face.

Peterson hesitated. He suddenly felt apprehensive about leaving Kon alone with this mad man. Stamatis took Peterson's arm and would have shoved him out of the curtained area, but the way was suddenly blocked by two men, who wore military uniforms and helmets and carried automatic weapons. Stamatis greeted them in Greek and pushed Peterson backwards into a chair. The men answered Stamatis in Greek, looked suspiciously at Peterson and approached the bed where Kon lay. As they turned their backs Stamatis raised his hand to his lips and signaled to Peterson to be quiet.

Peterson was getting used to the routine of keeping his mouth shut, and letting others do the talking. The soldiers asked Stamatis a lot of questions, but he seemed quite unconcerned. Peterson guessed that they were investigating some complaint about people escaping across the border.

Stamatis suddenly switched the conversation into English so that Peterson could understand. He was angry that Peterson had not left when he was told to go. He sensed that Peterson was not a part of what the others were involved in, but had somehow been caught up in it.

"We have no gunshot wounds here," Stamatis insisted to the police. "This man has pneumonia. See for yourselves how badly he breathes."

Stamatis had turned the oxygen delivery to one quarter the normal pressure when he placed the mask over Kon's face. After about thirty seconds Kon had felt the lack of air and his chest was heaving strongly. He gasped and struggled to pull in the small amount of oxygen. The soldiers watched him for a moment. He was obviously suffering some type of lung trouble, but because of the mask they could not get a good look at his face.

Stamatis appeared calm, but he knew that if he didn't turn the pressure up, in a matter of minutes Kon would suffocate. Peterson was terrified by the sudden bad turn Kon had taken, and wished the others would come. If the soldiers noticed the bandages on Kon they might force all of them back across the border. The thought of returning to prison made Peterson's heart and his mind race wildly. When one of the soldiers reached for the blanket covering Kon, Peterson jumped from his chair. Almost without knowing what he was doing he shouted, "Leave the man in peace! Can't you see he's dying?"

The soldier pulled his hand back abruptly. He did not really like investigating reports of illegal crossing. He was no supporter of the repressive Yugoslavian government. Poking about among the sick and dying was not his idea of defending the peace. He exchanged a glance with his companion and they stepped away from the bed. As soon as their attention was focused on Peterson, Stamatis' hand flew to the pressure valve. He cranked it wide open, and readjusted the mask over Kon's face. Kon's chest continued to heave, but at last he was getting results.

"What is your connection with this man?" the soldiers asked Peterson.

He stared at them then at Kon. What indeed, he thought. I can't claim a Greek as a relative and I can't even imagine I could have such a man for a friend. He wondered what Stamatis had said about Kon and why he was there. It would go badly if he said anything to contradict Stamatis' story. After a long pause he stammered, "He works for me."

"What work does he do?"

Peterson hesitated. "I'm sorry. I . . . I don't hear very well," he stalled, hoping to think of some reasonable answer. Stamatis was gesturing wildly with his hands. What is he doing? Peterson thought. He looks like a kid playing with a steering wheel. Suddenly it came to him. "He's my driver," he said aloud.

The soldiers seemed to accept his answer.

"What is your name?"

"Peterson," he said without thinking. Then it hit him. Damn, I should have lied! I'm no good at this game.

"What are you doing in Greece?" the soldiers questioned.

What could he say, he thought. What was it the others had made him out to be? A bookkeeper. No . . . what reason would a bookkeeper have for travelling about. The soldiers repeated the question impatiently.

Peterson glanced down, trying to think of something plausible. Well, he was wearing a suit, although on old one. "I'm a professor . . . from an American university," he began cautiously. "I'm here to study . . . your . . . your rock formations," he stammered, picking the one subject other than nuclear physics that he knew anything about.

The soldiers seemed satisfied for a moment, then began anew. "Let's see your papers!"

Peterson did not respond until they repeated the question.

"I'm sorry," he apologized nervously, "I don't hear very well."

"Your papers! Your papers!" the soldier shouted.

Peterson was almost trembling with fear. Each question was like some horrible riddle, and he was digging himself in deeper and deeper with his lies. "I don't have any," he said at last.

Stamatis was gesturing again. He had his pockets turned inside out and was holding them out from his sides. Peterson had never been good at charades, but he took a wild guess.

"They were stolen," he blurted out. Stamatis nodded.

"Who stole them?" the soldiers asked immediately.

Peterson felt he was in over his head, but there was no turning back. He rambled on, hardly knowing what he was saying.

"Some men stopped us on the road. They took everything — our papers, our money, even our car," he added for good measure. Stamatis nodded again.

"How many men and what did they look like?" shot back at him.

"There were four of them," he lied. "I didn't see them very well . . . one man knocked my glasses off."

The questions went on and on, and Peterson turned white. He was aware that he was shaking and thought he should offer some excuse. "I'm sorry," he said, "I must have a touch of the fever myself."

At that Stamatis came around the bed and pushed him into a chair. "You are right. You are not well," he exclaimed. "Make an end to your questions!" he growled at the soldiers.

The soldiers would not be put off, however. "Where did this robbery take place?" they demanded.

Peterson had run out of ideas, and stared at them mutely until Stamatis cut in to save him.

"Their car was stolen several kilometers south of town. He and the other man came in late last night. They were both exhausted from walking and that one collapsed," Stamatis said gesturing toward the bed.

"How did he get this strange pneumonia?" one soldier prodded Peterson.

Peterson could think of no answer for a moment, but then he recalled how cold he had been while hiding behind the buildings in Bitola. "It was very cold last night," he mumbled. "He was coughing when we began our journey. I . . . I thought it was from cigarettes. He's a heavy smoker."

The soldiers conferred together for a moment. "You must come with us and fill out a report for this robbery."

Peterson thought he would faint from fright. He could not go on with these lies any longer. His heart was pounding and he was sweating. Stamatis saved him again.

"Yes, yes, he will come," he told the soldiers, "but he must rest now. See how feverish he looks. He must have caught it from the other one."

When the soldiers stood firm Stamatis added a warning. "It would not be wise to expose yourselves to him for too long. We do not know exactly what this fever is that comes on so quickly."

The soldiers nodded and glanced again at Kon. "See that he comes to report when the fever is gone," one man growled and they left.

Peterson put his hands over his face and leaned forward in his chair. "I think I'm going to be sick."

"No! No! You did a fine job, my friend. A fine job!" Stamatis said warmly and put his huge arm around Peterson's thin shoulders.

Yiosiph and Jack stepped from the next curtained area. Yiosiph had caught Jack when he returned and they had heard everything.

"Yiosiph, bring brandy!" Stamatis called as they came around the curtain.

Brad came in a short time later and was not surprised to learn about the police investigation. He was impressed when Jack related how well Peterson had handled himself under questioning. So this skinny scientist has guts after all, Brad thought to himself. He turned to Peterson. "We have learned that the orderly who helped us last night has been arrested. We must go back to bring him out."

Peterson froze at the mention of going across the border again, and Brad put his hand on Peterson's shoulder.

"Please understand, I am not asking you to go with us," he said reassuringly. "Would you be willing to stay here with Geilla and keep an eye on Kon?"

Peterson thought for a moment, weighing his fears against his obligations. "I'll stay. I owe him that much," he said at last.

"Thank you," Brad responded warmly. "I must go make some calls to arrange for equipment. The orderly is being held at the military hospital so we must see what we can exchange for him. I will also notify your channels that you are free and in safe hands."

Shortly after Brad left, Geilla returned and took up her position by Kon's bed. When Paul came in, he tried to persuade her to get some rest, but she would not listen. He finally gave up and went to the hotel alone.

In a call to Carl, Brad explained the team's situation. Carl was not pleased to hear that Kon was down, but agreed with Brad that carting him off to London might do more harm than good. Carl promised support for bringing the orderly out. He would see that the team had equipment and would set up the necessary contacts on the continent. Their belongings would be sent immediately from Athens, where they had started, and a courier would deliver their paperwork by the following morning. In addition, Carl gave Brad the names of several contacts in Greece who would help coordinate arrangements locally. Before hanging up, Carl wished Brad luck in the rescue attempt and offered medical help for Kon if it later became necessary. Brad felt that his preparations for the rescue were in motion. He knew that Carl was completely reliable in supporting his operatives.

Brad made two calls in regard to Peterson and then put in a call to Mary, his wife. Although Mary never spoke about her concern for Brad, or tried to persuade him from going on assignments, he knew she would wonder about his delayed return. Mary shared all the aspects of Brad's special work, and he in turn tried to keep her posted on his whereabouts. That was how their marriage worked. Brad had tried not to marry, because his work was so hazardous, but Mary had persuaded him with her arguments.

"My darling," she had told him, "I love you and want to share your life completely. If you are captured or killed it will hurt me just as deeply if we are not married as if we were. Besides," she added in her practical, matter-of-fact manner, "if we are not legally married I will never be able to claim your body from those dreadful countries where you insist upon working."

The thought of Mary fretting over the rights to his dead body had made Brad laugh, and he gave in to her wish. He had never regretted his decision. Mary was Brad's anchor. She listened to his plans, rejoiced at his triumphs and shared his sorrow when things went wrong. Unlike Carl, she knew the members of the team personally, and welcomed them to the country home she maintained for Brad. She knew about Geilla's hopeless love for Kon and suspected her relationship with Paul. Although only a few years older than Geilla, she loved her like the daughter she was never allowed to have. Brad had agreed to marriage, but had stipulated that there must be no children to be left fatherless. Mary had kept the bargain, but she still hoped he would change his mind one day.

"Hello, my darling. What are your plans?" Mary said calmly when she got the call from Brad.

"The hiking was good, darling, but we had some rather bad luck," Brad answered after a slight hesitation.

"Are you all right, Brad?" she asked quickly.

"Yes, but our banker friend fell and is not doing very well. We have settled in at Florina." He paused. "Listen, darling, some of our group have business to settle about the trip. It's all rather complicated, but we'll be delayed a few days."

"I see," Mary responded. "How is everyone holding up?"

"Very bravely so far, but . . . could you possibly see your way clear to join us?"

"Certainly, darling. I will be there tomorrow. Is Florina on the rail line, Brad?"

"Yes, but it's a long haul from Athens."

"Very well, darling, leave the details to me," she added casually. "Will you be leaving before I arrive?"

"No, we need to get some things together and won't leave for 48 hours."

"Splendid," Mary added cheerfully. "I'll be able to see you off. Take care, Brad, and give my love to the others."

Mary hung up the phone and wrote out one of her many lists. Being married to Brad meant always being ready to go flying off somewhere at a moment's notice. She called the airport, packed a single bag, left word with a friend to cancel her appointments, gathered up her passport, and left.

Brad returned to the hotel after finishing his calls. Being careful not to disturb Paul, who was still resting, he removed his jacket and sank onto one of the beds. Once he was still, the strain of the long night came home to him, and extreme weariness crept over him. He closed his eyes, thinking only to rest, but in what seemed like a moment he heard Paul's voice. "Brad? Are you coming with me to relieve Jack and Peterson?"

Brad opened his eyes. He had not taken a turn with Kon all day. He must go now. "Right oh, Paul. Just give me a minute."

He forced himself off the bed and into the bathroom. As he splashed cold water over his face he caught a glimpse of himself in the mirror. You need a shave, old boy. You're starting to look as grubby as Stamatis, he thought. "Let's go," he said as he rejoined Paul.

Geilla was at her post when they came in. She turned her head in their direction, but did not speak. She looked exhausted.

"Geilla, please take some rest," Paul pleaded.

"No . . . I'm fine really. I can't leave him, Paul. I just can't," she answered faintly.

Paul placed his hands on her shoulders. He could feel her tension and fatigue through her blouse. Slowly he massaged her, moving his hands up her neck, then down her back. He kneaded her muscles firmly and deeply. She quivered slightly as he worked, but did not move to stop him. Only her iron determination kept her from falling asleep beneath his hands.

Neither Jack nor Brad took particular notice of Paul's action. Paul had a special gift for massage and they had all had occasion to be grateful for his skill. Brad wished that Geilla would yield to Paul's pleas and take some rest.

"I've asked Mary to come," he told Geilla and the others. "She

41

will be here tomorrow."

"Thank you, Brad," Geilla whispered.

Shortly after Jack and Peterson left, Kon stirred. He moaned softly once and turned his head. Brad went to the side of the bed.

"Kon, can you hear me?" he asked softly.

Kon's breath became irregular and he opened his eyes. He looked in Brad's direction, but Brad was not sure Kon really saw him until he whispered, "Brad?"

"Yes, Kon. I'm here," Brad answered. He took hold of Kon's hand.

"Brad?" Kon gasped again.

Brad felt encouraged. "How are you feeling, Kon?" he asked and smiled.

Kon drew in several short breaths before he spoke again. "Rotten, Brad," he gasped, "really rotten." He struggled to lift himself, but he grimaced and fell backwards.

The anesthetic must have worn off, Brad thought. "Get Stamatis up here!" he said over his shoulder to Paul, who was directly behind him.

Kon gripped Brad's hand and stiffened. "Brad, open the window, please. It's so hot in here, Brad . . . please, I can't breathe . . . very well," he panted.

"Hang on, Kon. We'll get you something for the pain. Can you hear me, Kon?" Brad raised his voice, but kept it calm.

"Yes," Kon gasped. "Please, Brad . . . open the window. Please . . ." His voice trailed off, but Brad could tell he was awake and hurting by the way he gripped his hand. He was trembling all over by the time Stamatis arrived a few minutes later. Brad was grateful for the speed with which Stamatis produced a syringe and plunged the needle into Kon's arm. Seconds later Stamatis took hold of Kon's shoulders. "The pain goes very soon," he said softly. Reaching for the oxygen mask, he opened the valve and lowered it over Kon's face. Kon drew in a few deep breaths and slowly relaxed his grip on Brad's arm.

"Kon, can you hear me?" Brad asked after several minutes. There was no response.

Stamatis removed the mask. "He will be quiet now . . . a little while." He checked the dressing over the incision, put a stethoscope to Kon's chest in several places and concluded sadly, "The fever comes yet."

Kon had not seemed to notice Geilla who still held his hand tightly in hers. She put her hand on his forehead now and felt how warm he was. "No wonder he wanted the window open, Brad. He's burning up!"

Stamatis gave her a damp towel to hold to Kon's face and instructed her to wipe his neck and arms occasionally. Paul, Geilla, and Brad waited and watched with Kon, but it was almost two hours before he stirred again. He became very restless and rolled from side to side. He called out to one of them from time to time, but would not be comforted when they tried to quiet him. As his delirium grew worse, he talked of many things, but none of them knew what he made reference to. Stamatis came to check on him, but declared he was not suffering pain, only fever. He would not drug him any more for fear of suppressing his breathing response which was already very weak.

Kon felt the fever not only in his body, but in his mind. As he struggled to breathe he remembered again the great weight of Zoel's body pressing him against the floor of the theater. He could almost feel Zoel's hands around his throat. Geilla's screams and Zoel's curses echoed in his ears and his mind swam with visions.

He recalled scenes from the trip north with Mario and Tina, and the other families from the theater. They had carried his limp body from the floor and lain him in one of their trucks. Mario and Tina knew Kon well and liked him. When Mario had discovered that Kon slept in the alley, he had insisted that Zoel find a place for him in the theater. It was Mario and Tina who bought Kon books, and sat with him by the kitchen table in their tiny apartment, patiently teaching him Italian and French grammar. Mario tried to enroll Kon in school by posing as his uncle, but since Kon had no identification, he was not accepted. Tina saw to it that Kon had one decent meal a day after he spent his meager salary on espresso and ices. Kon repaid the couple's kindness by minding their two small children while they went to rehearsals.

Mario and Tina knew how Zoel's mind had deteriorated and feared it would not be safe for Kon to stay at the theater. They had witnessed the ugly change in Zoel, and had been preparing to leave for some time. Watching Zoel attempt to strangle Kon had shocked them and crystallized their resolve to leave. It sickened them to think Zoel could be so brutal to Kon, who had been such a help to him.

Kon lay in Mario's truck all night without moving. Mario and Tina worried about his neck, but did not send for a doctor for fear the police would come and make trouble for everyone. Someone gathered a few of Kon's belongings and packed them in an old pressed cardboard suitcase they found abandoned in one of the dressing rooms, and long before dawn the caravan of four trucks was on the road north.

When Kon regained consciousness he could barely move without feeling pain in his back and shoulders and the right side of his face was badly swollen. The worst torment, however, was that his neck and throat had been so badly mauled he could not speak or swallow. He tried to protest when he realized that he was being taken away from Geilla, but Mario explained over and over that it would not be safe for him to remain near Zoel. Mario did not know about the single kiss shared by Geilla and Kon and therefore could not explain Zoel's irrational attack. He knew only that Zoel had become obsessively protective of Geilla. Although Mario did not say it to Kon, he guessed that Zoel was hoping for a richer, more cultured suitor for his only daughter.

The families travelled north for two days on their way to Switzerland to join another orchestra. They wanted to take Kon with them, but as he was not Italian, he would have to be smuggled across the border. If he was discovered, they would all be sent back. They determined that the best they could do for Kon was to find him a job in Milan.

Kon still could not speak when the group arrived in Milan, and his neck was discolored by a multitude of dark bruises. The women had applied various poultices to the bruises on his back and had reduced the swelling on his face with some strong smelling salve. They sat with him by the hour, coaxing him like a child, to get him to swallow even the tiniest sip of some bitter tasting herb tea. He tried for their sake, and held it in his mouth, but warm or cold, it was agony to swallow anything. They tried to put a salve on his throat, but when he winced and pulled away from the gentlest touch they gave up. They knew also that Zoel had hurt Kon in ways no salve or herb could heal.

The families waited one day in the city with Kon, hoping he would improve; but they were anxious to make their rendezvous at the other theater, and secure a contract. The following morning Kon was dressed in a clean shirt and his one suit. One of the women cut a piece from her only silk shawl and tied it around his neck like a cravat to hide the marks. The two oldest men went with him to speak for him and to bargain. It is not an easy thing to find a position for a young man with little schooling who cannot speak for himself, and Kon could not muster any enthusiasm for the project to make it easier for them.

They took him first to several theaters. He felt humiliated to be paraded before various employers to be poked and displayed like an animal at an auction, but he did his best not to wince when they asked him to lift boxes to demonstrate his strong back.

"Alas, he has laryngitis at the moment and cannot speak, but he knows French, Italian, a bit of English, and even Greek," they bragged for him. Unfortunately, Kon could only nod when he was questioned in the various languages, and in the end, the managers said they had no use for a man who could not speak.

After many rejections, they decided to take him to the hotels. There were more questions, more lies, and more parading before men with pitiless eyes. At length, the men got down to the noisy bargaining. Kon was taken out the door, and brought back again several times. Different people came in to see him and ask questions. Finally they brought glasses and opened the wine. As the "merchandise," Kon was not offered a drink. He thought he saw money passed to the man from the hotel, but he was not sure.

At last the deal was concluded and Kon signed the contract. He knew his friends had told their best lies on his behalf. He was led to the cellar where he would be allowed to sleep, without charge, and they brought his few clothes. The women had wanted to hold back the knife they had found in Kon's pocket, but the men thought it would be unforgivable to take anything more from him.

The men shook his hand very formally, but avoided his deep, dark eyes. The expression in them disturbed their hearts. The men assured him that the job was just temporary. Soon he would speak again and would find a better place. He was young, things would get better. They left him sitting on a cot in despair.

The men returned to the truck in bad spirits. "The bargaining did not go well," they told the women. "These greedy Northerners think only of money! They have no hearts!"

Kon's lack of speech had been taken as a sign that he was mentally defective, and the wages his friends had to accept for him were shamefully low. Worse yet, they had been required to post a cash deposit in case Kon broke or stole anything. The men wished they had been able to wait until Kon was well before they placed him, but they had their own children to feed and must find work soon.

CHAPTER FOUR

"Don't leave me here!" Kon called aloud in Italian. "Mario! Please! Don't leave me here!" Kon thrashed violently and tried to sit up. He fell back when he felt the pain in his chest, but moments later he tried again. He kept calling, "Don't leave me here," with haunting desperation. Geilla put her hand on his forehead and tried to soothe him. "We won't leave you, Kon," she answered in Italian. "Be still and rest. We won't leave you."

It did no good. Kon wrenched his hand from Geilla's, raised himself on one elbow, and immediately started to cough. Realizing that coughing caused him a lot of pain, Geilla redoubled her efforts to calm him.

"Who is Mario?" Jack asked as he came in for his watch.

"It could be Mario Visante," Geilla answered. "They met at the theater years ago, and I know they stay in touch."

Jack took hold of Kon's shoulders and forced him backwards against the bed. "Hey buddy — nobody's going to leave you here," he said softly. "You're with friends now — just take it easy. O.K.?"

Kon began to struggle against Jack.

"Hold his legs, Paul!" Jack called. "God, there's still a lot of fight left in him!"

"Geilla, you'd better get Stamatis," Brad called after a few minutes. By the time Stamatis arrived Jack had pinned Kon's arms and was holding him flat against the bed, while Paul and Brad tried to keep him from turning and kicking. Kon was panting for breath.

"Do something, doc! I don't want to hurt him," Jack pleaded. "The poor bastard doesn't even know it's me he's fighting."

Stamatis studied Kon for a moment then wedged himself between Jack and the bed. He brought out a small bottle and a syringe and injected a sedative into Kon's arm. Then he stepped into the next curtained area and returned with several pillows. "Enough, enough — let him up now," he ordered.

Paul and Jack held on to Kon a moment longer hoping the shot would take effect and quiet him.

"Release him — he won't give in," Stamatis shouted at Jack. Jack let go and stepped back. Immediately Stamatis took hold of Kon's left hand and bending the arm across Kon's chest he held the palm to Kon's right shoulder. An instant later he rolled Kon onto his right side, propping him against the pillows.

"Hush, hush — be quiet now, Kon. No more, no more," he repeated softly. Still holding Kon by the shoulder, Stamatis ran his hand skillfully across Kon's shoulders and down his back, gently massaging him and urging him to relax. Kon moaned faintly, but quit fighting. Stamatis pulled Kon's knees part way towards Kon's chest and continued rubbing his back until he was breathing more normally. Stamatis looked around at the others who were impressed by how quickly he had quieted Kon.

"A man feels too helpless pinned on his back. Sometimes you must let him up," he said to no one in particular. Carefully he arranged the covers over Kon and shook his head sadly. "When a man is conscious he is unafraid, but when he is like this . . . he is like the wild sparrow. He must not be confined. He frightens easily and will dash himself against the cage of his own bad dreams." He put his hand on Kon's forehead. "This one has too many bad dreams, eh?" He looked directly at Geilla, "Get some rest. You must be strong to help him," he said and left the room.

"You heard what the doctor ordered, Geilla," Brad said. "Please, take a break and . . ."

"Leave me alone, all of you," she said a bit too loudly. "I'm O.K.! I'm O.K.! I have to stay."

Paul went to her and put his hands on her shoulders. "Christ, Geilla, you're tougher to tame than Kon." He kissed her lightly on the forehead.

"Leave me alone, Paul!" she said frostily and pulled away. "I'm not tired. Go to bed if you want. Just leave me alone!"

"O.K.! O.K.! At least sit down over here." He led her back to the chair beside the bed. "Come on – relax a little bit." He massaged her shoulders briefly. "Kon's going to be O.K. I'll be back in a couple of hours," he said and left the room.

****

Two weeks passed before Kon was able to speak well again. By then he had learned that "Yes, sir" and "No, sir," was all that was required of him. He had also learned that life was going to be lonely for him in this new place. It became apparent that since he could not speak, the other young men he worked with took him for a half-wit. He endured their jeering and shoving calmly enough, but one day while he was eating, one of them took some bread from the plate in front of him. When a second boy tried the same trick, Kon's knife appeared instantly. He held the vicious looking thing defensively across his plate and glared at the boys with fire in his dark eyes.

They drew back and three of them went running to the cook demanding that Kon be ousted. The cook, who believed it bad luck to ill treat a half-wit, came over to the table, saw Kon hunched over his plate and instantly sized up the situation.

"Get out! Get out!" he yelled at the boys. "You taunt him to

47

madness! If you dare to take the food from his mouth again I will wave a knife at you myself!" he threatened, raising his long meat knife and slashing the air with it. The boys ran and he called after them. "Get back to work! You'll call the wrath of God on you by the way you treat a half-wit."

The cook went up to Kon and growled, "Put that knife away, boy. We don't tolerate that kind of thing here."

Kon glared at him a long moment before he silently folded his knife and put it in his pocket.

The cook put his large hand on Kon's shoulder. "You'll make much trouble for yourself if you show that thing again," he said more gently and turned away.

Kon knew he would now have his share of food, but he would eat alone. His action had set him against the only group he could hope to belong to. Without allies he would be totally isolated and defenseless. I must survive, he thought to himself. No matter what they think of me, I must survive. None of them are to be trusted.

And so Kon learned to clear the tables in the dining room, wash dishes, and carry luggage to and from the rooms. He noticed that all the young men would compete for the last job, because it sometimes was rewarded by tips. He did not leave his other duties to scramble for porter duty, but as he learned his way around the hotel and around the city, he was often sent to help with bags because he understood several languages and could answer questions more intelligently than most of the boys. Often he was sent to run errands because he never tried to cheat anyone for extra money. Gradually he learned where almost anything could be purchased in Milan, legally or on the black market.

Kon wrote to Geilla only once, to beg her forgiveness for kissing her and making Zoel so angry. It was a rather formal letter as there was so much he did not want to tell her. He was very lonely and received so little money that even though he let his clothes go to rags, he was often hungry. Although he was surrounded by food, he was allowed to eat only the leftovers and even those had to be shared with the other young men. All of them had family or friends who fed them and provided a place for them to sleep.

When Geilla wrote begging him to visit, he did not answer. He was ashamed to admit he could not afford even bus fare for the trip. There were hoards of unskilled young men in Milan, and he feared he would lose his place if he was absent for any reason. Mario wrote to Kon, and despite his own difficulties in supporting his two children and one on the way, he enclosed a small amount of money. Kon was so happy to have the address of his friends, he answered immediately. He thanked Mario for the money, and told him that he could speak once more. Mario and Tina were much relieved to learn that Kon's voice had returned. He had been so badly mauled, they had feared he would never be right.

Kon was not aware that there was no official record showing that he worked for the hotel. When his contract ran out after six months, he asked for more money. After much shouting and threatening, the manager gave in to Kon's argument that he could not live on his poor wage and would leave if he could not get more money. There was no contract for the new arrangement.

One day as Kon was loading luggage into the car of a Swiss family, who had been staying at the hotel, he heard the loud honking of a bus horn. Thinking a tour bus was arriving he came around the car. To his dismay he saw a small child dash from the door of the hotel into the street. The bus driver tried to brake, but he was going much too fast. Kon ran into the street, grabbed the child and jumped away with it just as the bus came crashing past. The bus came so close to them that the side mirror struck Kon on the back and knocked him to the pavement.

The child's parents had seen their child run into the street, but in their terror had not seen Kon dive after him. The mother ran to the curb just as the bus passed and would have been killed if her husband had not caught her arm. She screamed hysterically. After the bus passed, the child's father heard him cry, and expecting to find him crushed and mangled, he rushed into the street. Kon had pulled himself to his knees by the time the father came up. The man grabbed the child in his arms and cried for joy.

The street suddenly filled with people shouting and pointing. Someone from the crowd took Kon by the arm and pulled him to his feet. He felt dizzy and staggered a few steps towards the hotel, but the child's father stopped him.

"Are you hurt?" he asked in French. "You saved my son's life! I am very grateful."

"I am not hurt, sir," Kon answered in French. "Please sir, I must return to the bags." Kon turned away, but the man stopped him again. He took Kon by the arm and pushed him toward the curb.

"Please, you must meet my wife," he said excitedly as a woman came running toward them.

"Charlotte, this young man saved Charles' life!"

The woman took the child, who was about three years old, from the father, and hugged him to her breast murmuring, "My baby! Oh my precious baby!" After a moment, she smiled joyfully and offered her hand to Kon. "How can I ever thank you enough? I thought Charles was lost to me. You are a brave man to run in front of a bus."

Kon was still dazed and felt embarrassed by their attention. He ignored Charlotte's hand and bowed rather stiffly, self-consciously imitating the waiters at the hotel. He wanted only to return to his job before he was missed, but the child's father held him by the arm.

49

"Are you sure you are not hurt?" the man inquired again.

"I am well, sir . . . truly."

"Please, spend a moment with us," Charlotte asked. "This has been a terrible shock for us."

Her concern seemed so sincere that Kon stopped resisting and let himself be led to the chairs by the hotel cafe. The man made him sit by them. "Please, sir, it is not permitted to sit with the customers," Kon said with embarrassment. "I must leave or I will lose my . . ."

Just then the manager of the hotel, who had heard the story of the near accident and daring rescue, came out of the hotel. Seeking to capitalize on Kon's bravery and mollify the parents lest they blame the hotel in any way, he rushed up to them. Kon stood so abruptly he knocked over his chair. The manager seized him by the shoulder, "Sit . . . sit," he said expansively and smiled at all of them. "So you have met our brave employee. He is a fine young man . . . been with us for a long time."

The manager bowed smoothly to the parents. "I am Guido Barazini, the hotel manager. Let me offer you and your beautiful wife some wine to settle your nerves."

Without waiting for an answer, he called a waiter and ordered wine. "And a shot of brandy for our hero," he added slapping Kon on the back.

Kon was silent while the manager sat and talked glibly to the couple. The manager told such fantastic lies, Kon was fascinated until he realized the lies were about himself. He was humiliated and wanted to silence the manager, but he dared not speak. It was true that Mario had told a few tales on his behalf, but one friend has the right to brag about another to help him along. This man carried matters too far. At length the manager stood, bowed again and left.

The child's father turned to Kon, "You seem to be well thought of here, young man. Exactly what is your position?"

Kon did not hesitate. "I am sorry, sir, he spoke only lies. I work in the kitchen and carry the luggage, that is all. I have not been here one year yet. I swear he knows little of me and could not give my name if you asked him."

The man did not seem surprised. He looked straight at Kon noting his ragged clothes and rough hands. He liked Kon's rash truthfulness. "I can see he is no friend of yours, young man, but his lies were truly magnifique were they not?" he replied.

Kon looked him full in the face for a moment and then laughed. "Thank you, sir — perhaps his way with the truth has made him manager while I carry luggage."

"Nay, nay. No one likes a liar. He will fall, mark my words."

"And what is your name?" Charlotte asked pleasantly as she played with the child in her lap.

"I am known as Kon, Madame," he answered politely.

"Only Kon?"

He nodded.

"Where are you from, Kon?" the man asked.

"I came here from Naples. I worked in the theater there," Kon answered with just a touch of pride.

"What brought you here, Kon?"

Kon hesitated before answering, then said slowly, "I was hurt . . . in an accident. When I . . . when I lost my place in the theater, some friends brought me here." He fell silent.

Charlotte was suddenly seized by one of her "strange ideas" as her husband called them. She was a headstrong woman much given to moods and whims.

"Edgar," she said eagerly, "Could we not find a place for Kon with us? He could help the cook, and help with the boys, and perhaps we could train him to drive the car. Can you drive, Kon?" she asked eagerly.

"Yes, Madam, I often drove the trucks for the theater."

Charlotte warmed to her idea. "Oh, Edgar, we could use some extra help. He speaks Italian. That would be so helpful on our trips."

Edgar was dubious about the project. He had suffered through too many of Charlotte's whims over the years not to realize they often turned out badly. Charlotte had a mania for collecting things from paintings to antique furniture on their trips, and although Edgar was a kind, indulgent husband, he believed that collecting strange young men off the street was not to be encouraged. He did not wish to argue with his wife in public, but he had to put a damper on her idea as soon as possible.

"We can always use extra help, my dear," he told her gently, "but perhaps Kon likes it here and doesn't want to go running off to a strange country with us."

Kon caught the meaning of Edgar's words better than Charlotte, who did not want to be refused. She ignored Edgar's hints.

"Wouldn't you like to come to Geneva with us, and learn to be our driver?" Charlotte asked, already imagining projects for Kon to tackle.

The idea was too tempting to turn down, even to let Edgar off the hook, but Kon knew it was impossible. He looked over his shoulder before answering. "I would do anything to get away from this hotel, Madame, but it is quite impossible for me to leave."

Charlotte suddenly became more set than ever on her idea and even Edgar wondered about Kon's curious reply. "Why can't you leave, Kon?" Even as he asked the question, Edgar knew he had overstepped the bounds of politeness. Kon lowered his eyes and all the color left his face. Edgar felt very awkward. "You don't have to tell us, Kon. It is none of our business, really."

Kon did not look up. He took a breath as if to speak then held

51

back. At last he began, "You have been very kind, but . . ." he leaned across the table and continued almost in a whisper, "I am ashamed to say it, but I am not a citizen here. I have no papers, no identification, nothing. I came from Greece. I ran away very young. It is impossible to leave now, or I would have gone with my friends." His voice was full of sadness and guilt.

Edgar could not help feeling a touch of sympathy as he listened to Kon's explanation. He travelled a great deal for business and pleasure and viewed the freedom to come and go as his absolute right. After a pause he remarked, "Perhaps something could be done to get you a Greek passport."

Kon gave him a mournful look, "I have no contacts in Greece. I really do not know about these things. I never thought about it until my friends left me here," he confessed.

"Surely you can do something, Edgar," Charlotte put in. Although Edgar did not want to encourage Charlotte in her strange ideas, he was a kind man and did not like the idea of anyone being trapped by legal formalities. He had always had the wealth and power to circumvent these annoying difficulties. After all, Kon had saved his son's life at the risk of his own. Perhaps he could make some inquires, arrange a passport, and the boy could be on his way to join his friends. It shouldn't take too much effort, he thought. As he considered the necessary steps, Edgar warmed to the idea. He could do a favor for Kon, play the role of benefactor in Charlotte's eyes, and not have to take this rough looking young man into his home.

"Kon," he said at last, "I want you to give me your full name, birth date and place of birth. I may be able to help you."

Kon sat upright in his chair and responded eagerly, "Do you honestly think there is a chance I might be made legal, sir?"

"I won't promise, Kon, but we will see what can be done."

Edgar took out pen and paper and took down all that Kon could tell him. His face clouded momentarily when Kon admitted he did not know his exact date of birth. Surely it will be on record in his home village, he thought. As the last questions were asked, the child who had been so patient began to fuss, and the parents knew they must go. After Kon finished loading the luggage into their car, they shook hands all around and Edgar drove away.

Kon heard nothing from the family for two months. Then a letter arrived, informing him that a search had been made, but no birth record could be found in his village. Without some proof of his existence it was impossible to obtain a Greek passport. Edgar expressed his regret that he had been unable to help, and offered the suggestion that if Kon had some proof of how long he had been in Italy, he might be able to obtain Italian citizenship. Kon saved Edgar's letter carefully and wrote to Mario for advice.

Mario was quick to answer. Yes, he remembered when Kon had

come to the theater and he would write a letter or sign any forms Kon needed. He also enclosed an address for Geilla and mentioned that things were not going well for her and Zoel. Geilla had not written to Kon for months. She knew that he was being overworked and poorly paid, and she did not want to reveal her own troubles. She was very happy to receive his letter requesting her help to become a citizen. She answered immediately that she would be glad to help him, but he must come in person.

The pieces were fitting in place. Kon went to the hotel manager to tell him of his desire to become a citizen and get his statement that he was presently employed. The manager knew immediately what Kon had in mind. It was a common thing for the boys to go across the border to work. And why not? In Switzerland they could earn much more than the paltry wages he paid. He had not guessed that Kon was not a citizen, but he determined to make the most of the situation.

The manager told Kon he would sign the forms and even offered to arrange for the paperwork himself. He gave Kon permission to take a few days off, without pay, of course, to visit Geilla and Zoel and get their statements. Kon boarded the bus south, happily thinking that things were about to improve for him.

Geilla met Kon when he got off the bus two days later. He was so happy to see her he lifted her off the ground and swung her around and around calling, "Geilla! Geilla! My sweet little Geilla!" She laughed all the while never minding the stares of the people walking by. She had never seen Kon look so happy, or so handsome. He was full of excitement about becoming a citizen, and going to Zurich to work in the theater with Mario. Geilla wondered how she could ever have thought Kon's eyes were anything but fascinating dark pools that sparkled and flickered with life. He looked thinner, but he was as strong as ever. As for Kon, he thought Geilla even more beautiful than he had remembered. She looks thinner, almost frail, he thought. She needed protection. He must get her back in the theater.

When Kon had calmed down Geilla told him briefly about the changes the past year had brought to her life. Zoel had continued to drink and to fight with the performers. After Mario and his family left the others followed quickly. Zoel had lost his job as manager of the theater, and she was now working in a textile mill to support herself and Zoel whose health was gone. She had arranged for Zoel to sign his statement about Kon in front of two witnesses and gave the papers to Kon. To her amazement Kon insisted on seeing Zoel to make peace with him. Geilla was doubtful that any good could come from the meeting, but Kon wanted it so badly she could not refuse him.

Together they walked from the bus stop to the tiny flat where she and Zoel were living. Kon had never thought much about money while he had been working at the theater. There had always been enough to eat, he had slept in a regular bed, and had money for clothes. He had spent many happy hours with people from all over Europe discussing music, or playing and watching soccer games. Life had seemed so perfect then, he had never desired anything more. He had always known poverty, but after a year of working at a luxury hotel, he had become aware of the wealth that others possessed. When he entered the small flat, he knew at once how hard the past year had been for Geilla, for she and Alonzo had once lived in a fine house. He felt guilty that he had not been able to help her.

Zoel lay on the bed that Geilla had placed by the window so that be could watch the activity in the street below. He rarely went out anymore. Kon was shocked to see how gray and weak Zoel had become. He had been a strong, robust man only a year ago. As Kon looked down at him, he could hardly believe that this pathetic old man was the same one that had beaten him so badly. Truly the past year has not been good to any of us, Kon thought sadly. Things will get better, but first I must have Zoel's forgiveness so we can all be together again.

"Papa, someone's come to see you," Geilla said and shook Zoel gently by the shoulder. Zoel opened his eyes, but did not get up.

"Who is here, Geilla?"

"Papa, it's Kon. He's come back to us."

Zoel started at the mention of Kon. "Nay, nay, Kon is dead! I killed him long ago."

"No, Papa," Geilla said softly, "you did not kill him. He is here now." She helped Zoel to sit up.

Kon moved one of the straight chairs near the bed and sat down. "You did not kill me, Zoel," he said, and held out his hand. "Please . . . I would like us to be friends again."

Zoel stared at Kon for a long time. "So it is really you then, Kon?"

"Yes, Zoel, it's really me," Kon answered and smiled.

Zoel stared at him again and looked confused. "So if you are not dead, why did you go away and leave us? We needed you Kon. I treated you like a son and you left us."

Kon was not prepared for this illogical question and had no answer. Did Zoel really not remember what had happened? He could only sit and look at the old man.

When he received no answer Zoel continued again raising his voice. "Why do you come here? You are a worthless boy. I took you in and treated you well, and then you left us."

"Hush, Papa. Don't say such things," Geilla said, trying to calm her father. "Kon didn't want to leave us. He . . . he just had to go away for a while."

Kon was suddenly sorry he had come. He had hoped to make peace with Zoel, but he was getting nowhere. It troubled him that Geilla was forced to deal with Zoel alone, day after day. Perhaps if he tried again . . . He could not explain it, but it was important to him that Zoel accept him again.

"I am sorry I went away," Kon said taking Zoel by the hand. "Please forgive me. Don't be angry with me, Zoel," he begged, but it was useless. The old man just stared at him blankly.

At length Geilla ended Kon's misery. "Go back to sleep, Papa. You just had another bad dream." She covered her father with a blanket, and motioned for Kon to move away from the bed. "I'm going out for a while, Papa. I'll be back soon."

Geilla took Kon's arm and led him out the door. "His mind wanders, Kon. You must forgive him. After you left he became much worse. I think he felt so guilty about what he did to you, his mind would not accept it and he blamed you instead."

Kon did not answer and she could see that talking with Zoel had upset him. "Please . . . we have only one day," she said taking his hand. "Let's forget our sorrows just for a few hours. I've asked the neighbor woman to give Papa the dinner I prepared, so we can be together until you leave."

And so they walked the city together and sat for hours over espresso and ices at the cafes. They talked of good times in the theater, of Mario and his family, and of how someday they would all be together again. Towards evening Kon used all the money left from the bus ticket to buy them a meal. Geilla knew how little money he had, and ordered carefully. It pleased her to see Kon eat, however, for he looked so thin. Afterwards, they sat hand in hand, and watched the dusk turn to darkness. Then very softly, and very reluctantly, Kon told her it was time for him to leave. He would not let her walk to the bus stop with him, for it would not be safe for her to go home alone after he left. He walked to the flat with her. She knew by the time that Zoel would be asleep.

When at last he knew he could delay no longer, Kon put his hands to Geilla's face and kissed it gently. "I have missed you terribly, Geilla," he whispered to her.

"I have missed you too, Kon," she answered softly.

Suddenly the thought of having to leave again overcame him. He wrapped his arms around her and pressed her tightly to him. She could feel his breath on her neck. She raised her face to his and let him kiss her on the mouth. She liked the feel of his arms enfolding her, and the way his hands moved gently down her back. She had been so alone without him.

"Oh, Geilla, I hate to leave you," he whispered. "Wait for me, Geilla! Wait for me! I'll swear I'll make some money and come for you. I swear it!" Although he spoke softly, his voice carried the force of his determination.

"I'll wait, Kon. I'll wait," she promised.

****

It was almost 2:00 a.m. Jack sat watching Kon and talking to Geilla, trying without success to convince her to get a little rest. Paul came in from his break a few minutes early. "How's Kon? Any change?"

"He's been quiet, but he's still not breathing right," Jack answered.

Paul went closer to the bed. He put his hand on Kon's shoulder then felt across his chest. "Hey, this gown is wringing wet. Hell, let's get him something dry to wear. These sheets are soaked too. I'm going to find Stamatis," he said turning from the bed.

He didn't have to go far for Stamatis was coming up the hall in his usual slow manner. Yiosiph was with him, as ever, pushing a cart. Paul approached Stamatis. "Hey, doc, we need some dry sheets and a clean shirt for Kon. He's soaked."

"Yes, yes it's the fever," Stamatis answered calmly.

Paul glanced at the cart and saw a pile of sheets. Stamatis must have been making the rounds, he thought. He seems to prowl the halls at night. What was it he said about death and devils coming out at night? Well, they aren't going to sneak up on Stamatis. Paul followed him around the curtain.

Stamatis rolled Kon to one edge of the narrow bed and motioned to Jack to hold him from falling while he removed the wet sheets. They rolled Kon onto the dry side and Yiosiph put the wet sheets on the cart. Stamatis slipped the wet gown forward over Kon's arms and Jack lifted him so they could put a dry gown on him. As Jack lowered him, Kon opened his eyes and put his hand on Jack's arm.

"Jack! . . . Jack, put me off the train! Please . . . put me off the train!" he gasped.

"It's O.K., Kon. You're off the train." Jack put his hand over Kon's. "Relax. We're all off the train."

"Put me off, Jack. Don't get caught!" Kon gasped and his eyes closed again.

"Damn! I don't think he understood me, Paul," Jack said sadly.

"It's hard to tell. You'd better take a break, Jack. He'll be O.K. for a while."

Stamatis put another dose of penicillin into the IV tube, and turned to Geilla. "You still watch, eh. It is not good. You must rest."

"He's right, Geilla," Brad agreed as he came in.

"No, I want to stay," Geilla answered defiantly.

Brad looked at her pale, tired face. "Damn it! I'm in charge

56

here, Geilla," he said, raising his voice. "Go back to the hotel with Jack."

"No! I must stay, please," she pleaded and moved closer to the bed.

"Come on, Geilla. I'll go back with you," Jack said and tried to put his arm around her.

"Leave me alone!" she shrieked and raised her hand to slap Jack. He caught her wrist gently. "Let me go!" she wailed, then started to cry. Once the tears started, she could not stop them. Jack let go of her wrist, and she covered her face and sobbed uncontrollably.

Kon jerked at the sound, and rolled over on the narrow bed. "Geilla!" he called out, and strained to raise himself. He would have fallen if Paul had not caught him as he rolled over the edge. Kon struggled against Paul, calling, "Geilla! Geilla!" in a hoarse voice until he started coughing. He coughed from deep in his chest and he shook with the effort. Stamatis rolled Kon onto his side, but he continued to cough. He coughed up blood before he quieted down again, but he was panting so badly Stamatis held the mask to his face.

Geilla turned white and stepped backwards when Stamatis turned and bellowed at her, "Is this how you care for him? You cause needless suffering!"

Immediately Jack jumped between Stamatis and Geilla. "Leave her alone! She didn't mean to upset him. She's just worn out."

Stamatis shook his head. He could read the worry on both their faces. "No more tears, please," he said quietly. "You make more bad dreams for him."

Stamatis shot a look at Jack, who pulled himself straight. "You, big man," he snarled. "Hold the mask for him a while longer!"

"Sure," Jack answered coldly, glad to have something to do for Kon. Stamatis shook his head sadly and left.

Paul went to Geilla and put his arms around her. She was trembling. "Oh, Paul, I'm sorry I lost control. I don't want to hurt him," she whispered, and buried her face on his chest.

"I know. I know. This is hard on all of us," he said gently. "Geilla, if I bring a cot, would you take a little rest? Please."

Geilla nodded.

"Good girl." He kissed her on the forehead, led her to the chair and left. Returning shortly he set up the cot and made Geilla sit on it. He left immediately, but soon returned with a pot of tea and some cups.

"I think you need some tea, Geilla," he said gently and poured her a cup. She shook her head.

"Come on, drink it, please. You don't know how hard I had to beg to get this." He made a great show of adding milk and sugar, and stirring it for her. He presented her with the cup and she sipped the tea. "I think you overdid the sugar, Paul."

"You need the energy. Come on, drink up." He knelt in front of her as she drank and took the cup from her when she finished.

Geilla felt weary despite her protests, and hoped the tea would do her some good. The thought of leaving Kon was unbearable to her. If only he would not wall her out, she would tell him how much she cared about him. Suddenly she felt strangely dizzy. She looked straight at Paul who was still kneeling in front of her, but she could not focus clearly. She felt herself spinning and then she knew. "You bastard! You tricked me!" She raised her hand to slap him and he caught her as she fell forward.

Paul carried Geilla to where Jack was standing. "I'll take over on the mask. You take Geilla back to the hotel. You need a break too, Jack."

"Sure, I'll take her. She came close to losing it," Jack answered taking Geilla from Paul. She looked like a doll in his muscular arms.

"Yeah," Paul agreed, "she'll scratch my eyes out tomorrow, but she needs the rest."

CHAPTER FIVE

Kon returned to his job at the hotel in high spirits. He took the statements from Zoel and Geilla to the manager and again asked for his help in getting his citizenship papers.

"I can arrange this for you, but it will cost a lot of money," the manager began.

"I don't have a lot of money," Kon said simply. "You told me you would sign a paper saying that I work for you and I would become a citizen."

"These things are never that simple, Kon. There will be some investigation. I will have to use my influence and possibly pay some people to smooth things along. Yours is not the usual case, you know."

"How much money will you need?"

The manager named a figure. Kon had saved a little money by wearing his clothes thin and eating poorly, but he despaired when he heard the figure. "I have nothing like that amount," he confessed.

"That's too bad," the manager said with mock sympathy and got up from his desk.

Kon blocked his way. "But you promised to help me. I have all the signatures."

The manager seemed to reconsider. "Well, perhaps you could make a deposit and work off the rest."

"Impossible! I make so little money I could never save enough."

"But if you would agree to work without a salary . . ."

"Never! I starve now."

"Perhaps you could do some other errands for me."

Kon looked at him suspiciously. "What errands?"

The manager twisted the large ring on his right hand before he began slyly. "A number of gentlemen come to me asking to have some excitement while they are in Milan. They want to be entertained — but alas they do not know the city, and they do not dare to go alone. You know the city, Kon. You could be their guide. You could drive them where they want to go, bring them back here in the morning, and see that the police know nothing of their little games."

Kon did not like the sound of it. "I have no license to drive in Milan. What if I get stopped?"

"A license is an easy thing for one who is a citizen," the manager declared.

Kon looked at him in disgust. "I won't dirty my hands in your filthy business."

"Then nothing can be done for you," the manager said. He turned from Kon, walked to the door of his office, then hesitated. "By the way, Kon, do the police know you are in Italy illegally?"

Kon glared at him, but said nothing.

"Perhaps they would be interested to know about you. And if I tell them that certain things are missing from guest's rooms . . . it would not look good for you, Kon."

"You lie! I've never taken anything," Kon shot back.

"Perhaps, but which of your friends in the kitchen will take your side if I make a charge?"

Kon knew the manager had a point. The boys would all swear against him if the manager put pressure on them.

"How is the weather in Greece this time of year, Kon?" the manager asked maliciously.

Kon fingered the knife in his pocket, imagining how it would feel to draw the blade across the manager's throat. His hands shook in anger, but he fought the urge.

"It's your choice, Kon. Citizenship or deportation," the manager declared.

Kon was trapped. "You bastard! You greedy bastard! I could cut your throat!"

The manager laughed contemptuously. "You'll never get your papers if you don't hold your tongue, boy. I have to sign for you, remember?"

"If I agree to be a slave I must have a passport also."

"All right," the manager conceded, seeing the determination in Kon eyes. If I push this one too far he will cut me for sure, he thought to himself. He is the only one I have a hold over. "You must agree in writing to work for me for one year."

"A year!" Kon shouted. "You cursed thief! You suck the very life from me!"

"Enough of your insults! Sign the papers or I'll have you shipped away as a criminal!"

Kon was overcome by a hopelessness that was almost physical. He put his hand to his head and closed his eyes, but there was no escape. "I'll sign," he croaked at last as though the words choked him as he spoke.

When he could bring himself to do so, he wrote to the Swiss family and told them he was now an Italian citizen but that he had signed a contract to work at the hotel for a year. He said nothing of the terms of the agreement, or of his possible deportation. Only to Geilla and Mario did he reveal the utter misery of his situation. Geilla expressed her sympathy with great sweetness and told him she would wait for him. Someday they would be together again.

By placing his confidence in the wrong person, Kon had lost

what little independence he had, and was driven to work harder than ever. By day he worked in the kitchen and hauled baggage, and several nights a week he drove select customers to those haunts where they could enjoy their vices. Under the manager's direction, Kon learned where to take them to gamble, drink, and be entertained by loose women.

Kon hated the baseness of his clients, but he did his duty to them. He escorted them safely to various houses, guarded the door against police raids, saw that they had their papers, watches and money when they left and, if necessary, deposited them in their rooms at the hotel if they could no longer walk. He always waited for his clients in the car, silently watching for any sign of the police. Once he hauled a client out the back door just as the police came in the front. Occasionally he was called in to break up fights between his clients and other visitors.

Gradually Kon settled into a routine of patronizing only a few houses where he knew his clients would enjoy themselves and not be cheated too badly. After a time some of the girls became curious about the thin, quiet, young man with dark unruly hair and deep, sad eyes. They tried to entice him inside to join their revelry, but he would not go. It was his job to play the guard he told them; but still they wondered. When the weather turned cold, some of the younger girls took it into their heads to bring Kon coffee when they did not have customers. He was always grateful because it is hard for even a young man to have so little sleep. Once the girls brought him some food and they saw by his appetite how hungry he was. Thereafter they made it their habit to sneak him bread or fruit. Fiorenza, the manager, did not mind this small expense, because he brought clients and helped keep order in the house.

Sometimes, if they had no customers, the girls would sit and talk with him, and he would amuse them with tales of his life in the theater. The girls laughed, but did not really believe his stories. At times, when he was especially tired and lonely, he almost did not believe them himself. Thus he came to meet Tega. She was the youngest of the group and had long dark hair. Kon found her very attractive, although she was not the prettiest of the girls. She teased him mercilessly because he would not come inside and sample what the girls had to offer. He learned that she was Sicilian, but he did not know how she came to be in such a place. The girls tempted him many times, but he resisted until one time Tega invited him to visit her. "Just to talk and share some coffee," she promised. He put her off for several weeks, but one evening, when he had finished in the kitchen and had no clients to drive, he came alone on foot.

Tega was surprised, but pleased to see him and as promised she served him coffee, hot and sweet, the way he liked it best. They sat on the bed in her room; she relaxing comfortably against the pillows by the head and he remaining respectfully upright at the foot. They talked of many things. She told him of her large, poor family, and how she had run away to avoid being forced to marry a much older man. After many misfortunes, Fiorenza had found her in the streets and took her in. She was not happy with her situation, and he saw that like himself, she was very lonely.

"Is there no one you care for who waits for you?" he asked.

"There is no one," she answered. "And what of you, Kon?"

"I too ran away. I was thirteen. My father . . . drank too much and . . . then he would beat me," he hesitated over the story for even now it was painful for him to remember. "He would always be sorry afterwards and say he loved me, but he . . ."

"And what of your mother, Kon? Did she not protect you?" Tega asked quickly.

"She died when I was nine. Papa rarely beat me while she was alive, but after . . . he drank all the time and nothing I did pleased him."

Tega rose quickly and coming to sit beside him she put her hand to his lips. "No more, Kon. It is too bitter to remember these things." She could see he was sinking into dark thoughts.

"Tell me about the theater Kon," she said and took him by the arm. "What did you do there?"

He smiled and told her about the music, the beautiful costumes and the famous people he had met.

"It sounds like a fairy tale, Kon. Why did you leave such a wonderful place?"

"I did not want to leave . . ." he hesitated and she thought he would not tell her more, but suddenly the words rushed from him. "I fell in love with a girl there, but when her father saw me kissing her he cursed me and told me I was not good enough for her. Then he went crazy and tried to kill me with his bare hands."

"Oh, Kon, what a terrible story!" Tega cried and moved closer to him. "And what of the girl? Do you still love her?"

He did not answer, but put his hand up and held his head with it. "I don't know," he said at last. "I thought I did, but I have not seen her for a long time. She does not answer my letters."

"I could make you forget her," Tega said, and putting her hand to his face she traced the outline from brow to chin. She felt him tense, but his breath came more quickly. She let her hand slide gently down his neck, but he jerked his head back when she touched his throat. She held her hand in mid air after he pulled back.

"You do not like my touch, my sweet? Ah, it is true then. You are afraid of women. Are you still a boy, Kon?"

"No!" he whispered fiercely. Impulsively he took her hand and kissed it, moving his lips slowly from her fingers to her palm and then to her wrist.

"I am sorry. I did not mean to pull away." Putting his hand on her long hair, he stroked it seeming to absorb the softness of it with his large rough hand. "Touch me anywhere but there. I cannot bear any hand on my throat."

"I understand," she answered softly. She put her hand to his collar and slowly unbuttoned his shirt. His eyes were on her face and he studied her from beneath his full, dark eyebrows. Putting his hand under her chin he pulled her gently towards him and kissed her lightly on the lips.

The very tenderness of his kiss thrilled her. She put her hands on his chest and gently moved them over his shoulders and down his back. Her touch was like fire and ice on his skin; at once both soothing and exciting. He let her push him backwards onto the bed. Suddenly the loneliness he had fought for so long rose in him like a wave. He put his arms around her, and held her tightly as if to keep from sinking into total isolation. Then he kissed her passionately on her lips and on her neck. "Tega, you drive me crazy!" he whispered. "Could you even pretend to love me for a little while, like you do with the others?"

"No, Kon," she answered. "Not like it is with the others. With you it could be real."

"Love me then! Make me forget!"

Quickly she undressed, and then skillfully removed his clothes, before he could change his mind. She felt the fire in him and was surprised at the vigor of one who was so slow to be aroused. Clearly he was not afraid of women. She was not his first, Alonzo had seen to that, but she was more experienced and she taught him several ways to please a woman. Afterward, as he lay panting, but content, he smiled so broadly his whole countenance seemed to change.

"You are incredibly handsome when you smile, Kon. You should do it more often," she murmured, and dotted his face with quick, teasing, little kisses. He grinned self-consciously at her remark, but made no comment. No man had ever smiled so sweetly at her and she was touched. She did not take offence when he soon fell asleep as she knew he suffered constantly from fatigue. Enclosing her in his arms, he slept soundly all night, untroubled by the violent dreams that frequently plagued him; while she lay awake a long time, drawing strength from his very presence. Life did not seem so bitter while she was with him.

****

When Kon did not appear in the kitchen as usual the next morning, the cook went to search for him in the cellar. Finding that he was not there caused him to wonder for he had seen Kon leave the hotel the night before. Concerned that Kon had come to some harm in the streets alone, he locked the cellar door, and told the other boys that Kon had a fever and could not work. When Kon tried to sneak into the kitchen at 6:30, he came face to face with the cook who seized him by the arm. "Where have you been you lazy rogue?"

Kon was taken by surprise and said nothing, but for a brief moment fear flashed in his eyes. He stared at the cook waiting for him to bellow and betray him to the manager. Instead the cook hissed into his face, "Get to the cellar! I have already lied that you are too sick to work."

Still holding Kon by the arm the cook unlocked the door to the cellar and thrust Kon through. Kon was perplexed, but went to lay on the cot lest anyone come looking for him. The cook appeared shortly with a large cup of hot broth liberally laced with red pepper and ordered Kon to drink it. When Kon hesitated, the cook grabbed the cup and wrapping his arm around Kon's neck, he poured the broth down Kon's throat in great gulps that set him coughing.

"Ah, the cough is a good touch!" the cook said approvingly. "Now get undressed and stay under the blanket."

Moments later when the manager came crashing down the stairs cursing Kon for his laziness and demanding that he get up, he saw Kon's flushed face and the perspiration that dripped from his brow. The cook stood by the cot wearing a look of great concern. "See how badly he coughs though I bring him a special tea. He is useless in the kitchen until he is better."

"Then let him carry luggage," Guido shouted. "I don't pay him to lay in bed all day."

Kon was about to object that he was not paid at all, but the cook put his fleshy hand over Kon's face.

"Feel how hot he is, Guido. If you work him today he may faint, and you will have no work from him for several days. Even a dog must lie in a corner from time to time." The cook was a burley man and stood his ground between Kon and the manager.

"All right, I give him today, but he'd better get well fast or he will be sorry," Guido growled and stormed up the stairs.

After Guido left, the cook brought Kon coffee and bread. "This man holds the axe over your head for something, eh boy."

Kon nodded and silently sipped the coffee. Then, as the cook began to climb the stairs, Kon called to him, "Giovanni . . . I . . . thank you. You are my only friend here."

"Ha! Don't try to flatter me, boy. There must be at least one other, unless you have taken to wearing perfume."

Kon grinned and for a moment the cook saw that, indeed, he was still a young lad.

"Sleep now!" the cook boomed. "And I will pray to the Virgin for you, for at 4 o'clock today you will be miraculously cured and come to help me in the kitchen."

Kon smiled again and found it easy to obey.

****

Kon was kept very busy for the next several weeks and saw Tega only once when she brought coffee to the car while he waited for clients. Carla, one of the other girls, came also, so they had no private conversation. Tega kissed him on the lips and Carla teased her for being bold.

"Ah, Tega, you are too forward! You will frighten this little bird away." Carla ran her hand through Kon's hair to tousle it. "Have you not heard that he is afraid of women?"

Kon laughed and ignored her, but she kept teasing him.

"Why do you not come inside with your friends when you come? Surely it is no fun to sit all night in the cold."

"They are no friends of mine," he retorted. "It is my job to guard them. I deal with them only for money the same as you."

"So you do not enjoy it when we come to see you? It is only your job then to drink coffee and laugh with us?"

Kon looked directly at Tega as he answered. "I enjoy that friendship which is freely given. Can true feeling be bought for money?"

Tega said nothing, but Carla answered. "True feeling? No, but we sell make believe love. We learn to pretend very well."

Tega became impatient with her. "Oh be quiet, Carla!" she scolded, and put her hand to Kon's face. "I do not think this little bird is afraid of women. I think he just likes to choose carefully."

Kon took Tega's hand and put it to his lips.

"And I think we should leave him to sit by himself in the cold. Come, Tega, we must go and do our job also."

****

When Kon came alone a few nights later and asked for Tega, he sensed great agitation in the house. Even the girls he knew by name would not look at him, but hurried away on real or imagined errands. He stood in bewilderment until finally Fiorenza came and took him into the kitchen. "Sit down, Kon," she said quietly and lowered herself into a chair by the table.

"Where is Tega?" he asked, hesitantly taking the chair Fiorenza indicated. "I will wait outside if she is busy with . . ."

Fiorenza put her wrinkled hand over Kon's. "Tega is not here, Kon."

For the first time he noticed the tears in her eyes. "What has happened to Tega? Where is she?"

"They took her to the hospital, Kon, but there is little hope . . ."

"What happened, Fiorenza?" he asked growing agitated. "Tell me, please. What happened to Tega?"

Fiorenza pressed Kon's hand. "She was with a client . . . He was an evil man, Kon. I should have seen it on his face and not let him in," she moaned. Kon put both his hands over Fiorenza's.

"What happened? Please! Tell me!" he shouted.

"He stabbed her, Kon . . . she would not do something he asked and he stabbed her. She screamed so terribly we all heard it, but he had locked the door. It was too late for her by the time we came."

Kon jumped to his feet. "Who is he, Fiorenza? I will kill him for this!"

"We do not know. He had never come before. I should never have let him in. He was a madman." She put her head on her hands and sobbed.

Kon clenched his fists. "Merciful God this is too much to bear!" he cried aloud. "Where have they taken her, Fiorenza? I must see her."

Carla who had come into the kitchen answered him. "They will not let you in at this hour, Kon. You must wait."

"I cannot!" he shouted. "What if she dies? My God, she has not yet lived!"

Carla gave him the name and address of the hospital and he flew into the street.

"He was always so shy, Fiorenza, I never guessed he cared so for Tega."

"You cannot always read what is in a man's heart. My God, I should never have let that madman in."

Kon ran all the way to the hospital, burst through the entrance, and rushed to the information desk. "I must see Tega!" he exclaimed breathlessly to the woman behind the desk.

"I am sorry, visiting hours are over. You will have to come back . . ."

"No. I cannot wait. She may die! Please, I must see her now."

The woman hesitated. She was impressed by his earnestness.

"Well, perhaps I can give you some information about her condition. What is her name?"

"Tega," he answered quickly.

"Only Tega? What is her family name?"

Kon stared at her blankly. "She never told me her name only that she came from a large family in Sicily."

"I'm afraid that I can't help you, young man," the woman answered and started to turn away.

"Please," Kon pleaded desperately. "They brought her in only a short while ago. She was stabbed."

The woman drew in her breath. "You mean the girl from the bordello?" she asked, hesitating over the word.

66

"Yes! Yes! Where is she? Please!"

The woman's disapproval was evident in her voice as she answered, "She is on the ward, but you may not go in."

"Please, tell me where she is," Kon pleaded and raised his voice louder and louder as he became more frustrated. "She must not die alone. How can you keep me away? I am her only friend! Please!"

An older nurse who was passing by could not help noticing the shabby young man who was shouting and making a disturbance. "What is going on here, Marie? Who is this man?"

"He says . . ." the woman behind the desk started, but before she could finish Kon turned to the nurse. "Please, I came to see the girl who was stabbed at the bordello. She must not die alone." He took the nurse's hand. "I beg you, have mercy and let me see her. I go on my knees before you," he pleaded and threw himself down.

The nurse had seen much suffering in her life and was not easily shaken, but the intensity of Kon's pleas moved her.

"Get up, boy!" she said in a loud whisper. "Be quiet! You'll wake the dead with your shouting!"

"No! I will not go until I see Tega!" Kon cried from his knees.

"Mother of God, you are a trial," the nurse sighed and turned to the woman behind the desk. "Marie, where is the girl he seeks?"

"She is in the second floor ward, Irene."

"Thank you, Marie." The nurse turned back to Kon and seized his arm firmly. "Get up, boy! Get up!" Kon let himself be pulled up, but his eyes never left her face. "I will take you in, but you must control yourself and be very quiet. Do you understand?" she said sternly.

"Yes," Kon answered softly, "I promise. I promise."

The nurse led him up the stairs and down the long hall to the ward where eight beds with neat white linen were placed along the far wall. Tega lay in the third bed from the door. The nurse put her finger to her lips as a final warning to Kon before she went up to the bed. "Tega," she said quietly. "There is someone here to see you." She signaled Kon to come closer.

"Tega . . . it's Kon," he said very softly. Tega turned her head in his direction, and he saw the terrible paleness of her face. She opened her eyes, but there was no expression in them. He took her hand in his. "Tega, can you hear me?"

"Kon, is it you?" she whispered faintly.

"Yes, Tega, it's me. I went to the house to see you and they told me . . ."

"You came to me, Kon?"

"Yes, you are my dearest friend, Tega."

She smiled weakly at him. "So my little bird is no longer afraid."

"I have never been afraid of you, Tega. I swear it." He kissed her hand and held it to his cheek.

"Nor I of you," she whispered.

"Can I bring anything for you, Tega? Is there anyone you would like to send a message to . . . your family . . .?"

"No! Please," she said anxiously. "It is better they do not know how I came to die," she paused, "I have no one, Kon, no one."

He pressed her hand more strongly. "No! No! Don't say such a thing. You have me, Tega. I will stay with you."

She smiled at him, but did not speak. She lay very still and he held her hand and stroked her hair ever so gently. At last she moved slightly and he saw her wince. She drew in her breath sharply. "It's no good, Kon. I can't fight it away any more."

"I will get a doctor, Tega. He will make you well," he answered anxiously.

She gripped his hand. "No, Kon. It is too late for the doctor. I must have a priest and confess my sins. I will not die with this blackness on my soul." Her very desperation seemed to give her strength and she raised her head from the pillow and looked deep into his eyes. "Oh, Kon, I never meant to fall so low. I swear it! I did not want to live in such corruption."

"I know, I know," he assured her. "You did not choose it. You did only what you had to do to live. I understand, Tega. Truly, I understand."

"I must confess, Kon. I must confess my sins." She fell back on the pillow and closed her eyes.

"I will bring a priest if you wish it, Tega. Rest now, I will return soon." He kissed her on the forehead and left the room.

Kon went from church to church seeking a priest who would come, but when they learned that Tega was a prostitute they turned him away. They were comfortable in their beds and did not want to listen to this madman. He grew more desperate and his tale became more incoherent as he went from place to place. Finally, he found a young priest, not much older than himself, who would listen to his story.

"But she lives a life of sin," the priest chided Kon when he heard the story.

"Then she has all the more need of forgiveness!" Kon answered. "You must come with me, please. She has so little time."

So although it was late and Tega was obviously not of his parish, he went with Kon. When he returned, Kon rushed to Tega and gently took her hand. "Tega, I have brought the priest."

She opened her eyes and whispered faintly, "Thank you, Kon." The priest leaned over Tega and asked to hear her confession.

"I will wait in the hall," Kon told her. He started to release her hand, but Tega grasped his fingers before they slipped from hers. "No, don't leave me, Kon!" she gasped.

Kon looked at the priest who hesitated, then nodded yes.

Perhaps he did not want Kon to leave either. His seminary training had not prepared him to handle such a bizarre situation.

"I'll stay with you, Tega," Kon agreed. He took her hand more firmly, sat in the straight-backed chair by the bed, and bowed his head.

The priest walked around the bed, took Tega's other hand and she began the ancient ritual. "Bless me father, for I have sinned . . ." In the faintest of voices she listed her failings, and the many men she had known. She was vague about the number of men for she truly did not remember any of them.

"Are you sorry for these sins?" the priest asked coldly.

"Yes, yes . . . I have sinned. Forgive me, father," she begged. "I do not want to die with this blackness on my soul."

The priest looked at Kon and suddenly guessed his connection to Tega. Since this was to be Tega's last confessions, it should be as complete as possible, he thought. If he were to be judge, he must know all the evidence. "Have you had sexual relations with this man?" he asked, gesturing toward Kon.

"Yes," she answered faintly.

"And are you sorry for your sin?" he continued, carrying out the ritual.

"It was no sin, father. It was an act of love," she answered quietly.

Her answer was unexpected and the priest was in a quandary. He wanted to give her absolution, but he could not if she showed no remorse. Finally, he put it to her. "If you are not sorry, there can be no forgiveness."

Anguish stole across Tega's face, and she withdrew her hand from the priest's.

"You must forgive her," Kon demanded when he saw her look.

"I cannot! She will not renounce her sin."

Kon leaned over Tega and put his face close to hers. "Tell him you are sorry you gave yourself to me, my love, I will forgive you."

"No," she told him firmly. "It is the time for truth, Kon. I gave you my love. It was no sin."

Kon looked at the priest with eyes full of pain. "You must grant her absolution! I beg you, please have mercy on her," he whispered frantically.

"I cannot," the priest answered with great sadness.

Kon was crushed with despair and did not speak. The priest turned to leave, but suddenly Kon seized his arm. "Forgive her!" he shouted. "I take the sin for mine. I made her do it!" The priest looked at Kon and read the desperation in his eyes. "Say the words to give her peace," Kon implored still gripping his arm.

I am no Solomon to judge these hearts, the priest thought. She is so young . . . What do the books know of the misery of these two?

At length he nodded to Kon. "I will say the words and let God be the judge."

Kon relaxed, and his hand slipped from the priest's arm. The priest turned to Tega and he began the prayer. He signed the cross on her forehead and asked her to repeat the Ave with him, but as he began Tega gasped for breath. "Bless me, father, for I have sinned. Bless me, father, for I have sinned. Bless me . . ." she repeated over and over very faintly until her breath gave out.

"She's gone," the priest said sadly.

Kon did not seem to hear him and sat gazing at Tega.

"Would you like me to hear your confession also?"

When Kon did not respond, the priest came around the bed and put his hand on Kon's shoulder. He sincerely wanted to say something comforting, but no words came to him. He crossed himself slowly, and almost as an afterthought, he raised his arm and made the sign over Kon to bless him. "God be with you," he whispered and fled.

Over an hour later, the nurse who had led Kon into the ward came by as she was finishing her shift. She saw Kon sitting silently by the bed, faithfully holding Tega's hand and staring at her lifeless face. The nurse spoke to him, but he made no answer. She went to Tega and seeing that the girl was dead, she crossed herself quickly. She pulled the sheet over Tega's face and turned to Kon. "She's gone, son. There's nothing more you can do for her."

She touched his shoulder, and he turned and looked at her with an uncomprehending expression. His eyes were sad and circled with dark halos of fatigue. Noticing that he was still clutching Tega's hand, the nurse gently unfolded his fingers and slipped it away from him. "Come, it's time to go now." She took him by the arm, but he shook his head and pulled away, "No! No! I must stay with her. She is all alone. All alone," he moaned.

The nurse had faced grief before and closed her heart. She took his arm more firmly than before and pulled. "You must go now," she repeated sternly.

He did not resist. He was suddenly too tired to think or to feel. He staggered as she led him from the room.

CHAPTER SIX

Jack carried Geilla back to the hotel and placed her on one of the beds. He slipped off her shoes and thinking to make her more comfortable, he tried to remove her tight slacks. He found the zipper and opened it then pulled gently on the pant legs, but the slacks would not come off. He rolled her over several times as he struggled with them, then gave up for fear of waking her. Damn women's pants! How the hell did she get in them in the first place? He covered her with the blankets. No wonder she wears them on assignments, he mused to himself. They're a damn leather chastity belt! He went into the other room and fell on the bed.

The next morning the team's gear arrived from Athens as Carl had promised. As expected, Geilla was furious with Paul and lapsed into Italian three times in order to adequately express her low opinion of him. He was so happy to see her looking better again that he made the fatal mistake of letting a trace of a smile flit across his face as she completed her tirade. He saw her reaction coming well in advance, but he let her get off the slap she had started the night before. With that accomplished, she lost her anger and agreed to eat breakfast with him.

Throughout the day, various pieces of equipment for their return to Bitola arrived from Athens. Brad and Jack assembled most of it while Geilla and Paul took extra shifts with Kon. Kon's condition was not improving. In addition to his difficulty in breathing, he suffered more frequent fits of violent coughing which caused him pain and left him exhausted. He was still feverish and continued to rave, calling out in delirium. Geilla and Paul did their best to comfort him, but his mind kept conjuring up bad dreams for him.

****

Six weeks had passed since Tega's death, but Kon was still inconsolable. Guido was driving him relentlessly with more and more night work and secret deliveries. He rarely got more than a few hours of sleep at night, and when he did sleep, he had violent dreams and awoke with pounding headaches. The circles under his eyes grew darker, and he took scarcely any food except for strong coffee which he drank as often as he could. Several times Giovanni found Kon standing by a sink full of dirty pots, sound asleep with his eyes open and the water running over his hands. The girls continued to visit him when he drove clients to the bordello, but he no longer talked or laughed with them. They noticed he grew thinner by the week and tried to tempt him with fruit and little cakes, but he took only coffee.

One night when there was trouble at the house, Fiorenza called Kon in to protect the girls and put a client out. Everyone had been edgy after what had happened to Tega and Fiorenza kept a keen eye on every customer. As usual there was a lot of shouting on both sides, but this time the belligerent man pulled a knife and took a swipe at Kon. The girls screamed and Kon went insane. "You filthy bastard!" he screamed. "I'll teach you to pull a knife on me!" He drew his own knife and flung it at the man piercing him through the forearm. The man screamed and dropped his knife. Grabbing the knife from the floor, Kon hurled himself at the man, and knocked him down. In an instant he had a blade at the man's throat. He might have finished him, if Carla had not leaped at his arm, screaming, "No! Kon, no!"

Kon hesitated. His heart was racing and his headache rose to a blinding torment.

"Don't kill him, Kon! They'll hang you for it for sure!" Carla pleaded.

Fiorenza rushed to Kon and put her hand on his shoulder. "Let him go, Kon! Who will protect us if they take you away?" she cried in anguish.

Kon's hands shook in rage, but he slowly withdrew the knife from the man's throat. Holding the blade before the man's face, Kon stood. "Get up!" Kon growled and the man rose hesitantly. Suddenly remembering his own knife, Kon grabbed the man's arm and pulled the knife from his flesh. The man screamed again and Kon shoved him out the door and into the hall. "Get out you pig!" Kon roared in disgust. The man fled down the stairs, and they heard the outer door slam.

Kon leaned his head and hands against the wall and closed his eyes. He was sweating and his stomach burned. Carla came up beside him and gently put her hand on the back of his neck. "It's the headache again, isn't it?"

"Yes," he groaned. "I think it will drive me mad."

"I will bring you something for it if you wish," she said softly. She had offered him pills several times before, but he had always refused.

"Anything, Carla . . . please," he whispered wretchedly.

The clients Kon had brought were now uneasy. They were no longer in the mood for a night of rowdy drinking and lovemaking and demanded to be driven back to the hotel. Kon went slowly down the stairs and headed towards the door.

Carla came up behind him. "Are you sure you are well enough to drive back?"

Kon nodded "yes" but, suddenly she noticed the blood on the

sleeve of his coat. "Mother of Christ! That bastard cut you, Kon. Can't you feel it?"

Kon seemed to notice the blood for the first time. "It's nothing, Carla. Leave it."

"No, it bleeds too much, Kon. I will bind it for you." She turned and called over her shoulder, "Rita! Give me a hand. That son of a bitch with the knife hurt Kon." As Rita came up, Carla whispered, "Don't let him go until I patch him up. And get that coat and shirt off him."

Rita took Kon by the arm. "Come on, honey," she coaxed. "Let's go sit down over here. Carla will be right back." He started to pull away, but she locked her arm around his. "Come on, honey. I won't bite you."

He let her lead him to the sofa and sat beside her. She unbuttoned his jacket and slipped it over his arms, but he put his hand up to stop her as she tried to unbutton his shirt.

"Relax, honey," she said and pushed his hand down. "Some men pay me to do this for them. Come on now, let's fix you up before you bleed all over Fiorenza's new sofa."

Even as she spoke she unfastened Kon's shirt and finished pulling it off him. There was a gash across the width of his upper arm and blood was running down to his elbow. Kon looked at his bloody arm, but showed no interest or emotion. He laid his head back on the sofa and closed his eyes. "He took a real bad slice on you, honey," Rita said and wrapped Kon's shirt around his arm to catch the blood. Then she lay her hand on his shoulder and drew it across his chest in slow motion.

Carla came up as she finished the pass. "Keep your hands off him, Rita. He's not interested in your favors."

Rita made a face at Carla and tossed her head. "You just want him for yourself. He's too skinny for me anyway!"

"Go away, Rita. You make a poor nurse," Carla scolded, and seating herself on the other side of Kon she started to wrap his arm.

"I cannot mend his arm, but I could make him forget about it for a while," Rita answered and put her hand on Kon's chest. Carla slapped her wrist. "Leave him be, Rita! Can't you see he's not well? They kill him with work at that damn hotel."

"I see they do not feed him. Too bad. He has such nice shoulders. Make him put a little meat on, Carla."

Rita lit a cigarette and sat in silence while Carla finished binding Kon's arm. Gradually Rita noticed how little attention Kon paid to what Carla was doing. The poor bastard's exhausted, she thought and helped Carla put his coat on him again. "I will wash and mend your shirt, Kon. It is too bloody to wear," Carla told him gently. She handed him a small bottle. "Here are the pills. Wait till you get back and don't take more than two. They are very strong." She put her

73

hand to his forehead and gently smoothed his hair back from his face. "Wouldn't you like to rest here a while, Kon?"

He shook his head slowly. "No, I must take them back."

"Be careful then, my little bird, and get some rest."

Kon touched her hand. "Thank you, Carla," he whispered. "That was not the man I want to kill."

Carla watched as Kon led his clients out the door. She caught the arm of the last one and held him back. "You must be his eyes and ears," she whispered gesturing towards Kon. "I don't think he knows what he does."

Kon drove slowly back to the hotel, parked the car, and staggered into the kitchen. His head was splitting and his stomach felt queasy. He forced down two of the pills, groped his way down the stairs, and dropped onto the cot. He held the edges with both hands to keep from being thrown off as it spun round and round. Gradually it slowed to a stop and he was out.

At 5:00 a.m., Giovanni went looking for Kon and found him crumpled on the cot. He called to him in a loud voice and shook his shoulder. When Kon did not respond, Giovanni rolled him over, pulled him to a sitting position, and slapped his face several times. Still he could not wake him. Giovanni shook his head in anger and cursed. Tearing off Kon's jacket, he saw the bandage on his left arm and pulled it loose. "Mother of God! What have you been up to, boy?" He retied the bandage hastily and carefully examined both of Kon's arms. He could find no needle marks.

He laid Kon down, slipped his shoes off, and picked up the tattered blanket to put over him. "Mary Queen of Angels! Is this the only rag he allows you in this dank hole? Damn him! Even a beast deserves better than this!" Giovanni swore. He stormed up the stairs and sought out Guido. Finding him in the hall, he shoved him into the kitchen, and without prologue demanded, "What did you give the boy?"

Guido raised his eyebrows and looked offended. "Me? What are you talking about? What boy?"

Giovanni seized Guido's shirt in his fleshly hand and pulled him forward. "You know what boy! Your lackey! Your dog! The one who lies like a dead man in the cellar. What did you give him?"

Guido appeared cool and unconcerned although physically he was no match for Giovanni.

"You should know better, Giovanni. I never give my stuff away."

"Not even a sample to put the hooks in him?" Giovanni roared.

"Why would I go after a dog that has no money? If he had a fix, it was not from me. Maybe he's drunk. Did you know he went crazy last night and tried to kill a man with a knife? My clients did not like it and I don't like it either. I had to talk fast to convince them they had a great adventure they could brag about when they got home."

Giovanni was momentarily taken aback by Guido's statement and Guido shook himself free.

"That dog better remember who his master is, if he doesn't want to get hurt," Guido threatened. He straightened his collar and looked coolly at Giovanni. "I give the son of a bitch the day off! Let him cool down before he goes out again."

Giovanni glared at Guido. "Be careful, Guido. If you treat him like a dog, someday he may bite."

Guido blanched, but recovered quickly. "Ha! I have him on a short leash," he said contemptuously and left the kitchen.

Giovanni went to the storage closet and snatched a thick blanket from the shelf. He carried it into the kitchen, picked up a box of wooden matches, and went down to the cellar. Spreading the blanket over a box, he lit the matches, one by one, and carefully burned several small round holes in the blanket. "A curse on these rich bastards who smoke in their rooms! They ruin a beautiful thing with their carelessness," Giovanni muttered to himself. When he had finished, he nodded his head approvingly at his craftsmanship and took up the blanket. Folding it carefully in half, he lowered it over Kon, as gently as if he was creating a pastry.

When Giovanni returned to the kitchen, he busied himself with starting breakfast, but he collared the first boy who came into the room. "You boy!" he growled. "Make yourself useful. Go fetch Dr. Francini! Tell him Giovanni wants to collect a favor."

****

It was during this period that Kon received a letter from Edgar Marneé. The situation at the Marneé residence had changed and life was no longer running smoothly for the family. Albert had played some boyish prank on the au pair causing her to pack her bags and leave. The cook's helper had run off, and Charlotte had taken a fancy to having the garden dug up and rearranged. In short, they needed more domestic help and if Kon was still interested they would send someone to fetch him.

Edgar did not tell Kon of the long argument he had had with Charlotte over the matter. Charlotte sill pictured Kon as the young hero who had saved her son's life, and she was determined to make him a part of her household.

"This would be a wonderful way to repay him for his service to us," she argued.

"It would be better to hire someone from a local agency," Edgar answered.

"I hired Melina from Italy and she has worked very well as my maid. She has never given me a bit of trouble."

"Yes, but Melina comes from a good family. She works as a maid only because she is a student, and it gives her the opportunity to study in Geneva. Kon is a complete unknown."

"Well perhaps Kon would like to study in Geneva also," Charlotte countered, becoming a bit irrational in her determination.

"Don't be foolish — he has no ambition. He is perfectly happy where he is."

"That's not true! He told us himself he would do anything to get away from that hotel."

"But if we took him we would have to act as sponsors and be responsible for him."

"At least he could not run off and leave us without notice like the boy who just left," Charlotte retorted. "It would be nice to have some continuity in this household, Edgar." She paused to calm herself. "You are gone so much, my dear. I would like to have someone I could trust to look after the boys and to drive me to my meetings and social functions."

"And how do we know we could trust this young man we know nothing about?"

Charlotte hesitated, but she would not back down. "Well, I suppose we could send Francois to investigate him. He is an attorney. Surely he could find out if the boy is known to the police. He could also help to finalize the paperwork."

Edgar had no counter argument to that point and remained stubbornly silent. Charlotte sensed that she was winning and cleverly presented her final argument.

"Oh, Edgar, Kon would be such a help to us, and I'm sure he would work for very little. Would it not be less expensive to train him than to hire several different people?"

Edgar was taken by the idea that Kon would work for less than the going rate. He also knew that sooner or later Charlotte always got her way. "All right, my dear, I will write to Kon and see if he is still interested in coming to work for us."

Charlotte smiled sweetly at him. "Thank you, Edgar. You will see, Kon will be a great help to us. I will see to it myself that he is properly trained, and never gives you a minute of concern."

Edgar had his doubts, but he kept silent. Somehow Charlotte's projects always ended up making work for him, but there was no use in arguing with Charlotte once her mind was set on something.

Kon was happy to receive the letter, but wrote back that he still had four months to go under the contract he had signed. If they could wait, he would be happy to come when his contract was finished. Edgar answered Kon's letter, but it was somehow lost in the mail and Kon never received his answer.

Kon continued to work long hours and to suffer headaches as a consequence. Giovanni had made him solemnly swear never to take sleeping tablets again, and personally bought him all the aspirin he needed to keep going. Guido's repeated threats to have him deported, and his fear that the police were on to him about the drug deliveries caused Kon such anxiety that his stomach was in constant turmoil. His nerves were drawn to the breaking point by frequent threats of physical violence from the dealers he contacted. Despite his strenuous efforts to defend himself, he was occasionally beaten, and forced to crawl back to the hotel with neither money, nor drugs. Guido showed no sympathy for Kon, but the fact that he was Guido's agent afforded Kon a certain measure of protection from more serious harm. The dealers did not dare risk incurring Guido's wrath. Not all of Guido's agents were silent young men with only a knife for a weapon.

Kon grew more haggard by the week despite Giovanni's efforts to prepare extra food for him. "If you get any thinner, boy, your ribs will poke holes in your shirts!" Giovanni commented. He was becoming so concerned about Kon's failing health, that when Francini prescribed antacids, Giovanni bought them and poured them into Kon. He gave Kon a coat that had been left in one of the rooms. It was too large for him, but he needed something to replace the one that had been slashed with the knife.

Constant fatigue and headaches were affecting Kon's disposition and his temper flared more and more easily. The other boys had never been friendly towards him, but he usually ignored their snide remarks. Now he found it harder to keep his resentment in check, and frequently he became involved in fist fights. He won easily, but the others disliked him all the more. Most of them were younger, and had no idea of the activities in which Kon was forced to participate.

Early one evening after Kon had returned from a pick-up, Guido found the weight of the delivery a half ounce short. He immediately accused Kon of stealing. "You son of a bitch! You're holding out on me. How long has this been going on?" he shouted at Kon.

"You lie! The bag is sealed," Kon snapped back. "I just deliver it. I wouldn't dirty my hands in your filthy business!"

"You give me more and more trouble, Kon. You can be replaced you know," Guido growled.

"Like hell! Who else would do your dirty work for nothing?" Kon shouted at him.

"Shut up! I still can have you deported. One call to the police about your deliveries and you'd be shipped away like that," Guido said, snapping his fingers arrogantly.

"You wouldn't dare call the police! You're in this deeper than I am."

"But I have friends, Kon. Who would the police believe, some dumb immigrant, or a well known businessman?" Guido snarled contemptuously.

Kon became more and more angry in his frustration at forever being at Guido's mercy. "I'd rather die than go back!" he shouted. "I should have slit your throat long ago, you bastard" he said bitterly and drew his knife.

"Don't threaten me, boy," Guido warned, but he was alarmed.

"If I am to be dammed it might as well be for murder as for some lie," Kon screamed and rushed at Guido in a fit of rage.

Guido jumped from his leather chair and pushed it between himself and Kon. Kon was screaming curses at Guido so intently he did not hear Giovanni enter the room. He had heard them arguing and knew it was becoming more heated. As Kon sprang again at Guido, Giovanni struck him hard on the shoulder with a marble rolling pin. The force of the blow knocked Kon to his knees. Instantly Giovanni wrenched the knife from him and twisted his arm behind his back. Kon was stunned speechless.

"Forgive him, Guido," Giovanni said calmly. "He eats too many peppers and his temper heats up."

"The bastard's stealing from me, Giovanni! Then he has the nerve to pull a knife!"

"If the boy said he did not steal from you then it is true. He may be stupid, but he does not take what is not his. Look elsewhere for the thief," Giovanni pronounced.

"How can you tolerate such scum in your kitchen?" Guido said angrily. He pulled the chair aside and stood in front of Giovanni who was holding Kon down.

"He works harder than any three of the others, but you don't recognize it," Giovanni answered calmly.

Guido stood over Kon. "Someday Giovanni won't be around to save your neck and I'll finish you, boy. This is just a warning!" he growled, and smashed Kon in the mouth with his fist. Kon reeled backwards. Immediately Guido kicked him in the stomach and Kon groaned and slumped forward. Giovanni released Kon's arm, but made no move. He let Guido save face by venting his anger. "Get him out of here before he pukes on my carpet!" Guido shouted and kicked Kon in the ribs. Kon moaned, in spite of himself, and sank to the floor.

Giovanni bent and took hold of Kon's arm. He put it around his neck and pulled Kon to his knees. Kon groaned again as Giovanni half dragged, half carried him from the room. Giovanni lugged Kon into the hall, through the kitchen, and down to the cellar where he lowered him onto the cot. Leaving Kon doubled over with his head between his knees, Giovanni went up to the kitchen, and returned several minutes later with a tray.

Giovanni sat next to Kon on the cot, took hold of his jacket and pulled him upright. Throwing one massive arm around Kon's shoulders, he pinned him firmly against his huge chest. He wiped the blood from Kon's chin. Pouring some brandy into a glass with his free hand, he held it to Kon's mouth, and poured the liquid down Kon's throat. Kon coughed and tried to pull away, but Giovanni held him firmly. "Finish it! All of it!" Giovanni ordered. Kon swallowed as fast as he could although the brandy burned his throat and took his breath away.

"Damn it, Giovanni! I thought you were my friend. Why did you hit me?" Kon gasped between coughs.

"Because I am your friend! You don't know who you are dealing with, you little pup. If you cut that man he would shoot you down, or he would send his friends to do it for him."

"I could have killed him, Giovanni!" Kon screamed in frustration. "I would have done it if you hadn't hit me. You should have let me do it! You should have let me . . ."

"Mother of God, boy, do you want to be hung, or to rot in prison? You have no idea what it is like to be in prison. Believe me, you would not like it!"

Giovanni handed Kon some ice. "Here! Hold this on your lip," he said sternly. "I warned you not to show that knife around here. You didn't listen. Don't mess with Guido! He's bad news!" Giovanni said raising his voice.

"Why is it he never threatens you, Giovanni? Is he afraid of you?" Kon asked.

"I have a few friends too, boy. Do you think I was always a cook?"

"I didn't think . . ." Kon started, but Giovanni cut him off.

"You don't think at all! That's your chief problem. You just go crazy."

"I'm . . . I'm sorry, Giovanni," Kon said sadly. "I can't seem to hold myself in check anymore. I have less than three months to go before I'll be free of Guido, but I don't think I can make it. He's killing me, Giovanni! Bit by bit he's killing me." Kon lowered his head and groaned. His voice broke as he continued wretchedly, "I don't know what I'm doing half the time and . . . I don't even care!" His shoulders slumped and he put his hands over his face.

"Hey now! Don't start . . ." Giovanni began sternly, but checked himself. He put his hand on Kon's back. "Don't give up, Kon. Don't let that bastard win! You just need more rest," he said softly. "Come, let me take your coat," he said, and pulling Kon upright he slipped the jacket over his arms. "The time will go quickly, you will see. Be quiet now." Giovanni stood, and lifting Kon slightly he rolled him onto the cot. Kon groaned and clutched his stomach when he straightened out.

"Lie still," Giovanni said more softly than was his habit. He removed Kon's shoes then unfastened his belt and pulled the slacks off him. Carefully he felt across Kon's chest and down his ribs. "Nothing is broken," he announced at last.

The brandy was having its effect and Kon was feeling limp despite the pain in his stomach. Giovanni arranged the blanket over him and gazed sadly at his dark sunken eyes and his swollen lip. "Get some rest, Kon. You look like hell."

"I won't go back, Giovanni," Kon said drowsily. "I swear I'll kill him first."

"Don't give me more troubles, boy. Mother of God! I don't know why I bother to worry about you," Giovanni sighed, but he stood by the cot until he saw that Kon was asleep.

****

Giovanni was quite surprised when early one morning, about two weeks later, Francois came into the kitchen inquiring about Kon. He said very little at first thinking the Frenchman might be an undercover narcotics agent. Francois was both persistent and impatient, however, and was not shy about stating his business. He was there to fetch Kon to Geneva and he was determined to get the job over with as soon as possible.

Giovanni poured Francois some coffee and told him to wait by one of the small tables in the corner where the boys ate. Kon had been out driving clients until after 3 a.m., and was now laying out dishes in the dining room. Giovanni pulled him aside when he walked into the kitchen and told him about Francois. Kon was as surprised as Giovanni, and racked his brain thinking he must have forgotten what had been written to him.

Finally, he went up to Francois and introduced himself. He smiled and put out his hand eagerly, but Francois did not take it. He stared coldly at Kon, taking in everything from his shaggy, uncut hair to his worn out shoes. He was not impressed and did not attempt to hide his destain.

"So you're Kon, eh? Well, Madame Marneé has made a poor choice," he said rudely.

Kon stared steadily back at Francois. He wanted desperately to go to Geneva, but he was what he was. He had never pretended to Edgar or Charlotte that he was anything other than a cook's helper. His face betrayed no emotion, but his heart sank lower and lower under the Frenchman's gaze. "Monsieur Marneé wrote that he wanted me to work for him. Is it not so, sir?" Kon said at last.

"Edgar? Heavens no! He has more sense. It is Madame that is set on having you come."

It was not much of an offer, but Kon leaped at it. "Then I will come if Madame wishes it."

Francois shook his head. "You are right about that, boy.

80

Madame always gets her way." He stood up wearily, "Well, it is not my doing. I just want to finish with this job as soon as possible. Where is the man who holds your contract? I must deal with him."

Kon hesitated. It could go badly for him if anyone found out exactly what he did for Guido. Giovanni, who had been standing behind Kon, quickly stepped forward. "He is most likely in his office. I will show you the way." Giovanni pushed Kon aside and led Francois out of the kitchen. He returned a few moments later. "Go get cleaned up, Kon. Hurry! You must be presentable to meet this lady." He pushed Kon towards the cellar. "And change your shirt!" he called after him. Kon collected his things and headed for the one bathroom he was allowed to use.

As soon as he met Guido, Francois knew that he was dealing with a base character, who had somehow gotten a grip on Kon, and taken shameless advantage of him. Although he did not care about Kon, he wanted the relationship between him and Guido severed abruptly and totally. He offered Guido the tiny sum that Kon would have earned if he had completed the contract, plus a lump sum for his inconvenience. Then with great cordiality he had Guido sign a document releasing Kon from any obligation, past, present, or future. He demanded to have possession of Kon's citizenship papers, and his passport, and satisfied himself that they were complete. For his part, Guido was quite happy to be rid of Kon. The boy was becoming more and more difficult to dominate and might even be known to the police.

Having finished his business, Francois returned to the kitchen. Giovanni was waiting for him and barraged him with questions. Much to the Frenchman's annoyance, Giovanni insisted that he show him proof that he actually had been sent by Edgar Marneé. Giovanni's mistrust of Guido was such that he feared that Francois might have come to lure Kon away to be taken to the police, or murdered.

Convinced that Kon was truly escaping from Guido, Giovanni went to help him gather his meager belonging. Kon's two pairs of slacks, four shirts, and some underwear were quickly packed into the small pressed paper suitcase that he had arrived with. Kon was about to pack the bottle of aspirin and the stomach medicine that Giovanni had bought for him, but Giovanni stopped him. "You must not take them," he warned. "You go to live among foreigners, and must be on your guard. If these people even suspect that you are not in perfect health, they may refuse to have you. If you have a problem, blame it on the change of food. I have heard that complaint often enough from the Swiss."

Kon turned to Giovanni, "I have not said goodbye to Carla. Will you send word to her, Giovanni? She has been kind to me."

"Yes . . . yes, but you must forget her now and start a new, better life."

Kon hesitated, then put his hand out to Giovanni. "Thank you, Giovanni. I . . . I could not have survived here without your help," he said gratefully.

Giovanni took Kon's hand firmly, then suddenly he encircled him with his fleshy arms, and hugged him to his massive chest. "Mother of God, you have been a trial, but I will miss you, boy! Go now and work hard. I will pray to the Virgin that this fine lady keeps you."

Francois was impatient to be off, and there was no more time for good-byes. Kon put his small suitcase into the trunk of the car and climbed into the passenger seat. He had dreamt of someday leaving the hotel, but it was hard to believe he was actually doing it. He felt quite happy, until Francois told him he would have to undergo a health check and be given various inoculations. Kon did not have a very high opinion of doctors. He had not been awake when Francini had stitched up his arm, but he had not liked the man when Giovanni had insisted that he consult him about his stomach pains.

His only other experience with doctors had been with the man who had come to see him after the widow had pulled his battered body off her doorstep. His only clear memory was that the pain had been unbearable every time the man touched him. He had screamed and fought until the man held a cloth over his face. He still remembered the horrible smell of the cloth, and how he had clawed and struggled until he had fainted. He could never remember what had been done to him, he remembered only that he had hurt terribly for a long time afterwards. How was he to know what an incredible feat that back alley "doctor" had accomplished keeping him alive with only the most basic medical equipment, and no drugs other than chloroform to ease his pain. Perhaps it was just as well that Kon did not remember that he had been tied to a bed for days to keep him still while he was mad with fever, and that the widow had bound a cloth over his mouth to prevent his screams from alerting the neighbors to his presence. Kon should have been taken to a hospital, but the widow could not afford it, and she was afraid the police would take him away if they learned that he was a foreigner. No doubt the police would have given him up for dead if they had found him. Finding a dying boy in the streets was not an unusual thing in Naples. Who would pay to treat one more dirty orphan?

Francois drove to the clinic, and pushed Kon into the long line of noisy, jostling patients, while he went to fill out the forms. He had taken it into his head that Kon was incapable of reading or writing and was determined to have everything arranged as quickly as possible. Charlotte had stipulated that it was Francois' responsibility to see that Kon was given all the prescribed inoculations, and Francois took his job very seriously.

When Kon's turn came he was given a cursory examination, and pronounced fit. He was quickly inoculated against smallpox, typhoid, and para-typhoid. He took all the puncturing patiently enough, but objected when the doctor scratched his upper arm, dabbed something on it and refused to let him wipe it off. At that point the doctor took a closer look at Kon, and mentioned to Francois that Kon looked very thin and tired. He recommended that he return in a week for the remainder of his shots. In response, Francois raged in poor Italian, that neither he nor Kon were ever coming back to such a place, and that they had better get on with the job. So the doctor brought out more bottles, and more needles, and did his best to protect Kon from diphtheria, tetanus, and one other disease that no one could ever make out from the terrible scrawl on his health card.

After an hour and a half at the clinic, Kon was allowed to put his shirt on again and quickly ushered out the door. Francois took possession of his health card and kept it with Kon's other papers. Once again Kon felt that he was being treated like merchandise, but he was willing to do whatever was necessary to get to Geneva.

"It's a good thing I got the police check out of the way yesterday or we would be in Milan a full day. These people are so slow," Francois grumbled.

"Police check?" Kon asked in mild alarm.

"Yes. Did you think Monsieur Marneé would invite a total stranger into his home without doing some investigation?"

"I guess I did not consider the matter from his point of view. What did the police say?" Kon asked trying to sound only mildly curious although he felt his heart speed up.

"They had never heard of you, so, unfortunately, I am forced to take you with me."

"Good," Kon sighed and relaxed.

The original plan had been for Kon to help Francois with the driving on the return trip, but Francois had not been favorably impressed with Kon. He seemed almost unwilling to have him in his car much less to let him drive it. They started from the clinic at 10:00 a.m. and made good time on the road heading north.

At first Kon was happy to sit and watch the scenery, but as it came onto noon he felt his usual headache growing worse. Although the weather was only slightly warm, he felt hotter and hotter as time went past. Francois, who seemed only partially relaxed, had started smoking cigars, and the air in the small car soon became stale and full of smoke. Kon opened the window several times, but Francois objected to the breeze and insisted upon having it closed. By 1 o'clock, when Francois decided to stop for lunch, Kon's stomach was too unsettled to permit him any appetite, and he sat with his head against the back of the seat. He did not understand what was the matter with him, but he felt it had something to do with all the needles they had put into him at the clinic. Kon did not move when Francois got out of the car.

"Do you want anything to eat?" Francois asked gruffly.

Kon shook his head.

"What about a drink then?" Francois continued. Kon raised his head, then sighed. "I have no money," he said flatly.

Francois felt a slight pang of guilt as it occurred to him that Kon might have refused food for the same reason. "Edgar is paying for the trip. Any food we need is included. Look, I'm going to have lunch — do you want a drink or not?" he asked sharply.

Kon would not beg, but he was too thirsty to turn down any offer, no matter how rudely made.

"Some coffee then, please."

"Well, come on! Hurry up!"

Kon opened the car door and rolled himself off the seat. He walked with Francois toward the restaurant, but stopped when he reached the tables of the cafe. "I'll stay here, in the air," he said weakly.

Francois did not encourage him as he did not really like the idea of having Kon as a companion at the dinner table. "Very well, I'll send the waiter with your coffee." Francois turned and walked into the restaurant and Kon dropped into a chair by the wall. He leaned back, put his head against the wall and closed his eyes. When the waiter brought the coffee, Kon opened his eyes.

"Do you have any medicine for headache?"

"No, sir. You will have to ask the chemist," the waiter answered. Then seeing that Kon looked very tired, he added, "I could send someone for you if you tell me what you need."

Kon knew the waiter was hoping to make a little extra money for this service, and he shook his head. "The coffee will be enough."

The waiter nodded and left.

Although the coffee was hot, Kon drank it greedily. His mouth felt very dry. He stared out at the mountains with their lingering patches of snow, but their beauty did not stir him. He visited the rest room, threw some water over his face, then sat and waited for Francois to return. It was over an hour before Francois emerged from the restaurant. Seeing Kon almost asleep against the wall he rapped him on the shoulder.

"Are you ready to go?"

Kon did not answer, but rose and followed Francois to the car. Francois got in and leaned across to unlock the door for Kon. Taking a good look at Kon's face he noticed his unnatural color. "You're not going to be sick are you?"

Kon shook his head rather feebly.

"Good. I won't tolerate your being sick on my upholstery."

He started the car and grumbled under his breath, "God! Why

did I let Charlotte talk me into this trip? It is much more pleasant to make it alone." He drove on in silence and about a half an hour later he lit another cigar. The smell of it in the small, airless vehicle made Kon feel light headed, and the swaying of the car as they made their way around the mountain bends seemed to grow more violent at each turn. He regretted having taken the coffee. He swallowed hard twice, then suddenly put his hand on Francois' arm. "Please . . . stop the car."

Francois turned his head in surprise and seeing Kon's face he hit the brakes and pulled off the road. "Don't you dare soil my seat covers you son of a bitch! Get out!"

Kon flung open the door, and managed to hang his head out before the coffee came up with a violent rush. His stomach continued to contract, but since he had not eaten since the night before, there was nothing to force out. Slowly he pulled himself upright and leaned against the seat.

"Damn! What a nuisance you are! I should have put you on a bus. All this trouble to see that you are fit, and you throw up in my car."

Kon did not open his eyes, but responded irritably, "It is not my habit to be sick, sir. Perhaps if I could have a little fresh air I would do better."

Francois did not answer, but angrily snubbed out his cigar and waited to see if Kon was going to heave again. "Are you settled down yet?" Francois demanded after a few minutes.

"Yes, sir," Kon said defensively. Francois' attitude was beginning to make his temper rise.

"Then close the door and let's get going. You make my own lunch rise in my throat! I can't imagine what Charlotte hopes to do with a wretch like you!"

Kon thought he could not possibly feel any worse, but gradually he discovered he was wrong. His head continued to pound and he started to ache all over. He could not seem to hold his eyes open, but neither could he fall asleep or rest. Francois spoke to him several times, but he did not have the energy to respond.

A while later Francois shook him and shouted, "Wake up! Look alive! The border check is up ahead. You're supposed to be coming to Switzerland to work."

Kon opened his eyes and shook his head. He pulled himself as upright at he could. He opened the window half way and the rush of cool air on his face was a relief. Francois drove up to the gate and rolled down the window. When the guard stepped up to the car he showed his own papers and then handed over Kon's.

The guard glanced briefly at the papers, then at Kon.

"Looking for work, eh?" the guard asked him.

"No, sir. I am promised a job with Monsieur Marneé in

Geneva."

"What is your trade?" the guard inquired.

Kon hesitated. Kitchen helper didn't sound like much of a trade.

"He's a laborer," Francois put in. "Madame Marneé needs more domestic help." Francois noticed that the guard was looking closely at Kon.

"Are you sick, boy?" the guard asked.

Again Francois answered for him. "He's been car sick the whole trip – lost his lunch a while back. He's had all the shots and was checked at the clinic in Milan."

"Not very talkative is he?" he guard commented, still staring at Kon.

"He's not a prize as a travelling companion, but it is my duty to fetch him."

The guard took one last look at Kon's papers and handed them back to Francois. "Everything appears to be in order. You may be on your way," he said, and stepped away from the car.

Francois rolled up the window and drove through the gate. And so it was that free, but penniless and sick, Kon passed into Switzerland. The remainder of the trip was no better than the first part for Kon. When he found it too difficult to hold his head up any longer, he removed his oversized coat, and folded it several times. Placing it against the side window, he leaned against it. Francois at length realized that Kon was suffering from more than just motion sickness and mercifully allowed him to open the window part way.

Kon seemed unaware that the car had stopped when they arrived in the driveway in front of the Marneé home. It was almost 6 o'clock and Francois was hungry. He hoped that Charlotte would invite him to dine with the family as she often did. He shook Kon impatiently and insisted he put on his coat. He despaired of Charlotte's being favorably impressed with Kon, but he wanted things to go as smoothly as possible.

After a day of listening to Francois' criticism, Kon was not feeling confident about the meeting. He wondered if Edgar truly had not wanted him to come. Remembering Giovanni's words of warning, he struggled to pull himself from the car and stood looking at the huge house in the slowly fading light. Although it was only three stories high, it seemed immense as he gazed up at it from close range. Suddenly the house seemed to grow taller and loom ominously above him. His knees melted and he sank slowly downward into a gray pit. Something cold and hard struck him on the forehead and everything went dark.

CHAPTER SEVEN

Charlotte was in the library with Charles and Albert when she heard the loud knocking at the front door. The sound of excited voices and scurrying feet drifted in to her. She wondered at the commotion, but waited with the boys knowing that Edgar could handle any unexpected situation. Finally Edgar opened the door and rushed in.

"Our young helper has arrived, Charlotte, but he has fainted on the steps!"

"Good heavens! Is he so nervous to meet us again?" Charlotte asked in amazement.

"I don't think it was from nerves. Francois said the lad was acting strangely tired all day."

Charlotte left her chair. "Albert, be a dear boy and stay with Charles while I go with Papa," she said and hurried from the room just ahead of Edgar. She met Francois in the hall. "Francois, what have you done with the boy?"

"He is still on the steps. I was afraid to move him. He hit his head when he fell."

"Edgar said he was ill. Tell me what happened," she demanded.

Francois became defensive. "Well, he got out of the car, and was standing there looking at the house. Then he just sort of crumbled as he started up the stairs."

"Well, we can't let him lay in the street!" She turned to Edgar. "Edgar, would you please help Francois to carry him inside."

"Oh this is terrible! Just too terrible!" she kept repeating to herself as the men lifted Kon and carried him into the hall. "Turn him on his side, in case he has a fit or something," Charlotte said helplessly. She looked at Kon, but did not recognize him for the boy they had met almost nine months ago.

"Francois!" she said in alarm. "You have brought the wrong boy!"

"Madame, he is the one you requested. How many young men named Kononellos do you think work at that hotel?" Francois answered a bit impatiently.

"But he looks so much older. Look at his eyes. He looks positively awful!"

"It has been a long time since you've seen him, Charlotte. Perhaps you have forgotten," Francois said more politely.

"Oh, Edgar, we must call Carlin to have a look at him. He may have injured his head," she said anxiously.

"I will call him, Charlotte. Calm yourself. He probably was just dizzy from the drive, or ate something wrong for lunch." Edgar took Charlotte's hand for a moment before he went into the living room to make the call. He hated to see her get upset.

Charlotte seized upon the idea of poor food being the culprit. "Where did you eat lunch, Francois? What did he have?"

"We stopped in Aosta. I always go there. As for food, he didn't have any − only coffee."

"You didn't give him lunch?" Charlotte asked raising her voice slightly.

"He said he wasn't hungry," Francois added quickly. "His stomach was bothering him all day. He even brought up the coffee shortly after we left the restaurant. I tell you he was car sick. I don't know how you expect to make a chauffeur of him. The wretch came close to ruining my upholstery!"

"Oh, Francois, you were supposed to see that he was in good health," Charlotte wailed.

"They examined him at the clinic this morning. There was nothing wrong with him then," Francois said defensively.

Charlotte continued to fret until Edgar returned a few moments later.

"Carlin was in his office and will be here shortly. Please, don't get upset, Charlotte. I told you from the first this was a foolish idea."

Charlotte was beginning to think so herself, but she did not want to hear it from Edgar. She set her will against giving in to him. "There is no reason for all of us to stand and wait for Carlin," she said, trying to regain her composure. "We have held supper for your return, Francois. I will tell Anna to begin serving. Please, take the boys into the dining room, Edgar." Charlotte went into the kitchen and told the cook to begin serving the meal. When she returned to the hall, she heard the sound of voices coming from the dining room. She was about to join the others when she was suddenly struck by how forsaken Kon looked lying alone on the floor. She slipped up the stairs, and brought a blanket to put over him. As she covered his shoulders, she took a closer look at his face and touched his forehead. She knew immediately this was no simple case of motion sickness, and she rejected the idea of leaving him to lie alone in the hall. He might wake up and become confused to find himself in a strange place, she thought, remembering how her children sometimes became frightened when they were away from their familiar surroundings. She stepped into the dining room and asked Edgar to bring a chair into the hall for her. "I will wait with him until Carlin comes," she told Edgar.

Charlotte sat in the hall and wondered what she was going to do about the situation. She was sorry she had talked Edgar into letting her bring this young man from Italy. He looked so much older than she had remembered, and was so ragged and untidy with his ill fitting coat and long hair. How could she trust her children to such a person? She must either find something for him to do or send him back. If she were to send him back she would never hear the end of it from Edgar. And how was she to tell this young man that she did not want him in her home after he had left his job and travelled a long way to work for her. She was much relieved when Carlin arrived and interrupted her thoughts.

"Thank you for coming so quickly, Carlin," she said as she opened the door for him.

"What is the problem, Charlotte? Edgar said the boy you hired fainted on the steps."

"Yes, Francois saw him fall and hit his head. They carried him inside, but he has yet to wake up." She motioned to where Kon lay. "I felt his head, Carlin, and he is feverish."

Carlin hurried to Kon and turned him over. He felt his pulse, listed to his heart and looked at his eyes. "He does not seem to have a serious head injury. Where is he to stay? I would like to get him to bed and do a better examination."

"He was to stay in the room next to the boys," Charlotte started, but suddenly put her hand on Carlin's arm. "Oh, Carlin, I think I have made a terrible mistake in bringing him here. He is not at all as I remembered him. If he passes something to the boys, Edgar will never forgive me."

"Calm yourself, Charlotte. Just keep the boys away from him until I determine what is wrong with him. Now please ask Edgar to give me a hand to carry him upstairs."

Charlotte went towards the dining room, but before she reached the door Edgar and Francois came out of the room. Edgar was relieved to see Carlin taking charge of things.

"Good evening, Carlin. I am sorry to bother you with our little problems," Edgar said shaking Carlin's hand. "Francois swears the boy was checked at the clinic this morning and declared in perfect health."

"What did they do at the clinic?" Carlin asked turning to Francois.

"They gave him inoculations so he could enter the country, plus a few more. Charlotte had quite a list you know. It's all here on his health card," Francois answered taking the card out of his pocket and handing it to Carlin.

Carlin took only a minute to read it, then sighed. Before he could say more, Charles and Albert came running out of the dining room. They were startled to see Kon lying on the floor surrounded by the others. Albert who was eight came up to him, and stared down with wide eyed curiosity.

"Who is that man, Mama?"

"This is a young man I have hired to help Anna," Charlotte

answered, and taking hold of the child's arm she pulled him away from Kon.

"Why is he sleeping on the floor?" Albert continued.

"He is very tired, Albert," Carlin answered, "and he fell fast asleep before he got to his bed. We are going to take him there now. Will you help me carry him up the stairs, Edgar? Does he have any luggage, Francois?"

"Only a cheap little case."

"Would you bring it please?"

And so Kon was taken up the three flights of stairs and deposited on the bed in the room next to Charles and Albert. Carlin sent the others down to finish their supper while he undressed Kon and checked him over carefully. When he had finished he pulled the covers over him. To learn more about the boy, he opened his suitcase and unpacked his few belongings. Carlin left the light on the dresser turned on when he left the room and joined the others in the library for coffee.

"Well how is he?" Edgar was quick to ask.

"The injury to his head is minor, but he seems to be suffering from exhaustion. He's had a serious reaction to the inoculations and is running a temperature. He's really extremely thin and should not have been given so much in one day. His arms are badly swollen. It must have been a difficult trip for him today."

"He will recover though, won't he?" Francois asked, suddenly feeling guilty.

"Yes. I gave him something to keep the fever down, but he should be kept quiet for a few days." Carlin paused. "They must have worked him very hard where he was," he continued shaking his head. "I suspect he was beaten. He has the remains of some terrible bruises on his shoulder and over his ribs."

"How positively awful! Who would do such a thing?" Charlotte asked in dismay.

Carlin shrugged his shoulders. He did not want to upset Charlotte with tales of things he had seen. So they sat and talked of how they had met Kon, and looked over his papers. Carlin checked on Kon again before he left the house, but he had not moved.

When Carlin stopped at the house on his way to his office the next morning, he gathered that the boy had experienced a restless night. The blanket had fallen or been kicked onto the floor, and the sheets were damp and crumpled. Although it was nearly 8 a.m., Kon was still asleep. He lay sprawled on his back with his left leg drawn up and his right arm thrown over his head. Carlin thought he felt slightly cooler, but was still feverish. Kon did not move when Carlin checked his pulse, but when he lay his hands lightly on either side of Kon's throat to feel for swollen glands, Kon jerked violently. Then suddenly he sat bolt upright and seized Carlin by the arm. Realizing that this was not the dream, but that there actually was a stranger at his throat, Kon leaped backwards and a frightened cry escaped him. He stared at Carlin with wide eyes. Carlin noted his frightened response, but kept his voice as calm as possible.

"Good morning, Peter. I'm sorry I startled you."

When Carlin spoke, Kon drew back even farther and put his arm up as if to fend off a blow. "Who are you and what do you want with me?" he demanded.

"I am Dr. Carlin La Monde. I was sent by Edgar Marneé to take care of you, Peter," Carlin answered calmly.

Kon continued to stare at him in alarm. "Why do you call me Peter?" he asked uncertainly.

It was Carlin's turn to be surprised. "Peter is the name given on your papers. Is there some mistake?"

"My papers?" Kon repeated slowly. "No one has seen my papers . . . unless . . . Damn you! You stole my papers!" He lunged at Carlin and seized both his wrists. "Give me my papers, you thief! I gave nearly a year of my life for them!"

Carlin saw that he was becoming hysterical and did not try to pull away. "I have not taken your papers," he answered with as much calmness and authority as he could muster. "Edgar showed them to me. It was important that I know what treatment you were given at the clinic."

Kon stared at him suspiciously for a long moment before he relaxed his crushing grip and growled, "Give them to me then!" He let go of Carlin.

Carlin withdrew his hands slowly and walked to the dresser. He gathered all the documents, and returning to the bed he handed them to Kon. Kon took them eagerly and scanned them with growing dismay. The name given was clearly Peter, not Petros, and the signature, though very like his own, had not been made by his hand. He had never had a good look at the papers until now, as Guido had only passed them before his face to show that he had obtained them and kept his part of the bargain.

"My God! My God! He's cheated me again!" Kon moaned realizing that Guido had given him forged papers. Although he preferred to call himself Kon, Petros was his name, and he suddenly felt dishonored by having it stolen from him. "Truly you cannot bargain with the devil and win," Kon said dejectedly.

"Is there something wrong?" Carlin asked seeing the look on Kon's face.

Kon looked at him briefly, then put his hand over his eyes. He dared not tell anyone that his papers were forged. They might send him back to Italy. They might even send him to prison. He shuddered at the thought and Carlin wondered if the fever had affected him more seriously than he had suspected.

91

"Is something wrong, Peter?" he inquired again more gently. "It was Madame who decided to call you Peter. She thought it sounded more civilized than Kon. If that bothers you I'm sure she would call you whatever you wish."

Kon did not respond immediately, but slowly looked around the room. "What place is this? I don't remember coming here!" he asked apprehensively.

"This is the home of Edgar Marneé. You don't remember coming here because you collapsed on the steps and had to be carried to bed. You had a bad reaction from all the shots they gave you at the clinic. Do you recall anything from the trip?"

"I remember the terrible headache and being very, very hot," Kon answered thoughtfully. Then with determination, "If I have arrived in Geneva then I must go to work. Where are my clothes?" he said, seeming suddenly distressed at his nakedness. "I need my clothes! Why have you taken my clothes?"

Carlin feared he would become excited again and answered soothingly, "Your clothes are in the closet, but you are not ready to go to work yet. You still have a fever, Peter. You must rest."

The soothing tones did not work.

"I am not hired to rest. If I don't work they will send me back," he answered forcefully.

Carlin suddenly realized by the tone in Kon's voice that the fear of being sent back to Italy weighed heavily on his mind. How could he tell this poor, exhausted boy that Charlotte did not plan to keep him? It troubled him deeply, but he decided that for the moment his duty as a doctor was to keep Kon rested until he was physically stronger, and emotionally calmer.

"No one here requires you to work when you are ill, Peter. Edgar sent me to take care of you, and I order you to rest."

"I do not work for you. I must see Monsieur Marneé and know what he wants me to do," Kon answered stubbornly. Then wrapping the sheet around himself he got out of bed and went towards the closet.

Carlin was there before him and blocked the way. "Go back to bed, Peter, please. You can't see Edgar now. He has gone to the office."

"He left me no instructions? Does he know that I am here?" Kon seemed disappointed and confused, but would not back down.

"He knows you're here, Peter. I told him you need to rest and he agreed."

"I don't believe you!" Kon answered trying to push his way past Carlin. "No one gives a holiday to a man before he has worked."

Carlin put his hands on Kon's shoulders and tried to steer him back to the bed.

"Let me go! I will be dismissed if I don't work!"

"You will not be dismissed, Peter. I promise," Carlin said, looking Kon directly in the face.

"I don't believe you!" Kon shouted and tried again to push past him.

"Why won't you trust me, Peter?" Carlin asked calmly.

"How can I trust a man who attacks me while I sleep!" Kon snapped back.

Carlin was startled by his explanation, and had to think hard to see any reason in it. He finally understood. "I was not attacking you, Peter. I merely felt your throat to see if it was swollen. I meant you no harm."

Kon gave him a hard stare. He was not convinced. "If Monsieur Marneé is not here, I will go to Madame. She may have some work for me."

"Madame is not at home, Peter. She took the boys to school."

Kon did not answer, but again he looked disappointed and seemed to lose his determination. "It is not a good sign that they have no work for me," he said sadly.

Carlin was determined to hide the truth from him as long as possible. "It means nothing. They want you to rest and recover your strength before you begin. That is all. Now please, Peter, go back to bed. I will see that Madame visits you when she returns," he promised.

"But I need my clothes," Kon insisted stubbornly.

"Very well, I will get your shirt. Now please, go back to bed."

Kon retreated slowly to the bed, and Carlin brought him a shirt and a pair of shorts.

"Would you like some breakfast, Peter?" Carlin asked, trying to divert his thoughts.

"How can I prepare breakfast if I am not allowed to leave my bed?"

"You don't have to prepare it. I will ask the cook to fix something. Come, what would you like?" he asked cheerfully.

"Coffee."

"What, no food?" Carlin said with exaggerated surprise. "Please, you must eat something," he coaxed. "Aren't you hungry? When did you last eat?"

"I don't remember."

"Well, I will have the cook give us some rolls to have with our coffee. I haven't had breakfast yet either," he lied. He turned to leave, but stopped as he opened the door. "Peter . . . would you like to see where the toilet is?"

Kon nodded and followed him out.

Kon was standing by the window gazing out into the garden when Carlin returned with a tray of food and some clean sheets. It was a pleasant spring day and the garden was bright with many shades of green.

"It's very pretty here this time of year, Peter. The air is not as soft as in Italy, but more invigorating. Come, you must eat while the rolls are still warm!"

Kon sat and watched Carlin slice a roll and spread it thickly with some soft cheese. The sight of it reminded him that he hadn't eaten for a long time. He was surprised when Carlin put the roll on a plate and offered it to him. He had been used to fighting the others for even a share of what the customers had left. Carlin saw his surprised look, but ignored it.

"Come on, eat quickly before it gets cold!"

Kon ate it as slowly as his hunger would allow, all the while watching Carlin slice another roll and spread jam on it. Carlin poured them both coffee. "How do you like your coffee, Peter?"

"Very sweet."

Carlin spooned in the sugar and handed the cup to Kon. He sipped his own coffee slowly and watched Kon drain his cup in one continuous swallow.

"Do you drink a lot of coffee, Peter?"

"All I can get. I must have it to work."

"You don't get much sleep do you."

"Six hours some nights. Some nights . . . not as much."

"How much?" Carlin persisted.

"Maybe two hours," Kon answered slowly.

"How often did you get six hours during a week?"

Kon shrugged his shoulders. "Maybe twice," he said vaguely.

"What were you doing all night, Peter?"

"Working," he answered softly and looked away. Quickly he poured himself more coffee.

"How did you get that scar on your arm?"

Kon said nothing, but raised his chin slightly.

"And the ones on your abdomen?" Carlin persisted.

"They do not affect my work. What business is it of yours!" Kon snapped.

Carlin did not inquire about the bruises. He asked a few questions about what type of work Kon did and where he had been. At last Kon questioned him.

"Do you know this Francois, the Frenchman, who came to Italy for me?"

"Yes. He is Monsieur Marneé's attorney. Not really a pleasant fellow, but very clever. What about him?"

Kon hesitated and lowered his eyes before he spoke. "He told me several times that Monsieur Marneé was not willing to have me come. He indicated that only Madame wanted to hire me. Does he speak the truth?" There was a note of desperation in his voice.

Damn that man! Carlin thought to himself. Why couldn't he

keep his mouth shut? He looked at Kon and there was a long silence. "Francois has some very strong opinions, but he does not always speak for Edgar. Don't give too much weight to what he says." Carlin rose quickly, and taking up Kon's plate and cup he put them on the tray. "Here, give me a hand with this bed," he said abruptly, and tossed a clean sheet to Kon.

"Now you must rest, Peter," he said firmly when they had finished. "I will let Madame know as soon as she returns that you wish to speak with her."

Kon lay on the bed as ordered, but he frowned and stared out the window. Carlin knew he was worried about his job and would not sleep. He left him alone and went down to wait for Charlotte.

It was after 10 a.m. when Charlotte returned with Charles. She had been shopping and was surprised to find Carlin waiting for her. She sent Charles to the kitchen to see the cook so they could talk privately. Carlin told Charlotte how anxious Kon was to work, and how much he dreaded being sent back to Italy. He also told her that she must visit the boy, but that if she indicated in any way that she was disappointed with him, his recovery would be seriously affected. She agreed reluctantly to speak with Kon and assure him that he would be allowed to work once he was better.

Carlin entered the room first, and found Kon standing by the window which he had somehow forced open. His face betrayed his worry and unhappiness.

"Peter! You'll get a chill standing there. You should be in bed. Come, Madame is here to see you."

Carlin drew Peter to the bed and propped him against the pillows. He closed the window, and then opened the door for Charlotte.

"Good morning, Peter. How are you feeling?" she asked hesitantly.

"I am well, Madame," he answered. "So, am I to be Peter now?" he asked anxiously.

Charlotte was a little taken aback. "Well, it's a very good name. Don't you like it?"

"I . . ." he began and then he bit his lip and lowered his eyes. "You have hired me, Madame. You may call me what you wish," he said with resignation.

Charlotte hesitated and felt the silence was awkward. "Then I shall call you Peter."

He looked at her steadily trying to remember her from their last meeting. She did seem familiar with her small round face and pretty little mouth. She was not a tall woman, but had a trim figure.

"Madame, I am ready to work, but this man," he said gesturing towards Carlin, "tells me I must wait. What is your wish, please?"

Charlotte sat by the bed and studied the dark circles beneath his

95

eyes, but before she could respond, little Charles came running into the room. He had slipped away from the cook, and driven by curiosity, had come in search of his mother. He ran to her now, but hid behind her when he saw Peter. He tugged at her skirt. "Mama, who is that?" he whispered shyly.

Charlotte lifted the boy onto her lap. "That is Peter. I hired him to help Anna."

Charles stared silently at Peter, taking in every detail as only little children can do. "Why do you wear your shirt to bed, Peter?" he suddenly asked.

Peter did not know what to say. How could be explain to a child that it was not considered polite to appear naked before a lady. He felt awkward when he could think of no response. Carlin put a different meaning on Charles' question. "Peter forgot to bring his pajamas with him, Charles," he put in quickly and the child accepted his answer.

Charlotte looked at Peter and gave her answer to his question. "Peter, if Dr. La Monde says you must rest, then you must do as he says. His word is law in this house."

"Papa says we must all do as Dr. La Monde says, even Papa," Charles affirmed.

Peter smiled at the boy. Charles did not seem the least bit afraid of Peter as Charlotte had feared.

"But when will I work?" Peter persisted.

Charlotte hesitated and looked away. "Soon, Peter. When Dr. La Monde says you are better." Carlin had slipped out of the room while they were talking, but returned with a glass of water.

"You must get some rest now, Peter," he said firmly. "I will give you some capsules to help you sleep."

Peter's face darkened at the word capsules. "Will they make me sleep like the dead?" he asked in alarm.

"No, they are just to help you relax," Carlin answered. He produced two capsules and held them out to Peter along with the water.

Peter drew back. "No! I swore I would never take sleeping pills again." He stared at Carlin in defiance.

Carlin signed. "Who made you swear such a thing, Peter?"

"Giovanni. I promised him!"

"Who is Giovanni? Is he a doctor?" Carlin asked.

"No he is my friend. He said they are poison for me."

"Peter! I'm sure Dr. La Monde would not give you poison," Charlotte said with slight indignation.

Carlin was a very patient man, but he was growing tired of Peter's resistance to everything he prescribed.

"Please, Peter, don't set a bad example for the child. The medicine won't hurt you, I promise," Carlin said although he knew

Peter did not trust him.

Peter stared at Charles and Charlotte. If the child saw him refuse the medicine he might rebel himself, and the mother would be angry with him, but if he took it . . . He felt trapped.

"Please don't make me take them. Please . . . I swore." He looked at Carlin and pleaded, "I'll rest. I promise . . . I'll stay in bed as long as you like . . . please."

Carlin could see that Peter was becoming agitated. He shot a knowing glance at Charlotte as if to say, "Do you see how excited he gets?" He was convinced Peter was objecting because he did not trust him.

"Perhaps you have a milder medicine, Doctor," Charlotte offered. Sometimes the switch worked on the boys.

Carlin closed his hand over the capsules. "Well, we will try something else." He rummaged in his bag for a few minutes and came up with just one small tablet. "Come now, Peter, one tiny tablet won't hurt you." He held the tablet and the water out to Peter.

Peter stared at Charlotte, and she was moved to pity by the look in his eyes. He might seem hysterical to Carlin, but to her it was obvious that he was convinced they were asking him to take poison. She had never seen even little Charles get so upset over such a small matter, but she was too kind not to help him.

"Take the medicine, Peter," she said soothingly. "I will stay with you until you fall asleep. I promise nothing will hurt you."

Peter looked at her with resignation, but said nothing more. He swallowed the tablet.

"Now lie down and relax, Peter," Carlin coaxed and arranged the pillows.

Peter lay down, but kept his eyes on Charlotte. She sat calmly playing with Charles and telling him he must be quiet so Peter could go to sleep. After a few minutes Peter's eyelids began to flicker and close, but he shook his head and forced his eyes open.

"Don't fight it, Peter. Just relax," Carlin said softly. Sooner than Carlin had expected, Peter's breathing became quiet and slow and he knew he was asleep though his eyes were still open. His body had trained itself to sleep even when his will would not let his eyes close.

Carlin reached up and gently touched Peter's eyelids to close them. He sighed and shook his head. "What a fight to get him to quiet down." He put his medicines and equipment back into his bag. "I had better call my office, Charlotte. I did not expect to be here so long."

"Thank you for coming, Carlin. I'll sit with him just a moment longer. Charles, show Dr. La Monde where the telephone is."

Charles bounded off her lap and ran to the door. She knew that Carlin knew exactly where the telephone was, but Charles enjoyed playing the game. After they left, Charlotte sat quietly by herself listening to Peter's heavy breathing and wondering what she was going to do with him. She wandered absently to the dresser and opened the drawers. He certainly does not have many clothes and his shirts are gray with age, she thought. Well he was very poorly paid, she answered herself.

Planning to see Carlin out, she turned a final time towards the bed and noticed that she could not hear Peter's breathing. She bent low over the bed, but still heard no sound. Something was very wrong. She ran to the door, hurried along the hall and down the stairs. She called from the second floor landing. "Carlin, come quickly. Something's wrong with Peter. I'm not sure he's breathing!"

Carlin came up the stairs two at a time and rushed into the room. He felt for Peter's pulse, but it was very weak. He put his face close to Peter's. "He's still breathing, Charlotte, but just barely. He must be very sensitive to the drug. I can't risk having him sink any lower or it could be fatal." He took up his bag and prepared an injection, but at the last minute he forced more liquid over the end of the needle. He rolled Peter's sleeve back and pressed the needle into his vein.

I should have listened to him about the drug, he thought angrily to himself. Damn, I thought I was being so clever getting him to take that one little tablet instead of two capsules. He never suspected it was stronger than both the others. Carlin put the syringe away and looked at Charlotte. "I'm sorry this frightened you, Charlotte. I thought he was just hysterical, and I gave him a stronger dose to quiet him down."

Charlotte sank into the chair by the bed. "He took it to please me, Carlin. I knew he was frightened. I read it in his eyes."

She watched Peter closely and was relieved when a few minutes later he sighed and drew in a long breath. Carlin put a stethoscope to Peter's chest, and was pleased that his heart was beating stronger, but not racing. The smaller dose had been enough.

Peter turned his head and opened his eyes part way. His vision was blurred, and he could not tell if Charlotte was still there, or if she had lied to him. He uttered a single plaintive whisper, "Madame?"

Through her heart Charlotte suddenly perceived Peter not as older and rougher, but only as a very tired young man who needed care. Impulsively she put her hand on his forehead as she did to soothe little Charles or Albert when they were sick. She brushed the tangled hair out of his eyes, but it would not accept her guidance and fell back again. "It's all right, Peter. Go back to sleep," she said softly.

Carlin knew by the look on her face that she would not send Peter away and he was glad. Any young man who wanted to work as badly as Peter did, deserved a chance to prove himself.

"I will have to train him, Carlin. He is very rough material."

Charlotte sighed at the weight of the task.

"I can't think of anyone better suited to it than you, Charlotte," he said sincerely.

****

When Carlin returned at 7 p.m. to dine with the Marneés he looked in on Peter and found that he was still asleep. He went down to dinner with the family, but Edgar thought he seemed slightly preoccupied throughout the meal. When questioned, he admitted that he was concerned about Peter. "He should be awake by now. He has had so little to eat . . . he's so thin . . ."

"You are quite right, Carlin," Charlotte agreed. "I will ask Anna to heat some soup for him." She left the others to their dessert and went into the kitchen. She returned shortly with Anna who bore a tray with a bowl of soup, a glass of milk and a piece of cake.

"Shall I take it up, sir?" Anna asked Carlin pleasantly.

"Thank you, Anna, but I should go and see how Peter is doing." He took the tray and went upstairs. Peter was still asleep, but Carlin decided he must wake him. He sat by the bed and called him by name, softly at first, but then more loudly. He hesitated to shake him for fear he would startle him the way he had in the morning. He touched him lightly on the shoulder, then shook him and called again.

At last Peter rolled onto his stomach and raised himself half way. "I'm sorry, Giovanni. I must have forgotten to set the . . ." he mumbled drowsily, and jumped when he saw Carlin. He blinked several times and rubbed his eyes.

"I'm sorry to wake you, Peter, but I thought you should have more food."

Peter seemed very groggy so Carlin arranged the pillows behind him and gave him the food. He ate the soup willingly, but clearly he viewed the milk as an insult.

"I am not a child or an invalid, why should I drink milk?"

"Because it's good for you. Madame selected the food herself. She wants you to get well quickly."

Peter drank the milk silently.

Carlin remembered the robe and pajamas Charlotte had mentioned and brought them over to Peter. "Madame bought some clothes for you, Peter," he said, and spread the garments on the bed.

Peter showed no expression, but fingered the robe thoughtfully. Although it was only flannel it was of good quality and very soft.

"She means to have me stay then," he said looking at Carlin. Only the briefest smile showed on his lips, but his whole face suddenly looked more relaxed.

"Why there was never any doubt of it, Peter," Carlin lied.

"No, no. Something has changed her mind. She did not want me here this morning. I read it in her eyes."

99

CHAPTER EIGHT

Peter awoke early the next morning and as Carlin had predicted he was very hungry. He dressed quickly and hurried down the stairs to find the kitchen. Since he had done kitchen work before, he guessed that he would be expected to do it again. He didn't really care. As long as he was paid and given food he was willing to do any type of work.

When he stepped into the kitchen he saw a heavy-set woman with gray hair and a pretty dark haired girl, who he guessed was about his age, sitting at one end of a long oak table. They were drinking coffee and the aroma of it increased his appetite. He went closer to the table and stood watching the women for a few moments before he said softly, "Excuse me, I'm looking for Anna." The women looked up and stared at him in surprise.

"I am Anna," the older woman said after a moment. "Are you Peter?" she asked in disbelief.

"Yes, ma'am," Peter answered and took a step forward. "I've come to work."

Anna continued to stare at him. My word, Dr. La Monde is right! He is too thin, she thought to herself. She ought to know, she had raised three sons to manhood, and none of them had ever looked like this boy. Well, she would have to do something about the situation immediately. "Would you like some breakfast, Peter?" she asked getting up from the table.

"Yes," Peter answered truthfully. "But I could work first if you wish," he added promptly.

"No, no — no need to rush into it," Anna answered and smiled. "Are you feeling better, Peter? You gave Madame quite a fright when you fainted like that."

"Yes, ma'am. I can work now," Peter answered. Anna thought he still looked pale and drawn, but didn't question him. "Come, sit down, Peter," she smiled, and indicating the chair she had just vacated, she turned and went to the stove. Peter approached the table, but when he put his hand on the chair to pull it out, the girl gave him such an unfriendly look he withdrew to the opposite end of the table.

"Would you like some coffee, Peter?" Anna called cheerfully from the stove.

"Yes, please," he answered immediately. "I could get it . . ." he said and started to get up, but Anna was already at the table with a cup in her hand.

"No need to get up." She put the cup on the table in front of him. "Peter, this is Melina," Anna said, vaguely waving her hand in the girl's direction. "She is from Italy, also."

Peter looked at Melina as Anna went back to the stove. "Do you work here, too?" he asked politely.

Melina shot him a scornful glance. "I attend the university here," she said coldly.

"That's a good thing to do," Peter answered softly and took a gulp of coffee. He sat in silence until Anna returned with a plate heaped with eggs, sausages and bread. "Thank you, Anna. Is this all for me?" he asked in surprise.

"Yes, we've already eaten." Anna poured more coffee for herself and Melina, and they sat and watched Peter eat. He hunched over the table, held his left arm across his plate, and shoveled the food into his mouth as fast as he could with his right hand. Watching him from the corner of her eye, Anna marveled that anyone could eat so fast. Melina looked shocked, but Anna quickly put her finger to her lips to signal her not to say anything.

Peter glanced up as he finished and caught them staring at him. He looked warily from Anna to Melina and rose silently taking up his empty plate. "What would you like me to do?" he asked.

"I'll show you where things are," Anna said quickly to ease the awkwardness. She berated herself for her rudeness which had obviously made Peter uncomfortable.

About an hour later, when Carlin arrived, Peter was busy trying to repair the cranky old fan over the stove. Since it was Thursday and Carlin didn't have office hours, he had driven over to check on Peter's progress. He was a little dismayed to see Peter standing on a kitchen stool with his arm all but disappearing into the vent opening. He stood silently watching until Peter climbed down. "Who gave you permission to be up and working, Peter?" Carlin said sternly.

Peter jumped and turned to face Carlin. "No one, but I am well, sir, truly."

"Well, let us see. Sit down over here, Peter," Carlin said going over to the table. "Come on," he coaxed, "I want to check your temperature."

Peter didn't move until Anna came over to him. "Go sit, Peter. You can finish the fan later." She turned to Carlin. "I'm sorry, Doctor. I didn't realize you didn't want him up and about. He ate such a hearty breakfast I thought he must be feeling better."

"That's all right, Anna. I just want to check him over. He is a bit too eager to work." Carlin pulled a thermometer from his bag, and after much coaxing, convinced Peter to hold it in his mouth. He sat carefully watching Peter the entire time to see that he didn't remove it. "Well your temperature is almost normal, Peter. I guess I will have to give my permission for you to start work. But no heavy work and you must be in bed early tonight."

Peter looked relieved. He quickly went back to work on the fan, and Carlin went to talk to Anna. After several minutes Peter came up to Anna. "Excuse me, Anna," he said hesitantly, "I need a new wire to fix the fan. See . . . this little one is broken. If you know a shop that has electrical supplies I could finish the job very quickly."

Carlin looked at the fan and then at Anna. "I know a shop, Peter. I could take you there now if you like." Peter looked from him to Anna. "Is it all right for me to go, Anna?" No one has told me what . . ."

"It's fine, Peter. Dr. La Monde will see that you get back."

"Good! Let's go now, Peter," Carlin said eagerly.

Peter looked at him. "I'm sorry . . . I have no money, sir. Should I ask Madame . . . ?"

"I'll take care of it, Peter," Carlin said casually, and led Peter out to his car.

Carlin carefully pointed out various shops, the post office, Albert's school, and the bank Edgar managed as he drove Peter into town. They stopped at an electrical shop, and Carlin was impressed that Peter knew exactly what was needed to repair the fan. Afterwards he took Peter to the barber, but Peter refused to have his hair cut. After many questions he admitted to Carlin that he had no money, and that he had taken Edgar's offer of employment without discussing the terms. He refused Carlin's offer to pay the bill, for he was reluctant to be in anyone's debt. Carlin at last explained, as diplomatically as he could, that everyone at the house was offended by Peter's shaggy hair, and that things would go better for him if he would agree to have it cut. "Please, let me pay the bill, so I won't have to listen to their complaints," Carlin begged.

"I am sorry they bother you about my appearance," Peter answered. "I'll get it cut. I don't like it this way either." So the barber took up the task, being mindful of Carlin's instruction that the front be cut so that it could not possibly obscure Peter's eyes no matter how it fell. When Carlin approved the results, Peter smiled self-consciously for a brief moment and Carlin saw how different he could look. Charlotte will be pleased, Carlin thought.

Encouraged by the transformation, Carlin took Peter to a shoe shop, but he could not persuade Peter to accept a new pair of shoes as a gift. After much urging Peter reluctantly agreed to let Carlin loan him enough money for the shoes. Peter was suspicious, however, and wondered anxiously what Carlin would ask in return.

During the next week Peter was put to work helping Anna in the kitchen, and assisting Melina with the heavy cleaning. Unfortunately, the girl took every opportunity to ridicule Peter for his rough manners and lack of education. She would never have associated with such a person in Italy, and she was not about to do so in Geneva where she had pretensions of becoming an educated woman. When she discovered that Peter never balked or complained, no matter what she asked him to do, she quickly passed most of the cleaning chores onto him. She scornfully mentioned to Anna that Peter ate like an animal, and that he reminded her of a wolf. Anna disagreed. She saw no viciousness in Peter. He was more like some wild creature, she thought — thin, quiet, and wary, very wary.

Melina complained repeatedly to Charlotte about Peter's offensive table manners, and Anna was forced to confirm the reports. She had thought at first that Peter was just extremely hungry, but he continued to eat in the same manner, no matter how much she fed him. Charlotte got the notion that under the right circumstances and with a little coaching, Peter's habits could be improved. She decided that he should join the family at the dinner table on Friday evenings. When Friday came around, however, Charlotte yielded to Anna's suggestion that the boys be fed early so that they would not witness Peter's poor manners. Carlin was invited to dinner as a family friend, and because Charlotte valued his judgment in dealing with Peter.

Peter did not learn about Charlotte's decision until Charles and Albert came into the kitchen on Friday evening. Peter thought Anna was joking when she told him he was expected to eat with Charlotte and Edgar in the dinning room. He was not eager to go, and was suspicious of their motives. Anna had pressed Peter's jacket and insisted that he wear it, but he was painfully aware of how poorly it fit, and of how threadbare and stained his shirt was. Peter's appetite vanished completely when he walked into the dining room at 7:00 p.m., and faced the tribunal of Edgar, Charlotte and Carlin.

The meal was one, long, disastrous ordeal of spilling food, upsetting water goblets, dropping cutlery, choosing the wrong utensil, and retrieving runaway napkins. Peter heard nothing of the conversation except for the recurring comments, "Sit up straight, Peter; Take smaller bites, Peter; Keep your elbows off the table, Peter; Chew your food well, Peter; and never mind, Peter, Anna will clean it later."

If they had slapped him, he would have endured it, if they had dismissed him he would have left quietly; but they had humiliated him by exposing his ignorance, and in Peter's eyes that was an unforgivable injury. When at last Charlotte rose, and announced that dessert and coffee would be served in the library, Peter bolted from the room. He fled to the kitchen, and nearly collided with Anna as he burst through the door.

"Why must they humiliate me!" he shouted at her. "I would gladly stay in the kitchen, and not offend them with my coarse elbows and my clumsy hands. What have I done to deserve such a punishment?"

"They don't mean it for a punishment, Peter," Anna said in dismay. "They only want to teach you proper manners."

"I have been eating all my life and never was it such a complicated thing to put food in my mouth."

"Calm yourself, Peter. You'll give yourself indigestion," Anna said soothingly.

"I already have indigestion! The food sits in my stomach like a pound of nails!"

Anna felt sorry to think such a beautiful meal had made him ill. "I'll ask the doctor to give you something for your stomach, Peter," Anna said and started out the door.

"No, don't . . . please," Peter said laying hold of her arm. "I don't want to talk to him."

"But, Peter, it's his job to help people. Come on now, sit down and I'll go get him," Anna coaxed. Peter remained silent and she left, but the kitchen was empty when she returned a few minutes later with Carlin. "Now where has that boy gone?" she asked shaking her head. "I tell you, doctor, he was very upset at having to eat with everyone correcting him."

"I'll look for him, Anna. You go serve the coffee," Carlin answered and slipped out the back door into the garden. He searched the numerous paths and eventually spotted Peter pacing rapidly back and forth along the far end of the garden. Cautiously he went closer. "It's a nice night for walking, Peter. May I join you?"

Peter jumped, and looked up in surprise. "It is not my place to tell you what to do!" he growled. Carlin fell into step with him and paced silently for several turns before beginning softly, "Peter, I hope you understand that Madame did not intend to hurt you by asking you to eat in the dining room. She wants only to teach you some acceptable table manners so that you will be a good example for the boys."

"They think I am an animal! A wild animal! But I am not!" Peter exploded.

"No one thinks you are an animal, Peter," Carlin assured him calmly.

"Yes they do! I heard them!" Peter shot back.

"Surely you misunderstood. Who would say such a thing?"

"That girl — the dark haired one. I heard her tell Madame. She does not understand! None of you understand!"

"What don't we understand?" Carlin asked calmly, but Peter ignored him, and continued excitedly. "I am a fool! I should never have come here. I don't know what they expect of me. I never pretended to be anything more than a kitchen boy. I am not meant to be an example for anyone. You don't understand."

"What don't we understand, Peter?" Carlin repeated gently, but Peter could not bring himself to tell Carlin that he had been forced to fight for his food, that he had often been hungry, and that Guido had reviled him at every turn, for being nothing more than ignorant kitchen trash. He continued to repeat, "I should never have come!" until Carlin cut him off. "Peter, it's not so difficult to learn how to behave at the table. You could learn. I know it." Carlin stopped pacing, and laying his hand on Peter's arm he brought him to a halt. "You were just nervous tonight, Peter. It's understandable. You scarcely know the Marneés, but Charlotte is very kind. She would never intentionally hurt you . . . believe me. She wants you to learn the proper thing to do so that you can help train Albert and Charles."

Peter looked Carlin in the face. "I am not meant to be a teacher. They should have brought someone else!" he cried.

"I could show you how to sit and what fork to use, Peter. It's not hard, really," Carlin said quietly.

Peter took several deep breaths to calm himself. "I'll try, but everything here is so . . . so different from . . ." he sighed and lowered his head. "Even to speak in French, every hour of the day . . . I get the words crossed."

"I know it is hard, but you will learn," Carlin said and put his hand on Peter's shoulder. "How does your stomach feel, Peter?"

"I am . . ." Peter started, remembering Giovanni's warning, but he stopped suddenly, and raised his head to look at Carlin. What is the use to lie? he thought. Sooner or later he would let some crudity slip out, or choose the wrong fork, or drop one of those platters that was thinner than the shell of an egg. Then everyone would know that he didn't belong, and they would send him away. It was all too much to worry about when your stomach hurt so much. Perhaps, just this once, they would tolerate less than perfect health. How they must hate sickness, to keep a doctor always at their elbow. "It feels terrible, sir," he said almost in a whisper.

"Will you let me give you some medicine for it, Peter?" Carlin asked softly.

Peter hesitated. "I'm . . . I'm just not used to the change in the . . ."

"I'm sure that's all it is," Carlin agreed readily.

"If you think it will help I will take it," Peter said at last.

"Good! Come back to the house with me," Carlin said warmly and led the way. He was sorry that Peter was feeling ill, but glad that he at last trusted him enough to admit it. He realized that helping Peter to fit in was going to take more than a hair cut and a new pair of shoes.

****

Peter's abrupt departure from the dining room had startled Edgar. "My word! What a strange lad he is to run away before we've finished our meal. Perhaps you should see if he's sick," he said to Carlin just before Anna rushed in to announce that Peter was ill.

Carlin hurried out, and Edgar and Charlotte went into the library. Anna served them coffee and dessert, feeling sorry all the while that Peter was missing such a lovely cake.

"Well, Charlotte," Edgar began sternly as he sipped his coffee, "I hope you are satisfied with your decision to bring this skittish young man into our home."

"Perhaps I did underestimate how much training he would need, but I do want to give him a chance," Charlotte replied meekly, aware that her exercise in table manners had been less than successful.

"Well, if you insist upon bringing him to the dinner table, please see that he is properly dressed. Good Lord! He looks like some . . . some orphan!"

"I'm afraid Peter is an orphan, Edgar."

"Oh yes . . . I do remember that," Edgar muttered contritely. "But must he dress like a beggar? Get him some clothes that fit! Charge them to the household account. Take charge of him, Charlotte, before he shames us before the neighbors. If anyone should see him . . ."

"Yes, dear. I'll take him shopping early next week."

"Good. And perhaps next time we can have a simpler meal, with fewer dishes for him to knock over and spill. Is he so clumsy about everything?"

"Oh no! He's very careful, almost reverent with the dishes and the furniture. And he's willing. He does whatever Anna asks. He's quite clever too. He fixed that sorry old fan over the stove the very first day he was here. He's just terribly shy. He wants desperately to work for you, Edgar. He asks every morning if you have left any instructions for him. Couldn't you think of something?"

"What, some little chore? Should I trust him to wash the car? Never mind, I will ask him myself, so that I can show him the proper cleaner to use. Perhaps if I have a talk with him, he will calm down, and stop jumping out of his skin every time I speak to him. I do wish you had taken my advice about hiring some local boy."

"What is done is done, Edgar. I will do my best to make something out of him."

"I hope you can, but I don't envy you. Are you feeding him enough? He's terribly thin."

"Anna says he has a bit of trouble with his stomach. He's probably not use to the change in food. I think he was just nervous to be at the table with us."

"Judging by his manners, he hasn't had much practice in society. I suppose he can be taught. I hope the carpet won't be ruined in the process."

"It has survived Albert and little Charles," Charlotte responded philosophically.

"Yes . . . yes it has," Edgar said and smiled. "I imagine every generation must add a few spots to the family heirlooms. Are the boys asleep, or shall we call them in and let them help us with all this cake that Peter has left us?"

"Oh, Edgar, you'll ruin their teeth! I know they had dessert with their dinner."

"Well, just a small piece then, and I'll see that they clean their teeth again."

Charlotte smiled. "You do spoil them."

"It's a father's privilege. Must I always be the one who scolds and lectures?"

****

In the days that followed, Carlin instructed Peter in the intricacies of table manners, and Anna began to train him to serve as a waiter at the table. She thought he would be a great help to her when the Marneés gave formal dinner parties. Melina was always assigned to help her during these functions, but she tended to be lazy and spent too much time gossiping about the guests to be of much use.

Carlin enlisted Anna's aid to see that Peter took plenty of rest, and was allowed to eat as much as he wanted. Gradually the program had an effect and Peter was no longer troubled by severe headaches, and his stomach pains went away. Life did not seen so gray and hopeless to him, and he thought once again of Geilla. He had not written to her for months, because he could not think of a single cheerful thing to say; but now he wrote her a long letter telling her about his escape from Guido, and that he was settling into a new job. Geilla was overjoyed to receive his letter and answered it immediately, expressing her sincere happiness at his good fortune.

It soon became apparent that Peter could do more in the kitchen than peel vegetables and wash dishes. Watching him closely, Anna saw that he was a fairly accomplished cook. He was extremely quick with a knife, and bread dough came alive in his large strong hands. One afternoon, when he was caught up with his cleaning chores, and Melina was not around to give him more, he mentioned to Anna that he thought the bakery rolls she served were tasteless, and that he could do better. Knowing that he was not given to bragging, Anna gave him permission to try his hand at it while she went grocery shopping with Madame. Once she got over the shock of seeing her kitchen overflowing with dozens and dozens of rolls, Anna had to admit the results were delicious. "The rolls are wonderful, Peter, but this is not a hotel. Try not to make quite so many next time," she told him quietly. Although Edgar was very partial to good rolls, and did more than his part to reduce their numbers, Charlotte decided to donate the extra ones to a children's home.

When the rolls were wrapped Charlotte invited Peter to come with her to deliver them. He was disappointed that he was not yet allowed to drive, but made no mention of it. Charlotte was a regular patron of the home, and was addressed by name by the attendants when she arrived. She knew her way around the facility, and directed Peter to carry the rolls into the kitchen, where she introduced him to some of the staff. When she led Peter through the main play area on their way out, several of the children recognized her, and dashed forward calling and begging for her attention. She stopped to talk to them and satisfy their curiosity about Peter. He flashed his brief, shy smile at them, and they were his. He was happy that his mistake in the kitchen would help to feed these kids. He had seen so many thin, hungry children in Italy, and knew all too well how terrible it was never to feel full.

As Peter became more settled in the kitchen, new items began to appear at meal times, and Edgar was pleased with the variety. Charlotte was delighted that she did not have to warm leftovers for the family on Anna's day off. Gradually Peter came to understand why Giovanni had always been so critical of his work, and why he had required him to start earlier, and work later than any of the other boys. Peter realized that Giovanni knew from experience that a good cook was never without a job for long. The training had been Giovanni's gift to him, and he was grateful. He wrote to Giovanni telling him that his health had improved, and thanking him for giving him a trade.

Giovanni knew as soon as he saw the letter that Kon was feeling better, for it was addressed to 'Giovanni, the Fat Cook' in care of the hotel. Giovanni was not much of a correspondent, but he wrote to Kon relating a strange tale. Four days after Kon had left with Francois, a carload of federal narcotics agents had descended on the hotel, and arrested Guido on several charges of drug dealing. They knew that Guido had an accomplice, known as "The Skeleton" who acted as a courier, but had no other information about the man. Guido was forced to hold his tongue, for he knew that if the agents located Kon, Kon could inform them of the extensive network of dealers Guido supplied. So, in absentia, Kon at last had the upper hand, and Guido was sentenced to a term in prison.

Peter managed all his chores well, even though little Charles followed him everywhere begging him to read stories or play games. Albert sought him out when he returned from school, eager to play ball or hide-and-seek with him. Peter found a large ball that Carlin had given Albert, and he began to teach the boys to play soccer. Charles tired quickly and had to be carried on Peter's shoulders, but Albert thoroughly enjoyed the game.

One afternoon while Charlotte was writing letters at the desk in the library she heard the sounds of the boys playing on the lawn outside the window. She recognized the boys high pitched squeals, but there was another, deeper sound she could not place. Going to the window, she pulled the curtain aside just a bit so as not to be seen. She was astonished by the sight on the lawn. Peter was lying on his back on the grass, with Albert and Charles climbing and tumbling every which way over him, tickling and poking him, and shrieking, and Peter was laughing uproariously. It was a wonderful laugh that bubbled out from deep inside him. The three rolled and laughed for some time before Peter rose to his feet and a wild game of tag was suddenly underway.

Charlotte smiled with pleasure just watching them play, and was delighted to see that Peter could actually laugh. He was always so solemn she had feared he had forgotten how to smile. What surprised her most, however, was the way Peter could move, and the way he could run. She must see to it that he got some proper shoes, and set some time aside to practice seriously, she thought. She remarked to Edgar that evening that Peter was no longer so painfully thin, and that his athletic activities should be encouraged.

Charlotte had also decided that her children would be quite safe with Peter, and that it was time for him to learn to drive them to school. In her usual efficient way, she ordered a book of driving rules, and saw to it that Peter studied it from cover to cover. Peter was familiar with driving a large sedan, having had a lot of practice driving in Milan, and had no trouble getting his license.

Once he became the family's driver there seemed to be no end to the things he started to do for the household. He rose early to help Anna prepare and serve breakfast, drove Edgar to the office, dropped the boys at school, took Melina to class, and did the marketing for Anna, in addition to visiting the post office, and running any other errands that came up. In the afternoon he would fetch the boys from school, and take them swimming at the pool, for he was an excellent swimmer, or for a hike in the park. He drove Charlotte to meetings and luncheons, took Edgar to and from the airport, and in the evenings drove them both to either the symphony or a play. In addition, he washed and waxed both cars, kept them tuned up and saw that any major work was done without delay or inconvenience to the family. Edgar was forced to admit that he enjoyed having Peter around to handle so many of the irksome details of life.

CHAPTER NINE

In late July, the Marneés set off for a motor trip to Italy. Peter went along as their driver, and Melina was furiously jealous. She conveniently forgot that she had gone on many trips with the family, and that she had to remain behind this time to finish some required classes. Peter was caught up in the general feeling of adventure and excitement, in spite of a few anxious thoughts about crossing the border again with forged papers.

The holiday makers drove south, stopping at Aosta so that Peter could see that it really was a lovely place to have lunch. He recognized the restaurant where Francois had stopped before, but that experience seemed like something out of a dream. As he sat at the table with the family, he thought how pleasant it was not to have Francois carping at him. From Aosta Peter drove the family farther south along the coastal route, stopping over several times to make a leisurely trip of it. On the fourth day they came to Florence, and settling into their hotel, they left the car and went on foot, for there is much to see and enjoy in Florence, and it must be savored slowly.

The first day was spent sightseeing. Charlotte was pleased that Peter was along to carry little Charles when he got tired, and to sit and eat ices with Albert when the boy became bored with all the glorious cathedrals. Peter never minded being left to mind the boys for, like them, he preferred to take his "cultural education" in small bites. He thought it more enjoyable to sit in a cafe, sip espresso and watch the pretty young girls promenade past, than to wear out his shoes marching through musty galleries to look at one more pale, lifeless Madonna.

Now that he was back in Italy, and had the leisure to relax and daydream in the warm sun, he thought of Geilla and the last day they had been together so many months ago. He was writing to her again, and he longed more than ever to see her. He was making a little money now, but it was not enough to support a wife. They would have to wait.

The family's second day in Florence dawned warm and sunny, and Charlotte determined to devote the morning hours to shopping so that they could retire to the hotel and rest during the heat of the day. So off they went, with Charlotte taking the lead, followed by Edgar shepherding the boys, and Peter bringing up the rear. They pushed on through the shops so that they could be finished before lunch. After several hours, Charles grew tired and cranky, and Edgar had to take him on his shoulders, because Peter was all but buried under packages.

They had stopped at one shop where goods were tumbling out the door almost to the curb. Charlotte was engrossed in choosing some blouses with particularly fine handiwork when suddenly, out of the perpetual swarm of motor bikes on the narrow street, came a single rider who forced his noisy vehicle to jump the curb. With practiced skill, he drove up behind Charlotte, and seized the strap of her shoulder bag which she carried slung across her body. Charlotte felt a tug, then was spun around and yanked to her knees. Attempting to escape with the bag, the thief revved his engine, and began to drag Charlotte along the pavement. She screamed for Edgar to help her, but before he could put Charles down, Peter had dropped the packages and leaped at the thief with his knife in hand.

Peter caught the thief from behind. Holding his left arm around the man's neck, Peter swung his blade and stabbed the thief in the arm. The thief swore at Peter, but he released his grip on the shoulder strap. Instantly Edgar rushed forward and pulled Charlotte away from the bike. The thief attempted to turn the front wheel and drive away, but Peter held him by the neck and tried to pull him off the bike. After a violent struggle the bike suddenly tipped sideways, and both the bike and the rider crashed into Peter knocking him down. Peter still held his knife, and was about to stab the thief again, when the sound of a police siren pierced the air. Peter hesitated, then dropped the knife. He rolled free of the bike but continued to fight with the thief. Abruptly Peter rose to his knees, locked his hands together and smashed the thief in the jaw with his double fist. As the thief went down, Peter dove for his knife. He folded it and quickly slipped it up his sleeve.

"Albert, give me a hand!" he called out and the boy ran to him. Slyly he passed the knife to Albert. "Don't tell . . ." was all Peter had time to whisper before the police seized him by the shoulder and pulled him to his feet. He looked intently at Albert, and with his free hand quickly put his finger to his lips before the police twisted his arms behind his back, and slipped handcuffs over his wrists. Albert stared at Peter for a moment, then dashed away to stand behind his parents. Charlotte was crying hysterically, and clinging to Edgar as was little Charles.

There was a lot of confusion, but for a moment no one spoke to Peter except to ask his name. He blurted out "Kon," forgetting in his excitement that he was now Peter. Just then the thief, who had been hauled to his feet, started yelling at the police. "Leave me alone! He's got a knife! The bastard stabbed me."

"What were you doing to these people?" the police shouted back at him.

"Nothing! I accidently jumped the curb, and that son of a bitch leaped on me with a knife and tried to steal my bike!"

"Did you stab him? Where is the knife?" the police asked Peter.

"I don't have a knife," was all that Peter would answer. So they frisked Peter and made a lengthy search in the street, but they could not find a knife.

"Peter works for me!" Edgar told the police when he at last had Charlotte quieted. "He was trying to stop the thief from hurting my wife and stealing her bag." But alas, a simple explanation is never enough for the police. They must have evidence, and witnesses, and statements, and reports. So it was ruled that everyone must be escorted to the police station for further investigation, and the police called for another car to bring the Marneés. One man would wait with them, while the other took Peter and the thief to the station. One officer pushed the thief towards the car, and he went along sullenly; but when the second officer began to shove Peter, he broke away, and stumbled toward Edgar. "Monsieur Marneé! Don't let them take me! I've done nothing wrong," he pleaded to Edgar. Charlotte and Charles were clinging so tightly to Edgar that he could not reach Peter, but he called out, "Go along quietly, Peter, but don't say anything. Do you understand? Let me handle this. I'll send for Francois if necessary."

Peter did not have time to answer before the officer seized him roughly, and hauled him towards the car. Edgar noticed that Peter was limping. "Don't be so rough! He's hurt his leg," Edgar shouted at the policemen; but they paid no attention, and shoved Peter into the back seat of the car with the thief, who immediately began screaming, "Don't put him in here with me. He's a killer I tell you. Keep him away from me."

"Quiet down!" the policeman snapped back. "You're both going to jail until we get to the bottom of this, so sit back and be quiet!"

Peter experienced a terrible sinking feeling as he was driven away from the Marneés. It was bad enough to be handcuffed, and put in the same category as a thief, but if the police discovered his past he might never see the Marneés again. He was extremely defensive by the time he arrived at the police station, and the questioning began. Peter had no need of Edgar's admonition to remain silent. He knew the value of holding his tongue, and they could not have pulled an answer from him if they had put him on the rack. He admitted to being Peter Kononellos when they waved his passport in his face, but that was all.

When the police grew tired of asking Peter questions, they locked him in a cell and went away. He sat by himself, and brooded over what would happen to him if Edgar did not come. As the long afternoon turned to evening, his feelings of isolation and anxiety grew. A guard brought him food, but he had no appetite and ignored it. Time passed slowly, but Peter knew it had grown dark outside when the lights came on, and that it was very late when they went off again. He lay on his back on the bed, but his leg hurt no matter how he turned.

Someone asked if he wanted to see the doctor, but Peter only shook his head. He feared that if the doctor came, he would make him remove his shirt. It was his experience that a doctor could not treat a man who wore a shirt. If they saw his scars they would know he had been in fights before, and they would ask more questions.

In the early morning hours, Peter fell into a fitful sleep, which was haunted by the violent dreams he thought were gone from his mind. He awoke with a start to find his heart racing, and his breath coming in short gasps. Someone was holding his arms and shaking him, but when he tried to pull away, he discovered his back was pressed against the wall by the head of the bed. "Leave me alone!" he screamed in a strange blend of defiance and terror.

"Hey, hey now — quiet down!" the answer came back. "You're creating a disturbance with all your yelping. It's the middle of the night. For God's sake be quiet!"

Peter did not know the man, but he recognized the uniform in the dim light coming from the hall. "Have I no more time?" Peter croaked in a hoarse whisper.

"Time? Time for what? What are you raving about? You were having a nightmare," the guard answered gruffly, and released his grip on Peter's arms.

Peter exhaled audibly, and put his hand to his head. "I thought . . ." he started weakly, but caught himself and fell silent.

"Did you think I came to hang you?" the guard laughed rudely, but seeing the look on Peter's face he was sorry he had spoken. This kid is scared, really scared, he thought to himself. He had seen it before. They were almost all scared the first time they were brought in. After they had been in several times, they sort of died inside, and there was no more fear, and no remorse either. You couldn't do anything with them by the time they got like that.

"This your first time in here?" the guard asked in a more friendly manner. Peter nodded. The guard looked carefully at Peter. This kid is nicely dressed, he thought, everything neat and conservative, nothing cheap or flashy. He was not the usual hooligan. He touched Peter on the arm. "Listen, kid, go back to sleep, and try to be quiet," he said lamely and went to the door. Noticing that Peter was still sitting rigidly against the wall, he shook his head. "Relax, kid, things will look better in the morning," he called, but Peter could not shake the feeling that someone or something was at his throat.

Peter suffered a long night of isolation and worry, for he had no way of knowing how diligently Edgar was working to have him set free. He had given the police a complete statement when he had arrived at the station late the previous morning. However, the police knew the thief and wanted to build a case against him. Unfortunately, the one man who was assigned to the duty was at lunch, or off on another assignment, or with a woman, or God only knew where, so nothing could be done. Edgar pleaded to be allowed to see Peter, but since Peter was not being cooperative, the police were determined to keep him isolated until they could get a statement from him. They assured Edgar that the matter would be settled quickly, and that there was no cause for worry. Edgar was doubtful, but since the police had appeared to accept his statement about the incident, he left to find a doctor for Charlotte.

Edgar found that the Italian medical system was no more efficient or fast moving than the police system, and the afternoon slipped away before Charlotte had been treated and comfortably settled at the hotel. Fortunately, she was not seriously hurt, but her knees were badly scraped, and the condition was very painful. Although Charlotte could be very stubborn, she was essentially a meek person, and she had been thoroughly frightened by the attack. What seemed to horrify her the most, however, was the fact that Peter, a member of her own household, carried a knife and had actually stabbed a man. The fact that he had been defending her person and her belongings did not seem to carry any weight, and she closed her mind to any rational discussion of the matter.

She was so upset with Peter that she selfishly demanded that Edgar stay with her and the boys, rather than return to the police station. Edgar gave in to Charlotte's demands, as he always did, but he was troubled by the fear and despair he had seen on Peter's face as they hauled him away. He knew it was useless to argue with Charlotte, particularly when she was so upset, but he felt very grateful to Peter for having saved his wife from serious injury. Although his cultured mind disapproved of carrying a weapon, part of him secretly admired Peter's quick thinking and boldness in defense of Charlotte. Edgar knew he was man enough to do something to help Charlotte, but he doubted his effectiveness in dealing with the thief. Despite Charlotte's tears, Edgar could not abandon Peter to the police, so he arranged an early dinner to be brought for Charlotte and the boys, kissed them with a new appreciation, and returned to the police station.

The situation still had not been cleared up, as the man in charge of the case against the thief had not returned. "Yes, yes, we will be easy on Peter," the police assured Edgar. "No, he is still not talking. No, we will not let you see Peter, or send a message." Edgar waited for over an hour at the station hoping for something to happen, but nothing did. It was mealtime and everyone had gone to take supper. It was maddening to Edgar that no one seemed to care about the case or about Peter. At last, when he saw a man who was dressed like a cook, bringing trays of food for the prisoners, he scribbled a note on a scrap of paper, and offered the man a good sum of money to slip the note to Peter. The man quickly pocketed the money, and promised to deliver the note. Deciding that nothing more could be accomplished by waiting, Edgar went back to the hotel, and put in a call to Francois. The cook did search out Peter, and slip him the message on a tray, but since Peter refused the food, he never saw the message.

At 6:30 a.m., an officer brought breakfast to the prisoners, but when Peter saw that it was oatmeal porridge, he turned away. Left over oatmeal porridge was the one thing there had been an abundance of at the hotel, for after it had cooled on the table, no one was willing to fight for a portion of such a cold, sticky, gelatinous mess, and there had never been enough milk to make it slip down easier. Peter had eaten mountains of porridge at first, in order to keep from feeling so empty, but after a year, he found it stuck in his throat and he could no longer force it down.

When the officer returned to collect the tray, he noticed that Peter had not touched the food. "What's the matter, boy? Isn't this as good as mama's cooking? Or are you on a hunger strike? That won't get you anywhere in here. Nobody even knows you're alive."

Peter did not answer, but the man's remark struck deep. By 9 a.m., he felt totally empty, and it was not just from lack of food. He knew that Edgar had not wanted him in the first place, and he had given up hope that Edgar would help him now. By the time the officers came to take him from the cell at 10 a.m., Peter was totally despondent, and did not even ask where they were taking him. It passed through his mind that there should have been a trial before they sent him away, but he felt it didn't matter, for there was no one to speak in his behalf. As he stood and tried to walk, he discovered his right leg had stiffened during the night, and he could barely hobble. He was leaning heavily on the guard as he was brought into the main room.

Edgar was touched with sympathy when he saw the hopeless expression on Peter's face, and the way he was limping. "Peter! Didn't they bring a doctor for you?" he demanded indignantly.

Peter looked up in surprise and saw Edgar, flanked by Francois. "Sir . . . I thought you would never . . ."

Edgar strode swiftly across to Peter, and grasped his hand. "I wouldn't abandon you, Peter. I'm terribly sorry this has taken so long to sort out, but Francois has come up with an acceptable solution. You have only to sign a statement, and we can all go home."

Peter was still mistrustful of Francois, and he read the statement several times before he put his signature on it. It stated only that he was Peter Kononellos, that he lived in Geneva, and that he was sponsored by Monsieur Edgar Marneé. Francois had suggested that all charges against the thief be dropped, thus avoiding a trial, and any further investigation of Peter and his knife. Edgar's formal statement also made no mention of a knife. "This time Barabis will not be the only one to be set free," Edgar explained, and Peter knew he meant the thief. "But we must not tell Madame what has been arranged. She is very upset with you, Peter. She and I will have to discuss your situation very seriously when she is calmer."

Peter did not understand Charlotte's feelings, but he made no comment. He turned to Francois, "I thank you for your help, sir," he said formally and offered his hand. He was not surprised when Francois refused it saying, "I knew you would be nothing but trouble. I only wish Edgar had listened to me."

"Please, Francois," Edgar said abruptly, "I have heard enough about this dreadful situation!" He took Peter's arm rather briskly. "The car's outside, Peter. I will drive us to the airport and Francois will bring the car back to Geneva."

"But I should drive it, sir," Peter objected.

"Don't be absurd, Peter. You can scarcely walk and we have no time to find a doctor," Edgar countered.

"But it is my duty to . . ." Peter started, but Edgar raised his voice and cut him off. "Don't give me an argument, Peter! Just do as I say!"

"Yes, sir," Peter answered with resignation, suddenly realizing that Edgar was upset with him also. He wished that he could walk without Edgar's assistance, but his leg could not take the weight. It seemed to take forever to reach the car. Charlotte turned her head away as Peter approached the car, and did not speak to him; but as Edgar opened the back door, little Charles appeared out of nowhere, and flung himself at Peter, shouting, "Peter's back! Peter's back!" Never had the child's pure devotion been so welcome. As Peter put one arm around Charles and hugged him, Charlotte called sternly from the front seat, "Charles! Stay away from Peter. Remember what I told you."

Peter had never heard Charlotte speak so coldly, and it distressed him. He turned to Edgar, "Sir, perhaps I . . ." he began, but Edgar cut him off curtly.

"Get in the car, Peter — just get in."

Peter let go of Charles. "Do as your mother says, Charles," he said in a lifeless tone. Charles pouted, but retreated to the far end of the seat as Edgar helped Peter into the car. Edgar closed the door, and got into the front seat with Charlotte and Albert, while Francois walked around and got into the back next to Charles.

It was a long silent ride to the airport. Peter thought he saw Charlotte dabbing her eyes with her handkerchief several times, but she did not turn her head in his direction. He sensed that he had caused a rift between Charlotte and Edgar, and it added to his misery. Things had been going so well, and now suddenly everyone was angry with him. The silence in the car was so oppressive that

116

while they were waiting for a light to turn green, Peter thought of opening the car door and leaving them to go on without him. He put his hand on the door lever, but discovered that Edgar had locked it from the driver's seat. Knowing he was a still a prisoner did nothing for his unhappy state of mind.

As usual, the airport was crowded, and they waited a long time in the car while Edgar went to fetch an attendant and a wheelchair for Charlotte. Peter was annoyed and embarrassed when Edgar returned with a wheelchair for him, but he knew from Edgar's frown that any objection would be immediately overruled. No sooner had Peter settled into the chair than Albert began pleading repeatedly to be allowed to push Peter up to the terminal. Charlotte objected at first, but when Albert kept on about it, she at last consented. Seeing that Albert considered pushing his chair great fun lessened Peter's vexation considerably.

They were all hot and tired by the time they had boarded the plane and were actually in the air. Charlotte, who sat by Edgar, put her seat back, and was asleep before the flight attendant could serve the first drinks. Edgar was glad for he knew that Charlotte hated to fly. It was the first flight for Peter and although he was not overly nervous, he was curious about all the strange sounds that thump and whir on an aircraft. Flying was old hat for Charles and Albert, however, and the seat belt sign was barely dim before they were crawling over Peter, demonstrating the light switch, the air outlet, the seat back tray and the reclining seat. After a little while, however, they settled down and Charles began to pester Peter to read him a story from one of the seat pocket magazines. Hoping to keep him quiet, Peter let him pick the article and started to read it aloud. Since such articles are totally devoid of interest, Charles quickly began to squirm and demanded to sit on Peter's lap.

Peter was a little reluctant, but since Charlotte was asleep, and Edgar did not say anything, he let Charles climb into his lap. Not to be left out, Albert craftily showed Peter how to lift the seat arm, and inch by inch, he snuggled in next to Peter. Peter dutifully read on about silk worms and mulberry leaves to the end of the article, but then the steady droning of the engine, and the friendly warmth of two sleepy little bodies overcame him and his head began to nod. He had slept very little during the night and he felt drained. He fought the drowsiness for a while then chose to escape into the oblivion of sleep. With Albert at his side and little Charles on his chest, he was not bothered by nightmares.

When Edgar looked around the seat back a short while later, he saw the three of them fast asleep in a blissful tangle of arms and legs. Seeing how dearly his children loved and trusted Peter, Edgar could not bring himself to believe he was the terrible threat to civilized society that Charlotte suddenly thought he was. However, it was not

117

easy to get through to Charlotte once she got one of her whims.

When they arrived in Geneva, Edgar hired a cab and they drove to Dr. La Monde's office. He was surprised to see them, but unfortunately he was involved in some other emergency and could not see Peter immediately. After a brief discussion, it was decided that Peter would stay with Carlin, who promised to drive him home later when he came to check on Charlotte, and the Marneés went home in the cab. Carlin rearranged his busy schedule as best he could, but it was over an hour before he was able to treat Peter.

As Peter expected, Carlin asked him to strip to his shorts and get on the table. His leg and ankle were swollen, and there was an angry red laceration down the front of his shin. "Did the bike fall on you, Peter?" Carlin asked, having heard a brief explanation from Edgar. "Yes, sir," was all that Peter would answer.

"Didn't the police bring a doctor for you?" Carlin asked in surprise.

"They asked me . . . but I didn't want to see him."

"For heaven's sake, why not, Peter? It must be painful."

"I was . . . I was afraid he would see the scars and know I had been in fights before."

Carlin wanted to ask Peter exactly what had happened in Florence, but he doubted that he would tell him everything. He took a different tack. "Tell me about the scars, Peter. I am your doctor now, and I should know."

Peter said nothing at first, but then asked, "Does Monsieur Marneé know about the scars?"

Carlin saw that Peter was testing him. "Not unless you told him, Peter. As a doctor, I learn many private things about my patients, but it is my duty not to reveal them."

Peter had never told anyone about what had happened to him when he first came to Italy alone at thirteen, but he decided to trust Carlin, and slowly, with much hesitation the story came out. He told of the vicious attack by the gang of boys, of the widow's kindness, of the horrible pain, and of his long slow recovery. When he was well enough, the widow taught him to speak Italian, and told her neighbors that he was her nephew. He felt very grateful to her and did all he could to repay her kindness. He cleaned and repaired her house, and did all her shopping, walking all over town to find and bargain for food at a cheaper price to stretch her meager income. He took every job he could find to bring her a little money.

Kon had no plans in life except to survive. Although he had always carried his knife, as soon as he was well, he began to practice with it during every free moment. He practiced holding it in either hand and throwing it with great accuracy. He would have been happy to stay with the widow, for life was better for both of them since he arrived; but she was old, and despite all he did for her, her heart

118

gave out one day while he was working.

Word of her death seemed to spread on the wind, for before he had time to overcome his grief and provide for a decent burial, the tiny house was full of relatives, crying and wailing and grasping at the widow's few belongings. Kon was unceremoniously pushed into the street by people he had never seen at the house before, and the neighbors instantly forgot all he had done for the widow. He was not invited to the funeral, but he went to the church anyway to pay his respects. He was the only one there whose grief was not just a show. After the Mass when everyone filed out of the church, he clenched his fist around his knife and returned to the streets.

Carlin sat and listened to Peter's story with amazement. He kept his tongue, however, and only shook his head sadly when Peter talked about his memory of the pain. "It must have been terrible for you, Peter, but I am glad you told me. Perhaps now you can let it go from your mind."

"I will never forget that gang," Peter said fervently. "I thought it would be different once I left my village and no one knew me, but I was wrong."

"Peter, I'm sure those boys went after you only because you seemed different. Many people fear what they do not understand," Carlin said sympathetically.

"No . . . it was more than that," Peter said quietly. "The boys in my village used to chase me. They would shout things about my mother. I never understood any of it, but they hated me."

"What did they say, Peter?" Carlin asked gently.

"I don't remember. I don't want to remember!" Peter blurted. "I only remember being afraid. They chased me whenever I was alone, until one time I . . ." Peter stopped abruptly, and stared silently at Carlin, his eyes aflame with suspicion and fear.

Carlin saw the look and knew that he had learned more than Peter was willing to share with any living soul.

"You tricked me!" Peter hissed. "You filthy bastard, you tricked me! I should never have trusted you." Peter lunged forward, and Carlin feared he would leap off the table. He seized Peter by the shoulders. "It was not a trick, Peter, I swear. You don't have to tell me any more. Some things are best forgotten."

Peter struggled with Carlin for another moment, and then sat rigid, staring at him. "Please . . . I have said too much," he whispered guiltily.

"Don't be troubled, Peter. You have my sacred word that I will not repeat anything you have told me."

Peter bit his lip. "I have never told . . ."

"I understand," Carlin assured him quickly. "We will never speak of it again."

Peter hung his head and Carlin released him. "Will you let me examine your leg?" he asked gently.

Peter nodded.

Carlin felt he knew Peter better for having heard his story, and he was more determined than ever to see that things went better for him. He took an X-ray of Peter's leg, but it showed no fracture. Carefully and very gently, Carlin cleaned the long gash on Peter's leg, and treated the various scrapes he found on his back. Carlin knew that the mark on Peter's arm was from a more recent fight than the scars on his abdomen, but he did not pry for details. He perceived that Peter had often been exposed to violence, and at last he understood why Peter was so reluctant to trust anyone. He chose not to ask Peter about what had happened in Florence.

"Have you had lunch, Peter?" he asked, and Peter shook his head. "Well, I will send my nurse to get something for you. I'm afraid you will have to wait here until I can finish with my other patients. Then I will drive you home." Peter nodded. He was not looking forward to facing the Marneés.

When Carlin drove Peter home, Edgar was waiting at the door to meet them. He greeted Carlin briefly, and then turned to Peter. "How is your leg, Peter?"

"It is fine, sir."

"Good. I am glad to hear it is not serious. I think you had better go to your room, Peter," Edgar pronounced solemnly.

"Sir, I don't understand . . ." Peter began, but Edgar interrupted him impatiently.

"I will discuss the matter with you later," he said raising his voice. Peter stared at him, and Edgar saw the fire in his eyes. Edgar sighed, "I'm sorry, Peter. I didn't mean to shout. Please — just go for now." He turned to Carlin. "Carlin, would you please help Peter up the stairs, and then join Charlotte and me in the library."

"I don't need any help," Peter snapped, and limping across the hall he started up the stairs.

"I'll be there shortly, Edgar," Carlin promised, and following after Peter, he took him by the arm. "I don't need your help!" Peter snarled, but he didn't pull away, and he found it was easier to get up with Carlin's assistance.

"Don't be angry with Edgar. He's worried about Charlotte, and about you," Carlin offered, but Peter did not respond.

When Carlin joined Edgar and Charlotte in the library, Edgar gave him a detailed account about their encounter with the thief, and Peter's reaction. Charlotte remained silent while Edgar talked, but quickly voiced her objections when he had finished. "I cannot have this . . . this assassin in my house! He's not to be trusted," she exclaimed.

It was obvious to Carlin that Edgar did not share her opinion when he quickly responded, "We can't put him in the street like a dog, or some discarded souvenir you've collected. You were the one who was so anxious to have him come."

"He was so quiet and polite and willing. I never dreamed he had a knife!" Charlotte shot back.

"He is still all of those things, Charlotte. He may have acted rashly, but it was for your sake. He had no thought for himself. He could have run away and left us."

"Carlin, you know Peter better than either of us. What did he tell you about what happened?" Charlotte asked in bewilderment.

Carlin hesitated. He did not want to betray Peter's confidence, but he felt they should be made to understand that Peter's background was vastly different from theirs. "I didn't push him to tell me what happened in Florence, but he did tell me some very shocking things about where and how he grew up. Peter has had to deal with violence all his life and he was forced to learn to protect himself. I see no viciousness in him, but if he believes he is being attacked, he will fight to protect himself. I believe he has included yourselves and the boys in the select number that he will defend."

So the discussion went on for another day, and Peter remained isolated and miserable. Anna brought him his meals for it was too difficult for him to climb the stairs. She saw how unhappy he was to be kept like a prisoner and she did her best to cheer him. Since Peter was in disgrace, Charlotte had forbidden the boys to visit him, but late in the evening of the second day, long after everyone had gone to bed, Albert snuck to Peter's room and rapped quietly on the door. Although Peter was in bed, he was still awake, and made his way to the door. He was surprised, but happy to see Albert, and quickly pulled him into the room, closing the door behind him. After a totally uninhibited greeting, Peter remembered that he was supposed to set a good example for the boys. "Albert, you should not be here. Your parents will be angry if they find out," he cautioned.

"Would you tell on me, Peter?" Albert asked incredulously.

"Of course not, Albert. I keep a secret until death," Peter assured him.

"Well, so can I," Albert answered with pride, and unrolling an extra fold in the waist of his pajamas, he produced the knife.

Peter was greatly relieved to see it, and took it from Albert as if it were made of gold. "You are a good boy, Albert," Peter sighed. "I thought I would never see it again. You told no one — not even your papa?"

"I did not dare, Peter. I was very frightened when the police took you away. I thought they might take me too, so I hid the knife. Later I put it in my shoe, and no one found it."

"You are a good friend, Albert. Many a man could not have done as well," Peter said sincerely, and put his arm around the boy. Albert smiled and felt glad to be counted as Peter's friend, and to be free of the burden of the knife.

"What did they do to you in jail, Peter? Did they hurt you?"

"No, they didn't hurt me, but I was scared. When your papa did not come for me, I was afraid he had found the knife and that the police would hang me. I would not want to go there again." Peter fell silent for a moment. "You must go now, before anyone learns you came," he told Albert, and still with his arm around him he limped to the door.

"Good night, Peter," Albert whispered.

"Good night, Albert and thank you."

On the following day when Peter hobbled down the stairs, and came looking for something to do, Anna felt sorry for him for she knew that idleness was poison to him. So she sent him to sit in the garden with several cans of polish, and a huge bundle of rags. Then she carried every silver or brass item in the house out to him to be polished, from the smallest spoon to the largest vase. He worked away as he tackled every task, with great diligence and determination.

As Anna had anticipated, Melina took Peter's fall from grace as an opportunity to inveigh against him to Charlotte. She compared him to the street gangs she had seen throughout Italy. The fact that he came from Milan gave her the material to paint an even blacker picture of him. But the more Melina vituperated against Peter for his background, lack of education, and poverty, the more Charlotte came to see that she was wrong to judge Peter by her own strict standards. He was, after all, an orphan, and as Melina had pointed out, he came from the lowest class in one of the roughest cities in Europe. She thought of what Carlin had said about Peter, and for the first time she began to form a more realistic picture of him.

Charlotte did not decide what to do about Peter until the following morning, when Albert, who had finally put together enough of what he had overheard to realize that Peter might be sent away, announced at the breakfast table that if Peter left he was going with him. Of course little Charles immediately declared that if Albert and Peter were going anywhere, he was going along too. It was quickly decided that the best solution was not to make any more fuss about the incident, and that Edgar would make Peter give up the knife. However, what seemed logical and proper over the breakfast table was not so easy to accomplish when Edgar called Peter into his office to discuss the matter. Peter knew full well that his job, and his future with the Marneés were on the line, but the knife was his security in a very insecure world, and he adamantly refused to part with it.

"Peter, you are making this very difficult for me. I don't want to send you away, but Madame does not approve of your carrying a knife. What am I to do, Peter?" Edgar concluded in exasperation.

"I do not know, sir. I don't want to leave, but I must be able to defend myself."

"But, Peter, you are with us now. We live in a civilized country. We have rules and laws, and we have the police to protect us. We don't need to carry knives."

"I saw how the police protected you in Florence, sir. They were nowhere to be seen when that thief hurt Madame, and they put me in jail when I tried to stop him. I have no use for that kind of protection!"

Edgar saw that he was getting nowhere in his efforts to change Peter's mind about the knife, but he admired Peter's truthfulness in stating his opinion. Another boy might have given in quietly and then replaced the knife in secret. Peter was close-mouthed to the extreme, but there was no deceit in him. Edgar remembered how Peter's honesty had appealed to him the day they had met in Milan. "Peter, what am I to do with you? You can be so stubborn. What would your father have done if you refused to do as he asked?"

Peter was startled by the question. He stared at Edgar for a moment, then lowered his head and bit his lower lip. He did not look at Edgar when he finally answered, "When . . . whenever I displeased my father . . . he would beat me until I could no longer stand."

Edgar was shocked by Peter's answer. He said nothing for a long time before responding, almost in a whisper, "Peter! I had no idea . . . I am terribly sorry . . ." Then he added decisively, "That is not an option for me, Peter. I'm afraid I will have to bow to your stubbornness and let you keep the knife. But you must never, ever let Madame or the boys know that you still have it. Do you understand me, Peter?"

"Yes, sir," Peter answered swiftly.

"One more thing, Peter," Edgar began, "When the fall semester starts next month, you are to be enrolled in the night school in town. Charlotte will get you a schedule and help you to decide what to study."

Peter was affronted, and objected immediately. "Sir, I am not a child! I am too old to be sent to school."

"Nonsense, Peter. It's a night school. Everyone there will be your age or older. I thought you wanted to learn things."

"I do, sir, but . . . " he started, but Edgar was in no mood for excuses.

"Good. Then it is settled. We will pay for the school, and we expect you to work hard."

"Yes, sir. Thank you, sir. I will try," Peter answered, and seeing that Edgar had taken up some papers he turned to leave.

"Peter," Edgar said and hesitated. "Yes, sir?" Peter answered apprehensively, wondering what new ordeal Edgar would announce.

"I do appreciate what you did to protect Madame."

Peter turned to face Edgar. "I would not let anyone hurt her, sir. No matter what."

And so when September came around, Peter was officially enrolled in school. Charlotte thought he should begin with French literature and modern history for she noticed that he seemed to enjoy reading stories to the boys, and she imagined those subjects would be easier for him than mathematics or science. However, about a third of the way through the semester she received a call from the school notifying her that Peter was failing both subjects. She was surprised and dismayed, for she knew he was devoting hours to reading and doing his assignments.

She scheduled a meeting with both teachers, and found it a new and unpleasant experience since Albert had always done so well in school. The teachers were in agreement that Peter was not adjusting well to being in class. He would not volunteer any answers, and when called on by name, he became so nervous he could not express himself clearly in either French or Italian. He never asked a question of the teachers, and avoided the other students. His written homework in history was acceptable, but his reports on French literature indicated a total lack of comprehension. Since Peter was clearly not enjoying either course, it was suggested that he be withdrawn, or transferred to other classes.

Charlotte went home feeling very discouraged, and decided to confront Peter the next afternoon. Although she thought she was being unusually kind and patient, she could tell that Peter was upset that she had found out how poorly he was doing. He was so defensive that only after much prying and questioning did she manage to piece together that Peter lacked confidence about his ability to learn, and found it humiliating to be corrected in front of the group. He was so afraid of being ridiculed by the teacher or the other students that he could barely concentrate in class. As for the literature, he said he could not understand why any of the people did or said what they did, for he had never known anyone even remotely like any of the characters, and anyway, it ruined a story to ask so many questions about it.

Charlotte struggled to overcome Peter's reticence and was shocked to discover that Peter had not been allowed to attend school regularly as a child, because his father believed education was unnecessary for a fisherman. He had been kept out of school to mend nets, and haul fish, and when he did go to class, the other boys had made fun of him because he was always so far behind. It was only because of Mario's efforts that he had learned to speak and write properly.

Charlotte sensed that Peter would have been happy to withdraw from school, but she was determined not to give up on his education. After a conference with Edgar and Carlin it was decided that Peter would switch to mathematics and geography. Although the work might be more difficult, he would not be required to express any opinions. It was also arranged that the teachers would phrase their questions in class so that Peter could get by with a very brief answer.

And so Peter started in again, and although he was behind the class, he did fairly well with his assignments. In order to gain some extra credit in geography, he took on a project of designing and creating a system of colored overlays on the map of Europe to show the various areas by population density, language, mineral production and so forth. It involved a great deal of time and effort, but he received an excellent grade, and demonstrated that he could produce quality work when left on his own.

Some of the basic principles of mathematics were still eluding Peter, however, and he continued to struggle. Edgar found him in the library late one evening. "Peter, are you still working at this hour?"

"Yes, sir," Peter sighed, "but it is useless. None of my answers match those in the book."

Realizing that Peter was about to give up for the night, and possibly forever, Edgar asked to see the lesson and quickly determined where Peter had gone wrong. Peter was so grateful for his help that Edgar made it his habit to oversee all Peter's homework. Although Peter was very much in awe of Edgar, he had nowhere else to turn. When he discovered that Edgar would never belittle him for what he did not know, he began to ask all the questions that he feared to ask in class.

After several weeks of working with Peter, Edgar mentioned to Charlotte that he wished he had more time to himself in the evenings. However, when Charlotte suggested they engage a tutor for Peter, Edgar immediately dismissed the idea. He laughed, and admitted that it made him feel good to see Peter learn and improve. Albert had always done so well in school he needed little extra attention. With Edgar's help, Peter was able to complete both courses on time with passing grades. The experience gave him a sense of accomplishment, and greatly improved his outlook about school. He had not overcome his dislike for being surrounded by a large group of strangers, however, and he never would.

CHAPTER TEN

It was Thursday morning, and Peter was on his way to the Children's Home laden with a basket of rolls. He claimed he had accidently made too many again, but no one was fooled. Both Anna and Charlotte knew Peter enjoyed going to visit the children. The time he spent with them was his time to relax. With the children he never had to worry about his manners, or his posture, or if his shirt had a smudge on it. Something else drew him, however. It was the knowledge that these kids did not have anyone else to visit them. Their loneliness and his formed a bond between them.

On this particular day he began to play some board games with several of the older children when he became aware of a commotion in the next room. When he saw several of the staff disappear, he slyly put himself out of the game, and slipped through the door to see what was happening. On a folding table stood a metal tub full of hot water, and a stack of clean towels. One of the assistants, a husky woman wearing a white uniform, was holding a boy about five or six years old. The boy was calling "mama" in Italian and trying to pull away from her.

A young staff assistant recognized Peter, and spoke to him. "The police just brought this little one in. The nurses are trying to give him a bath before they put him to bed. He's really filthy, but the little devil won't cooperate."

As Peter watched, two of the male attendants went up to the boy. While one tried to help the woman hold the boy, the other tried to pull the child's ragged shorts off. When the attendant got the shorts down to the boy's knees, Peter saw that the boy had no underwear. The boy started crying more loudly, and the attendants tried to hush and console him. He would not listen, however, and continued to struggle as they pulled the shorts over his feet. His yelling became louder and more frightened as the attendants tugged at his shirt and finally pulled it over his head. The boy almost squirmed free as his shirt came off, but the attendants caught him again.

The boy's frightened screams made Peter uneasy. Without taking his eyes off the boy, he pushed his way towards the table. A moment later when the nurse and one attendant lifted the boy, and tried to put him into the tub, the boy's screams rose to a new pitch that went beyond hysteria to sheer animal terror.

Something in the sound stirred a dormant memory in Peter. He felt strangely light-headed. He no longer merely heard the child's screams, he resonated with them. Peter heard himself shout, "No!" Then he leaped onto the table, punched the male attendant in the face, and snatched the screaming child from the startled nurse. Peter held the naked boy against his chest for only a moment before the rickety table crashed to the floor, shaking the tub, and splashing the hot water in all directions. While everyone scurried to keep their feet dry, Peter, who was still holding the boy, jumped off the table, and isolated himself in a corner.

Peter heard the boy's screams ringing in his ears, and felt the boy's fists pounding furiously on his arms. He held the boy's legs tightly against his body, to protect himself from being kicked. The staff shouted at Peter, but he did not hear them. He had crossed the barrier and jumped into the child's private hell, to keep him company in his terrible loneliness and fear.

Peter sat on the floor with his back to the others, and rocked the child back and forth. The staff heard him talking softly to the child, but they could not understand what he was saying. Some of it was Italian and some of it was Greek, but the message was the same, "Don't be afraid. I will never let them hurt us again." Gradually the screaming subsided, and there was only the sound of muffled sobbing, and a few frightened whispers. Peter kept talking to the child, but no one heard what he said.

Holding the boy with one arm, Peter moved slowly toward the nearly empty tub of water. Still talking to the boy, he picked up a towel and dipped it into the water. He pressed the wet towel over the boy's back and along his skinny, dirty arms. Ignoring the water on the floor, Peter sat by the tub. Balancing the child in one arm, he continued to dip the towel and rub the boy. He made soft coaxing noises until the boy turned his face, and let Peter hold the towel to it. It was not a thorough washing job, but by the color of the towel, it was more than the boy had been given in a long time. Peter wrapped the child in a dry towel, and stood up, lifting him in his arms. Peter looked at the staff with a wary expression. "He needs some . . ." he began in a southern dialect, but quickly switched to French. "He needs some bread."

The staff stared at Peter, but no one moved. Finally the resident doctor, who had been called into the room spoke. "Someone get some bread — and some milk," he added as an afterthought.

"No milk," Peter corrected. "Bring a little wine with water."

"That's not good for a child," an attendant objected.

"Do you think he has anything that is good for him?" Peter snapped. "It is only you rich Swiss that worship the cow."

Peter turned his back to the others and talked softly to the boy until the food was brought. When it came, Peter sat on the floor. He tore the bread into little pieces, and offered them to the boy. Seeing the boy hesitate, Peter put the plate on the floor beside him. He took one of the pieces and started eating it with exaggerated pleasure. After a few minutes the boy snatched a small piece, and stuffed it into his mouth. Seeing that Peter did not object, he grabbed another, and another until he had eaten them all.

Peter took up the wine and sipped it. The boy's eyes were on him like black searchlights. Peter offered him the cup, and he gulped the wine with thirsty slurping noises. Peter didn't turn his head as the boy drank, but he called in French, "Is there a shirt for the boy?"

There was some shuffling and a cotton undershirt was passed to Peter. It didn't seem to take much coaxing to get the boy to let Peter help him put it on. It was long and hung almost to the boy's knees which seemed to please him.

"Where is he to sleep?" Peter asked, taking up the child and turning towards the others.

"In the small room with the younger children," the doctor said coming forward. Immediately the boy started screaming again, and Peter stepped backwards abruptly, holding the boy's face against his chest. Peter spoke to the boy in an Italian dialect, then to the doctor in French, "I know the room." Ever talking to the boy in soft tones, Peter carried him into the sleeping area, and leaning over the metal railings on the bed he tried to put him down. The boy would not let go of Peter, however. He clung to Peter's neck, and cried in frightened words that only Peter could comprehend. Peter tried to soothe the child, but he did not succeed. At last Peter gave up and lifted the boy out of the bed. He gathered up the blanket and the pillow, and taking the boy into a corner, he made a make-shift bed for him on the floor, using the pillow as a mattress.

"The child should be in the bed, not on the floor!" one of the assistants exclaimed with indignation.

"He's not used to a bed! A child can get a good sleep on the floor. I know. I have done it!" Peter answered impatiently.

"At least give him the luxury of another pillow under him, Peter," the doctor said softly and handed Peter another pillow.

"Yes, it is better with two," Peter admitted.

The doctor did not fully understand Peter's response to the child's screams, but he could see that the child reacted more positively to Peter than to any of the staff. It reminded him that sometimes the staff tried to fit the children to the rules rather than seeing each child as a defenseless, frightened little individual. Peter seemed to have unusual insight into the children's fears. The doctor watched Peter now as he sat on the floor next to the boy. He made it seem quite natural that a boy should sleep on the floor.

Peter wrapped the boy in the blanket, and although it was obvious that the boy was tired, he was too frightened to sleep. "Don't let them put me in the soup! Don't let them cook me," he whispered to Peter in a frightened little voice.

Peter smiled at him. "That was not a soup! That was a bath! It is very nice once you get used to it."

"Don't let them cook me!" the boy repeated.

"I won't. I won't. They don't mean to hurt you. They will be very kind, but you must not scream at them."

"They stole my clothes. They tried to cook me!"

"They will give you new clothes, and they only wanted to wash you. Go to sleep now. I'll keep watch. I won't let them hurt you."

Peter sat with the boy for a long while. The doctor sent everyone back to their duties and the room became quiet. At last Peter rose and left the room. The doctor caught him in the hall and tried to talk to him, but Peter didn't really hear what the doctor said. Peter looked at the doctor with bitterness in his dark eyes. "He is too young to be so alone! Much too young!" he said mournfully, and walked out the door.

Charlotte was in the library and saw the car when Peter pulled up. Wondering why he was so late getting back, she went into the hall to greet him. She was shocked to see the disheveled state he was in. Peter's shirt was soiled and hanging over his belt, and his slacks were dirty and wet. If it wasn't for his grim expression, she would have guessed that he had been in some rowdy ball game with the boys.

"Peter! Where have you been?" she asked in astonishment.

"At the Children's Home, Madame," he said softly.

"What happened to your clothes?"

Peter looked down, and appeared surprised that he was so wet and dirty. "Forgive me, Madame. I got into some water," he said, and started up the stairs.

"Peter, what happened?" Charlotte called after him.

He turned and looked at her, opening his mouth as if to speak, then he lowered his eyes and bit his lip. "It is not good to remember such bitter things, Madame," he mumbled and continued up the stairs.

"Peter, what's wrong?" she called, but he did not answer.

Charlotte went into the kitchen to talk with Anna, but Anna could only report that Peter had strode into the kitchen wearing a gloomy expression, and had passed her by without a word. Charlotte waited almost an hour, thinking that Peter would come down, but he stayed in his room. Surmising that the morning's visit had not been the usual happy occasion for Peter, Charlotte called Dr. Brencic, the Chief Physician at the Children's Home, and got the story. She was in the kitchen with Anna when Peter came down to fetch the boys from school. He had changed his clothes, but not his grim expression.

"Peter, the boys have missed your company since you've been going to school in the evenings. I would like you to stay home this evening and spend some time with them," Charlotte told him.

"If you wish it, Madame," he said evenly.

"I do, and I would like you to eat in the dinning room with the family this evening."

"It is only Thursday, Madame," Peter reminded her.

"I know, but I have invited Dr. La Monde and he hasn't seen you for a while."

Peter thought it was a strange excuse, since Carlin had been at the house on Monday, but he didn't argue. He actually felt relieved; he was not in the mood to face the teachers and their endless questioning.

When Melina came in from class, Charlotte announced that as a special treat, she had arranged for some friends to take Melina to a concert. Melina was to have an early dinner with Anna, and be prepared to leave the house at 7:00 p.m. After Peter returned, Melina boasted that while he would be worrying over his "sums," as she mockingly called his math class, she would be attending a concert. She could not resist throwing the fact in Peter's face, for she knew he was fond of music. She had overheard him telling Anna about the concerts he had heard for free by standing in the back of the theater after the last intermission. Sometimes he went after class, and sometimes when he drove Charlotte and Edgar.

Evening at the Marneés began with a leisurely dinner, and Charlotte carefully drew Peter into the family circle, even as she had done for Carlin five years earlier after his beloved wife had died. The group ate and talked, played games and listened to music, and Charlotte created an atmosphere of harmony, and barred the doors against the hostile elements of hunger, want, and loneliness.

As the evening progressed, Peter sensed the significance of the occasion, and realized that Charlotte had staged it especially for him. Even the absence of Melina had been arranged, lest any discord spoil Peter's pleasure. The boys had been allowed to stay up later than usual, but at 9:00 p.m. Charlotte called for them to get ready for bed. Peter stood by the library door silently watching Albert and Charles perform their nightly ritual of kissing their parents, and being wished a good-night. Charlotte came up to Peter as he went out the door with the boys. "Good-night, Peter. Sleep well, and don't stay up all night reading," she said, putting her hand on his arm.

When he paused and flashed her a brief smile, she saw that the sadness was gone from his eyes.

"Good-night, Madame, and thank you," he said warmly.

In the morning, as Edgar was preparing to leave for the bank and Peter was helping the boys get ready for school, Charlotte received a telephone call. After a short conversation she went to look for Peter and called him in from the car.

"Peter, I've just had a call from Dr. Brencic at the Children's Home." She saw a shadow cross Peter's face, but she continued without a pause. "He says that the little boy you met yesterday is hysterical again. He asked if you could come and talk to the boy. Perhaps you can get him to calm down and eat."

Peter put his arm against the door and leaned into it, covering his face. "He asks too much, Madame. It is so hard . . . I can't bear the screams."

"You are the only one who can stop them, Peter. The child is terrified of everyone else." Charlotte could see he was reluctant to face the child. "Please try, Peter. He needs you. You understand him," she pleaded.

"I understand him too well, Madame . . . but I will go if you wish it. You have been very kind to me."

"Thank you, Peter. I know you will do your best. And, Peter," she said as he turned to leave, "while you are at the Children's Home, you must apologize to the attendant you struck. I will not tolerate such vulgar behavior. Now . . . don't frown. You must learn to be more controlled."

"Yes, Madame."

"Good. Do be careful driving. I know I've made you late. "

"Yes, Madame."

"Don't forget to stop at the cleaners on the way home. Have you – stand straight, Peter. You'll ruin your shoulders if you slouch like that."

"Yes, Madame. The clothes are in the car."

"Good. Thank you for going to help the boy, Peter."

Peter returned to the Children's Home, calmed the boy, fed him, and learned what little he could about him. He discovered that the boy's name was Julio Bertoni, and that he had not been abandoned intentionally. Little Julio had been left to mind a younger sister and baby brother, but while his parents were gone, some people came into their apartment, and took the children away. He had fought to defend his brother and sister, but they had all been put into a car and driven to a large building. In the process of being transferred from the car to the building, Julio had made his escape by biting the hand of one of his captors. Being a spry little fellow, he made a wild dash for freedom and hid in some trash bins. He had been on his own for over a week, and was nearly starved, when a shop-keeper caught him trying to steal some fruit. At that point he was turned over to the police.

Peter related Julio's tale to Dr. Brencic, and was told that it had probably been the welfare inspectors who took the children. The doctor notified the police and an official search was made, but no one came forward to claim the boy. Peter visited Julio every day and carefully introduced him to the attendants so that he was able to be moved to a bed, and accept his food from the regular staff. Peter pleaded with Dr. Brencic to contact the welfare people, and eventually Julio's younger brother and sister were located and brought to the Children's Home.

Although Peter did not discuss the matter with anyone, he was determined to locate Julio's parents. He haunted the poorer sections of the city asking question about Italian families and their children. Peter even borrowed Albert's camera, and took pictures of Julio and the others, to carry with him when he made his rounds. After weeks of searching he finally located Julio's parents, and brought them to the Children's Home. Although he was pleased to be present at the joyous family reunion, his triumph was short-lived. Dr. Brencic told Peter that the welfare authorities had declared that since both parents were forced to work away from home to support their children, they could not be allowed to take the children until they could show that someone would be available to watch them.

Peter was furious and could barely calm himself enough to explain the situation to the parents. When she heard the news, Julio's mother began to scream hysterically and clasped her three children to her breast refusing to leave. Julio's father immediately started shouting at Dr. Brencic in Italian, calling him rude names. Peter felt angry and betrayed. He had worked very hard to bring the parents and children together only to have them separated again. He hesitated, and then began complaining bitterly to Dr. Brencic in French.

Dr. Brencic was very unhappy. He agreed with Peter that the children should be with their parents, but it was his responsibility to carry out the welfare regulations. He pleaded with Peter to help him calm the parents, and ask them to be patient until a solution could be found. Now that their parents had been located, the status of the children had changed, and they were no longer eligible to stay at the Children's Home.

Peter did not understand the intricacies of the regulations, but he recognized that all the crying and shouting was very upsetting to the children. He did his best to explain matters to the parents, and in the end Dr. Brencic agreed that since the reunion had been so emotional, the parents could spend the night with their children. Peter felt very involved with the family, and quickly consented when they asked him to stay. He called Charlotte to request permission to spend the night, and promised that he would be back in time to take Edgar to work in the morning.

Charlotte had become accustomed to the fact that although Peter never actually lied to her, he never volunteered any information about his activities. Rather than cross-examine Peter over the telephone, she insisted on speaking to Dr. Brencic, and was able to get the whole story. She had to admit that she had no idea that Peter had been searching for Julio's parents. At length, Peter was allowed to stay, the parents and the children were quieted down, and Dr. Brencic went home to worry over how he was going to resolve the situation.

When Dr. Brencic returned to the Children's Home in the morning, however, there was no sign of Peter, the children, or their parents. He immediately called Charlotte only to learn that Peter had not come home as promised. Dr. Brencic hung up the phone is dismay. Things had gotten out of hand. Children he was responsible for were missing, and Peter had never told him where he had located Julio's parents. Reluctantly, Dr. Brencic picked up the phone and called the police.

****

When Peter walked into the hall at 8:30 a.m., Charlotte was waiting for him with her arms folded and her pretty little mouth drawn into a tight line.

"Where on earth have you been, young man?" she demanded sternly.

"I . . ." Peter started hesitantly, but Charlotte cut him off.

"Do you know that the police are looking for you? Have you any idea of the uproar you have caused? What have you done with those children?"

Peter stood silently while she asked her questions and looked her straight in the face when he answered. "The children and their parents are on a bus headed for Salerno. You Swiss with all your stupid regulations have driven them away! They return to poverty, but they are together!"

Charlotte was shocked. "Peter! Was this your idea?"

"Yes. Those welfare people would not let them keep their own flesh and blood. It was their only choice."

Charlotte was momentarily at a loss for words. She frowned and shook her head before continuing. "You had better go to your room, Peter. You are in very serious trouble."

So once again a storm raged around Peter, and as before Peter staunchly defended his actions and would not back down. After the police in Salerno verified that Julio's family had arrived safely, a conference was held with the welfare officer on one side and Dr. Brencic, Carlin, Edgar, Charlotte and Francois on the other. After much deliberation, it was determined that having the family reunited and removed from Switzerland was the cheapest, best solution for everyone involved. Since the children had been returned to their parents no one could be accused of kidnapping them. However, the welfare officer felt that Peter should be punished for being a public nuisance and causing everyone extra paperwork. He suggested that Peter be banned from the Children's Home, but Dr. Brencic objected on the grounds that the children would miss the personal attention Peter gave them.

133

So it fell on Edgar to summon Peter and deliver a long, serious lecture on the responsibility of being a good law-abiding citizen. While Edgar was delivering his carefully prepared speech, he suddenly remembered Charlotte's promise that if she was allowed to bring Peter into the household, he would never cause a moment of trouble. He sighed thinking that once again it was his duty to discipline the boy.

"Peter, you have caused a lot of people a great deal of trouble and anxiety. What do you have to say for yourself?"

"I am sorry to cause you trouble, sir," Peter said sadly, "but a child should not be alone."

Peter stood respectfully silent while Edgar began his lecture, but before he was finished Edgar came to the conclusion that he had no right to tell an orphan that it was a crime to keep a family together. "Peter, I see there is no way to convince you that what you did was wrong. Just promise me that in the future you will discuss things with Madame and I before you do anything rash."

"I will try to remember, sir."

CHAPTER ELEVEN

Late one Saturday evening, Peter was at home studying. Earlier he had driven Edgar and Charlotte to a concert, returning home about 12:30. He knew that Melina had gone out with Richard, and it bothered him that she was not home yet. Melina claimed that Richard was a student at the University, but Peter was skeptical. Richard seemed so much older than Melina. Peter usually didn't take any notice of Melina's friends, but there was just something about Richard he didn't like. Maybe it was the way Richard looked at Melina.

Peter worked until almost 2:00 a.m. on a report that was due the following week. He had carried his papers into the kitchen and was working at the table, in order to be closer to the coffee pot. Despite Carlin's many lectures, Peter continued to hit the caffeine heavily when he worked late. When Melina still had not shown up by the time Peter put his work away about 2:30, he poured himself another cup of coffee, drank it hurriedly, and decided to go look for her.

Peter got his jacket and took the keys for the small sedan. He headed into town by the main route, hoping to spot Richard's car returning. When he didn't meet Richard, he cruised around the downtown area for a while, thinking the couple might have gone to one of the more popular clubs. Peter knew Richard liked to show off by spending money. When he didn't find them, he circled out from the center of town. At last he spotted Richard's car parked outside a row of low rent apartment buildings favored by students. Richard's car was easy to spot. In this section of Geneva a brand new, jet black Porsche stood out from the other vehicles.

Peter parked the sedan and surveyed the apartments. He hoped for Melina's sake that there was a party going on somewhere. After a quick tour of the block he knew that there were several loud, raucous parties to choose from. He approached the building nearest the Porsche, and going from door to door, his ears told him where the party was. He rapped firmly on the door several times before it was opened by a tall blond girl, who smiled at him, and immediately offered him a drink. The din in the room was so loud, it was a long time before Peter was able to make the girl understand that he was looking for someone in particular. She didn't seem to know who was in the room, but invited him in with a wave of her hand. She tried to slip her arm around his waist, and offered to escort him, but he pushed past her, and made his way around the crowded room. Satisfying himself that neither Melina, nor Richard were in the room, he made his way back to the door.

"Did you find your girlfriend?" the blond asked, as he pressed past her to get to the door.

"No, but thanks for letting me look."

"Stay and have some fun. I'll see that you have a good time," she offered.

"Some other time," Peter mumbled and pushed out through the crowd.

Once on the street again, Peter checked that the Porsche was still parked at the curb. Melina has to be around here somewhere, he thought, and approached the next apartment block that was blaring forth loud music. This time the door was opened by a heavyset young man with a bottle of wine in his hand. He didn't offer Peter a drink. "What do you want?" he asked curtly.

"I'm looking for a certain girl," Peter explained politely. "Really! There are lots of girls here. What does she look like?"

"Slim build, dark hair – she's wearing a blue blouse and long silver earrings."

"She's not here," the man with the bottle grunted, and tried to close the door in Peter's face.

"I would like to look for her. Her father will be very angry if she isn't home soon," Peter continued, undisturbed by the man's rudeness.

"I told you, she's not here. Now get out!" the man said. Something in his tone convinced Peter that he was lying.

"I think I should look for her myself. Just in case you've made a mistake," Peter said calmly, and pushed his shoulder against the door.

The heavy set man suddenly gave the door a shove and Peter would have been pushed into the hall if he hadn't quickly braced himself against the door jam with his feet. Using his legs as a lever, Peter forced the door open, and a moment later the heavier man saw a flash of steel coming towards him. It stopped just short of his stomach. "I think I should look for her myself," Peter repeated.

"O.K.! O.K.! Hey, I don't want any trouble. You look around all you want."

"Thank you," Peter said, and instantly the knife vanished.

Peter passed the man with the bottle, and pushed his way into the room. It took him only a few minutes to locate Melina. She was sprawled on a sofa in the corner. Richard, who sat close beside her, was pawing her, and trying to unbutton her blouse. Melina was obviously very drunk, and was having a hard time keeping ahead of Richard's hands.

"Stop it Richard! Leave me alone!" she repeated several times, but she was giggling and not putting up much resistance. Richard kissed her on the neck, and began to slide his hands under her skirt.

A moment later Peter gripped Richard's arm with his large powerful hand. "Let her go," he said coldly.

Richard looked up at Peter and frowned. "Hey! What the hell do you want here? Mind your own business!"

"Melina is my business. Take your hands off her."

Richard let go of Melina and stood up. He was slightly taller than Peter, and a good deal heavier.

"I've seen you before," Richard growled. "Who the hell are you anyway?"

Peter knew that Richard had seen him at the Marneés, and he was betting that Melina had not bothered to mention who he was. "I'm Melina's brother, and I'm here to defend the family honor," Peter announced.

Richard looked first surprised and then angry. "You're a liar! She never told me she had a brother. I ought to break you in half for coming in here," Richard threatened and took a step forward.

Peter's hand hardly seemed to move, but before Richard could take the second step, Peter passed his blade under Richard's chin. "The family does not mention me," Peter said softly. "I'm a blot on their good name. I've been in prison — for cutting a man."

Recovering herself, Melina stood up and saw the knife in Peter's hand. "Peter! I thought they took your knife!" she said in alarm.

"They tried to," Peter answered, and deftly tossed the knife from his right to his left hand and back again.

Richard looked from Peter to Melina, and then stepped backwards raising his hands in front of him. "I wasn't trying to hurt her. I swear. She's a nice girl," he said apologetically.

"You're damn right she is, and I don't want to see you bothering her ever again!" Peter said coolly and took Melina by the arm. "What would Papa say if he knew you were with a man like this?" he demanded sternly.

Melina was startled. She shot Peter a guilty look and put the back of her hand over her mouth.

Still brandishing the blade, Peter backed away from Richard, taking Melina with him. The music had stopped and everyone moved aside as they made their way to the door.

They were on the street before Melina reacted. Angrily she shook herself free and raised her arm to slap Peter's face. He was too quick, however, and caught her hand. "You've got a lot of nerve barging into a private party like that, and embarrassing me in front of my friends. Who do you think you are anyway?" she shrieked.

"Friends?" Peter shouted back at her. "You call those people friends? You were about to play the wife to Richard, and they would have let you do it!"

"What business is it of yours? I don't have to answer to you!"

"You're right! And I don't give a damn what happens to you!

137

But Madame is responsible for you. As long as you are a part of her household, I will not let you bring shame on her. You're always bragging about your family, why don't you think about them before you make a fool of yourself? What would your father say if he knew you were drunk?"

Without waiting for her answer, Peter yanked the car door open and pushed Melina into the seat. He slammed the door shut and went around to the driver's side.

Melina was visibly subdued. "I would not have to wait for my father's anger," she said slowly. "My brothers would kill me. Oh Peter . . . was I really that close to letting him . . .?" She suddenly looked so ashamed Peter lost his anger.

"I don't know," he said brusquely, "Maybe you have more sense than I think."

Peter started the car and drove in silence until Melina started to giggle.

"What's so funny?" Peter challenged.

"I was just thinking how fierce you looked, standing there with that knife, Peter. And that line about being in prison — really!"

"I'm sorry I couldn't think of anything better to say," Peter snapped.

She laughed again, and Peter grinned in spite of himself. "I guess I was stupid to claim to be your brother, but I needed some authority to back me up. Richard would have torn my head off if he knew I push the vacuum cleaner for you."

"Well it was very kind of you to come after me. I know I've not been very friendly to you," she said contritely.

"You are a very foolish girl, Melina. I was trying to avoid a scandal. Madame has enough grief from me."

"Well it was still very nice of you. I guess I never appreciated you." She shot him a strange glance and smiled. "It's funny, but I never noticed until tonight — you really are handsome, Peter."

Peter laughed. "You have never been so drunk before, Melina. You'll think differently in the morning."

"No, it's not just the alcohol. I guess I always thought of you as scrawny and shaggy, but you're not like that anymore, Peter."

"So I am no longer the wolf, eh?" he said turning to face her.

She laughed. "You're right — I am a foolish girl. I should never have said such a thing. Will you forgive me?" she asked, and abruptly put her hand to Peter's cheek.

Peter jumped, but was surprised that her touch could be so gentle. He looked straight ahead. "I accept your apology," he said formally.

"Why, Peter, I think you are afraid of me," Melina taunted. When Peter ignored her, she reached over and teasingly ran her fingers up and down his arm.

He tensed and tried to shrug her off. "You're drunk, Melina. Go sit where you belong!" he snapped. "And button your blouse! Mother of God, you have no shame!"

"Don't you like me, Peter? Why did you come to rescue me if you don't like me?" she teased and put her head on his shoulder. "I think you are jealous of Richard . . . admit it?"

"I am not jealous of Richard! I just don't think you should go out with him. He's too old for you, and I don't think he has good intentions."

"And who should I go out with, Peter? You?"

"Your family would really be pleased with that, wouldn't they," he said scornfully.

"Why do you worry so much about my family? They mean nothing to you!"

"A person's family is important! You don't appreciate what you have. If I had a family, I would never disgrace them."

When they arrived in the driveway at the Marneés, Peter stopped the car and went around to help Melina. As he opened the car door, Melina leaned out, threw her arms around Peter, and kissed him on the mouth. He was taken by surprise, and a current of sensuous pleasure rippled through him. She was so close, and so incredibly feminine and soft against him, that his judgement wavered. It would feel so good to . . . he thought. He started to put his arms around her, then abruptly pushed her away. "You're drunk, Melina. You don't even like me!" he said in a hoarse whisper. "Dio mio! Life was so much easier when you hated me!"

"But I do like you . . ." she insisted.

"Be quiet, Melina. You'll wake Madame," he warned.

He took her arm to lead her towards the kitchen door, but she stumbled. He caught her and held her against him.

"Oh Peter, all of a sudden I feel awful. I need to lie down."

"Not now, Melina! Not yet!" he whispered loudly, but she slipped and fell on her knees. Suddenly she gagged, then her stomach rebelled and began to empty itself. She groaned and Peter held her from falling. "Oh Peter, I think I am going to die."

Peter shook his head. "It's very unlikely, Melina, but you won't feel very good tomorrow, that's for certain. Bring everything up, if you can manage it," he coaxed.

When she had finished heaving, Peter helped her to her feet, and struggled to unlock the kitchen door. He had barely got her through the door when she went limp, and fell against him in the dark. Picking her up, he held her in his arms while he groped for the light switch. "Melina? Melina! Wake up you stupid . . ." he whispered excitedly. Without warning the light snapped on, and he froze.

Anna stood staring at him in astonishment. "Peter! What happened?"

"I think she fainted!" he blurted out.

"I thought she was home hours ago. Didn't she go out with Richard? Where is he?"

"They were at a party. Richard was drunk . . . I made him take his hands off her."

Anna shook her head and looked worried. "I knew that young man was not to be trusted! Did he . . .?"

"No," Peter answered quickly. "I found her in time."

"I suppose Melina has been drinking too," Anna said sadly.

"Yes . . . she was sick just now."

"Will you take her upstairs, Peter? I'll take care of her."

"Yes," Peter said, and silently carried Melina up the stairs.

"Madame will be very upset when she learns what Melina's been up to," Anna said as she opened the door to Melina's room.

"Anna! Please don't tell Madame," Peter pleaded, and set Melina on the bed.

"But Madame is responsible for her, Peter."

"Please, Anna, you know how Madame feels about drunkenness. If she finds out, she'll never allow Melina to go anywhere again. Please — can't you tell Madame that Melina has a headache or . . . or some woman's problem?"

Anna looked steadily at Peter. "Why do you want to protect Melina? She goes out of her way to make trouble for you."

Peter shrugged. "She's just trying to make a life for herself. If her father found out she was drunk he would force her to go home and marry some man he picked for her. Besides, I don't want Madame to have any more worries. I am always such a . . . a disappointment to her. Please Anna! Don't tell Madame. I'll see that Melina never goes out with Richard again. She's a good girl, really."

Anna sighed. "All right, Peter. I won't mention Melina's behavior to Madame, but if she asks, I will have to tell her the truth."

"Thank you, Anna, thank you," Peter answered, and flashed her that half-pleased, half-shy grin of his that she found irresistible. Peter was not at all like the three brawny, boisterous boys she had raised, she thought to herself; but he worked very hard for her, and did everything he could to make her work lighter.

"Peter, I never knew a boy with as many secrets as you," Anna said and laughed. "Did you put the car away?"

"Not yet. I will go do it."

"Yes and you'd best get to bed. It's late and you have to drive Monsieur and Madame to church in the morning."

"Dio mio, you're right," he moaned. "Perhaps I will have a headache tomorrow myself," he said and grinned at her.

"Be gone you rascal!" Anna scolded and closed the door behind him.

CHAPTER TWELVE

Geilla was writing to Kon once again, but she told him very little. She did not want to burden him with her problems. Although she was working long hours at the textile mill, she was paid so little, that she was forced to sew some piece work at home. Her days were gray and featureless, and she felt as though she never got to sit down or rest. Even when she went home there was her father, or rather the shadow of the man who once was her father, to care for. Zoel had grown worse, and sometimes did not even recognize her. The neighbors had found him wandering in the street on one occasion, and Geilla feared he might fall on the stairs. She had asked a doctor to come several times, but there was nothing he could do for Zoel's mind.

Life was hard for Geilla, for unlike Kon, she was not used to fending for herself. She had always been well cared for, and after her mother died when she was eleven, Zoel and Alonzo had spoiled and pampered her in every way. Now she was lonely and vulnerable, and did not dare to go anywhere except to the mill, or occasionally to church. She was young and beautiful, and men bothered her in the streets, and especially at work, brushing against her or grabbing her when they thought no one was looking.

The person who annoyed her the most, however, was Servio Magagnini, the owner of the mill. Initially he did not visit the mill every day, but when he came he always tried to engage Geilla in conversation. At first she smiled and was polite to him, for he was her employer; but when he started coming every day, and invented excuses to call her into his office, it began to bother her. He was always a gentleman, and never said or did anything improper, but he was very persistent in asking her to go to dinner or to the theater with him. Geilla felt embarrassed at being singled out for his attention, for he was in his sixties, and held no attraction for her.

When Servio learned that Geilla was supporting herself and her father, he arranged for her to have a raise. Unfortunately, the net effect was to bring down a rain of venom from the other workers at the mill. They started calling Geilla dirty names, and insinuating that she was giving her favors to Servio. The women scorned her and the men became even more vulgar in their attempts to paw and touch her.

Once when Zoel had a fever and Geilla was forced to stay home with him, Servio came to her flat with a doctor. She was reluctant to accept any favors from him, but since she was very worried about

Zoel, she finally agreed to let the doctor in. Geilla was embarrassed about the bareness of their flat. She had grown up in a large house with beautiful furnishings, but she had been forced to sell everything to pay a lawsuit the owners of the theater had brought against Zoel. Kon had always seen that the bills were paid on time, and that the performers received the money, publicity, and respect they had been promised in their contracts. After he left, Zoel let things slide, and the owners lost money.

Servio began to send special food to Geilla, for her father of course, and it was impossible to send it all back. Sometimes beautifully wrapped baskets of fruit would be delivered while she was at work, and she had no money to pay for a messenger to send them back. After several months of being turned down when he asked Geilla to dinner, Servio reminded her that she owed him as least something in return for his gifts. Geilla had feared Servio would call in the debt someday, and now she was caught. Reluctantly, she agreed to go to dinner with him. Servio took her to one of the best restaurants in Naples, but she was embarrassed that she did not have clothes that were fine enough for the occasion. As always, Servio was a gentleman, and throughout the meal he treated her kindly and tried to make her feel at ease. Nevertheless, she felt very nervous and could not enjoy herself. At last when the meal was over, and she thought she would be allowed to go home and be alone, Servio began a conversation that became a nightmare for her.

"Geilla, I have visited you every day for months. You are so beautiful I cannot stay away. You must know I care deeply for you." He paused and put his hand over hers on the table. She could barely hide her dismay.

"I would like to make you my wife, Geilla," he continued. "It would make me very happy to have you with me always."

Geilla recovered enough to make a response. "Signor Magagnini, I am sorry, but this cannot be. You have been very kind, and I appreciate what you have done for my father, but this cannot be."

She tried to withdraw her hand from his, but he held on.

"I know I am much older than you, Geilla, but I am very well off. I would take very good care of you. I could give you anything you want."

Geilla pulled more forcefully, and Servio let go of her hand. "Please, Signor Magagnini, I want nothing from you. I want only to go home, please."

Even in his ardor Servio could see that Geilla was getting upset by his attention and he decided not to press her.

"Very well, Geilla, I shall take you home, but please think about my proposal."

All the way home in Servio's car Geilla shook while Servio talked quietly of his family home in the country. He tried to interest her in going to visit it with him. When at last they arrived at her flat, Geilla forgot all the formalities of thanking Servio for the meal, and made a mad dash from the car. Servio got out to escort her to her door, but she was gone too quickly. He cursed himself for having spoken so soon and frightening her, but he was not about to give up. He would be patient – she would come around, he thought.

And so it went. Servio was forever coming to see her, and she could not escape him. Everyone at the mill thought she was already sleeping with him, and even her neighbor, Signora Marcucci began to encourage her to accept him for his money.

"A girl could do worse than to marry a rich man," she told her.

"But I am waiting for Kon. He's the one I love."

"Where is this young man of yours? Why is it he never comes?"

"He is working in Switzerland."

"Switzerland! Why does he go so far away if he loves you?"

"He has a good job there. He is trying to save some money for us."

"And has he asked you to marry him?"

"No . . . not yet. He has so little money."

"Why do you waste your time on a poor boy when you could marry a rich man? Who will take better care of you and your father?"

"But I love Kon and he loves me. I know it, even if he doesn't come."

Kon had been sending her a little money, but it seemed to disappear so quickly. Geilla wrote to him, but said nothing of her problems with Servio. She was happy that Kon at last was with people who looked after him, and she hid her own misery from him. She tried to find another job, but she had few qualifications, and was so frail, no one would hire her. She was offered a position as a live-in child's attendant, but she could not accept it, because she had to look after Zoel. As she grew more and more tired, the world lost its interest for her, and she wrote to Kon less and less often.

Geilla had not been eating properly for several months. One day as she worked at the mill, she either fainted, or fell asleep, and her sleeve got caught in the fabric rollers. When she realized what had happened, she screamed in terror, and tried frantically to free herself. Several women rushed to her and tried to help, but before the men could stop the machinery, three of her fingers and her wrist were smashed. Geilla was still screaming when they pulled her free, and Servio, who had been in the office, came running into the work room. Seeing that it was Geilla who had been hurt, he forgot his years, and quickly lifted her in his arms. He carried her to his car, and drove like a madman all the way to the hospital, calling aloud to God and the Virgin to save and protect his beloved. Geilla fainted before they arrived.

Hours later, Geilla awoke to find herself in an unfamiliar bed, surrounded by white sheets, white curtains, and strangers dressed all in white. She felt very weak and was frightened to be alone. She tried to sit up, but as she did, she felt a severe throbbing in her hand. It felt so heavy, she did not know if she could lift it. Someone was standing by her bed, and she imagined it was Zoel.

"Papa?" she called weakly. "What has happened to me?"

"You fell into the machinery, my dearest," a voice answered, and she suddenly realized it was not her father, but Servio, who was standing by her bed.

"I thank God you were not killed! They tell me you will heal well, Geilla. I will find the best doctors for you. Anything you need I will get for you . . . anything!"

Geilla looked at Servio for a long time and saw that he really was worried about her. She remembered his loud woeful prayers on the way to the hospital. She was grateful to him, but she wished fervently that it was Kon standing before her. She had been waiting and waiting, but he never came. He was never there to hold her, or to comfort her, or to love her. Suddenly she wondered if Kon ever even thought about her any more, now that he had a new life, and she began to weep. She wept for Kon who was so lonely, and she wept for herself that she was always so tired, and she wept that there was only Servio to comfort her.

Servio mistakenly thought Geilla was in pain, and anxiously taking her hand he assured her again that he would bring the best doctors for her. Then he raced into the hall, calling loudly for help.

Poor Servio, she thought, he has such a good heart. If only I could feel anything at all for him . . . but I love Kon, only Kon. Oh Virgin of Virgins will he never come back to me?

Servio returned, dragging the doctor, who looked at Geilla's hand and asked a lot of questions, but she could not stop her tears and continued to sob. Finally the doctor put a needle in her arm, and after a short while she stopped crying. She still felt very sad, but she was so tired, she could not pull away when Servio held her hand. She fell asleep wondering who was looking after her father.

Several unhappy days later, the doctor said Geilla could leave the hospital. Servio was there to drive her home. It seemed to Geilla that he had been with her all the time she had been in the hospital, but she had been so groggy she could not recall much of what happened to her. She did not remember that she had cried so uncontrollably whenever she was awake that the doctors had kept her sedated so that she could rest.

Geilla leaned on Servio's arm as they went down to his car. She realized that he was very attentive and kind and fussed over her like a mother hen, but she wished fervently that he would leave her alone. She found it very difficult to control her tears for even the short ride home. Thankfully, Servio had the good sense to bring Signora

Marcucci to take Geilla into her flat.

"You are not to worry about anything, Geilla. I will see that you are paid your regular wages until you are well again," Servio promised her at her door.

"And as for the doctors, they have been taken care of," he concluded, smiling at her as if paying her bills were a great privilege.

"You are very kind, Servio, but I can't accept . . ." she protested, but Signora Marcucci cut her off. "You are most generous and thoughtful Signor Magagnini. Your help is deeply appreciated." Signora Marcucci took Geilla by the arm rather forcefully, and rushed her into the flat.

Servio walked sadly down to his car. He had spent many hours at the hospital, worrying over Geilla and he was tired. The years he had cast off when he rushed to her aid came back to him in full measure. Perhaps I am a fool to love someone so young, he thought, but love her I do, and my heart is as full of longing as any young man's.

Although Signora Marcucci scolded Geilla for even thinking of refusing Servio's offers of help, Geilla managed to convince her to help her write a letter to Kon. It was a plaintive appeal in which she poured out her heart, telling him of her love, and begging him to come to see her. Against Geilla's wishes, Signora Marcucci added that Geilla had been injured and could not work, and was in desperate need of money.

When Peter received Geilla's letter, telling him that she could no longer work, he was frantic. His first thought was to take the money he had saved and hurry to Naples to be with Geilla. However, as he calmed down, he realized that the money would not last long, and that his chances of finding a good job in Italy were very poor. Meeting the Marneés had been a lucky break, and he did not want to abandon a rare opportunity. He longed to see Geilla with all his heart, but he realized that he would be of very little use to her in Naples. He therefore decided to approach Edgar about a raise.

Although he was anxious to get money to Geilla as soon as possible, Peter waited until after the family had dinner and were gathered in the library. Then he paced the hall impatiently, hoping he could catch Edgar alone.

"Sir, I must talk to you immediately," he said abruptly as Edgar came out of the library.

Edgar could see that Peter was agitated. "What seems to be the problem, Peter?"

"Sir, I've been here over a year. I've worked hard and done everything you've asked of me. I . . . I must have more money!"

"So, you want a raise," Edgar said and smiled. "Well you certainly have done good work for us. I will discuss the matter with Madame and we will see . . ."

"I must have it now, sir! As soon as possible!"

145

"Peter, what's the rush? I thought you were happy here."

"I was . . . I mean, I am. I'm sorry, but . . . I need the money now, sir."

"Are you in trouble, Peter? Tell me the truth. What is this all about?"

Peter hesitated. "The money is for a friend," he began reluctantly. "She . . ." he paused, and Edgar drew the wrong conclusion. "Peter, have you made some girl pregnant?"

"No, sir!" Peter growled and glared at Edgar. "Whatever you may think of me, I do have control of myself!"

"I'm sorry, Peter. I had to ask. You are a young man and . . ."

"And what? You think because I come from Italy, I have fire in my blood and can only think with . . ."

"Peter! Please, I never intended to insult you."

Edgar put his hand to his head in frustration. "I believe we were discussing your raise," he continued quietly.

"Yes, sir. I must have more money."

"Why is this woman asking you for money, Peter? Is it because you have a good job? I hate to see you being taken advantage of."

"What I do with my money is my own affair! I did not come to beg, sir. I thought you were pleased with my work and would help me."

"I am pleased with your work, Peter. I just don't want you to throw your money away. You must think of the future."

"You don't understand . . . when you have no money, you have no future!" Peter said raising his voice.

"Calm yourself, Peter. I will give you a raise, but I will hold half of the increase in trust for you."

"What good is money I cannot spend when I need it?"

"I am only trying to keep you from doing something foolish."

"The only foolish thing I did was to ask for your help. I should have known you would not understand. Keep the money for the future, I don't care. Use it to bury me!" Peter shouted and stormed away leaving Edgar with his mouth open.

"What was that all about?" Charlotte asked. She had heard the shouting and came out of the library just as Peter turned and left.

"I don't know what's gotten into Peter! He rushed up to me a minute ago, and insisted I give him a raise immediately so he could send money to some woman. Then he got angry and stalked away when I said I would hold part of the increase in trust for him."

"Why does he need to send money? Oh Edgar, has he . . . ?"

"Don't even say it! That was my first thought, but when I asked him, he was terribly insulted and lost his temper. He never did tell me why he needed the money."

"Calm yourself, Edgar," Charlotte said talking his arm. "I have found that the more important a thing is to Peter, the less he will say

146

about it."

"Why must he be so secretive about everything?"

"It's become a part of his nature. He just doesn't trust people."

"I am disappointed, Charlotte. I thought Peter knew me well enough to tell me the truth."

Charlotte patted his arm. "I think he trusts you, Edgar. He just doesn't like to have anyone make suggestions about how he should run his life."

"Perhaps I should have given him the money, but I do wish he would have told me who the woman was."

"He may tell us more when he calms down. I could tell something has been bothering him all day."

"How can we help him if he won't tell us anything?"

"We can't, Edgar, we can't and it breaks my heart."

****

Immediately after he stormed away from Edgar, Peter was sorry he had lost his temper. Edgar certainly had been very kind and generous to him, and he was grateful. Why had be been so defensive about telling Edgar why he needed money? Asking for a raise is too much like begging, he told himself. It was humiliating to have to tell anyone that the girl he loved and hoped to marry had to work in a textile mill. Geilla deserved better than that. She had not grown up in poverty like he had. If only he had a better job, he could be more help to her. Zoel's curse still rang in his ears. Peter wondered if he would ever be good enough for Geilla. He felt he could not approach Edgar again, so he determined to find an extra job.

****

Three weeks later Peter was fighting exhaustion, and everyone in the house noticed that he was moody and ill-tempered. At 7:15, on Friday evening, Carlin was in the dining room with the family when Peter entered. "I'm sorry I'm late," he mumbled, and quickly took his place at the table.

Even at first glance, Carlin could tell that Peter was not well, but he kept quiet and studied him. Throughout the meal, Peter ate very little, said almost nothing, and hardly seemed to hear the conversation that was going on around him. When at last the family moved to the library for dessert and coffee, Carlin managed to corner Peter.

"How are you feeling, Peter?"

"I am well, sir," Peter answered and looked away.

"Anna tells me you've been eating poorly and drinking too much coffee. I thought you agreed to cut back."

"I did . . . and I have. I just need a little extra sometimes. I've been doing a lot of studying lately."

Edgar heard Peter's remark and came up beside Carlin. "What are you studying, Peter? One of the teachers called yesterday and informed me that you haven't been to class for almost three weeks."

Peter stiffened, shot a startled look at Edgar, and averted his gaze. Carlin saw immediately that Peter was embarrassed to be caught in a lie. He was curious, for he knew Peter was always careful to tell the truth, even when the consequences were unpleasant. When Peter didn't respond, Edgar pressed the point.

"Why have you stopped going to school, Peter?"

Peter shifted his weight and looked guilty. "I've . . . I've been very . . . very busy lately, sir," he stammered.

"Busy with what? What could possibly be more important than your education?"

"I took a night job. I need some cash!" Peter suddenly shouted.

Edgar looked surprised but said nothing. Peter took a step backwards. "May I be excused, sir. I really must be going."

"No. You may not be excused," Edgar said quietly. "I pay you to be on call as our driver and to look after Albert and little Charles. What if one of the boys got sick during the night? What if the house caught on fire? I thought I could rely on you when I go away. You disappoint me, Peter. I forbid you to continue this other job!"

"You can't do that! I am entitled to a life of my own."

"Not when it interferes with your duties to Madame and the boys."

"It's not interfering! I've done my work."

"That's not true! Charles said you were too grumpy to play with him, and Anna mentioned that certain things have gone undone."

"I'm sorry. I'll try a little harder to . . ."

"Look at you, Peter. Your making yourself sick trying to work another job. You missed the turn driving home tonight, and you could barely stay awake at the dinner table."

"I'll do better, I promise. I'm just a little tired."

"How long do you think you can keep this up, Peter?" Carlin asked abruptly.

"As long as I need to. It's none of your damn business anyway!" Peter snapped.

"Peter! It is his business," Edgar said raising his voice. "I want Doctor La Monde to take a look at you. You don't look well."

"I don't need a doctor. There is nothing wrong with me!" Peter shouted.

"Dr. La Monde will be the judge of that. He is in charge of the health of everyone in this family, Peter."

"I don't belong to your family! I only work here. I can do as I wish."

Edgar was losing his patience. "If you want to continue to work here you will do as I say!"

Charlotte quickly stepped between Peter and Edgar taking Peter by the arm. "Please, Peter. Let Carlin check you over. Do it for me . . . please."

Peter pulled away. "There's nothing wrong with me," he said trying to gain control, but Charlotte noticed that his hands were shaking.

"Please, Peter," Charlotte continued. "I am concerned about you. Admit it — you haven't been yourself lately."

Peter put his hand up and held his head with it.

"All right, all right! I am a little tired, but that's my business! Leave me alone! All of you!"

Peter tried to back away, but Carlin caught his arm. He could feel that Peter was extremely tense. "Peter, you're on the verge of a collapse. None of us want to see you get sick again. Please, come upstairs with me. It won't take long."

Peter stared from Carlin to Edgar and then to Charlotte. "No. I'm just . . . I'm just a little tired," he said weakly.

"I know you are, Peter. I can see it," Charlotte said quickly. "Go with Dr. La Monde. Let him help you."

"But I need the money . . ."

"We'll talk about it, Peter," Carlin said gently pulling him towards the door.

"Come up to your room, and tell me why you need the money. Please, I want to know all about it."

Peter let himself be pulled forward, but hesitated again as he reached the door.

"There's nothing wrong with me, truly. Nothing," he insisted.

Carlin grabbed his bag, which Charlotte had suggested he bring, and led Peter up the stairs. By the time they reached the third floor, Peter was moving with difficulty and clutching the railing. Supporting him by the arm, Carlin maneuvered him into his room and made him sit on the bed.

"I need you to take your jacket and shirt off, Peter," Carlin said, but Peter didn't respond. "Peter? . . . Come on. Let me take your jacket."

Peter let Carlin help him with his jacket, but when Carlin tried to untie Peter's tie, Peter put his hand up and pulled away. "Leave it! I'll do it, myself," he said sharply.

"All right, Peter . . . let me help you with your cuffs." Carlin unbuttoned Peter's shirt cuffs and noticed his wrists. "Peter, where is your watch?"

"I . . . I must have lost it somewhere."

"It's not like you to be careless with your belongings. What did you do with it? Oh, Peter, have you sold it? Madame will be very hurt if you did."

Peter lowered his head. "No, don't tell her, please. I need the money. I only pawned it. I hope to get it back. I needed the money."

Once Peter had his shirt off, Carlin took his pulse, listened to his heart, and took a blood pressure reading.

"Well, it's obvious you're pushing too hard, Peter. You really must get some rest. I have to stand behind Edgar and forbid you to continue this other job. Where have you been working anyway?"

Peter gave him a vague look. "At a warehouse . . . a big warehouse . . . lots of trucks."

"Oh Peter! Why did you pick such heavy labor? It's not good for you."

"I'm strong. I can do it!"

"But you're not built for it. You're too light."

"Well it pays! I need the money, doctor! I need the money!" he shouted.

"All right, all right. Don't get upset. Tell me why you suddenly need more money."

Peter hesitated and then the words came rushing out in a torrent. "It's for a friend. She's in terrible trouble. She hurt her hand and can't work. Her father is sick. She's all alone . . . all alone."

"It's very generous of you to want to help her, Peter, but is she so important to you that you will make yourself sick to give her money?"

Peter looked at Carlin in disbelief. "Of course she's important to me! I plan to marry her."

Carlin was surprised. He had no idea Peter had become so serious about a girl. He was not aware that Peter even had a social life.

"What is this girl's name, Peter? Where does she live?"

"Geilla — her name is Geilla. She lives in a small flat. She deserves better. She used to live in a house, a beautiful house with lots of furniture and rugs and nice things . . . expensive things."

Carlin put his hand on Peter's shoulder.

"Where is the flat, Peter?"

"The flat? In Naples."

"Naples! When were you in Naples, Peter?"

"Two years ago."

"And you haven't seen her in all this time?"

"No," Peter mumbled and started to get up from the bed.

"I have to get to the warehouse. If I don't . . . they will hire someone else."

Carlin caught a hold of his arm. "Peter, you are in no condition to do heavy work. Your heart is beating too fast as it is."

"You don't understand anything do you! I need the money. Let me go."

"No! Listen to me. Did you ask Edgar for money? You must be due for a raise by now."

Peter shook himself free. "I asked him! I asked him three weeks ago! He said he would keep the money for my future. Geilla is my future. I couldn't make him understand. I can't make you understand."

"All right, Peter. All right. I do understand that this is important to you. Look, I'll loan you some money. I'll give you some money! How much do you need? Whatever it takes to get you to quit this other job. I know you'll hurt yourself if you try to work tonight. Please, let me help you."

Peter was silent and looked intently at Carlin. "Why would you do this? What do you expect to get from me?"

"I don't expect anything from you. My God, Peter! You were a wreck when you came here. I just don't want to see you get sick again, that's all."

"You would really care if I got sick?"

"Of course I care, Peter. Edgar cares too, but you wouldn't tell him why you needed the money."

"He insulted me! He asked if I had made a girl pregnant. He doesn't think I can control myself!"

"Peter, it was a logical question. He was only trying to find out what kind of trouble you were in."

"Well, I am insulted. I would never ask such a thing of him. Just because I come from Italy . . ."

"Peter, calm down. It has nothing to do with where you come from. Listen to me, Peter. Will you let me help you?"

"Will you make me sign a contract?"

"Only if you want to, Peter. Let me know what you need."

Peter named a figure and Carlin was surprised it was so little. "Perhaps you could work it off doing some jobs for me," Carlin offered, knowing Peter hated to be in anyone's debt. Peter stiffened and immediately became suspicious.

"What kind of jobs?"

"Relax, Peter — nothing difficult. I was thinking you could wash and wax my car, or maybe fix the window in my office."

Peter nodded. "I could do that for you."

"Good. Then you agree to give up this night job and let me help you?"

Peter thought for a long time before answering. "You are right . . . I have no energy to work. I ache all over, and everything spins when I stand up. It was very hard to drive home tonight. Edgar spoke the truth, I missed the turn. I truly did not recognize it."

"It's O.K. You just need to rest. Why don't you get undressed for bed. I'll be right back," Carlin coaxed.

Carlin left Peter sitting on the bed, and went into the bathroom to fetch a glass of water. When he returned he saw that Peter had not removed his clothes.

"Come on, Peter. Let me help you. You really aren't up to much, are you."

Peter looked up and rubbed his hand across his eyes. "What did you say?"

"I said you need to get undressed and into bed. Come on, take your shoes off. Yes . . . now the slacks, that's it. O.K. now, Peter, I want to you to take these tablets."

"No! No pills . . . what are they?" he said stubbornly.

"They're muscle relaxants. They will help take the soreness away."

"I don't need them."

"Yes you do, I insist."

"No. I won't . . ."

Carlin was suddenly stern. "Peter! Let's not go through this again. Take the tablets!"

"No, I swore . . ."

"Oh I give up!" Carlin said in disgust and put the pills away. He left the room and Peter wondered if he was angry, and would withdraw his offer of help. He thought of trying to get dressed, but he could barely summon the energy to move. Peter was struggling with his shirt when Carlin returned.

"What are you doing?" Carlin asked sharply. "Were you going to sneak out?"

"I thought you were gone. I thought you had changed your mind."

"You have no faith, Peter. Here, drink this," Carlin said offering Peter a glass.

"What is it?"

"Just some wine to help you relax."

"What did you put in it?"

"Nothing. Come on, drink it."

Peter took the glass and sipped cautiously. He didn't detect any strange taste. "You swear it's only wine?"

"I swear it, Peter. Come on, drink up. I'm not going to poison you."

Peter drank. "It's good wine," he commented. "Do you always prescribe it?"

"No. It's only for stubborn patients who won't take their medicine."

Peter smiled briefly and handed the empty glass to Carlin. "Sometimes it pays to be stubborn."

Carlin shook his head. "Why must you always give me an argument?" He pulled the covers back and helped Peter into bed. "Lie face down," Carlin said, and began to run his hands over Peter's

152

shoulders.

"What are you doing? Leave me alone!" Peter growled. He tried to roll away, but Carlin pushed him down.

"Just lie still. Put your arms down," Carlin ordered, and wrestled Peter's arms to his sides.

"Let me go. Don't do this to me!"

"Be still, Peter. I'm not going to hurt you. You don't trust anyone, do you?"

Carlin sat on the bed beside Peter and firmly massaged Peter's shoulders and back. "You're very tense, Peter. Try to relax."

"Don't . . ." Peter started to object, but he quickly realized how good it felt to have Carlin rub his tired muscles. He stopped squirming and lay still.

"Haven't you ever had a back rub, Peter?"

"I don't remember," Peter mumbled. "It feels . . . good." His muted grunts told Carlin he appreciated it.

"How soon can I have the money?" Peter asked, suddenly reminding Carlin of his promise.

"How soon do you need it?"

"Tomorrow. Can you come tomorrow? I must mail it before noon."

"So soon? All right. I will come at 9:30."

"Promise me you'll come. Swear it!"

"I promise, Peter. You would be impossible to live with if I forgot."

Peter sighed. "Tell Charles I am sorry I was cross with him. I didn't mean to be . . . I am just so tired . . ." his voice trailed off and he was asleep. Carlin rolled Peter onto his back and pulled the covers over him. Gathering up his bag, he turned out the light, and went down to talk to Edgar and Charlotte.

****

Almost two months had passed, but Peter still had not told Edgar or Charlotte any more about who he was sending money to. They knew that Carlin was supplying him with extra cash and that he anxiously checked the mail every day, but they had no details. Peter seemed to be more on edge every week, and Charlotte had put him to work turning over the garden, thinking that the extra physical activity might drain off some of his nervous energy.

Late one Thursday evening, Charlotte and Edgar returned from attending a Schubert and Brahms concert. Peter had driven them as usual, but Charlotte had not been pleased with him. She had commented several times during the trip home that he was going too fast, but he didn't seem to pay attention. After Edgar went into the library, Charlotte waited in the hall, while Peter put the car away. She scolded Peter again when he came in from the garage.

"I'm sorry," Peter mumbled absently, and without really looking at Charlotte, he started up the stairs. Charlotte caught something in his expression, but could not put it into a thought.

"Peter, aren't you feeling well? You didn't say if you enjoyed the concert tonight."

"I am well, Madame," he said without turning towards her. She thought it strange that he was almost rude to her. She took a step towards him. "Peter, look at me when I'm speaking."

He turned and she noticed he look tired. "Are you sleeping well? You're not worried about your final exams, are you?"

"No, Madame," he mumbled and turned away again.

"Is something bothering you, Peter?" she said gently. "If there is anything we can help you with . . ."

"There's nothing wrong with me, Madame," he answered sharply.

"All right, Peter. Goodnight then."

"Goodnight, Madame."

Charlotte watched Peter climb the stairs, then went in to join Edgar. About an hour later when she went to check on the boys before she retired, she noticed that the light was still on in Peter's room. She did not disturb him, but made a mental note to ask Carlin to talk to him when he came for dinner the following night.

CHAPTER THIRTEEN

Melina, whose bedroom was on the second floor, awoke with a start. She sat up in bed and tried to place the sound she had heard. When everything was quiet, she was almost convinced that she had been dreaming. She thought to lay down again, but changed her mind. She rose, put on her robe, and turned on the light. She knew she had heard a noise, and although the boys were primarily Peter's responsibility, she decided to check on them. She stepped into the hall, switched on the light and was shocked to see Peter laying face down at the foot of the stairs.

"Dio mio! Peter! What happened?"

When he didn't respond she bent over him and caught the smell of alcohol. "Peter, you bastard, you're drunk! Oh God, if Madame finds you, you'll be in the street again."

She shook him and whispered loudly. "Peter, get up! Get up! Oh how could you be so stupid?" She was thoroughly dismayed when he didn't move. She turned and dashed down the stairs to Anna's room by the kitchen. Anna was surprised to hear that Peter was drunk. She thought Melina was exaggerating, but she threw on her robe, and hurried out the door behind the girl.

"Oh, Anna, we've got to get Peter up to his room before Madame finds out," Melina said in an excited whisper.

Anna knelt over Peter. She saw the broken glass, and noticed the unnatural way his arm was bent under him. "We'd better not move him, Melina," Anna cautioned. "I think the poor boy's broken his arm. We'd better call Dr. La Monde. There's no telling what else may be wrong with him from a fall like that."

"But if Madame finds out he was drunk . . ."

"This is serious, Melina. Peter needs a doctor right away." Anna struggled off her knees. "You go call Dr. La Monde," she said, taking Melina by the hand for a moment. "Tell him to send an ambulance. I must tell Monsieur Marneé."

By the time Carlin arrived about thirty minutes later, the Marneé household was gathered anxiously around Peter. Melina was in tears, fearing that Peter would be dismissed, Charlotte was wringing her hands, and Edgar was pacing. Carlin confirmed that Peter's arm was broken, and that he had hit his head on the banister post.

"What happened to cause him to drink like this?" Carlin asked the others.

"Something was bothering him all day," Charlotte commented.

"I asked him about it just before I went to bed, but he wouldn't tell me anything."

"A letter from Italy came for him today," Anna added. "The news must have upset him. He didn't eat any dinner tonight."

"A letter, you say — I'll check his room," Carlin said, and hurried up the stairs and into Peter's room. He found the letter on the small desk Charlotte had installed for Peter. Carlin read the letter and his heart sank. When he found an empty bottle and the seal, he was more anxious than ever to get Peter to the hospital. He stuffed the letter into his pocket and hurried down the stairs.

"The young fool finished off a whole bottle of brandy, and God only knows how much of the bottle he was carrying when he fell," Carlin told Edgar quietly.

"I'll get dressed and join you at the hospital," Edgar replied.

"Don't tell Charlotte how much he drank," Carlin warned.

When the ambulance arrived a few minutes later, Carlin supervised lifting Peter onto a stretcher and rode with him to the hospital. It was a long, hard night for Carlin. He set Peter's left arm, which was fractured in two places, and realigned Peter's shoulder, which had been partially dislocated. He stayed to observe Peter, lest he stop breathing, and inserted an IV tube to administer fluids to guard Peter from dehydration. When morning came, Peter was still limp and unresponsive, but he was alive and Carlin was relieved. Seeing how exhausted Carlin looked, Charlotte suggested that he go with Edgar to have some coffee while she sat with Peter. Carlin agreed knowing it might be a long wait before Peter woke up.

****

Geilla had seen to it herself that her letter to Kon was properly mailed, but she was dependent on Signora Marcucci to do the cooking and cleaning for her. Signora Marcucci took on the job eagerly, for she was convinced that Geilla was not eating properly, and was only too glad to "feed her up," as she called it.

One day while Geilla was away buying food with Signora Marcucci, Zoel staggered to the stove, and somehow managed to set the tiny cooking area on fire. When Geilla returned, the other tenants were pouring buckets of water on the still smoldering floor of her apartment, and the apartment manager was in the midst of a tirade about careless tenants. The moment the manager saw Geilla, he began to shout and scold about what a nuisance her father was to the neighborhood. Geilla pushed past him without hearing a word he said, and ran into the flat. She called aloud, and searched everywhere for Zoel, and was reaching a state of panic by the time she found him sitting calmly in a corner. Before she could discover if he was hurt, the manager was behind her, ranting and raving.

156

"I'm finished with you and your idiot of a father! He wanders in the streets like a lost dog. He sets fire to my building. Who knows what he will do next! I'm finished! Through! I want you both out!"

"But, Signor Cerruti, please. He is not well! Where will we go?"

"I don't care where you go! You don't pay the rent on time here. I cannot give my rooms for free."

"But I paid the rent last month. I am only a little late. Please, Signor Cerruti, I have been in the hospital. Give me a little more time. Please."

"No! You frighten the others by setting fire to the place. I cannot have this disturbance!"

"I will watch him more closely, please . . . let us stay. I beg you."

The manager was tempted to give in to Geilla. She looked so young and beautiful with tears forming in her liquid onyx eyes, but the other tenants were watching. If he showed any weakness, they would take advantage of him. He had to keep the upper hand. He was not a rich man. He could not afford to have a kind heart, he thought, and turned an impassive face to Geilla.

"I give you until tomorrow evening to move your things."

"Signor Cerruti, please . . ."

"Enough! I am not a priest to listen to your troubles. Get out and leave me in peace!" the manager shouted and forced his way through the crowd, which had gathered by the apartment door.

"What will I do, Signora Marcucci?" Geilla cried as she sank into a chair.

"You will help me fix a meal, and then we will send a message to Signor Magagnini. He will help you, I am sure."

"But I can't accept his help, Signora Marcucci. I am already too much in his debt."

The older woman straightened herself and gave Geilla a hard look. "Unless your adventuresome young man has wings, and a pocket full of gold, who else is going to help you?" she shouted as if she were scolding a stubborn child. "You must face facts, Geilla. A young man easily forgets! You have a wealthy, stable man who wants to take care of you. He is even willing to take your father in the bargain. What more do you want?"

Geilla started to object, but the woman cut her off.

"And don't speak to me of love! Does love put a roof over your head? Does love pay the butcher? Signor Magagnini will be good to you. You can learn to love him. Forget about this foolish young man with the empty pockets!"

Geilla did not have the strength to argue. It had been so long since Kon had come. He had sent a little money, but he had made no mention of marriage. Perhaps he had changed his mind. Perhaps he had found a Swiss girl to keep him from being lonely.

Signora Marcucci could not tell from Geilla's silence if she had

157

won her point or not, but she let the matter drop. It was not to her liking to have to force Geilla to face the ugly truth. It is pleasant to have dreams, she thought, but life is not made of dreams. Life is made of struggles. But, if a woman could marry a rich man . . . now that is a worthwhile dream.

"Come, Geilla," she said softly, "leave this mess the others have made. Get your father and come across to my house. We must cook for the men."

So Geilla got her father and left the flat. She helped Signora Marcucci as best she could with her one good hand, and after the meal, Signora Marcucci sent her youngest son to take a message to Servio.

Geilla did not feel comfortable taking Servio's hospitality, but he was delighted to serve her in any way he could. He took her to his country home, and provided separate, but adjoining rooms, which opened onto an exterior, paved courtyard, for herself and her father. Servio had the servants arrange outdoor benches with cushions so Zoel could lie in the sun, or the shade, and enjoy the air without Geilla having to worry about him falling down the stairs, or wandering into the streets. Geilla told herself it was only a temporary situation, and was careful to notify the post office where to forward any letters. It was a respectable arrangement because Servio's younger, widowed sister also lived in the villa.

When at last the letter from Switzerland arrived, however, it was not Geilla who opened it, but Servio. Reading Kon's pledge of love for Geilla, he realized why Geilla's heart had been closed to him. In a fit of jealousy he burned the letter, and all Geilla's hopes were destroyed with it. Servio began to press his case more ardently with Geilla, and after a month of constant pressure Geilla lost hope and agreed to marry him. She felt she had been abandoned by everyone she had loved. Her brother had died, her father had destroyed himself with drinking, and Kon had deserted her.

The banns were read and the wedding was quickly arranged. It was a strange affair, as Geilla took no interest in the plans and left everything to Servio and his sister. Even when her dress was selected for her, she made no objection. People commonly cry at weddings, but to see a bride in tears is not a good omen. Since her father was again stricken with fever, and her friends from the theater had scattered, Geilla was alone at her own wedding. She wept before the ceremony, she wept during the ceremony, and she wept afterwards, which made a gloomy affair of the small reception Servio had arranged. Supported on Servio's arm, her face as white as her gown of lace and pearls, Geilla had barely a word for Servio's guests. She was now mistress of the estate, but she felt more like a prisoner.

Geilla wept for three days after the wedding and Servio, being a temperate man, left her alone. However, on the fourth day he came into her room unannounced.

"Geilla, I love you, and it breaks my heart to see you weep, but you have agreed to be my wife, and you must keep your vow. I have been patient long enough. I demand the presence of my wife at my table and in my bed."

Geilla looked at him for a long time in silence. Although his words had been harsh, his eyes pleaded with her. She suddenly was struck by the realization that all the tears she could ever weep could not change the fact that she was now a married woman. All her youthful dreams were shattered, all her hope had been stripped from her, she had only her honor. She straightened herself and rose with controlled dignity.

"Forgive me, Servio. I forgot my place."

****

It was almost 4:00 p.m., and Edgar had taken Charlotte home to rest, by the time Peter regained consciousness. He opened his eyes, looked around, and felt a moment of panic before he recognized Carlin who was standing by the bed. "Doctor La Monde? What are you doing . . . what place is this?"

"You're in the hospital, Peter. You fell on the stairs."

"Hospital? No! I can't stay here!" Peter tried to sit up and discovered that his left arm was completely useless. "What's the matter with my arm, doctor? Why can't I move it?" he asked anxiously.

"Calm down, Peter. You'll be all right, but I'm afraid your arm is broken. I had to put a heavy cast on it."

"Broken? Oh God no! I can't bear to be a cripple! I'd rather be dead!" he moaned.

Carlin patted his hand. "Peter, it's not as bad as all that. It will heal."

"No! No! I have seen the crippled ones in Naples, and even in my own village. No one will hire them. They must beg in the streets. No woman will . . ." he moaned and closed his eyes. "Dio mio! Anything but this. I cannot bear it."

"Peter, don't carry on like this. You'll get well again, I promise. You won't be a cripple."

Peter opened his eyes and stared at Carlin. "Can I believe you? Don't deceive me!"

"I swear you'll get well again, Peter. I'm a doctor, I know about these things. Trust me."

"I will hope you are right, but how can I work with only one arm? What will I do? I owe you money. I knew I should never have taken the money from you."

"Peter, don't get upset. It doesn't matter about the money. Just relax and try to rest. It's been a rough night. I wasn't sure you were going to make it. You know, you nearly poisoned yourself with all that alcohol."

"You should have let me die! I was only trying to forget. All the money I had from you, everything I sent — it was all in vain. Geilla has married another man — someone with lots of money. Her father was right. He said I was worthless. I tried to help her, I tried to save some money, I tried to learn, but I failed. You should have let me die."

"You are not a failure, Peter. She never got the money you sent. The letters must have gotten lost. You tried your best."

"How do you know these things?"

"I saw the letter," Carlin said softly.

"You read my letter? How dare you to speak to me! You have no honor! Oh God, have I no privacy?"

"Peter, I went to your room because I had to know how much alcohol you had taken. I saw the letter and I wanted to know why you had suddenly started drinking."

"You had no right . . ."

"I do have a right. I loaned you money. I have a right to know about my investment. Besides, I am your doctor. If anything upsets you and makes you ill, I have a right to know about it."

"You carry your duty too far to pry into my private affairs!"

"Peter, when your so called private affairs cause you to get drunk, and tumble down the stairs in the middle of the night, frightening everyone in the house half to death, it becomes my duty to find out why."

"So now I am a fool before everyone in the house!"

"No one else knows about the letter, Peter; but yes, everyone knows you got drunk and fell down the stairs. Melina wanted to drag you to your room before Charlotte found out, but when Anna saw you were hurt she would not let you be moved."

"Melina tried to cover for me? I cannot believe it. She has been against me from the start."

"Well, she was very worried that Madame would be angry with you for getting drunk."

"And I suppose Madame is angry with me. I have ruined everything, doctor. I truly am worthless."

"You are not worthless, Peter; perhaps a trifle foolish, but only because you are young. And don't worry about Charlotte, she was more worried about you than angry. Try to get some rest now. Are you in any pain? Does your shoulder hurt?"

"My shoulder? I don't know . . . nothing feels right . . . everything hurts."

"It's from all the alcohol. It will wear off. Try to sleep now, all right?"

"Sleep? Here? No! I want to go home. I have to look after Albert and Charles. I have to . . ."

"You're not ready to go home yet, Peter. I want you to stay here a while longer."

"But it's my duty . . ."

"Anna will look after the boys. You must rest."

"You're not going to leave me here, are you?"

"Of course not. You can go home very soon. I'll stay here until you fall asleep, and Madame will be back later."

"I don't want to stay here," Peter declared stubbornly.

"I understand, but just this once, you must do as I say. I promise that no one will hurt you. Now relax and go to sleep."

"I don't want to stay . . ." Peter said wearily. He didn't really want to submit, but he was too tired to fight any longer. He closed his eyes for just a moment and sleep won the battle.

Peter woke again about 8:00 p.m. His shoulder was aching, and he could not find a comfortable position. He moved restlessly and did not notice Charlotte, who was sitting by his bed, until she spoke to him.

"Peter, are you awake?"

"Yes," he said turning his head towards her.

"How are you feeling?"

"I am well," he said rather uncertainly.

"Is your arm hurting you?"

"No," he said weakly, but she could read the pain on his face.

"Are you sure?" she said and reaching up she stroked his forehead and pushed his hair from his eyes. "Tell me the truth."

Now that he was awake the pain seemed to be increasing rapidly.

"Where does it hurt?" Charlotte coaxed.

"My shoulder . . . where is the doctor?"

"Carlin went home to get some rest. He was up all night with you, and had a busy day with other patients. He left some medicine for you though."

"No pills! I can't take pills."

"They aren't sleeping tablets, Peter. They're only for the pain."

"No pills, please. He knows I don't take pills! Why did he leave them?"

"He knew you would need them sooner or later. Won't you take them for my sake? I hate to see you suffer. You're in the hospital, Peter. There are lots of doctors and nurses here. I'm right here. I won't let anything happen to you."

Even as Charlotte coaxed, the pain had grown worse and was now in his arm. Suddenly he clutched at Charlotte's hand. "Don't leave . . . everyone leaves . . ."

"I won't leave," she said softly. "I'll stay right here."

He was silent for a few moments, then, "It grows worse, Madame."

"Take the medicine, Peter. There's no need to suffer. Would your friend Giovanni make you suffer like this?"

"No, he was kind to me. He bought me medicine and made me drink it. He was a good friend to me."

"You miss him, don't you?"

"Sometimes . . . yes. He took care of me when I was in trouble."

"Let me take care of you, Peter. Take the medicine, please."

"All right," he said softly.

Charlotte sighed with relief, and quickly handed him the capsules and a glass of water. He swallowed the capsules, settled back against the pillow, and was quiet. Charlotte hoped the medicine would take effect rapidly.

"I am sorry I got drunk and caused a disturbance in the house, Madame."

"Something made you very unhappy, Peter. What was it?" Charlotte asked gently.

He hesitated. "It is a long, sad tale, Madame. I will not bother you with it."

"I am ready to listen, Peter. Tell me what disturbs you. Please, I worry about you."

"I am not worth your trouble, Madame."

"Don't say that, Peter. Someone has hurt you. Tell me who. It's that girl, isn't it? The one you sent money to."

Peter bit his lip. "Yes."

"Tell me about her. When did you meet her?"

Peter looked at Charlotte. Would she believe him? Could a woman like Charlotte understand? He thought not, but his misery was overwhelming, and she was the only person he had left. He told her the whole unhappy tale.

"Peter, you must not think you are worthless. If the poor girl never got your letters, she had no choice. You must forgive her and go on with your life." Charlotte stroked his forehead again. "You are a very good looking young man, Peter. There will be lots of girls who will be interested in you."

"No! It is not easy for me to make friends."

"Well, you must try harder. Your teachers tell me you never even speak to the other students. You must smile a bit more, and let people get to know you. You are too secretive. You hardly tell me anything."

Peter smiled a weak smile. "No one else is as persistent as you, Madame, or as kind. Geilla was the only girl who truly knew me and loved me the way I am."

"That's what love is all about, Peter. None of us is perfect. You will find the right girl."

"I had the right girl. I just didn't have enough money."

"Well, we must see what can be done about that."

"Nothing can be done, Madame," he said sadly. "I have wrecked myself and cannot work. I can't drive, I can't dig. I can't cook. I can't even wash dishes. What's to become of me?"

Charlotte could see he was close to tears.

"Don't get upset, Peter. You'll get well again. Just be patient."

"Patient! How long will anyone tolerate a man who can't work?"

"Long enough, Peter, long enough. You must rest to get well quickly. And you must promise me you'll take your medicine."

"I promise. You were wise to make me take it. It does help."

"Good. Now see if you can get some rest."

Peter slept, but in the morning he was extremely depressed. When Edgar came to see him, Peter turned his head away and could not bring himself to speak to him. He imagined Edgar would accuse him of being a fool to send money to Geilla, and he dreaded being dismissed for getting drunk and making himself useless.

Carlin had told Edgar of the letter from Geilla, and Edgar believed Peter was suffering from a disappointment in love. He had no idea Peter was so distressed about having injured himself. He asked Peter how he was feeling, and was dismayed when Peter responded vehemently, "My life is ruined! I wish I were dead!"

Peter would make no other answer to Edgar's questions or assurances that things would improve, and Edgar concluded it would be best to leave Peter alone for a while. He went out and sat in the waiting room. He knew Carlin had been very tired the night before, but nevertheless, he hoped he would come soon to deal with Peter's negative state of mind.

Carlin arrived about 10:30, and was immediately besieged by complaints from the staff that Peter would not eat any breakfast, refused to let them take his pulse or temperature, and would not take his medicine. When Edgar added his bit about Peter's depression, Carlin was not pleased. He understood the source of Peter's depression. Carlin had felt his own life was over when his wife had died, and he had suffered such severe, incapacitating depression that he had undergone months of treatment with drugs and counseling. What had saved him in the end was his ability to bury himself in his work. Carlin wanted to save Peter from the terrible descent into hopelessness, but since Peter was unable to work, it would not be an easy task.

Stopping by the kitchen, Carlin picked up a pitcher of orange juice and a glass, and marched to Peter's room in a determined mood. He strode through the door and drew back the curtain around Peter's bed. Peter had rolled himself into a ball which Carlin recognized as an "I'm ignoring the world" posture.

"Good morning, Peter. How are you feeling?" Carlin asked in his most jovial manner. When Peter ignored him, Carlin ruthlessly pulled the covers off of him.

"I hear you have refused to eat anything. That's not the way to get better. I want you to sit up and drink some juice." He took Peter by the arm, but Peter jerked away violently.

"Leave me be," he snarled, but Carlin detected more misery than anger in his tone.

"No I won't," Carlin said forcefully. "Charlotte told me you promised to take your medicine. Come on, sit up and take it. You're only hurting yourself."

"I don't want your damn pills! That's your answer to everything, isn't it?"

Carlin straightened himself. "I won't let you do this to yourself, Peter," he said coldly and stalked into the hall. He returned in a few minutes with a very sturdy, athletic looking male nurse. Together they wrestled Peter into a sitting position.

"I'll give you one last chance to drink this," Carlin said holding up the glass of juice. Peter glared at him and growled, "I'll fight you, you bastard!"

"And you will lose!" Carlin threatened. "Don't make me do this."

Peter set his jaw defiantly, but did not answer.

"I am sorry to do this Peter, but I will not let you hurt yourself with your stubbornness."

Carlin nodded to the nurse who forced Peter's one good arm behind his back and held him so he could not jerk away. Carlin took Peter by the jaw and tried to force his mouth open. He was not prepared for the wild struggle that Peter put up as he jerked and fought, but he hung on. "Damn it, Peter, give in!"

Carlin pressed more firmly and managed to pour some juice down Peter's throat. At last the glass was empty, but there was so much juice on Carlin, on the nurse, on the bed and all down the front of Peter's gown that it was impossible to tell how much Peter had actually swallowed. Carlin knew that the battle had become a test of wills, and that if he gave in now, he would lose all hope of being able to help Peter.

While the nurse held Peter, Carlin refilled the glass. He held it in front of Peter.

"I have gallons of this stuff in the kitchen, Peter. You can either give in and drink some, or I will strap you down and put a needle in your arm."

Peter lurched, but he saw it was hopeless. He had misjudged Carlin's determination. His left arm had been hurting all along, and now his right arm was beginning to bother him. Carlin steeled himself for another battle. "Hold him while I get the restraints," he told the nurse. He moved to set the juice down.

"Wait! Don't tie me down, please. I'll drink."

Carlin hoped Peter would not see how relieved he was. "Will you take your medicine?" he asked as fiercely as he could manage.

"Yes," Peter agreed meekly.

Seeing Peter's defiance turn to submission, Carlin suddenly hoped he had acted correctly. If he had lost Peter's trust, it was an empty victory.

"Let him go," Carlin said quietly to the nurse. The nurse let go, but seeing that Peter was about to fall backwards, he put his arm behind him. Carlin was not sure Peter could hold the glass by himself, but he managed to get all the juice down and swallow the capsules. The nurse caught the empty glass as Peter dropped it and Peter fell back onto the bed.

"I knew I should never have trusted you!" Peter said bitterly. "I can't trust anyone. Everyone turns on me in the end – even Geilla."

"That's not true, Peter. I'm only trying to help you," Carlin said soothingly. "Look, it's almost lunch time. If you sit up and eat some soup and bread, I'll get you some coffee. Fair enough?"

"You treat me like a child!" Peter complained.

"You are worse than a child when you get stubborn, Peter. Come on, wouldn't you like some coffee?"

"Yes," Peter admitted reluctantly.

"Bread and soup first . . . agreed?"

Peter put his hand to his head. "I have no choice . . . you are my jailor."

"Come on, cheer up," Carlin coaxed. "It's good soup."

Despite Carlin's best efforts, however, Peter remained depressed and Carlin was forced to continue to use threats and bribery to get him to eat or take medication. On Sunday, Carlin decided that Peter was well enough to leave the hospital, but he thought it might be wise not to send Peter back to the Marneés immediately. Instead he helped Peter get dressed, and took him to his own home. He reasoned that a new location might prevent Peter from brooding about all the things he was unable to do. Peter was installed in a large room on the second floor, and Carlin offered him the run of his house, including his library, his extensive music collection, and his garden. When Carlin left for his office on Monday, however, he took the precautions of locking his liquor cabinet, and removing the knife he had found in Peter's pocket. Carlin asked his part-time housekeeper to prepare lunch for Peter, but when he returned in the evening he found the food uneaten. Peter had made no effort to get up and get dressed. When the same thing occurred on Tuesday, Carlin became worried about Peter's deepening depression. On Wednesday morning he charged into Peter's room.

"Peter it's time to get up! Charlotte is coming to visit you. Come on, get cleaned up and dressed."

Carlin hauled Peter out of bed, pushed him into the bathroom and laid out some clothes for him to wear. Peter moved very slowly, however, and Carlin continued to prod him. "For heaven's sake, go back and shave, Peter. You look positively awful. Go on. Don't let Charlotte see you like this!"

Carlin helped Peter into his clothes, buttoning his shirt over the cast on his left arm. Peter stood sullen and silent while Carlin tied his shoe laces, and buttoned his shirt cuffs for him. Then Carlin took Peter down the stairs and into the living room. Charlotte and the boys arrived a short time later, but Peter barely responded to their questions. Without enthusiasm, he let the boys put their names on his cast, and looked at some of Albert's school papers. At last little Charles became impatient, and tugging on Peter's arm, he demanded, "When are you coming home, Peter?"

Peter looked at Charles with depths of sadness in his dark eyes. "I don't know, Charles. I don't know where to go."

Charlotte gave Peter some books, and made him promise to do whatever Carlin asked. Then she took him by the hands and looked directly into his face. "You must get over this mood, Peter. You have to get better and come back to us."

When Peter made no reply, Charlotte shook her head, and took the boys into the hall to talk to Carlin.

"I am worried, Carlin. I have never seen Peter so despondent. It's not like him to be so unresponsive."

"I know. I would much prefer to have him swearing and growling at me than to be like this. If he doesn't come out of it soon, I am afraid I shall have to send him to a clinic near Luzern. They've had good success treating patients for severe depression. I hesitate to start Peter on drug therapy. He is so sensitive to medication, he would be a difficult case."

"Oh Carlin, I hope it doesn't come to that. I would hate to send Peter so far away. He is a terribly lonely person, despite all we do to make him feel at home with us. I wish we had known sooner how deeply he felt for this girl."

"Don't let the situation upset you, Charlotte. He is young yet. He'll get over this. I'll call you on Friday to report any progress."

"Thank you, Carlin. I had better get Albert to school. I must say, the house is coming apart without Peter to help us."

Peter had sat in the living room alone while Carlin and Charlotte were talking. He had overheard only snatches of their conversation, but in his negative state of mind, he had focused on key words and constructed a radically different meaning. When Carlin entered the living room, and came up to the chair Peter was sitting in, Peter seized his arm.

"Don't send me away, sir, I beg of you! I can no longer make a living. Have mercy, don't send me back . . . please. I can't even defend myself."

Carlin was momentarily shocked by Peter's outpouring.

"Peter, what is this all about? No one said anything about . . ." he started, then suddenly stopped himself. It struck him that Peter had overheard his conversation with Charlotte and that he had misinterpreted the words. "You heard what I said to Charlotte, didn't you?"

"Yes . . . I'll do whatever you wish . . . please don't send me away. I beg you!"

"Will you promise to do whatever I ask?"

"Yes, yes, I promise . . . anything . . . just don't send me back to Greece."

It was hard for Carlin not to try to comfort Peter, he looked so miserable, but he remained firm. "All right then, the first thing I want you to do is come and have some breakfast."

"Yes, sir," Peter answered numbly.

"And one more thing, Peter."

"Yes, sir."

"If you are going to stay here, I would like you to call me Carlin."

"Yes, sir," Peter responded mechanically.

"We'll have to work on that one," Carlin said and smiled as he led Peter into the kitchen. Peter ate what was put in front of him, but Carlin could see that his appetite was still poor. He was glad that he now had some way to get Peter to do what he asked, but he could not help feeling distressed that after having lived with the Marneés for over a year, Peter could believe that they would be so callus as to send him back to Greece. Carlin wondered if Peter would ever learn to trust anyone.

Later, Carlin took Peter to the office with him, found some papers for him to sort, and then set him to work calling patients to remind them of appointments. He asked Peter to log some payments, and was impressed by how neatly and accurately Peter tallied the entries. Peter explained that Alonzo had taught him to keep the accounts at the theater when he was a boy.

The following day at breakfast Carlin broached a new subject to Peter.

"Peter, I had a call from Dr. Brencic at the Children's Home. He would like you to come and help with the children."

Peter's face clouded. "What can I do for them? I have made myself a cripple! I can't even button my own shirt or tie my God damn shoes."

"You are not a cripple!" Carlin almost shouted in his exasperation. "And for heaven's sake, stop feeling sorry for yourself for one minute, and think of the children. They need attention, Peter. You can read to them, and play games with them the same as you always did."

Peter was about to object when Carlin silenced him. "Besides, you promised to do what I asked."

"How can I forget! You keep at me every minute," Peter snapped.

Carlin ignored the outburst. "I think you are well enough to go, Peter. I'll drive you there after breakfast."

"Whatever you say," Peter mumbled.

Carlin went into the Children's Home with Peter. He wanted to talk to Dr. Brencic in person to ask him to keep an eye on Peter, seeing that he ate lunch, and took his medicine when his shoulder hurt. Carlin did not admit to Peter that actually he had been the one to call Dr. Brencic about Peter coming to the Children's Home. Carlin knew it was an experiment, but he hoped that being with the children would be good for Peter.

Dr. Brencic greeted Peter warmly and ushered him into the large play area. Several children recognized Peter, and immediately ran up to him with great exuberance, jumping up and down and pulling on his sleeve. He was barraged with questions.

"Where have you been, Peter? What happened to your arm? Does it hurt? Can you play a game with us?"

Dr. Brencic saw that Peter was reserved in his greetings, and a little put off by all the questions. "Peter's been in the hospital," he said to cover Peter's awkwardness. "He fell down the stairs and broke his arm. It still hurts, so you must not climb all over him and pull at him."

Dr. Brencic guided Peter to a chair while he continued to give instructions to the children. "Francis, go get some story books for Peter to read! Michael and Linda . . . get some cushions so the others can sit on the floor here. That's it . . . make a big circle. Very good! Betsy, bring that chair over here next to Peter. Now, you may all take turns sitting next to Peter, and helping him turn the pages. No, Lisa you may not sit in Peter's lap." And so Dr. Brencic organized the children and made Peter comfortable, and left him to read the stories the children never tired of hearing. At lunch time, the children were eager to help Peter with his food, and he ate to please them. Dr. Brencic made a point of giving Peter his medicine in front of the children so that he was obliged to take it in order to set a good example.

****

A week had passed and Peter was standing outside of Edgar's office at the Marneé residence. Carlin had driven him to the house, but had not told him why Edgar wanted to see him. Peter wished Carlin had stayed with him, but he had driven back to his office. Peter imagined it must be 2:00 p.m., but he was not sure. He missed having the watch Charlotte and Edgar had given him. It had been very plain, but it kept good time.

When he could bear the waiting no longer, he opened the door and stepped into the room. As soon as he saw Edgar seated behind his desk, Peter knew it would be an official meeting.

"Good afternoon, Peter. It's good to see you. How are you feeling?" Edgar said warmly.

"I am well, sir," Peter answered politely.

"And how is your arm?"

Peter hesitated. Had Edgar called him here to remind him that he hadn't done a day's work since he got drunk? He had no defence. "It is still useless, sir. I am sorry."

Edgar's expression didn't change. "That's to be expected, Peter. You had a very bad fall. Is it still painful for you?"

"Not as much, sir. Carlin . . . I mean, Dr. La Monde insists that I take tablets every time he sets eyes on me."

"If he advises it, I recommend you do as he says. He's a very good doctor, you know. He took a lot of trouble over you, Peter. You came very close to killing yourself."

"I'm sorry sir . . . I didn't mean to cause anyone any trouble. I should have been more . . . more . . ." He stopped, trying to remember the word Charlotte always used to scold him — "responsible," that was it. "I should have been more responsible."

"Well I hope you won't do anything as foolish in the future. You are no longer a boy, Peter. Madame and I have discussed your situation, and we have decided to make some changes in your position here. On Monday morning . . ."

Peter didn't hear anything else. He suddenly felt a tightening in his throat, and he could hardly breathe. So this was it, he thought. They were sending him away. Carlin had lied to him. He could almost see himself back in his village. Where would he go? What could he do with only one arm? He would have to beg. What scorn they would heap on him — Petros, sent home in disgrace, penniless after all those years.

He had been ignorant when he left Greece, but now he knew what it was like to sleep in the street, to lie awake from hunger. Why hadn't Carlin let him die? He could hear them now, shouting at him, and chasing him with sticks and rocks the way they used to. They had him by the arm.

"Peter? Peter? Are you all right? Are you in pain? Sit down before you fall."

It wasn't the gang who had him by the arm, it was Edgar. He was pressing a glass of water into his hand. "Here, drink this! My God, Peter, you look so white. Put your head down for a few minutes." Peter realized he was sitting in a chair in Edgar's office and Edgar was standing next to him, pushing his head onto his knees.

"Peter, I know this will be a change for you, but I think you can do the work. You've done well in school. You will be training with several other young men."

Peter raised his head. "Training, sir? Training for what?"

"Peter, didn't you hear anything I said?"

"Only that I had to go. I did everything Carlin asked . . ."

"You don't have to go if you don't want to, Peter, but it would be a start at a good career."

"A career?"

"A career in the bank, Peter. It can be very profitable if you work hard."

"At the bank? You want me to go to the bank?"

"Yes, Peter. Are you sure you are all right?"

"Yes, sir, but how can I work with only one arm?"

"You will get well again, but in the meantime, you can study and learn the routine. You will have to learn to use your brain, Peter, not your back."

Peter wasn't sure what Edgar expected of him, but he would do anything to avoid being sent back to Greece. "I'll try it, sir. Whatever you say."

CHAPTER FOURTEEN

"Peter is in love," Charlotte told Edgar in answer to his question of why Peter had been acting so strangely.

"In love!" Edgar sputtered. "Nonsense! With whom?"

"With Claire, his little pupil. Haven't you noticed the way she looks at him with adoration when he brings her to tea?"

Edgar's mouth fell open. "You mean that little blonde girl who can't do arithmetic, let alone algebra?"

"The very one," Charlotte answered with a laugh.

"But she's just a child!"

"She's eighteen, Edgar — almost a woman."

"Come to think of it," Edgar continued, "Peter has never brought anyone else to visit us. Do you mean this has been going on under my nose and I never knew it?"

Charlotte smiled. "I don't think Peter realizes yet that he's been totally smitten. He imagines that all the time he spends with Claire, even the hours he spends gazing dreamily at her while she plays that flute of hers, is strictly to improve her mathematical skills."

"Well, Peter certainly does love music," Edgar declared. "It's a pity we didn't see that he took lessons on some instrument. It would have done him good."

Charlotte shook her head. "You forget, my dear, that even mentioning the word 'lessons' would send Peter into a panic. Getting him educated was the greatest challenge of my life." She laughed as she remembered their past struggles. "Do you remember all the times we took Peter skiing, and told him there was no time for him to have instructions, because he had to help Albert and Charles with their lessons? It was so easy and natural for him to learn when he thought no one would be watching him."

"Yes, he would pick up every comment when he thought it was meant for Albert."

"No, Edgar, I can't see how we could have fooled him about playing the piano. He would have guessed when he had to practice." She laughed at the thought and Edgar joined in.

"Yes that's true. I'm glad he's taken such an interest in studying languages, though. I've never seen anyone with such a knack for developing a perfect accent."

It was more than a knack, however. Peter worked at it. He had been attending classes at the university ever since he started working at the bank six years ago. It had not been an easy transition for Peter to go from being Edgar's chauffeur to being an apprentice bank clerk. He had begun his training with four other young men, who were the well-educated sons of wealthy families. Although they were no more capable than Peter, and none were as hard working, they made it clear to Peter that they believed he was socially inferior. Unfortunately, almost everyone at the bank, except for Edgar and Mademoiselle Flambert, one of the secretaries, held the same opinion.

Whether from personal judgment, or because she was thoroughly professional, Mademoiselle Flambert always treated Peter with respect. She did not hesitate to focus her most formidable, unyielding-spinster frown on anyone who called Peter names behind his back. Even the combined favor of Edgar and Mademoiselle Flambert could not shield Peter completely from poison tongues, however, and he often overheard the names, Edgar's protégé, Charlotte's lap-dog, or The Greek. The barbs hurt, but Peter did his best to ignore them. He concentrated on his work, and reminded himself that working at the bank was a tremendous opportunity. He was determined to prove to Edgar that he was worthy of his trust.

The social encounters that Charlotte insisted Peter participate in were even more distasteful to him. He grew tired of attending parties and dinners where he knew he was accepted only because of Edgar's influence. He felt he was the well-dressed, well-mannered, social pariah among the banking families. Even if he met a girl who had not heard of him, after they went out a few times, she invariably invited him home to meet "papa", and it was always the same. Her family would be extremely polite and refined, while they dissected Peter with their questions. "Where do you come from, Peter? What does your father do, Peter? Who are your people, Peter? Where did you attend university, Peter?" How was he supposed to answer? "My father was a penniless fisherman, sir. He came from a long line of ignorant drunkards, and was killed in a brawl. Please, sir, I am probably no better than he was, but I want to marry your daughter."

So Peter polished his manners, learned to smile while he was being humiliated, and as ever, he gave his trust to very few. He frequented the theater alone, and made occasional social contacts with the performers who were passing through town. These girls never asked to see his credentials before they went out with him, and when they invited him home, it was not to meet "papa." Peter was always discreet in order that no hint of scandal would taint Edgar, or the bank, and he was extremely careful not to father a child. He knew full well that the world would not be kind to a half-Greek bastard.

Peter had met Claire when Edgar had sent him to attend an accounting course that was not offered at night. It had been her first week at the university, and she had asked Peter's help after she had become hopelessly lost and disoriented. Peter noticed that she was close to tears when he told her that the class she was already late for was on the other side of the campus. He offered to take her there in his car, but she reacted as though she were afraid he would eat her on the way.

Although he was not gallant in a flashy sort of way, Peter could not bear to see a woman or a child cry. He was not quite sure in which category this girl belonged. She had soft blue eyes, and long blonde hair, which hung down her back in a single glorious braid. She must be old enough to attend university, he thought, but her expression is so childlike. Seeing that she was upset, Peter told her he knew the professor she was looking for, and said he would walk her to class, and personally offer an explanation as to why she was late. When she meekly agreed, Peter took her books from her, and strode rapidly across the campus, with her trailing several steps behind him the entire way. Peter in fact, did not know the professor, but he offered such a beautiful formal apology in Claire's behalf, that she was not marked late. Little did the professor, or Claire, realize that while living with the Marneés, Peter had on numerous occasions been sent to make formal apologies to people. Often it was over some cultural difference he did not understand, but he had learned to dutifully recite whatever Charlotte told him he must say.

Peter forgot about the girl until several weeks later, when he saw her in the crowded lunch room at the university. She was looking for a place, and he gestured that there was a seat across the table from him. She smiled and appeared to light up when she recognized him.

"Oh, I am so happy to see you," she said shyly as she sat down. "I never had the opportunity to thank you for directing me to class. I would have been terribly embarrassed if I had been marked late."

Peter nodded silently, but when she kept looking at him with such an eager, expectant expression in her soft blue eyes, he wondered if he had forgotten a required social response.

"It was my pleasure," he answered formally, picking the phrase from his mental catalog. Her smile grew even brighter, and he found it very pleasant to look at. "How are you doing in class?" he asked, risking a spontaneous remark.

Her smile disappeared suddenly and he was sorry.

"I'm afraid just getting to class on time is not enough. I am a total dunce at mathematics, and I won't be able to hide my failure much longer. My father won't be at all pleased," she sighed.

"I'm sorry it goes so badly for you," he said sincerely, remembering how upset Charlotte had been over his failures.

"Oh, I guess I didn't really think I could do well at mathematics. I am a musician by inclination, but father thinks I should learn something useful."

Peter would have let the conversation drop, since he had

finished eating; but suddenly she brightened again and asked, "And what about you? What are you studying?" She looked at him so earnestly he felt it was not just an idle remark.

"By day I study accounting, and at night I study languages," he answered slowly.

She looked horrified. "Accounting! What a terrible burden for you!"

Peter could not help laughing at the face she made to indicate her distaste.

"Accounting is very useful to me. I work at a bank," he said, suddenly feeling he had to justify what seemed to her a terrible choice.

"Oh," she said looking a bit stunned. "I've never met a banker. You seem too nice to . . . Oh, I am sorry . . . " she stammered. "It's just that my father always said . . . " she faltered and blushed with embarrassment.

Peter wanted to laugh, but she looked so upset he was afraid he would hurt her feelings. He wished she would flash her pretty little smile again.

"Did you think all bankers have long teeth and bite little girls?" he asked with a smile.

"Oh no! Please forgive my terrible manners! I . . ." her blush deepened to crimson.

"Well it takes many years to grow big teeth, and I must not be much of a banker for mine haven't grown at all yet," he responded.

She started to giggle. "Oh, now you're making fun of me."

"Yes I am, and I'm sorry," he said and laughed. "It's just that most people aren't nearly so frightened of me."

"Oh, I'm not really frightened . . . you must think I'm a terrible nuisance." She blushed again, and saw him stand to leave.

"No indeed. I think you're very sweet," he said simply and he was gone.

Peter was a long time in getting to know Claire, for she was shy and seemed so young he did not take her seriously. He could not bear to see her failing in school, however, and when she asked him if he could recommend a tutor, he cautiously volunteered. His own studies left him little time, but he offered to meet her wherever she wished once a week to help her. Since she lived with her parents, he went there. He learned that she was the youngest daughter of a wealthy industrialist, but he rarely met her parents, who classified him as an older student working his way through school and therefore of little consequence.

It was almost a hopeless task to teach Claire mathematics, for her mind was not bent towards numbers, but Peter kept going to her house. He began to go more often, and when one evening Claire insisted on playing the flute for him, to demonstrate that she was good at something, he knew he had to keep going, whether she ever learned mathematics or not.

Although Claire would easily have been overlooked in a crowd, her sweetness and innocence were very compelling to Peter. After years of being rebuffed in Swiss society, because of his lack of family connections, or because he was Greek, he found it impossible to ignore a girl who thought he was the perfect embodiment of wisdom and sophistication. Peter knew he wasn't the perfect being Claire thought he was, but it was a heady experience to bask in such adoration and he became addicted.

Eventually Peter was successful in imparting enough mathematical wisdom to Claire that she passed the course, although just barely. When she triumphantly told him that she has passed, Peter was jubilant. No poet or painter was ever more proud of his "creation" than Peter was of Claire. Seeing her happy childlike face beaming up at him, he totally lost his head. Clasping her to his chest, he lifted her feet off the ground, and swung her around in a full circle. He set her down lightly, and still full of excitement, he kissed her on the forehead. He was about to kiss her on the lips when he suddenly drew back. What had gotten into him? What was he thinking to be tempted by such an innocent child?

"I'm sorry, Claire. I . . . I got carried away," he apologized. "I am so very proud of you, I lost my head."

Claire was young and innocent, but she was not a child. She felt a surge of pleasure she did not quite understand from Peter's physical presence.

"I would gladly endure a thousand terrors of mathematics to see you so happy, Peter," she told him with simple sincerity.

He took her hand in his. "We must celebrate! Will you go to dinner with me?" he asked. It was their first purely social visit.

Claire's father was pleased when he learned that Claire had passed the course, and was more kindly disposed towards Peter. He thought Peter certainly must be a very studious, dedicated young man to implant any discipline to Claire's vague, romantic mind. In truth, Claire's father really had a very poor opinion of Claire's mental ability. He wished to keep her in school only until he thought she was mature enough to be married off to the properly ambitious son of some other family in the chemical business.

Although his excuse for coming to see Claire now no longer existed, Peter was seen more and more often at her house, and her parents got quite used to him. He took Claire to concerts where they shared their mutual love of music, and he took her to visit Charlotte and Edgar. Surprisingly, Charlotte was more nervous than Claire, for Peter had never brought anyone to visit before, and she wanted everything to be absolutely perfect.

Claire enchanted the Marneés with her sweetness, and her

devotion to Peter. Then, to complete the charm, she played her flute for them, and they realized that whatever talent she lacked for mathematics, she more than made up for in musical ability. Claire was incredibly gifted, but had no conceit, and would only dare to play after much prompting from Peter.

Charlotte thought it a waste that Claire's parents had put her into mathematics rather than sending her to the conservatory, but if they had, Peter would never have met her. After that first visit, it was not long before Peter realized, as Charlotte had correctly guessed, that he was in love with Claire, and could not think straight when he was around her. Although she was as quiet as Peter, no evil, or sadness had touched her young life, and she was light-hearted and open. It was no surprise to Charlotte when Peter mentioned several months later that he had presented Claire with a ring, and that her parents would give a small party to announce their official engagement. Peter had never actually asked Claire's father for permission to marry his daughter. Somehow, things just seemed to happen and no one said "no", so Peter kept quiet, and let Claire and her family arrange all the details.

Charlotte and Edgar were invited to the engagement party since they were the only people Peter had any connections with. Claire's parents were very quiet, conservative people, and were relieved to see that the people who were backing Peter were from the best in the old-line Swiss society. They knew little about Peter's background, but seemed satisfied that he would accept the child they viewed as a rather useless, dreamy, romantic girl. Claire's artistic ability had always been somewhat of a mystery to her parents, who had produced three other offspring who were serious-minded and industrious. Peter thought of Claire's family as colorless drones, and often wondered how gay, creative little Claire had sprung from such work-a-day soil.

Peter had a secret dream that when he and Claire were married, he could provide Claire with the encouragement and opportunity she needed to fully develop her talents. He was not selfish enough to think that Claire's talent should be lavished on himself alone. Perhaps he hoped that through her musical ability they could both escape from the structured lives they both found themselves living, but which was so unlike their more free-spirited natures.

After they were engaged, Peter was bolder about taking Claire places to be alone with her. She never told her parents that she went to Peter's apartment for she knew they would object. Usually they just talked, or she would play the flute for him while he lay on the floor by her feet. Peter was past the barrier of thinking of Claire as a child, and his longing for her grew with each visit. He knew she was a virgin and was saving herself for her wedding night, but he still wanted her. He started increasing the distances he ran, trying to slow down his urge, but it didn't work. Even in the sleep of exhaustion, he dreamt of her. He quit drinking even wine when they went out for fear he would lose control of his will.

When Peter thought he could not restrain himself any longer, he made his plans, and one night he coaxed Claire to his bedroom. She was hesitant, but he could not help himself. She was soon to be his, and he could no longer wait. He did not turn the lamp on in the bedroom, and in the dim light from the hall, he slowly and lovingly undressed her. She made no move to object, but hid herself with her hands when he bared her breasts.

Sensing her overwhelming shyness, Peter pulled the covers back, stripped the sheet from the bed, and draped it gently around Claire. Feeling beneath it, he finished undressing her, and carried her to his bed. In growing excitement he quickly tore off his clothes, and rummaged in the dresser drawer. Then he lay next to her and caressed her through the sheet. She trembled when he touched her, but he did not know if it was from fear or excitement. Although he was burning with desire and breathing heavily, he waited for her to raise the sheet and invite him to come to her. He had never been with a virgin, and he felt it was his responsibility to see that she blossomed to womanhood with all the tenderness he could manage.

"I am on fire for you, Claire, but I won't force you. You must want to give yourself to me," he said softly.

She hesitated, and he thought he would die of agony if she would not yield to him. Finally she lifted the edge of the sheet and whispered, "I want to be yours, Peter. Show me what to do."

Slowly he moved towards her, and gently put his arms around her. He realized he was shaking from the strain of holding himself in check. Trying his best to tame the wildness in himself and be gentle, he caressed her and finalized their union.

Claire made little response, but she accepted him, and willingly let his fire consume her. Timidly she moved her hands over his body, and he felt the warmth of her love in the incredible lightness of her touch. It was so gentle, so like Claire herself. He needed her gentleness, her caring. Then he again lay quiet, holding her in his arms.

"Did I please you, Peter?" she asked shyly.

"Yes, my dearest Claire, you pleased me very much," he said, and kissed her lightly. "Your pleasure in our union will grow, I promise you."

"I like the feel of your body close to me, Peter, but . . . I am afraid . . ." she broke off suddenly.

"Oh, Claire," he sighed. "You're not afraid of me are you? I tried so hard to control myself."

"Oh no, Peter. I'm not afraid of you. I'm afraid I might . . . what if I get pregnant before we are married? My parents would be so angry with me. They raised me very strictly. My mother could never show her face to the neighbors if I disgraced myself."

He sighed with relief that he had not terrified her with his vigor. "You are not to worry about having a child before you want one, Claire" he assured her. "I took care to protect you. Perhaps I should have told you but . . . I did not want you to know how long I had planned for tonight. I've wanted you for a long time, Claire."

"Oh, Peter, I will be so happy when we are married. I won't have to answer to my parents every time I go out. We can be together all the time, and I will have as many babies as I want. You do want to have children, don't you, Peter?" she asked suddenly alarmed that he might not share her dreams for a family.

"Yes, I want you to have babies. I don't know that I will be a good father, but I will try very hard. I must make up to my sons for all the suffering my father gave to me."

It suddenly occurred to him that once he and Claire were married he would have someone to call his own. He would no longer be the outcast. He would actually belong with Claire and she would belong with him − forever. The idea charged him with such an incredible sense of happiness and contentment that he seized Claire to him and whispered passionately, "Claire, you are my magic charm. You have given me everything I have always wished for. I cannot tell you how much I love you!" In that moment he felt she was everything a woman could be for him. She was his friend and his lover, his mother and his child.

Several months later Peter was in his office at the bank. He had not been able to keep his mind on his work all day for thinking of coming events. That evening he and Claire were to take part in a rehearsal for their long awaited wedding. Afterwards, they would be guests at a dinner given by Charlotte and Edgar for the bridal party and a few friends. Peter had wanted to keep the wedding arrangements simple, but Claire's family were controlling the wedding, and it had grown into a large formal affair. Peter never enjoyed meeting hordes of strangers, but he had let Claire's family have their way in every detail, except one. He would not agree to take communion, and become a member of the Strom family's church. He had had little opportunity or inclination to practice his Greek Orthodox religion since he had left home, but he felt it would be a slap at his mother's memory to reject it. Peter had few clear memories of his mother, but he remembered she had taken him to church at every opportunity.

As Peter glanced at his watch for the hundredth time, his secretary buzzed with the message that he had a visitor. She said the woman would not give her name, but indicated repeatedly that the matter was very urgent and that no one else could take care of it. Since it was almost 3 o'clock, Peter decided he could use an interruption to hurry the day along. As his secretary ushered the woman into his office, Peter recognized her as Claire's older sister Ingred.

"Why didn't you give your name, Ingred? I would not have made you wait if I had known."

Ingred looked at Peter with the rather stern glance he had come to recognize as a characteristic of everyone in Claire's family, except for happy little Claire. "I did not want anyone else to know I came here," Ingred answered quickly.

"Why so secretive, Ingred? Everyone knows I am to be married tomorrow. I have been so excited lately they would have thought me mad if I didn't give some explanation," he laughed, but his mirth faded abruptly when he noticed that Ingred was staring at him.

"What's wrong, Ingred?" he suddenly asked in dismay. "Has something gone wrong with the wedding plans? You know it wouldn't matter a bit to me if Madame La Rouche has another engagement and can't sing at the wedding, or if the florist gives us the wrong color flowers."

"Peter, stop joking!" Ingred commanded coldly, and his heart froze.

"I don't know how to tell you this, but there isn't going to be a wedding."

"No wedding," he repeated dully. "But why? What has happened?" Suddenly Peter looked horror stricken. "Has something happened to Claire?"

"No," Ingred answered slowly. "She's not hurt or anything like that . . ."

"Ingred, for the love of God, tell me what's wrong then!" he shouted at her.

Ingred turned away from him. She could not bear to see the look on his face. In her own severe way she had taken a liking to Peter. She knew he was devoted to Claire which made her tale all the harder to tell.

"Peter, perhaps you should sit down," she said more gently.

He staggered backwards and collapsed into his chair. "Please tell me what's wrong," he pleaded mournfully.

"My grandfather arrived for the wedding last night. He is quite old, but he still has a controlling interest in the family business, and the family fortune. When he found out you were Greek he was furious and threatened to cut my father off financially. Father tried to convince him you were financially stable on your own and were not marrying Claire for her inheritance, but . . ."

"Her inheritance! I never knew she had one!" Peter shot back.

"I know you never considered Claire's money, Peter, but grandfather got his money from his father and he is very protective of it."

179

"So I am damned because I am a Greek. Why didn't someone tell me this before? I never made a secret of the fact!"

"It's not just that you're Greek, Peter. It would be the same if you were French, or English, or even a Swiss from the wrong canton. We Stroms have always married within a select social circle, and grandfather is very class conscious."

"But why did your father agree to the marriage if he thought I was so . . . so dammed inferior?"

"Father has always known that Claire was a little different from the rest of the family. At first he had hoped that she would get over her childish infatuation with an older man, but when she didn't, and he saw how comfortable she was with you he was willing to go along to make her happy. You know, we are all very strict and unyielding with ourselves and others, but Claire is the one bright fairy-child we all love. She makes us be happy in spite of ourselves. When father saw how good you were to Claire, and how you seemed to understand her dreamy side, he knew he could never find a better match for her from within the acceptable circle of families. He had hoped grandfather would yield for the sake of Claire's happiness, but the old man will not budge."

"I want to talk to Claire and hear what she has to say about all this nonsense," Peter said with determination. He suddenly got up from his chair and took a long stride towards the door.

"You can't talk to her, Peter," Ingred called after him. "Father has sent her away."

"Sent her away? Where?"

"I can't tell you, Peter. You weren't supposed to learn anything until this evening. A messenger was supposed to come to the church with a letter for you, but I thought you deserved better than that."

"I don't believe this is happening, Ingred. This is not the twelfth century. Claire has a mind of her own. Where did she go?"

"I can't tell you, Peter. Father doesn't want you to make any trouble."

"Trouble! Does he think I will sit by and let you people steal Claire away from me?" Peter suddenly grabbed Ingred by the arms and shouted, "Where is she, Ingred?"

"Peter, let go. You're hurting me!"

Peter glared at Ingred in silence, and only gradually became aware that he was crushing her arms. He let go, and dropped his hands. "Forgive me, Ingred. I forgot myself. Don't play games with me or I may lose control!"

Ingred had never seen such a black look on a man's face and it frightened her. "Father took her to Spain this morning," she confessed.

"To Spain! Where in Spain? Tell me, Ingred!" Peter raised his hand and she thought he might strike her.

SELECT THE DESIRED FUNCTION

FOR PROBLEM ASSISTANCE SSA

A. MASTER FILE QUERIES/IN...
B. RSDI / SSI CLAIMS
C. PR01
D. PR02
E. PR03
F. PR04
G. PR05
H. PR06
I. PR07
J. PR08
K. SECURITY ADMINISTRAT...
L. PHOENIX

"I don't know, Peter. I can't tell you any more."

"I can't believe Claire would leave like this . . . without an explanation . . . without even saying good-bye."

"She was very upset and confused, Peter. She was brought up to obey, and she can't bear to go against father. You don't know what a tyrant grandfather can be. Even father is still afraid of him."

"I know what it is like to be bullied — but a son can only be afraid of his father for so long and then he must make his own decisions!"

"You don't understand, Peter. Father would lose his business if he stood up to his father."

"Damn it, Ingred! If a man becomes a sniveling coward over money, I'm glad I never had any!"

Ingred could see that Peter was becoming more and more angry, as he realized the full impact of the situation and she was eager to get away.

"I must go Peter. I'm terribly sorry to have been the one to tell you the news, but I wanted to spare you the embarrassment of waiting at the church with all your friends."

"Embarrassment!" Peter echoed loudly. He turned from her and slammed his fist against the wall in frustration. "Embarrassment doesn't begin to describe the desolation I feel. Your father's decision has ruined Claire's happiness, and destroyed my life. I hope to see him in hell surrounded by all his precious money!"

Ingred never heard Peter's curse for she had slipped out the door while his back was turned. When he turned back and saw that she was gone he covered his face with his hands. "My God, what a family of spineless worms!" he said aloud. "My dearest Claire, I had expected more from you, but one can't fight what runs in one's blood. If only I could have gotten you away from them . . ." With shaking hands he picked up the brass paperweight from his desk and threw it against the wall. He stood alone for a few moments, and then he suddenly felt he had to get away.

He stormed out the door and ran straight into his secretary who had heard the crash and come hurrying in to see what had fallen.

"Excuse me, Monsieur Kononellos," she said straightening herself. "I came to see if anything was broken."

"Only some vows, Mademoiselle Flambert. Only some vows," Peter said bitterly, hardly stopping as he rushed past.

"Monsieur Kononellos, wait!" she called after him. "The tickets for your wedding trip have arrived."

Peter turned and looked at her. She had always been so cool and efficient in arranging everything for him. Although she was a proper middle-aged spinster, and he felt he was a social misfit at the bank, she had always been kind to him. Even when he had first started and was not entitled to a secretary, she had treated him with respect, and had discreetly corrected some of his glaring blunders. If only she could arrange his life the way she arranged his schedule, everything would run smoothly, he thought. He took a faltering step towards her.

"I'm afraid I won't be needing the tickets after all, Mademoiselle Flambert. Please cancel them. Please cancel everything!"

Mademoiselle Flambert had the distinct impression he wanted to say more, but he turned abruptly, and ran through the lobby and out the door. Although she was always careful to pretend she took no notice of anyone's personal life, she knew from the anguished look on Peter's face that he was extremely upset. She was no busybody, but she felt that Edgar had a right to know that something serious had gone wrong with Peter's wedding plans. She stole into Peter's office, replaced the paperweight, stacked his papers, and then slipped quietly into Edgar's office.

Peter drove rapidly to Claire's house, and pounded on the door in a blind fury, but there was no answer. At last he was forced to face the fact that he was never going to be allowed to marry Claire. The finality of being exiled from his every dream of happiness left him totally numb and empty. He wandered back to his car in a daze, and scarcely without willing it, he drove to the apartment he had leased for his bride.

He unlocked the door, went in, and threw himself on a chair. As he sat gazing at the furniture his despair grew deeper. What care and love had gone into selecting each piece, he thought. As a wedding present, Edgar and Charlotte had given him and Claire a sizeable allowance for household furnishings. Not trusting his own untutored tastes, he had elicited Charlotte's aid in furnishing the home he was preparing for Claire. By day Charlotte guided Claire through the quality shops, and helped her settle on the most enduring, classic styles; and by night, Peter acted as arbitrator to break any ties, and settle differences of opinion. It had amazed him how well Charlotte and Claire worked together to furnish the apartment in the most tasteful, inviting manner. Both women agreed that the apartment should be presentable for entertaining the business clients that Peter would acquire as his career moved forward. Charlotte had been impressed by Claire's natural good taste, and Claire felt content to express her more fanciful nature in the purchase of several bright impressionistic paintings. Claire knew her parents would disapprove of such "outlandish decorations," and she was relieved when Charlotte assured her that it was permissible for young people to display a few bright things in their home.

Looking at the pictures now, reminded Peter of Claire's gaiety, and the apartment seemed dreary and forlorn without her. Everything in the room reminded Peter of Claire, and the longer he sat, the more miserable he felt. What was he to do with the apartment and all its furnishings? Without Claire he would not enjoy it. Without Claire he would never entertain clients. Without Claire he was alone. He put his head in his hands and the silence of the empty rooms flowed over him in waves. It penetrated him to his soul and washed away every spark of hope.

At last the apartment was engulfed in lengthening shadows. Since the electricity had not yet been turned on, there would be no relief from the darkness. Peter could think of only one source of help – Charlotte. She would tell him what to say to everyone who had sent gifts. She would know what was proper and polite. She would know what to do with the useless pieces of his life. He must get to Charlotte as soon as possible.

Peter did not remember leaving the apartment. He did not remember driving his car. He remembered only a screech of tires, the sound of metal clashing against metal, and the jolt of being thrown against something hard. Gradually he became aware of a horn blaring loudly, but he did not realize that he was slumped over the steering wheel. He tried to straighten up, but he felt so dizzy when he lifted his head, he gave up and closed his eyes.

Suddenly the car door was yanked open, and someone was shouting at him in poor French. It was the driver of the truck that had smashed his car. He was a wiry, dark-haired man in his late thirties. "What in God's name is the matter with you pulling right in front of me like that? You imbecile! Don't you pay attention to red lights? Are you crazy or just drunk?"

Peter had no idea what the man was talking about. He kept his head down and hoped the man would go away. The noise of the horn was beginning to give him a headache.

"Hey, are you all right?" the man shouted over the noise of the horn.

Peter felt hands on his shoulders and he was lifted backwards. Mercifully the horn stopped blaring.

"Oh my God!" the driver said. Peter could hear other voices, but they seemed far away.

"Go call an ambulance! This guy's bleeding all over the place!" the driver said in French.

"Relax it's just a bloody nose," someone answered.

"No, he's cut his head too. Have you got a handkerchief?"

"No. Use his shirt. Keep his head back."

Peter felt hands pulling his shirt loose, and then the hateful cloth was over his face. He lurched sideways. "No! Don't!" he tried to shout, but his voice was too weak and they thought he was moaning.

"Hey, hold still! Come on, let me wipe your face."

Peter could feel the cloth, but there was no chemical smell. He tried to turn his head away, but someone held it. The taste of blood was on his lips.

"Where the hell were you going in such a hurry?" the driver asked, and drew Peter's head back against the head rest.

"Spain," Peter mumbled vaguely.

"Oh sure — no wonder you were in such a damn hurry. God, I hope you have insurance!" the man said to himself in Italian. Then he shouted in French, "What's your name? Your name — what's your name?"

Peter misunderstood. "Claire," he whispered.

"Claire, my ass," came back in Italian. Then Peter heard in French, "Where do you live? You must be rich. That's an expensive suit your ruining with your damn bloody nose. Where do you live?"

"Claire's gone. I can't stay there . . ." Peter mumbled. He could hear the sound of a siren coming closer.

"Who the hell is Claire?" the driver shouted. "Was there someone else in the car? Did your girlfriend get thrown out?" He started to shake Peter in frustration. "Where's Claire?" he yelled again.

"She's gone! She's gone! I'll never see her again," Peter moaned.

Just then two men from the ambulance came up.

"I can't get a straight answer from this guy," the truck driver shouted. "I think he's drunk! He didn't stop at the light — never even slowed down, the bastard! I'll be out of business for weeks!"

"Let's have a look at him," the ambulance attendant said, and motioned to the truck driver to move away from Peter.

"Good luck! I'm going to put out some flares," the driver said and stalked away.

The attendant leaned into the car. "How do you feel, monsieur?" he asked in French.

"I am well," Peter answered faintly.

"Nothing hurts?" the attendant asked, and held a clean cloth to Peter's face. Peter did not answer.

"What's your name, monsieur? Can you give me your name?" Still no response.

The first attendant looked at the second man. "I think he hit his head. He didn't have his seat belt fastened. You'd better get the stretcher." The second man shook his head and left.

"We're going to lift you out, monsieur. We'll try to be careful, but let us know if you feel any pain, O.K.?"

"Yes . . . O.K."

The attendants began to lift Peter out. "O.K. now, slowly . . . that's it. Watch his neck. Feel any sharp pains, monsieur? Monsieur? Can you hear me?"

"Yes, I hear . . ." They had Peter on his feet, and were bracing him from both sides. "Good, good. Now, can you stand by yourself?"

One man let go for a second, and Peter swayed dangerously.

"That's what I thought. We'll have to put you on the stretcher, monsieur."

The attendants tried to take hold of Peter again, but his attention was suddenly attracted by the sparkle of the bright flares lying in the dark street and he pulled away. "There's been an accident! I should move my car!"

The attendants got a grip on him again. "It's not necessary. Your car is fine where it is."

Peter looked at them in confusion. "Who are you? What do you want with me?"

"We're from the ambulance. You need to come with us."

"Ambulance?" Peter repeated slowly. "Was someone hurt?"

"We're not sure yet," the attendant said evasively. "It's not safe here. You must come with us."

"Where are you taking me?"

"To the hospital to check you over."

"But my car . . ."

"It's O.K. where it is. I promise it will be taken care of," the attendant assured him.

"I don't want to go to the hospital," Peter said stubbornly. "I have to see Charlotte."

Peter tried to pull away, but the men hung on. Peter's nose was still bleeding and blood was running down his face. The attendants were struggling to get him on the stretcher when the truck driver came up.

"Say, give us a hand here, would you? He's not cooperating."

"I told you he was crazy or drunk," the driver answered, and grabbed a hold of Peter. "Hold still! You're getting blood all over me."

Peter tried to fight them, but his movements were slow and uncoordinated. They forced him onto the stretcher and quickly strapped him down.

"Why are you doing this? I don't want to go to the hospital," Peter said and tugged at the straps.

One of the men from the ambulance searched through Peter's coat pockets and pulled out his wallet. "Here it is," he said quietly to the others. "Peter Kononellos. Let's get him in the ambulance."

"I'm going with you," the truck driver declared boldly. "I want to find out if he's insured. Somebody's got to pay for my truck!"

"What about the police?" the ambulance attendant asked.

"Tell them I hurt my back! I'm going with you!"

"O.K., O.K.. Get in the back, but keep your mouth shut. He doesn't even know he's the one who's been in the accident."

"I don't want to go to the hospital! I want to see Charlotte. Let me go!" Peter kept repeating as they lifted the stretcher into the ambulance and drove away.

One attendant leaned over the stretcher and tried to wipe the blood from Peter's face. "Hold still, Monsieur Kononellos. You're only making it worse!"

"Why must I go to . . ." he started again, but the attendant cut him off.

"Because the doctor wants to see you, Monsieur Kononellos."

"Carlin? Carlin wants to see me?" Peter quit struggling.

The attendant put his elbow in the truck driver's ribs, and put his finger to his lips. "Yes, Carlin. He told us to find you and bring you to the hospital."

"Why?"

"I don't know, monsieur. You'll have to ask him when we get there."

"I want to see Charlotte," Peter mumbled.

"You can call her from the hospital." The attendant held Peter's head back and after a few moments his nose stopped bleeding. "Have you been drinking, monsieur?"

"Drinking? No. I don't drink anymore. Don't want to lose control with Claire. I must be careful for her sake."

"Who the hell is Claire?" the truck driver asked loudly.

"Be quiet! I told you to be quiet!" the attendant hissed. "Don't set him off again." It was too late.

"My bride! My bride! My poor little Claire," Peter moaned.

"Where did she go, monsieur?" the attendant asked without real interest.

"To Spain — they took her to Spain."

"Is she on holiday? She'll come back."

"No . . . no . . . her father took her away. He won't let me marry her. She never even said good-bye. We were to be married. They left me to explain to everyone . . . I am so humiliated . . ."

The attendant shot a glance at the truck driver.

"When were you to be married, monsieur?"

"The 30th of May."

"That's tomorrow!" the truck driver said, slapping the attendant on the arm. "What a terrible thing!" he said to himself in Italian.

"Terrible," Peter repeated, and switched from French into Italian. "They took my bride . . . all the little children we were to have . . . everything. I have no life left!"

"Why would they do such an evil thing?" the truck driver asked in dismay.

"They say I am not good enough. I am not a Swiss. I have no family. Why did they let me believe I could be happy? Why did they wait until I could taste it before they snatched my happiness from me? Why? I never lied about myself. How could they be so cruel!"

Peter's voice broke and he started to sob.

The attendant had not understood what Peter said and was at

a loss, but the truck driver reacted with sympathy. He had often been humiliated by the Swiss. Shoving the attendant out of the way, he took Peter's hand between his own.

"Hush, hush — don't let these Swiss bastards see you weep. They have no hearts. Don't . . . don't," he said and began wiping Peter's face using his own shirt.

"They took everything — I will never forgive them. Never!" Peter sobbed.

"I know . . . I know," the driver said. "Be strong . . . be strong. It is better to curse them than to weep," he said, but tears were running down his face as he remembered his own humiliations.

"My God, have you both gone crazy?" the attendant asked. "What's the matter with him?"

"You filthy Swiss have torn his heart out! You've stolen his sons!" the driver shouted in his poor French which had became worse now that he was upset.

The attendant stared at him in amazement. "What are you talking about? I've never met the man before!"

"It doesn't matter! You Swiss are all alike. You think you are so superior. You disgust me!"

"Hey, settle down back there!" the second attendant called from the cab. "We're almost at the hospital. Let's not have another bloody nose."

The attendants acted swiftly and efficiently when they reached the hospital. Peter was wheeled inside and in a matter of minutes a doctor came to look at him. Peter had stopped sobbing, but was clinging to the truck driver's hand as if to draw courage from him.

"We hauled this one out of a wrecked car," the ambulance attendant said quietly to the doctor. "Name's Kononellos. He must have smacked his head. He's totally confused and started bawling on the way in."

"I see," the doctor answered. "Any problems with motor control?"

"He couldn't stand by himself when we hauled him out."

The doctor nodded. "Confusion, loss of coordination, emotional instability — sounds like a concussion. The police will want a test for alcohol though. Thanks for bringing him in."

The doctor stepped up to the stretcher. "Good evening, Monsieur Kononellos. My name is Doctor Ebersole. How are you feeling? Does your head hurt?"

"I am well," Peter said faintly. "I don't know why they brought me here."

"You were in an automobile accident, Monsieur Kononellos. We think you might have hurt your head." The doctor took a light to look at Peter's eyes.

"Hold still. It won't hurt. Hold still, Monsieur Kononellos, please. Hold still. Can you tell him to be still?" the doctor asked, looking at the driver.

The driver put his hand on Peter's shoulder and addressed him in Italian. "Be brave. Let him take a look so he'll go away."

Peter lay still, but the driver felt him tense and press himself against the stretcher. The doctor made a few more notes and looked at the driver.

"Are you a friend of his?"

The driver laughed a dry laugh. "Not until a moment ago," he said, and motioned the doctor to lean closer. "It was my truck that smashed his car," he whispered into the doctor's ear. "The poor bastard doesn't realize it's been wrecked!"

The doctor raised his eyebrows in surprise.

"He needs a friend real bad. His bride-to-be just left him. Almost at the altar."

The doctor made a few more notes. "What's your first name, Monsieur Kononellos?"

"My name?"

"Yes, what is your first name?"

"Peter. I am called Peter now."

"Do you remember where you were going when you had the accident?"

"I didn't see the accident . . . only the flares."

"Yes, hmm . . . I see"

"They told me Carlin was here. Where is he?"

"Carlin? Who is Carlin, Peter?"

"Carlin La Monde. They told me he wanted to see me."

"Who told you he was here, Peter? Do you remember?"

"Of course, I remember! The men from the ambulance told me. That's why I came."

The doctor looked at the driver. "What is he referring to?"

The driver leaned forward and whispered in the doctor's ear again.

"Is Carlin La Monde your doctor, Peter?"

"Yes, yes, of course! Why did they lie to me if he's not here? Let me up!" Peter said, and suddenly letting go of the driver he pulled at the straps. "Let me up! They lied to me. Carlin isn't here is he? You're all lying to me."

Peter rocked himself violently and fought against the straps, and his nose started to bleed again.

Doctor Ebersole remained calm, but the driver was upset. "Have a care, Peter. You're making it worse for yourself. Lie still! Lie still!"

"Leave me alone! Leave me alone! I can't trust any of you."

"Talk to him. See if you can get him to lie still. I'll see if I can locate Dr. La Monde," the doctor said and retreated hastily.

"Mamma mia! Why did I have to hit a madman? Hey! Hey! Be

quiet now. You've scared him away. He's gone to find your friend Carlin. Hush. God what a beautiful suit and you insist to bleed on it!"

Peter paid no attention and continued to shout, "Let me up! Let me up! Leave me alone!"

He was still struggling and bleeding when the doctor returned a few minutes later with a tray of supplies.

"Doctor La Monde is on his way, Peter. Please lay still."

"I don't believe you! They lied to me. Everyone's been lying to me."

The doctor attempted to hold some gauze to Peter's nose, but Peter kept jerking his head away. When the doctor tried to loosen Peter's tie, Peter became frantic. He began to scream and swear, and fight against the straps, pouring forth the most vile vindictive language in his rage and frustration. Luckily the good doctor understood only the rudiments of Italian and was not offended; and the truck driver who did understand, only laughed.

"Ah ha! He has been in Naples. Only in Napoli do they swear so magnificently! It is music to my ears to hear such wonderful foul curses again! Bravo Peter! Bravo! Here — let me loosen your collar so you can roar louder." With a quick motion he tore Peter's shirt open at the neck. Peter was surprised by the man's strength.

"I need to pack his nose to stop the bleeding, but there's no way I can do it when he's struggling like this," the doctor said helplessly.

"You cannot put him to sleep? I thought you have drugs for these things."

"It is too risky with a possible head injury."

"He is very much afraid of what you might do to him," the truck driver said. "He swears to hide his fear. Someone must have hurt him. You see he goes crazy when you try to touch his throat."

"I only want to stop the bleeding, but he must lie still."

"Leave it to me," the driver said, and turning back to Peter, he suddenly seized him by the shoulders, and bellowed into his face at the top of his lungs, "Enough, Peter! Shut up!"

The force of his action startled Peter, and he ceased swearing and struggling, and stared at the driver.

"You're bleeding badly, Peter. Feel it on your face! Taste it! You will be very sick if you continue to bleed. You and I know these Swiss are a bunch of bastards, but they are very good doctors. This one wants to put some cotton in your nose to stop the blood. It is only cotton, Peter. Here, feel it!" The driver thrust some cotton into Peter's hand. "You must lie still while he puts it in, do you understand? If you can't lie still, I will have to hold your head," the driver threatened, and quickly wrapped his hairy arm around Peter's neck. Peter started to choke and gasp and the driver let go. "Will you lie still, or must I hold your head?"

Peter made no answer and the driver moved to hold his head.

"No, please . . . don't. I'll be still."

"Good. You may begin doctor, and try not to hurt him."

The driver moved around behind Peter's head, and kept his hands on Peter's shoulders, partly to restrain him, and partly to comfort him. Peter drew his head back, and trembled visibly as the doctor started to put the cotton in his nose. The driver tried to calm him. "It's only cotton, Peter. It's only cotton. It won't hurt you."

"Close your eyes, Peter, and breath through your mouth," the doctor suggested gently, but Peter's eyes followed every move he made. Despite Peter's best efforts to be still, his head jerked a few times and his body twisted beneath the straps. He was wet with sweat, and gasping for breath by the time the doctor finished. The doctor took advantage of Peter's relative stillness to examine the cut above his eye and the bump that had formed on his head. "I'm finished, Peter. You should not lose any more blood," Dr. Ebersole announced after what seemed to Peter a very long time. Peter closed his eyes. He shook violently several times and the driver patted his shoulder. "You did very well, Peter. If you were not under this good doctor's care, I would buy you a whiskey!"

"Will you release me now, or do you wish to torture me again?" Peter asked bitterly.

"Dr. La Monde will release you when he comes, Peter. He will take care of you."

"You lying son of a bitch! He's never coming. You tricked me!"

"Why would we want to trick you, Peter? Dr. La Monde is on his way . . . believe me. Try to rest a little now. Will you stay with him?" the doctor asked turning to the truck driver.

"Sure . . . Peter and I are friends now, aren't we, Peter?"

Peter didn't answer. He was confused and unwilling to trust anyone.

"Relax, Peter," the driver said after the doctor left. "He's poked you enough for one day. He won't be back. Tell me how you came to speak such beautiful Italian and to curse with such gusto. Even I could not follow all your gutter talk, and I am no gentleman like yourself."

Peter's eyes remained closed and he did not answer. The driver sat quietly for a while then he gently touched Peter on the arm. Peter jumped nervously. "You are not resting, Peter. How will you get well? Tell me about this Charlotte you are so anxious to see. Is she another of your girlfriends? Is she pretty and willing?"

"Shut your mouth you pig!" Peter suddenly growled. "Don't dare to speak that way about Madame. Be glad that I am tied down or you would have a knife in your throat!"

"So you do have a tongue," the driver laughed. "I thought the good doctor took it with him when he left. I apologize if I have offended a virtuous lady. Tell me about her. It will pass the time until your doctor friend comes."

"You mock me! He is never coming."

"But he is. He is. You must believe. I would not let them keep you strapped down if I did not believe it myself."

"Why should I believe you? I don't even know you. Why are you here, anyway?"

"I am Giorgio Vittorini, truck driver, at your service. As to why I am here . . . it's a long story, Peter. I will tell it to you some day, but not right now. Come, tell me about Charlotte. I promise to be more respectful."

"Madame Charlotte Marneé is the wife of the man I work for. She arranged for me to come from Italy. She trained me to work for her, and in spite of my great stupidity, she saw that I was educated. I owe her a great deal."

"So you are Italian then!"

"No, I am Greek, but I ran away when I was very young. I worked in Italy for many years and was granted citizenship."

"If you loved Italy enough to become a citizen, why did you leave?"

"I had much poverty and sorrow there and no hope for a future."

"You are truly an Italian then. That is the price we must pay for the privilege of living there."

Peter was silent and the driver thought perhaps he was getting some rest and was glad.

CHAPTER FIFTEEN

It was nearly 10 p.m., and Carlin was at the Marneés. No one had seen Peter since he had flown from the bank at 3 o'clock and everyone was worried. Charlotte had called the Strom residence repeatedly, but there was no answer. She had begged the minister to delay the rehearsal as long as possible, but at 9 o'clock he had closed the church and locked the doors, muttering that "young people have no respect or responsibility any more". Charlotte knew something dreadful had happened, for it was not like Peter to forget appointments. She called the few people from the Strom's social circle that she knew, and made some discreet inquiries, but no one had seen Peter or Claire.

Charlotte was sitting in the library with Edgar, Carlin and the boys, drinking endless cups of coffee, when Anna announced that there was a call for Dr. La Monde. Carlin went into the hall to take the call, but returned in a few minutes. Only those who knew him would have known that he was agitated, but Charlotte saw it immediately.

"The call was about Peter, wasn't it?"

"Yes. His car was struck by a truck and he's at the hospital. Dr. Ebersole says he isn't badly hurt, but might have a head injury."

"We'll go with you," Charlotte said immediately. "Albert, you and Charles may stay up until I call you from the hospital, but don't give Anna any trouble."

"But mother, we want to see Peter."

"I know, dear, but the hospital might not allow many visitors at this hour. I promise to give him your love. Be a good boy and look after Charles."

"Go ahead in your car, Carlin. I will drive Charlotte and myself. We might need to come and go separately," Edgar commented as Carlin made for the door.

"Good idea. I'll see you in a few minutes."

Carlin dashed into the hospital, but stopped for a hurried conference with Dr. Ebersole before be went in to see Peter. Even after what Ebersole had told him, Carlin was shaken when he saw Peter lying strapped to the stretcher, his shirt torn open and covered with blood. Peter's eyes were closed.

"Peter, are you awake?" Carlin called softly as he came up to the stretcher. Peter's eyes opened instantly.

"Carlin? Oh God, Carlin! I thought everyone had lied to me. Please, Carlin, let me loose — please! I can't bear these straps another minute . . . please." Peter started to squirm and struggle.

"Stay quiet, Peter. I'll have them off in a minute. I'm sorry they had to restrain you, Peter, but Dr. Ebersole tells me you would not cooperate when they tried to help you."

"They forced me to come here, Carlin! I was on my way to see Charlotte. They pulled me from my car, and forced me to come here! They lied to me! They said you wanted to see me. They . . ."

"Calm down, Peter. Calm down," Carlin said soothingly and took Peter by the hand. "You were in an accident, Peter. Your car was wrecked. Try to remember."

"No! No! It was someone else! It was someone else! I saw the flares . . . I wanted to move my car, but they wouldn't let me. They pulled me away and tied me down!"

"It was you, Peter. Look at your shirt. You're covered with blood."

Peter looked totally bewildered. "I had a nose bleed, Carlin — just a nose bleed. They threatened to choke me if I didn't lie still while they stuffed my head full of cotton. Now I can't breathe, and I have a terrible headache."

"Listen to me, Peter. Dr. Ebersole put a little cotton in your nose to stop the bleeding. You lost a lot of blood, Peter. Don't you remember?"

"I remember the taste of blood. My face was wet. Everyone was trying to put things over my face. I thought they were going to smother me . . . just like before. I fought them, but they tied me down . . . just like before . . . they tied me down!"

"It's all right now, Peter. You're not tied down any more. Tell me, does anything hurt besides your head?"

"My arm . . . no my shoulder."

"Which one hurts?"

"I think my left one hurts . . . yes, the left one."

Carlin felt up and down Peter's arm.

"I'll have to take some X-rays, Peter."

"Don't tie me down again, Carlin! Please. I couldn't bear it."

"Relax, Peter, no one's going to tie you down. Just relax. Charlotte will be here in a minute. She's very worried about you."

Carlin had noticed the dark-haired man sitting in the room with Peter, but had been too occupied with trying to keep Peter calm to speak to him. "So you're the truck driver. Tell me what happened."

"Shh . . . he doesn't know who I am," the driver whispered, gesturing towards Peter. "I'll tell you about it later. You'd better stay with him. He doesn't really understand what's happened to him."

Their conversation broke off as Charlotte and Edgar came in. Charlotte didn't have the benefit of advanced warning, and was shocked when she saw Peter's bloody shirt.

"Peter! What happened?" she cried, and rushed up to the

stretcher.

"Oh Madame! I have been trying to get to you for hours. You must help me. Claire's gone!"

"Gone? Gone where?"

"To Spain. Her father took her to Spain. They won't let me marry her. Everything is over . . . our wedding, our children, our future . . . everything."

"Tell us what happened, Peter," Edgar put in. "Who was the woman who came to your office today? What did she tell you?"

"It was Ingred, Claire's sister. She told me the wedding was canceled. It's true! I went to Claire's house and no one was there."

"Did Ingred explain what happened to change Claire's mind?" Charlotte asked.

"No one has asked Claire. Her grandfather came for the wedding. When he found out I was a Greek, he turned everyone against me. He thought I was after Claire's inheritance. I swear I never knew she had an inheritance."

"This is preposterous! Why did they wait until the last minute to decide that the wedding was off?" Edgar asked.

"They are all afraid of the grandfather. He controls the money. My poor Claire is too weak and innocent to fight them all."

"Claire's family have treated you shamefully, Peter. They have humiliated us all!" Edgar said indignantly.

"They said I'm not a Swiss . . . I am not good enough . . ."

"How dare anyone say the Marneés are not good enough!" Edgar shouted so loudly they all were quiet.

"Peter is not a Marneé," Charlotte reminded Edgar quietly.

"Damn it! I am the head of this household, and I say he is a part of it," Edgar roared. The room was silent. None of them had ever seen Edgar so angry.

"Perhaps it is all an excuse. Perhaps Claire never loved me after all," Peter said softly.

"Don't even think such a thing, Peter. She worships you," Charlotte said firmly.

"Perhaps when she found out I wasn't as perfect as she thought, she was disillusioned!"

"You're wrong! She loves you, Peter. I know it," Charlotte assured him.

"Charlotte is right, Peter," Edgar said, calming himself. "Don't ever doubt that Claire loves you. Perhaps we can convince her family that you and Claire belong together."

Carlin was distressed about the canceled wedding, for he had been looking forward to acting as Peter's best man. More than any of them, he knew how much Peter needed a wife and family, to settle him down and give him support. At the moment, however, he was concerned about Peter's health.

"I really must get some X-rays," he told Edgar. "That man is the truck driver who smashed Peter's car. Perhaps you'd better have a talk with him. The police will want a report, but Peter is in no condition to make a rational statement. He insists it was someone else who had the accident."

"I'll talk to him, but I wish Francois was here to handle things."

So while Edgar talked with the truck driver, Charlotte called the boys, and Carlin took Peter to have X-rays taken of his arm and his head. Carlin decided that Peter should stay at the hospital overnight, but Peter did not agree. He argued with Carlin all the way back from the X-ray department, and all the while Carlin tried to get him undressed and into bed. Carlin was not having much success when Edgar came in a short time later.

"I can't reason with him, Edgar. He's over excited and irrational, but if I sedate him, I won't be able to gauge his physical state. Maybe he'll listen to you."

Edgar nodded and bent over the stretcher. "What's all this fuss you're making, Peter?" he said quietly. "If Dr. La Monde says you should stay here tonight, then you must do as he says. You know his word is law in our house."

Peter's annoyance with Carlin had turned to anger, and he focused it on Edgar. "This is not your house, Edgar! I'm a grown man, and I thank you to stay out of my affairs!"

"We're only trying to do what's best for you, Peter. You're not well. You need . . ."

"I am sick and tired of all of you telling me what to do! You people think you are so superior and know everything. Well you don't! You filthy Swiss have made a shambles of my life. I can't tolerate any more! I'm going back to Italy where at least a man knows who his enemies are!"

Suddenly Peter sprang from the stretcher, pushed his way past Carlin, and took three long strides towards the door, before he was overcome by the most violent wave of nausea and dizziness he had ever experienced.

"Catch him, Edgar!" was the last thing he heard as everything went dark.

Carlin stayed with Peter all night, waking him frequently to ask him simple questions. Peter gave a variety of answers to the question, "What is your name?" ranging from Peter, to Kon, to Petros, but he was always definite about being Kononellos. Peter usually remembered his correct street address, but sometimes he gave the Marneés' address by mistake. When he gave his name as Kon, he responded that he lived in the cellar, a damp, cold cellar. If he answered that his name was Petros, however, he became anxious, and had no answer concerning where he lived. To dispel Peter's anxiety, Carlin suggested that Petros lived with the Marneés. Peter quickly

195

agreed, and gave the names of everyone in the house.

Carlin accepted all of Peter's answers as evidence that Peter's mind was functioning normally. He knew that Peter had some traumatic memories buried deep within him, but Carlin believed that like shrapnel in flesh, it was better to hope the wound would heal over it, than to dig it out and do further harm. Toward morning, however, he took Peter for another X-ray, and concluded that surgery was not necessary.

Peter woke naturally at 10 o'clock the next morning. When he tried to open his eyes he discovered his right eye was not working. His throat was dry from breathing through his mouth and his body ached as if it had been crushed. Although it did not register in Peter's mind, it was May 30th, his long awaited wedding day.

Charlotte had been up early calling as many people as she knew who had been invited to the wedding to tell them of the cancellation. Edgar staunchly insisted that the social disgrace should fall strictly on the shoulders of the Stroms, for they had been in charge of hiring the hall, the caterers, the musicians, the florist, and the photographers. He did agree to call the minister, only to find that Ingred had conveyed the message. Charlotte was tired and worried as she sat by Peter's bed hoping he would wake in a calmer state of mind.

"Good morning, Peter," she said and forced herself to smile when she saw him trying to open his eyes. "How are you feeling?"

"I am well, Madame," Peter croaked and wet his lips.

"Would you like some water?"

"Yes," he said quickly, but his head felt split-in-two when he moved to raise it.

"How clever of Carlin to provide a straw. Just turn your head, Peter. I'll hold the glass."

Peter drank eagerly for he felt as though he had been desiccated. "What's wrong with me, Madame?" he asked sorrowfully after several minutes.

"You were in an automobile accident, Peter. Carlin says, that judging by the bruises, you were thrown against the door, and then fell onto the steering wheel, hurting your face. Luckily nothing is broken, but your poor nose took a terrible blow and is quite swollen."

"Have I lost an eye?" he asked anxiously.

"Heavens no! It's just swollen shut. Carlin said you would probably feel weak and sore all over, but you should recover quickly."

"So I really was the one in the accident. How strange. I truly don't remember being in the car."

"Well, there were several witnesses. Apparently you were going very fast and drove through a red light. A truck struck your car."

"Was anyone else hurt?"

"No, only you."

"That's fortunate."

"Yes, in a way, but I'm sorry you were hurt."

Before Peter could answer, Carlin came into the room and approached the bed. "Well, good morning, Peter!" he said cheerfully, and examined Peter's two black eyes and swollen nose. "If you will forgive me for being a Swiss, I will be happy to take the cotton out of your nose."

"I don't see why you need to be forgiven for being Swiss," Peter remarked, and Carlin surmised that Peter remembered nothing of his angry outburst.

Peter found it unpleasant to lie still while Carlin worked on his swollen face, but he trusted Carlin enough to know that he would not intentionally hurt him. Although Peter agreed to Carlin's suggestion that he eat a light meal, he felt very tired and fell asleep again before Carlin could bring it.

"I think the storm is over, Charlotte," Carlin said quietly. "I only hope we can help Peter pull his life together again. Marrying Claire would have been so good for him."

"I'm not sure that things haven't turned out for the best, Carlin. Claire is very sweet, but perhaps Peter needs someone with more fiber. He has a more tumultuous side to his nature than he usually allows us to see."

"Perhaps you're right, Charlotte, but it won't be easy for Peter to get over Claire."

Later in the day when Peter was again awake and had eaten, Giorgio came to see him. "And how are you feeling, Peter? Do you remember me?"

Peter took a long hard look at him and a memory came to him as if from some ancient time. "Yes, you are Giorgio Vittorini, the truck driver."

"The same."

"It was you who ran into my car wasn't it?"

"Yes, it was an unfortunate thing, Peter. You went against the light — I could not stop. I am sorry you were hurt."

"The fault was mine, Giorgio. I was not myself. You were a friend to me when I was alone."

"It was a small thing, Peter, to listen to a man's troubles."

"You did more than that for me, Giorgio. You gave me courage, and prevented me from making a total fool of myself. You saved my pride which is all I have left."

"You will find life again, Peter. It comes and goes."

"For me it is gone — but what of you? Will you have a new truck from it all?"

"Nay, nay! The good gentleman would give it, but I could not afford the insurance and the taxes. Also it would ruin my sleep to worry that some bastard might steal it. I will be content to have the old one fixed."

"Is that all you will get?"

"No, the gentleman was very generous. He gave me enough cash for a full load of oranges. I shall have a nice profit when I sell them. But we must not tell why he gave the gift."

"It is not right that Edgar should pay for my mistakes, but I am glad for you. Do you have a family, Giorgio?"

"Can there be an Italian without a family? I have a patient wife and seven little ones. Thank God, most of them look like me. I am gone a lot, but luckily I don't count too well. They could all be my doing. They wait for me and treat me like a king when I come. I go there now, with a friend, while they fix my truck."

"You are a wealthy man, Giorgio. I regret the loss of my sons."

Peter suddenly looked at Giorgio with a sorrowful expression. "I was always so careful with her, Giorgio. She wanted to save herself for the wedding night, but she yielded to me. I was careful of her, but if I had given her my child, they would have forced me to marry her. I was a great fool! For the sake of her honor, I have lost her."

"Don't brood on these things, Peter. You acted with honor. What more can a man do?"

Peter was silent, and then turned, and began to search in the drawers of the cabinet by the bed. "They have taken my wallet, Giorgio. I wanted to send a gift — for the children."

"It is not necessary, Peter."

"I want to, Giorgio. Please. Wait . . ." Peter found a piece of paper and scribbled a note. "Here, give this to Dr. La Monde. He will see that you get something spendable."

Giorgio took the note and glanced at it. "Even a scoundrel like myself cannot accept this much from you, Peter."

"I have no need of it, Giorgio. My life is over. Take it to please me. Take it for your sons."

"No, I cannot. It would shame me to accept so much." He shoved the note back at Peter.

"Very well then," Peter said taking the note. He scribbled on it again and handed it back to Giorgio.

"Please . . . as a gift between friends. Use this to take your family to dine . . . all of them . . . and remember me when you raise the glass."

The driver took the note, read it and smiled. "You are very kind. We will drink a toast to our patron."

"I am no patron, Giorgio. I am Kononellos, the cook's helper."

"No! No! You are a Marneé now. I heard the good gentleman say it!"

"It was a figure of speech," Peter protested.

"No! It was more. He loves you like a son, Peter. I saw it. No Florentine nobleman ever roared with more furry at having his son slighted. He may not tell you in words, but you are like his own flesh and blood."

"A man could be proud of such a father as Edgar, but mine was a drunken brute."

"Why can't a man have a second father? He can have more than one son. Think about it! I must go. My family and I will drink a toast to you, Peter, and I will pray to the Virgin that you will mend quickly."

"Thank you, Giorgio. No one has done that for me for a very long time."

****

Charlotte received the call on Monday afternoon. A friend had seen the article in a Zurich newspaper she subscribed to. The name of Strom was well known in Zurich and the headline had caught her eye. She had only to check a few details to know it was about Claire.

Perhaps if Claire's family had taken her to Spain there would have been a happier ending, for the beauty and excitement of the country might have caught her interest, and given her some pleasure. However, they were much too prosaic; they took Claire to Zurich. Monsieur Strom had even lied to Ingred about it, fearing she would tell Peter the truth. The harsh bareness of her grandparents' town house depressed Claire and the thought of spending the rest of her life without Peter to teach and encourage her was unbearable. She had tried, when she felt she wasn't being watched, to call Peter at his apartment, but there had been no answer. How was she to know that Peter was in the hospital?

No one guessed that Claire would have the resolve to do what she did. She had not been brought up to defy her parents, and she could not do it now, even for love of Peter. There seemed to her only one way out, and she took it. She flung herself out of the fourth story window and brought her brief life to an end.

Carlin agreed with Charlotte that they should not tell Peter right away. They had brought him home from the hospital on Monday morning and sent him directly to bed in a first floor room. Peter was still experiencing bouts of dizziness, and it was feared he might fall down the stairs. Claire's father called for Peter on Wednesday, and Charlotte took the call. She explained to Monsieur Strom that Peter had been in an automobile accident, and could not come to the phone. Speaking to Charlotte as a parent, Claire's father confessed that he had completely misjudged the depth of Claire's feelings for Peter. He was heartbroken that he had caused his own child to become so despondent as to kill herself. He asked that Peter come to Claire's funeral on Thursday, for he felt that as a father, it was the last thing he could do for Claire. Charlotte promised to do what she could, but could not guarantee that Peter would be physically able to attend, or that he would want to.

Charlotte felt she bore the responsibility of breaking the news to Peter. She went to his room and sat by his bed. Carlin had predicted that Peter would require a great deal of sleep for his nervous system to recover from the double jolt of physical and emotional shock, and he had been right. Peter seemed to have great difficulty staying awake or focusing his attention for more than a short period of time, and Charlotte suspected that Carlin had not told her the truth about the seriousness of Peter's head injury. As she gazed at Peter now, her mind was drawn back to that morning when she had first seen him as a ragged, exhausted boy. She and Edgar had worked hard to train Peter and give him everything he needed for a good life. She wished she could have protected him from this terrible unhappiness. Carefully, so as not to startle him, she reached out and gently pushed the hair back from his forehead. It would not stay put and she smiled at the stubbornness of it . . . so like Peter himself. She stroked his forehead gently and he stirred and opened his eyes.

"How are you feeling, Peter?"

"I am well, Madame," he said drowsily, but he looked at her steadily. She was smiling at him, but her eyes were full of sadness.

"You look tired, Madame," he said softly. "I think you spend too much time fussing over your kitchen help."

"It's not fussing, Peter, it's caring, and I want to do it," Charlotte began. "Peter, I'm afraid I have some very sad news to tell you. I told you that Claire loved you very much and it is true. She loved you so much, Peter, that when her parents took her away, she could not bear to be apart from you and . . ." Charlotte faltered and pressed his hand.

"Charlotte . . . tell me the truth," Peter said evenly.

"I am so sorry, Peter but . . ." Charlotte stifled a sob. "Claire has killed herself."

Peter's fingers went limp in Charlotte's hand and she thought she heard him moan, but he quickly turned his head aside. "My poor little Claire. My poor little Claire. Such sweetness gone from the world." He turned back to Charlotte and grasped her hand. "Oh Charlotte, was it a sin for me to love her? I would have given her up if I had known she would die because of me. I have been the ruin of such a beautiful creature!"

"It's not your fault, Peter. It's not your fault. Claire made her choice. She did not want to live without you. She was not strong-willed. She could not go against her father."

"If only I had been able to get her away from her father . . . I could have made her happy. I know it!"

"Her father wants you to come to the funeral, Peter. It's tomorrow morning."

"My God! He has the gall to invite me to the funeral? So I am allowed to stand by Claire at the grave, but not at the altar! What a mockery!"

"You don't have to go, Peter. You still aren't well . . ."

"I will go. I will go. There must be someone there who understood her," Peter said sadly.

"Edgar and I will go with you, Peter. We loved Claire too."

"Thank you, Madame, thank you."

The following morning Edgar came to help Peter get dressed. Since the accident Peter had suffered frequent memory lapses, and they became more apparent when Edgar tried to get him ready to go out. Edgar had to select Peter's clothes and prod him to put them on. Edgar also brought Peter a pair of dark glasses, because his eyes were still black and blue.

Walking unsteadily between Charlotte and Edgar, Peter entered the church where he and Claire were to have been married. Throughout the brief ceremony he sat rigid and still, and Charlotte wondered if Peter even realized where he was. The minister never mentioned that Claire had intended to be married or that she had taken her own life. After the funeral, Edgar drove Charlotte and Peter to the cemetery, purposely choosing the last place in the line of vehicles, so that Peter would not have to stand and wait at the grave.

A large group was assembled at the grave when they arrived, and they took a place in the rear. Charlotte caught only a glimpse of the coffin through openings between the many shoulders in front of her. It struck her as being unusually heavy and ornate to contain spritely, gentle Claire. She wondered if Peter had even seen the coffin.

Peter stood with his head bowed, but Charlotte could hear him whispering sorrowful, beseeching prayers in what she guessed was Greek. She could not tell if he was praying for Claire or for himself. Suddenly he began to cross himself repeatedly. Charlotte did not want to interfere with a ritual she did not understand, but when he kept at it, she gently slid her arm around his and held it still. Peter looked at her and she saw that tears were running down his face.

"I can't remember . . . I can't remember the words, Charlotte," he mumbled sadly. "I said them . . . for my mother. I thought I would never forget them, but God forgive me, I can't remember the right words."

She pressed his hand. "It's all right, Peter. Just listen to the minister," she answered trying to calm him.

"But I am a Greek. I should pray in Greek."

"Well the prayer is for Claire and she spoke French. Just say a prayer in French, Peter."

"Will it be right? I must get it right, for Claire's sake."

Charlotte had never thought about the differences in the

languages. Although she could speak German fluently, she thought in French, and she prayed in French. She was not in the mood for a theological discussion, but she could see that Peter thought it was important. "Say the prayer however you can, Peter. Let God sort it out. These things are easier for him."

"Yes, yes – you must be right," he said, but when he began to pray again it was in Greek. It was the only way he knew how to pray.

Charlotte could feel that Peter was shaking, and she began her own silent prayer that the minister would finish before Peter collapsed. She blamed herself for allowing him to come. He was not well enough to be put through this ordeal. She was lost in her own thoughts when Edgar put his arm around her. She looked up in surprise and noticed that the service was over and everyone was moving toward their cars. She clutched Edgar's hand firmly. "I'll be all right, dear," she said softly. "I think you'd better help Peter. This has all been very hard for him."

Edgar nodded his head and took Peter's free arm. "It's time to go, Peter."

Peter looked at him blankly. "Go? Go where?"

"Let's go home, Peter. The service is over."

"Everything is over, Edgar, everything."

They began heading towards the car when Charlotte caught a glimpse of Claire's father coming towards them. She quickly turned her head, and pretended not to see him. She tried to hurry Peter forward, but Monsieur Strom was determined. He followed after them, and called out to Peter. Charlotte thought that Peter had not heard him, but when he called again Peter halted abruptly.

Monsieur Strom rushed up to Peter, and tried to put his hand on his arm. Peter jerked away even though Edgar and Charlotte had hold of his arms. "I have nothing to say to you, sir!" he growled.

Monsieur Strom ignored the obvious rebuff. "Peter, I am so sorry this has happened," he said quickly.

Peter pulled loose from Charlotte and Edgar. He stood glaring at Claire's father, his sorrow transformed to wrath. "Sorry! Do you think you can just apologize, and make everything right again?" Peter thundered. "By God, I swear you are a murderer and a thief! You have killed your own child, and stolen my life and my happiness!"

"Peter, please . . ." Charlotte said meekly, and tired to take his arm. Peter shook her off. The look on his face turned blacker, and he continued to rage. "You never understood Claire. She tried her best to please you, but you were never satisfied, were you? You always made her do things she didn't want to do. She never wanted to study mathematics! She never wanted to go away. She wanted to play the flute! She wanted to marry me, and have lots of babies – my children! Now she has nothing but a grave!"

Peter made a lunge for Strom, but suddenly Claire's older

brother, William, appeared out of nowhere. He stepped in front of Peter shouting, "This is all your fault! You filled Claire's head full of nonsense and dreams!" Without warning he struck Peter in the face. Peter staggered backwards, and Charlotte saw blood streaming from his nose. Before she could reach to help him, Peter lashed out at William, knocking him to the ground. Edgar caught Peter's arm for a moment, but he couldn't hold him. Peter jumped on William, and began to batter him with his fists. Before he could seriously injure William, however, several of Claire's cousins arrived, and grabbed Peter by the arms. Peter glared at Claire's father, and struggled against the men who held him in check. "You deserve the lowest place in hell for what you did to my poor Claire!" he roared.

"Please forgive him, Monsieur Strom. He is not well," Charlotte cried to Claire's father.

"I see my father was right!" Monsieur Strom said arrogantly. "You are not fit to marry a Strom. I am sorry Claire ever became involved with you."

"I think you had better go, sir," Edgar said with icy formality. "You have caused my family enough grief."

Claire's brother was on his feet and would have struck Peter again, but his father called him back. "William! Enough! Don't dishonor yourself by fighting with this son of a Greek whore."

The remark infuriated Peter. He twisted violently, almost breaking free from the men who held him. "How dare you defile my mother's name you murderer! Murderer! I will shout until God himself hears me and strikes you down!" he screamed at Claire's father.

Monsieur Strom turned away, but William took one last revenge. Seeing that his cousins had a secure hold on Peter, he rammed his fist into Peter's stomach. Peter tried to dodge the blow, but he was restrained. "Damn you, you cowardly Strom! Damn all of you!" Peter cursed as he dropped to his knees.

Edgar was aghast. He raised his arm as if to strike William, but he checked himself. "Get out of my sight!" was all he allowed himself to say, although William had his fists up. When Edgar turned he saw that Peter had been released, and that Charlotte was trying to stop his nose bleed with her tiny handkerchief.

Peter's anger had sustained him, but now he felt dizzy and sick to his stomach. He sank down on the grass, and felt its moist coolness against his cheek. He heard buzzing and talking all around him, but he could not understand the words. "We commend this soul into the hands of God," he repeated over and over in Greek. Gradually the sounds sorted themselves out, and he recognized Edgar's strong, calm voice. "Peter! Peter, you must get up. Let me help you to the car." He felt hands lifting him, supporting him. He stumbled forward, but everything was black, and he kept tripping over his own feet.

"He lied, Edgar, he lied! My mother was not a whore. Believe me, Edgar, believe me," Peter kept whispering, but he spoke in Greek and Edgar did not understand. Edgar held Peter from falling, and cursed the Stroms for not accepting him. He felt ashamed that he shared a common nationality with such a family.

When Peter awoke, he was back in his own bed at the Marneés, and Edgar was sitting with him. Peter asked why he was there and Edgar told him that he had passed out at the funeral. Peter could not recall anything about the funeral, and seemed only vaguely aware that Claire was dead. Edgar had to explain what happened to Claire again and see the pained look on Peter's face. And so it went for several days, Peter would wake and ask about Claire, and then Edgar, or Charlotte, or Carlin would explain that she was dead. Peter would seem to understand them and talk rationally, and then he would fall asleep again and forget.

Carlin assured Charlotte that it was all part of the trauma of a head injury, and that Peter would eventually recover; but Charlotte began to think that if she had to tell Peter about Claire, and see that look in his eyes, one more time, she would have a nervous collapse.

Summer was drawing to a close before Peter was able to return to work, and resume any sort of normal schedule. Despite Charlotte's pleading, he moved back to his own apartment. However, when Edgar discovered that Peter spent all his free time listening to tapes of Claire playing the flute, and drinking himself senseless, he demanded that Peter return to the house. Peter went back without an argument. He didn't care. He didn't care about anything anymore.

CHAPTER SIXTEEN

Seven months had passed since the wedding had been called off, and Peter was in Rome, acting as Edgar's representative at an international banking conference. Although Peter had spent a good part of his life living and travelling in Italy, he had never had the opportunity to visit Rome, and he was excited by the ancient city. Since it was December and the weather was chilly, the streets and cafes were no longer overflowing with tourists.

On the second night, after being honored by an invitation to a rather tedious and boring formal dinner given by some of the older delegates, Peter was invited to a private party. He pleaded fatigue and tried to excuse himself, but when the host persisted, he gave in and went along with the group. Charlotte would be proud of my party manners, he thought to himself. These people never suspect I am painfully bored with them.

Peter had made it through the dinner reasonably well, due to the fact that he had been seated directly across from a very smooth-talking man, who kept everyone amused with tales of his many travels. Although Peter was highly qualified and confident in even the most delicate dealings with clients on a one-to-one basis, he did not shine in large gatherings. He could manage to recite the necessary social pleasantries at a dinner party where he was required to make conversation with only a few people, but he usually hid behind formal reserve to the point of stiffness at cocktail parties.

On this occasion, the hostess, Nadia d'Alessandro, was particularly anxious to gain the favor of the man who worked so closely with Edgar Marneé. She had her beautiful white arm wrapped python-like around Peter's, before he had scarcely taken off his overcoat, and with effervescent hospitality she led Peter around for introductions. Gauging Peter's nervousness by the stiffness of his arm, Nadia stopped frequently to see that he was properly fortified with champagne. She managed the conversation so adroitly that no one seemed to notice that Peter only smiled, and shook everyone's hand. Peter could not understand why even his most inane comments called forth peals of laughter from Nadia, but it was a congenial laugh, and after several glasses of champagne, he was content to let her lead him around, and pretend that he was a smashing social success.

However, when Nadia pulled him into a group that included a small, slim woman who wore her dark hair trimmed boyishly short, Peter forgot even to smile and shake hands. Suddenly he became totally rigid, and appeared rooted to the floor. He stared at the woman, and in a matter of seconds he turned so pale, Nadia thought he might drop at her feet. She thought to cover for his rudeness, and smiled conspiratorially at the woman. "Please forgive Signor Kononellos, Geilla," Nadia said in a hushed tone. "I think I have fed him too much champagne." Nadia chuckled, but caught herself when she saw the look on Geilla's face, and the way she was staring at Peter. Nadia was afraid they would attract attention standing there like two plaster of Paris statues. Quickly releasing Peter's arm, she took Geilla by the hand, and pulled her forward. "Geilla, I have a feeling you've met my dear Peter before. Please entertain him while I see to my other guests." Turning abruptly, Nadia bubbled a greeting to a guest who had just arrived, and slid away gracefully.

It was Geilla who eventually realized how awkward she and Peter looked, standing there staring at one another. "So they call you Peter now. That seems very formal," she said trying to sound nonchalant, although she felt her heart speed up.

"Yes," Peter stammered. "Charlotte thinks it sounds more civilized than Kon."

"Charlotte?" Geilla repeated numbly. "Is that your wife's name?"

"I have no wife," he confessed with a trace of bitterness.

It was Geilla's turn to stammer. "Oh! I thought . . . someone told me you were engaged."

"I was . . . last spring . . . but, the lady . . . the lady withdrew her consent. It was . . . a great shock to me."

"I'm terribly sorry, Kon," Geilla answered, seeing that it was still painful for him to talk about the matter. She was surprised at how glad she was that Peter was still unattached. She studied him for a moment. He has changed, she thought. He looked taller to her, but she had no way of knowing how often Charlotte had disciplined him to stand straight and keep his head up. Although Kon was just 5' 11", he appeared taller because of his excellent posture. Geilla thought he looked older, and that the sadness which once was only in his dark eyes now showed on his face. Somehow it was not unattractive on him, and gave him an air of distinction. His hair was the same though, dark, thick and falling gently across his forehead. She thought it gave him a look of boyish impetuousness, and balanced the hard set of his mouth. She wondered if his smile was still as enchanting, the way it would flit across his face to soften and light his features. Suddenly she longed to see that rare smile once again. It was a need as immediately important as air to a drowning man. "I think I've had too much champagne," she said abruptly. "Kon, would you take me somewhere to get some coffee?"

Peter looked at her with a blank expression. "What about your husband, Geilla? Shouldn't you go with him?"

Geilla stared at Kon, then sighed deeply. "My husband has been dead for over a year, Kon," she said softly.

He was shocked. "Forgive my rudeness. I did not know . . . I am truly sorry. I . . ." She took him by the arm. "It's all right, Kon. I am over my grief," she said soothing his awkwardness.

Nadia caught them at the door as they were putting on their coats. "I'm sorry you're leaving so soon, Peter. I did so want to talk to you."

"Perhaps some other time," Peter mumbled. "It has been a most interesting . . . a most memorable evening. Thank you for inviting me." He took her hand impulsively, and although he could not remember her name, he bowed gracefully and kissed her hand. She stood speechless with surprise as Peter whisked Geilla out the door. Was that the same reserved, stiff, board of a man that had come in a little over an hour ago? she thought to herself. Was it just the champagne that had made him so gallant? She doubted it.

The air was chilly, but Kon did not seem to notice. He was feeling a strange sensation of warmth and lightness coursing through his veins. Was it the champagne? he thought. No, he had tried too many times to get this feeling from alcohol to know it was not possible for him. Enough alcohol could dull the pain, but it could not make him feel good.

Kon hailed a cab, and Geilla gave directions to a small restaurant she knew kept late hours. They sat over coffee and talked, awkwardly at first, then more freely, about all the good, and some of the bad things that had happened in their lives since they had last met. Kon saw that Geilla had adjusted well to the death of her husband, but that the loss of her only child was still a painful memory for her. He envied her having had the opportunity to have a family of her own, as he always felt he occupied a strange position in the Marneé household — more than a servant, but not really a son.

Kon felt quite happy to be with Geilla. He tried hard to impress her with his success and his sophistication, not realizing that most of what he said involved Claire, and his emptiness without her. Geilla could see that Kon had been deeply in love with Claire, while she had developed only a lukewarm fondness for Servio after several years of marriage. She envied the depth of Kon's passion, even though she recognized that he now suffered more severely than she did.

At last when the proprietor came by the fourth time to ask if they needed anything else, they knew it was time to go. Kon hailed a cab. Geilla insisted she could get home by herself, but he would not hear of it, and accompanied her to her apartment. She was living in Rome almost full-time, and although she did not have to work, she had taken a job as an interpreter for an international company. It was through that connection that she had been invited to the party at Nadia's. Years of acting as hostess to Servio's friends and clients had transformed Geilla from a shy young girl into a confident, cosmopolitan woman. As Servio's wife, she had been assured of a prominent position in Italian society.

Kon left the cab and walked with Geilla to her door. He did not really expect to be invited in, because it was so late, he just wanted to stay with Geilla as long as possible. For her part, Geilla knew the conference would be over in another day, and she did not want Kon to walk out of her life again. He finally realized he would have to say something if he wanted to see Geilla again. "May I call you sometime?" he asked, abruptly retreating behind his formal facade.

"Yes. Yes, of course," Geilla responded eagerly. "Here, I'll give you my number," she continued, pulling a card from her bag, and rapidly writing the number. She was disappointed that Kon lacked the courage, or the desire, to say anything more definite. She took the plunge. "How long will you be in Rome, Kon?"

"I had hoped to finish tomorrow and then fly back to Geneva."

"And you have never been in Rome before?" she questioned.

"No. This is my first visit. I wish . . . I wish the bank did more business here."

She took his arm casually. "Let me show you the city, Kon. I know it well, and I promise not to bore you with too many Madonnas."

He laughed and she saw the hint of his special smile. "I accept. I don't think I will have a better offer."

"Good," she said, and flashed him a full lingering smile. "Pick me up here whenever you can get away."

"I will do my best to hurry the negotiations, but Edgar is depending on me. In the past, he has always attended the conference himself."

"I'm sure you will charm them all into accord," Geilla said, sensing the burden of responsibility Kon felt as Edgar's representative.

"Until tomorrow then," he said, and vanished before she could answer.

Geilla entered her apartment and sighed. She would have to go over the place very carefully, and remove every trace of Angelo before Kon arrived tomorrow. She had made up her mind that she was finished with Angelo last week, but she had not told him. Angelo was in Paris, and she did not want him to hear the news over the telephone. Geilla had planned in her mind how, when he returned, she would break the news to him gently, and ask him to remove his things. She had packed most of his clothes and personal items, but there were still some pictures scattered about. She did not want to hurt Angelo, but after living with him for three months, she had decided she did not love him. She had been infatuated with him for a while, but there was no substance to the man. After he left the last time, it came to her that the only thing Angelo gave her was the physical passion that had been totally lacking in her marriage to

Servio. However, having lived for six years with a man who showered her with kindness and consideration, and sought every opportunity to express his deep love and respect for her, Geilla was seeking more than pure animal lust.

Geilla wondered if she could rekindle anything with Kon. He had been very formal with her all evening, but he never had been one to show his feelings openly. She would have to feel him out carefully, since he was obviously still hurting from his disastrous engagement. Geilla was glad that Kon had Charlotte to care for him, and give his life some stability. Her life with Servio had not been exciting, but at least she had been part of a family.

Even after Kon returned to his hotel, he still felt a sense of lightness. The doorman was astonished when Kon answered his perfunctory greeting with a smile. He had judged Kon dour, even for a Swiss. Kon scanned the agenda for the next day's meeting, and decided that if he could get several of the delegates to come to terms, he could conclude his business by the 1 o'clock lunch break. He knew he could not bear to sit through another boring luncheon speech, even if Geilla was not waiting for him. Kon scribbled some notes, arranged his clothes, put his shoes out to be shined, and called the airline to cancel his flight to Geneva. He was not sure what would develop when he met Geilla again, but he wanted to give himself enough time to see it through. The bank could get by without him for another day or two, and Edgar had been after him for weeks to take a vacation. Kon went to bed reluctantly, prepared for the nightly ordeal of staring into the darkness until he was exhausted, but it seemed he had barely pulled the covers under his chin when he drifted off.

Surely the morning session had not been changed, but it seemed to Kon that it included more than the scheduled number of uninspired speakers. When Kon finally got down to negotiating judiciously with a few senior delegates, he found himself smiling and thinking of Geilla. Indeed, while the other junior delegates were obviously nervous, and fawned on the older men, Kon appeared confident and relaxed. The senior delegates liked the way Kon cut to the heart of matters, and expressed himself with as few words as possible. After signing a deal very much in Edgar's favor, Kon flashed his shy smile, and even the most experienced delegates recognized Kon's latent talent.

After a dull, but successful morning, Kon jumped into a taxi, and headed for Geilla's apartment. He felt relaxed and satisfied about settling the business deal, light-hearted and full of anticipation about seeing Geilla again, and to his amazement, ravenously hungry. Kon was quite impressed by the elegance of Geilla's living quarters. At least financially things had improved for both of them over the years.

"Have you eaten?" Geilla asked as he looked around her living room with approval. "No, I stole out as soon as the rest went in to lunch. As a matter-of-fact I'm famished."

"Good! I have just the place in mind. You'll love it. Their veal is excellent." Geilla kept up a rapid fire chatter until they were comfortably seated at a table in a small picturesque restaurant, which had not yet been listed in the foreign tour guides. It was the kind of place where the waiters were fat and friendly, not skinny and snobbish. Kon noticed a large Italian family celebrating some event at a nearby table, when the sounds of their lively conversation and good-natured laughter drifted over to where he and Geilla were seated. Kon closed his eyes, rested his chin on his hand, and sighed.

"Are you tired?" Geilla asked quickly.

"No, not at all," Kon answered slowly. "I am just absorbing the sounds of the language, and the smell of garlic in oil. This place is perfect, Geilla. You won't scold if I forget and put an elbow on the table will you?" he asked with a sheepish grin.

"Absolutely not," Geilla laughed. "The day is yours to do with as you wish!"

"I do feel it is mine, Geilla," he responded eagerly. "I could not believe how well the negotiations went this morning. The delegates agreed to my every suggestion." Again she saw his brief grin, but not the smile she longed for.

So they ordered wine, and toasted both the past and the future, and lingered long over their food; and Kon felt that all the glories of Rome surely could wait, while he feasted on the beauty of Geilla's smile. When at last Geilla suggested that if Kon wanted to see anything at all, they must go quickly while the light lasted, he agreed reluctantly. They hailed a cab and made a dash for the Colosseum. Dodging the small groups of hearty tourists, they moved about the structure, and climbed to various levels. Kon was excited to be surrounded by the living presence of history and would have been satisfied to see nothing else, but Geilla prodded him, and they moved on to see the ruins of the Roman Forum just as the light was fading.

Kon had been captivated by the horse drawn carriages he had seen passing, and although it was rapidly turning cold, he was eager to share the experience of riding in one with Geilla. Perhaps it was a hold-over from the time when he could not have afforded the pleasure, or perhaps it was the excuse he wanted to sit close to Geilla, and keep her tiny fingers warm in his broad hand. Whatever the reason, Geilla acquiesced and Kon requested a long drive.

"Ah, the lover's tour! I know it well!" the driver answered knowingly, and Kon laughed.

Hoping to stretch the day, Kon suggested they attend the opera, for he was a lover of music, and the passion of Italian opera was not lost on him. It was difficult, but not entirely impossible, to get tickets, if one was willing to pay the price, and Kon was willing. Lack of money had banished him from Geilla once, but he would never let it happen again. He had money now and, by God, he would show Geilla what a success he was. The performance of "La Tosca" was thrilling. By the end Geilla was in tears, and Kon was stirred by mixed emotions, remembering how his own love affairs had always ended in tragedy. Geilla knew the love duets had stirred Kon deeply, for he had held her hand throughout the performance and she had felt the intensity of his involvement. When he announced that late supper and floods of good wine were necessary to restore their battered feelings, Geilla quickly agreed. She chose the restaurant again, and this time selected a more elegant, and consequently a quieter one. They settled into a corner, and she tried to draw from Kon what his life had been like in Milan. He would tell her very little. She spoke of her marriage, but he really did not want to know the details of her life with Servio. However, when Geilla again told of the accidental death of her three-year-old son, he was very sympathetic. She was struck by his compassion which was in sharp contrast to Angelo's cold indifference. Lest Geilla give in to bitterness, Kon tried his best to cheer her, and told her of the many adventures of Albert and little Charles, both during the time he looked after them and later. She laughed freely and realized how attached he was to them. Perhaps in sharing their childhood he had captured a part of the joy and innocence he had been denied in his own youth.

Once again they were the last patrons to leave the establishment, and the proprietor smiled a benediction on them as he closed the door. What a lucky man to have such a beautiful young woman cling so amorously to his arm, he thought as they departed. Although the night had become wet and raw, they were foolishly oblivious of the weather. At last they came to Geilla's apartment and she invited Kon in for coffee. She removed her coat and hung it in the closet, and taking his overcoat and scarf, she hung them beside her own. Before she could turn and shut the door, he was close behind her, encircling her with his arms. Gently he ran his hands across her breasts and slid them down her sides. She drew in her breath excitedly as she felt his lips on her neck. "Geilla," he murmured. "I thought I would never feel alive again."

"Kon," she sighed, imparting beauty and strength to the name she had once bestowed on him in scorn.

"I thought you were lost to me forever," Kon said turning her towards him. "I thank God for sending you back to me!"

"I have never stopped thinking about you, Kon. During all those years . . . I wept a thousand times for what might have been."

He held her face between his hands, and gazed lovingly at her. "No more tears . . . ever again . . . I promise you," he whispered between kisses.

They held each other in a long passionate embrace. "Stay with me, Kon," she implored. "Don't ever go from me again!" And thus entreating him, she took his hands in her own, and led him to her bedroom. There they began to undress each other slowly, taking pleasure in revealing themselves to each other with confidence and trust. But as Geilla began to unbuckle his belt she felt Kon tense and hesitate. "What is wrong, my love?" she asked in dismay.

He took her hands from his waist. "I am a fool!" he blurted. "I did not anticipate . . ." She looked at him in confusion, until he gripped her hands. "Geilla, I would not curse you with my bastard child. I must go — now, before I lose my will." He turned from her, but she held him and smiled at his naivete.

"There is no need to go, Kon. I will prepare myself." He looked at her in surprise. He had always taken the responsibility of protecting Claire from the consequences of his ardor. Geilla felt a brief pang of guilt. "I am no longer seventeen, Kon."

He smiled, embarrassed that she had read his thoughts. "Forgive me," he said. "I have no right to ask perfection. In my dreams you have never changed, but there is no satisfaction in dreams. I loved you then, as a girl. I love you now as a woman." He embraced her and held her tightly to his chest. "Geilla, you are the one beautiful thing in my life!"

And so she prepared herself, and loved him all the more for his thoughtfulness and restraint. Again she compared him to Angelo, who in the heat of passion, would not have cared about the consequences. Kon's pent up longings for Geilla were like tinder that exploded into a fire of passion. He caressed her soft flesh as if her gentle roundness was the perfect complement to his own angularity. He reveled in the freedom of letting his emotions drive him, without the need to restrain himself, and gently coax a timid school girl. Geilla rapturously accepted him and matched his intensity. She molded herself to Kon and his very leanness aroused her. She felt as if there were no barriers of flesh to isolate her from his deepest feelings.

Afterwards as they lay together, Kon smiled a blissful smile of contentment, and it was as if years had been lifted from him. He is so enchanting when he smiles, Geilla thought. In the tranquility that follows passion, she ran her fingers caressingly over his scars, and inquired about each of them. He gave her only a brief description of the incidents that had caused them, and she kissed each mark in turn, as if to erase the cruelty and pain others had inflicted on his flesh. She wondered if her love were great enough to heal the scar Claire had left on him. Her tenderness and concern affected him deeply, but he hid his feelings. "If I had known you would kiss my scars, I would not have fought so vigorously," he said lightly. Then they slept, happily cradled in each other's arms, for it was almost dawn.

212

In the morning when Geilla awoke, she turned and reached for Kon, but he was gone. She rose from the bed, and seeing that his clothes were also gone, she slipped on a robe and went into the living room, calling his name softly. He was not there, but she smelled the aroma of freshly brewed coffee. She hurried through to the kitchen, and found Kon deftly slicing mushrooms into paper-thin slices.

"Kon, what on earth are you up to?" she asked in greeting.

He turned abruptly and smiled broadly. "Good morning, my love! Did you sleep well?" he inquired happily.

"Wonderfully!" she answered and put her arms around him. He kissed her hair.

"What are you doing in here, Kon?"

"I am getting ready," he said with mock solemnity, "to prepare you the most fantastic omelette you have ever eaten. Unless, of course, you have been to Milan and tasted Giovanni's work. I admit his eggs have a better texture than mine, but he does not have the skill to slice the mushrooms as thin."

She laughed at his remark for it was so unlike him to boast.

"Are you ready for coffee, my love?" he asked with a smile. "Yes I am, but you don't have to wait on me," she answered.

"Perhaps I do not have to, but I want to. It is something . . . something from myself!" he said seriously. "Yesterday the day was mine, and today it is yours," he concluded, handing her a cup of coffee, with just a touch of cream, for he had noticed how she liked it. She beamed at him and he smiled that special smile of his. Oh, God, what I wouldn't do to see that smile, she thought as she took the seat he held for her.

"Are you ready for your omelette?" he asked.

"Not yet," she answered dreamily. "Come, sit and drink coffee with me. Let me look at you, so I can believe you are really here. Tell me this is not all just a dream."

He poured himself coffee and sat across the table from her. Suddenly she noticed that he was wearing a different suit from the one he had worn last night. "Yes I went back to the hotel to shower and change my clothes," he admitted when she asked. "I have never acquired the ability to sleep late."

She studied him thoughtfully. She could see that the cut of this suit was slightly different from the other one, but it was the same shade of dark grey. She wondered just how tight a mold he was forced to live in, in order to work at a bank. She would never have guessed that the ragged, wild looking boy who had come to the theater in search of work would become a banker, and a very successful one at that.

So they drank coffee and talked, and delighted in each other's company, and at last he prepared the omelettes. Geilla knew that Kon had worked in the kitchen at the hotel, but she had never

213

guessed how well he could cook. She declared the omelette superb, and was touched that he had prepared it with his own hands. Angelo always sat while she cooked for him, and Servio would have sent a servant to do such a menial task.

After they had eaten, Kon agreed to let her help clean the few dishes. They made a game of it, laughing and stirring up soap bubbles, splashing one another with water, and chasing each other around the kitchen. They were perfectly spontaneous, and kissed and touched, and Kon was relaxed and could laugh. He did not have to hide any part of himself from Geilla – not even his scars. What freedom not to have to pretend that he had always been rich, and well-mannered, and successful.

When the dishes were done, Kon lifted Geilla off her feet and carried her into the bedroom, where they let the warmth of their laughter and mutual delight heat to passion. They expressed their feelings for each other by joining their bodies and uniting their hearts. All the pain of their long separation, and all the magnificence of Rome were forgotten in their bliss. At length after they had expended their energy, and slept again in each other's arms, Geilla remembered her promise to show Kon the wonders of Rome. He was content just to be with her, but he agreed to go wherever she chose to please her. So they dressed and went out. Although it was still chilly, the sun came out, as if drawn by their happy mood.

They began their journey at the Spanish Steps, walked southwest to Barcaccia Fountain, and then farther south to see the famous Trevi Fountain. At that point, Kon rebelled and declared that he would not go a single step farther unless they stopped for coffee, and Geilla consented. They found a suitable spot, and their coffee break expanded to include lunch. The day was passed seeing the sights, and stopping frequently for refreshments, for the weather had turned unusually cold. Although Kon actually saw very little of Rome, he felt that it was the most beautiful city in the world. Just being there with Geilla made it so.

They went to dinner early, and Geilla noticed that although Kon seemed happy and relaxed, he said very little. She would not have worried if she had known how busy he was, making plans to incorporate this wonderful dream with Geilla into his everyday life in Geneva. Certainly Kon was in a position to support a wife, but he doubted that he could match the affluence that Servio had provided for Geilla. Kon wondered if Geilla would be content to share his colorless life in the role of wife to a junior banker. Geilla was not the shy, self-effacing girl that Claire had been. Geilla seemed almost too brilliant to fit into his rather Spartan way of life. Perhaps she would help him to at last enjoy the fruits of his success; but he must not speak of these things yet, for he dared not risk losing her.

After dinner they went to a concert, and again Kon held Geilla's

214

hand throughout the performance. They returned to Geilla's apartment about 11 o'clock, and settled lazily onto one of the huge luxuriant sofas to sip wine and talk. Feeling relaxed in each other's company, they slipped off their shoes, and Kon threw his jacket and tie over the back of a chair. All day he had been close to Geilla, and they had talked and laughed as friends, but now he wanted more. He wanted to hold her in his arms, and feel her soft, sweet skin next to his. Gently he took the wine goblet from her hand, and set it on the table next to his own.

"There is no need for wine, Geilla. Your eyes alone excite me." She smiled and he took her in his arms. In a flush of desire, he opened his shirt, and began to unzip her dress. Suddenly he heard a voice behind him, and Geilla turned to stone in his arms.

"Playing little love games on the sofa are we? You certainly didn't waste much time after I left, Geilla!"

Kon drew back, and saw that Geilla's face was ashen.

"Angelo! I didn't expect you . . ." she stammered.

"Obviously not! How dare you bring another man here, you faithless witch!"

Kon stood abruptly, and stared mutely from Geilla to Angelo. Angelo carried a suitcase, and obviously he had a key to Geilla's apartment. Suddenly Kon was overcome with rage at being humiliated and betrayed. He turned to Geilla. "Fidelity never was your strong point, was it, Geilla?" he growled in disgust.

Geilla was shaking. Remembering the years she had cloistered herself in order to remain true to Servio, she was infuriated by Kon's remark. "How dare you say that to me!" she shrieked, and rising from the sofa like a fury, she slapped Kon's face with more force than she intended. Instantly Kon raised his hand, but he caught himself. Clenching his fist, he lowered it slowly to his side. It was not in him to strike a woman, no matter how he was provoked. Kon glared at Geilla, and for a moment he hated her for making a fool of him, but he could not sustain his anger. Even now his desire for her was unquenched. His heart was rent. It seemed clear to him that she had not left him for lack of money. She had never loved him. She didn't love him now. She wanted only to tease and torment him.

Geilla had regained control. "Forgive me, Kon! I didn't mean to . . ." she cried, but Kon turned away. Straightening his shirt hastily, he gathered the shreds of his shattered dignity, and addressed Angelo with studied formality. "My deepest apologies, sir. I was mistaken that the lady was free. I have taken that which is not mine." Immediately Kon snatched up his shoes and jacket and made for the door.

"Kon! Wait!" Geilla cried, but Kon ignored her. Tearing open the closet door, he pulled his coat forward so roughly that both the hanger and his scarf fell to the floor. Without stopping Kon whirled around and came face to face with Geilla.

215

"Kon, please don't go! I'm finished with Angelo. I . . ."

Kon glared at her, his eyes aflame with resentment. "I'm finished with you, Geilla. Find someone else to humiliate!" he said in such a low menacing growl that she backed away from him.

Kon raced out the door, flew down the stairs, and was in the lobby before he realized that he was holding his shoes in his hand. He threw his coat and suit jacket on the floor in a rage, and jammed his feet into his shoes. He yanked at the laces so furiously that one snapped in his hand, and he hurled it across the lobby. Kon took up his jacket and thrust his arms through the sleeves with angry jerking motions. He dashed towards the outer door, but the doorman, who had been observing Kon from just inside the door, caught his arm. "Your coat, Signore!"

Kon gave him a blank look. "What?"

"Don't forget your coat, Signore," the doorman repeated. He walked over and calmly picked up Kon's overcoat. He had seen Kon come in earlier, with Geilla on his arm, and had greeted Angelo as he came in later. The doorman was a keen observer of the habits of the tenants of the building, and he surmised what had happened in Geilla's apartment. Seeing the anguished look on Kon's face, he gently placed the coat over Kon's shoulders. "Women can be very fickle, Signore, but there are many others to choose from," he said and opened the door for Kon.

Kon looked at him. "I'll never trust a woman again!" he vowed and stormed out the door.

Immediately an icy gust of wind lashed at him, and he felt a cold drizzle on his face. He guessed that the temperature had dropped close to freezing. Turning his collar up, he plunged his hands into his pockets. Fingering his knife, he was doubly glad that the doorman had given him his coat.

Kon was furious and walked rapidly for blocks without any thought as to where he was going. How could she do this to me? he kept asking himself. How could she lie there beside me, and pretend she was happy, when all the while she was waiting for another man? I have got to be the greatest fool that ever walked God's earth! Damn! Damn! Damn her to hell!

It was several hours before Kon's anger faded, and a sense of emptiness assailed him. He had no idea how long he had been walking or what part of town he was in. Since he was unfamiliar with Rome, he determined to find a busier street and flag down a cab. As he walked he noticed that ice was forming on the pavement. He pulled his coat tighter, and cursed himself for having left his scarf in Geilla's apartment. Meeting her again had stirred so many memories and emotions his mind was in a turmoil. He had just begun to pull his life together again. Why did she have to show up and kick it apart?

216

CHAPTER SEVENTEEN

Kon was lost in dark thoughts when he came to the cross street. Two cars were approaching, and he waited for them to pass. As they came nearer, he noticed that the first car carried an embassy flag, but he could not identify it as it flashed past. As he watched, the car in the rear accelerated, and pulled alongside the first car. Then it moved to the right and crossed into the right lane. At first Kon thought the car had skidded on the wet pavement, but as he watched, he realized that the driver of the second car was deliberately trying to force the first car to the curb. He watched with growing interest as the second car pulled directly in front of the first, forcing it to stop abruptly.

As the two cars came to a halt, three men ran from the second car and approached the first. Kon saw them smash the side rear window, tear open the rear door, and pull the passenger from the car. The passenger began calling frantically for help. While the men who held the passenger started to haul him towards the second car, the driver of the first car jumped out, and began to struggle with them. As Kon approached the scene at a fast walk, he heard a blast, and saw the driver jerk backwards and fall. Remembering the embassy flag, he knew this incident was not connected to the Black Hand.

The passenger began to scream and struggle violently, and one of his assailants struck him savagely across the face. Kon could sense the victim's fear and helplessness, and his anger flared. He felt as if he was witnessing a reenactment of the attack by the gang. This time he was prepared.

With knife in hand, Kon charged at the man with the gun. Striking him from behind, he drove his blade into the man's kidneys, once, twice, three times in quick succession. The man screamed and dropped to his knees. Instantly Kon swung his blade into the man's chest. He fell at Kon's feet. Without pause, Kon leaped at one of the men holding the passenger, and drove his blade into the man's back. The man bellowed. He let go of the passenger and lunged at Kon. Kon dodged, and swung his knife upwards into the man's stomach. The man doubled over, and Kon stabbed him again. Kon shoved the man's body aside and it dropped silently to the street.

The terrified screams of the passenger rang in Kon's ears. He was about to go for the third man, when he heard a blast and felt a fiery stab in his right shoulder. Kon turned, and in the light from the street lamp, he had a clear view of the man who had shot him. Still clutching his knife, Kon staggered forward until he felt his ribs explode.

Kon heard the fourth man shout an order, but he could not make out the words. He tried to hurl his knife at the man, but his arm had lost its strength. The forth man stepped forward to fire at Kon, but lost his footing on the icy pavement just as he pulled the trigger. Kon saw a flash and felt his head snap back. He never heard his own final cry as he dropped in the street.

The man with the gun regained his balance, and looked around nervously. He barked some commands to the man holding the passenger, and together they began to drag the passenger towards the car. Overcome with terror, the passenger continued to scream and struggle. He could hear the faint wail of a siren and clung to the hope that some passing motorist had called the police.

He was right about the call, but it had come too late to help him. The man with the gun suddenly brought it down on the back of the passenger's head. He sank forwards and the kidnappers shoved him into the car. They sped away just as the police arrived.

The police surveyed the scene with professional curiosity. They found the body of the driver, who was wearing an official embassy uniform, and surmised that he had been killed while trying to defend his passenger. They found the bodies of the two kidnappers, and thought it strange that they had been stabbed rather than shot. And they found Kon.

"Hey! This guy's still alive!" an officer called as he rolled Kon over. "He's really bleeding! Look's like somebody tried to blow his brains out! I'll call for an ambulance."

Police Sergeant Trigilio came to look at Kon. He noticed that Kon's coat collar was turned up, and that his coat was sodden, as if he had been laying in the street much longer than the others.

"How come he's the only one wearing an overcoat?" he asked aloud. He found Kon's knife and wondered.

"Any I.D. on those two?" he asked the other officers as he began to unbutton Kon's coat.

"Nothing on either of them," the answer came back.

"Christ! Where's that ambulance? This guy's not going to make it if they don't hurry!" Sergeant Trigilio said as he saw the blood on Kon's suit. Hastily he went through Kon's pockets, and pulled out Kon's passport. "Says here he's a banker from Geneva. What the hell's he doing here? There's something funny about this guy. I can't figure where he fits into the picture. I want him alive until we can get some answers. Jesus! What's keeping that ambulance?" Sergeant Trigilio shouted and pressed his palm into Kon's bloody shoulder.

****

Charlotte was alarmed when the Italian Police called the next afternoon to check Peter's identity. They had traced Peter to his hotel, and thus to the financial conference and to Edgar. Charlotte told the police that Edgar was in London, and begged them to tell her what had happened to Peter. She was frantic when they informed her that he had been shot, and was under police guard at the hospital in Rome. Charlotte called Carlin and Francois immediately; but Francois was on holiday, so Carlin flew to Rome alone.

It was early evening by the time Carlin arrived at the hospital. When he identified himself, and asked for Peter, he was told to wait. In a few minutes a tall, harried-looking young man dressed in white came to meet with him.

"How do you do, Dr. La Monde? I am Dr. Garbolino," the man said warmly, and offered his hand to Carlin. Carlin shook it, and although he was anxious for news of Peter, he resigned himself to endure the social formalities.

"Please — come into my office where we can talk privately," Garbolino said, and led Carlin to a small partitioned enclosure that was overflowing with medical books, papers and files. "Not very spacious, but I am never here," Dr. Garbolino apologized. "This is so awkward, Dr. La Monde," he began hesitantly, "but may I see some identification."

Carlin was surprised, but complied. "Certainly," he said, and pulled out his passport.

Dr. Garbolino glanced at it briefly. "I am deeply sorry for this precaution, Dr. La Monde, but the police are guarding this particular man very carefully. No one has bothered to tell me if they are protecting us from him, or him from us, but we must comply with the regulations."

"I understand security measures," Carlin commented. "I just don't understand what the police want with Peter."

Dr. Garbolino sat back in his chair and surveyed Carlin for a moment. "What knowledge do you have of Signor Kononellos?" he asked at last.

"I have been Peter's personal physician for many years. What is his present condition?" Carlin asked anxiously.

"It is still critical," Dr. Garbolino answered. "He was shot three times, and has lost a lot of blood. He was very fortunate in that the bullets did not hit any vital organs. One bullet grazed the right temple, one cracked a rib, but did not penetrate the lung cavity, and one went through the right shoulder. The major complication is that while he was in surgery, he had an adverse reaction to the anesthetic, and suffered temporary heart failure. He's on the heart monitor, but we are having difficulty stabilizing his condition."

Carlin shook his head. "Peter is highly sensitive to drugs. Whatever I prescribe has to be low dosage of short duration."

"I'm pleased that you have come, Dr. La Monde. Frankly I welcome your experience with this patient." Dr. Garbolino leaned a little closer to Carlin. "The police are anxious for me to restore Signor Kononellos to consciousness, but I do not wish to take too great a risk."

"What do the police want from Signor Kononellos?" Carlin asked.

Dr. Garbolino sighed. "I really do not understand the details, Dr. La Monde. Apparently there have been several murders, and they think he is mixed up in it somehow."

"Peter? Involved in murder! That's preposterous! Who made such ridiculous accusations?"

"The police have been in and out of here all night. I'm afraid they found Signor Kononellos in the street along with several dead bodies."

Carlin's eyes grew wide in amazement and he shook his head. "There must be some terrible mistake," he gasped.

"I do not know, Doctor. You must talk to the police yourself. I will tell you one thing – this matter must be of some importance. A Mr. Bradley Cover-Rollins has come all the way from London to make inquiries."

"I don't know what to make of all this, but I would like to see Peter," Carlin answered.

"Certainly," Dr. Garbolino said, rising from his chair. "I see that in addition to being a patient, Signor Kononellos is a personal friend of yours."

"You are quite right. I have tried to be of assistance to Peter whenever I could."

"Come then. Perhaps he will respond to your presence."

Dr. Garbolino led Carlin from his office. They took an elevator to the third floor intensive care unit. A police officer was stationed outside the door, but fortunately he recognized Dr. Garbolino.

"This is Dr. Carlin La Monde," Dr. Garbolino told the officer. "He has arrived from Geneva to take charge of Signor Kononellos. I have checked his identification myself, so please do not hinder his access to his patient." Without pause Dr. Garbolino pushed open the door, and led Carlin inside.

Peter was still unconscious, and lay surrounded by equipment. Dr. Garbolino introduced Carlin to the nurse in attendance in the unit, and she left to attend another patient. Carlin studied Peter's chart, and then checked the bandages on Peter's head, shoulder, and ribs. At length he seemed satisfied that everything was being done properly. Carlin took Peter's hand and called to him. "Peter? Peter, it's Carlin. Can you hear me?"

Peter's head jerked slightly, and he turned towards Carlin. His eyelids fluttered, and his eyes half-opened. "Carlin?" he responded faintly.

"Yes, Peter, it's Carlin. You're going to be all right. Charlotte sent me to look after you."

Peter shook his head weakly, and looked distressed. The blips on the heart monitor increased in intensity, and became more rapid.

"Kidnapping!" Peter gasped. Carlin leaned closer to hear him. "Stop . . . kidnapping . . . get police . . . must stop kidnapping!" Then his eyes closed, and he was still once again.

"Peter? Peter? Can you hear me?" Carlin asked, and pressed Peter's hand. There was no response.

"What was he trying to say?" Dr. Garbolino asked.

"Something about a kidnapping. But he might be hallucinating from the drugs."

"It's possible, but under the circumstances I think you should talk to Mr. Cover-Rollins."

"Very well. I am curious as to what this is all about. However, I must put Peter's arm in a sling before he wakes again. He can be very stubborn about accepting treatment. I would also like to move him to a private room."

Dr. Garbolino nodded and went to speak to the nurse.

Carlin didn't learn much from Mr. Bradley Cover-Rollins. In fact, he was the one to supply most of the answers. Carlin was impressed, however, that the matter was of international importance, and that somehow Peter held a vital key.

It was approaching midnight before Peter again became aware. He felt a heightened sense of anxiety, but could not focus on the source. He rolled his head from side to side, and tried to sit up, before Carlin put a hand on his chest to restrain him.

"Lay still, Peter. It's Carlin," he said soothingly.

Peter jumped and Carlin got the impression that Peter didn't recognize him.

"Carlin?" Peter repeated numbly.

"Yes, Peter. How do you feel?"

"Feel?" Peter echoed weakly.

"Yes, how do you feel, Peter? Are you in pain?"

"My head hurts. Where am I, Carlin?"

"You're in the hospital – in Rome."

"Rome?"

"Yes, you came to a banking conference. Do you recall it?" Carlin asked casually, trying not to betray his mounting concern for Peter's memory.

"A conference?" Peter mumbled.

"Yes. You went, but you didn't come home after it ended. What happened, Peter?"

Peter was very slow in answering.

"The conference! Yes the conference . . . and afterwards I was walking . . . it was so cold . . . Oh my God, Carlin! Carlin, there was a kidnapping! I saw it," he gasped. "Three men dragged another man from a car and were beating him. He was screaming, Carlin! I couldn't allow it! I went to help . . . there was a shot. I jumped at the man with the gun . . . I stabbed him . . ." Peter's anxiety had increased as he talked, and suddenly he raised himself and seized Carlin by the arm.

"I killed him, Carlin!" Peter said, half choking on the words. "There was no one to stop me, and I killed him. It was terrible! The man kept screaming for help, but no one came. I tried to save him. I fought with the men, but . . . but there was an explosion in my head. My God! What have I done?" he asked in horror. "I've killed one man . . . and maybe another. God forgive me! . . . he just kept screaming!"

Carlin was shaken, but remained in control. "Calm yourself, Peter. Try to remember. Who were the men? What were you doing there?"

"I don't know. I think the man who was kidnapped was from some embassy."

Just then Dr. Garbolino came in. "Ah, your patient is finally awake. The police will be very anxious to talk to him."

"Must he talk to them immediately?" Carlin asked.

"I am afraid so," Dr. Garbolino answered wearily. "They have been hounding me all day."

"Very well," Carlin sighed, "but only briefly."

Carlin turned quickly to Peter. "You don't have to tell them anything, Peter. I will send for Francois."

Suddenly Police Sergeant Trigilio burst into the room, and pushed his way past Dr. Garbolino. "If you know what's good for you, you'll confess right now," he snapped impatiently, and pulled a tattered notebook from his pocket. "Why were you after that man? Where have they taken him?" And so the ordeal began, and Sergeant Trigilio assailed Peter mercilessly with questions.

Peter was guarded, but truthful in his answers, but the more he denied being in league with the kidnappers, the more Trigilio badgered him. Finally Peter lost his temper. "You stupid bastard!" he shouted. "Why don't you look for the kidnappers instead of harassing me?" He set his jaw and glared at Sergeant Trigilio, and all the threats Trigilio threw at him fell on deaf ears. At length Sergeant Trigilio gave up in defeat and left. Peter exhaled slowly and closed his eyes. "Why won't he believe me, Carlin? I swear I did not want to kill anyone."

Shortly after Sergeant Trigilio left, a nurse told Carlin that a man was waiting for him in the hall. Carlin went out, and Brad approached him about talking to Peter.

"Please, no more questions," Carlin pleaded. "He's very tired."

"I understand, but this is urgent. I'll try to be brief, but I need all the information I can get," Brad answered.

"Very well," Carlin assented. "I'll introduce you, but please don't upset him. He needs rest."

Carlin led Mr. Cover-Rollins into the room. Peter's eyes were closed, and Carlin thought perhaps he had fallen asleep.

"Peter?" he called tentatively. "There's someone here to see you."

Peter opened his eyes slowly.

"Peter, this is Mr. Bradley Cover-Rollins. He's come from London to investigate the kidnapping."

Peter turned his head away. "No more questions," he said weakly. "I have told all I know. I don't know who the men were. I am not working for them. I . . ."

Brad stepped closer to the bed. "Relax, Peter," he said in French. "I don't have many questions, but I need your help to locate the man who was kidnapped."

Peter turned towards Brad. "I swear I don't know where they took him or why. I never saw them before."

"Just relax and try to remember, Peter," Brad said softly and reached into his coat pocket. "I would like you to look at these pictures, and tell me if any of the faces seem familiar."

Peter looked distressed, but Brad held up the photos for him to see. Peter shook his head at the first three photos. "It's no use. I don't recognize any of these people. Carlin, please . . ." he called. "My head hurts. Have you nothing to help me?"

"Of course, Peter," Carlin answered. "I'll get you some tablets. Please hurry your questions, sir. He is not well," Carlin said to Brad as he left.

"I really am sorry to bother you, Peter," Brad said, "but a man is in grave danger. Do you recognize any of these photos?" he asked holding them up more quickly. Peter looked at the pictures and struggled to focus.

"Wait! Wait . . . that last one. May I see it again?"

"This one?" Brad said holding the picture closer to Peter.

"Yes. That's him! That's the man who shot me! There was a pain in my shoulder, and I turned. I looked directly at him."

"I see," Brad said in a noncommittal tone. "Do you recognize any of the others?" he continued, and held up the pictures again.

"That one! That's the man who was taken."

Brad silently gathered the pictures and put them back into his pocket.

"Peter," Brad began very quietly. "Why did you get involved with these people?"

Peter stared coldly at Brad. "I am not involved with them!" he declared in exasperation. "I told you, over and over . . . I saw what was happening and I tried to stop it. They were beating a man . . . three against one. I couldn't allow it!"

"And how did it come about that you just happened along at the right minute?" Brad asked.

"It was a coincidence. I was out walking. I wish to God I had taken some other turn!"

"Why were you walking in that part of town? No one had seen you at your hotel for a day and a half. Where were you all that time, Peter?"

Peter glared at Brad. "That is my private affair!" he answered, raising his voice.

"Peter, I am trying to help you remember." Brad said earnestly. "You must have some alibi for the police."

"It's none of their damn business!" Peter shouted.

"Peter, there were several telephone messages from Geilla waiting for you at the hotel," Brad continued patiently. "Who is she? Is she involved with the kidnappers?"

"Stay out of my private affairs! You hound me to death with your questions!" Peter snapped, and Brad concluded that he had hit a sensitive nerve.

"Peter, calm yourself. You must have an alibi for the police, or it will go very badly for you. You could be charged with murder. Tell me who Geilla is. What is your relation to her?"

"Get out! Leave me alone!" Peter roared. "No more questions! I can't bear it!"

Carlin returned to see Peter struggling frantically to get out of bed. Brad had a hold of his arm. "Peter! It's all right. Calm down," Carlin said, rushing to the bed. He put his hands on Peter's chest and gently pushed him down.

"I must insist that you leave, sir." Carlin said coolly to Brad.

"I will go," Brad answered quickly, "but I wish to speak to you again."

"Very well . . ." Carlin started, but Peter grabbed his lapel.

"Don't tell him anything, Carlin! Please! Nothing!" Peter begged anxiously.

Carlin gestured for Brad to leave, and Brad retreated silently.

"Relax, Peter. Just relax. He's gone."

"Don't tell him anything, Carlin! Please! She mustn't get involved — I can't trust her. She lies to me! What if she lies to the police?"

"Hush, hush, Peter. Calm down. What are you talking about? Who mustn't get involved?"

"Geilla! I was with Geilla! She made a fool of me. She lied to me. She never loved me. It wasn't the money! She never loved me. Never!"

"Calm down, Peter. You're upsetting yourself. Listen to me. I'm going to give you something to help you sleep."

Carlin pried Peter's fingers loose from his coat. He stepped away from the bed and got his bag. Quickly he prepared an injection and returned to the bed. "This is a very mild sedative, Peter . . . just enough to help you relax so you can sleep naturally," he said, expecting the usual argument from Peter. He was startled when Peter suddenly flung out his arm and pleaded, "Make it the full dose, Carlin! Make it an overdose. No one will ever know. It could be a natural mistake."

"Peter! What are you saying?"

"End it for me, Carlin! Please! No one will ever know."

"Peter, don't talk like that," Carlin said in dismay. He took Peter's arm, and gently slipped the needle into it. He discarded the syringe quickly, and taking Peter's hand he held it reassuringly, and stroked Peter's arm.

"You'll be all right. I will forbid any more questions. Just relax."

"My life is cursed, Carlin!" Peter whispered hoarsely. "Claire is dead! Geilla has betrayed me! The police think I am a murderer! End it for me, please — end it now!" Peter begged, and clutched at Carlin's wrist.

"Shh . . . shh, Peter, relax . . . relax. You're just overtired. You'll feel better when you wake up," Carlin said quietly.

"No! No! It's hopeless! It's hopeless! I can't bear it any longer! End it . . . end it, please," Peter continued to beseech Carlin until he lost consciousness.

Very gently Carlin folded Peter's arm across his chest. Carefully he pulled the covers over him, arranging the folds with painstaking precision. He brushed the hair from Peter's forehead, and then wiped his own eyes with his hand. A moment later Brad was at his side. "Dr. La Monde? Are you all right?"

Carlin shook his head slowly. "Life can be so unfair . . . so cruel. What lie can I tell him tomorrow to make it any easier?"

"I don't know," Brad sighed. "I am truly sorry I set him off. Sometimes I hate this bloody business! But come, you look like you could use a drink, and I still need to ask you some questions."

Carlin shook his head, and then reconsidered. "Well, maybe some coffee. It's Peter's trick to drown his troubles in alcohol, but it never really helps him."

"We'll make it coffee then. I think you can tell me all I need to know about Peter."

"Very well, but let me leave instructions with the nurse. He must be carefully tended in my absence."

Carlin was reluctant to leave Peter for long, so they chose a small restaurant near the hospital. After they ordered, Brad pulled out a small notebook.

"Did Peter mention to you where he went after the conference ended?" Brad began.

"Yes," Carlin answered slowly. "It is against my principles to betray a patient's confidence," Carlin answered, "but in this case I feel

I must, to spare Peter from more questioning. You cannot imagine what he has been through. I fear he is on the verge of a mental breakdown."

Brad sighed. "I am sorry to put him through this, but I must have an explanation for the police. They do not understand the international implications of this incident. Unless I can establish Peter's whereabouts he could be tried for kidnapping or for murder."

"It must not come to that," Carlin responded. "It would destroy him. Peter must never learn that I told you . . . he was with a woman named Geilla."

"I suspected as much. Do you know who she is?" Brad asked.

Carlin rested his head in his hand. "Yes," he said sadly. "She is someone Peter knew a long time ago. He was in love with her, but she married another man. It was a terrible blow to Peter. I thought he had forgotten her, but somehow, she has hurt him again."

"Do you know why she would be calling him now?"

Carlin shook his head. "Peter has not mentioned her for years. Perhaps he met her by accident."

"Do you have any idea how I might find her?"

Carlin sighed and sipped his coffee.

"Peter came to Rome for a financial conference. He is not an outgoing person. He must have met her through someone at the conference."

"I found the list of the delegates in Peter's hotel room, but there are hundreds of them, and they have all dispersed. Can you give me any clue to the ones Peter might have contacted?"

"I can't, but Edgar Marneé, the man Peter works for, would know."

"Where can I find Marneé?"

"He was in London, but he has no doubt heard about Peter, and returned to Geneva. Please . . . let me talk to Edgar first. Peter is more than an employee to him, and he will be very upset about Peter's difficulties."

"All right, but I am anxious to locate Geilla, and see if she can tell me anything about Peter."

"She may not cooperate," Carlin warned. "She must be a wicked, conniving woman. She has positively bewitched Peter, and has wreaked havoc with his life."

"She is my only lead. I have to check her out. I want to believe Peter's story, but there are several things that puzzle me. If he is indeed a Swiss banker, why does he carry a knife, and why was he so willing to risk his life for a total stranger?"

Carlin shook his head. "That's so like Peter. He was attacked as a boy, and he has carried a knife ever since. Edgar and I have tried to get him to put it aside, but he won't part with it. As for risking his life — Peter has tremendous compassion for anyone who is being victimized. This is not the first time he has come to someone's aid. He got into more than one scuffle at the university. Once he defended a foreign student from some bigots, and another time he saved a policeman from a group of angry students."

"I see," Brad replied. "I would like to talk to Peter again when he is calmer."

"That might be arranged, but please, never mention Geilla to him. I can assure you he won't tell you anything, and it only upsets him."

"I can see he does not like to volunteer information."

"You are quite right. I have been friends with Peter for over eight years and there are still many things he won't tell me."

"Well, let us hope this Geilla will fill in the details I need."

"Yes," Carlin said and rose to leave. "I will call Edgar first thing in the morning. I would like to get Peter back to Switzerland as soon as possible. Do you think you can arrange it with the police?"

"As soon as I can establish his whereabouts after the conference, he will be free to leave."

"Then I sincerely hope you can locate Geilla. One more thing — promise me you will not tell her where Peter is. I don't want her to interfere in Peter's life again."

"He is your patient, doctor. I will not go against what you advise."

After their meeting Carlin returned to the hospital, and Brad went back to his hotel to confer with his associates. He verified that Peter had positively identified the victim and one of the kidnappers. In the morning Carlin called Edgar, and gave him a detailed report on Peter's physical and mental health, as well as explaining his precarious legal situation. Edgar gave Carlin the names of several of the delegates that Peter would have met. Edgar also reluctantly agreed to search through Peter's private papers for a particular name and address, after Carlin convinced him that the information was essential to Peter's welfare.

Later in the morning when Peter awoke, he was very subdued, and Carlin thought that perhaps Peter did not recall his desperate pleas of the night before. When he talked to him, however, he realized that Peter was seriously depressed.

"I am sorry I spoke like a coward, Carlin, but the thought of being hung for murder does not appeal to me. I am at last convinced that Francois is right. I am nothing but trouble."

"Don't think like that! Francois has not said that in years!" Carlin objected heatedly.

"What's it like to be hung, Carlin? Is it like being strangled? I'm afraid I will not die well if they put a noose on my neck."

"Peter! Stop it! Do you hear me!" Carlin suddenly shouted. He took a hold of both of Peter's hands and pressed them. "No one is going to hang you! Do you understand? No one!"

"It doesn't matter, Carlin. I don't care anymore . . ."

"Well I do!" Carlin insisted. "And so do Charlotte and Edgar! We were very worried when you didn't come home after the conference."

Peter was silent for a moment. "What a disgrace I am to Charlotte. She will despise me when she learns what I have done. God help me! I never intended to kill anyone."

Peter turned his back to Carlin, and would not respond to any words of comfort. Carlin sat by the bed and hoped that he would soon hear from Edgar and from Mr. Cover-Rollins. After a long time Peter spoke, but he refused to look at Carlin. "Carlin, I have remembered something about the kidnapping. When the car passed, I saw the license plate. I can't remember all of it, but the first three numbers were 573. You must tell Mr. Cover-Rollins. He is the only one looking for the man who was taken."

"Excellent idea, Peter. I'll call right away!" Carlin said, and hurried from the room. Unfortunately, Brad was out so Carlin left a message.

"What time is it?" Peter asked when Carlin returned.

"It's almost 11:00 a.m."

Peter sighed. "Go and rest, Carlin. You don't have to guard me. I promise I won't do anything foolish while you are away."

"I'm not guarding you, Peter. I'm just trying to keep you company," Carlin answered gently. "It is very difficult to help a man who turns his back to you."

"I am sorry I disrupt your life," Peter said softly. "Please go eat and rest. I'll be here when you get back."

"All right, I'll go, since you are so anxious to get rid of me. Can I bring you anything? Are you hungry?"

Peter shook his head. "I'm not hungry . . . I suppose cognac is forbidden."

Carlin smiled. "Yes, but I will allow a little coffee if you would like."

Peter nodded and Carlin left. Once Carlin ordered his food, he discovered he was hungry, for he had not taken much time to eat since he arrived. As he was leaving the restaurant, he spotted some fruit filled pastries on the counter. He bought several kinds, hoping he could tempt Peter with one. In the past he had tackled Peter's black moods with stern authority, but Carlin sensed that sternness might push Peter over the edge this time. This time he would coax him back softly, gently like a wounded, wary creature.

While Carlin was tending Peter, Brad was busy trying to track down Geilla. Using the list of contacts Carlin had given him, he was able to trace Peter to Nadia d'Alessandro, and thus to Geilla. Nadia eagerly gave Brad Geilla's address and telephone number. She sensed a scandal in the making, and was piqued when Brad would not give her any information to satisfy her curiosity. He was careful not to mention Peter, but Nadia could not resist telling her tale of how Geilla and Peter had reacted upon meeting.

Pretending to be an insurance investigator for the international firm that Geilla worked for, Brad called upon Geilla. He worded his questions carefully, not telling Geilla that Peter was the one who was being investigated. Thinking she had to account for herself, Geilla gave Brad a complete itinerary, but discreetly omitted Peter's name from the conversation. When Brad had obtained enough facts to verify Peter's movements and activities, he slyly let slip that Peter was the one he was actually investigating.

Brad was surprised by how quickly and vigorously Geilla came to Peter's defense. She confessed the true emotional parting she had with Peter, and did her best to pry information about Peter's location and the nature of his troubles from Brad. Brad felt at a loss to judge whether or not Geilla really cared about Peter, but he could see that she could easily have convinced Peter that she loved him. Brad did not reveal that Peter had been hurt.

On the way out of Geilla's apartment building, Brad spoke to the doorman, who confirmed Geilla's story that Peter had left in an angry mood.

Putting together Geilla's story about when Peter had left, with the fact that Peter's overcoat had been completely sodden when he was found, Brad concluded that Peter had been exposed to the weather for several hours. Brad also knew that the route the car took after it left the embassy was chosen at the last minute. There was no way Peter could have been waiting at a pre-selected rendezvous. Having made up his mind that Peter's connection with the kidnappers was coincidental, Brad notified his superiors, who arranged with the Italian police to call off any further investigation of Peter. Brad called Carlin to inform him that Peter was free to leave Rome, and was pleased to learn that Peter had remembered part of the license plate number.

Carlin had made a great many telephone calls during the day, but Peter barely noticed when he came and went. He scarcely responded to Carlin's questions, and refused to take any food other than coffee. Around 6:00 p.m., Carlin noticed that Peter's wounds were causing him pain, and he coaxed Peter to take some capsules. Peter was so unresponsive he did not question what Carlin handed him. He swallowed the capsules and after a short while his eyelids became heavy and he felt dizzy.

"What have you done to me, Carlin?" Peter mumbled.

"Nothing drastic, Peter. The medicine sometimes makes people drowsy. Don't fight it. You need the rest."

Peter tried to voice an objection, but he nodded off before he could finish.

As soon as Carlin was satisfied that Peter was fully sedated, he stepped into the hall. The police guard had been removed earlier in the day, but another man was standing outside the door. He was in his late thirties, and his pleasant, round face was partially hidden by a short, dark beard. He looked up anxiously when Carlin approached.

"He's finally out," Carlin announced. "I hated to trick him, but it's better this way. He's too depressed to make decisions for himself."

"We will do our best to help him," the man responded.

"He needs care, but he's too upset over all these killings to face Charlotte right now. One word of disapproval and he will crumble."

"He'll see things differently when he gets away. He did the right thing to try to help that man."

"Come. Help me get him ready," Carlin said, and led the way into Peter's room. The man followed Carlin in, and together they transferred Peter onto a rolling stretcher, covered him, and strapped him down. Carlin gave the man Peter's suitcase and valise, which had been sent from the hotel.

"This should be enough to last him a few days. He really shouldn't be allowed out of bed very often," Carlin cautioned.

"We'll see that he behaves," the man assured Carlin.

"Good. Dr. Samuels will meet you when you arrive," Carlin said.

"Don't worry, Dr. La Monde. We'll take very good care of him."

"I hope Peter won't be too angry with me for doing this. We will all miss him, but I'm convinced it is the right thing to do."

"We'll do our best," the man repeated, and Carlin wheeled the stretcher out the door and down the hall. Carlin rode to the airport in the ambulance with Peter. He supervised transferring him to the private charter plane, and then stood by the stretcher, as if reluctant to send Peter away alone.

"Don't look so worried, Dr. La Monde. He'll be fine," the younger man assured him.

"I sincerely hope so," Carlin said sadly. Then turning abruptly he added, "You have my instructions. I shall be there in four days to check on his progress. Please watch him carefully."

"We'll do our best," the man answered warmly.

Carlin started to exit the plane then hesitated.

"Is there any other thing we should know?" the man asked quickly.

"It's just a minor thing," Carlin said hesitantly. "Don't feed him oatmeal. He won't eat it."

The man smiled. "I'll remember," he answered and put his hand on Carlin's shoulder. "He'll be fine. I promise. You'll see him in four days."

"Yes. Yes, of course. Thank you for coming for him," Carlin said and left.

As Carlin had predicted, Peter did not regain consciousness until the next morning. He awoke slowly and looked around him in confusion. This is not the hospital room, nor is it a prison cell, he thought. "Carlin?" he called several times. When there was no answer, he had the frightening thought that his memory had failed him, and that he was losing his mind. He searched the room carefully, trying desperately to find a single item he recognized. It was a pleasant sitting room, with long rich draperies at the windows, an ornate fireplace, and light colored paintings hanging on the walls. He was lying in a fold-out sofa bed.

Where was he? he kept asking himself. He put his hand to his head and felt the bandage. Yes, he remembered that. He struggled to sit up, and only then did he remember that his right arm was immobilized. He pushed himself up with his left arm and looked around. Suddenly he noticed a young girl standing by the door. She was wearing a yellow dress, and had matching ribbons in her long dark hair. Peter guessed that she was six or seven years old. She was staring at him with curiosity in her dark eyes, as if she had been watching him for a long time.

"What place is this?" Peter asked quietly in French. The girl did not answer, but turned and fled from the room.

"Papa! He wakes! Papa!" Peter heard her call in Italian.

Something strange has happened, he thought wildly. I must get up! I must defend myself! The knife – I must have my knife! No! No more killing! Peter was standing by the bed when the man who had taken him from the hospital burst into the room.

"No! No! You must not get up! Doctor's orders!" he said quickly in Italian, and rushed toward Peter.

Peter tried to step away, but the man caught his arm. "By God it's good to see you again, Kon! It's been a long time!" he said warmly.

Peter looked at the man in bewilderment. Slowly memory flooded back to him. "Mario?"

"Yes, Mario! Have I grown so fat you don't recognize me? Speak to me! Let me know you have a voice again!" the man shouted in his excitement.

Kon was suddenly overcome with emotion and could say nothing more than, "Mario! Mario! Dio mio Mario!"

Mario embraced Kon with exuberant affection. He could feel Kon's shoulders shaking, but he could not tell if Kon was sobbing or laughing. Indeed Kon could not decide how he felt. At last Mario released Kon and guided him back to bed. "Enough excitement! I promised Dr. La Monde I would not let you up." Kon clutched at Mario's arm as if he feared he might disappear.

"Carlin? You met Carlin? Where is he?"

"He flew back to Geneva after he put you on the plane to Zurich."

"But the police . . . ?"

"It's all been settled. Mr. Cover-Rollins has some very highly placed friends," Mario answered.

"But . . ." Kon started.

"No more worries, Kon! You are here! You need some food, and Tina and the children are anxious to talk to you."

"Tina!" Kon answered in dismay. He rubbed his hand over his unshaven chin. "I must shave and get dressed before . . ."

"Nonsense! This is not Geneva. This is a bit of Italy, and you are with family."

Before Kon could object, Mario had stacked several pillows behind him. Kon noticed that he was wearing his own pajamas. "Where did these come from?" he asked in wonder.

"They were in your suitcase. Mr. Cover-Rollins had it sent from the hotel in Rome."

"I see I can hide nothing from that man," Kon responded with irritation.

"Stop fretting! He is a busy man to act as your valet. He saved you from serious trouble, Kon. But enough of that, let me call Tina."

Mario stepped to the door and called aloud, "Tina! Nonna Louisa! Come! Kon is awake. Bring some coffee!" Mario waited by the door, and moments later Tina entered carrying a breakfast tray. Kon recognized her immediately. Aside from being a few pounds heavier, she hadn't changed a bit.

"It's good to see you again, Kon!" Tina said warmly. Taking Kon by the hand, she kissed him lightly on both cheeks. "How are you feeling?" she asked stroking his hair which was still matted with blood.

"Much better, Tina. So much better! I'm sorry I'm so disheveled. I don't usually come calling dressed like this," he added with slight embarrassment.

"Give it no thought. We are so happy to have you with us again," she said and squeezed his hand.

Peter did not remember that Mario and Tina had been in Geneva for his wedding. Learning of its cancellation, they had hurried to the hospital to see him. Unfortunately, Peter had been asleep every time they came, and they were forced to return to their family obligations without ever talking to him.

Tina went to the door and called, "Mama! Where are you hiding? Come and see Kon!"

A stooped, old woman, dressed in black came out of the kitchen. "Don't yell at me, daughter! I'm coming! Someone must stir the soup," she grumbled.

"Leave the soup, Mama. Come! Kon will fall asleep again before you see him." Tina took the woman by the arm and tried to hurry her along.

"What's the rush? He's not going anywhere. I've got all his socks soaking in the laundry tub."

"Mama!" Tina scolded, and then laughed. Nonna Louisa ambled slowly towards the fold-out bed. Kon recognized her, although she looked smaller and more shrunken than when she had sat with him in the truck on the way to Milan. She had always been kind to him. Indeed Louisa mothered everyone, and had insisted that Kon call her "Nonna" or "Grandma" as Tina's children did.

"Good morning, Nonna Louisa. How are you?" Kon asked and smiled.

"Ah, the Good Lord keeps my bones together for another day. But what of you, my son? My God how they have hurt you!" she said putting her wrinkled hand on his shoulder.

A sorrowful look crossed Kon's face. "It's nothing. I was a fool to be so careless," he said lightly.

Mario did not like the turn the conversation was taking and acted swiftly to change it. "Well, Nonna Louisa," he said jovially. "What do you think of our boy Kon? He's grown to be a famous banker and a gentleman," Mario bragged.

"No! No! hardly a famous banker! I'm barely more than a clerk," Kon corrected.

"That's not the story Dr. La Monde tells!" Mario countered.

Nonna Louisa studied Kon carefully, missing nothing as she scrutinized him with her wise, all-seeing eyes. She frowned.

"I see he's learned to keep the hair out of his eyes, and no longer chews his fingernails to the quick, but he's still too thin!" she announced at last.

Kon smiled sadly and shook his head. He knew he had been losing weight steadily since Claire's death. "I am cursed with the title of 'skinny'. Don't scold me for something I cannot change."

"Well, we will do our best to put some flesh on you while you are with us," Nonna Louisa answered. "But beware! Tina has done too good a job on Mario!" She laughed, and they all joined in, including Mario.

"Perhaps now that you have practiced on me, you will do a better job with Kon, and not put all the bulk on his middle," Mario said patting his ample stomach fondly.

And so Kon was settled with the family. Although Mario's fortune had improved over the years, he was still far from wealthy. His family had grown to include five children, and his modest house seemed to be continuously overflowing with the family and their friends. The older children did not remember Kon, but he quickly made friends with them. With the three older children home from school, and the two younger ones off for the holidays, there was always someone visiting Kon, bringing him food, or asking him to play cards. He was touched by their attention, and did not suspect that the children had been given strict orders that he was never to be left in the house alone.

Even the family dog took it upon himself to check on Kon. More than once he appeared in Kon's bed, to wake him from his dreams of violence. One night Mario came when he heard Kon call out in his restlessness. He brought some wine, and sat with Kon, trying to comfort him. Mario encouraged Kon to talk about the dreams, but Kon would say nothing. Mario thought it tragic, that a man who knew nine languages, could not express his deepest feelings in any of them. Although Kon was not able to give voice to his loneliness and despair, he was able to accept the family's love. Gradually it lessened his isolation, and helped heal his pain. He knew he could receive from these people, and not fear that they would present the tally sheet at some future time.

The rhythm of the house revolved around Tina and Mario's performance schedule. The family came to life only at late morning, and chaos reigned far into the night. Despite the fact that Mario and Tina were occasionally forced to go out for performances, the group spent a happy time gathered together. Nonna Louisa filled her days by cooking the specialty dishes and sweets the family loved, and even Kon, who was often indifferent about food, ate well. As might be expected, Mario and Tina's offspring were all talented musically, and many hours were devoted to family musicals. Though Kon did not play an instrument, he was an eager, appreciative listener.

When Carlin arrived as promised, he was given a gracious reception. He was pleased that Peter's wounds were healing well, and satisfied that he had made the right decision in sending Peter to relax among old friends. Carlin knew that as much as Peter loved and admired Charlotte, sometimes it was a strain for him to live up to her expectations. Peter missed seeing Charles and Albert, but he was relieved to know that his injuries had not caused the cancellation of their skiing holiday.

After the holidays, Peter returned to Geneva, full of determination to absorb himself in his work. He was disappointed that he was not fit enough to ski, and that Carlin had forbidden him to start running until his side had healed. He was in his office at the bank when he got a call from Carlin, asking him to join him for lunch. Peter was a bit surprised, for Carlin was usually quite busy during the day. Peter suspected that Carlin was checking on him. Carlin had been keeping close watch on him ever since he had returned from Zurich.

When Peter arrived at the designated restaurant, he was surprised to find that Carlin was not alone. He approached the table and Carlin had stood to greet him, before he recognized the man who was with Carlin. Peter hesitated, but it was too late to retreat.

"Peter, do you remember Mr. Cover-Rollins? He asked me to

arrange a meeting," Carlin said, taking Peter's hand.

"What am I accused of now?" Peter said coldly, and remained standing.

"Nothing, Peter," Brad assured him quickly. "Please, sit down. I need to talk with you."

"Let me have your coat," Carlin said quietly.

"I have nothing further to say to him, Carlin. Why did you plot to bring me here?" Peter said suspiciously.

"It is not a plot, Peter. Please, sit down before you attract attention," Carlin answered.

Peter glanced around quickly. Grudgingly he let Carlin take his coat and hang it on the rack.

"Thank you for coming, Peter," Brad began in a friendly tone. "I wanted to speak with you, but I felt it would be better if I was not seen at the bank."

Just then the waiter came to replenish their coffee, and Peter ordered whiskey.

"Peter, you shouldn't — not with the pills," Carlin cautioned.

"I'm off the pills, Carlin. It's time I had my life back!" Peter snapped. They sat in silence until the waiter had brought the whiskey.

"Peter, I wanted to tell you in person that we have located the man who was kidnapped. He is alive and well, and the men who staged the kidnapping are in custody."

"Really?" Peter said flatly.

"Yes. The man who was taken speaks very well of your bravery in trying to prevent the kidnapping. He is very appreciative of your help."

"So, I am now the hero, where before I was a murderer for slaying two men. I am sorry, but I cannot feel pride in something so shameful as killing!" Peter said bitterly, and tossed down the whiskey.

"It is not a matter to boast of, Peter," Brad continued calmly. "In my business I have learned that evil must be destroyed to protect the innocent. It is not a matter of pride, but of duty."

"Duty can be a heavy burden," Peter said thoughtfully. Then added more cheerfully, "but I am glad the man is returned. All was not in vain."

"I thought you would be more pleased to hear the news, Peter," Brad put in.

"I am pleased for the man, but . . . I prefer not to think about the incident."

"I'm sorry you feel that way. I came to ask your help. It would strengthen the case if you would be a witness at the trial."

"You mean in court . . . before all those people!" Peter asked in alarm.

"Yes, the trial has been set for early next month. Your testimony would seal the case against the kidnappers."

Peter remained silent as Brad continued. "The man who was kidnapped was with a Dutch trade mission. He was using Rome as a neutral ground to arrange some financing for a South African company. A group of Arab terrorists heard about the deal and thought that they could embarrass the Italian government into releasing some terrorists they are holding. You came walking into quite a tangled web, Peter. The Italian government was very anxious to keep the kidnapping quiet lest Italy get a bad reputation as an international meeting place."

"It all sounds incredibly complicated, and now you want me to become more involved," Peter answered.

"Your testimony would be very helpful, Peter," Brad said, and settled back in his chair. The waiter came to take their order. Peter would have been satisfied to have only another whiskey, but Carlin shot him such a disapproving look, he added soup to his order. Carlin was only partially mollified.

They sat and discussed the case, and in the end Peter agreed to testify. Perhaps there are weapons other than the knife with which to extract revenge, he reasoned.

CHAPTER EIGHTEEN

Less than a week later, Peter got a call from Brad notifying him that the kidnappers' defense lawyer had been informed that there was a witness who was willing to testify. Brad knew that Peter would now be in jeopardy, and wanted to take him into protective custody. Peter refused vehemently, declaring that he was not a criminal, and he would not hide like a craven dog. Brad had been powerless to change Peter's mind, and the conversation ended with Brad warning Peter to be extremely alert and cautious.

Peter stubbornly kept to his regular routine, and appeared at the bank every morning on schedule. He usually arrived at 7:00 a.m., long before the bank opened. It was his habit to wake early, and he preferred driving in before the traffic became heavy. He was in his car on Tuesday morning waiting at a traffic light. The traffic was still light, and he was third in line from the intersection. As he mentally reviewed his presentation for a meeting later in the morning, he noticed that the cars in front of him had begun to move.

He took his foot off the brake, and slipped the car into gear. Just as his car began to move forward, however, he felt a jolt as the car behind him rammed into the rear of his car. Peter heard metal crunching and glass breaking, and his car shot forward several feet. He regained control promptly, however, and brought it to a stop by the curb.

Looking into the rear-view mirror, Peter saw that the car behind him had been hit by the car behind it. He opened the door, got out, and looked back at the cars behind him. To his amazement Peter saw a vehicle two cars behind him, pull out of line and speed away. He noted that the front end of the car was smashed and the radiator was leaking. Damn! There goes the son of a bitch that caused this pile up, Peter thought. He tried to get the license number, but the car was gone too fast. Someone called the police, and the next hour was taken up with making sure no one had been hurt, and exchanging information with the other drivers.

Later in the morning, Peter went to a body shop to have the damage to his car appraised. As the mechanic finished writing his estimate, he came inside and approached Peter.

"Do you want to replace those windows now, or later? I'm not sure I can make them look like the result of the accident, but I can try," he told Peter.

"What windows?" Peter asked, thinking the mechanic was trying to pad the bill.

The mechanic looked up from his clip board with a peevish expression. "The side rear windows – the ones with the holes in them," he growled.

"What holes? What are you talking about?" Peter asked impatiently.

"The bullet holes! Don't tell me you didn't notice them?"

Peter's amazement was written on his face.

"Well, come out and look! How could you miss them? You've got a perfectly matched pair – in one side and out the other."

Peter followed the mechanic out, and walked around the car with him. "It's a good thing the bullet didn't hit about eight inches to the left or you wouldn't be standing here," the mechanic commented.

Peter suddenly felt his stomach turn acid, and start to gnaw itself. Those holes were not there when I left this morning, he thought.

"Replace the windows! Both of them! I'll pay any extra charge out of my pocket," Peter told the mechanic. Turning on his heel, he hurried inside and called a cab. Before he returned to the bank, however, Peter made one stop. He bought a knife to replace the one he had lost in Rome.

On Thursday Peter rented a car. He drove in at the usual time and parked across from the bank. He was standing next to the car, gathering up his briefcase, when suddenly he heard the persistent blaring of a car horn. Peter looked up to see a refuse truck bearing down on him at high speed. It seemed as if the truck was out of control, and would strike him before he could reach the curb. With only seconds to spare, Peter sprang onto the front hood of his car. He felt a jolt as the truck crashed into the side of his car, and he was thrown off the far edge. Peter was on his feet in time to see the truck speed away. He stared after it, trying to spot the license number, but the truck bore no plates. A moment later, a car that had been parked several car lengths behind Peter pulled away from the curb and raced after the truck. In a flash Peter realized that the incident had not been an accident.

Peter straightened his clothes, and retrieved his smashed briefcase from the street. Placing it on the hood, he removed the contents. Since the driver's side of the car had been thoroughly crushed, he opened the door on the passenger side, and threw the battered remains of his briefcase inside. Hoping that no one from the bank had seen what had happened, he crossed the street and entered the building. Edgar was not in yet, and there was not much activity in the lobby. Peter stopped at Mademoiselle Flambert's desk.

"Good morning, Monsieur Kononellos," she said cheerfully as always.

"Good morning, Mademoiselle Flambert," he answered a bit distractedly. "I have some pressing business this morning. I am not to be disturbed for about an hour."

"Yes, Monsieur Kononellos. Would you like me to bring your coffee?"

"Not now, Mademoiselle Flambert," he said aloud. It occurred to him that what he really wanted was a shot of whiskey to calm his nerves, but he rejected the idea. It would be too easy to let this one incident send him sliding downhill. He turned and went into his office. The rental company is not going to be happy about this, he thought, then spent the next half-hour making calls to arrange for having the car towed away. Peter sat for a few minutes trying to calm himself, but he could not relax. At the end of the hour, he buzzed Mademoiselle Flambert and asked her to please bring him some coffee. Mademoiselle Flambert was quick to oblige. She knew something was grievously amiss when Monsieur Kononellos did not take his morning coffee.

Peter stopped by Edgar's office later in the morning, and casually mentioned that the car he had rented had been the victim of a hit and run driver. Edgar questioned Peter repeatedly to assure himself that Peter had not been hurt, and then let the matter drop. He did not connect the incident with the fact that Peter was a crucial witness.

After three tense, watchful days, Peter received a mysterious telephone call at his apartment. The caller did not identify himself, but he indicated that he was watching Peter's every move. He spoke in crude Italian with a terrible guttural, rasping accent, that grated on Peter's nerves. The caller threatened that if Peter dared to appear at the trial, he would be slaughtered on the courthouse steps. Peter sat up all night. He was no coward in a face-to-face encounter, but how could he defend against a sneak attack? The following morning he made excuses when Edgar invited him to come home for dinner to visit with Charlotte and the boys. He dared not risk getting them involved in his problems.

That very morning Peter changed his routine. He made a list of all the taxi companies in the city, and never called the same one twice in a row. He began to place the calls under a fictitious name, and made the driver come and ask for him by that name. Peter watched constantly to see if he could detect whether anyone was following him. He rode taxis to various shops and restaurants, entered, and then slipped quietly out the rear door. The telephone threats continued.

Two mornings later Peter called a taxi to take him to work. He dared not drive his own car for fear it might have been tampered with. He decided to wait for the cab in the lobby of his apartment building. He went downstairs, and about ten minutes later he saw a cab pull up in front of the door. Stepping through the door, Peter hurried toward the cab. Suddenly something heavy crashed into him from behind. He was hurled to the pavement, and his head was forced down as he struggled to rise. He heard a blast followed by the sounds of glass shattering and tires screeching. Seconds later he was pulled to his feet. He found himself gazing up at a tall, extremely well-built young man with short blond hair.

"I am terribly sorry, Monsieur! Pardon my clumsiness!" the man apologized hastily in French. Peter's discerning ear detected a slight American accent in his pronunciation.

"Why don't you watch where you're going you clumsy bastard!" Peter shouted, brushing the dirt from the front of his coat. Peering around the wall of muscle in front of him, Peter saw that the plate glass doors of his apartment building had been shattered.

"What the hell . . . ?" he mumbled and took a step toward the door.

Instantly the driver of the cab was at his elbow. "Monsieur! Did you call for a cab? I cannot wait all morning."

"A thousand pardons, Monsieur!" the huge young man apologized again. "Please . . . let me pay for your cab," he said quickly, and thrust some bills into the cab driver's hand. He took Peter's arm and turned him toward the cab. Peter glanced over his shoulder at the shattered door. Abruptly he wrenched his arm free, and backed away from the cab. "I've changed my mind! I'll walk!" he snapped.

"But Monsieur! The fare!" the driver called, but Peter took off at a run.

Peter arrived at the bank overheated and disheveled. His uneasiness was not diminished when, at late morning, he received an unsigned telegram from London, advising him to be more cautious, and warning against going to work on foot. It must be from Cover-Rollins, he thought, but how could he know what had happened so quickly? What really had happened anyway? Was someone trying to scare me off, or had it been a kidnap attempt? How many people are watching me? he wondered.

Edgar noticed that Peter had become extremely nervous, and asked Carlin to have a talk with Peter. Carlin called Peter, but as usual, Peter would not tell him anything. Worried that Peter was succumbing to depression, Carlin went to the bank to see him. Peter almost ran to shake Carlin's hand when he came into his office, but his words contradicted his action.

"You should not have come here, Carlin!" he said excitedly.

"For heaven's sake why not, Peter? Don't I have the right to visit a friend?" Carlin answered in dismay.

"It's too dangerous!" Peter blurted.

"Why? Peter, what's wrong?"

Peter turned abruptly and paced across the room. "I'm being watched, Carlin. I didn't think they could find me so fast!"

"Peter! You must call Mr. Cover-Rollins. Make him honor his pledge of protection."

"No! I am not a child! I can take care of myself!" Peter declared stubbornly.

"Peter, you don't know these people. You can't deal with this alone. Please, I beg you! Get some help."

Peter paced around his desk twice, and Carlin hoped he was getting through. "I'll think about it, Carlin," Peter said at last. "Just stop hounding me!"

Carlin could see that the tension was wearing Peter down. "All right. I won't say any more, but please be careful."

"I will. I will. Please give my love to Charlotte and the boys. I can't risk going there until this thing is settled."

"That's probably the wisest course, but they miss you." Suddenly Carlin put his hand on Peter's shoulder. "If there's anything I can do, please call me. Good-bye, Peter."

"Good-bye, Carlin. Thank you for coming."

Peter thought long and hard about what Carlin had said, and finally realized that Carlin was right. He could not handle this situation alone. He had only the vaguest idea of who was after him. He checked the calendar on his desk, and rummaged in the drawer for his telephone list. Slipping out of the bank, he hurried to a small shop a few blocks away. He found the public telephone, and called the international operator. After a long wait, a familiar voice came on the line. "This is Giorgio Vittorini. Who asks for me?"

"Giorgio, it's Peter Kononellos."

"Peter! How good to hear from you. We got your letter. Thank you for remembering Carmella's birthday!"

"Giorgio," Peter began hesitantly. "I'm sorry to interrupt your visit with your family . . . I need help, Giorgio! No one here understands."

"Consider it done, Peter. Whatever it is!" The answer came back immediately.

"Thank you, Giorgio. I am deeply in your debt. This is what you must do."

Carefully Peter outlined his plan to Giorgio. Giorgio was promptly caught up in the craftiness of it, and added a few embellishments of his own. Peter added a cautionary note as their conversation ended.

"This is not sport, Giorgio. It could be dangerous. I will forgive you if you put your family before me."

"Nonsense, Peter, you are my friend, and I have much to thank you for. Forget the danger! I have not lived and worked in the shadow of the Sicilians all my life without learning a few tricks. I will come."

"Thank you Giorgio. I will not forget your loyalty."

Peter made one other call, then returned to his office. He hoped another strike would not come until his plans were in place.

On the following Saturday, Peter was in his apartment after another night of waiting and watching. He had hardly slept at all during the past week except for a few hours he had caught at his office. The telephone threats had become so loathsome, he had unplugged his phone to silence its incessant ringing. Those who were watching Peter, and there were several of them, had seen him enter his apartment building on Friday evening, but had not seen him come out again. The only signs of action at the apartment building were the usual Saturday activities of people coming and going from shopping, an occasional delivery of laundry, and someone coming to pick up a load of carpets for cleaning.

About 1:00 p.m., a delivery truck arrived from a local furniture shop. The driver went up to the door and buzzed one of the apartments. A few minutes later the truck driver and his assistant began to carry a large sofa into the building. They had some trouble getting it into the elevator, but when they stood it on one end, there was just enough room for it and the driver, who rode up to the floor above Peter's floor with it. The assistant, who was a tall man with huge shoulders and a belly to match, was forced to take the other elevator. He was the only person going up in the elevator. When the driver arrived at the desired floor, he flipped on the hold switch which effectively tied up one of the elevators in the building.

If anyone had been watching from the lobby it would have appeared that the driver and his assistant found it as difficult to get the sofa out of the elevator, as to get it into the elevator. Actually, the driver and his assistant had hurried down one flight of stairs and raced to Peter's apartment. Peter was waiting by the door and quickly let them in.

Immediately the tall man removed his cap and loose jacket to reveal the thick padding he had fastened over his shoulders and down his front. He quickly unfastened the padding, and Peter slipped into it. The driver buckled the shoulder and chest pads onto Peter. The assistant exchanged his work pants and shoes for Peter's dress clothes, and helped Peter into the coarse jacket. Next the assistant removed his fake mustache. The driver quickly produced a duplicate, and glued it in place on Peter. Peter placed the assistant's cap on his head, pulling the brim down in the front. The driver nodded his approval of the final effect, which disguised Peter's face, and made him appear about fifty pounds heavier.

As the three men left Peter's apartment, Peter locked the door behind them. They hurried up the stairs, and Peter helped remove the sofa from the elevator. Abandoning that prop in the hall, the driver and his new assistant rode down to the lobby in the elevator. Peter kept his head down, as he and the driver walked toward the waiting truck.

Shortly after they drove away, a tall, but bent old man with grey hair came weaving his way out of the building by the back door. He pulled a bottle from his coat, and looking quickly behind him, he put it to his lips. Stealthily he put the bottle back in his pocket, and walked slowly down the street, staggering as he went. Once he was out of sight of the apartment building, he hailed a cab and gave the driver the address of the furniture store that had sent the furniture truck.

Peter had discarded his mustache and padding, and was waiting with Giorgio, in Giorgio's truck, when the grey-haired man arrived. Forgetting to stagger or stoop, he dashed for the truck, and jumped in next to Peter. Giorgio started the engine and pulled away immediately.

"By God, Giorgio, we did it!" the grey-haired man shouted.

"That we did, Vito! That we did!" Giorgio answered excitedly. "Vito! May I present Peter, my good friend and benefactor," Giorgio continued, reaching over and thumping Peter on the back.

Peter could not help laughing from the sheer exhilaration of feeling free. "I owe you both a great deal for saving me from that wolf pack. How did you come to think of the mustache and all this padding, Giorgio?"

Giorgio laughed. "In my youth I fancied myself a singer, and spent one season carrying a spear at the opera. It was there I learned the art of disguise. Look how quickly Vito aged, and grew young again."

"What became of your musical career?" Peter asked.

Giorgio laughed again. "To my chagrin, my face was prettier than my singing, and I was always relegated to the chorus. One day I got bored with holding my spear forever upright, and the devil took hold of my mind. I was standing behind the soprano, as usual, when suddenly I had an unholy desire to know if all that bulk belonged to her, or her bustle. I steered the tip of my spear up behind her and gave a gentle inquisitive probe. Alas, she wore no bustle, and she let forth a shriek that echoed to the highest balcony. So ended my singing career!"

Peter roared with laughter as Giorgio finished his tale. "Giorgio, you are either the greatest rogue, or the greatest liar I have ever met. I am honored that a man of your broad experience counts me as a friend."

"Giorgio!" Vito laughed, "I can guess that it was not a spear that you used to poke the soprano!"

"Vito! You defame my good character!" Giorgio objected. "And in front of my friend, Peter. For shame!"

Peter laughed again.

"And look at you, Vito," Giorgio added, "you are always ready for a little sport, for your pants are open even now!"

"It is not from lust, but from necessity that I keep them open! You did not tell me that Peter was such a bean pole. I can't get this zipper closed to save myself. Even to sit down in these pants runs the risk that I will sing the high C myself!"

"Then I will stop immediately," Giorgio declared. "We cannot sacrifice a good baritone voice for the sake of a pair of pants!"

So Giorgio stopped the truck and the switch was made.

"Ah wait until we get to Naples, Peter! The three of us shall have a grand time. You will meet my brood, and Carmella will be delighted to show how beautiful she looks in her new frock."

Peter shook his head sadly. "I would truly love to meet your family, Giorgio, but I dare not put them at risk. I must stop in Milan."

"But, Peter," Giorgio objected quickly, "they are expecting you!"

Peter looked even more disappointed than Giorgio. "I am sorry, Giorgio, but I cannot go. I have asked too much of you already." He paused, and Giorgio nodded his head in resignation. "If you will have me," Peter began, "I promise to come another time. Sometime when I can relax and make a holiday."

Giorgio brightened. "That would be good. When the weather is warmer we can sit in the garden, and invite the neighbors."

"Yes, and I will play 'uncle' and bring presents for all the children," Peter added.

"Good! Good! It is set then for the spring, and I will tolerate no more excuses."

And so Giorgio told more tales, and they laughed all the way to the border. After they crossed into Italy, they stopped to eat, and Giorgio insisted that they have wine to celebrate. Peter had been strictly avoiding alcohol, in order to stay alert and watchful, but the taste of it appealed to him now, and the wine flowed freely at dinner. The wine relaxed Peter enough for him to realize how exhausted he was. Even as he left the restaurant, he began to stagger and sway.

Ignoring Peter's repeated protests that he was all right and could manage on his own, Giorgio and Vito helped him to the truck. They rolled him in some old blankets Giorgio kept for those times when he grew too tired to drive, and laid him in the back of the truck. Despite the bumping and rocking, Peter immediately fell into the first good sleep he had had in ten days.

"Ah, Vito," Giorgio said gesturing towards Peter. "It pains my heart to see a man with Peter's education and money driven to sleep in a truck with only empty orange crates for companions."

"Has he no family, or friends to help him?" Vito inquired.

"There are a few who care about him, but they would make him a Swiss, and he has too much fire in him. So we must look after him, and make him laugh to forget his troubles."

It was dark by the time they reached the outskirts of Milan. Giorgio stopped the truck and went around to the back. He pulled on the lever to raise the metal door, and even as it rattled and scraped open, he could hear the sound of crates crashing and falling. Giorgio turned on his flashlight, and directed the beam into the truck.

"Don't come any closer!" he heard Peter warn.

"You're safe, Peter. It's Giorgio! We've reached Milan."

Giorgio slowly played the beam of light along the sides of the truck until he spotted Peter, wedged between the stacks of crates. Peter's legs were still tangled in the blankets, but his knife was drawn and ready. He had a wild, alley cat with his back up look about him.

"Peter, it's Giorgio Vittorini! You're in my truck. You fell asleep," Giorgio called quickly, and lowered the light.

"Giorgio?" Peter gasped. "Why did you tie me?"

"I didn't tie you. We rolled you in some blankets to keep you from freezing to death back here."

Giorgio heard Peter let his breath out, and watched him sag back against the crates.

"Don't ever startle me like that again, Giorgio. I nearly lost my wits when I heard that door go up."

"I'm sorry, Peter," Giorgio said, scrambling into the truck. "Are you all right?"

"Yes," Peter answered a bit uncertainly.

While Peter fumbled to free himself from the blankets, Giorgio rummaged among the crates, and uncovered a rusty tool box. Opening it, he pulled out a bottle, removed the cap, and passed the bottle to Peter. "Don't tell Vito . . . I think you need a jump start to get your heart going, Peter."

Peter took the bottle, sniffed it, and grinned slyly. "A man needs a little anti-freeze in his blood sometimes," Peter commented and took a swig. "You're a good man, Vittorini," Peter said, handing Giorgio the bottle.

Giorgio took a quick swallow and recapped the bottle. "It gets cold and lonely in the mountains, Peter. A man must be ready for anything." He put the bottle back in the tool box, and put his finger to his lips. "Come, show me how to find your friend."

Peter followed Giorgio out of the truck, and climbed into the cab next to Vito. Vito glanced at him as he closed the door.

"Well, are you set for 30 below, Peter?" he asked knowingly.

Peter laughed a throaty laugh. "I'm set, Vito! I'm set!"

Vito turned to Giorgio. "You sneaky son of a bitch, how come I never get a taste from your private stock?"

Giorgio rapped Vito lightly on the arm.

"Be quiet, Vito! Peter's been freezing his ass off for hours back there! Wait till we get to Naples, then I'll quench your thirst!"

"You heard his promise, Peter. I'll hold him to it too."

245

Peter gave directions, and shortly they pulled up in front of a small restaurant. A sign carefully taped to the door read, "Closed."

"Perhaps it would be better to go in the rear door. Can you find an alleyway?" Peter asked.

"We will look," Giorgio answered. "Does your friend know you are coming?"

"Yes. He knows I hoped to come today."

Giorgio found the alley and parked the truck a half block from the restaurant.

"I will wait until I see that you have found your friend," Giorgio announced as Peter got out.

"Thank you, Giorgio. Don't leave until I signal," Peter answered. Peter crept up to the door and rapped softly. When there was no response, he rapped again, and immediately the door was pushed open. Peter stood staring at a burly man in his mid-sixties. The man gaped back at Peter for almost a minute before recognition lit his face. "Kon? By God is that you? I did not expect you at the back door!"

"It's good to see you, Giovanni," Peter said slowly.

Suddenly Giovanni flung his arms around Kon and pulled him against his chest. He hugged Kon warmly, and then shoved him out to arm's length to look at him again. Noticing the scar on Kon's temple he frowned. "Who has done this to you?" he shouted touching the place where the bullet had left its mark. "I sent you to a good family, and look how you return to me! What has happened? Have you lied to me about your success?"

"No! I'm fine! Stop fussing, Giovanni. It's an old wound."

"Old wound, he says! What? All of three weeks? Mother of God, boy, are you in trouble with the police?"

"No! I just need a place to stay for a while," Kon answered, growing impatient.

Giovanni shook his head. "Well, come then, and we will eat," he said gruffly.

"I must signal my friends first," Kon said.

"You brought someone with you?"

"I got a ride with some friends."

"And you make them wait in the cold? Have the Swiss taught you no manners? Why didn't you bring them in?"

"It is not my place to offer hospitality when I come asking help," Kon said defensively.

"You are no beggar at my table, Kon. Call them in!"

Kon went to the door and waved to Giorgio and Vito, beckoning them to come in. He made brief introductions, mentioning that Giorgio and Vito were from Naples.

"Come, we eat now," Giovanni said by way of welcome.

Giorgio and Vito looked a bit hesitant. "We don't mean to

trouble you. We ate a while ago."

Giovanni stared at them. "I cannot say what the custom is in Naples, but there is no shortage of food at Giovanni's table for any friends of Kon."

Giorgio smiled. "We accept the honor – to celebrate a successful adventure!"

"Good! Good! Let's move out to the dining room," Giovanni said, ushering Kon and his guests out of the kitchen.

"Lucia! We are ready to eat!" Giovanni called over his shoulder to an attractive middle-aged woman who was working in the kitchen.

"Yes! Yes! It comes," she said good-naturedly to the men's backs. She smiled and nodded to Kon when he glanced back at her.

So the men sat and ate a meal fit for any dodge in his palace. And though Lucia served the meal, Kon knew that Giovanni had cooked it himself. Giovanni is truly a master of his craft. He is wasted in this simple eatery, Kon thought as he ate. Kon said little during the meal, but Giovanni watched his face and his plate. He knew his talent was displayed before a knowledgeable judge.

After the meal, the men settled back in their chairs, and Kon waited in anticipation for the carefully orchestrated bragging to begin. Although bragging was not his game, he was curious as to how Giovanni would fare against the combined efforts of Giorgio and Vito. Kon had barely refilled his glass when he was rudely put out of the game.

"Kon, go help Lucia clean the plates!" Giovanni ordered as if on a whim.

Kon shot him an offended look.

"What are you waiting for? Did you think you could accept my hospitality and give nothing in return? Have you become too good to do honest work?"

Kon looked annoyed, but he bit his tongue, and took up the empty plates. Lucia welcomed him in the kitchen, and immediately began to ask him questions about his life in Switzerland. She seems to know a great deal about me, Kon thought. He discovered that Lucia had such a friendly, cheerful nature, that he felt at ease with her, and quickly forgot his irritation. She noted that Kon addressed her respectfully, as few younger men did anymore, and he would not let her lift the heavy pots. Kon rolled up his sleeves, and dove into the soapy water with no complaints, but she saw that his hands were not used to such rough work.

After Kon left, Giovanni leaned back in his chair. Giorgio studied him slowly, craftily. "You have a nice business, Giovanni. You are a lucky man."

Giovanni smiled with self-satisfaction. "I am a lucky man indeed. The boy arranged the loan for me. He is clever with figures. Somehow he made it look as though I could afford this place!"

"It is good to have a banker for a friend," Giorgio answered.

Giovanni suddenly leaned towards the truckers. "Tell me of the boy. He is truly a banker, or is he involved in some crooked business?" he demanded, lowering his voice.

"Of course he's a banker!" Giorgio exclaimed with indignation.

Giovanni looked perturbed. "I can't speak of Switzerland, but in Milan a banker wears an expensive suit, and a fine tailored shirt. Why does Kon come so poorly dressed?"

Giorgio laughed. "His dress is only a disguise to help him escape. He has many beautiful suits."

Giovanni seemed only partially satisfied. "And what of this Swiss family he writes to me about? Have you met them?"

"Yes, I have met the banker and his wife. They think well of Peter, and treat him like a son. I have also seen another well-dressed man and his wife, who came all the way from Zurich, when Peter was in the hospital," Giorgio bragged.

"You lie! When was Kon in the hospital?" Giovanni asked raising his voice.

"I am no liar," Giorgio answered heatedly. "They took him to the hospital after the accident. I rode in the ambulance with him myself!"

"What accident? He told me nothing of an accident!"

"I see he tells you nothing! He was in a car accident the very day his wedding was canceled. I know, because it was I who smashed his car."

"You smashed his car, and he calls you a friend! Has he gone mad?"

"It was an accident! He was overcome by grief for his lost bride. He ran a red light and I hit his car. He did not take it amiss. Why do you find fault with me now?"

Giovanni pounded the table with his fist. "That boy would not tell a priest his sins! I will wring the truth from him." Giovanni suddenly bellowed, "Kon! Get in here!"

Kon came out of the kitchen wiping his hands on a towel, and stood silently before Giovanni.

"When were you in the auto accident?" Giovanni demanded.

Kon was startled. He looked at the three men sitting at the table. "Last spring," he answered quietly.

"Why did you hide it from me?"

"I didn't hide it! I guess I forgot to tell you. I had some trouble with my memory."

Giovanni was not satisfied with Kon's answer. "How could you forget to tell me such a serious thing?" he shouted.

"Damn it, Giovanni, I just forgot!" Kon shouted back. "Some days I could hardly remember who I was. What does it matter now?"

"It matters because I think you lie to me. Why must you disguise yourself, and sneak out of your own home? Why do you run all the way to Milan? What kind of filth are you involved in, Kon?"

Kon glared at him. He had planned to tell Giovanni about the terrorists, and ask his advice, in his own good time; but not like this.

"How dare you call me a liar!" Kon roared. "I came here seeking help. If I wanted to be questioned and accused, I would have gone to the police. I will not be treated like a criminal! I am sorry I disturbed you. I will have more privacy at a hotel!" Kon turned and stormed into the kitchen.

"Kon!" Giovanni called after him, but he did not stop.

Giovanni sat looking stunned, but Giorgio leaped from his chair and flew after Kon. He caught his arm before he reached the door.

"Peter! Don't be a fool! Where will you go?"

"Take your hands off me!" Kon growled. "You're as bad as he is, sitting there like an old crone telling tales about me. I should never have trusted you!"

Kon jerked his arm, and Giorgio released him without a word. Kon stepped towards the door, but as he tried to open it, Giorgio jumped him from behind. Throwing his left arm around Kon's neck, he seized Kon's right arm and twisted it behind Kon's back. Immediately he took his arm from Kon's neck and jammed the palm of his left hand into Kon's right shoulder, at the place where the bullet had entered. Kon cried out and fell against the door.

"Do you think I don't know that you've been hurt, and that someone is trying to kill you?" Giorgio hissed into Kon's ear. "Giovanni asks questions because he needs to know what you are going up against."

Before Kon could answer, Lucia came rushing up. "Let him go, please!" she begged.

"He drives me to it!" Giorgio shot back at her. "It's the only way I can make him stop and listen."

"Don't hurt him, please. He is a guest here."

Giorgio let go of Kon and watched him clutch his right arm, pulling it against his body. "Who told you I had been shot?" Kon demanded.

"No one," Giorgio snapped back. "I saw you were hurt when you tried to lift the sofa. When does a right handed man lift with his left arm?"

Lucia put her hand to Kon's cheek. "Don't leave in anger, Kon, please! You will break the old man's heart. He spoke of nothing but your coming for three days . . . please."

"If he is so eager to have me come, why does he treat me so poorly? Why must he know all my business?"

Lucia stepped closer to Kon, and put her hand on his sore shoulder. "Because he cares for you. He brags about you constantly."

"He has a poor way of showing it, to send me to the kitchen like a dog, in front of my friends — or the men I thought were my friends."

"It is just his way. He worries about you, Kon, although he tries not to care."

Kon made no answer, and Lucia stepped closer, and whispered in his ear. "Giovanni lost two sons to the Sicilians, Kon. He always hoped for a better life for you. He tried to keep you away from the drugs, and the killing when you were a boy. It scares him to see you running from trouble now."

"How do you know all this?" Kon whispered to Lucia.

"A man reveals more to his wife than he knows, Kon."

"His wife! Dio mio! He never mentioned a wife!"

Lucia smiled. "Like you, he does not tell all his business. Please, open your heart, and apologize."

"Why must I apologize? He's the one who called me a liar!" Kon said aloud.

"Because you are the younger man and can bend. It is the old way. Please. . . do it for my sake," she implored.

"She is right," Giorgio added quickly. "You must be the one to apologize. It need be only a gesture."

"Oh, all right! I'll do it," Kon agreed. He thought over all the eloquent, formal phrases that Charlotte had ever taught him, and dismissed them as inappropriate. This had to come from his heart. Kon straightened himself, and headed for the dining room. He stood before Giovanni, who looked at him expectantly. "I . . ." Kon stammered and stopped. He lowered his head, then raised it, and looked Giovanni in the eye.

"The food here is very good. I could not find its equal at any hotel."

Giovanni smiled, and motioned for Kon to sit. "Next time I won't make the food so hot. It ruins your disposition."

250

CHAPTER NINETEEN

Carlin tried all day Sunday without success to reach Peter by telephone. Becoming anxious for Peter, he called Edgar, and together they went to Peter's apartment building. When they could not gain access to Peter's apartment, they buzzed the manager and voiced their concern. The manager had met Edgar during the past summer, when Edgar had made one of his frequent visits to check on Peter. The manager knew that Edgar's concern for Peter was genuine, and he agreed to let Edgar and Carlin into Peter's apartment.

The apartment was empty; and aside from the telephone, which had been unplugged, all of Peter's belongings, including his suitcase and valise, were in order. The manager re-locked the door as they left, and Carlin took Edgar home with him. He immediately put in a call to Mr. Cover-Rollins.

"What!" resounded over the line from London when Brad heard the news. "But my men have been watching him day and night! We'll start a search immediately."

Monday morning, before Edgar left for the bank, a young man arrived at the Marneé residence by car. Stealthily he placed an envelope by the door, rang the bell, and departed as mysteriously as he had come. By the time the maid got to the door, the man was gone. The envelope was addressed to Charlotte, and the maid took it in to her. Charlotte recognized Peter's strong, precise hand, and tore open the envelope. Inside she found a brief message from Peter stating that he was well, and had left town of his own accord.

"Really, Peter!" she declared in vexation. "This is quite inadequate." Nevertheless she was glad to have the note, and shared it with her equally anxious husband.

"Did Peter honestly think this brief note would prevent us from worrying?" Edgar said in exasperation after he read the message.

Charlotte shook her head and smiled. "I believe my lectures are having some effect, Edgar. I can remember when Peter would not have told us even this much."

Jack, too, was relieved when he learned that Peter had not been abducted, for Brad had come down hard on him and Paul for not keeping closer tabs on Peter.

"I didn't think he had it in him to escape," Jack told Brad defensively when he put in a call to London.

"Well now you know! Get on his trail immediately. I want Kononellos alive, in Rome, in two weeks!" Brad ordered.

"We'll find him," Jack promised confidently.

Jack hung up the phone, and went back to the hotel to break the news to Paul. Paul could tell by the look on Jack's face as he burst through the door that he was in a foul mood.

"What's up?" Paul asked in his usual imperturbable manner, after Jack hurled his coat onto a chair.

"Brad's annoyed with us!" Jack exclaimed. "Kononellos wasn't kidnapped! That skinny little shit gave us the slip!"

"Damn! We'd better find him fast!" Paul said shaking his head.

"I wish Brad would just come out and say 'You screwed things up'!" Jack said smacking his fist into his palm. "His blasted diplomatic innuendos cut deeper than any ass-kicking I ever got from a drill sergeant. I hate it when he says he's 'annoyed' with me."

"I know. He's dressed me down with a few expressions no one in Chicago would even recognize as an insult. Hey, relax. It's my fault. I should have realized that Kononellos would make a run for it."

Jack and Paul made inquiries at the apartment building, and learned that the sofa delivery had been faked, but Peter's trail went dead at the furniture store. Brad was not pleased.

Two weeks later, Brad was surprised to receive a telephone call from Peter. He was ready to testify. Brad named the meeting place and Peter agreed to appear in two days. Brad didn't ask Peter how he was, or where he had been. He suspected that one incautious word would cause Peter to clam up or bolt.

Peter was at the meeting place well before the appointed time. For twenty minutes, he stood across the street from the hotel, watching the door. When he didn't spot Brad, he decided to go in and wait. The hotel's spacious lobby had a lofty ceiling from which hung two huge crystal chandeliers. There was an ample selection of chairs and couches with marshmallow soft cushions in the room, but Peter chose to stand against the wall to the left of the door. From there he had a clear view of the front door, the bank of elevators directly across from the door, and the registration desk to the right of the door. He could also see into the bar to the left of the front door, and watch the passageway to the right of the elevators. By 10:40 a.m. the lobby was almost empty.

Peter felt tense and clutched his knife in his hand. He did not like surrendering his safety to a stranger. He wished he had been able to learn more about the elusive Mr. Cover-Rollins before coming to Rome, but none of Giovanni's sources had been able to help him. Peter wanted to believe that Brad was what he claimed to be, but Giovanni had told him so many tales of deceit and betrayal in the Brotherhood that he was skeptical.

At 10:43 the elevator doors opened and Peter saw Brad and another man step out. Peter picked up the small suitcase he had brought with him, and began to move toward Brad. Suddenly Peter recognized the man who was following Brad. It was the same tall, muscular American with blond hair that had knocked him down in Geneva. Peter cautiously edged towards the front door as Brad walked to the middle of the lobby. Brad was scanning the lobby for Peter and saw him to his left. As Brad strode forwards, Peter saw the American reach into his coat.

"Look out!" Peter yelled to Brad, and sprang forwards. He shoved Brad aside, and lunged at the American with his knife open. Before the blade struck, however, a slender, dark-haired, man appeared from nowhere, and deftly kicked the blade from Peter's hand. Peter was startled, but quickly spun to his left and rammed the American in the stomach with his left elbow.

"Run, you fool!" Peter screamed at Brad, who had stopped and turned.

The American seemed to absorb the blow with no apparent ill effect, and instantly brought his fist up under Peter's chin. Brad heard Peter's teeth snap together from the impact, and saw him reel backwards.

"Peter! Calm down! Jack works for me!" Brad shouted, but Peter ignored him. He regained his balance, and tried to kick Jack, but the dark-haired man grabbed him from behind. Peter began to struggle and twist so violently, that Brad feared he would break his own arm trying to escape from Paul's grip.

"Peter! Take it easy! These men work for me," Brad called again.

Peter turned towards Brad with a shocked looked on his face. "You set me up, you lying son of a bitch!" Peter roared. "I should never have trusted you! Jesus Christ! A set up and I walked right into it! God Damn!" Peter screamed in frustration. Brad noticed that people were beginning to come out of the bar and stare.

"It's not a set up, Peter. We're trying to protect you," Brad said, taking Peter by the arm; but Peter was wild with a combination of fear and rage. "I'll get you for this!" he screamed at Brad. "I swear I'll get you for this!"

"Take him down, Paul, before he creates an even bigger scene," Brad said quietly. Swiftly he snatched Peter's knife from the floor, and hurried to the registration desk. He grabbed the phone seconds before the desk clerk could put his hands on it.

"Police!" Brad declared, flashing a badge before the clerk's startled face. "We'll take him away quietly."

"But I must call the manager!" the clerk objected excitedly.

"Don't make a scandal for him. His wife has no idea what he's involved in. Just keep it quiet. We'll take him out," Brad said, as if revealing a confidence.

The clerk looked confused. "What's he involved in?" he asked with morbid interest.

"Embezzlement. He came to turn himself in, but he panicked at the last minute. Pretend it never happened. Publicity would ruin his family."

The clerk nodded his head knowingly. "All right, but get him out of here!"

Brad turned away from the clerk just in time to see Jack and Paul haul Peter down the passageway that led to the rear door. Brad picked up Peter's suitcase, which was lying abandoned in the middle of the lobby, and hurried after them.

"I'm sorry, Brad. I had to really clobber him," Paul apologized, as they loaded Peter into the back seat of the car. "He was struggling so violently I was afraid I might break his neck if I tried to use a head lock."

"It's O.K.," Brad answered, getting into the driver's seat. "We had to get him out of there. He went absolutely berserk when he saw Jack."

"Yeah. I think he recognized me, and figured we were all after him," Jack commented as Brad started the car. "He sure knows how to fight! I thought you said he was a banker."

"He is," Brad answered.

"Well what the hell was he before he became a banker?" Jack asked. "You don't learn to fight like that in any posh men's club."

"That's the strange thing about him, Jack," Brad answered glancing over his shoulder as he drove. "I can't find any record of him until he showed up in Geneva. No birth certificate, no school records, no work papers . . . nothing. His citizenship papers look genuine enough, but I don't know where or how he got them. I hope you didn't bruise him too badly, Jack. We've got to make him look like a peaceful, law abiding citizen at the trial."

****

Peter felt something cold and damp on his face, and raised his hand to push it away. The right side of his face was numb, and his neck hurt clear down to his shoulder.

"Watch it! He's coming to!" he heard a voice say from miles above him. Peter forced his eyes open, and found himself gazing up at a calm, comely, masculine face with gently slanted, dark eyes.

"Hello, Peter. How's your jaw?" Paul asked in an offhanded manner. "I think I kept the swelling down with the ice."

Peter glared at Paul, then raised his head and looked around. He was lying on a sofa in a sitting room with large glass doors which led to a garden. Brad and the American were standing by the sofa watching him intently. Without warning Peter lunged and tried to roll himself off the sofa.

Paul grabbed his shoulders and pinned him down. "Whoa! Calm

down, Peter! You're not going anywhere just yet!"

"Take your filthy hands off me!" Peter tried to shout, but his jaw didn't cooperate, and the garbled sounds that came out didn't sound very menacing.

Brad leaned over the sofa. "Listen to me, Peter," he began earnestly. "I did not set you up. I am trying to protect you. I *want* you to testify at the trial. These men work for me. You are perfectly safe here with them."

"You lie!" Peter hissed. "I saw that one in Geneva. He knocked me flat, and then tried to push me into a cab."

"I was only trying to keep you from getting your head blown off," Jack protested. "Someone threw a bomb at you when you came out the door. Don't you remember the shattered glass?"

"I remember!" Peter said vehemently. "I also remember somebody took a shot at me while I was waiting for a light!"

"I know, Peter," Paul put in. "I was following your car. I saw two guys, two lanes to your left pull up even with your car and aim a rifle at you. I rammed the cars behind you as hard as I could, hoping the jolt would push you out of the line of fire. I chased after the guys with the rifle, but they got away while I was trying to untangle my radiator from the bumper of the car in front of me."

Peter was unconvinced. "What are you planning to do to me now? Try to break my arm again?" he snapped.

"I'm sorry, Peter," Paul answered. "I wasn't trying to break your arm. I was just trying to keep you from slicing up my partner. If you hadn't struggled so much I would have let go sooner."

"How long are you going to keep me pinned to this God damn couch!" Peter snarled at Paul.

Paul looked at Brad for an answer.

"Let him up," Brad said quietly. Paul released his hold on Peter, and Peter sat up with a jerk. A moment later he learned that it is not wise to sit up fast, when your jaw is as big as the Colosseum. Instinctively he grabbed his chin to keep it from falling off his face.

Brad walked over to the sideboard, poured some whiskey into a glass, and returned to the sofa. "I think you could use a drink," Brad said offering Peter the glass.

"I don't want anything from you, you bastard," Peter said with disgust. "I just want to get out of here."

Brad shook his head sadly. "I'm sorry, Peter — even if you refuse to testify, I can't let you leave until after the trial. It's just too dangerous."

"So I am a prisoner! I knew it!"

"You're not a prisoner," Brad said calmly, although Jack could see that his patience was wearing thin. "Peter," Brad began, and opened his jacket slightly, so that Peter could see he was wearing a shoulder holster and a pistol. "If we had wanted to hurt you, we could have done it long before now."

Brad nodded his head and Jack and Paul drew open their coats to show that they too were armed. Peter stiffened and looked suspiciously from one face to another. Paul closed his coat briskly with a flick of his wrist. "Come on, Peter," he coaxed. "We're all in this together. Why don't you just relax and make the best of it. We've got a nice private room for you. We even stocked your favorite brand of whiskey."

"How long?" Peter asked sharply.

"Just until the trial is over . . . less than a week," Brad answered quickly and held out the glass of whiskey.

"What choice do I have?" Peter grumbled.

"You can stay, and work with us to prepare your testimony to put these guys away, or you can stay, and snarl, and swear at us, and make us miserable for a week," Brad answered.

Peter put his elbows on his knees, and held his head with his hands. "I'll testify. That's why I came," he affirmed at last and took the whiskey.

"Good! Good! Let's all have a drink," Brad said with relief. "I'll let Dr. La Monde know that you are safe."

Peter looked up from his drink. "I suppose he did wonder where I went," he mumbled.

So they drank, and Brad made official introductions. Peter finally gave in, and reluctantly shook hands with Jack Barrons, and Paul Artier. Peter wondered silently if his shoulder would ever have a chance to heal if people kept trying to twist his arm off.

That very afternoon, the team began to prepare Peter's testimony. The prosecuting attorney had given Brad a list of the questions he would ask Peter, as well as a list of the questions he anticipated the defense attorneys would ask. Paul and Jack took turns asking the prepared questions, but Peter was so defensive about supplying any information about himself, that they were forced to ask five or six questions for every one the attorney proposed.

At first they allowed Peter to pace and move about while they laboriously pulled answers from him, but after several hours, they decided that he must learn to sit still while he answered. So Peter sat and gripped the arms of the chair, but when he judged a question too personal, or too insulting, he bounded from his seat, and was across the room before they could stop him. By 6:00 p.m. Jack was threatening to handcuff Peter to the chair, and Paul was beginning to wonder if they would ever get beyond the basic questions of who Peter was, where he resided, and what he did for a living. When Brad returned from consulting with the attorneys, he stuck his head into the room, and motioned for Paul to come out into the hall.

"How is it going?" he asked cheerfully.

"Very slowly," Paul replied. "Kononellos is the most secretive, stubborn, suspicious . . ."

"Have patience with him, Paul," Brad said putting his hand on Paul's arm. "He's trying to cooperate."

"It's hard to tell, Brad. Getting information from him is like pulling teeth."

"Maybe you should take a break and have dinner," Brad suggested.

"O.K. I'll tell Jack."

Paul went back into the sitting room, and announced that the questioning would be suspended for a while, in order to have dinner. Paul invited Peter on a tour of the villa, and he agreed readily. After being confined to a chair for hours, he was anxious to move freely, and stretch his legs. Paul made an effort to engage Peter in a conversation about the old villa. He could see that it was easier for Peter to talk about topics unrelated to himself. Paul learned that Peter was very interested in history, and also knew a good deal about art.

About an hour later, the men assembled in the dining room. Although the cook had prepared a lavish meal, Peter didn't show much interest in the food. Only after watching Peter toy with his food for a while did Paul guess that Peter's jaw was still sore from the blow Jack had struck. After dinner they returned to the sitting room, and Brad took over asking Peter questions. He had only slightly better luck than Jack in getting Peter to answer.

Shortly after midnight Brad called a halt to the questioning. "I think we could all use some sleep. Let's start again in the morning. Paul, you take the first watch," he said briskly.

Peter shot Brad an angry look. "Are you afraid I will slip out during the night?"

"No, Peter, but I'm not sure who might try to get in. We can't be too careful."

Peter was slightly alarmed that Brad did not feel he was completely secure even at the villa.

Brad guessed Peter's feelings. "By the way, you might sleep better for having this," Brad said, and tossed Peter his knife. Peter caught it and clenched it in his hand. "Thanks, I . . . I'm glad to have it back."

"Good night, Peter. Get some rest. We'll be getting to some tougher questions in the morning."

Peter nodded, but he did not leave the sitting room when the others went out. Instead he went to the sideboard and poured himself a glass of whiskey. Why bother going to bed, he thought. He knew he wouldn't sleep. Worse yet, if he did fall asleep, he would probably have another horrible nightmare. The last thing he wanted was for Jack, or Paul to see him sweating and screaming over nothing. Mario hadn't said anything about the dreams, but then Mario had known him as a boy. Peter knew that Jack and Paul would agree with his father that having nightmares was a sign of weakness, more suited to women and children than to men. More than once his father had slapped him awake for crying out in his sleep. He had tried to master the dreams, but he couldn't. He had learned not to show any weakness when his father whipped him, but when he slept he lost control.

So Peter sat and drank, and thought back to the first time he had been in a court room. He had been eight years old. The boys in his home village had caught him alone on the beach when he was going from his father's boat to his house. School was out for the day, and a group of them were waiting. Seeing the boys stoop to gather rocks, he had begun to run, hoping he could outrun them as he usually did. He stood a head taller than anyone his age, and had long gangly legs that carried him along the stony beach like some strange shore bird. He ran that day, faster than ever before, but the boys split into three groups, and cut him off from the path to his house. He felt the sting of the pebbles pelting him as he ran, and was panting breathlessly by the time they overtook him.

"Leave me alone!" he gasped defiantly, as they seized him, and began to strike him on the legs with sticks.

"Why weren't you at school today, Petros?" they asked, taunting him. "Are you so smart from mending nets that you don't need lessons? Why do you run wild, while we are cooped in a stuffy classroom?"

They shook him and pulled his ragged clothes. How could he tell them how badly he wanted to go to school – how much he longed to learn to read and write? They would not listen. They were the sons of fishermen like himself, but they were allowed to learn.

"Look! He has new shoes!" one of the boys sneered. "He's too good to come to school with us!"

"So you think you are better than us now, you dirty little beggar. We will see. Take the shoes!" an older boy commanded.

"No!" he screamed. "They're mine. My mother . . ."

"Your mother's a whore, Petros. Where did she get the money?"

"She scrubbed . . ." he began, but someone struck him in the mouth.

"She's a whore, Petros. Everyone says so!" the older boy insisted.

"No! You lie! She's not . . ."

"My mother says your mother brings shame on the whole village!" another boy jeered.

"Why did she come here? She's not one of us," the older boy sneered. "And you, you skinny bastard, look how she brings you up. You don't come to school, and you fall asleep in church! A wicked boy like you does not deserve new shoes. Take them!" he commanded again.

"No! Not my shoes! Please!" he begged, but they ignored his pleas. He knew his father would beat him if he lost his only pair of shoes. When the boys grabbed him, and started to pull on his shoes, he was filled with panic. Suddenly he pulled one skinny arm free, and groped for the fish knife he carried in his pocket. Grasping the knife, he slashed out blindly, and the blade caught one of the boys on the arm. The boy cried out, more from surprise than pain, but seeing the blood, the others released Petros and backed away.

"Watch out! He's got a knife! He's gone crazy!" one of the boys shouted.

Half dazed at his own audacity, he brandished the knife in front of them.

"My father will set the police on you, Petros. You have gone too far. You must be punished!" the boys threatened, but to his great amazement they turned and fled.

He stood alone. He knew he could not go home. He had committed a terrible sin. In terror he ran along the beach, going farther away from the village than he had ever been. He ran on, though his shoulders ached, and the pain in his side stabbed deeper and deeper into his middle. He ran until he collapsed.

It was dark by the time they cornered him behind some rocks. In the dim light from their lanterns, the faces of the men from the village looked bizarre and evil. He feared that his father would make good his threat to cast him into the sea, and he fought when they tried to hold him. So violently did he struggle against his own father, the other men thought he had been seized by a fit. Hoping to calm him, someone threw a piece of old canvas over his head, and tied him in a bundle. It was hot and airless under the canvas, and the more he jerked and kicked, the harder it was to breathe, but he would not give in. He struggled until at last he fainted.

In the morning they brought him before the magistrate, and if their objective had been to strike terror into the heart of one young, wayward boy, they had total success. He was so afraid of being locked up, or sent away, that his legs could barely hold him erect. When his name was called he could not force his feet to move, and when his father pushed him forward, he fell. Someone held his arms, but so great was his fear, he could not tell his own name. He heard nothing that was said to him except "fine" and the word struck him like a blow. A fine meant his father would have to pay money, and he would be very angry with him.

After his parents brought him home, his father had lashed him viciously with a heavy hemp line. His mother had wept, and tried to protect him, but his father had knocked her down. Although it took tremendous effort, he did not cry out while his father whipped him. When his mother hauled him before the priest the next day, he confessed his sin, but could not bring himself to say he was sorry. It would have been a lie.

He had been surprised that the old priest had not been angry with him. Indeed the priest seemed to know more about him, and his family than he knew himself. He did not mind when the priest told his mother that as a punishment, he must come every week to read the scriptures with him, and write out long passages by hand. How could a father object to such a proper Christian punishment? And if there happened to be a history, or a geography book open on the table when Petros arrived, they would read from that, for who would expect such an old man to make an extra trip to fetch a bible. And so Petros learned to read, and to form his letters.

****

Shortly before 4:00 a.m., Paul came in from patrolling the grounds of the villa. Remembering that he had seen the light on in the garden sitting room, he went in to turn it off. He caught the strong odor of whiskey as he came into the room. He was first startled, then disgusted, to find Peter passed out on the couch. Peter was still clutching the empty decanter of whiskey, but the matching crystal glass lay in pieces on the floor below his out stretched hand.

"God, what a mess, Kononellos. Not only are you impossible to work with, you're a God damn souse!" Paul said, picking up the glass, and tossing it into a waste basket. He opened the glass door slightly to freshen the room. "Why the hell didn't you go to bed!" Paul said aloud, and snatched the empty decanter from Peter. Peter groaned slightly, and put his left hand to his right shoulder.

Paul was struck that even when Peter was obviously dead drunk, he behaved as if his shoulder was hurting. Paul was used to dealing with sore muscles. His mother and his uncle had taught him volumes on various oriental methods of massage and body alignment. Without a second thought, the way some people would straighten a picture frame, or Jack would tighten a loose screw, Paul put his slender, graceful hand on Peter's shoulder. He let his strong, well-trained fingers probe Peter's muscles. It took only seconds for him to feel the weakness. His natural curiosity was aroused. Unbuttoning Peter's shirt, he pulled it open and exposed the still vivid scars on Peter's shoulder.

Damn! he thought, suddenly feeling a healer's sense of universal sympathy. I wish I had known about this. Skillfully he began to run his hands over Peter's shoulder and down his arm. Paul stopped his work only momentarily when he heard Jack come into the room.

"What's with our skinny friend? Was he getting rowdy again?" Jack asked with a wry grin.

Paul shook his head. "No. Looks like he just sat and drank until he passed out. Look at this though," Paul answered, pulling Peter's shirt open further.

Jack stepped over to the couch and looked over Paul's shoulder. He let out a low whistle. "Damn! Must have gone clean through. Brad mentioned that he talked to him at the hospital, but I didn't know what had happened."

"I wish I had known about this before I started wringing the hell out of his arm."

"He didn't give you much choice he put up such a struggle," Jack commented.

"Yeah, but I could have brought him down with another technique if I had known his shoulder was like this. After all, he is a witness. He's not one of the terrorists." Paul ceased massaging Peter's arm and deftly rebuttoned Peter's shirt.

"It's really going to be fun working with him tomorrow," Jack said. "He's a big enough nuisance as it is. I hate to think what he'll be like with a hangover."

"I know what you mean. His answers are so guarded, I am beginning to suspect that something besides the kidnapping happened to him in Rome. We have to rehearse him enough that he can make his statement without so much hesitation. If the defense lawyers catch on that he is hiding something, they will be on him like jackals. Well, I'd better get some sleep," Paul concluded.

"Should we put him in his room?" Jack asked.

"No," Paul said thoughtfully. "Let's leave him here. When I showed him around earlier, he was very upset to see that we had brought his clothes, and some of his gear to Rome. He doesn't like to have strangers messing with his stuff. Better not mention that I worked on his arm."

"O.K. I'll put a blanket or something over him," Jack answered. "Brad's going to be unhappy that we let him get drunk. God, I'm getting sick of baby sitting this guy!"

Jack flicked the light switch off as they left the room. Paul went to his room and Jack went to Peter's room to get a blanket. A few minutes later he returned to the darkened sitting room. Without turning on the light he unfolded the blanket and laid it carelessly over Peter. Turning from the sofa he felt the draft of cold air blowing in from the slight opening between the glass doors. I'd better close that, he thought. If this guy so much as catches cold, Brad will be upset. He likes to deliver a witness in perfect condition.

Jack closed the glass door and left the room. He decided to make a tour around the villa wall, and went out through the front door. Turning to his right, he crossed the lawn in front of the house, passed through the garden, and followed the wall around behind the house. There was no sound from the property directly behind the villa. The rear of the villa the team occupied was not well lit, but anyone who came in from the neighboring villa would have a long, difficult route back to the street.

Jack continued his tour around the house, and followed the wall down to the front gate. He rattled the lock on the ornate metal structure, and scanned the street through the gate to satisfy himself that no one was parked along the curb. Everything's tucked in for the night, he thought.

Jack reached into his coat pocket for his pack of cigarettes, and lit one using his fake gold lighter, a gift from Linda. He gazed at the cheap lighter, then squeezed his fist around it, and checked the street again. Why do I bother to keep this lighter? he wondered. Maybe because it reminded him not to get sentimental about Linda. The lighter was just one more cheap trick she had played on him, before she cleaned out their joint bank account, and ran off with some other patsy. She hadn't even bothered to file for divorce, so he could have been free of her sooner.

If only Linda had stayed in Germany with me, things might have been different, Jack often told himself. She hadn't liked Germany — it was too different, too foreign, she had whined. Well that was the very thing Jack had liked. He wanted to see something different. He had had his fill of raising corn and hogs in Kansas. He took a drag on his cigarette, and slipped the lighter back into his pocket. That damn lighter had lasted longer than the marriage, Jack thought bitterly. He began another circle through the grounds. Maybe after the trial I can get to see more of Rome, he told himself.

****

Contrary to Jack's expectation, Brad didn't come down on him and Paul for letting Peter get drunk. All he said when Jack told him was, "I should have anticipated as much. I'll handle it."

Shortly before 8:00 a.m. Brad stormed into the garden sitting room carrying a pitcher of ice water. Peter was still asleep on the sofa, lying on his left side, with his back to the room. Without prelude, Brad poured half of the ice water down the back of Peter's neck. Peter groaned and rolled onto his back, and Brad promptly flung the remainder of the water in Peter's face. Peter sputtered and sat up with a start. "What the hell . . ." he began, but Brad grabbed the front of Peter's shirt so forcefully he jerked Peter's head.

"Listen Kononellos!" Brad shouted. "I've had enough of your nonsense. I've got two good men tied up on this job. I'm not going to let them risk their lives while you get drunk and make yourself useless!"

"I am not useless!" Peter roared at Brad, but the sound of his own voice made his head split.

"Good!" Brad snapped. "We have a lot of work to do today, and

I expect your full cooperation. Now get cleaned up, and let the cook know what you want for breakfast!"

"No food — just coffee!" Peter grumbled, pulling himself off the sofa.

"All right! I want you back here at 9:00 a.m. sharp," Brad said and left.

When the team assembled again, Brad commenced asking questions, and Peter answered them in a low, monotone voice. When it came to explaining why he had been walking so far from his hotel, Peter claimed staunchly that he had gone to a concert alone, then gone to eat. He declared that he had decided to walk back to his hotel, and had gotten lost. Brad knew that Peter was lying, but no matter how many times he asked the questions, he could not get Peter to change his story. Brad finally decided that he could trust Peter not to reveal where he had really been. The fact that he had been with Geilla actually had no bearing on the kidnapping.

After several hours, Paul took over on the questioning, and pried and probed trying to force Peter to trip up. Aside from a few angry outbursts, however, Peter stuck to his story. Brad was genuinely pleased that Peter had been able to invent a plausible explanation concerning his activities. He would be able to hold to his story much more tenaciously than if the team had been forced to suggest a solution for him. Brad was determined to see the kidnappers sent to prison, but he was glad he did not have to humiliate Peter to achieve his goal. What had happened in Geilla's apartment that night was of no significance to him.

Shortly after 2:00 p.m., Brad noticed that Peter's nerves, and his hangover, were getting the best of him despite his attempt to cooperate. His resentment flared when questioned about why he carried a knife, and he started to swear and curse the kidnappers, the victim, the police, the courts, and himself for getting involved in such a mess. Brad called for a break. "Why don't you take a walk around the grounds before lunch, Peter. It's a bit chilly. You might want to wear . . ." he stopped in mid-sentence, for Peter was out the door like an excited hound.

The others decided to leave Peter to himself for a while. When the food was ready, however, Paul stepped into the garden to look for him. He found him studying some brown, shriveled looking bushes.

"Looks like that frost in December killed a lot of the plants," Paul remarked casually.

"Yes," Peter responded, "but these bushes could have been spared if they had been wrapped with burlap. Madame Marneé always had me wrap hers."

Paul was suddenly intrigued. He was always eager to talk to anyone who knew about plants. His own knowledge of gardening and herbs was extensive, but he was continually searching for new varieties, or interesting plant lore.

"I didn't know you were a gardener," Paul commented.

Peter laughed a mirthless laugh. "I was more like a human rototiller than a gardener. Madame was always setting me to dig up something, and plant it somewhere else. And pruning, Dio Mio, everything had to be just so — no higher, no wider." Peter gestured with his hands to illustrate items in a row.

They talked about various gardens, and Paul named a few of the plants for Peter, mentioning that many of the plants were common to the U.S. and Europe.

"How did you learn so much about plants?" Peter asked, as they moved about the garden.

"My mother taught me," Paul answered. "She was very interested in herbs, for cooking and various cures."

"You're an American aren't you. I recognize the accent."

"Yes. I'm from Chicago."

"I see," Peter answered hesitantly.

Paul smiled at Peter's politeness.

"My mother is from Thailand. I guess I take after her. Hey! I think lunch is ready. Let's go in," Paul added, abruptly changing the subject.

"I'm not hungry," Peter said, but Paul did not believe him. He could see the discoloration on Peter's chin.

"Well, come in and have some coffee. Maybe you'll change your mind. I asked the cook to make some soup."

Peter looked at Paul, and seeing his sly grin, he chuckled.

"Soup might be good. I seem to be having some trouble with my teeth lately."

Paul laughed aloud. "How strange! Maybe it's the climate."

"You might be right. The last time I was in Rome, I landed in the hospital."

Paul laughed again, and led the way back to the house. Brad was pleased to see that Peter looked more relaxed as he entered the dining room with Paul. Now, if we can just get him to go easier on the booze, we may all survive this trial, Brad thought.

****

The trial had been in session for several days, and it was time for Peter to appear. The team had prepared him as best they could, and it was Paul's estimate that if Peter could hold his temper in check, he would do O.K. Brad thought that was a big "if", but they had run out of time.

Peter had been up since early morning. He hadn't slept well. Actually he hadn't slept well since coming to Rome, but he was used to operating with too little sleep. He was nervous. He didn't like to interact with large groups of people, and the thought that someone might try to kill him, before he even got to the witness stand, did not make the situation any more inviting. Peter was dressed, and imagined he was ready to go, until Brad came into his room with a vest. It was not the type that bankers need to wear.

"I think you should wear this under your shirt," Brad said offering Peter the vest.

Peter pulled back. "What's that for? You told me I'd be surrounded by police."

"You will be, and we'll be guarding you. It's just a precaution. Go ahead, put it on!"

"No! I'll look like a fool sitting up there with that on. Everyone will take me for a coward! Look I'm not afraid to . . ."

"Just shut up, and put the bloody thing on!" Brad said wearily. "We're all wearing one, and no one will ever suspect, if you keep your mouth shut. Now put it on before you get killed, and everyone sees what a stubborn fool you really are!"

Before Peter could respond, Paul came into the room. He saw Brad holding the vest. "Is there some problem with the fit?" he asked calmly.

"Oh it will fit well enough," Brad said sarcastically. "I think Peter just needs a little help getting into it. Maybe you can help me 'explain' it to him."

"Sure," Paul said, and taking the vest from Brad, he advanced on Peter. "I'll try not to leave any bruises where they will show," Paul said in a matter-of-fact tone.

Peter stepped back. He tried to read the expression in Paul's eyes. They were calm, but determined. "You really intend to force me into that thing, don't you," Peter said defensively.

"Yes," Paul answered in a very business like manner. "I don't want you to take any unnecessary risk. It's my job to deliver you in good condition, even if I have to break you in half to do it."

Paul stepped forward and held out the vest. Peter took another step backwards, but Paul saw his neck muscles tense.

"Why don't you just put it on. I really don't want to hurt your shoulder again," Paul said quietly.

Peter hesitated. He didn't quite know what to make of Paul. He had been friendly enough and had seen that he was well taken care of; but Paul was obviously ready to kick the shit out of him, if he didn't wear the vest. Peter surmised that Jack and Brad would add their muscle power to Paul's if he resisted. The three of them worked as a team, and he couldn't fight all of them without getting hurt.

"Come on! Be sensible," Paul coaxed. "You were lucky last time. The bullet might hit a little lower next time. You don't want me to lose my job do you?"

"I guess not," Peter said warily.

"Thanks for seeing it my way," Paul said and smiled. "Catch!" he said suddenly, and tossed the vest to Peter. "I'll just wait here . . . in case you have any trouble figuring it out," he said and sat on Peter's bed.

"Thanks," Peter said wryly, and slowly unbuttoned his shirt. He turned his back to Paul. He was always reluctant to show his scars. They were ugly reminders of his past defeat and humiliation. When Peter had retied his necktie, Paul stood, and held Peter's suit coat for him as a good will gesture. Peter was about to snatch his coat, but suddenly changed his mind. Turning slowly, he let Paul ease the coat up over his arms.

"Thanks for letting me keep my job," Paul said airily.

Peter did not answer. A moment later Jack put his head around the door. "I brought the car around. Is everyone ready?" he asked cheerfully.

"We're ready!" Brad answered. He led the way out of the house, and the others followed him to the car. Peter sat in the back, looking tense and somber. He kept going over his testimony in his mind.

"Remember, just don't get hot, no matter what they ask you," Paul advised him, but he had little hope that his words would stick.

When they pulled up by the plaza in front of the Palace of Justice, they noticed that there was a crowd gathered outside the building.

"Who are all these people?" Peter asked in dismay as he looked out the window.

"Mostly reporters and curious spectators," Brad answered casually. "I'm afraid the case has attracted a lot of attention in the press."

"I didn't realize there would be so many people," Peter said hesitantly. "I never agreed to this. I never agreed to make a public spectacle of myself!"

Brad could see that Peter was having second thoughts about getting out of the car. "I assure you, no reporters will be allowed in the court room, Peter. We will be with you to block their access. You will just have to ignore them until we get into the building."

"Ignore them! Damn! There must be a hundred of them!" Peter snapped. He held his head with his hand. "Oh God! Edgar will be appalled if word of this gets to Geneva. Edgar hates gossip and publicity!"

"Well, you can't back out now. Here they come!" Brad said, opening the car door. Brad signalled with his arm, and suddenly a uniformed policeman appeared, and slipped behind the wheel. Instantly Jack jumped out of the car, unlocked the rear door, and pulled it open. Peter looked up, and saw that Paul was standing beside Jack.

"Just don't say anything to them," Paul warned. "They can't print what you don't say."

"God what a nightmare!" Peter muttered, and stepped out of the car.

As the first of the reporters arrived, the team surrounded Peter in a phalanx formation. Paul stood on Peter's right, Jack on his left, and Brad slightly ahead of him. Slowly they pushed their way toward the building. Peter looked straight ahead as the reporters began to shout questions at him.

"Did you really see the kidnapping? Tell us what happened! Who killed the driver? Did you kill any of the terrorists?"

The shouting became louder, and more persistent as the team inched their way forward. Despite the team's efforts to shield Peter from the crowd, someone managed to shove a microphone into his face.

"Is it true that you belong to a secret terrorist organization? Are you involved in some kind of drug deal?" a shrill voice shouted.

Peter turned abruptly and glared at the questioner. He clenched his fist, but before he could raise his hand, Paul grabbed his right arm.

"Just keep walking," Paul said calmly under his breath. "Ignore them – nothing to it – ignore them. Just keep moving." Paul turned his shoulder forward, and pushed his way through the crowd. He kept talking to Peter, and pulling him along. Paul seemed perfectly at ease, except for his dark eyes which darted rapidly from side to side, scanning the scene for any sign of trouble.

Flash bulbs lit up all around them, and the police shouted orders to the crowd. The noise grew louder, and the questions became ruder as the press realized that Peter was not going to cooperate. Suddenly Peter lurched forward, and Paul feared he might attempt to charge for the building. "Take it easy. Just take it easy," Paul said aloud, and tightened his grip on Peter's arm.

Progress was slow, but they were nearing the entrance to the building. They were almost even with the row of massive pillars, which formed a colonnade around the building, when Peter jerked his head to the left. Without warning he slammed against Paul, and shouted, "Get down!" Peter dove for the ground, pulling Paul with him, and thrusting Brad forward. Three shots rang out, and Peter felt the impact as one bullet hit his vest. Immediately a woman directly behind the team began to scream and the reporters scattered.

Peter raised his head, and saw the terrorist who was still holding the gun. The man looked wild-eyed and confused, and was staring at something on the ground behind Peter. Peter glanced back and saw a woman lying on the pavement. She was bleeding and moaning. Peter's hand flew to his knife. He turned and saw the terrorist raise his gun shakily and aim at him.

"You filthy son of a bitch!" Peter screamed, and lunged for the man. Before Peter could reach him, however, Jack leaped forward and tackled Peter's ankles throwing him to the pavement. The terrorist fired, but the shot went over Peter's head.

"Stay down!" Brad shouted, and fired at the terrorist. The shot hit the man in the arm, and he dropped his gun. Peter struggled to crawl toward the terrorist, but he suddenly felt a shooting pain in his hand as Paul caught him in a vice-tight grip.

"Drop it! Now!" Paul commanded quietly. "You're just a witness! Remember?"

Peter fought to hold on, but his hand went dead, and Paul twisted the knife away from him.

"Get him inside!" Brad ordered, and before Peter could clutch his wrist, he was pulled to his feet. He could still hear the woman's horrible screams. He tried to get a look at her, but Brad stepped in front of him. As they hauled him away, Peter had a glimpse of two men who were holding the terrorist by the arms. One of the men was Sergeant Trigilio.

Paul and Jack pulled Peter through the massive doors, and into the lobby of the building. Peter was struggling and screaming curses at them, as he stumbled along. Two plainclothes men arrived, and Peter was ushered into an empty office, and pushed into a wooden arm chair. Everything had happened so fast, he was unaware that he was breathing rapidly and shaking. He heard several voices asking him questions in Italian and in English, but for a moment he could not sort out what they were saying. Paul had found the mark on Peter's shirt, where the bullet had struck, and he was searching for any signs of bleeding.

"Are you O.K.? Are you hurt?" Paul kept repeating, until Peter finally shouted, "Leave me alone!" He tried to push Paul away from him. "What happened to that woman? Where is she?" Peter asked excitedly.

At that moment Brad came in, and shot a meaningful glance at Paul and Jack. "She's O.K." Brad said quickly to Peter. "They took her away. It was just a scratch."

"No! She was bleeding! I saw her! God damn it! That bastard shot her! Isn't anyone going to help her?"

"She's O.K., Peter," Brad answered. "The police are with her. She'll be O.K."

Peter seemed to relax a little.

"I think he needs some nerve tonic," Paul said to Jack, who magically produced a small silver flask from his coat pocket. Paul removed the cap and offered the flask to Peter. "Here! Calm down."

Peter reached for the flask, but his hand was still numb, and he could not hold it. Paul caught the flask as Peter fumbled with it, and pressed it into Peter's left hand. Peter took a long draught and was grateful. He held his right hand protectively against his chest as he drank.

"Let me see your hand," Paul said quietly.

"No!" Peter growled and pulled away. "Leave me alone! Just leave me alone!"

"Come on. I just want to see how much damage I did."

"No!" Peter repeated adamantly.

Paul shot a glance at Jack, who immediately reached down and snatched the flask from Peter. Putting his hands on Peter's shoulders, he pulled them against the back of the chair. "Come on," he coaxed. "Let him have a look. Paul's good at fixing things."

Peter stared at Paul with a venomous look, but said nothing.

"All right! All right! Have it your way," Paul said at last. "Give him another drink," he said to Jack and turned away.

Peter was surprised, but kept his eye on Paul as he drank. Paul seemed to be having a conference with Brad. Peter wondered anxiously if they were planning to take him by surprise.

Actually, Brad was informing Paul that the woman who had been shot was dead. She had bled to death before an ambulance could be summoned. They decided not to tell Peter. It would only upset him. Finally Brad came up to Peter.

"Peter, I think I can arrange a delay, and have you testify tomorrow, if you don't feel up to it," Brad said sympathetically.

Peter glanced up at him. "No! No more delays! I won't go through that mob again."

"Are you sure you feel O.K.?" Brad asked.

"Yes! Yes, I'll testify. Let's just get this over with!"

"O.K. You'll be called in about fifteen minutes," Brad answered. He turned to Paul. "Take him down to the men's room, and throw some cold water on him. See if you can get his suit cleaned off. He looks like he's been rolling in the mud."

Paul nodded, and together he and Jack lifted Peter to his feet, and helped him out the door.

"And for God's sake comb his bloody hair!" Brad called after them as they started down the hall.

A few minutes later, a tall, thin, slightly pale, but respectable looking banker took the stand to testify against the kidnappers. It was hard to tell who was more nervous, Peter or the team members, as each question was posed.

The defense tried to belittle Peter's efforts to prevent the kidnapping, but even the way Peter sat, unconsciously clutching his sore wrist, convinced the jury, far better than words, that the injuries he had received in defense of the victim, were not yet healed. Later the defense attorney tried to disparage Peter's character by forcing him to admit that he had killed two men during the kidnapping. His dramatic attempt backfired, however, when Peter covered his face with his hands, and leaned forward in his chair. In a voice choked with remorse Peter whispered, "Yes! Yes! God forgive me. I killed them!"

The jury felt in their hearts that Peter Kononellos was not a man who could easily take a life. The defense attorney recognized his mistake immediately, but it was too late. The jury's sympathy swung towards Peter and he was allowed to step down without further questioning.

Peter was solemn and withdrawn, as he made his way out of the court room. Brad and Jack were quite pleased with the way his testimony had been received, and Paul was his usual calm, analytical self.

"Well, it's back to the car, and then you can forget about all of this, Peter," Brad commented.

"Yes . . . back to the car," Peter mumbled.

"Sergeant Trigilio has promised me two extra men as an escort. It should go easier on the way back," Brad added.

Peter didn't answer. Once again the team surrounded him as he stepped out the door. The reporters were still there, and seemed even more anxious to get a word from Peter. The shouting of rude, prying, personal questions continued all the way to the car, but Peter turned a deaf ear to them. He tuned out everything, but the sound of Paul's voice telling him calmly, and quietly that it would soon be over, and he could go back to his normal, private life. Peter was glad that Paul was with him. Paul was quiet, and calm, and always seemed to have everything under control. Peter was thankful that all of them were there, to keep this mob of strangers from stripping away every shred of his privacy, pride and dignity.

When they reached the car, Sergeant Trigilio was waiting for them. Peter hesitated, but Trigilio eagerly put his hand out.

"Thank you for coming to testify Signor Kononellos. I know this has not been easy for you, but it has been a great help," he said and smiled.

"I'm glad it's finally over," Peter mumbled and shook Trigilio's hand. He felt relieved that Sergeant Trigilio finally believed his story.

Jack opened the front door of the car for Peter. "I think the celebrity should sit in the front," Jack said with a wink.

Peter suddenly grinned. "I'll be glad to get back to Geneva where I am not as 'famous'," he said as he got in. He looked at the clock on the dashboard, and was startled that it was only 11:00 a.m. He felt as if he had been on public exhibition for hours.

Brad drove the team back to the villa, and Peter headed for the shower. He hoped it would help him relax, and he wanted to get some heat on his wrist. Afterwards, he joined the team in the garden sitting room. They were enjoying a pre-lunch drink as a celebration. Using his left hand, Peter poured himself a drink and flung himself into a chair.

"I thought it went very well today, Peter," Brad said. "Soon you'll be able to get back to the bank."

Peter sipped his drink and smiled. "Actually, I thought I might take a few days off and go skiing. I haven't been yet this year."

"Skiing! Sounds like a great idea!" Jack responded eagerly. "I've always wanted to learn to ski, but I never got the chance. I guess you have to learn when you're a kid though."

"Not really," Peter answered slowly. "I . . . I had never even seen a pair of skis until I got to Geneva."

"No kidding!" Jack exclaimed. "What did you do before you became a banker?"

The question was innocent enough, but Jack could see little doors slam shut in Peter's mind. He didn't answer for a long time. "I wasn't much of anything," he said at last.

Paul jumped in to change the subject. "Well, if you plan to go skiing, you'd better let me have a look at your hand," he said.

"No need . . . it's feeling better," Peter answered evasively.

"Oh," Paul said with mock surprise. "I was just wondering how you were going to hold a ski pole, when you can't even hold a glass."

Peter glared at Paul, embarrassed to be caught in a lie.

"Come on," Paul said, "let me look at it. What are you afraid of?"

"I'm not afraid," Peter snapped. "I don't need your help. I have my own personal physician."

"So you admit it still hurts," Paul answered.

"Of course it hurts, you bastard! You nearly broke it! I'd be a fool to let you near me again!" Peter suddenly shouted and stood up.

Brad stood also, and going to the sideboard, he came back with the decanter of whiskey.

"Please, sit down and have a drink with us, Peter," Brad said diplomatically.

Peter sat down.

"You should consider letting Paul work on your hand," Brad continued. "He's very good at massage. It might make your skiing go better."

"I prefer to consult with Doctor La Monde," Peter answered testily, and they could tell by the set of his jaw that he was not about to change his mind.

This time it was Jack who changed the subject. "Say, how the hell did you know that guy was behind the pillar this morning?" he asked abruptly.

Peter shifted in his chair and his jaw relaxed. "Someone must have stepped in front of him because I heard him growl, 'Get out of my way!'. I recognized his accent. He was the same man who kept calling my apartment and making threats."

"You never told me that you had received threats," Brad said.

"What did he say?"

Peter sipped his drink before answering. "His Italian was very crude and hard to follow . . . it was something about butchering me on the courthouse steps."

Brad's eyebrows went up in surprise. "You should have told us, Peter."

"Why? What would you have done about it — take me to the courthouse in a tank?"

Brad smiled, "Well no, but we might have been able to trace the call."

"I'm sorry. I didn't think about that," Peter said evenly.

"Well, it came out right in the end. Say, I have an idea. After lunch, why don't we take a drive to Vilerbo. We could see the sights, have a meal and spend the night. What do you say, Peter? Wouldn't you like to get away from the villa for a while?"

Peter looked disturbed. "I expected to return to Geneva tomorrow."

Brad cleared his throat, "Well, yes but . . ."

"But I'm still your prisoner!" Peter snapped.

"I wish you wouldn't think of it that way!" Brad said letting his diplomacy slip for a moment. "We've gone to great lengths to make this as pleasant as possible for you. It's still not safe for you to go trotting off to Geneva alone."

"Why did you lie to me? I hate being lied to!"

"It was very important that you testify, Peter," Paul said calmly. "We were afraid you would back out, if you knew how much time was involved."

"You were right about that! I'm sorry I ever got mixed up in this mess!" Peter growled. No one said anything for a minute, and then Peter sighed. "What the hell! I am sick of this place. Where did you say you wanted to go?"

"Vilerbo," Brad responded quickly. "It's about 60 miles from here. They have some interesting ruins, and it's quieter than Rome."

"All right, I'll go, but don't lie to me. I hate . . ." Peter broke off and bit his lip.

Brad sensed how difficult it was for Peter to let his guard down. "We're all on your side, Peter," he said seriously. "You have my word on that."

CHAPTER TWENTY

After lunch the group packed and Brad drove them to Vilerbo, to stroll through the cobbled stone streets of the old medieval town. Brad was satisfied that Peter had at last resigned himself to being closely followed. They were wandering casually through the curio shops, and Peter seemed to be enjoying himself, until suddenly he heard a thunderous boom behind him. He reached for his knife, and was about to dive for the floor when he heard a frightened voice say, in German, "I'm sorry! I'm sorry! It was an accident. It slipped out of my hand!"

Peter looked around to see a young couple standing stock still, starring at a huge copper pot, which was lying on the floor. Peter exhaled and felt embarrassed about overreacting, until he noticed that Paul was standing at his elbow with his gun drawn. Peter saw Jack flick his coat closed and step over to the couple. "You must forgive them," Jack said, in flawless German. "They are American. They watch too many gangster films and it makes them jumpy."

The couple smiled nervously, and Jack handed the man the copper pot. "Very good quality − you see it is hardly dented," Jack assured the couple, and nodded to the shopkeeper, who stood looking on in fright. Jack turned, and saw that Brad and Paul had edged Peter out the door.

"Why did you tell those people I was an American?" Peter demanded, when Jack joined the group on the street.

"People will overlook the most outrageous behavior from Americans. They think we don't know any better. Europeans imagine we all drive big cars and pack guns."

"Don't all Americans carry guns? They do in the films," Peter remarked.

Jack looked at Paul and grinned. "Not all Americans do. I met a guy once in a bar in St. Louis that didn't have one."

Peter laughed. "Do you expect me to believe that?"

"No, but who would believe that a distinguished Swiss banker would dive under the table because someone dropped a pot!"

"I didn't dive under the table!"

"But you went for your knife," Paul put in.

"Yes, and I didn't find it," Peter complained.

"If you promise to keep it out of sight, I'll give it back," Paul answered.

"I promise you won't see it, unless I need to use it," Peter declared.

"That's good enough. It's our job to see that you don't need it." Paul handed Peter his knife and smiled. Peter laughed, but he understood from Paul's performance in the shop, that Paul and the others took their job of protecting him very seriously.

In the evening after dinner, the group sat and talked over drinks. They were all content and relaxed except for Peter. He was reserved and contributed little to the conversation. Listening to Brad, Jack, and Paul talk, however, he envied their camaraderie, their closeness. They worked as a team and obviously enjoyed each other's company. As they laughed and related stories about their numerous assignments and travels, Peter realized how varied and exciting their work was compared to his. He was strictly Monsieur Kononellos at the bank – at least that's what they said to his face. He had gotten used to ignoring all the other names he heard. It was a job, and he did it, and did it well; but he could never relax at the bank. Aside from Edgar, no one there was his friend.

Peter's hand still hurt. He was reluctant to approach Paul, but it dawned on him that if he showed it to Carlin, Carlin would tell him he wasn't ready to ski. Well, to hell with Carlin. I want to get away from all this . . . this publicity and questioning and prying, he thought. I just want to be by myself for a while, out on the slopes where no one knows who I am, or what I do, or what I used to be. He slammed the door shut on his memories. He would not allow himself to even think about Geilla.

Shortly after 11 p.m., the group split up. Paul went to his room, and had barely taken off his coat and shirt, when he heard a knock on his door. He went to open it, and was surprised to see Peter standing in the hall. He looked uncertain, as if he didn't really want to be there.

"I . . . er . . . I wasn't sure you were still up," Peter began hesitantly. Even as he spoke he felt foolish, for he had followed Paul out only moments before.

"I'm still awake. Come on in," Paul said, casually motioning for Peter to enter. Paul closed the door, and backed into the room to give Peter more space. He had observed that Peter became uneasy when people got too close.

Peter was struck by how athletic and muscular Paul looked without his shirt. With more than a touch of envy, he stared at Paul's well defined deltoids, and solid-looking biceps. Peter had felt the power in Paul's deceptively graceful looking hands, but he was awed to realize how totally well-developed Paul was.

"Did you want to see me about something?" Paul said, seeming indifferent to Peter's silent admiration.

"No . . . well, yes," Peter stammered. "About my hand . . ."

"Is it acting up again?" Paul asked in mock surprise.

"No . . . I just thought perhaps . . ."

274

Paul quickly discerned that it was pure emotional torture for Peter to ask for help.

"Sit down, Peter," he said quietly, and waved Peter towards the bed.

****

By the following morning Peter's hand was feeling better. Aside from one excruciating moment, when he thought Paul meant to yank his arm off, the treatment had not been unbearable. Paul had requested room service to send some ice, but they apparently had misunderstood, and delivered a bucket of ice complete with a bottle of champagne. Paul and Peter had laughed about the mix-up, then shared the champagne, while holding the ice on Peter's hand. After Paul talked with him for a while, Peter lowered his guard enough to admit that his shoulder still bothered him from time to time. He agreed reluctantly to let Paul work on it, and truly appreciated that Paul didn't ask about his scars, and never alluded to how thin he was. Maybe it was just the champagne, Peter thought, but he had found himself wishing that he could trust Paul.

After breakfast the group made the short drive to Bognaia to visit Villa Lante. Paul was eager to explore the famous gardens, and Jack was intrigued by the engineering of the waterfall and the fountains. Peter strolled though the scenery, thankful for the peacefulness of the location. He was glad that he had come.

At lunch time, Brad put in a call to Sergeant Trigillio. He learned that the two kidnappers had been found guilty, and sentenced to life imprisonment. Peter was understandably elated to hear that he was free to return to Geneva, and ordered a bottle of champagne to celebrate. In a sudden rush of bonhomme, Peter announced that if Jack still wanted to learn to ski, he would be happy to meet him in Villars, and introduce him to the greatest ski instructor in Switzerland. When Jack accepted with instant enthusiasm, Peter seemed surprised at his own rashness. Returning to form, Peter admitted that perhaps Rudy was not the greatest ski instructor in Switzerland, but that he was the only one he claimed as a personal friend.

Although not quite as enthusiastic as Jack, Paul agreed to go along. He mentioned that he had been skiing several times, but not recently. Brad conceded that a vacation was in order, but stated that he was anxious to get back to London.

"Mary has really clipped your wings, Brad," Jack remarked with a laugh.

"On the contrary," Brad replied with his most British of accents. "She always mends and preens them after an assignment, and I rather enjoy having her do it," he concluded smugly.

Jack and Paul laughed knowingly, and Paul explained that Mary was Brad's wife.

Later the group returned to the villa in Rome, and Peter put in a call to Rudy von Steiger, to arrange rooms for himself and his guests. Although February is considered the high season for skiing in Switzerland, and resorts were fully booked months in advance, Rudy always had access to rooms. Years before Rudy had risen to his present position as ski instructor, he had worked at Villars as a waiter in one of the large hotels. Rudy and Peter had met when the Marneés first introduced Peter to skiing.

Seeing Rudy on the slopes, Peter had been filled with admiration for his skill and grace. Peter learned that Rudy was from Germany, and worked as a waiter in order to have access to the slopes to train. Rudy had fallen in love with a beautiful Swiss girl, who had come to Villars with her parents. Their romance had progressed smoothly until, on the last night of her stay, Rudy was assigned duty at a banquet. Peter had overheard Rudy on the phone, begging every waiter in Villars to take his place for the evening. Rudy pleaded desperately in German, French, Italian, and English, but no one was both willing and able to help him. Peter watched as Rudy went from anxiously dropping coins into the phone and begging, to waving bravely to the lovely girl who waited hopefully in the hotel lobby.

When at last Rudy had exhausted his long list of friends and turned from the phone in despair, Peter hesitantly approached him and volunteered to work in his stead. Rudy was skeptical at first, but Peter convinced him that he had served many dinners at the Marneés where the set-up was much more formal. Rudy left with the girl, silently hoping that he would still have a job when he returned, but willing to risk all for love. Edgar had been angry that Peter had taken on other duties without his permission, but Charlotte thought Peter had made a gallant gesture on behalf of young lovers, and quickly forgave Peter's rashness. She wisely suggested that she and Edgar take the boys elsewhere to dine that evening, so as not to make Peter nervous.

The evening had gone well for both Peter and Rudy, and Rudy showed his sincere gratitude by offering to coach Peter on the slopes. Although Peter had balked at Edgar's attempts to enroll him in ski classes, taking help from Rudy, who was barely two years older than himself was a different matter. Peter eagerly accepted Rudy's help, and thus began their friendship. On subsequent trips, Charlotte noticed that Peter appeared more confident on the slopes. She would have been appalled, however, if she had discovered that Rudy was taking Peter over the novice jumps.

It was several hours before Rudy could be located, but once he was on the line, he promised to locate rooms for Peter and his friends, if he had to turn away Prince Charles himself. Knowing that he could rely on Rudy's word, Peter packed his bags and said good-bye to the team. He was about to call for a cab, when Jack insisted on driving him to the airport. Paul went along also. As Peter shook hands with Jack and Paul, it occurred to him how hard they had worked to help him through a very humiliating and dangerous period. Later, while standing in the crowded waiting lounge, staring at the faces of the strangers, Peter made up his mind to go straight to the Marneés when he got off the plane. It was Friday and Carlin would be there for dinner. Peter suddenly longed to see them all again.

****

Three days later, Peter met Jack and Paul at the airport in Geneva, and they boarded the train for Villars. Rudy had not let Peter down, and they were directed to a luxury apartment in a private chalet with a magnificent view of the mountains. Rudy, who addressed Peter as Kon, was personally disappointed that neither of Kon's guests was a woman. He felt that Jack and Paul must be very important to Kon, however, for Kon never came skiing with anyone but the Marneés.

Knowing that Kon was a dismal failure at bragging and showing off, Rudy determined to do the honors himself. He apologized profusely to Jack and Paul, implying that the rooms were far inferior to what Kon was used to. He also insisted on arranging for his best assistant to give Jack private skiing instruction. Kon could hardly keep from laughing at Rudy's show, but Jack and Paul were impressed.

"By the way," Rudy cautioned as he left, "if anyone asks, all of you work for a group called 'New Dimension Travel' in New York."

"We get it," Jack replied with a grin.

The weather that first day was exceptionally fine, and the party got in hours of excellent skiing. Jack was properly fitted out, and took up Alpine skiing with the energy and joy of an overgrown child. Seeing how wild Jack was about sports, Kon was inwardly pleased that he had invited him to Villars. Kon smiled to see Jack having so much fun, even though at the moment, he was totally devoid of skill. Jack was strong, and fit, and obviously very determined to learn. He would do well, Kon mused. For his part, Paul took to the lengthy cross-country trails. Although Kon estimated Paul's skill level at the lower range of intermediate, Paul displayed a natural grace in all his movements. As long as he stays on the right trails, I won't have to worry about him, Kon thought as he headed for the lift. Kon's game was downhill, fast and furious, to the point of doing timed runs over a measured course. Kon was absolutely fearless on skis, attaining a sense of personal freedom on the slopes he never experienced anywhere else.

Rudy believed that Kon could have won medals and money in competition, if he had been allowed to put more time into his training, but it was Edgar's choice that Kon become a banker. Rudy knew that Kon was fiercely loyal to Edgar, and would not go against his wishes for any amount of glory.

On the second day at Villars, Kon again took to the steepest slopes, while Jack and Paul went their separate ways. Rudy saw Kon briefly, several times during the day, and noted that Kon's usual controlled courage and resolve were missing. In their place was a frantic drive that verged on recklessness. Rudy warned Kon to slow down and relax, but Kon shrugged off his advice. It was late afternoon before Rudy had finished giving lessons, and was able to devote his full attention to observing Kon as he practiced some jumps.

Rudy saw Kon go into that last jump. He knew immediately that it would be bad. Kon's approach was wrong, his timing was off, and he wasn't leaning into it far enough. Not only was the jump bad, Kon was not able to maintain his form, and Rudy knew his landing would be difficult.

Kon's landing was disastrous. He hit hard, and careened wildly down the slope until he lost control completely and fell. His momentum carried him downward, and he tumbled, rolling over, and over, until finally he jolted to an abrupt stop.

Kon was still lying motionless, face down in the snow when Rudy reached him several minutes later. Kicking off his skis, Rudy dropped to his knees beside Kon. Rapidly he clawed the snow away from Kon's face and called out to him.

"Kon! Kon! Are you all right? Kon! Answer me!"

At last Kon raised his head slightly. "I've lost it, Rudy. Everything was wrong! The approach was wrong. I couldn't hold the position . . ."

"It wasn't your best . . . forget it . . . are you hurt?"

"I don't know," Kon muttered weakly and struggled to turn over. "I'm . . . all tangled up," he continued, and then suddenly became annoyed. "I should have been able to do it, Rudy. Damn! I should have been able to do it!"

"Calm down! Tell me if this hurts," Rudy said, as he carefully straightened first one of Kon's legs, and then the other. "You'll do it, Kon," Rudy assured him. "You just weren't ready for it today. You missed a lot of practice this year. It will come. Can you sit up?"

Kon didn't seem to hear him. "I can do it, Rudy. I know I can do it! I have to do it!" Kon uttered with almost fanatical determination.

Rudy detected the unfamiliar tone in Kon's voice. "What's gotten in to you, Kon?" he asked, slowly pulling Kon into a sitting position. "Why are you pushing so hard? You've been doing crazy stunts all day."

"What do you mean?" Kon shot back defensively.

"It's as if you've been trying to show off. That's it, isn't it? You've been trying to impress those two Americans, haven't you?"

Kon stared at him. "Oh God, Rudy," he said suddenly realizing the truth. "Have I been that great a fool? I am ashamed to face them."

"Hey, it's human to want to display your talents. And they are impressed, believe me. Are you sure you are all right?"

Kon nodded "yes" and struggled to his feet. He took a faltering step, mumbled, ". . . still dizzy," and sank to his knees.

"Sit still a minute longer," Rudy suggested firmly as he caught hold of Kon. "I'll get a toboggan for you."

Kon seized Rudy by the arm. "No! Don't do that to me! Please!" he pleaded. "I'll ski back — just give me a minute. Please!"

"O.K. O.K. I understand. I'll help you back, but that's it for today. Do you understand?"

"Yes," Kon nodded submissively. They sat in silence for a few minutes, and Rudy offered Kon some chocolate. He wondered who Jack and Paul were, and where Kon had met them, but he didn't ask. He knew Kon was touchy about personal questions.

"You really are an excellent skier, Kon," Rudy said at last. "They aren't in your class at all. Remember that. You're just no good at showing off."

Kon nodded. "You're right. I was an idiot to try. I just wanted to . . . They're just so dammed . . ."

"Hey, my obstinate friend, there's more to life than big muscles," Rudy commented quickly. "You've got brains, and talent, and a lot of good qualities. They'll see it in you, when they get to know you. Besides, you're a lot tougher than you look, Kon."

"Oh save your breath, Rudy," Kon protested with a self-conscious grin. "You've got to get me back to the lodge before I make an ass of myself."

"Well, come on then," Rudy said pulling Kon to his feet. "You never listen to a damn thing I say anyway!"

"That's not true," Kon protested. "It was you who taught me to jump in the first place. I never would have thought of it myself."

"Yes, I taught you to jump — as a skier — not as some fool acrobat!"

"I'll behave myself tomorrow," Kon promised as Rudy helped him put on his skis.

"Tomorrow? You'll be lucky if you can walk tomorrow. Take it easy, Kon."

Kon considered Rudy's advice as he crawled out of bed the next morning, but he refused to sit quietly, nursing his bruises, while Jack and Paul were up and about. He stood in the shower for a long time, hoping the hot water would dissolve the stiffness in him, but the result was minimal. Fortunately for Kon's pride, neither Jack nor Paul had witnessed his horrible fall.

Jack was also feeling tired in the morning, but it had been his idea to go skiing, and he wasn't about to admit to Peter that he couldn't keep up the pace. He had been astounded by Peter's speed on the slopes. Watching Peter soar off the jumps with effortless grace, increased Jack's determination to learn to ski as fast as possible.

Paul would have been satisfied to go for a swim and relax a bit, even if it meant enduring a razzing from Jack, but somehow the thought of Peter soaring effortlessly through the air egged him on. Letting his feelings overrule his judgement, Paul dressed and went out with Jack and Peter. He watched them go their separate ways, then headed for the cross-country trails. He passed few other people as he went, and was soon absorbed by the beauty and peace of the mountains.

****

By 3:30 in the afternoon Paul was beginning to feel weary. He had been out on the prepared trails since early morning, and had been too far away from the main lodge to stop for lunch. He regretted that he hadn't taken Peter's suggestion to carry some chocolate with him. The scenery had been so enchanting, Paul hardly realized that the trail wound gradually uphill. He knew he was puffing more, but he put it off to the strenuous activity.

When he came to an unmarked fork in the trail, Paul went to the left, thinking to make a sweep around the next peak, and then head back to the lodge. The bright afternoon sunshine had disappeared, and the temperature began to drop rapidly as the sky turned dark. After Paul moved several hundred yards farther along the trail, it became clear that the trail wasn't going to turn back as he had hoped. He felt disappointed. What had been fun was rapidly becoming an effort. The wind had picked up, and he felt it's biting chill, even through his jacket. He pictured himself back at the lodge, sitting by the fire, sipping brandy with Jack and Peter. Just keep going, he told himself, and for a little while it worked.

Farther along the trail, the scenery changed, and Paul could see a village far below him in the valley. The houses looked snug and inviting, as more and more lights began to glow a rich, warm ocher against the somber grey sky. If only I could get to one of those buildings, I could rest and escape this terrible numbing cold, he thought longingly. Surely someone there would know how to get back to the lodge.

Paul kept his eye on the edge of the trail, hoping to find a path leading down to the valley. He began to breathe harder as the trail became steeper. His ankles and knees ached with every stride, and he began to wonder if the trail would ever turn back. The trails are all loops, aren't they? Did I made a wrong turn somewhere? Did I miss a marker? The realization that it would soon be dark made him vaguely uneasy. Paul no longer perceived the trail as tranquil and beautiful. It had become empty and hostile. Is it stupid to keep going? Should I turn back? What am I doing out here alone?

Suddenly Paul saw a break in the edge of the trail. Something, or someone had taken a short cut down to the valley through the trees. Paul should have realized he was not equipped for back country trails, but he no longer cared. He was hungry, bitterly cold, and tired, so terribly tired. He had to get down to the valley now, before this bone-chilling wind blew him off the mountain, or the growing darkness enveloped him completely.

Someone had made this trail down to the warmth of the valley, and if they could do it, so can I, he reasoned. This trail I'm following must lead to Italy, or France, or God knows where. I don't know how, but I must have made a wrong turn. I've got to do something, or I'll never get back.

Paul turned and left the main trail. This new trail was easy at first; the snow was just a little deeper that was all. The descent was gradual, winding gently down through the trees. It felt good to slide downwards without having to push at every stroke. Paul was pleased with his decision to take a short cut. This was so much easier. It was going to be fun to slide down to the valley. He felt exhilarated, as he started to gain speed. I'm going to make it! he thought. I will be safe and warm in some cabin before my strength gives out completely. I should have thought of this before.

Paul's euphoria grew as he gained speed, and for a brief moment, he imagined that if he could just gain enough momentum, he could leave the trail, and soar out over the trees like Peter did. Hell! Peter wasn't all that clever – all you needed was enough speed and . . . By the time Paul noticed that the trail had taken a sharp turn to the right, it was too late. He raced forward unchecked, breaking a path as he went. He tried to slow his progress, but his right ski caught on the tip of a rock protruding through the snow. Suddenly he pitched forward over his skis, and was thrown head first into the underbrush. He was aware of dried leaves and twigs slapping at his face, and clawing at his clothes, as he descended. Paul felt a shaft pierce his left forearm, and then an icy wall struck his chest with such force that his breath was snatched away.

Almost ten minutes had passed before Paul floated back to consciousness. He lifted his head slightly, and saw blood dripping into the snow. Something's hurt, he thought absently. A rabbit? A deer? He didn't like seeing the blood drip right before his eyes. He raised his head slightly higher, and saw that his blood soaked sleeve was caught on a branch. He tried to pull his arm towards him, but let out a cry, as he felt his flesh tearing. Fighting down his rising nausea, he tried to crawl forward, but he felt a shooting pain in his right knee. Laboriously he dragged himself forwards, but from his position on his stomach, he could not raise his arm high enough to lift it off the broken branch. Steeling his nerve, he tried again to yank his arm free, but once again he felt his arm being torn apart. One more excruciating pull was all he could manage, before he sank into oblivion.

CHAPTER TWENTY-ONE

Shortly before 3:00 p.m., Kon swallowed his pride, and started back to the lodge. He could no longer ignore the throbbing of the massive bruise on his left hip. No matter what Jack or Paul might think, he was weary and didn't dare risk another run. He stopped by the beginners slope, and silently observed Jack for a few minutes. Jack didn't look as eager as he had on the first day out. In fact, he was spending more time flat on his back than upright, and he seemed to be fighting his equipment.

Shaking his head, Kon skied over to where Jack had once again fallen. "You've learned a lot, Jack, but don't you think it's time to go in?" he said, and extended a hand to Jack.

"Damn! I think I'm getting worse instead of better. I can't seem to keep my feet untangled," Jack answered from the ground.

"Maybe you're trying too hard. Why don't you stop for a while," Kon suggested. He saw that Jack was puffing.

"What time is it?" Jack answered and accepted Kon's extended hand.

"It's nearly 3 o'clock."

"Hey, it's still early. I can't quit yet."

"Why not? You don't have to learn everything in one day," Kon replied. He smiled, remembering how often Rudy had said that very thing to him.

"Yeah, but . . ." Jack started, but stopped. "Well, I was just fooling around until Paul got back. Have you seen him?"

"No. Did he come back for lunch?"

"No. I haven't seen him since this morning."

"Did he say where he was going?" Kon asked, suddenly feeling concerned.

"He said he wanted to try one of the ridge trails. He likes to get off by himself. You know, he should be back by now. Maybe I should look for him."

"You can't, Jack. He might be miles from here and you haven't even tried cross-country. I'll go."

"Well, I'll come with you. What can be so difficult about cross-country?"

"It's quite different, and I don't think you are up to learning it right now. Why don't you go back to the lodge and wait for us?"

"No! If Paul is in trouble, it's my responsibility, not yours."

"Listen, Jack," Kon began politely. "You are both here as my guests, and I feel responsible for your safety. You've learned a lot in the past two days, but you're not ready for this. You'll only slow me down. Please – go back to the lodge and wait. I don't want to worry about your breaking a leg while I look for Paul."

Jack grudgingly admitted the truth in what Kon had said.

"O.K., O.K. I'll go back, but shouldn't you get more help?"

Kon was about to say no, but reconsidered. He looked at his watch, and then at the darkening sky. Chances are that Paul's already on his way back, he thought. But if Paul is in trouble, I might not be able to find him before dark.

"You're right," Kon said aloud. "I'll alert the ski patrol. Paul could have gone a long way by now."

Kon gave Jack a hand with his equipment, and they hurried towards the lodge. They met Rudy on the way.

"Have you seen Paul today?" Kon inquired anxiously.

"As a matter-of-fact, I did," Rudy replied. "He asked me about some of the ridge trails. I showed him several on the map. Isn't he back yet?"

"No, and it's getting dark early. I think I should go look for him," Kon answered. "I could use some help from the ski patrol. There's a lot of ground to cover."

Rudy frowned. "That won't be so easy. A group of English skiers have been smacking into trees on the higher runs, and there's been a minor avalanche on the trail to the next village. Most of the ski patrol is tied up for the next hour or so. I'll tell you what," Rudy added, seeing the distressed looks on Jack's and Kon's faces. "I'll show you the area that I recommended to Paul, and I'll let you take one of the portable radios. If you start now, I'll call some men from town, and they can be on the trail in less than an hour."

Kon looked at his watch. It was already 3:20 p.m.

"I hope Paul is on his way back, but I'd better get going. Can I borrow some equipment, Rudy?"

Rudy nodded, and selected some skis for Kon from his own collection. He knew what would suit him.

"Jack, why don't you take a look around the lodge while Kon gets ready. Check the restaurant area. No sense going out if Paul is sitting in the bar with a beer."

Jack chuckled, and made a rapid tour of the lodge, checking all the seating areas and the rest rooms.

"He's not in here, and I can guarantee he wouldn't go back to the chalet without letting me know," Jack said when he returned.

Kon had changed boots and was about to dash out the door.

"Kon! Wait!" Rudy called after him. "Take a pack – just in case." Rudy handed Kon a small backpack, and turning away from Jack, he lowered his voice to a whisper. "Are you sure you feel up to this, Kon?" he asked.

"Yes! Yes! I'll be fine. Just don't let Jack go out."

"O.K." Rudy said reluctantly. "I wouldn't let you go, if I had anyone else. Be careful, and be sure to check in on the radio. I'll coordinate things from here, and send more men as soon as they are available."

"Thanks, Rudy. I should have kept a closer watch on Paul."

"Hey! He's pretty independent. Here, take these," Rudy added, slipping several chocolate bars into Kon's pocket. "Good luck!"

Jack watched Kon leave. He studied the trail map, estimating the distance Paul could have covered since morning and felt useless. He was not used to the sensation, and it rankled him.

It was almost 3:45 by the time Kon was on the trail. He knew that there were 19 miles of groomed trails at Villars, but with Jack and Rudy's help, he had eliminated the trails Paul had taken on the first two days. That still left 10 miles of trails to be searched, assuming that Paul hadn't left the trail for some reason.

Kon took the first trail that Rudy had suggested to Paul. It was slightly more than 3 miles long, and relatively easy going. Kon thought that Paul might have taken that trail after a day of more vigorous skiing. Kon had done cross-country racing in the past, and could cover ground fast. He worked up a sweat on the trail, but didn't find Paul.

With two remaining trails to choose from, Kon chose the longer, higher trail. If Paul was determined to get away from it all, that would be the trail to pick. Kon knew the trail well, and decided to make a reverse loop to the recommended traffic flow. Although going in that direction meant he was immediately forced to climb two steep hills, most of the trail would be down hill.

Kon was puffing, and his thigh ached by the time he reached the top of the second hill. When he stopped to rest, he remembered that he had forgotten to check in after completing the first trail. He radioed Rudy to let him know where he was. Blaming the wind for his breathless sounding transmission, he tried to hide the fact that he was tired. Kon ate one of the chocolate bars, pulled his collar up, and felt a little better for the moment.

Even though the trail was now mostly a gentle downhill grade, it took effort to move along with any speed. There weren't many tracks in the snow, and Kon had no way of telling which, if any, were Paul's. He pushed onward, and about a mile and a half down the trail, he saw an indication that someone had left the trail. There were a lot of ski tracks in the snow, as if someone had found it difficult to turn and head into the trees. The tracks were fresh.

It was 5:15, the sky was dark, and it was cold. Kon gazed at the lights in the village far below and thought of the warmth coming from the many fireplaces. He shivered slightly and was glad for the protection of the Norwegian ski jacket Charlotte had given him two years ago. She knew he was always the first to get chilled on a ski outing. He had come down with bronchitis one year, and she had never let him forget it.

There was no way for Kon to know if it had been Paul who had taken this cut through the trees, but if he didn't search the area now, it would be too black to search it later. Standing at the summit of the narrow trail, Kon shouted Paul's name several times. The sound carried down the valley on the wind, but there was no answer. Kon radioed back to the lodge. Paul had not come in yet, and Rudy was having trouble rounding up enough men to make a search. He promised to keep trying. Kon sized up the dark trail, and gave his position to Rudy, in case he couldn't make it back again in the dark. Rudy advised Kon to wait for a team with lights, but Kon shut off the radio without responding. If Paul had left a well-marked, groomed trail, for a path through the woods, he must have been confused and irrational. Kon had seen skiers behave that way when they got extremely cold. If that had happened to Paul, he needed help soon.

Moving cautiously, Kon glided down the trail. He followed the tracks, and several hundred yards later the narrow trail grew steep. Kon hoped fervently that these were not Paul's tracks he was following. Paul had no business being on a trail like this. The trail swung to the right and Kon started to turn. Suddenly he noticed the tracks heading straight ahead. Someone had missed the turn. Kon halted abruptly and scanned down the slope. He could see nothing but the dark shapes of trees. It seemed hopelessly futile to call into the darkness, but he did. He shouted Paul's name again and again, but the wind mocked his efforts.

Carefully sidestepping down the hill, Kon followed the ski tracks, until they vanished mysteriously. Kon was seized by the sinking thought that he too was a victim of the cold, and that his mind was playing tricks on him. No! Those were ski tracks I was following. Where did they go? Kon stood a moment, and then shoving his poles into the snow, he removed his backpack. He struggled with the zipper, until at last it slid open. He pulled out a long metal flashlight, and held it between his knees, while he closed the pack, and slung it on his back.

Holding the light, Kon slid forward very slowly, straining his eyes to see ahead. Several yards in front of him was a stand of young trees, and he moved towards them, until his ski clinked on something metallic half hidden in the snow. He stopped to pick it up. It was a ski pole. He slid forward, looking up and down the line of trees. Then he saw the dark shape on the ground, between the trees. It was too dark to recognize the color of the clothes, but it was a body. Anxiously, Kon kicked off his skis, planted them and the poles as a marker, and ran forward.

Whoever it was, was lying flat on the ground, except for one arm that appeared to be suspended in the air. Kon focused the light on the arm, and felt his stomach turn, as he realized that the arm was impaled on a broken branch. Hurriedly Kon leaned over the form, and saw that it was Paul. There was blood on his face.

"Paul! Paul! Merciful God, don't let him be dead!" Kon prayed aloud. He dropped to his knees beside Paul. Hastily he propped the flashlight upright in the snow, and tore off his gloves. He fumbled with Paul's sleeve, and held Paul's wrist. Paul's skin was cold to the touch, but Kon felt a slight throb beneath his fingers. Quickly Kon slipped off his backpack, and zipped it open. Reaching in, he groped for the first aid kit. Purposefully he moved around Paul's head, and very cautiously he tried to lift Paul's arm from the branch. He had barely moved it when Paul groaned.

"Oh God! I'm sorry, Paul," Kon whispered. "I'm sorry. I didn't mean to hurt you." Kon picked up the light, and tried to examine the wound, but he could see nothing but blood. "I can't see what's holding it, Paul. Paul? Can you hear me? I can't see a damn thing!"

Kon put his hand on Paul's cheek and wiped the blood away. He dare not move Paul's head. "Paul! Please . . . answer me," Kon called several times.

Suddenly Paul called faintly, "Jack?"

"No, it's Peter. I'm trying to help you."

"Peter?"

"Yes, Peter Kononellos. I came to look for you."

"Where's Jack?"

"He couldn't come . . . he . . . he had another job."

"Oh . . . he didn't tell me. My arm is stuck, Peter. I can't lift it."

"I know. It's caught on a branch. I can't see well enough to pull it free. I'll have to cut the branch."

"It's bleeding, Jack," Paul mumbled. "I saw it dripping. I thought it was a rabbit . . . or something."

"You'll be all right — I've got some bandages," Kon said, trying to sound confident. "I'll fix it. Just let me get it free."

Kon propped the light in the snow again, and reached for his knife. He began to cut the branch, trying to hold it as still as possible, but he heard Paul suck in his breath as the branch gave way.

"I'm sorry! God, I'm sorry!" Kon said, as he caught Paul's arm. "I'll get a bandage on it."

Kon opened the first aid kit and felt for the thick soft packages. He opened one, and began to work, but it seemed an impossible task to hold Paul's arm, unwrap the bandages, place the bandages over the wound, and tie them in place. He worked carefully, so as not to drive the branch deeper into Paul's flesh. The wind whipped at the bandages, and Kon's fingers grew numb and stiff. He attempted to adjust the light several times, but it kept falling over, leaving him in the dark. Kon talked to Paul as he worked, and tried to assess the extent of his injuries. He was relieved that Paul's neck was not broken, and that Paul could move his right arm. Paul was conscious, but not really alert, and kept asking about Jack. He seemed extremely concerned about him.

"Don't worry. Jack's fine," Kon assured him. "He's at the lodge with Rudy. He's helping coordinate a search team."

"Good . . . good. I was afraid he would hurt himself. He's over enthusiastic sometimes."

After what seemed like hours, Kon had the bandages in place around Paul's arm. He wished he had more bandages, but he was glad to have the bleeding under control.

"It's not a very neat job," Kon apologized. "Does anything else hurt? Can you turn over?"

"Something's wrong with my knee," Paul muttered. "It hurts to move it."

"Which knee hurts?"

"What?"

"Which knee hurts, Paul?"

"Right . . . the right one."

"Can you move your left leg? No pain anywhere else?" Kon questioned.

"No . . . it's . . . it's just the knee. I tried to get to the branch, but I couldn't push . . . I can't tell if it's broken," Paul answered, and struggled to move.

"O.K., O.K. Don't move it!" Kon responded excitedly. "Just stay there, O.K.? I've got to find something . . . my ski, that's it . . . O.K., I've got to get my ski to make a splint. I'll be right back. Don't move, O.K.? I'll be right back."

"I'll wait," Paul muttered.

Kon snatched up the light, and followed his footprints back to his skis. So much for leaving a sign, he thought. As least I can leave the poles crossed. He put the skis over his shoulder, and hurried back to Paul. He knelt in the snow, and planted the light again. The beam flickered, and Kon swore and rapped the case. The beam steadied. "I'm going to have to straighten your leg, Paul," Kon said, taking hold of Paul's foot.

"I know. Go ahead . . . just be . . . oh damn! I really messed it up. Are you finished?"

"Yes. Hold still while I brace it with my ski." Kon rummaged in the backpack. "Shit! There's nothing to tie it with! What kind of God damn, stupid emergency kit is this anyway? Damn it to hell!" Kon shouted in frustration and threw the backpack aside. "God damn! I must have used the wrong stuff on your arm," Kon muttered in disgust. "There must be something to tie . . . hold on . . ." Kon mumbled, and reaching up he opened the neck of his coat, and pulled his scarf free. Cutting the edge with his knife, he tore the scarf in half lengthwise. "All right, I think this should work," Kon said more calmly, and began to fasten his ski along the back of Paul's leg. "There, unless I've forgotten something, you should be O.K. now. Doesn't look very good . . ."

"It'll be O.K., Peter. I appreciate . . ."

"It's nothing," Kon said, cutting Paul off.

Paul strained to roll over, and Kon turned him on his back. It bothered Kon to see blood marring the perfection of Paul's handsome face. He wiped the blood away several times, and wished he had something to put over the cut.

"I'd better call for some help to get you back," Kon said and radioed Rudy. He gave his assessment of Paul's injuries, and tried to pin-point their location. Rudy scolded Kon for being so late to call in, but promised to send a snowmobile with a toboggan as soon as possible.

Kon turned back from the radio, and noticed for the first time that Paul was shivering. It's no wonder he's cold, Kon thought; his hat is gone, his sleeve is soaked with blood and who knows how long he's been lying in the snow.

"Paul?" Kon called, seeing that Paul had closed his eyes. "I called Rudy. He'll get someone up here right away. Don't worry. We'll get you back."

"Thanks, Peter," Paul answered weakly. "Rudy always calls you Kon? Is that your nickname?"

"I suppose so," Kon answered slowly. "People used to call me that when I was a boy."

"I like it. It fits you better than Peter."

"I never have liked being Peter, but I didn't have much . . . That's just what I'm called at the bank."

"Would you mind if I called you Kon?" Paul asked.

"I guess not. People call me all sorts of names, especially behind my back."

"Like what?" Paul asked.

"Just forget about it," Kon snapped. "I'm not supposed to hear what they say."

"O.K . . . O.K., but Kon's a good name."

Kon didn't answer. He watched Paul shiver for another few minutes, and then quickly unzipped his heavy jacket. He pulled it off, and laid it on the ground beside Paul. Kneeling next to Paul, Kon lifted him and laid him on the jacket. Gently he placed Paul's bloody arm part way into one sleeve. The jacket was too small to wrap around Paul's jacket, but it came far down his back. Kon pulled the zipper together at the bottom and closed it up as far as possible.

"You shouldn't do this, Kon. You'll catch cold," Paul objected weakly.

"I'll be all right. I've got a heavy sweater. Here . . . let me fix your scarf," Kon added, and unzipping Paul's jacket he pulled Paul's scarf out, and wrapped it around Paul's head, covering his ears. He zipped Paul's jacket closed again, and tucked the ends of the scarf in. "There . . . how's that?"

"Much better," Paul said with a weak smile. "You're good at this doctor stuff, Kon. You must have a string of little brothers."

"No . . . I never had a brother," Kon said sitting down next to Paul. "I . . . I used to take care of two boys for a family. I guess it was like having brothers. But don't expect anything else. I don't wipe noses for anyone over six."

Paul chuckled. "Six! Boy are you a soft touch. I cut 'em off at four. With seven noses to look after, I wouldn't have had time for anything else."

"Seven! You have seven brothers?" Kon said in disbelief.

"Yeah. My mother just likes kids, I guess."

"Your father must have been rich. My father . . . my father used to complain that I ate him out of house and home."

"He complained about you? I just can't picture you being a big eater. You're so damn . . . I'm sorry . . . I shouldn't have said that," Paul apologized.

"Never mind," Kon answered numbly. "I'm used to it. I hear it all the time. Tell me about your father. Does he like kids too?"

"I guess he must have. He certainly could have done something about it if he didn't. He was a doctor."

"A doctor . . . that's nice," Kon said, suddenly feeling the emptiness he always felt when people talked about their families. Mentally, he drew away from Paul. He hoped Paul wouldn't ask him about his father.

Paul was too groggy to see the change in Kon, however, and rambled on without stopping. "Yeah, he wanted me to follow in his footsteps . . . college, med school, the whole bit. I wasn't too interested . . . but then he died and everything changed – everything," Paul ended sadly.

"Yes, I know what you mean . . . what happened to your father?"

"At first my mother told us it was a heart attack. I didn't believer her. He had never had any trouble with his heart. And the police kept coming around. I was seventeen. I was a bit wild, but I wasn't stupid . . . we lived in Chicago. So I asked the police. They put me off . . . but I kept asking questions. Then they told me to quit snooping around or I would wind up the same way. Stay out of it they said . . . my mother needed me . . . I finally wormed it out of them. My father had been murdered."

"Murdered!" Kon gasped. "Mother of God! How? Why?"

"He went on an emergency call on the south side. He was good about that. He always went when people needed help. It was a bad neighborhood. He didn't care, he went whenever people needed him. They shot him! Right through the head. Christ! He never had a chance."

"But why? Who would kill a doctor?"

"Mistaken identity, the police said. There was a gang war going on, and he got in the middle of it." Paul's voice had grown fainter, and he seemed to be losing his concentration. Kon was anxious to keep him awake.

"What a loss! Chicago must be a terrible place. Paul? Paul?" Kon shook him gently. "Tell me about Chicago, Paul. What is it like?"

"It was pretty tough," Paul responded vaguely. "I had joined a gang myself. I wanted to be big time stuff — I wanted to be accepted."

"But your father was a doctor. You must have had a good life. Doors would be open for you."

Paul hesitated, as if reluctant to verbalize his secret thoughts. Then he talked on. "Not if your mother is a foreigner, and you have slanted eyes. Christ! I didn't fit anywhere. I wasn't white, I wasn't black, or Hispanic. It wasn't even an Asian gang. It was just a bunch of creeps, but they let me join. God I was stupid . . . so stupid. They never fought my battles, but I got pulled into theirs. I was always in a fight."

"I know the feeling," Kon answered, suddenly feeling that perhaps there wasn't such a gulf between himself and Paul. "What happened after your father . . .?"

". . . . had to get a job . . . didn't leave much money. It takes a lot to raise eight kids. My dad was never rich. He wasn't a surgeon or a specialist. He just took care of people . . . patients . . . my mother . . . and all of us. It was pretty hard after he died."

Paul stopped talking, and Kon feared he had blacked out. He knew he had to keep Paul awake, but it was getting more and more difficult. Kon could feel his own energy ebbing away, and he was bitterly cold. He touched Paul's face and called to him.

"Paul? Paul? Stay awake, Paul . . . please. Someone will be here soon." He put his hand on Paul's shoulder.

Paul's voice came back faint, but determined. "Kon . . . things are looking pretty desperate here. I won't be able to stay . . . to stay awake much longer, and you're shaking. God, you must be cold . . . shouldn't have taken your coat off . . . stupid idea."

"No! No," Kon objected. "I'm fine. Rudy should be here any minute. Just hold on."

"Listen to me, Kon. I think it's time we tried something to . . . to preserve our body heat. You've got to lay down on top of me so we can help each other keep warm."

"That's crazy!" Kon objected immediately. "I'll only hurt your arm. I'm fine where I am."

"Don't be stubborn, Kon . . . please. Just try it. I could use a little more heat . . . please."

"Oh all right! What am I supposed to do?"

"I'm not sure . . . just lay down here, and pretend you're a blanket."

Kon moved closer to Paul, and slowly lowered himself over Paul's body.

"Are you sure this is supposed to help?" Kon asked irritably.

"Yes . . . it's an old boy scout trick."

"What's a boy scout?"

"You've never heard of the boy scouts? Where the hell have you been?" Paul asked in surprise.

"Here and there," Kon said vaguely. "I must have missed them."

"Do you feel any better?" Paul asked after a few minutes.

"A little . . . at least this keeps the wind off one side."

"You're still shaking," Paul said flatly.

"I can't help it," Kon snapped. "Hey, this was your idea!"

Kon regretted his temper when Paul didn't answer. "Paul? Tell me about these boy scouts. What do they do besides lay on top of each other in the snow?"

Paul sighed. "They're sort of a club for boys. They teach you how to build fires . . . and how to survive in the wilderness and . . . and stuff like that. Jack was a boy scout."

"I never learned any of that. Do they teach you how to fight?"

"No . . . No . . . Boy scouts aren't supposed to get in fights. They're supposed to be honest and . . . and trustworthy . . . and honest . . . and patriotic and help people . . . yeah . . . that's it . . . they're supposed to help people."

"Who do they help?"

"Well, they help old ladies . . . and little kids . . . and . . . each other."

"Would they help a Greek?"

"I suppose so. I don't remember the list . . . Greeks must be in there somewhere."

"That's good. Nobody ever helps a Greek," Kon said wearily.

"Are you Greek? I thought you were Swiss."

"Ha!" Kon laughed bitterly. "Ask the Swiss. They never let me forget it. Were you a boy scout, Paul?"

"No . . . I was . . . I was a 'Green Dragon'"

"A 'Green Dragon'? What did they teach you?"

"They taught me to smoke . . . and spit at cops . . . and to hot wire a car and . . ."

"Did they teach you how to fight?"

"No . . . my uncle taught me. He's good . . . really good . . . even today he can kick me around like dirt."

"You were lucky," Kon responded enviously. "I had to learn on my own."

". . . did a good job, Kon," Paul answered with conviction.

Kon lay across Paul's chest, and put his head down. He was

292

tired, so tired, and so bitterly cold. I must not go to sleep, he warned himself. He could hear nothing save the sound of the wind. The flashlight had quit working.

"Paul? Are you awake?" Kon asked, snapping himself awake. "Don't go to sleep, Paul . . . please."

"I'm awake," Paul mumbled. "I think there's a bear coming, Kon. I hear growling."

"There aren't any bears in Switzerland, Paul. It's just the wind."

"No, it's a bear . . . getting closer. You better . . . you better run, Kon. I . . . I just don't have the strength . . ."

"There aren't any bears, Paul. Don't worry. I wouldn't leave you here if there were."

"Listen, Kon. It's a bear . . . must be a big one . . . it's growling. Run Kon! . . . Run!" Paul gasped.

Suddenly Kon heard the sound. He pulled himself upright. "It's not a bear, Paul! It's a snowmobile! They're coming Paul! Paul?" Kon shouted, and shook Paul. He didn't answer. "Paul! Paul! Wake up!" Kon shouted again and again, and felt a terrible loneliness creeping over him. Before it gripped him completely, he heard a call. "Kononellos? Kononellos is that you? Where are you?"

Kon inhaled and fought off his despair. "Down here! Behind the trees! Hurry!" he shouted. Kon kept shouting and calling into the blackness, afraid to leave Paul for fear he would never find him again in the dark.

At last the searchers found Kon's crossed poles and followed his footprints. They located Kon sitting next to Paul, holding one arm protectively across Paul's chest. "He was afraid of bears," Kon mumbled. "I told him there weren't any, but he didn't believe me."

"It's O.K. It's O.K. You did a good job keeping the bears away. We'll take over now," one of the search team said. He wrapped a blanket around Kon, and helped him to his feet.

"He hurt his leg," Kon said. "The right one . . . at the knee. I tried to fix it, but there wasn't any . . . there wasn't any . . ." Kon mumbled as the searchers knelt over Paul. "Be careful of his arm. It was torn . . . on a bush. He was awake until just a minute ago, but I lost him. He was afraid of bears. I tried to tell him . . . but I lost him."

"He'll be fine. He's still breathing O.K. Don't worry."

Kon didn't recognize any of the searchers, but they seemed to know what they were doing. One man stood with him, supporting him, and holding the blanket around him.

"Where's Rudy?" Kon asked, momentarily coming out of the fog that had engulfed his brain.

"He's still coordinating things back at the lodge. It's been a busy day for accidents. Rudy said to tell you he was staying behind to keep Jack out of trouble."

"Good . . . good. He's terrible on skis . . . never saw a man fall so many times. He wanted to come . . . he really wanted to come, but I was afraid he'd kill himself."

The rescuers had fastened a smaller splint for Paul's leg, and arranged the blankets in the toboggan.

"I think you should get in first and hold him," one man said to Kon.

"No! I don't need to ride," Kon answered sharply. "I'll ski back. Where are my skis?"

"I don't know," the man lied. "Come on, it's a long way back. You don't even have a jacket."

"I've got a jacket! It's under Paul. I can ski. I don't need to ride in that thing!" Kon said raising his voice, and slowly backing away from the men. "Where are my skis? I must find my skis!"

One man caught Kon by the arm, and made vague promises about searching for his skis, while the other two had a brief conference. After a few minutes, they came toward Kon.

"Look, we know you can ski back, but what about your friend? What if he wakes up and starts to worry about bears again? He'll be scared to death by himself. You don't want him to be afraid, do you?"

Kon looked warily from one man to the other. "Paul's not afraid. I don't want Paul to be afraid," he said weakly.

"Of course you don't. So if you get in first, and kind of hold him, he'll stay calm, and sleep all the way back. All right?"

"All right. I'll go with him," Kon agreed. He limped toward the toboggan, and got in stiffly. His hip was hurting badly, his shoulder ached, and his feet were icy.

The rescue crew lifted Paul, and laid him in front of Kon.

"I'll bring his skis," one of the crew said quietly.

"Good. I'm glad Rudy warned us how pigheaded this guy can be."

"He's not a problem," the first man responded. "A lot of guys get a little strange when they're half-frozen. He can't even remember that he used his ski to make a splint. He did a nice job, but he's in bad shape now."

Kon was barely awake during the ride back to the lodge, but he stayed with Paul, as promised, and followed him into the ambulance without comment. When they arrived at the hospital, Paul was still unconscious, and was quickly wheeled away, while Kon was ushered into a curtained treatment area to be checked by a doctor.

Rudy and Jack, who showed up a few minutes later, had no trouble locating Kon. They could hear him disclaiming at the top of his lungs, "God damn it! There is nothing wrong with me! Leave me alone! Where is Paul? What have you done to him?"

They hurried down the hall, and discovered Kon, his back to the wall, his fists up, threatening to strike down the next man who tried to take his clothes from him. One of the two attendants with him was wiping a cut lip. Rudy stepped into the treatment area without hesitation and stood in front of Kon.

"Paul's fine," Rudy said calmly. "They took him to surgery to stitch up his arm. You're behaving very badly, Kon," Rudy continued, shaking his head in disgust. "They just want to get the wet clothes off you. You'll catch pneumonia if you stand around like that. Come on, I brought you some dry clothes."

"Get them out of here, Rudy!" Kon barked, still holding his fists up.

"All right! Don't get so upset. They were only trying to help you. Christ, you're making a scene over nothing," Rudy answered, and waved the two men out of the area.

"Go get him some hot coffee. I'll look after him," he told them quietly.

They hesitated. "Are you sure you'll be all right?" one man asked, obviously convinced from Kon's aggressive stance that he was not to be trifled with.

"Go on. I'll be O.K. Kon's just a little shy about taking his clothes off in front of strangers."

"Shy! The man's a raving lunatic!" the attendant with the cut lip shot back.

"No, no," Rudy assured them, flashing his good natured smile. "He's just a little upset, that's all."

The men left, and Rudy moved closer to Kon. "How are you feeling, Kon?" he asked with sincere concern.

Kon slowly lowered his fists, and his aggressive facade vanished, revealing his extreme fatigue. He shivered violently.

"I'm cold, Rudy," Kon whispered wearily. "I'm so cold it burns." He slumped against the wall to steady himself.

"I thought so. Come on, sit down over here," Rudy said, taking Kon by the arm. "Jack, bring me those clothes, will you?"

Rudy helped Kon to the treatment bench. "Look at you, you're all wet under that sweater. The sooner you get it off, the better you'll feel."

"I can't get it off, Rudy. My hands won't work. I couldn't even get my knife."

"And it's a good thing, too. You'll get yourself in trouble. You'll be O.K. Just sit still a minute," Rudy said, and grasping Kon's sweater, he pulled it over Kon's head. He started to pull on Kon's cotton shirt, but it was wet, and stuck to Kon's skin. "Give me a hand with this, will you, Jack," Rudy called over his shoulder.

"No . . . don't," Kon started.

"Oh shut up, Kon!" Rudy said, and pushed Kon onto the table, squelching his objections. "You're becoming a nuisance. I'm sure Jack has seen a scar or two in his time."

Rudy continued to pull the clothes off Kon, but he raised his eyebrows when he saw the marks on Kon's shoulder and on his side. "Christ! What have you been doing to yourself?" he exclaimed.

"Things got out of control in Rome," Kon said evasively. "It's nothing."

"Nothing! Edgar told me at Christmas that you had been in the hospital, but . . . Jesus, Kon! Stick to skiing. It's not so dangerous!"

Kon turned his head aside, and closed his eyes, but he remained passive as Rudy and Jack finished stripping his wet clothes off. He was always intensely embarrassed to have anyone see his scars, and he felt utterly shamed to be naked and helpless in front of Jack. Jack sensed Kon's feelings, however, and kept his opinions and his quips to himself. You can tell a lot about a man from his scars. This guy's been in one hell of a fight somewhere, Jack thought. But where? And why?

"Here, Peter, get these on before you turn into an icicle!" Jack remarked, and pulled a pair of his own baggy sweat pants over Kon's legs.

By the time Rudy and Jack had Kon dressed, and wrapped in a blanket, the hospital attendant had returned with the hot coffee. Rudy dumped two packets of sugar into it and brought it to Kon. Kon was shaking so badly, however, that Rudy had to hold the cup for him. When Kon continued to shake, even after the coffee was down, Jack reached into his coat pocket, and slyly pulled out his serviceable silver flask.

"Forget the coffee!" Jack remarked. "You need a real drink before you shake your mountings loose." Supporting Kon with one arm, Jack carefully held the flask for Kon.

"You take that thing everywhere?" Kon mumbled.

"Sure," Jack said and smiled broadly. "Boy scout rule – be prepared!"

"You really are a boy scout, aren't you?" Kon whispered. He swallowed a few more sips, and felt a sensation of warmth coursing through him. He closed his eyes and relaxed, no longer loath to accept Jack's help. Paul had been right, Greeks must be on that list somewhere, he thought, and fell sound asleep.

"Well, he's out," Jack announced. "I'd better go see about Paul."

"Go ahead. I'll stay with Kon," Rudy said, as Jack left.

A few minutes later, a doctor came to check Kon over. "I can't find any indication of frostbite," he remarked. "Let him sleep for a couple of hours, and I'll check him again before you take him home."

"What about this?" Rudy asked, showing the doctor the massive bruise on Kon's hip. "If you want to get an X-ray, you'd better do it now. He can be very uncooperative when he's awake."

"So I've heard!" the doctor chuckled. "Let's do it to be on the safe side."

So Kon was taken to the X-ray department, but nothing serious showed up on the films.

Jack had to wait for over an hour before he was allowed to see Paul, who had been taken to surgery. Luckily Paul's leg was not broken, but his knee had been severely twisted, and his ankle was sprained. He was still in shock from loss of blood and extreme cold, but the doctors gave him a unit of blood, and assured Jack that he would be coming out of it soon.

Jack got some coffee and sat in the waiting room. So much had happened, he couldn't believe it when he looked at his watch, and saw that it was only 7:30. He thought about calling Brad, but he decided to wait until Paul came around, and he had a more definite idea of how he was. Besides, he had other reasons for not wanting Brad to learn that Paul was going to be out of commission for a while. Shortly after 9:00 p.m., a nurse came into the waiting room, and told Jack that Paul was awake and asking for his friends. Jack smiled and hurried after her.

"You may stay only a few minutes," the nurse told Jack as she turned and left. Paul was lying flat on the bed. His left arm was swathed in bandages from his wrist to his elbow, and his right arm was connected to a bottle of saline solution. His color was better than when he had been wheeled in, but he looked limp and tired.

"Hey, Paul! How's it going?" Jack said heartily.

"Hi, Jack," Paul responded slowly. "I'm O.K. I guess. They must have given me something . . . I can't keep my eyes open. Are you O.K.? I was worried . . ."

"I'm fine," Jack answered, and gave Paul's outstretched hand a firm squeeze. "Doc says you'll be O.K. soon. Nothing's broken."

"Good," Paul muttered sleepily. "Where's Kon?"

"He's asleep in a corner somewhere around here. He wore himself out searching for you. He'll be O.K. once he gets warmed up."

"Good . . . good. He's a strange guy, Jack. You know he still doesn't trust me. He came to ask me about his hand the other night. Nearly broke his heart to ask for help . . . but he gave me his coat. I told him it was a stupid idea . . . told him he would be cold. I had to get that guy half drunk before he let me lay a hand on him . . . but he gave me his coat — right off his back — like I was his best friend. Weird huh?"

"Yeah, he's weird all right," Jack agreed. "But it's a good thing he found you when he did. He might have saved your life. Hey buddy, you'd better get some rest. You almost look like I could take you down."

"Never, pal . . . never," Paul whispered, and he was out.

The nurse returned and shooed Jack from the room. "Go home," she told him in English, tinged with a heavy French accent. "He will sleep a long time now."

Paul seemed to be in good hands, so Jack decided to take her advice. He went to find Rudy, and together they woke Kon, and helped him out to the car. Kon asked about Paul several times, and Jack kept repeating that he was O.K. until Kon finally believed him. Rudy drove Jack and Kon to his home where Karina, his wife, had a pot of soup waiting for them. Seeing the tired group gathered around her table, Karina silently brought out extra bedding and insisted that Jack and Kon spend the night.

CHAPTER TWENTY-TWO

In the morning, the household conspired to stay quiet, so as not to wake Kon, who was sleeping much later than usual. On his way to work, Rudy dropped Jack off at the chalet, where he hurriedly cleaned up, before taking a cab to the hospital. Although visiting hours did not begin until 11 a.m., the nurses found it impossible to turn away the smiling, blond giant whose relaxed, yet determined, stance reinforced his quiet statement that he had every right to visit his business partner and friend. Sensing that nothing short of a good measure of physical violence would deter Jack, the nurses allowed him to sit with Paul who was still asleep.

Kon awoke shortly after Jack and Rudy left, but sat for a long time, drinking coffee with Karina. Although she had not seen him for almost a year, Karina reserved a special place in her heart for the man who had been so instrumental in bringing about her happy marriage to Rudy. Kon had spent many a pleasant evening relaxing with Rudy and Karina, and now he permitted her to pull the details of his broken engagement from him. She assured him sympathetically that he should not give up on Swiss girls, because of one bad experience.

"You are much too eligible to quit looking, Kon," she teased. "You're young, and good looking, and have piles of money. Lots of girls would rate you as a real prize!"

"A prize?" Kon asked caustically. "Is that all I am? Is it only a game for women to entice me and make me crazy, and then humiliate me?"

Karina understood intuitively that Kon's sudden bitterness involved someone other than sweet little Claire. He had shared his grief with her, but she dared not question him about the source of his bitterness. She sensed that this wound was too deep, and too raw to tolerate probing. Impulsively she put her hand over his.

"Real love exists, Kon. Don't close your heart to it," she said softly.

Kon enfolded her soft hand in his and squeezed it affectionately.

"Be good to Rudy, Karina. I need the inspiration."

"Be good to yourself, Kon. You're a dear friend to us both," she said, and stood abruptly. "Now, enough coffee. You must eat! You're getting too thin!"

"Blast! I hear that at every turn," he said impatiently.

"Well, do something about it!" she answered with a friendly laugh.

"All right, all right. If I am to play the prize goose, I suppose I must be stuffed."

"With pleasure," she laughed and went to the stove.

****

Kon arrived at the hospital shortly after 11 a.m. and was directed to Paul's room. He approached hesitantly, for he felt partly to blame for the fact that Paul had been injured. He wondered apprehensively what Paul might say. Stepping quietly into the room, he overheard what sounded like the tail end of an argument between Jack and Paul.

"No! You are not to go alone," Paul said with authority.

"But it will throw everything off schedule if I don't show. It doesn't take two people. I just have to meet the boat from Milan," Jack countered.

"Absolutely not — not without a backup — oh hello, Kon," Paul added, abruptly terminating his conversation with Jack.

"Good morning, Paul. How are you feeling?" Kon responded shyly.

"Better! Much better — thanks to you. The doctor said you probably saved my life," Paul said warmly and extended his hand.

Kon was a little embarrassed, but shook Paul's hand formally. "I didn't want . . . I wouldn't want to ruin the reputation the Swiss have for hospitality."

"Far from it! Say, how are you? Have you thawed out yet?"

"I am fine. I slept well and long."

"Great! Pull up a chair and stay as long as you like. Jack's got these nurses totally cowed."

So Kon sat, and Jack noted that he was more talkative than usual, and even smiled a bit. Maybe Kon's suspicious, thorny shell is beginning to crack, Jack thought.

Early the following morning, Jack and Kon went to meet Paul, who had demanded to be released from the hospital. Although barely able to hobble with the aid of a cane, he preferred the quiet and privacy of the chalet to a hospital room. Kon had packed for his return to Geneva and delayed only long enough to say goodbye to Paul.

"Goodbye, Kon. It's been a great trip despite my little incident," Paul said, shaking Kon's hand. "I'm glad Jack is spending the day in Geneva with you. It will keep him out of trouble. He wanted to . . . well, never mind. He's like a big kid sometimes, and I have to rein him in. He's very interested in your work at the bank."

"Yes . . . yes he is," Kon stammered. He hoped Paul hadn't noticed his surprise. Kon was shocked that Jack would lie to Paul, but he bit his tongue. What good would it do to betray Jack and cause a rift between friends?

"Well, I'd better be going," Kon said taking up his coat. "Call me if you are ever in Geneva."

"Goodbye, Kon and thanks again for everything."

Kon met Jack in the hall as he was leaving. "What are your plans for today?" Kon asked casually.

"Actually, I thought I would ride in to Geneva with you. I have to follow up on a few leads Brad gave us."

"Then we'd better get going or we'll miss the train," Kon answered looking at Jack with a quizzical expression.

"O.K.," Jack answered quickly. "Just let me tell Paul that we're off."

Jack disappeared into Paul's room, and Kon wondered again, exactly what Jack had told Paul. It is none of my business really, he told himself.

****

Kon's a bit strange, but he's bright, Jack thought, as he shook hands with him after they got off the train in Geneva. As soon as Kon had hailed a cab and disappeared, Jack bought another ticket, and took the train to the airport. Once there he headed for the general aviation terminal, and the Zeno Airlines office.

"Good morning," Jack said in French, as he walked up to the counter. "Is Stephin here today?"

"I believe so, Monsieur," a clerk answered and stepped behind some partitions. Several minutes later a short, youngish man, with dark bushy hair and a forty-eight hour growth of beard came up to greet Jack.

"Where to?" he said curtly.

"Lugano," Jack answered.

"Just yourself?" Stephin asked, giving Jack a sharp glance.

"Yes. My friend has been delayed."

"O.K. The plane is on the apron. It's the one with the wide yellow stripe on the nose. Any baggage?"

"I am to pick up a package here," Jack answered.

"The name?"

"Whitman. David Whitman," Jack answered.

"Yes, it's come," Stephin muttered, and reaching under the counter, he handed Jack a small parcel. "Go out that door," Stephin said gesturing with his thumb. "I'll be out in a few minutes."

Jack opened the door and was immediately hit by a blast of cold air. He strode rapidly toward the plane, happy to see that it was a high performance four seater. Being a pilot himself, he didn't mind a bumpy flight, but anything smaller might not be allowed to take off under such gusty conditions. Jack unwrapped the package Stephin had given him, and put on the clothes it contained. Not very smart, but at least the sleeves are long enough this time, he thought. He reached for the holster with the .38, and strapped it on.

After a short, but rough flight, Stephin set the plane down as if the runway had been hand polished.

"Three hours – no more," Stephin said curtly.

"I'll be here," Jack agreed, wondering if Stephin had ever heard the legend of Swiss hospitality.

The taxi was waiting as expected, and the driver handed Jack the keys.

"No dents, Signore, please," he pleaded anxiously in English. "It looks bad if you make the dents. The customers think I am reckless."

Jack grinned, remembering that he was in the Ticino area – almost a part of Italy. "O.K. – no dents. Relax! I won't be long."

Jack pulled a map from his pocket, and checked the route he had studied earlier. He slipped the vehicle into gear, and the taxi pulled away, with a shudder and a belch of smoke.

"Oh great! Just what I need, a built-in smoke screen," Jack muttered. "I hope I don't have to make a fast get away, or I'm out of luck."

Jack drove to the pier, parked the cab on the street, and checked his watch. The tour boat was not due for another twenty minutes, but already cabs were jockeying for curb space. Some were disgorging passengers, who were making a day-trip to shop in Italy. Others were waiting to take the Italians to the two busiest places in town – the banks and the casinos. The concepts of borders, and political jurisdiction, and currency controls are very nebulous in Lugano, and many interesting practices occur there that would not be tolerated in other parts of Switzerland. Occasionally these petty illegalities become more blatant, and official intervention becomes necessary. Jack was there to investigate one of these interesting situations.

Just as the tour boat pulled in and dropped the gang plank, Jack got out of the taxi. He strolled casually around to the passenger side, lit a cigarette, and leaned leisurely against the rear fender. His insolent manner did nothing to make him attractive to the first wave of passengers who came off the boat, and he studied the crowd. There were several men carrying suitcases, but Jack recognized Tony from a photograph Brad had shown him. He cast his cigarette away as Tony came by.

"Come to play a little baccarat, Signore?" Jack asked in Italian.

"No," Tony answered. "No pleasure for me today. I come on business."

"Ah, to the bank then," Jack said and nodded knowingly. "I know the way," Jack added, and opened the back door for Tony. There was no need to ask the name of the bank, for Jack knew.

"Don't pull away yet. I think I am being followed," Tony said apprehensively, as Jack got behind the wheel. "Some guy kept circling me while I was on the boat."

"No problem causing a delay in this thing," Jack said, and starting the cab he deliberately stalled it out. Pounding the steering wheel in mock anger, he got out of the vehicle and pulled up the hood. While Jack pretended to fiddle with the engine, Tony surveyed the thinning crowd for the man he suspected was tailing him. After a few moments he opened the car door and started to get out. Jack rushed over to block his way. "Please, Signore," he begged. "Give me another minute. I will have it going very soon."

"Be quick about it, you fool!" Tony shouted at Jack, then dropping his voice to a whisper he added. He's sitting in a dark grey car across the street. Let's go!"

"Patience please, Signore. I need the fare." Jack pleaded, and pressed the car door closed. Quickly he dashed around to the front of the car and slammed the hood down. He jumped into the car and started the engine. Pretending to check for traffic, he glanced at the car across the street, and pulled away from the curb.

"Anyone we know?" Jack asked.

"No, but De Bernardi runs a big operation."

"Have you got the list?" Jack inquired.

"Yes. Account numbers and amounts, but no names," Tony answered.

"That would be too easy. We'll have to investigate their connection. This is just the first step."

"Unfortunately my usefulness is over if they are on to me."

"Let's go to the bank and see what your 'friend' will do. You have to make those deposits, or De Bernardi will suspect you're up to something."

Jack drove straight to the bank. Checking his rear view mirror frequently, he saw that they were being followed. When they arrived, Jack waited in the cab while Tony entered the bank. Jack lit a cigarette and appeared to smoke casually, but he noticed when the dark grey car passed by and circled back. He had finished his cigarette before Tony came out of the bank.

"I've made the deposits. What now?" Tony asked getting into the taxi.

"You can't go back to Milan. It's too risky," Jack responded.

"But if I don't go back, De Bernardi will know something's wrong."

"We'll have to keep him guessing," Jack shot back. "I suggest you lay low for a few days. Take the first train out of here, and then call De Bernardi. Tell him you spotted the tail and you think the Italian authorities are on to you. Make excuses that you can't go back without tipping them off."

"O.K.," Tony drawled doubtfully. "I hope he falls for it."

"We just need to buy a little time so we can find out who owns those accounts. Be sure to check with me before you go back to Milan."

"O.K. I'll make the call," Tony agreed.

Jack consulted the map and drove the taxi to the train station. He thought he spotted the grey car tagging along, but to be certain they were not being followed he executed a series of unannounced left turns and doubled back several times along the way.

"I'll follow you in, just to make sure you get on the train," Jack said as he parked the taxi.

"Thanks," Tony mumbled and got out of the cab. He opened his wallet, and pretended to ask Jack the fare. Jack pretended to name a figure, and Tony appeared to become angry. After a loud exchange of insults, Tony stalked away, and Jack followed him demanding more money. Jack tried to step in front of Tony several times, but Tony did not look at him and kept going. He glanced quickly at the departure schedule and stormed up to the ticket counter. Fortunately there was no line and Tony purchased a one-way ticket to Zurich. The train was due to leave in eight minutes.

Pushing past Jack, who had dogged his heels persistently, Tony went through the turn style, and hurried toward the train. Jack called a rude insult after him, and shook his fist in the air. In apparent disgust, he lit a cigarette and leaned against a post to brood about the lost fare. From the corner of his eye, Jack scanned the train platform for Tony's "friends", but he didn't see them. He stood and smoked until after the train had pulled out, then started back to the cab.

He was on the crowded walkway outside the station when he felt steel being pressed into his back. He started to turn.

"Keep moving!" a voice snapped in Italian. "Go to the left!"

Someone put a heavy hand on his right arm and he knew there were two men behind him. Jack didn't speak much Italian, but he knew what these bastards wanted. He kept walking, wondering when he would have a split second to reach for his gun. If they found the list of account numbers, he was dead.

Jack walked stiffly along the pavement toward the curb. He recognized the dark grey sedan even before the muzzle in his back nudged him towards it. All his senses were alive, hoping to catch one unguarded moment. He kept walking until he was alongside the car. When he stopped, the man on his right reached forward, and opened the rear door on the passenger side. Turning his head slightly, Jack caught a glimpse of the man, and recognized him as the driver of the sedan. He was taller and thinner than the other man. The driver let go of Jack and stepped around behind the door. At that moment the man with the gun shoved Jack toward the car and barked, "Get in!

We want to talk to you."

Jack stooped and turned, as though he intended to get into the car, but at the last minute he reached into his coat. Before he could grab his gun, however, he heard a shout. He turned in time to see a cartload of luggage slam into the man with the gun forcing him against the open door. Without warning heavy bags and briefcases began sailing through the air in all directions. One flew, or was intentionally thrown, over the car door, striking the driver in the face. He staggered backwards, fell against the car, and slid to the ground.

The man with the gun recovered his balance, then stiffened abruptly, as a voice threatened in Italian, "Drop the gun, or you'll feel the full length of this blade!"

The man moved to raise his arm, but suddenly winced and dropped his gun.

Jack jumped to catch it before it hit the street. "Jesus, Kon! Don't skewer the guy in broad daylight!"

"Relax, Jack. I barely scratched him," Kon answered quietly. "He's got two inches of mozzarella protecting him. What do you want to do with them?"

"Get them in the car," Jack whispered. "I bet the other one has the keys. Let's get out of here before we start attracting attention."

"Get in the car!" Kon barked in Italian and pushed the man toward the open door. Immediately Jack brought his gun down on the back of the man's head, and thrust him into the car. Kon spun around the door. Searching rapidly through the pockets of the man on the ground, he found the car keys. Kon opened the front door, and had bent to pick up the fallen man, when Jack appeared, and ordered, "Start the car! I'll take care of this!"

Kon hesitated.

"Move!" Jack growled.

"All right!" Kon snapped, and was around the car in a flash. Kon had the engine running, and the car in gear, when he heard both side doors slam in quick succession. A moment later Jack tore open the door behind Kon.

"Let's go!" Jack commanded as he jumped in. Kon let out the clutch, turned the wheel, and the car shot away from the curb without a tell-tale squeal.

"Where to?" Kon asked, checking the rear view mirror.

"I don't care! Just get off the main street!" Jack answered sharply, and turned to look out the rear window. No one seemed to be following them, but he saw several people gathered around the pile of luggage.

"What are you doing here!" Jack asked, turning back to Kon.

"I thought you might need a chauffeur," Kon answered drily.

"Don't get smart! You should have stayed in Geneva. You're in a real mess now. Shit! I should have listened to Paul."

"You should have. He's very level headed," Kon answered.

"Oh shut up and let me think!" Jack snapped. "I've got to decide what to do with these two now that we've got them."

"Who are they?" Kon asked.

"I don't know, but I'm going to find out right now. Pull up over there – behind that van."

Kon parked the sedan, and imitating Jack, he began searching through the driver's coat.

"You shouldn't accept rides from people who carry guns, Jack," Kon said, pulling a .38 from the driver's holster. "It's apt to be a one way trip."

"Yeah, yeah . . . any I.D. on him?" Jack asked.

"Only an international driver's license . . . Enrico Parise . . . bad picture . . . very bad picture of him, or whoever it really is," Kon grunted. "What are you going to do with them?"

"I haven't decided. I want to keep them out of circulation for a while. This one followed our agent from Milan. I prefer to leave his boss in the dark about what happened to him."

"Where did your friend from the bank go?"

"You saw him?"

"Yes, I saw you pick him up."

"How did you know where I was?"

"I overheard you mention something to Paul about meeting the boat from Milan. There is only one place the boat from Milan stops that is of any interest. Lugano is not exactly unknown in the financial world."

"So you followed me?"

"Yes. I chartered a plane, rented a car, and waited at the pier."

"Why you cunning little fox!" Jack exclaimed with surprise tinged with admiration.

Kon grinned. "You almost fooled me with that taxi, but once you got out, you were the biggest thing around."

"Well, I'll be dammed if you aren't the slipperiest . . ." Jack stopped abruptly. "Hey! This guy's got a boat ticket. He obviously expected to go back to Milan today. I've got an idea. Start driving. We need to find a quiet part of town!"

"You mean somewhere you can dump a body without being noticed?" Kon asked in dismay.

"Hell no! Just some out of the way place we can leave the car."

"All right," Kon said and started the car. "The old town has some secluded areas."

"Great! Let's get there before these guys wake up."

Kon drove into a winding maze of narrow streets and alleys, far from the banks and fashionable shopping areas that attract tourists to Lugano. They went deeper and deeper into the maze until they were in the hidden, run-down sections no city father likes to admit having in his jurisdiction.

"This is good! This is just what I was looking for. You must have been here before," Jack commented.

"I've been to Lugano on business. I do happen to know a bit about the town," Kon answered.

"Lucky for me then. Pull up over there," Jack said, gesturing with his head.

Kon pulled over to the curb alongside the windowless brick wall of a small warehouse. "What now?" he asked stopping the engine.

"Empty that guy's pockets. Take everything — then open the trunk."

Kon did as he was told, placing the driver's wallet and keys in his own pockets. Then he got out and opened the trunk. Jack, who had followed after him, immediately began to rummage in the trunk. Pulling out the tire iron, he smashed the rear light on the driver's side of the car, making sure the bulb was broken along with the cover.

"O.K. Now keep a look out," Jack said quietly.

Kon nodded. He watched the street, while Jack carried the driver from the front seat, and deposited him in the trunk. Jack removed the driver's belt, and used it to secure the driver's hands behind his back. Then he removed the driver's tie, and wound it around the driver's face as a gag. Emptying both guns, Jack carefully wiped them with his own handkerchief, and put them in the trunk. Pulling the hem of the driver's coat from under his body, Jack draped it over the edge of the trunk, and closed the lid. Part of the coat was still visible, and gave the impression that something had been thrown into the trunk in great haste. As a last measure, Jack pulled a small plastic cylinder out of his pocket, opened it, and removed one of the metal bits. He snapped it onto the end of the cylinder forming a small screwdriver, and used it to remove the rear license plate.

"O.K. Give me the key to the ignition," Jack ordered and Kon obliged. Jack carefully wiped the key, and placed it in the ignition. "Let's get out of sight," Jack said, as he closed the car door on the driver's side.

Kon shot Jack a puzzled look, but followed him into an alley across the street from the car.

"As long as you're here, you might as well make yourself useful," Jack commented. "Go call the police while I keep an eye on the car."

"The police!" Kon objected. "What should I tell them? And why me? Why don't you call them?"

"Christ! Do I have to explain everything? You're the damn Swiss! I want the call to sound like an anonymous tip from a local resident. Tell them you saw two men stealing a grey sedan from in front of the train station. Tell them you think the car was headed for the pier."

"What if they don't believe me?"

"It doesn't matter. Look, I figure this guy is going to wake up any minute. He won't know where the driver is. His money is gone. His gun is missing. All he has is a ticket for the boat to Italy. My guess is he'll think the ticket was overlooked, and head home as fast as possible. If he moves the car anywhere, he's bound to be spotted by the police. When they find the guy in the trunk, both of them will have to do a lot of explaining. Even if he dares to call his boss, they'll be off the street for at least a day!"

"It sounds reasonable," Kon agreed, "but what if he decides to leave the car and go on foot?"

"Then I'll have to shoot him in the leg, or come up with some other plan!" Jack shot back impatiently. "Will you just get going and leave the rest to me!"

"All right! I just hope they believe me. Dio mio, I wish I had stayed in Geneva! I hate dealing with the police."

"I know I can count on you not to say too much to them," Jack added.

Kon grinned. "So . . . silence is golden after all," he muttered, and slipped silently down the alley.

"Did he take the bait?" Kon asked when he returned about twenty minutes later.

"Yep! He's gone. What took you so long?"

"I don't carry a telephone in my pocket!" Kon snapped. "It's not easy to find a quiet place to make an anonymous call."

"O.K. O.K.! Speaking of calls, I'm going to have to call Brad, and tell him things have changed. He'll have to arrange for you to investigate that bank. Have you ever audited a bank?"

"No, but I've seen it done several times and . . . wait a damn minute! How did I get involved in this? This is your job!"

"Well, you came waltzing right into the middle of it! Following me like some damn bloodhound. Where in hell are we going to find another banker who's worth shit in a fight?"

"I don't know, but you can't just commandeer me. I've got my own work to do!" Kon responded indignantly.

"Well you can't back out now! How do you expect to become a boy scout if you won't help a friend?"

Kon stared at Jack and his dark wary eyes narrowed. "Are we friends?" he asked flatly.

Jack looked at Kon in disbelief. "That's a hell of a question! First you freeze your ass off hauling Paul down a mountain, and then you risk your neck to save me from extinction. Doesn't that count as a little bit more than Swiss hospitality? Hell! I have relatives who wouldn't do that much for me. What do you need — an act of Congress? Some damn certificate on the wall? Why did you bother to come after me?"

"Because I wanted to know what was so God damn important that you would lie to Paul! I thought you were his friend!" Kon shouted.

"I am!" Jack shouted back. "Look, he's my partner. We had a job to do, but because I was so damn hot to go skiing, Paul got hurt and couldn't come with me. He didn't want me to come alone, but I didn't want Brad to find out that we had missed a contact. He'd come down hard on Paul for botching a job. I figured I could do the job myself, and Brad would never know."

"But Paul told you not to go alone. I heard him!"

"I know, but Paul treats me like I was his kid brother sometimes. He worries too much. Anyway, you're here, and I need your help. I admit it! O.K.? I need your help! Brad's going to be very upset with me for disobeying orders, and he'll be on Paul's case for not keeping me in line."

Kon looked silently at Jack for a long time. "I'm not very good at taking orders myself," he said at last. "What do you want me to do?"

Jack smiled conspiratorially. "It's very straightforward — no weapons — nothing risky. You'll just have to go to the bank, and search through their records to find out who owns a series of numbered accounts. Brad will set you up with all the credentials you need. Believe me, he can pass you off as a member of the Swiss Banking Regulatory Agency."

"What are you trying to prove from the accounts?"

"We hope to establish some connection between the accounts, and the various shell companies run by Luigi De Bernardi. We know he's laundering drug money through Switzerland, but we need a concrete connection before we can get the Swiss and Italian authorities to cooperate in a thorough investigation of his dirty operation."

"I see. How long will all this take?"

"You tell me! How fast can you sift through that financial garbage? One day, two days, a week? Whatever it takes, but we have to get you in there before De Bernardi can close out the accounts."

"I should be able to get the information you need in an hour, but I'll have to do a sham audit to satisfy the bank managers who will probably want to look over my shoulder the entire time."

"Not if we arrange a diversion — say a group of English investors who want to establish a currency trading account."

Kon smiled a sly grin. "Is there nothing you can't arrange?"

"Probably, but I'm sure Brad is working on it right now."

Kon laughed his deep throaty laugh, and Jack was glad to hear it. He knew Kon was ready to help him.

"Let's get back to Geneva," Jack said.

"I've got to pick up my rental car. I hope I didn't get a ticket by leaving it at the train station."

"Stop worrying. I'll pay for it myself if you did. Why don't you turn the car in, and fly back with me?"

"You have your own airplane?" Kon asked in amazement.

"Yes, but I didn't bring it with me. I've got a very sullen charter pilot waiting for me," Jack said, looking at his watch. "If I don't hurry, the son of a bitch will leave without me."

"I must tell you one thing before we go," Kon said earnestly.

"What's that?" Jack questioned.

"I'm not really Swiss."

"Hell, I knew that! So what?"

Kon looked at Jack and saw that his expression had not changed. He shrugged. "I forgot. You people know all about me."

"Not everything, but enough to know you really are a banker and a man we can trust in a tight spot. Hey, what do you know about me?"

"Only that you are a boy scout."

"Used to be . . . used to be. That was a long time ago."

Kon shook his head, "No . . . you still are."

"Oh cut the shit! Use your superior local knowledge to find us a cab!"

Kon laughed. He knew he was going to like working with Jack. "What are you going to tell Paul?"

"Nothing. I thought I'd leave it to you to explain what happened."

"Me? Why me?"

"Because you'll say so little, Paul will get completely frustrated trying to find out what happened, and drop the whole thing. Unfortunately, Brad's a different animal. He'll need a written report, and he'll tell me he's displeased with me."

"You should be able to handle that."

"Oh yeah, just don't ever let Brad get displeased with you. It's very unpleasant."

Paul was not so easy to put off, however. He was furious with Jack for going to Lugano alone, and he did not bother to couch his anger in diplomatic phrases. Brad was quick to see the opportunity to use Kon to get information from the bank. As soon as he stopped threatening to throw Jack off the team, he set to work arranging papers for Kon. When the work was finished, Kon's credentials as a Swiss bank examiner could have passed even the most critical test.

****

The team had assembled in Lugano in order to make the foray on the bank. Unable to accompany the team because of his injury, Paul made his contribution by deftly applying makeup to Kon's dark hair to add a distinctive touch of grey. Thus properly aged, Kon took a cab to the bank. As he stepped out of the taxi, he had a moment of doubt about his ability to carry off his role as bank inspector. He took a deep breath, and bolstered himself by remembering the admonition Charlotte had given him the first time she had sent him off to the bank with Edgar. "Stand up straight, and look them all in the eye, Peter . . . and for heaven's sake stop pulling at your tie as if you were a donkey in a halter!" she had told him. Kon squared his shoulders and entered the bank.

Ten minutes later Brad arrived with his entourage of British investors. Jack was strategically placed in the group to cause the maximum disturbance. The group effectively distracted several senior officers at the bank with their self-important demands for attention, and their endless questions. Under the guise of checking various numbered accounts at random, Kon quickly identified the owners of the accounts on his list. Several of the accounts were listed as businesses, but most had the name of one Jacobie Sozani listed as treasurer.

Carefully shuffling through enough ledgers and receipts to draft a cursory report, Kon bid the bank managers a formal good-bye late in the afternoon. Returning to the hotel, he reported his findings to Paul and they talked until Jack and Brad arrived a short time later. Brad was impressed by the thorough and professional work Kon had done at the bank. Kon obviously had an eye for details, a head for figures, and a flair for intrigue, for in addition to presenting Brad with a list of all the names on every signature card for all the accounts in question, he gave Brad copies of deposit and withdrawal records for most of the accounts.

"Splendid job, Peter! Thoroughly splendid!" Brad concluded as he scanned the information. "Your assistance has been invaluable."

Kon's only response was to show a flicker of a smile, but he was pleased that his extra effort had not gone unnoticed.

That night, after Peter had flown back to Geneva, the team gathered to discuss strategy for a complete investigation of all the companies listing Jacobie Sozani as treasurer. It would require months of tedious work poring through the records, both public and private, to sift out a common connection. The hunt would be worth it, if they could get De Bernardi convicted, but it would take hundreds of man-hours from a highly skilled, dedicated professional to accomplish the task. Even as Brad spoke, Paul knew that Brad would nominate Peter Kononellos for the job.

"He certainly knows the banking business!" Jack commented when Brad asked for his opinion of Peter.

"Paul, what's your estimate of Peter, or Kon, as you say he prefers?"

"He's got a sharp mind, no doubt about that. He's resourceful and determined. He's just a bit . . . impetuous."

"Impetuous? That's an understatement if I ever heard one!" Jack sputtered.

Brad smiled. "That's true, Paul, but I think he would settle down after he worked with you for a while. Jack used to fly off more in the beginning."

"Well, thanks for the vote of confidence!" Jack said sarcastically. "I may have showed a little temper, but I never was as suspicious, or as defensive as Kon."

"That's also true," Brad assented, "but that's not all bad in our business. Kon's obviously been in some sticky situations and he's learned to look out for himself."

"The killing bothers him," Paul added. "He's carrying a load of guilt about those two kidnappers, and he was upset about that woman at the courthouse."

"Yes, I saw that," Brad agreed, "but I would not want a man who could kill without remorse guarding my back on a mission."

"You're right about that," Paul said.

Suddenly Jack spoke out with conviction. "Hey, I think he was handling it just fine until that sniveling shit of a lawyer twisted everything to make it look like Kon had done something despicable. Christ! He acted to save a man's life! You can't sit around debating morals while somebody is being murdered!"

Paul smiled. "Well said, Jack! He'll be O.K. I think that once Kon is on the team, he would be very loyal. I've seen the way he acts. When we met him at the hotel in Rome and he thought you were going to hurt Brad, he pushed Brad aside and leaped at you without a second thought."

"He's certainly not a coward," Jack added. "When he saw that guy with the gun at the courthouse, he purposely moved away from me, and it was no accident that he pushed you two down. He meant to save us. He could have stepped behind me to save himself."

Paul and Brad nodded their agreement.

"So it's agreed that I should ask him to join the team," Brad said in summary.

"Sure! We could use his skills. I'm no good at the paper work stuff," Jack affirmed.

"Paul? How do you vote? He'll be working directly for you. Can you handle him?"

Paul remained thoughtfully silent and it occurred to Brad that Paul might opt for a more easy-going personality in the group.

"I think Kon would be a good addition, but on one condition," Paul said at last.

"And that is?" Brad asked.

"I've got to have the authority to do something about those skinny arms of his."

Jack snickered, and Brad was surprised by the personal nature of Paul's request. "This is business, Paul! I'm not running a health club," he objected.

"I know, but Kon's right arm is not healing well. He tore it up trying to break away from me. He's too proud to mention it, and by the time that personal physician of his finds out, it may be too late. If he joins the team, my life may depend on him some day and I want him as perfectly tuned as possible."

"I don't like to interfere with a man's personal life, Paul. What if he won't agree? We need his brains, not his brawn!"

"I appreciate that, Brad, but I can't believe that Kon enjoys being so thin. I think he's just resigned himself to it."

Brad sighed. He knew there was no way Peter would ever be as well developed as Paul, or as massive as Jack, but he understood that it was important to Paul to cultivate Peter's potential.

"I can't make his muscular development a condition of employment, Paul, but I will give you a free hand to coax, beg, bribe or bully Kon into better condition. However, please be diplomatic."

"Of course, of course. I know it will be difficult, but I'll think of something."

"Sure you will, but how can he do a bench press if you have an arm lock on him?" Jack asked drily.

"Cut it out, Jack!" Paul ordered. "I'll need your help with this. I don't want to hurt his pride."

"O.K. O.K. I'll shut up!" Jack drawled. "Paul's right, Brad. Kon is too thin, and I know he hates it. He'll never be a heavyweight, but we could put a little more muscle on him."

"All right! Do what you can with him, but don't hurt his arm or his pride. I don't want him to quit."

"Thanks, Brad. You won't be sorry. He'll need a gun too," Paul added. "Jack can show him how to use it."

"He doesn't need to be armed to sort through records," Brad commented.

"I agree, but he's got spirit, Brad. Let's get him some equipment to back it up. We'll find other things for him to do."

"Right! I guess that makes the vote unanimous. I'll convey the invitation," Brad concluded.

****

"Why does Peter want to get involved in such dangerous work?" Edgar ranted to Carlin, who was sitting across from him in his office at the bank. "Don't I pay him well enough? Have I hurt his feelings?"

"It's not the money, Edgar," Carlin answered. "It's his way of setting the world right. Peter has very high ideals about how the world should be."

"We all have ideals, Carlin, but we learn to be realistic about what we can change. We don't go running off to risk our lives helping people we've never even met!"

"No we don't. But we each have developed a way to serve our fellow man in some quiet, socially acceptable manner. Peter is neither a builder nor a healer, he's a fighter."

"Well, I wish he would find some other way to right the wrongs of the world," Edgar grumbled. "I know he hasn't been completely happy at the bank. I've tried to protect him from the jealous criticism, and find a social niche for him, but I've failed. Perhaps I should have adopted him years ago. Perhaps he would get the respect and attention he deserves if his name was Marneé instead of Kononellos."

"It might have helped in some ways, but it would have been too great a burden for both of you. Peter holds you in the highest esteem, Edgar. He struggles constantly to be what you want, but it's against his nature to be patient, and orderly, and sedate. If he were your son, you might feel obliged to change him to fit your image, and it would break him."

Edgar smiled. "Do you actually think I could ever succeed in controlling Peter's temper, or taming that wild streak in him? The tremendous passions of love and despair that mark Peter's life terrify me. However, I must confess, I do envy him his very un-Swiss spontaneity."

"I have seen too many healthy Swiss males destroy themselves to think that we Swiss have our emotions under control, Edgar. I believe we must allow Peter more . . . more uncertainty than either of us would find comfortable, in order to save his sanity. If you could have seen the state he was in when I went to Rome . . . Working with this group has been so good for him. When he came home after the trial, he was relaxed and full of enthusiasm about going skiing with them. He hasn't shown so much enthusiasm about anything since Claire died."

"You're right about that. Charlotte and I both noticed the change in him. I suppose I must give my blessing to this new undertaking, but it will mark the end of my restful sleep for worrying about him."

"I realize it will be difficult, but you must never indicate that his decision will cause you anxiety or inconvenience, Edgar. Peter won't go if he thinks you need him."

"Of course I need him! I've come to depend on him, but I can't be so selfish as to shackle him for my benefit. Do you realize, Carlin, that this is the first time Peter has ever asked my advice or permission before he acted. It has always been my responsibility to punish him after he acted without thinking. Guiding him in this decision is a tremendous burden."

"You must not doubt his total loyalty and gratitude to you and to Charlotte."

"I know. A man could not ask more from his own son. And to think I was against having him come . . . How I will miss him, Carlin!"

"But I understood it was not to be full-time," Carlin said anxiously.

"No, no. I couldn't allow that — for Charlotte's sake. And Peter said that working here will provide a perfect 'cover' for his covert activities. Covert activities! Oh, Carlin, the very sound of it . . ."

"Peter is very capable, Edgar, and Mr. Cover-Rollins is thoroughly trustworthy and professional."

"Yes, I realize Peter is capable, and for that very reason I have decided to send him to France to work in the Paris branch."

"Paris! Have you mentioned it to him?"

"Not yet."

"You must broach the subject very carefully, or he may think you are displeased, and are exiling him."

"It is not a punishment! It is a wonderful opportunity. When Peter goes to Paris he will at last escape from working with the young men he trained with. No one there knows his origins, and they will accept him at face value. Besides, I will suggest that working in two cities will provide him an excuse to absent himself for extended periods."

Carlin smiled. "Then that is the very argument to use. When is he scheduled to start with Mr. Cover-Rollins?"

"He waits on my decision. The group wants him in London as soon as possible. Apparently they plan to give him some indoctrination, and some physical training. He seemed quite eager for it. It has always bothered him that the Swiss government won't accept him in the home guard until be becomes a citizen. You must never tell Charlotte, but Peter was so downcast about being excluded that I took him to the target range and taught him to shoot my pistol."

"Edgar!" Carlin said in mock surprise. "And you kept it from Charlotte?"

"Oh yes. Peter is an excellent marksman . . . steady hand, good eye, and all the rest. And we swore an oath, 'to death' as Peter put it, never to tell Charlotte or the boys. I suppose it was foolish, but I think Peter finally began to trust me after that."

"I'm so glad you took him. For years Peter lived in mortal fear that you didn't want him, and would send him away."

"Oh, Carlin! I never seriously considered it, even when Charlotte was upset with him. We couldn't have gotten along without him! Melina was lazy and spiteful, and left all the cleaning to Peter, and though Anna was a dear woman, her cooking was monotonous. It was Peter's creations that made our meals interesting. We have missed him at home now that he works here." Edgar paused, lost in thought, and then continued, "Shall I call him in then and end his misery?"

"Yes, it's time," Carlin replied softly. "I'll just slip out quietly before . . ."

"Oh no! Don't leave me to deal with him alone! I need you here, to see that he does not misunderstand my intentions, and to strengthen my resolve to set him free."

"Very well, I'll stay. Call him in."

CHAPTER TWENTY-THREE

Mary had arrived at the hospital in Florina as promised, and the team was glad to see her. They each felt that she functioned as a silent member of the group. She never participated directly in the missions; the danger, the action, or the violence. Her job came later. When the team returned victorious, Mary shared their accomplishments, and was the adoring audience that the secret nature of their work never allowed. And when any of them returned tired, or injured, or discouraged, she commiserated, and consoled them, and tended to their ills. Optimistic, calm, efficient, and matter-of-fact, Mary displayed qualities that were invaluable to the team.

With Mary's arrival, all the preparations were in order for the team's return to Bitola. Peterson stayed with Kon so that Mary and Geilla could see the team off. It was late morning. Geilla thought it was unusual, but not without precedent, for the men to be so tired at the start of an assignment. She felt a strange sense of loss, coupled with a slight pang of guilt as they drove away. Perhaps I should have left Kon in Mary's care and gone with them, she thought briefly. No, with my mind on Kon, I would only be a liability. Brad understood that before I did.

Brad drove Artukovich's truck which had been painted a dark shade of blue, and now bore an inscription in large gold letters, which translated to "Institute of Advanced Medicine". Paul rode in front with Brad, and the back was heavily loaded with equipment. Jack had left about an hour earlier, driving a truck which was the same model as Artukovich owned. It had also been painted dark blue, but was unmarked.

It was interesting for Brad to retrace the route the team had travelled only two nights before. Although neither Brad nor Paul had seen much of the road on the previous trip, they could tell by the look of it, that it had not been easy for Geilla to keep them out of a ditch. The countryside was not unpleasant to look at, and Brad kept the speed down to avoid shaking the equipment loose.

Brad and Paul pulled into Bitola just under an hour after they left Florina. They circled past the market square, parked, and waited. About ten minutes later, Jack drove in and parked his vehicle beside several other trucks.

"Any trouble?" Brad asked, as Jack came up to the marked truck.

"None," Jack answered shaking his head. "I found the spot Artukovich's friends recommended, and slapped on the explosives. I hope those guys had an up-to-date timetable, or a lot of people are going to be blown to dust."

"Relax, Jack, I checked it," Brad assured him. "The charge will go off ten minutes before the train arrives. These guys have done this kind of thing before. Climb in the back!"

In the daylight, the town looked much larger, but they had no trouble locating the military hospital. Brad drove boldly up to the front door, parked the truck and got out. He strode up to the guard and said in English, modulated with his best French accent, "I have a delivery for the commandant."

"Who are you and what do you deliver?" the guard demanded.

Brad drew himself straight, "I am Monsieur Gerald Petrand of the Institute of Advanced Medicine in Paris. I have brought the X-ray equipment that my institute is donating to this hospital."

"Wait here," the guard snapped and stepped inside. Immediately another guard appeared to take his place. Brad endeavored to engage the guard in a conversation, but he stood silent, and eyed Brad with suspicion. After several minutes the first guard returned. "The commandant wishes to see your papers, and the requisition for the X-ray equipment."

"This is most unusual, but I will be happy to show them to him if he insists." Brad drew his passport from his coat pocket, and handed it to the guard. "The other papers are in the truck, Monsieur." Brad walked back to the truck, and made a show of looking for the papers in his briefcase. "This is a copy of the letter to the commandant notifying him that this hospital has been selected by the review committee," Brad said, as he handed a letter to the guard. "You can see his name at the top."

The guard snatched the paper from Brad's hand and took a brief glance at it. "Wait here," he snapped and stepped inside again.

This time the wait was considerably longer. Jack climbed out of the truck, and came up to Brad. "What's all the fuss? Do they want this thing, or not?" he said in English.

"Patience, George, there must be some mistake. Please wait in the truck."

Jack sauntered back to the truck, leaned against the side, and lit a cigarette.

Finally the guard reappeared, but if possible, he was even less polite than before. He seemed surprised to see Jack. "The commandant wishes to see you, and the others inside," he said, and motioned for Paul and Jack to come forward. When they were all together, the guard shoved Brad through the door.

"Hey, watch who you're shoving!" Jack called to the guard. "Monsieur Petrand is a very important man."

Once inside, the guard directed them down a short hall. He followed, waving them forward with his weapon when they hesitated.

The guard rapped sharply on the first door to the left, then opened it, and waved them inside. Brad recognized Commandant Smrcek immediately from the pictures Artukovich's friends had shown him. Smreck sat behind a large mahogany desk. Pictures of various grim-faced government leaders hung on the wall behind him. There was a long silence before Brad took the initiative.

"Monsieur Commandant, I am Gerald Petrand of the Institute of Advanced Medicine in Paris. I have the honor of personally delivering the X-ray equipment the Institute has decided to give to your hospital, and seeing that it is properly installed."

The commandant did not respond, but made an elaborate display of shuffling the papers on his desk. Finally he looked up with a frown. "Monsieur Petrand, I have never heard of your institute, and I have no idea why they would send this hospital an X-ray machine. Is this some trick you have arranged to put me in your debt?"

Brad put on a haughty air of offended dignity. "I assure you, Monsieur Commandant, this is no trick on my part, but a gesture of peace and good will, from my country and it's citizens to your good people."

"Why was I not informed of this 'gesture' as you call it before?"

"Have you not received the letter from the Institute announcing your hospital as the chosen candidate of the Board of Directors?" Brad asked in surprise.

"No sir, I have not, but I intend to get to the bottom of this matter at once. I will put in a call to General Jakupak and ascertain if he has any knowledge of this donation."

Brad looked uneasy for a moment, then cautioned the commandant, "Monsieur Commandant, that may not be a wise thing to do."

The commandant raised his eyebrows in question. "Please explain yourself, sir."

Brad hesitated, then began as if divulging a confidence, "You see, Monsieur, there are a number of people who did not want this equipment to come into your hands. They wished to keep it for themselves. It would not be good to involve these people until the equipment is permanently installed."

The commandant looked directly at Brad. "Are you insinuating that General Jakupak might try to keep this equipment for himself?"

Brad lowered his voice, and continued, "I can say nothing for sure, as I am not a member of the selection committee . . . but one does hear rumors, Monsieur." Brad let this idea sink in, before he said in a more normal tone, "But I am sure you know General Jakupak's mind better than I do on these matters."

The commandant did not answer, but stood contemplating Brad suspiciously. "Perhaps you are right, Monsieur Petrand," he said at last. "I will go directly to your institute, and get to the bottom of this."

319

Brad remained confident under Smreck's penetrating gaze. "A wise decision, Monsieur. I have the number right here," Brad answered coolly, and pulled a card from his coat.

The commandant took the card, glanced at it briefly, and walked to the door of his office. As the commandant pulled the door open, Brad saw that a guard was waiting on the other side.

"Ring this number in Paris, and connect me as soon as you have them on the line!"

"Yes, sir!" the guard answered, taking the card. He saluted, and the commandant closed the door.

The commandant returned to his desk and sat behind it. "Gentlemen, please sit down. You must be tired after your long journey. May I offer you some of our local wine?"

Monsieur Commandant is feeling magnanimous at the thought of getting the upper hand on Jakupak, Brad thought, and nodded politely. Paul and Jack sat quietly at the far end of the room, while Brad sat closer to the commandant, who served them from a liquor cabinet cleverly hidden in a bookcase near his desk.

"Now," the commandant began, sitting back comfortably in his chair, "tell me about your institute, and how I come to be the lucky recipient of your peace offering."

Brad carefully sipped his wine. "Excellent wine, Monsieur. It is a credit to your country. As for the Institute, we are a small, but well known group, which promotes the idea of bringing the highest level of medical care to remote areas. We have a committee which travels across the continent, gathering information about hospitals and clinics. They submit the names of worthy facilities to our Board of Directors. Since we are privately funded, we can award a donation only every third year. Your hospital was chosen in the hope that the equipment would be used for the benefit of all the citizens in this region. It is my understanding that there was once another hospital in this area which was absorbed into this regional one. It is the Institutes's wish that the largest number of people be served."

The commandant smiled at Brad's naive account of the government's takeover of the local clinic. He warmed to the idea of playing the role of benefactor. Here was a chance for him to gain the gratitude of the otherwise hostile local populous at no cost to himself. "Tell me about the equipment you have brought," Smreck said genially, as he poured Brad another glass of wine.

Brad smiled and nodded. "We have brought a most sophisticated piece of modern equipment. It scans the entire body, and can make very precise films of all the internal workings. These two talented gentlemen are my assistants, and are well trained in the installation and use of the equipment. May I introduce Monsieur Conrad and Monsieur Marshall."

Paul and Jack nodded formally in turn, as Brad introduced

320

them. "They are from the United States, but they have had much of their training at our Institute."

The commandant seemed very interested, and asked several other questions about the equipment before the phone rang. The call to Paris had finally gone through, and it was obvious from the one side of the conversation they could hear that Carl had set things up well. The commandant seemed quite satisfied with all the answers he received. He smiled at Brad as he hung up the phone.

"I beg your pardon for my misgivings, Monsieur Petrand," he said warmly to Brad. "It seems all my objections have been answered. Please proceed with the installation as quickly as possible. You shall have my assistance in every way."

"Very good, Monsieur Commandant. I should like to see the site you have chosen as the X-ray room."

The commandant looked surprised. "I have not yet chosen a site, but I will be happy to show you our facility, and you may choose as you see fit." He stood up and graciously waved them towards the door. "Please allow me to show you around. I am sorry that Dr. Kusalo, the head of our hospital, is not here to meet with you, but he was suddenly called away to a medical conference in Belgrade.

"I am sorry to hear that, Monsieur Commandant," Brad said aloud, knowing that Artukovich's friends had arranged Dr. Kusalo's timely departure. As they left the office, Brad stayed close to the commandant, while Paul and Jack took a minute to get out the door.

The commandant kept his word about showing them around. As they made the tour, Jack carefully noted the location of the electrical switch boxes, and traced the power supply.

"You must understand, Monsieur Commandant, that this machine requires a great deal of power," Brad said. "It will be necessary to wire it directly to the main power supply to prevent voltage fluctuations."

"I see," the commandant nodded.

"We'll have to shut everything down briefly while we wire it in," Jack added. "What kind of emergency power source do you have?"

"We have a small generator, that will run all the essential equipment and some lights," the commandant answered.

"Good! Good! I would really like to see what you have," Jack continued, showing great professional interest.

The commandant added the generating plant to the tour and Jack was lavish in his praise of the efficiency and orderliness of the dilapidated, inadequate equipment. He ran his hands appreciatively over it, and asked several questions about the fuel supply. When the Commandant turned his back, Jack loosened one of the fuel lines.

The commandant introduced the team to the two doctors, who were on duty during the day, and in passing, the team noted the room where Artukovich was being held. At length they chose a site

321

on the first floor, near the operating room, and adjacent to the ambulance exit. The area had once been a ward, but had been taken over for storage. It measured about 15 by 20 feet and was the only area that was large enough for their needs.

Explaining that it would be necessary to build a separate, isolated area for the equipment, the team moved their truck around to the ambulance area, and began to carry in their supplies. The three of them worked all day, setting up partitions, laying out areas for X-ray, for film development, and patient observation.

Only late in the afternoon did they begin to carry in the components, and start to assemble the monster X-ray machine itself. When they had finished placing it in the room, the commandant was very impressed with its huge size, and gleaming metal surface. Banks of switches and dials, contained in a separate console unit, added an air of advanced technological mystery.

From early evening until after dark, Jack and Paul worked at pulling wires through conduits, and tying into the main power supply. The building itself was old, and the wiring was inadequate, which fitted their plans very well. It seemed to the staff on duty that the team had been underfoot all day, carrying parts around, or hauling wires into and out of corners and through walls. They were quite a nuisance to the staff, but their presence soon became commonplace, and mostly they were ignored.

At 9 o'clock Brad announced to the commandant that they were ready to test the machine. They called for a volunteer from among the staff, but the machine was so huge and ominous looking, no one would come forward. At last, at Brad's suggestion, the commandant selected a tall, stalwart, young soldier to be the subject for the first X-ray.

"Monsieur Commandant, I invite you to join me in the observation room. From there we can safely view the proceedings, and not be harmed by any stray radiation," Brad assured the commandant.

"Good, I am anxious to see it work," he answered.

"Perhaps you should give orders that the test is not to be disturbed. Any extra light, while the technicians are handling the films, could ruin the results. The preparations are lengthy and delicate and we would not want to have to repeat them at this late hour," Brad warned.

"Yes, of course. It must go well the first time," the commandant answered. He walked to the door, and spoke to the guard on duty. When he returned, Brad led him to the observation area on one side of the room. From there they could look through a glass panel to view the proceedings.

Jack and Paul had put on white gowns and gloves, and appeared to be making final adjustments to the machine. Jack came up to the soldier. "You will have to undress for the test. Please put on this gown and lie on the table."

The soldier took the gown, but seemed a little hesitant.

Paul came up. "Don't worry. Everything will be fine. You may change there, behind the screen."

The soldier seemed relieved, and hurried behind the screen which stood in front of the wall which was perpendicular to the observation room. Jack and Paul stood by the bank of dials, and lowered their voices slightly, knowing the soldier would do his best to listen. They were fairly certain that a soldier in a multi-lingual country would understand enough English to comprehend what they were saying.

"Are you sure the beam is finally adjusted," Paul whispered.

"Yes, yes," Jack answered. "I fixed it after that guy in Frankfurt. That will never happen again."

"I hope not. He was a mess! One more like that and you'll lose your job," Paul responded.

"Listen, don't point your finger at me. You've made a few mistakes yourself."

"I tell you that was not my fault. The switch . . ."

"Quiet! Here he comes," Jack said, and quickly stepped away from Paul. He went up to the soldier who looked quickly from him to Paul.

"Are you certain everything is working properly? Perhaps you should try it once first," the soldier said nervously.

"No, no. Everything is fine," Jack responded. "You won't feel a thing. Come on, get up on the table."

The soldier complied, but continued to look around apprehensively. When Paul came forward with a syringe and a large gauge needle, the soldier's eyes widened and he bit his lower lip.

"Nothing to be afraid of," Paul said briskly. "We're just going to inject some harmless dye to make your insides show up better on the film. Hold out your arm."

The soldier looked quickly in the direction of the commandant, and against his better judgment, he put out his arm. Paul had the needle in his vein instantly, and the soldier was relieved that despite the size of the syringe, it didn't seem to take long for the liquid to go in. The soldier had no idea that it was not dye that Paul had injected, but a solution of nicotinic acid.

In the observation room, Brad explained to the commandant what the technicians were doing.

Jack came up to the table. "Now you just relax a minute while the dye gets into your system. You won't be able to feel it, but it will show up on the film."

Paul and Jack went to the dials, and began to adjust them. After a moment, a slight humming sound came from the table beneath the soldier. He lay on his back and did his best to relax, but he could not. Slowly the feeling of apprehension in the back of his mind grew to a strange anxiety. His heart rate increased, and he started to quiver slightly. Watching the soldier from the corner of his eye, Paul rolled a screwdriver off the edge of the counter. When it hit the floor with a bang, the soldier jerked violently, and Paul knew the chemical was taking effect. He turned a few more dials and increased the pitch of the hum coming from the table.

"Does that sound O.K. to you?" Paul whispered just a bit too loudly to Jack.

"Yeah, yeah. Come on, let's give it a shot. We can always do it again," Jack answered.

"Sure we can — but not on him if this doesn't work," Paul insisted.

The soldier had heard their remarks and began to shake. Jack stepped up to the table. "Well, are you ready for the scan?"

The soldier turned his head towards Jack. "Are you sure you know what you're doing?"

"Yes, I'm sure. There's nothing to it, but you've got to lie still. You can't be jumping around like that." Jack went back to the console and touched some switches, and a huge metal arm began to descend over the soldier. Although it came to a halt several feet above him, he suddenly had an intense desire to get up from the table and flee.

Paul came over to where the soldier lay. "What's the big deal? Why can't you hold still!" he shouted at him.

Jack threw up his arms and walked in a circle. "We're ready to go and you can't be still. What's the matter with you?" he growled.

"I don't know, sir. I'm nervous. I don't want to do this," the soldier admitted.

Paul went to the microphone hanging over the console. "Monsieur Commandant," he said calmly, "we are ready to proceed with the test, but this man won't lie still."

From inside the control room Brad instructed the commandant to push the proper button to activate his microphone.

"Soldier!" the commandant's voice boomed through the speaker, "I command you to control yourself! Lie still!"

"I'm sorry, sir. I can't," the soldier pleaded. "Perhaps someone else can be calmer."

"It would take more time to find and prepare another man, Monsieur Commandant," Brad explained. "I think the man is overwhelmed by the size of the machine. Perhaps if they gave him something to relax him, he could lie quiet for the twelve minutes the technicians need. He need not be alert during the test."

The commandant was becoming impatient. It was well after 9 p.m., and he wanted to go off duty and relax. He nodded to Brad.

"Do whatever you must to make him be still."

Brad switched on the microphone. "Monsieur Marshall, please sedate the subject, and proceed with the test."

The sedative was ready, and Paul had it in the soldier's arm before he knew what was happening. "This is just to relax you so you can lie still," Paul said in a friendly manner. After a few minutes, the soldier closed his eyes and was still. Paul signaled Brad that they were ready to begin. He went to the control panel, set the switches, and the huge metal arm suspended over the soldier began to move slowly over his body travelling from head to foot. Paul and Jack slipped behind the shielding screen, where Jack quickly exchanged his civilian clothes for the soldier's uniform complete with revolver.

Inside the observation room, Brad continued to explain the use of the machine to the commandant, keeping his attention fixed on the man beneath the machine. While Brad talked, Paul and Jack opened a ventilation panel they had installed in the wall they had built to separate the X-ray room from the storage area, and slipped through. They hurried through the storage area, and cautiously opening the door to the hallway, they stole through the door without being observed. Jack moved quickly to the commandant's office, and finding it unguarded, he slipped inside. Separating from Jack, Paul moved warily down the hall, and crept up the stairs to the second floor. Looking quite official in his white coat, he strode boldly down the hall towards the soldier who was stationed outside Artukovich's door. Paul mumbled, "Medication," and pulled a syringe from his pocket. The guard stood aside.

Paul pushed the door open and went in, closing the door behind him. A man was lying on the bed, but Paul could not tell if he was awake or asleep. He lowered his head as he went up to the bed, then suddenly clamped his hand over the man's mouth. It was Artukovich, and he immediately began to struggle.

"Don't make a sound!" Paul whispered. "Vidosevich told us you were here. We've come back to take you out."

Artukovich became still.

"Will you be quiet and do as I say?" Paul asked quickly.

Artukovich nodded his head and Paul released him. "Good man! Let me get rid of the guard."

Paul went to the door, put his head out, and grunted, "Come hold him down."

The guard did not speak, but entered the room, and came up to the bed. Paul pulled a syringe from his pocket, and mumbled, "Hold his arm."

As the guard leaned forward, Paul struck him sharply with the side of his powerful hand, and he collapsed onto the bed. Paul pressed the needle into the guard's arm, and pushed the plunger. "O.K. let's go!" Paul whispered. Slipping his arm around the orderly's back, he helped him out of the bed, and over to the window. Unbuttoning his loose lab coat, Paul removed a harness from around his waist, and fastened it around Artukovich's body. Next, he uncoiled a nylon line which was wrapped around his ribs and fastened it to the harness. As he looped one end of the line over the radiator, the room went dark. "O.K.! Out you go," Paul said, and pushed up on the window.

Artukovich sat on the ledge in the darkness. "I can't walk. How am I to get away from the building when I get down?"

"Don't worry. Someone will be waiting to help you. Now go before they get the emergency power on."

Paul took up the slack on the line, and braced himself as Artukovich left the ledge. Slowly and smoothly, Paul let out the line. Artukovich descended gently downward, keeping himself away from the wall with his hands. Paul held on a few minutes longer after he had let out all the line, and he felt three distinct tugs. He removed the line from the radiator, pitched it over the ledge, and closed the window. Hurrying back to the bed, Paul set up a small flash light on the stand by the bed. He stripped the holster and pistol from the soldier, and rolled him onto his side.

As Paul was covering the soldier with the sheet and blanket, he heard the voices of two men in the hall outside the door. He could not understand much of what was being said, but one man was asking a lot of questions. Paul surmised that they were wondering where the man who was supposed to be guarding the door had gone. Quickly Paul grabbed the flashlight from the bed stand, and switched it off. He flattened himself against the wall, and edged his way towards the door. Without warning the door opened and one man stepped into the room. Rapidly he played the beam of his flashlight around the room. Even in the poor light, the body of the soldier was visible on the bed. The man stepped farther into the room, and Paul silently raised his arm, getting ready to strike. If the man with the light saw the guard's boots, he would give the alarm.

Suddenly Paul heard the sound of someone hurrying down the hall. A man was shouting excitedly, but Paul could make out only one word, "generator". That's it! Paul thought, they can't get the emergency generator started. Someone stuck their head into the room, and focused the beam from their flashlight on the first man. Paul pressed his back against the wall behind the door, held his breath, and waited with his arm raised and ready. After a moment, the men turned and left as quickly as they had come. Paul let out his breath. He sprang to the bed, and wrapped the blanket over the bottom edge, tucking it in neatly. Still holding the flashlight, he hurried across the room and crept soundlessly out the door.

The commandant had not been pleased when the power went off in the X-ray room. "What has happen to this wonderful machine of yours?" he shouted at Brad.

"Monsieur, I do not know," Brad answered with a mixture of confusion and indignation. "This has never happened before. I will ask the technicians."

The commandant heard a click, and thought it was the button on the intercom. "Monsieur Marshall, what has happened to the machine?" Brad said into the microphone. The answer came back over the speaker. "I do not know, Monsieur Petrand! Everything has stopped. I think something has burned out!"

"How is the young soldier?" Brad asked with concern. Again the voice came back, "He is fast asleep, but unharmed. We are here with him."

"Monsieur Commandant, I can assure you nothing like this has ever happened before. We will locate the failure, and repair the machine as soon as possible."

"I certainly hope so, Monsieur Petrand," the commandant shot back. "I am losing my patience with you, and your colossal machine. This is a hospital! We cannot function without power, and I will not tolerate anything that interrupts it!"

"Yes, yes, you are quite right," Brad agreed humbly. "I apologize from the bottom of my heart. This will not happen again. Please allow me to light your way to the door," Brad continued. Removing a small flash light from the back wall, he escorted the commandant from the observation booth to the door.

"We will look after the man who volunteered, and return him to duty as soon as possible," Brad promised.

"See that you do!" the commandant snapped in Brad's face. He opened the door, and Brad knew from the dim light shinning down the hall that the building was operating on emergency power. "I want that machine repaired, Petrand. I am fed up with this delay!" the commandant growled.

"Yes, Monsieur Commandant! We will go right to work on it, but may I ask that we have no interruptions. Now that there has been a failure, we do not know if there has been a radiation leak. We must take all possible precautions. There must be no unauthorized personnel in this room until we know that it is safe."

"As you wish," the commandant grunted. "I will post a guard at the door."

"Thank you, Monsieur Commandant. We will do our very best to repair the machine quickly," Brad said with dignity. Turning he closed the door, and locked it from the inside. He went to the console, and threw the switches to disconnect the X-ray machine from the main system. It won't take long for the commandant's men to get the regular power supply operational now, Brad thought. Even before the lights came on in the room, Brad switched the tape in the recorder, and his voice plus that of Paul and Jack echoed through the room. He stepped behind the screen, and exited through the air vent, snapping it in place as he retreated.

It was 9:47 p.m. when Brad entered the ambulance bay. Paul was holding a gun on the two ambulance attendants who where against the wall. "Good work, Paul. Any sign of Jack?"

"He should be here any minute."

The phone on the desk rang, and Brad picked up the receiver. Although the person who was calling talked very fast, Brad understood that the caller was requesting an ambulance. Brad made a few responses and hung up. "Right on time," he said glancing at his watch. "Get these two attendants in the vehicle!"

Paul nodded, and pressing the muzzle of the gun against the back of one of the attendants, he ordered him to get behind the wheel. Paul stepped back, and prodded the second man with the gun. "Get in the back!" he said coldly.

As they were getting in, Jack arrived. He was supporting Artukovich who could barely stand. "The call's come already, Jack," Brad said. "We'd better get going. Those explosives you planted went off right on time, but it will be several hours before anyone here realizes that no one was hurt." Brad went up to Artukovich. "So we meet again, my friend!"

"I am more happy to see you this time than the last," Artukovich responded, and put out his hand. Brad took it firmly, and helped Jack lift the orderly into the back of the ambulance. Paul handed the gun to Brad, and went to open the bay doors. Jack, who was still wearing the soldier's uniform, was seated in the front when he returned. Paul climbed in the back, and closed the door. Brad shoved the gun against the neck of the man behind the wheel. "Start the engine!" he ordered. "Now drive! No tricks, or I'll pull the trigger!"

The driver was smart. He kept both hands on the wheel, and did what he was told. As they passed through the market square, Brad ordered the driver to stop, and Jack got out. Paul got into the front seat, and Brad ordered the ambulance attendant to drive on. Brad checked his watch again. It was 10:05.

After they had gone about 10 miles, Brad told the driver to stop. He held the gun on the two attendants, and Paul tied and blindfolded them. After a short time Jack drove up in the unmarked truck. While Brad and Artukovich held hand lanterns, Paul and Jack carefully applied a decal with the gold lettering of the "Institute of Advanced Medicine" to the side of the truck. Leaving the two attendants tied in the ambulance, the team helped Artukovich into the truck, and the group continued south as rapidly as possible.

"Your friends know their business. They called in right on time," Brad said to Artukovich.

"So you have met Vidosevich then."

"Yes. You work with an interesting group."

"How is it for the one that bleeds so much?"

"He was alive when we left, but he's not doing well."

"He is with Stamatis?"

"Yes."

"Have more faith. Stamatis does not like to lose."

By 10:45 p.m. they were close to the border area, and Brad brought the truck to a stop. Paul went to the rear of the truck, and gave Jack a hand to conceal the orderly behind the false panel between the cabin and the cargo area. It was a narrow slot, and Artukovich would have to stand; but once in position, he was completely hidden from view from either side. Once Artukovich was in place behind the driver's seat, Jack positioned himself in the coffin-like space behind the passenger seat, and Paul snapped the cover panel in place. When Paul returned to the cabin, Brad continued towards the border at a slower speed.

When they reached the gate, Brad had his passport ready and passed it through the window. "Good evening, Monsieur," he said pleasantly to the guard. The guard gave Brad an icy stare, and looked at Paul, who quickly produced his passport, and handed it to the guard.

"You've had a very short visit," the guard said, noticing the entry stamp from the afternoon. "What is your business in Yugoslavia?"

"We have just returned from delivering some medical equipment to Commandant Smrcek at the military hospital in Bitola," Brad volunteered.

The guard studied both passports closely, then said suspiciously, "Open the back!" Brad got out, and going to the rear of the truck, he pulled back the canvas flap. The guard studied the inside carefully. When he was satisfied that the truck was empty, he turned on his heels, and went into the guard house. Paul felt for the gun and holster he wore under his white lab coat. "Steady, Paul," Brad whispered.

The guard returned shortly with the stamped passports. "I hope you have enjoyed your visit," the guard said in a professional manner.

"Thank you. I have gained a lot from my visit to your country," Brad responded. The guard opened the gate and Brad drove through. That was the way things were supposed to work, he thought to himself. If only the last trip had gone as smoothly, Kon would not be lying in the hospital.

"Our friend, Commandant Smrcek is going to have to do some fast talking when General Jakupak gets that telegram from the Institute stating that the X-ray equipment intended for the hospital in Belgrade was stolen while the truck was parked in Bitola," Brad said to Paul. Paul smiled slyly. "Yeah, and Smreck is never going to be able to explain what happened to Artukovich, or the dossier of evidence on him."

CHAPTER TWENTY-FOUR

Stamatis was there to meet them when they arrived at the hospital. He smiled to see them all return, but positively beamed when he saw Artukovich. Stamatis threw his sturdy arms around him, and all but swept him off his feet with an exuberant bear hug. "So you are here at last, Artukovich! It is good!"

"Good for you Stamatis, but my work is finished," the orderly responded sadly.

"Nonsense! There is much for you to do from this side," Stamatis answered. "But come, you need to rest. These mad men will exhaust you with their incessant dashing about at all hours." Keeping one arm around Artukovich to support him, Stamatis turned to the others who had stood watching the meeting. "Come, we will have some food to celebrate your safe return. Then you must sleep."

"Food sounds good, Stamatis, but how is Kon? Has he improved?" Brad asked hopefully.

Stamatis looked at the three tired faces in front of him and his smile faded. "He lives yet, but it does not go easy for him," he said softly. "Come," he continued gently when he saw their anxious looks, "I will tell the others that you have returned. Yiosiph will stay with Kon while you eat together."

"I want to check on Kon," Paul said, and turned to leave.

"Paul, wait!" Stamatis called after him. "There will be time for him. Eat first, and celebrate your safe return. You must be strong with life to help a weaker one."

"I'm not in a mood to celebrate anything," Paul insisted. "You go ahead and eat. I'll get something later." Without waiting for an answer, he walked away with his usual feline grace.

Jack started after him, but Brad caught his arm. "Let him go, Jack. He's too worried about Kon to relax, but Stamatis is right. We can't help Kon if we're exhausted."

"O.K., Brad, but let's eat fast. I want to check on Kon myself."

Supporting Artukovich, who was now limping badly, Stamatis led them to the same room they had sat in three nights ago, and told them to wait. The young boy, who had led them to the waiting room before, arrived shortly with a cart loaded with bread, cold lamb, several types of cheese and some fruit. After a few minutes, Mary, Geilla and Peterson arrived.

Mary rushed to Brad, and he pressed her tightly against him.

"Mary, my darling!" he said simply, as he drank in the fragrance of her perfume, and felt the softness of her hair.

"I'm so glad you're back!" Mary said with deep emotion. "I know I am not supposed to worry, but sitting there by the hour with Kon, I could not help but be reminded of what could happen to you."

"Please don't worry, Mary. Please don't ever worry." Brad drew her away from the others, and continued in a whisper as if he was filling her ears with rapturous words of love, "How is Kon?"

She held her lips to his ear. "He's getting weaker all the time. I would suggest we take him to London, but I don't think he could survive the trip."

Brad looked grim, and quickly turned his back to the others. "What is Stamatis doing for him?" he whispered anxiously.

"He's pumping him full of antibiotics. He has tried three types, but nothing works. Kon has been absolutely mad with fever all day and is nearing exhaustion. He started calling for Alyce shortly after you left, and hasn't let up all day. Geilla is frightfully upset. Against my advice, she put a call in to Alyce, and begged her to come. It was the most awful experience for her to go through, but she will do anything to see Kon well again."

"Is Alyce coming?" Brad asked in dismay.

"I'm afraid so. She was very reluctant to make such a long trip, but Geilla finally convinced her that Kon might never make it back to Paris. Oh Brad, I know Kon would not want Alyce to see him like this, but it broke my heart to hear him calling for her."

"Perhaps she will do him some good," Brad said, trying to soothe her. "He always seems happy when he is with her, and she did manage to get him to cut back on the heavy drinking."

"I know, but Alyce has no idea about the dangerous work he does. It will be a shock for her to see him. He looks awful, Brad, positively awful. I do hope she can keep her head," Mary concluded mournfully.

Just then Stamatis came in, gleefully waving two bottles of wine. "Come, let us celebrate the return of my good friend, Artukovich," he called.

Brad and Mary turned and rejoined the group. The boy had brought a wheelchair for Artukovich, and he was seated by the table of food.

Geilla stood talking with Jack and Peterson. She looked weary and very alone. Stamatis poured wine for everyone, and encouraged them to eat and relax. He seemed quite happy and at ease as he circled the table trying to cheer everyone. He came up to Brad, and throwing his arm around Brad's shoulder, he pulled him away from the group. Pouring more wine into Brad's glass, he said in a loud voice, "Drink! Celebrate a safe return!" Then suddenly turning his back to the others, he lowered his voice and said seriously, "I know you go to make some report on your mission." He put his hand on Brad's arm. "I ask you, please, if you have any connections at all, you must get me a supply of a new drug I have read about. Your friend was so weak when you brought him . . . the surgery was a success, but the infection is spreading. It resists everything I have tried. He struggles so to breathe, his heart will give out if we can't find something to help him."

Brad glanced at his watch and was silent for a long moment. "I'll go at once and make my report. Give me the name of the drug."

Stamatis quickly slipped Brad a piece of paper with a single word printed across it. "Do not leave too suddenly and alarm the others," Stamatis cautioned. "They do not know how bad it is."

Brad nodded, then forcing a smile he raised his glass to Stamatis and returned to the table. His appetite was gone, but he ate, and encouraged the others to eat and relax.

Finally Stamatis called for everyone to go and rest, and wheeled Artukovich away to bed. Brad issued his orders.

"Jack, you go back to the hotel with Geilla and Peterson. Mary, would you take some of this food up to Paul and see that he eats. I've got to send a report to Carl."

Jack shot Brad an inquisitive look, but Brad put his hand on Jack's arm. "Get some rest. I'll be needing you later." Jack nodded and escorted Geilla and Peterson down the hall.

Mary put some food on a tray, and climbed the stairs to the ward. She found Paul sitting by the bed, holding the mask to Kon's face. Paul looked up as she came in, and she was dismayed to see the stricken look on his face.

"He's not getting any better," Paul said sorrowfully. "I really thought he would be better. I can't let him slip away like this. I just can't . . ."

Mary's heart sank. She was glad that Geilla was not there to hear such talk from Paul.

Dear God, what can I say? she thought. Silently she set the tray of food on a chair. Taking a deep breath, she walked calmly to Paul and put her arm around him.

"Don't give up on Kon," she said softly. "You know better than any of us how tough he is. We've sent for Alyce. You'll see, he'll rally when she comes," she said with forced cheerfulness.

Paul did not answer, but Mary felt him lean against her. Abruptly he straightened himself, and Mary sensed he felt embarrassed that he had allowed himself to seek even a moment of comfort from her. Don't worry, Mr. Tower of Strength, she thought, touching his arm lightly. I won't tell anyone you're human.

"You're right, Mary. Kon is tough. He'll be glad to see Alyce," he said.

"Yes," Mary answered slowly. "I brought you some food. Brad said you scarcely had time to eat all day."

"I guess I don't feel hungry right now."

"You should take something. We need your strength, Paul – all of us," she said softly. "I'll take over on the mask." She put her hands over Paul's, and gently took the mask from him. "Go on – get something to eat," she told him firmly.

"Yes, mother," he drawled sarcastically, but he smiled at her.

Paul forced himself to eat, but the food was like straw and cotton to him. He kept thinking of Kon, and remembering all the things they had done together. He recalled the last time Kon had pulled him out of a tight spot. It had been the most daring, foolhardy thing he had ever seen Kon do.

The team had flown to the mid-East to rescue a hostage, but the mission had been aborted when the hostage was killed and Paul taken prisoner. There was no publicity about Paul's arrest. He was an unknown and had been herded in with the general criminal population at one of the smaller jails.

While sitting in a hot, crowded cell with a group of Arabs, he heard the firing start. He guessed that another truce had broken down, and that rival factions had started shelling each other again. Most of the soldiers left the jail when the commotion started.

Suddenly, Paul heard shouting outside the cell. He looked up, and to his surprise there was Kon, wearing a uniform complete with head gear, and an automatic slung over his shoulder. He was holding a soldier from behind with his revolver pressed against the soldier's back. The soldier was screaming in Arabic, and Paul guessed he was begging the other soldiers not to fire at Kon. Three soldiers stood together. They were armed, but did not move.

"Paul! Where are you?" Kon called aloud, as he hauled the man backwards from the main room down the passageway to the cells.

"Here, Kon! First cell on your right."

Still holding his gun against the soldier, Kon ordered him to remove his weapon and hand it to Paul. As the man did as he was told, one of the other soldiers made a move for his weapon. Kon snarled in Arabic and fired a single shot, hitting the man square in the chest. The man screamed and fell forward, and the others froze where they stood. Still holding the one soldier in front of him, Kon kept the others at bay while Paul blasted the lock off the cell door. The prisoners began pushing Paul from behind as they made a wild rush from the cell. They quickly overpowered the two remaining guards, took their weapons, and started towards the street door. Suddenly it flew open, and four soldiers rushed in with their weapons raised. Paul pulled the trigger. Two soldiers went down and two dropped their weapons and backed off. The prisoners seized the weapons and started firing out the door at random.

Kon struck his hostage on the side of the head with the butt of his revolver, and shouted for Paul to make for the door. As the prisoners charged through the door shooting wildly in all directions,

Kon caught up with Paul, and led the way around the side of the jail. They made a run across the street, and Paul saw a jeep in the shadows. The sound of heavy artillery reverberated close in front of them. As they leaped into the jeep, several blasts from automatics roared from behind, and Paul heard Kon curse in Italian. Paul swung around to return the fire, and felt a searing pain in his right shoulder. With determination he raised his gun, and sprayed the area behind him from left to right. He saw several men fall, but could not tell how many were still standing.

Kon had the jeep moving before Paul finished his sweep and they sped away, zig-zagging through a maze of narrow streets. Even after they were certain that no one was pursuing them, Kon drove at top speed.

Paul looked over at Kon. "That was the stupidest stunt you've ever pulled, Kon."

"Shut up, Paul," Kon snarled. "It worked, didn't it?"

"Yeah, but only because no one would expect a sane man to walk in there alone. I'm surprised Brad would authorize such a scheme."

"He didn't," Kon snapped. "I'm afraid our friend Bradley is going to be very displeased with me."

Paul laughed a dry laugh, "Displeased! Hell! For once he'll be really pissed!"

"To hell with Brad! I couldn't leave you there, Paul," Kon answered heatedly.

Kon drove to a small, badly scarred airfield where Brad and Jack were waiting. When Kon had disappeared earlier, Brad had been angry. He had told Jack he would give Kon one hour to show, or be left behind. He was in favor of having Carl pull a few strings to have Paul released. When the hour was up, Jack had pleaded for a fifteen minute delay, then for another five. With three minutes to go, Jack was pacing when Kon and Paul pulled up.

Jack ran to meet them, and noticed Paul's bloody arm as he helped him out of the jeep. "God it's good to see you again, Paul! Let me do something for your arm," he said throwing his own arm around Paul. They started towards the plane, but stopped when Kon didn't follow. Thinking that Kon was reluctant to face Brad, Jack turned back.

"Come on, Kon. Brad will be glad to see you, even though he is angry."

"I'm not worried about Brad. The bastards got my leg, Jack! Haul me out, will you!"

Jack opened the door and saw the blood dripping from Kon's left thigh. "Don't move," he said in what he hoped was a calm voice. "I'll get the stretcher."

Jack dashed toward the plane, and returned shortly with Brad.

334

Together they lifted Kon out and laid him on the stretcher. He had been hit twice. Jack had their emergency kit and knelt to take a closer look at Kon's wounds.

"Forget the first aid crap, Jack!" Kon shouted. "Let's get the hell out of here. I've held things up enough."

Jack shot a look at Brad who nodded. "Shut up, Kon. Where's your knife?" Jack shouted back at Kon.

"Right pocket," Kon grunted and moved to reach for it.

"Lay still! I'll get it," Jack warned. He cut through Kon's pant leg and pulled it away. "How the hell did you drive with a leg like this?"

Kon did not answer.

"Must have been some fight. Wish I'd been there," Jack continued as he put a tourniquet around Kon's thigh and tightened it. The bleeding let up.

"Let's get him on the plane," Brad said to Jack. "Are you all right, Paul?"

"Sure, go ahead. I can get myself to the plane."

After takeoff, Brad came back to where Kon lay, and began to bandage his leg.

"You knew it was a terrible risk to go in there alone, Kon."

"Yes, yes, make it short," Kon answered, clenching his teeth as Brad took up on the bandage. "Paul's already told me how stupid I am. I wore a Point Blank, Brad. They weren't supposed to shoot my God damn leg!"

"You should have thought of Paul! You could have gotten him killed."

"Damn it, Brad, I had to risk it! Those bastards might have hung him while you and Carl were screwing around with your damn diplomacy."

Brad wanted to say more, but it didn't seem right to chew out a man while you were patching him together.

"God I need a drink, Brad! Where's that bottle I brought?" Kon asked anxiously.

"I don't know," Brad lied as he finished tying the bandages on Kon.

"What do you mean, you don't know?" Kon snapped. "For God's sake, look for it, Brad! I need it!"

"No," Brad answered calmly. "No alcohol right now. I recommend a shot of morphine."

"What are you – some damn doctor! I need a drink, Brad," Kon shouted and grabbed Brad's arm.

"Not now, Kon, not now! It will only make you bleed faster. Take the morphine. It's better."

"Oh all right!" Kon grumbled. "Remember to cut the dose. You know I can't . . ."

"I know," Brad said as the needle hit Kon's arm. "It's all premeasured for you."

"You sneaky bastard!" Kon muttered. "Give one to Paul too. He must be feeling pretty shaky." He turned towards Paul, who was slumped against the wall near his head. "Sorry they shot up your arm, Paul."

"It's O.K., Kon." Paul muttered. Then after a pause, "Kon . . . thanks for getting me out. I wasn't looking forward to being hung."

"I couldn't leave you there, Paul . . . just couldn't." His voice trailed off and he fell silent.

Brad didn't lecture Kon any more about being irresponsible, but in his official capacity, he suspended him from the team for six months. That was just enough time for Kon to take sufficient physical therapy to enable him to walk without a noticeable limp. Kon eventually went back to running and skiing, but after that incident, Paul could always tell when Kon was pushing himself too hard on an assignment by the way he walked.

****

Mary sat with Paul, waiting for Brad to return from making his report to Carl. She wondered if it was really taking a long time, or if she was just tired. She was glad that Geilla had not given Brad an argument about going back to the hotel. She needed the rest.

Kon had been quiet, but after a time he became restless again. He rolled his head, and called softly for Alyce several times. Although his voice was barely above a whisper, Kon's plaintive calling pierced Mary's heart. He had been calling all day and neither she, nor Geilla had been able to comfort him. Mary felt guilty when she did not respond to Kon immediately, and she was glad when Paul went to him.

"Alyce will be here soon, Kon," Paul said softly, and touched Kon on the arm. Paul poured some water into a glass, and lifting Kon he offered it to him. Kon tried to pull away, but Paul held his shoulders. "Come on, just a sip, Kon," he coaxed.

Sensing that it was Paul who was with him, Kon opened his eyes, "Paul?"

"Yes. It's O.K. Alyce will be here soon. Try to take some water."

"Water? It tastes like blood, Paul. I can't swallow . . . Put me off the train, Paul! Now . . . before it's too late. It's worse than I thought," Kon gasped.

"You're off the train, Kon. We're all off," Paul answered quickly. "Try to drink."

"We're off?"

"Yes, we're all off. Peterson is safe! The mission is complete."

Kon was silent, and Paul poured some of the water into his mouth. Kon swallowed a little, and tried again to pull away. "It's blood, Paul. I can't . . ."

"I swear it's water, Kon. Drink it . . . please."

Kon took a few hesitant swallows and looked at Paul. "Put me off, Paul . . . don't get caught," he mumbled, and closing his eyes he went limp against Paul's arm.

"Kon! Kon! You're off the train," Paul said softly. Then raising his voice, "Christ! Why can't I get through to him? I can't even ease his mind about that stinking train!"

"It's the bloody fever. You did all you could," Brad said as he came around the curtain. "Why don't you get some rest, Paul?"

"Rest? Hell! How can you expect me to rest?" Paul answered sharply.

"Take some tablets! You're the chemist!" Brad said irritably.

Mary saw Paul glare defiantly at Brad, and expected to hear an invective tirade, but Brad put up his hand.

"Just for a few hours, Paul, please. Geilla is going to need you tomorrow. Don't start a mutiny," he said quietly.

Paul bit his lip and stared at Brad. Then he nodded. "You're right. Promise you'll call me if he gets any worse."

"Yes, yes of course," Brad agreed and Paul left.

"He's taking it very hard," Mary said, going up to Brad and putting her arms around him.

"I know. He's trying to will Kon better, and put on a brave show for Geilla, and he doesn't have you for an anchor. I love you, Mary," Brad said clutching her to his chest. "I couldn't stay in this business if it weren't for you."

Mary raised her head, and he kissed her lightly on the lips. And how I wish you would quit, she thought, but she knew it was in his blood. "You should get some rest, too," she murmured.

"I know. I will later, when Jack comes back."

"You were a long time making your report," Mary commented.

Brad took her hand. "I didn't want to say anything in front of Paul, but I was trying to contact Dr. La Monde. I know Kon insists upon keeping his work on the team completely separate from his personal life, but Carlin would never forgive me if I let Kon slip away without telling him."

"What did he say? Is he coming?"

"The situation is dreadful, Mary. Young Charles has been hurt in an automobile accident and is in a coma. Carlin was terribly upset to hear about Kon, but he said that he can't possibly leave Geneva. Charles is hanging between life and death, and Charlotte is nearly hysterical. Carlin said that he would talk to Edgar, and asked me to call him again. When I assured Carlin that everything was being done for Kon, he begged me not to let him sink into despair. Oh, Mary! He was so distressed, I was almost sorry I had called him."

"You had to, Brad. You gave your word to Carlin. How terrible for him to caught in the middle!"

Mary sat with Brad, and was thankful that Kon was quiet until Brad left again to call Carlin. Then she sat alone. She held Kon's hand, listened to his labored breathing, and prayed that she would have the strength to bear up. She was startled from her reverie when Yiosiph came around the curtain, and spoke to her in Greek. She thought at first that he was upbraiding her for not talking to Kon, and she felt a pang of guilt; but when he produced a pot of tea, and continued to jabber at her, she realized he was expressing his concern for her. She smiled and accepted the tea. She explained that she was waiting for Brad, knowing that Yiosiph understood more English than he let on.

Brad was surprised, but relieved to see Yiosiph sitting with Mary when he returned.

"Any news?" Mary asked when she saw Brad.

"Carlin talked with Edgar and he agreed that Albert should come. He will be on the flight to Athens later this morning. I have arranged with Carl to have someone meet him at the airport and bring him here."

"I'm so glad," Mary sighed. "You need to get some rest, Brad." Mary poured some tea for Brad, and watched him sip it. They were both relieved when Jack showed up a few minutes later.

CHAPTER TWENTY-FIVE

Alyce hung up the phone after talking with Geilla. She was almost sorry that she had agreed to go to Greece. Perhaps sorry was too strong a word, but she certainly had misgivings about meeting Kon in such a strange place. Somehow she felt she held the upper hand in their relationship, because Kon always came to her. He kept returning to see her and it was exhilarating to be with him; but after three years, his visits were no more frequent, and he had never asked her to marry him.

She thought back to the last time she had prodded him towards a commitment. The evening began as usual, with Kon sitting attentively in the front row of the audience, watching her with that unsmiling, almost analytical look he often wore. He was quite familiar with the workings of the theater. If the sound was not absolutely clear, or the lighting effects were less than perfect, he always noticed.

He had come backstage to her dressing room after the performance, bearing an enormous bouquet of white roses, tied with a deep blue satin ribbon. She smiled at him as she took the flowers, thinking how handsome he looked in formal evening dress. Although no one had ever been able to get Kon into a ruffled shirt, the very whiteness of his plain shirt set off his dark eyes and his dark hair. Somehow Kon's untameable hair offended her rigid sense of order, the way it invariably defied control and slipped across his forehead spoiling his otherwise sophisticated appearance.

"You were magnificent tonight, my darling," he said, presenting her the roses and kissing her lightly on the lips.

"You say that every time you come, Kon. You are not a true critic." She laid the flowers on her dressing table and sat before the mirror with her back towards him.

"Is it any less true because I say it often? I have said 'I love you' many times, but I meant it as much the last time as the first," he answered and kissed the back of her neck. "Must I think of a new way to tell you my feelings?" he continued. Unzipping her tight costume, he bent and kissed her back as he slowly revealed it.

Alyce straightened and pulled away. "Don't, Kon. I am still wet from the performance."

"Then I will dry you," he said, and taking the silk scarf from around his neck, he started to rub it across her shoulders.

"Don't be absurd. You'll soil your scarf," she protested. Turning to face him, she put her hands on his shoulders, and pushed him away. "You must be patient until I take my shower and get dressed."

"All right," he sighed. He took off his coat and sank into an armchair across from the dressing table.

"Where would you like to go for supper?" he asked as she picked up a towel and started towards the shower.

"Gabriella is having a few people in. I thought we might join them."

"Anyone I know?" Kon asked quickly.

"Oh, Georgette and Andre . . . I think you've met most of them," she called from the shower. Then very casually she added, "My father said he might stop by later. It would be a good opportunity for you to meet him, Kon. He's anxious to make your acquaintance."

Kon stiffened, but said nothing. He did not look up when she came out of the shower a few moments later. Alyce took one look at him and knew. "You don't want to go, do you?" she said petulantly.

He raised his head. "Let's just go alone. I don't want to share you with anyone tonight."

She stood before him, still wearing only the large towel. "Why won't you agree to meet my father, Kon? This would be the most natural way. I have told him all about you and he is curious."

"So you've told him all about me, eh? And what did he say?"

"He would like to meet you himself."

"I can imagine he does," Kon mumbled almost to himself.

"Please, darling, do this for me," Alyce begged in her most engaging manner.

"Some other time, perhaps, not tonight, Alyce."

"You say that every time, Kon!" she responded angrily. "What can my father possibly say that would be so terrible?"

"I don't know, Alyce and I am unprepared," he answered vaguely. "Fathers have a way of holding me up to the light and exposing my flaws."

"You're just being stubborn, Kon. You care nothing for my feelings!" She turned and started to walk away.

He jumped from his chair and forcefully took her in his arms. "That's not true! I do care. Please forgive me, Alyce, but in this one thing I am a coward." He held her close against his chest, oblivious to the dampness of the towel she still had wrapped about her. "You are my jewel, Alyce, my beautiful jewel. I could not bear to lose you."

She usually reveled in the strength of his impetuous embraces, but tonight she was angry because she could not manipulate him. She was used to having her own way, but neither her tears, or her smiles could move Kon once his mind was set.

"Be sensible, Kon. You'll ruin your jacket," she said irritably and tried to pull away.

"The jacket is nothing, Alyce. You are important to me."

She let him kiss her, but she did not respond. He released her and she silently went behind the screen and began to dress.

Damn! there never is a way around this father problem, he thought. Sooner or later I will have to meet the man and endure the verbal vivisectioning. God, how I dread it!

Alyce was in a brighter mood when she came from behind the screen. She had failed this time, but some day she would win. Meanwhile she did not want to drive Kon away. He was much too eligible. Although not as smooth as some of the others she dated, he was good looking and very vibrant physically. Kon had a way of controlling his excitement and desire until she was ready for him. Then she surrendered to the strength and fire in him, that started as a glowing ember, and grew into a cloud of flame, devouring every feeling but her desire for perfect union with him. No one had ever made her feel as totally dominated, or as free, at one and the same time, and it was a thrilling experience.

Kon also had a respectable position in a bank, and judging from the gifts he brought, he was quite well off. His other work took him away quite often, but that gave her the freedom she enjoyed. The situation could be very nice, if only she could get him to marry her.

Alyce was on the plane before she let her mind drift back to Kon. She was wearing the necklace he had given her last Christmas. It was fashioned of five perfect sapphires in a graceful, white gold setting. Kon knew her favorite colors were blue and white and chose them for everything he gave her. Thinking about him now, she wondered if he had a favorite color. He had never mentioned one.

She remembered the night he had given her the necklace. After her performance they had gone to supper at one of her favorite restaurants. He had been in an unusually happy mood and displayed that rare smile that lit his face and gave him an almost enchanting attractiveness. They had returned to her apartment early and settled themselves comfortably on the sofa to sip a new wine he had brought for her. Suddenly, he took her hand and held it gently.

"I have a gift for you," he announced happily.

She was intrigued. He usually presented his offerings when he first came into her dressing room after a performance. "I knew you were hiding something all evening. What is it?" she asked gaily.

"A Christmas present for my jewel," he answered, and getting up, he went to his coat which lay across a chair. He pulled a long, thin box from the pocket. Her smile froze when she saw its shape. It was the wrong size to hold a ring. Nervously she opened the box and saw the five glorious sapphires.

"Oh, Kon, it's beautiful!" she gasped.

She lifted the neckless in her hand and the stones sparkled with deep blue fire.

"You should have given it to me earlier. I could have enjoyed wearing it all evening," she complained.

He sat by her on the sofa. "I wanted you to wear it first for me alone. I designed it myself. See, this way it is 'A' for Alyce and this way," he said turning it, "it is 'K'. Here, let me fasten it for you," he offered, and gently slipped it around her neck. He gazed longingly at her for a moment, then added, "I would like you to come to Villars with me for the holidays. You wouldn't have to ski with me. You could just sit by the fire and look beautiful, and warm my ears with your hands when I come in. I have reserved a chalet for us. It would be so perfect, Alyce, so peaceful. Just the two . . ." he stopped suddenly when he saw her look.

"I'm sorry, Kon. I've made other plans," she whispered. "You should have let me know sooner."

"I see I was a fool to keep it as a surprise!" he said bitterly. He got up, paced the length of the room, then stood with his back to her.

"I had hoped that this year we could spend the holiday together." He paused and unconsciously brushed his errant hair from his forehead. "No matter, there will be another time," he said casually, but his smile was gone.

"I must go," he said bruskly.

"But, Kon," she protested, flashing her most engaging smile. "Aren't you staying? I haven't expressed my thanks for your gift." She reached for him, but he slipped away.

Picking up his glass, he tossed down the remainder of the wine. "It is only a trinket," he said caustically. "I must go. I'm expected in Geneva tomorrow."

He picked up his coat and hurried out, but she caught up to him as he was putting on his coat in the hall.

"I'm sorry about the holiday," she murmured demurely and slid her long fingers gently under the lapels of his overcoat. "I'll make it up to you," she promised, gazing up at him and smiling seductively.

He looked at her impassively. "Perhaps with the new year, I will discover what will put me at the head of the line," he said coldly and he was gone.

Perhaps I should have canceled my plans and gone with him, Alyce thought, as she gazed out the window of the plane. Kon had invited her to join him on trips several times, but she had never made the time. However, a trip to Villars was an exclusive invitation into his territory and his private life. She knew the Marneés were often there and they were the closest Kon had to any family. Inviting her there might have meant he was making plans for their future. She almost regretted having turned him down, but Andre had asked her first. Though more polished than Kon, Andre was not as well off or as generous. He was not as exciting to be with either, but she could manipulate Andre, and he never suspected when she cheated on him. Somehow Kon always knew when she had slept with another man. He never reproached her for it, but she could not conceal it from him.

Andre had come to see her just after Kon left Paris four days ago. Seeing them both in such a short time made her realize that Andre was not half the man Kon was; but on his last visit, Andre had hinted about marriage. She was hoping Kon would speak out when she arrived in Greece. She did not fully understand why he had sent for her. He should have called her himself instead of asking Geilla to do it.

Alyce was tired by the time she arrived at the hospital in Florina. It had been a long ride from Athens in an old railroad car with a group composed of several rough looking men, a few old women and one young pregnant woman with a shrieking child. Alyce was irritable as she stood in the wind swept street watching the taxi driver struggle to unload her mountain of luggage. She did not quarrel over the fare, but presented him with a handfull of the unfamiliar bills, and dashed into the comparative warmth of the hospital.

Taking just a moment to get her bearings, she strode up to the information desk in her usual confident manner. "I am here to see Monsieur Kononellos. He is a patient of Dr. Stamatis," she said, in French, to the woman behind the counter.

"Stamatis, eh," the woman replied rudely. Then, "Wait." The woman left the desk and walked slowly down the hall. Opening one of the doors off the corridor, she shouted to someone in Greek. Alyce caught a glimpse of a young boy as he scurried from the room and disappeared up the stairs. The woman returned to the desk, but ignored Alyce, and continued slowly checking over a stack of papers. Alyce removed her coat and sat in one of the wooden chairs lining the hall.

After a short wait, Alyce saw a tall, well-built man coming towards her with long strides. She recognized Brad as he came closer. He took her hand formally, but his words were full of emotion. "Thank God you've come, Alyce. Kon has been calling your name for hours."

"What has happened, Brad? I could scarcely make sense out of what Geilla told me over the phone. She said Kon was very ill and that he was never coming back to Paris. What is he doing in this horrid place?"

"I'm afraid it's very serious, Alyce," Brad said slowly. "We were on a rescue mission and Kon got hurt. He lost a lot of blood. He was very weak by the time we brought him to the hospital, and now he has a severe lung infection." Brad watched Alyce's face as he spoke, and he sensed that she did not really comprehend what he was telling her. "I know this is all very strange to you, but Kon's in bad shape, Alyce. He needs your support."

"I'll do what I can, Brad," she responded after a long pause.

"Good. I'll take you up. Let me take your coat," Brad said and

343

took her by the arm.

Paul saw them as they came down the length of the ward and understood immediately why Kon was so hopelessly fascinated by Alyce. She seemed to float as she moved, and her features were strikingly beautiful. Her skin had the color and luster of rare pearls and her long ebony hair was piled high on her head. She was wearing a white, raw silk suit and a pale blue blouse open at the neck. There at her throat hung the sapphire necklace that Kon had given her just before Christmas.

Paul recognized the necklace immediately as the one Kon had spent three months designing and having crafted to his exact specifications. The jeweler had been forced to cast the setting twice before Kon was satisfied that it was perfect. It was an exquisite, but very expensive trinket, and Kon had been in debt for several months because of it. Kon always had been a sucker about spending money on women, Paul thought; but who could blame a man for being a fool over a woman like Alyce. How thoughtful of her to wear the necklace today.

Alyce was surprised to see so many people waiting at the end of the ward. It suddenly occurred to her, that aside from Brad and Geilla, she had never met any of Kon's friends. Brad quietly introduced Alyce to the others who were gathered outside the curtain. Their eyes were all on her, but she was used to attention and nodded formally to each of them. At last Brad took her arm again and led her around the curtain.

Stamatis had been holding the oxygen mask to Kon's face, but he hid it immediately when Alyce came around the curtain. Stamatis eyed Alyce critically and motioned for her to come up to the bed. Alyce stepped forward, but stopped suddenly and drew in her breath when she saw Kon. She stared at him, but froze where she stood. Despite Mary's and Geilla's best efforts, Kon looked ghastly. His face was ashen and his eyes were dark sunken hollows. The thought that she was too late and that Kon was already dead flashed through her mind.

Brad slipped past her, and taking hold of Kon's hand with his left hand, he put his right hand on Kon's shoulder and shook him gently. "Kon, wake up," he said softly. "Alyce is here."

Kon rolled his head, but did not open his eyes.

"Kon, can you hear me?" Brad continued. "Alyce is here."

"Alyce?" Kon gasped, and opened his eyes part way.

"Yes, Kon, it's Alyce. She has come," Brad said quickly.

Kon opened his eyes and blinked several times before he recognized Alyce. "Alyce!" he called softly.

Brad let go of Kon's hand and moved aside, motioning Alyce to come forward. She didn't move. She could only stand and stare at this body that was not at all like the strong, vital man she knew as Kon.

This was not her barbarian – her conqueror. This man had the mark of death on him, and she was horrified.

"Alyce!" Kon repeated, and stretching his arm forward, he held out his broad hand.

Jack was standing directly behind Alyce and saw her pull back when Kon put out his hand. Suddenly he took her by the arm and pushed her forward. "Say something to him, or I'll break your arm!" he hissed into her ear.

She opened her mouth to speak, but nothing came out save, "Kon?"

That one poor offering brought a smile to Kon's face. "Alyce, my jewel," he said weakly and strained his arm to reach her.

Alyce suddenly regretted that she had ever left Paris and her own familiar world for this man she really knew so little about. This was not the same man who had set her passion on fire. She could not bring herself to touch this . . . this stranger.

Jack saw Kon straining to reach Alyce, and her lack of response infuriated him. He tightened his grip on her arm. "God damn you! Take his hand!" he snarled into her ear.

"Let me go!" she cried to Jack, but Kon heard her. He stopped struggling to reach her, and studied her face. "Is Andre the winner then?" he said faintly. Alyce started and stared at him. Slowly she straightened herself, and her face took on a determined look. She had made her choice. She could never live with a man who could read her the way Kon could. "Yes!" she answered almost defiantly.

Kon looked at her for another moment, then said faintly, "So, I am still the fisherman's son." He turned his head aside and closed his eyes. "Ashes . . . all ashes," he muttered so faintly that only Geilla, who had been standing faithfully by his right side, heard him.

There was an overpowering silence in the room until Brad spoke. "Let her go, Jack."

Jack pushed Alyce away from him, and looked at her in disgust. "Damn! I can't see what Kon saw in a heartless bitch like you," he growled and strode angrily out of the curtained area.

Alyce looked from one to another of the group and felt their hostility. She looked once more at Kon, then slowly reached up and unfastened the necklace from around her neck. She lay it in Kon's outstretched hand, but it slipped through his limp fingers and fell to the floor with a crash.

"I think you should go, Alyce," Brad said coldly. He took her arm with courtly correctness, and escorted her from the room.

Geilla tightened her grip on Kon's hand and shook as she began to sob uncontrollably. "You were right, Mary. I should never have asked her to come. I've killed him, Mary. I've killed him!"

Mary hurried to her, and putting her arm around her, she pried her hands loose from Kon. "Hush! Hush! It's not your fault, Geilla.

You were only trying to help him. Don't cry! Don't cry! You know it disturbs him. Let him rest. Come away for a bit until you are calmer." Slowly Mary coaxed Geilla away from Kon and took her to the hotel where she could release her sorrow without upsetting Kon. Mary found it hard to control her own tears, but it would not do to break down. Brad was depending on her.

CHAPTER TWENTY-SIX

Almost immediately after Alyce left, Kon took a turn for the worse. His blood pressure dropped and his temperature rose alarmingly. Although Stamatis increased the dose of antibiotics and shot him full of drugs to control the fever, Kon became increasingly restless and cried out in delirium. The members of the team took turns trying to calm and reassure him; but he did not recognize them, and struggled frantically whenever they touched him.

Shortly after 4 o'clock the young Greek boy, who haunted the wards at all hours, acting as eyes and ears for Stamatis, appeared and announced to Brad that two men were waiting for him in the lobby. Brad began following the boy down the long ward, but he flitted out of sight before Brad reached the stairs. When Brad entered the lobby, he saw two young men waiting at the reception desk. As he came up to them, the older one, who was wearing an American Air Force uniform, stepped forward with a take-charge air. "Mr. Cover-Rollins?" he asked briskly.

"Yes," Brad responded.

"I am Major William Allensworth, U.S. Air Force."

"It's a pleasure to meet you," Brad answered as they shook hands.

"This is Albert Marneé," Allensworth said, stepping aside.

The younger man came forward and shook Brad's hand with a firm, confident grip. Although Albert appeared to be about twenty, Brad recognized him as the same tall, slender, sandy-haired boy, whose likeness he had seen smiling out from a plain silver frame in Kon's apartment in Paris.

"It's good of you to come, Albert. I was sorry to hear about Charles. Has there been any improvement?"

"None," Albert responded sadly. "We were at the hospital all night, but he is still unconscious. I hated to leave, but someone had to come for Peter. How is he?"

"I'm afraid it's not good, Albert. The fever . . . but we must not hold up Major Allensworth," Brad said turning toward the major. "Thank you for bringing Albert so quickly."

"Anytime!" the major answered and smiled. "I'd better go. This flight was logged as a test run. Good luck, Albert!"

"Thanks, Bill," Albert said. "I really appreciate . . ."

"Hey, nothing to it!" Allensworth said as he hurried out.

"Kon's fighting a terrible infection, Albert," Brad said seriously after the major had left. "It started in his lungs, but it seems to be spreading. He's absolutely tormented with fever and delirium. I don't mean to frighten you," Brad added when he saw the look on Albert's face, "but he may not recognize you."

"Carlin told me he was very bad. That's why I came."

Remembering the assurances that Alyce had uttered only hours before, Brad wanted to be sure that Albert was not shocked by Kon's appearance. "You must prepare yourself, Albert. Kon looks dreadful, absolutely dreadful!"

"I imagine he does," Albert answered knowingly. "He was in an auto accident once. I saw him when they brought him home."

"Let's go up then. The rest of the team are waiting to meet you."

Albert nodded, and Brad led the way up the stairs and down the long ward. Albert's face betrayed his growing dismay as he noticed the out-dated equipment and stark atmosphere of the hospital. Since Mary and Geilla were still at the hotel, only Jack, Paul and Peterson were with Kon when Brad led Albert around the curtain. Paul stood to greet them. Brad began introductions, but Albert hurried past Paul, and rushed to the bed.

"Peter! Oh my God!" he exclaimed and touched Peter on the arm. Peter was struggling and gasping for breath. "Peter? Peter, can you hear me? It's Albert," Albert called softly, but Peter did not respond.

"Can nothing more be done for him?" Albert asked, appalled by Peter's suffering.

"The doctor is giving him antibiotics, and we are trying to locate a new drug," Paul answered, trying to sound hopeful.

Albert touched Peter's hand and felt the virulence of the fever from the heat of it. Peter tried to pull away, but Albert tightened his grip and touched Peter on the shoulder.

"Peter? Peter, don't be afraid. It's Albert. You're safe here, Peter. I'll take care of you."

Peter turned his head and gasped, "Albert?"

"Yes. I've come."

"Albert?" Peter whispered faintly. "Is it really you?"

"Yes, it's me, Peter. I had to come."

"Oh Albert, I had another terrible dream. Don't tell your papa, Albert . . . please . . . swear you won't tell him!"

"I swear, Peter. I swear. He'll never find out."

Peter appeared to relax momentarily. "You're a true friend, Albert . . . a true friend. Don't tell your papa . . . please . . . he'll send me away . . . I'll take you skiing, Albert . . . soon . . . just you and Charles."

"Yes, yes I want to go, Peter," Albert agreed eagerly.

"Promise me you'll look after Charles, if they send me away. Promise, Albert."

"I promise, but I won't let them send you away."

"Promise me, Albert . . . Charles is not as brave as you. He's too young to understand . . ."

"I promise, Peter, I promise," Albert repeated, but Peter would not be comforted and kept mumbling incoherently.

Noticing Albert bite his lip and fight back his tears, Paul laid his hand on Albert's shoulder. "Don't let it upset you. He doesn't really know what he's saying."

Albert hung his head in despair. "Oh God, what if I lose both of them? I couldn't stand it!"

"Hey! Hey! Don't talk like that. Kon's a fighter. He'll be O.K.," Paul responded almost mechanically. "Would you like to meet some of Kon's friends?" Paul continued, and coaxed Albert away from the bed. Paul introduced Jack, and Peterson, and then repeated his own name, which he knew Albert had not caught when Brad had tried to make introductions.

"Have you eaten, Albert? Would you like some coffee?" Paul asked solicitously.

"I'm not hungry. Well, maybe some coffee, if it's not too much trouble," Albert answered quickly.

"It's no trouble. How do you like your coffee?"

"Black, with lots of sugar."

"Fine, I'll be right back," Paul answered and walked quickly down the ward.

Albert was sitting with Kon, trying to make sense out of his delirious raving, when Paul returned a few minutes later carrying a tray loaded with cups of coffee.

"Take a break, Albert. I'll sit with Kon," Brad said, taking a cup from the tray.

Albert looked up when Paul handed him the coffee.

"I wish I could do more for him," he said sadly.

"You did more than you realize. He focused on you for quite a while. Come and sit down. Tell me about the dreams."

"You know about the dreams?" Albert asked in surprise.

Paul nodded. "Yeah, I know. He won't talk about it, so I just ignore them."

Albert smiled faintly. "I guess . . . he makes quite a row sometimes, doesn't he?"

"He certainly does. I thought it was from the kind of work we do. We all get a little uptight sometimes. I didn't realize he's had them for so long."

"He's had them since he first came to live with us. He slept in the room next to Charles and myself, and I could hear him call out in his sleep. I roused my father the first time I heard him. I was sure someone was trying to kill him. Peter was very upset when my father woke him. He was terrified that my father would send him away, and made me swear that I would never call him again. I couldn't believe that anyone would be frightened of my father, but I swore.

It's strange. Peter always came to comfort Charles and me, if we had bad dreams. Sometimes he slept on the floor in our room all night if we were afraid, but he was terribly ashamed that he had nightmares. He didn't have as many after he was with us for a while, but they never went away completely."

"I know for certain that doing the work we do has added a few more horrors to his mental collection. I've woken up in a cold sweat a few times myself. I'm glad you've come, Albert. Kon is not one to brag, but he is extremely proud of you and Charles. I appreciate anything you can do to keep his spirits up."

"I'm happy to meet some of Peter's friends. He never tells us about his work . . . doesn't want us to worry, he says. But we do, especially my mother. She worries about all of us. She nearly went to pieces about Charles. Poor Charles, I hope . . ." Albert broke off and gulped his coffee which had grown cold.

Paul patted Albert's arm. "Come on. I want you to meet some more of Kon's friends," he said, seeing that Mary and Geilla had returned from the hotel.

****

As the hours passed, Kon's fever persisted and grew worse, until shortly after midnight he began to have convulsions. Albert, who had been sitting by the bed, turned white-faced with alarm.

"Peter? Peter? What's wrong?" he asked anxiously as Kon jerked his hand free.

Jack, Paul, and Brad rushed to the bed and tried to keep Kon from falling, or jerking out the IV needle, while Geilla dashed down the ward to find Stamatis.

"Leave him alone!" Albert cried to Jack and Paul as they took hold of Kon's shoulders and legs.

"What are you doing? You're hurting him!" Albert protested.

"Stand aside, Albert," Brad ordered when Stamatis limped in a moment later.

"No! You're hurting him! Let him go!" Albert pleaded and started to pull on Paul's arm.

"Get out!" Stamatis roared at Albert, but Albert stood rooted to the floor, prepared to defend Peter from everyone, particularly from this stranger with dirty, rumbled clothes and a grubby beard. "Leave him alone!" he shrieked.

"Get him out of the way, Jack," Brad ordered, straining to remain calm while he struggled with Kon.

Jack let go of Kon and lunged at Albert, grabbing him by the arm. He pulled him away from the bed, hauled him over to the cot and pushed him down onto it.

"They're hurting him!" Albert shouted.

"No they're not," Jack said softly. "They're his friends. They'll be gentle, but Kon has to be controlled, or he will hurt himself."

"What's wrong with him?" Albert asked in confusion. "He was quiet and then all of a sudden . . ."

"It's convulsions," Jack shot back, "from the fever or the medication. God only knows. Kon is so sensitive to drugs."

"Who's that old man?" Albert wailed.

"That's Doctor Stamatis."

"Doctor? He doesn't look like any doctor I've ever seen. Let me go! He's hurting Peter! I wish Carlin had come," Albert cried and struggled to stand up.

"Sit still!" Jack barked, annoyed that he was sidetracked from helping Brad and Paul. "You haven't seen everything, Albert! You're still a kid. Stamatis is a field surgeon. He's very good with Kon."

"I know a doctor when I see one. He's not even . . ."

"Shut up!" Jack hissed, doing his best to keep an eye on what Stamatis was doing.

Stamatis had injected Kon with a sedative and the violent contractions gradually subsided as it took effect. Paul and Brad released their tight grip on Kon, and tried to lay him in a comfortable position. Stamatis arranged the covers over him and held the oxygen mask to his face.

"Let the boy come now," Stamatis called.

Jack helped Albert to his feet and he approached the bed hesitantly, surveying Stamatis critically.

"You show a good heart to defend a friend who is down, but your fear is misplaced. We try only to keep Kon from hurting himself. Here . . ." Stamatis said, pulling the chair closer to the bed, "sit and hold the mask for him. Let him draw on your courage."

Albert did not know what to make of Stamatis, but he was glad to see Peter lying quietly again. He touched Peter on the arm and called anxiously to him, "Peter? Peter, are you feeling any better?"

Albert bit his lip when Kon did not answer.

"It is enough to let him know that you are with him," Stamatis said quietly and walked away. Geilla silently took up her vigil on Kon's right. She looked at Albert, but could not find any words of comfort for him. She was weighed with guilt about having asked Alyce to come to Florina, and blamed herself, more than Alyce, for hurting Kon.

No one could think of sleeping. Although heavily sedated, Kon continued to experience mild, but persistent tremors that caused his limbs to twitch, as if his brain were losing control. Kon was failing, and they all feared he had lost his will to live. It was Saturday night and the ward had become more active as the remains of drunken brawls and silent stabbings began to trickle in. Stamatis seemed to draw energy as the carnage piled higher, however. Watching him move slowly among the moaning bodies, Brad admired his steady nerve.

"You seem to have a heavy load tonight," Brad commented as Stamatis passed by the end of the ward.

"This?" Stamatis said gesturing towards the beds. "This is my regular work. Who do you think comes to Stamatis for help? The women won't come. The children won't come. They are all afraid of me. I am too rough, too crude. Anyone who can walk goes to someone else," he cried, throwing up his hands. "What do I get? I get the pieces when everyone else has given up hope!"

As he came closer, Brad could smell the alcohol on his breath. "Well, I spit on those men in their fancy offices and their lily white coats!" Stamatis said vehemently. "This is my work — sewing life back into these pieces."

Stamatis limped away and Brad's heart sank a little lower. I should never have left Kon in this God forsaken place, he thought. He will be dead by morning, and I won't be able to face the others. They depend on me and I've let them down. I won't be able to hold the team together if Kon dies. Brad wandered back to the others and could not help noticing how exhausted and discouraged they looked.

Stamatis came in a short time later to check on Kon's oxygen supply. Turning from the bed, he looked from face to face. Sensing their collective discouragement he exploded in anger.

"Why do you stand and watch if you no longer believe he will live? Get out! Get out! Is the boy the only one with a backbone? Tell him you need him!" He took Geilla by the arm and shouted at her, "Tell him you love him! Be strong! Share your life with him. If you don't have the courage, get it from the bottle."

Stamatis limped to the end of the curtain and bellowed in a voice that rang through the ward, "Yiosiph! Bring the ouzo!" Turning back to the team, he growled, "Don't bury him yet! I am not beaten!" Then he stalked down the ward.

Yiosiph arrived a few minutes later with a cart of equipment, a bottle of the clear, strong liqueur and several shot glasses.

"For once I agree with that mad Greek," Jack said pouring himself a shot of ouzo. "I could use a little liquid courage."

"He's right," Brad said, going to the cart. "We're not helping Kon by standing around feeling discouraged. We've got to keep ourselves together and draw him back."

Brad poured a glass of ouzo for each of the others and everyone took theirs except Paul.

"Come on, Paul, you could use a good belt," Jack encouraged.

"I don't . . . it just doesn't seem right to stand around boozing while Kon . . ." Paul objected.

"The hell it doesn't!" Jack countered. "If you were lying there, and Kon was waiting for you to come out of it, he sure as hell wouldn't turn down a drink. He'd probably be better by now if we put whisky in that IV instead of glucose."

Paul smiled at the thought. "Yeah, he sure can down a few, can't he?" Paul walked over to the cart and Jack put his muscular arm across his shoulders. "Don't give up on him. Like the doc says, let's not bury him yet."

The team kept a sorrowful, anxious vigil over Kon all night. About 3:00 a.m. a courier arrived by helicopter from Athens with a supply of the experimental drug that Stamatis had asked Brad to secure for him. Carl had tracked it down in Sweden and arranged for it to be flown out as soon as possible. Ignoring the catalog of precautions and contra indications that arrived with it, Stamatis hurriedly prepared a syringe and gave Kon a large dose. He repeated the injections hourly and checked on Kon's progress; but if he detected any change, he didn't mention it. Around 9:00 a.m. Stamatis gave Kon another dose and indicated that he was going to taper off on the injections, but that he should be called immediately if Kon's condition changed in any way.

At 10:00 a.m., Albert was sitting on the cot, trying valiantly to stay awake, when a tall stately Greek priest strode purposefully around the curtain and moved quickly to the foot of Kon's bed. The team looked up in surprise as he came into their midst. His long, white, carefully trimmed beard stood out against his traditional black robe and headdress. He had the positive air of a man who had a mission to fulfill.

"Is this the man with the pistol wound?" he asked in crisp, precise English.

Brad stepped up to him. "Excuse me, Father, there must be some mistake. This man has a lung infection."

The priest looked directly at Brad. "Do not lie to me, my son. I know how this lung infection began."

"Who are you, and what is it you want here, Father?" Brad asked coolly.

"I am Father Léon. I have come to hear this man's confession and administer the last rites. He is Greek Orthodox is he not?"

Brad looked startled. He didn't have the faintest idea what Kon's religion was. "I really don't know," he answered, feeling embarrassed that he knew so little about a good friend.

Geilla came up and quickly supplied the answer. "He was raised Greek Orthodox, Father, but I don't know if he still . . ."

"And what is his name, please?" the priest asked before she had time to finish.

"Kon," Geilla answered quickly.

"Kon?" the priest replied, raising his eyebrows to indicate he thought her answer inappropriate. "I mean his true name, his

353

Christian name."

"It's Peter. No, Petros really. Petros Kononellos."

"Petros?" Brad repeated. "I never heard him use that name."

"I used to tease him about it when he was young," Geilla confessed guiltily. "I think I made him ashamed and he stopped using it."

Jack was having difficulty associating Kon with this very foreign looking priest. He walked over and addressed him almost belligerently. "What the hell difference does it make what his religion is? He's a good man. He deserves to be left in peace. He doesn't need your damn voodoo crap."

Brad quickly put his hand on Jack's chest. "We really don't know what Kon believes, Jack. At a time like this, would you deny him anything that might give him some consolation?"

Jack looked from Brad to the priest. "I guess not," he said at last. "What the hell! Nothing else has worked."

The priest looked directly at Jack with a steady calm gaze. "I will give the peace of God to any man that repents and asks for it, but a man of peace does not die from a bullet wound."

Jack suddenly thought of Kon's quick temper and his heavy drinking and wondered what the priest would think of him if he knew. "Well, if he's not a man of peace, he is a man of justice," Jack muttered.

Peterson, who usually was quiet and stayed in the background, suddenly found his tongue. "Don't judge him too harshly, Father. He got hurt saving me from the communists. He stayed behind to find my eyeglasses and they shot him. He was trying to do a good deed and . . . they shot him," he said sadly.

Paul came away from the bed. "He's an honest man, Father, and trustworthy. He saved my life — more than once."

Father Léon looked carefully at each face in the group, reading the love and concern they shared for Kon. Surely an evil man could not claim so many loyal friends, he thought. "Although I do not know him, I will bless him," he said and stepped up to the bed.

Father Léon took Kon's left hand between his hands and called in a soft, but commanding voice, "Petros! Petros! Can you hear me? Look at me Petros!"

Kon turned his head slightly. Father Léon leaned forward until his thin ascetic face was only inches from Kon's and called again. "Petros, can you hear me? I have come to hear your confession."

Kon turned his face towards the priest and opened his eyes. The priest looked deep into Kon's dark eyes as if he could read all the secrets of his heart. "Petros, unburden your heart — confess," he commanded.

Kon moved his lips as though he were trying to speak, but he could only gasp.

Father Léon saw that Kon was too ill to recount his sins, and asked, "Petros, are you repentant and truly sorry for your sins?"

Kon's eyelids closed, but the priest pressed his hand.

"Speak to me, Petros," he commanded in Greek. "Speak! Are you repentant and truly sorry for your sins?"

Kon heard Father Léon's rich majestic voice tolling in his ears. Opening his eyes he saw only the calm, slightly sorrowful face of a man who knew and understood all the follies and frailties of men. There was compassion in his eyes, and forgiveness, blessed forgiveness. Kon read the question in them even as the priest asked again, "Are you repentant and truly sorry for your sins?"

Kon drew in a labored breath. "Yes, Father," he whispered in Greek. His eyelids fluttered and closed again.

Lifting the ornate, silver crucifix which hung on a heavy chain around his neck, Father Léon touched it to Kon's forehead. Kon welcomed its soothing metallic coolness on his feverish flesh. The priest chanted a prayer in an ancient, stylized Greek that even Kon did not fully comprehend; but he took comfort in the prayer. He knew his sins had been absolved.

Father Léon raised his hand and traced a large cross over Kon's body, touching him lightly on his head and both shoulders as he formed the cross. Twice again he formed the cross, chanting a prayer as he performed the ritual. Then taking a small vial of oil the priest anointed Kon's forehead forming a small cross. He anointed each of Kon's eyes, his nose, mouth, and hands, calling down a blessing on him. When he was finished, he moved solemnly to the foot of Kon's bed. Rolling back the covers, he anointed Kon's feet. When he had completed the anointing, he again took Kon by the hand and called to him. "Petros, listen to me. You must not forsake your friends. They need you. They love you, Petros. You must not abandon them. Do you understand?"

There was no response from Kon.

Father Léon called again. "You must not give in! Turn away from sin, Petros. Turn away from death. Do you understand?"

Kon opened his eyes and the team could hear his ragged breathing. "I understand," Kon whispered faintly.

Father Léon laid his hand on Kon's forehead.

"Sleep now, Petros," he continued. "Sleep a peaceful sleep and awake well and whole. Believe, Petros! Believe! Let God forgive and heal you. I give you the kiss of peace." And so saying Father Léon leaned forward and touched his lips lightly to Kon's cheek. "Peace be to you, Petros."

"Peace," Kon repeated after him and then his head fell sideways and he was still.

"I have done all I can. He is in God's hands now," Father Léon said turning from the bed.

For a moment Brad feared that Kon was dead, but suddenly Kon twitched. Brad sighed. Nothing has changed, he thought bitterly.

Seeing that Brad was lost in thought, Mary came up to the priest as he prepared to leave. "Thank you for coming, Father. I'm sure Kon is grateful to have your blessing."

Father Léon nodded. "Pray for him, all of you. Pray!" he said in the same commanding tone he had used with Kon.

Jack stepped over to the curtain as the priest left the bed, and Father Léon looked directly into his eyes.

"I'm sorry . . ." Jack began haltingly, "I think he really was glad to see you."

"Never lose faith in God's mercy, my son. Prayers are answered."

"I'm too angry to pray! I just keep hoping . . ."

"Your hope is your prayer, my son. Hold to it. God be with you!" he concluded, and touching Jack on the forehead he left.

Jack stood alone for a moment. "Shit! I need some air!" he croaked and hurried down the ward.

About twenty minutes after Father Léon had left, Paul noticed that the horrible twitching that had plagued Kon all night had stopped and he lay perfectly still. His breathing was quiet and easier and his face looked relaxed. There was no trace of the suffering that had marred his features for days. Paul slipped away from the bed and sought out Stamatis. He found him hunched over a cup of black Turkish coffee in the staff room. He looked red-eyed and worn and his powerful shoulders sagged wearily. He did not hear Paul approach.

"Don't you ever sleep?" Paul asked quietly, so as not to startle him.

Stamatis made a sound indicating disgust with Paul's question and mumbled something in Greek.

"What's that?" Paul asked, but Stamatis only waved his hand as if brushing Paul away. "There is little comfort in the bed of the man whose woman has flown," Stamatis growled. "But you come about your friend. There is a change?"

"The twitching has stopped and he is quiet. I hope to God he's just asleep."

"We will see," Stamatis said abruptly and stood up. He straightened himself and led the way back to the ward. He checked Kon over carefully and put another dose of the new antibiotic in the IV. "He sleeps. The fever is broken," Stamatis announced at last. "He must have a dry shirt."

Stamatis had barely turned from the bed before Yiosiph came in, carrying an armload of sheets and a clean shirt. He said something to Stamatis in Greek, but Stamatis dismissed him with the same disgusted grunt he had used on Paul. Working together silently, Stamatis and Yiosiph replaced the wet sheets and put a clean gown on Kon. Kon moaned softly when they lifted him, but slept on in peaceful oblivion.

"Go rest now," Stamatis said to Geilla as he passed in front of her. "You must have a smile for him when he wakes. Go!"

Geilla covered her eyes with her hand and turned to Mary. "Oh Mary . . . just to see him smile one more time . . ."

"Shhh . . . shh . . . he's right. Don't let Kon see you cry. He can't bear tears." Mary put her arm around Geilla and prayed that Stamatis was right about Kon waking up. She was about to lead Geilla away when she noticed Albert shaking his head in an effort to stay awake. He's a very determined young man, she thought to herself. But he's also very tired.

"Albert?" she called aloud. "Why don't you come back to the hotel with us. You could use some rest."

Albert looked up and shook his head. "No, I'll stay with Peter. I'll be all right."

"Mary's right," Brad put in. "You were up all night with Charles before you even got here. Go back to the hotel for a while."

"No! I'll stay. Carlin would want me to. I wish he had come. He would have been able to do something for Peter."

"You're doing a lot for Peter," Brad answered. "Look, I'm in charge here, Albert, and I say you should go back to the hotel with Mary . . . just for a while."

"No! I'm not going," Albert repeated firmly. "You have no authority over me. I don't work for you, and . . . and you're not my father!"

Brad smiled to himself. It's easy to see that Kon had a hand in bringing this lad up, he thought. Poor Edgar, having to raise Kon and Albert. I wonder if Charles is as stubborn.

"You're right, Albert. I can't order you, but I strongly recommend that you get some rest."

"No! Carlin and father both . . . I can't let them down."

Paul walked over and stood between Brad and Albert. "Leave him alone, Brad, He's got his orders. All he needs is a cup of strong coffee. I'll get some for him. Would you like that, Albert?"

Albert nodded, relieved that someone understood that he had to stay. Paul walked out with Mary and Geilla, but returned shortly with a tray loaded with coffee cups. He passed them around to Jack, Brad, and Peterson.

"You like your coffee black and sweet the way Kon does, don't you, Albert?" Paul said.

"Yes," Albert mumbled.

Paul spooned sugar into one cup of coffee, mixed it and handed it to Albert. Taking the last cup from the tray, Paul stood next to the cot.

"Kon has stopped twitching and he's breathing better. I think

357

he's going to make it."

"Good. I was afraid . . .,"

"He's tough, Albert, and I think your being here helped."

Albert swayed forward slightly and Paul immediately set his own cup down.

"Albert, are you O.K.?"

"I . . . I don't feel very well, Paul."

Paul gently took the cup from Albert and put his hands on Albert's shoulders.

"You haven't eaten much, Albert. Maybe you should put your head down for a few minutes."

Albert looked uncertain. "Maybe . . . just for a minute . . . I feel kind of . . . dizzy."

Albert fell sideways and Paul quickly lifted Albert's legs and laid him on the cot.

"You won't tell Dr. La Monde, will you?" Albert asked drowsily.

"Of course not. You'll be up in a minute," Paul assured him.

"I hope Charles is O.K. Mother is . . ." Albert whispered and he was out.

"Good job, Paul," Brad said as he walked over to the cot. "He never guessed."

"It's all in the brew," Paul answered. "He is so worried about letting Carlin down. Hell! Carlin would have sent him to bed hours ago. I'll see if I can find a blanket. He'll be out for a while."

Paul walked slowly away from the cot and disappeared down the ward. I wish I could sneak some of that stuff into Paul, Brad thought as he watched Paul leave.

When Paul returned he spread the blanket over Albert, then pulled up a chair and sat on Kon's left. "One of you should get some sleep," he commented to Brad and Jack.

"Naw . . . I'm O.K.," Jack answered. He stepped closer to Brad and lowered his voice. "Peterson looks about done in. Maybe you should take him back to the hotel."

Brad observed Peterson who was standing by the window. "I think you're right, Jack. I'll walk back with him. I could use some air. I won't be gone long."

Brad moved towards the window. "Henry, I'm going back to the hotel for a while. Why don't you come with me?"

Peterson looked at him a bit absently. "I kind of wanted to see if he was going to wake up or . . . something."

"I know, but he could be out for a long while. You've been up all night. It won't hurt to take a break."

Peterson gazed towards Kon. "I guess I'm not doing a whole lot of good here anyway," he mumbled.

Brad put his arm across Peterson's bony shoulders. "You've been a great help. We all appreciate it."

358

Peterson shook his head and sighed and Brad edged him out of the curtained area.

Jack sat and talked quietly with Paul while Kon slept on. A while later Brad returned and the three of them made a conscious effort to keep each other awake. Well over an hour passed before Jack stood and stretched. "I'm going to get some more coffee. Can I bring any back for you Paul? Brad?"

"Sounds great," Paul answered, stifling a yawn and Brad agreed. "I'll see what I can rustle up," Jack said and strode down the ward.

Paul was fighting to stay awake and wishing that Jack would hurry with the coffee, when he thought he heard a faint whisper. He stared at the bed. Yes! It was Kon who was calling to him! Kon's eyes were open and he looked alert.

"Kon! Are you awake? How are you?" he asked excitedly.

Kon struggled to answer and managed a weak throaty whisper. "Tired . . . so tired . . . didn't sleep well . . . strange dreams . . . so many strange dreams."

"You've had a high fever, Kon."

"Is there any water here?" Kon asked weakly.

"Sure, Kon! I'll get you some." Paul quickly poured a glass full of cool water from the pitcher Yiosiph had placed by Kon's bed. Kon struggled to raise himself, but he was so weak he could hardly lift his head. Paul put his arm under Kon, and lifting him, he put the glass to Kon's lips. It was an effort for Kon to take a few small swallows, but Paul was delighted to see him show any sign of life.

"Had enough?"

"Yes. Thanks, Paul," Kon answered in a weak whisper and coughed several times. When Paul lowered him, his head fell to the right and he saw Brad standing by his bed.

"Hello, Brad. Are you here too?" Kon asked in surprise.

"All the time, Kon," Brad answered warmly.

Kon suddenly noticed the high curtainless window and the barren white walls. "Have I been arrested?" he asked in a toneless voice.

"No! No!" Brad assured him quickly. "You're in a hospital — in Greece."

"Greece?" Kon mumbled. "How the hell . . . the train! We were on the train . . ."

"It's O.K.! You're off the train," Paul put in quickly.

"Peterson?" Kon asked.

"He's O.K. We got him out," Brad replied.

"Good," Kon sighed with relief. "What time is it?"

Brad looked at his watch. "Almost 1:00 p.m."

"Then I didn't hold things up too badly after all. When are we scheduled to fly out?"

Brad smiled and shook his head.

"Not for a while, Kon," Paul answered. "You've been very sick for the past five days."

"Five days! No! You've got to be kidding!"

"He's right, Kon. You had a terrible infection," Brad told him.

"Five days . . . I had some strange dreams. I dreamt my father came. He was nice to me . . . so kind . . . not at all the way he used to be. He was . . . gentle . . . wishful thinking huh?"

"Sounds like a good dream to me," Paul answered softly.

". . . had another dream," Kon began slowly. "Alyce was here. She . . ." he stopped abruptly and studied Paul's face. In his exhaustion Paul had momentarily let his expression reveal his thoughts.

"It wasn't a dream, was it?" Kon whispered.

Paul didn't answer. He looked at Brad, his eyes pleading for one of Brad's smooth diplomatic cover-ups. Finally Brad gave Kon his answer. "She came . . . but she couldn't stay."

"You mean she didn't want to. She lives in a perfect make-believe world and I don't fit in. I'm not some damn dancing prince." He looked thoughtfully at Paul. "You look tired, Paul. You should take better care of yourself," Kon said softly and closed his eyes. He was asleep immediately.

Paul shook his head sadly. "Jesus! Look who's talking!"

Jack came in a minute later and saw the pained look on Paul's face. "Oh God! He's not dead, is he?"

"No! No!" Brad answered quickly. "Kon woke up while you were gone. He is really weak, but he was clear headed and calm."

"That's great! Why the long faces? He is going to make it, isn't he?"

"I think so, but it will be a while before he's on his feet again," Brad answered.

"He knows about Alyce," Paul said mournfully. "I had hoped he wouldn't remember."

Jack handed Brad a cup of coffee and then gave one to Paul. "Come on, Paul. The sooner he's through with that bitch, the better. I don't know how she fooled him for as long as she did. She obviously didn't give a damn about him."

"He wanted her to be the right one so badly he let himself be fooled," Paul answered. "Damn her! She lied to him so often. Why couldn't she lie when he needed it?"

Brad put his hand on Paul's shoulder. "Don't be bitter, Paul. Kon's going to need a lot of cheering up. He's right about your being tired. Why don't you go back to the hotel and rest. You know that as soon as Kon can lift his head he'll be chafing to get moving and we'll have our hands full keeping him in bed."

Paul smiled weakly. "You're right. I'd better rest before he starts to recover. At least now I can relax and sleep. Have you got a key,

Brad?"

"Yes," Brad answered, and pulling the room key from his pocket he tossed it toward Paul. Paul reached for it with his right hand, but he missed it and caught it with his left. Brad pretended not to notice that Paul had fumbled the catch. "See you in a few hours, Paul," he said casually.

"Right," Paul responded, but as he turned to leave he smacked his left knee on the chair and nearly stumbled. He recovered quickly and walked slowly down the ward.

Brad turned to Jack. "You'd better go with him, Jack. See that he gets to the right hotel. I've never seen him this tired."

"Got it," Jack answered, and hurrying after Paul, he slipped his watch off his wrist, and dropped it into his pocket. "Hey, Paul! Wait up!" he called. "I'll walk back with you. I forgot my damn watch!"

****

When Mary and Geilla returned to the hospital, Brad told them that Kon had been awake. Mary saw that Brad was still worried about Kon and coaxed him into going back to the hotel to rest. Jack went with him, but returned about 7 p.m. in order to let Paul sleep.

Kon woke again about 8 p.m. and was surprised to see Albert sitting by his bed.

"Albert?" Kon called weakly as he came around.

"Hello, Peter. How are you feeling?"

"Not so great, Albert. What are you doing here? I thought . . . am I still in Greece?"

"Yes, I heard you were sick," Albert said simply.

"How long have you been here?"

"Oh . . . a day or so. I've lost track of time."

"So have I . . . Dio Mio, what's this thing doing on me?" Kon asked suddenly as he felt the chest tube with his hand.

"Hey! Don't pull on that!" Jack said, coming up to the bed. "It's to drain the fluid out of your chest. Leave it alone!"

"Jack, are you here? Help me get this thing out. I don't need it."

"Yes you do! Now stop pulling on it. Mary, you'd better find Stamatis."

Mary hurried out before Kon saw her. By the time Stamatis arrived, Jack was holding Kon's arm to keep him from pulling the chest tube out.

"So you are awake! Stamatis boomed in Greek as he came up to the bed. "How goes it for you?"

Kon made no answer, but looked in dismay at Stamatis, noting his unshaven face and soiled clothing. He was too weak to pull away when Stamatis leaned over him, and began to palpate and listen to his chest, but clearly he did not like it.

361

Kon turned to Jack. "Who the hell is this guy? Get him off me, Jack! Albert! Give me a hand!"

Jack grinned. "Take it easy, Kon. That's Dr. Stamatis. He's done a good job keeping you alive."

"Doctor!" Kon gasped. "God damn! No wonder I feel so rotten! Couldn't you find anyone else in this God forsaken place? Albert? Why didn't Carlin come with you?"

"Hey! Hold your tongue. He was highly recommended," Jack insisted.

"Carlin wanted to come, but he had another emergency. Mr. Cover-Rollins told him you were being well taken care of," Albert explained cautiously.

"You mean Brad turned this guy loose on me? Jesus! Where the hell is he? Brad? Brad? I'm annoyed, Brad! I'm displeased! I'm . . ."

"You're a damn nuisance!" Jack said firmly. "Relax, will you? You're still breathing and yelling. You weren't doing either when we brought you in here. Just take it easy and let Stamatis get on with the job. O.K.?"

"He's right, Peter," Albert put in. "You were in terrible shape. We were all ready to give up, but Stamatis pulled you through. I wouldn't let anyone hurt you, Peter. You know that."

Kon stopped struggling. "I know that, Albert. I just . . . I just don't trust any doctor except Carlin."

"Well, Jack and Paul trust Stamatis, so I trust him," Albert argued.

"Paul thinks he's O.K.? Where is Paul anyway?"

"He's asleep. You told him to get some rest," Jack commented.

"I told him? I guess I did, didn't I. He looked so tired."

"He was awake a long time worrying about you, Kon, so just relax and let Stamatis take care of you. O.K?"

"O.K. I'm sorry. I'll be quiet."

Stamatis listened to Kon's remarks in silence while he completed his examination, then remarked to Jack in English. "So he does not like the service eh? I see he is ungrateful as well as stupid! What a poor Greek to let a Slav get the better of him!"

Kon was taken aback when he realized that Stamatis had understood what he had said.

"When will you take this 'thing' out of my chest?" Kon demanded.

"Right now, if it pleases your majesty," Stamatis answered with mock humility.

"Get on with it then! And take this junk out of my arm!" Kon growled.

"The IV stays!" Stamatis growled back at him. "For now," he added softening his tone.

"All right! All right! I am at your mercy," Kon sighed.

362

Kon remained silent while Stamatis called Yiosiph and together they removed the chest tube and put a dressing on Kon.

"I suppose I should say 'Thank you'," Kon mumbled in Greek when Stamatis had finished.

"It is not required," Stamatis answered flatly. He turned and left.

Yiosiph stayed behind to hang a fresh bottle of glucose for Kon. Kon was silent, but submissive while Yiosiph took his temperature and felt his pulse.

"You should show more respect for Stamatis," Yiosiph scolded in Greek. "Without his skill you would not be alive to act so rudely."

"Was I truly so close to death?" Kon asked in Greek.

"So close that your friends despaired. So close that even Stamatis sent for the priest lest you slip away without repenting."

"The priest . . . so it was the priest and not my father who was so kind to me. I thought it was a dream."

"Of dreams I know nothing, but you owe your life to Stamatis."

"I am sorry, Yiosiph. I will try to be calmer, but it goes against my nature to lie so helpless."

"If you do as Stamatis says and don't fight him, you will be well soon," Yiosiph commented. He lifted Kon and held a glass of water for him to drink.

"I will try," Kon said. "It is hard for me to obey the doctors. I do not like to take orders."

Yiosiph smiled a kindly smile. "I will not order then, I will only 'suggest.' Go back to sleep. You need much rest."

"Hey, what are you two plotting with all this jabbering in Greek?" Jack asked as Yiosiph left.

"I have learned how much worry I have caused my friends," Kon answered in English.

"You know, you really did have us scared this time, Kon," Jack said seriously. Then he grinned. "Once you stopped cussin' and started talking to that priest, Paul and I were ready to flip coins for the Ferrari."

Kon turned to Geilla who was standing faithfully at his right. He smiled and pressed her hand. "How often have I told you! The car goes to Geilla! Neither of you Yanks is man enough to handle it."

"What about me?" Albert cried before Geilla could answer. "I would love to have that car!"

"Your father would have a stroke if I gave it to you, Albert. He gave me a long lecture about responsibility when I first bought it. He rode in it only once when he was desperate to get home to dinner. I swear he would have taken a cab, but it would have been rude, because your mother had invited me to dinner. He sat tense and silent all the way home, absolutely refusing to enjoy the ride."

"Yes, that sounds like papa," Albert laughed.

"Dear Mademoiselle Flambért was the only person at the bank

who didn't think I was being disgustingly extravagant and brash to drive it. I gave her a ride home one night and the faster I drove the more she smiled. When I pulled up in front of her apartment building, she asked if we could drive around the block again, because she was sure her sister was watching from the second story window."

They all laughed. "Go back to sleep before you insult anyone else, Kon!" Geilla admonished.

So Kon slept, but in the morning he was no stronger. Stamatis came to see him and he and Yiosiph propped him against pillows. They tried to feed him some broth, but Kon was annoyed because he was too weak to hold the spoon himself, and he ate very little. Finally Mary told Kon in her matter-of-fact manner that the sooner he ate, the sooner he would get better, and the sooner they could all go home. Having it put to him that he was causing everyone inconvenience, Kon swallowed his pride and swallowed whatever was spooned into him. Once Stamatis saw that Kon could handle the food, he removed the IV.

Brad put in a call to Carlin early in the morning and was relieved to learn that Charles had regained consciousness. He was able to speak and recognize his family, and the surgeons had been able to save his leg. He would be immobilized for a while, but Carlin predicted a complete recovery. It gave Brad great pleasure to report to Carlin that Kon had survived the crisis and was recovering.

Albert was overjoyed when Brad told him the news about Charles. "I wish I could tell Peter the good news, but he'd kill himself to get to Geneva if he knew Charles was in the hospital."

"Yes, it's better not to tell him. I'm sure your parents would agree," Brad advised.

"I'm glad to see that Peter has so many friends. Knowing that he won't be alone makes it easier to leave. I don't know why, but no one at the bank ever liked him. I think he had trouble making friends at school too. He's very shy, you know. But it was wonderful to have him take care of us when we were growing up. He let us do all kinds of rough and dirty things that no one else would. He washed all our clothes himself, so that no one would know how filthy we got. He even started washing our bed clothes after Charles accidentally wet the bed one night. We trusted him with all our secrets. We knew he would never betray us even if he were boiled in oil."

"He's still that way, Albert!" Brad laughed. "It's incredibly annoying sometimes, but I admire him for it."

"You may not believe it, but even though he's so quick tempered, he never laid a hand on us. He always conveyed the idea that we were so fortunate to have such kind parents that we should never do anything that would make them unhappy. Keeping up the family name was like a sacred trust to him. He said that without it we would be defenseless, and scorned, and ashamed for the rest of our lives. He certainly kept us in line. I don't know why I'm telling you all this. I'm just so glad I didn't lose him."

"We're all glad, Albert."

Albert felt torn between staying with Peter, and going home to be with Charles and his parents. He didn't want to lie to Peter, but he didn't want him to know the truth either. Peter solved the dilemma for him, however, by insisting that Albert was taking too much time from school and should go home on the next flight. So Albert left early in the afternoon, sent off by grateful hugs, and handshakes, and promises of future visits.

Later in the day, Peterson came to see Kon.

"I've put off leaving as long as I could, but I must get back to my work. I've come to say good-bye and thank you. I'm deeply sorry that you got hurt, but I'm thankful that you didn't die because of me."

"Please don't feel guilty about my getting shot, Mr. Peterson. I was just doing my job. Usually I'm not so stupid about it. I should have been paying more attention when I came out of that cell. I appreciate that you stayed to help take care of me. I understand it was a harrowing experience for you."

"I admit I was scared when those soldiers came, but I think I learned something about myself. You know, I never served in the military . . . my eyesight was too bad. I always wondered how I would have behaved in combat. It has been inferred that I am a coward, but now I know better. I'm not very assertive or aggressive, but when I had to, I kept my head and didn't shit my pants. That's not a bad record for a bookworm."

Kon smiled and extended his hand. "That's not a bad record for any man, Henry. I'm glad we were able to get you out. I wish you luck in your work."

"Good-bye, Kon, and good luck to you."

Once Albert and Peterson were gone, Kon became obsessed with the desire to leave the hospital. Before he could roll himself over in bed, he began to pester Stamatis about when he would be free to depart. At last Stamatis told him that when he could walk to the toilet and back, alone, without falling, he could leave. Kon's mind fixed on the goal and he struggled with determination to gain independence. All too soon Brad's prophesy came true, and the team had to guard Kon carefully to see that he did not try to get out of bed by himself.

Once the IV was out, Stamatis had no convenient way to sneak medicine into Kon. When Kon balked at letting him inject antibiotics, Stamatis resorted to deceit. Craftily hiding a small syringe in his huge hand, he caught Kon unawares and jammed the needle into Kon's arm. Kon was furious.

"You bloody bastard!" he bellowed. "If you even dare to try that again – doctor or no doctor – I will put you through that God damn window!"

Stamatis immediately seized both of Kon's wrists, and pinned them against the bed. Kon was too weak to resist and Stamatis held him down for several minutes to drive home the point.

"When you are strong enough to throw me out the window, I will be the happiest of men! But until you are well enough to do it, you will do as I say!" Stamatis roared back at him.

And so the battle of wills began, with both men willing Kon to get well as soon as possible. The following day, when Kon announced that he wanted out of bed, Stamatis agreed that if one of the other men went with him, he could take a wheelchair to the toilet. Kon was dismayed when he learned that the toilet was at the far end of the long ward, but he did not give up.

Disdaining all offers of help, Kon hauled himself into a wheelchair and propelled himself down the length of the ward. When he returned, however, his legs gave out before he managed to climb into bed. Jack lifted him into the bed and he remained quiet and moderately submissive for the rest of the morning. The same scene was repeated, with Kon walking part of the way before he fell, until after three days he insisted he was ready to attempt the trip alone.

Calling Stamatis to witness the test of his strength, Kon began the long walk down the ward. Despite Kon's protests, Paul followed solicitously behind him. When Kon reached the end of the ward he turned slowly and hesitated, as if mentally measuring his stamina against an insurmountable objective. Paul could hear Kon's labored breathing and noted when he began to limp at every step. Paul knew that Kon would not give up and he added his will to Kon's, trying to keep him going by mental determination alone. Brad could see the intently stubborn set to Kon's chin while he was still far down the ward.

Kon moved the length of the ward with no trace of his usual light gait. His face was grim, but resolute as he approached Stamatis.

"I have passed your test. Release me!" he gasped and began to cough.

Stamatis shook his head sadly. "You will not yield to wisdom?"

Kon hid his clenched fist behind his back and continued to cough.

"No," he gasped at last.

Stamatis sighed. "Then I will keep my word. You may leave tomorrow, at midnight."

"Midnight!" Kon croaked. "You extract another full day!"

"No, Kon, I do not steal a day. I give you one, to rest and to heal."

Kon made no reply and Stamatis turned quickly and limped down the ward. He hesitated, but did not turn back when he heard Kon hit the floor with a thump.

Shortly after the team got Kon back into bed, Brad went to search out Stamatis. He found him sitting with the young boy who followed after Stamatis like a shadow. Stamatis spoke to the boy in Greek, and he disappeared immediately.

"Why did you agree to let Kon leave the hospital?" Brad began angrily. "Even I can see he is not well enough . . ."

"Sit, sit," Stamatis said cutting Brad off.

Brad stood for another moment and then sat across the table from Stamatis. The boy appeared with a tray and two cups of the coffee Stamatis drank so often, and then vanished again.

"We Greeks like to make our coffee strong and black, and then we must sweeten it to hide the bitterness," Stamatis began thoughtfully and slowly sipped the scalding liquid. "It is like life. We would not have it watered down for us, but we must add a little sweetness to make it palatable!" He rubbed his head with his hand and sat back in his chair. "I know your friend is not healed, but he is a very stubborn man. He has fought me from the beginning. It is very hard to help him. I think I must sweeten life a little for him and loosen the bonds, no?"

Brad sighed. "You are quite correct. Kon is exceedingly stubborn. It's the only thing that sustains him sometimes. I was afraid he had given up when Alyce left him, but he pulled through."

"Has he spoken of her?"

"Only once."

"I think he hides his feelings from you."

"I wouldn't doubt it. He usually has a very rough time of it after these broken love affairs."

"It has happened before?"

"Yes, all too often."

At that moment the boy arrived with a glass of milk and Stamatis poured a little of his coffee into it to flavor it for him.

"Is the boy your son?" Brad asked.

Stamatis smiled and ran his hand carelessly through the boy's hair. "Not by blood, only by choice. His parents were lost in a fire. He barely survived, he was so badly burned. I cared for him a long while. I tried to find a home for him once or twice, but who will take a boy who needs so much medical attention? So he stays to sweeten my life."

The boy grinned and Brad guessed that he was content with the arrangement.

"Do you have a wife to help look after him?"

"A wife? No! Only Father Léon says I still have a wife — she has flown back to the city."

Brad remained quiet, sensing that Stamatis was in a pensive mood.

"I found her in the city. She was a nurse in Athens. I brought her here as my bride," Stamatis continued. "She tried . . . she worked with me . . . but then the children came and she stayed at home and I got involved with the political movement across the border. I was injured and I became full of anger. I wanted to solve all the problems of the world. I spent more and more time away, more and more time with the soldiers. She asked little of me, but I was healing the world. I had nothing left for her. One day she took the children and left."

Brad sighed, "I am truly sorry. Do you ever see your children?"

"Ah yes, once in a great while. I have a son in Athens. He is honored as an eye specialist." Stamatis laughed. "Very learned, respectable man — white coat, big office — everything! I should be proud to have fathered such a scholar, but if he had to sleep one night, hidden in a ditch, he would die of pneumonia. Only my youngest daughter ever loved the mountains as I do. She became a teacher for handicapped children. She married . . . but enough history! You are worried about your friend. He is a fool to choose such a hard woman over one who would die for him," he said philosophically.

"I agree," Brad commented, "but there is no way to tell him. He must learn for himself."

"Yes, he is not a man to listen to advice. Too bad, too bad. He wastes his strength fighting against me. Perhaps once he feels free, you can make him relax and rest."

"It won't be easy," Brad answered and smiled. "He fights me too."

"Then we must plot together. You must not let him go far when he leaves here. Make whatever excuse he will believe. I will supply you with drugs if necessary, but he must be kept still. This brave show of strength he put on exhausted him. It must not happen again."

"Even if we all stay with him, we can control him for only a few days."

"Perhaps he should stay in Greece for a while and renew his heritage."

Brad shook his head. "Kon is not comfortable with being Greek. He has fought it for a long time."

"Why? Is he so ashamed of his own people?"

"I gather from the little he will tell me, that his father was an ignorant, brute of a man. Kon left home very young. He knows only that being Greek means being poor, and overworked, and beaten as a child, and being beaten, or scorned everywhere he went. He has suffered so much prejudice, he has never gotten over it."

"It is not right that he should feel this way. I will talk with him," Stamatis announced decisively.

Brad doubted that anything Stamatis could say would have any influence on Kon, but he kept his peace. He knew Stamatis had a force of will no less powerful than Kon's.

CHAPTER TWENTY-SEVEN

Despite frequent pleas that he remain in the hospital, Kon insisted upon leaving at midnight as Stamatis had agreed. To everyone's relief, however, Kon accepted Brad's excuse that Mary and Geilla were too tired to travel, and the team settled into rooms at a larger hotel in Florina. Paul was able to slip Kon a sleeping potion only once, for afterward Kon became extremely suspicious, and Paul feared Kon would refuse to take any food or medicine if he tried it again. After two relatively quiet days, during which Stamatis checked on Kon several times. Kon's restlessness returned to plague him. Rather than permit Kon to go off on his own, as he threatened to do, Brad took Stamatis' advice and arranged to hire two cars to move the group to Kastoria to experience the beauty and peace of the lake.

Paul drove the first car, taking Kon, Geilla, and Jack with him. Brad drove the second car, taking Mary. The road was steep and winding, but the scenery was beautiful. Although Kon had appeared to enjoy the spectacular views of the lake as they approached Kastoria, Brad suspected Kon was weary by the time they reached the hotel, because he didn't argue about being put in a room that shared a bath with an adjoining room. When Paul and Jack made a show of flipping a coin to decide who would take the other room, Paul made the call, and Jack did not question him. He knew Paul wanted to keep an eye on Kon.

During the night Paul heard Kon moving about in the next room. He heard him go into the bathroom, flush the toilet, run water in the sink, and then the bathroom door clicked open. Kon was coughing. He had been coughing since he woke up in the hospital. It was to be expected, Stamatis had said, but he had warned that uncontrolled violent coughing could reopen the wound and cause hemorrhaging. Paul heard a crash, a thump, and then a moan. He jumped out of bed, and went into the adjoining room at a run. The room was dark.

"Kon? Are you all right? I heard a crash," Paul called.

"I am well. I turned too fast and hit the dresser," Kon's answer came back, punctuated by rasping coughs.

Paul felt his way towards the night stand, and turned on the light. Kon was lying on the floor just outside the bathroom. "Let me give you a hand," Paul said, bending over him.

"No! I am well, truly," Kon insisted, but he didn't get up. He just kept coughing.

Paul got his arm around Kon, and pulled him to his knees. Kon was gasping for breath as Paul hauled him over to the bed. "Don't you have some cough syrup?"

Kon shook his head "yes" and continued to cough.

"Where is it?"

"On the floor . . . knocked it off the dresser," Kon gasped.

Paul got down on his hands and knees, and searched the floor. "Got it!" he called after a minute. "You're lucky it didn't break." Paul twisted the cap off, and handed the bottle to Kon, but Kon was coughing so violently it was several minutes before he succeeded in swallowing any of the medicine.

"You should have stayed in the hospital, Kon. You're not really up to speed yet," Paul scolded, and took the bottle from Kon. "Did you take those antibiotics Stamatis gave you?"

"No . . . shit! I went into the bathroom and . . ." Kon answered, and started to get up.

"Stay put! I'll get them." Paul ordered. "You should have asked for help," he commented, coming back with the capsules and a glass of water. "You're so damn independent . . ." Paul held out the medicine, and Kon snatched it impatiently.

"Get off my back, Paul! I made a mistake in the dark, that's all. I'm not Mr. Perfect like you," Kon said testily and swallowed the capsules. "I'm sorry," he said more calmly when Paul didn't answer. "I hate taking pills. You know that."

"I know," Paul said sympathetically, "but you'll have to keep at it until the infection clears up."

Kon coughed a few more times, and lay back on the bed.

"Feeling any better?" Paul asked, sitting down on the bed.

"I'm tired, Paul. I'm just so damn tired."

"It's a natural reaction, Kon. You were seriously ill. You still have a long way to go to get on your feet."

Kon was silent for a moment, and then sighed heavily. "It's more than my lungs. I just don't know if I can go on now that Alyce . . . I thought we had something together, something to build on. Why the hell can't I get it together? What's wrong with me anyway?"

"Nothing, Kon, nothing. You just picked the wrong woman."

"Well, I've had a string of them, and it turns sour every time. I used to think it was because I didn't have any money, but no matter how much I spend, I can't keep a woman."

"You can't buy what you're looking for," Paul commented, but Kon didn't seem to hear him.

"I spent a lot on that woman, Paul. I gave her everything I could think of . . . stuff I couldn't really afford, and she walked out on me."

"She was a bitch, Kon, and you knew it. That's why you never married her."

"Don't speak of her like that! I won't tolerate it! Not even from you."

Paul grew impatient. "She kicked you when you were down, Kon. That makes her a bitch in my book!"

"No, no, you don't understand. She wanted me to meet her father and I never would go. She must have asked me a dozen times, and I never would go. I was afraid, Paul. Can you imagine? I was afraid of some dried up old man . . . a dried up old man with a lot of money. I was afraid he would find out who I really am, and then it would be over for me with Alyce."

"You should have gone to meet her old man, and told him to bug off. She's a grown woman, Kon. She did not need her daddy's permission to marry you."

"Maybe I was afraid to take the risk. Every time I think I've found the right woman, I get kicked in the teeth."

Paul knew it was true. Kon had been involved with some insufferable women. Alyce had been one of the better ones. At least she was respectable, and didn't have a jealous husband stashed away. That little surprise of Lillian's had created a dreadful scandal for Kon. It was strange, Paul thought, Kon was usually very suspicious, but sometimes he let women tell him outrageous lies, and walk all over him. He believed he was in love every time. Unfortunately, the women didn't always feel the same way, and when they walked out, Kon was disillusioned and bitter.

"Well, maybe you've been chasing the wrong woman, Kon. You need a woman who cares about you, not your money."

"Right, sure, sounds great . . . and where the hell am I supposed to find her?" Kon grunted.

Paul looked at him and shook his head. "God! I never dreamed you could be so stupid for so long."

"What are you talking about?" Kon snapped.

Paul hesitated. I hate being in the middle of this, he thought. I'm pulling out. Geilla will have to find some other shoulder to cry on. It's too hard to support both of them. I've got enough to worry about. "Never mind," Paul said out loud. "Trying to give you advice is like talking to a wall." He got up from the bed and went into his room without another word.

Kon lay awake for hours, trying to sort out his feeling for Alyce, and Paul, and Geilla, and himself. He hated to admit it, even to himself, but he knew Paul was right about Alyce. She was so beautiful, so talented, so refined, I just didn't want to see that she didn't care about me, he concluded. She never wanted to know me as I really am. My God! It wasn't her father I was afraid to face. It was Alyce I was hiding from. How could I have been so blind? Was that what Paul meant about my being stupid for so long? Well, it's over, but what the hell . . . now I can spit when I want to, Kon reflected sadly. Geilla certainly had that right about Alyce. I should have listened to her. At least Geilla stuck by me while I was sick. Her concern had seemed genuine, he thought, but maybe it was just another wishful dream, like the one about my father. What does it matter though, she is not meant for me. Paul has the right attitude. He doesn't let women get to him. I just wish . . . Why did Alyce have to discard me in public? That's the worst part — looking like a fool — and having to start over with someone else.

In the morning Kon awoke when the door to his room opened. "Paul? Is that you?" he called.

"No, it's Brad," the answer came back. "I just came to see if you were all right."

"I am well," Kon answered wearily, and sat up. "Where's Paul?"

"Paul's gone. He woke me early this morning with some tale about having to get back to Chicago immediately. He was visibly disturbed about something, so I sent Jack with him. Any idea what happened?" Brad asked.

"No, he didn't say anything to me. His family lives in Chicago. Could something have happened to one of them?"

"That's possible. I wish he would have told me what the urgency was. Sometimes he's as bad as you for being tight lipped!"

"Maybe I should try to call . . ." Kon offered.

"No . . . if he needs us, he'll call. Jack will give me a report if it's serious."

"You're right. He's entitled to a personal life," Kon said and paused. "I want to go back to my village, Brad. I need to get some answers and settle some . . . some feelings, I guess. I'll need a car."

Brad studied Kon. He understood that he was searching for something, but he could see that he was not well enough to make the trip alone. "I can't let you go until you're stronger, Kon," Brad said slowly. "These roads are difficult to drive and it's a long way."

"Oh for God's sake! I'm well enough to drive, Brad. I don't need to be coddled."

"But you do need to be reined in. You push yourself too often. What if you got a coughing fit while coming around one of those hairpin turns?"

Kon knew it was highly probable, but he refused to concede the point. "Who do you think you are to order me around? I thought I left my keeper behind when I left Florina."

Brad recognized Kon's impatience with his physical condition, and answered calmly, "I am the leader of this team. As long as you are on the team, it's my responsibility to keep you alive and functional. I do the same for everyone who works for me."

"So . . . I am just a tool you polish and keep tuned up! Well, maybe I'll quit, and make life easier for you!" Kon snapped.

"You're not a tool," Brad said in exasperation. "You're my friend, even though you are the biggest pain in the ass I've ever met. Look, if you'll rest here for a few days, I'll drive you to your village myself."

"No!" Kon objected and started to cough. "I want to go alone. God damn it! Must my entire life be a circus? I can't even be cast aside in private like any other man!"

Brad suddenly caught a glimpse into the depths of humiliation Kon had been hiding since being rejected by Alyce. Brad realized that all the friendship and support the team had given to Kon was fine, but in their concern, they had denied him the opportunity to grieve, and lick his wounds in private. "I understand, but you'll have to wait," Brad said quietly. Kon flashed him a poison look, but he was coughing so violently he could not respond.

"You prove my point. Take your medicine," Brad coaxed, and handed Kon the bottle of cough syrup. "Maybe you'll fool me and get better fast."

Kon took a swig of the syrup. "God, I hate this stuff! It tastes like fish guts."

Brad smiled. "I'll bring you some coffee."

"Thanks, Brad. I . . . I really don't want to see anyone right now."

****

"Geilla, will you go to Mitikas with me?" Kon asked the following afternoon, when he found her in the hotel lobby after lunch. "It seems I have been forbidden to make the drive alone."

She looked at him closely. It was not like Kon to obey any rule that stood in his way. Perhaps he at last realized that he was far from well. She wondered how the trip would go with just the two of them, alone for several days. Kon had said very little to her since he awoke in the hospital. It was almost as if he was avoiding her. She suspected he was still upset over Alyce. Mary had warned her that he might not be himself for a while.

Mary had witnessed some of the terrible moods and drinking binges Kon had gone through after broken love affairs. Geilla herself had seen how hard Kon had taken it last Christmas when Alyce had not accepted his invitation for the holidays. He had not joined the rest of the team at Mary and Brad's house until Christmas Day. Then he had been totally dispirited and drank so heavily he passed out before dinner. They had all been totally disgusted with him, but forgave him when his hangover turned into a terrible case of the flu. It was almost as if he didn't want to be alone for the holidays, yet couldn't bear to let anyone near him.

"I'll go with you," she said at last. "I'll even do the driving if you want."

"Thank you," he answered with obvious relief. "Mitikas isn't much of a town, but it's important for me to go."

373

"Do you still have family or friends there?" she asked casually.

He shook his head. "No. There were only my parents. I just want to track down some information about myself. I would like to leave tomorrow morning if that is convenient."

"Yes. I can be ready," she answered cheerfully.

Geilla hoped he would stay and talk with her, but he seemed preoccupied and left again as silently as he had come. She finished her tea and went to tell Mary that she was going to Mitikas with Kon.

"You must wear a dress," Mary advised when Geilla told her the news.

"But I didn't bring one with me," Geilla answered.

"Then you shall have to buy one. The people in these little villages are very provincial. Kon would never say it, but you would shame him if you wore those leather pants!"

"But he likes them on me."

"Yes, in Rome, or Paris, but not in Mitikas. Charlotte has made him very conservative socially. Wear a dress – with sleeves. You can always leave it behind when you leave."

"Come with me then to see that I choose something modest and ugly," Geilla pleaded.

"I didn't say you had to look ugly, only modest. A peasant girl can be very fetching while pretending to be demure," Mary laughed, and they set off for the shops.

Kon's furrowed brow relaxed and he grinned broadly, although briefly, when Geilla came down to breakfast the next morning. He had almost forgotten how delightfully sensuous Geilla looked when she walked. Whereas Alyce had appeared to glide statuesquely as she moved, Geilla seemed to skip with life and energy. It must be the skirt, he thought, watching it sway and flutter as she came towards him.

"New outfit?" he asked casually.

"Yes," she drawled. "It's my sweet, innocent, peasant disguise. Do you approve?"

Kon chuckled. "Why do I have the feeling that no matter what I say I may get my face slapped?"

She raised her eyebrows.

"It's very pretty," he said lamely.

Geilla smiled. Mary was right about the dress, she thought. A modest dress was always a good investment. You could dress it up, or dress it down – who am I kidding? I will have to lower the neckline a foot and a half, not to be mistaken for a nun when I get back to Rome. But Kon had smiled, that was worth the price of a dress.

****

374

Geilla didn't mind driving through the mountains to Mitikas, but it bothered her that Kon was still coughing so much, and showed no appetite when they stopped to have a picnic with the food she had packed.

"Did you take your medicine?" she asked as she poured coffee for him.

"I took some this morning," he mumbled, then coughed.

"You should take some more. Stamatis said you need frequent doses."

"He only said that so I would remember. He had no idea how many people would take pleasure in reminding me," he responded testily and continued to cough.

"Why must you always be prodded to do what is good for you? Why are you so eager to get to Mitikas anyway? You should have rested and gone another day."

"No. I have to get to the town hall. They will not be open on Sunday. I must get there tomorrow."

"Is there something special you are looking for?"

"Some record of my birth, and perhaps something about my mother. Edgar made inquiries once, but he could not learn anything."

"Does it matter now, after all these years?"

"It does to me. I am Greek, Geilla. I will never be a Swiss, despite some scribbling on a piece of paper. I have tried . . . I have really tried, but I do not think like they do. I cannot be so controlled and so . . . so orderly."

Geilla noticed that he had barely tasted his food.

"I know you did not have an easy childhood, but why did you finally leave?" she asked and poured him more coffee.

"Because of my father."

"He was never good to you. What happened . . ." she began carefully, but he cut her off.

"He was killed . . . murdered! . . . with a knife. I found him in the house. He . . ." Kon halted, and she waited anxiously, wondering what he might confess. "I never knew what had happened. I had been working alone on the boat, cleaning equipment, as usual. I came home by the path. It was late and I was tired. I went into the house and . . . it was dark. I thought my father was at the taverna. He always went there when he wasn't working the boat. I remember starting for the kitchen area when I heard a noise behind me. I called out, but as I turned, something hit me on the side of my head.

The blow must have knocked me out, because when I woke up, I was lying on the floor. I pulled myself up and staggered towards the kitchen, but I stumbled over something on the floor. My head was bleeding and it hurt so badly I felt sick to my stomach. Somehow I managed to light the lamp, and I noticed that some of the furniture had been overturned. Then I saw my father lying face down on the floor. I thought he was drunk. I bent . . . and turned him over . . . then I saw the blood . . . great rivers of it. It was horrible!"

Kon shuddered involuntarily and Geilla saw that the passage of time had not diminished the intensity of his revulsion. "He was always in some brawl," Kon continued. "No one liked him, he was a beast. But I never expected . . . he was a powerful man . . . he always beat everyone else. If only he had let me come home with him . . . I could have helped him. I could have fought beside him. But he made me stay on the boat. He always made me work on that damned boat. I hated it! I wanted to have a home like other people. I wanted us to be . . ." Kon stopped abruptly and ran his hand through his hair in agitation. Seeing how painful it was for him to speak of his long buried memories, Geilla touched his hand sympathetically, "You don't have to tell me any more."

He turned his face from her momentarily. Then he lowered his head and stared into his coffee cup. "No. I can't keep it hidden any longer. It rises to choke me. You know who I am, Geilla. There is no need to pretend in front of you. I often wished that Alyce . . . but it was not meant to be."

So he is still grieving for Alyce, Geilla thought. I cannot find it in me to comfort him about her.

"My father's death was a terrible shock to me," she heard Kon continue, after a pause. "I didn't know where to turn. I didn't have a single friend in that village. I was afraid they would think I had killed my father, because I always carried a knife. God knows I had the motive . . . but I didn't kill him. There were times when I wanted to, but . . . don't you see . . . he was the only person I had. I kept hoping that someday I would find a way to please him . . . some small thing that he would notice.

I was confused and afraid. I didn't know who had killed my father or why. Perhaps they meant to kill me also. I went to the priest and told him about my father. The priest believed me . . . he knew my father's habits. He advised me to wait. He said the police would find the murderer, but I left. There was nothing for me among those people. I was marked as an outcast. I wrote to the priest once and learned that the police had arrested some man for killing my father. I was living with a widow in Naples at the time. She was very kind to me. I didn't want to go back to my village. I wrote one other time, but the old priest had died."

He fell silent and she saw that he had become downcast from remembering the past. "Why do you return to such an unhappy memory? Forget it. Let's go to Lefkos instead," she said brightly. "You could rest and . . ."

"No! I must go back. Stamatis said I would never be completely free of it, but that I must face it. He is right, I must deal with my legacy. I have been ashamed for too long."

She sighed. "Then I will go with you, Petros, for it was I who made you ashamed of your own Christian name. Come it's getting late."

Kon gave her a hand putting the food away and they returned to the car. He said little during the afternoon, but seemed to enjoy watching the scenery. They stopped in Ioannina for the night and found a small hotel. Although he was nearly overcome by a violent fit of coughing, Kon arranged for two rooms, and a silent young boy carried their bags to the second floor. As the boy left, Geilla saw Kon pass him a lavish tip and whisper to him. She forgot it immediately, knowing that Kon always gave generous rewards for any personal service.

"I am sorry to leave you on your own, Geilla, but I cannot hold my head up any longer. I will see you in the morning," Kon apologized and disappeared into his room.

Geilla felt disappointed. She had a simple dinner alone at the hotel and reminded herself that she was there on business, not pleasure. After she ate, she asked the waiter to bring her a pot of tea and some bread on a tray, explaining that the food was for her friend who was too ill to come down for dinner. She also asked the waiter to give her a key to room twenty-seven. The waiter looked annoyed, but hid his frown when she pressed a handsome tip into his pocket.

Geilla took the tray and went to Kon's room. She heard him mumble in Greek when she knocked, but he didn't come to the door.

"Kon? Are you all right?"

"Yes . . . just leave me be," he grumbled, but she heard him coughing.

"Kon? May I come in? I brought you some food."

"Leave me . . . . alone. I'm not . . . hungry," he gasped, punctuated by coughs.

Geilla sighed and was about to turn away when she heard glass breaking.

"Kon? Are you sure you are all right?" she called again. He didn't respond and she hesitated. She was worried about him. In addition to her deep personal feelings, she felt a responsibility towards him as a member of the team. They all knew he tended to be careless about his health. She thought how she would behave if she suspected that Paul or Jack were lying ill behind that door.

"Kon, I think you should try to eat something," she said and unlocked the door.

The room was dark, but by the light coming from the hall, she fumbled toward the night stand. She heard something crunch beneath her foot as she switched on the lamp. Noticing a nearly half empty bottle of whiskey on the night stand, Geilla understood why Kon had given the young boy so much money. Kon was lying on the bed and appeared to have collapsed without undressing after he had removed his coat and shoes. For a brief moment she felt angry, thinking that Kon was trying to drown his unhappy memories, but then she remembered that whiskey helped quiet his cough.

"I see you've had dinner," she said with a sharp edge to her voice. "Why don't you sit up and try some food."

He turned his head to look at her. "Nothing . . . please . . . I will be sick if I eat anything."

She was determined to see that he didn't drink himself into oblivion. "You must try," she said firmly. "You haven't eaten all day. Come on . . . at least turn over," she continued, taking him by the arm. When he did not move, she shook him gently. She thought of her father and all the times she had cared for him. She hated to see Kon heading the same way. "Come on, Kon. Sit up and eat," she said again.

At last he rolled over and she was alarmed by how totally spent he looked. "I can't eat, Geilla. Leave me be," he protested numbly.

She put her hand on his forehead and felt the heat. God help him! His temperature must be up again, she thought. "Kon, are you hot?" she asked more gently. He did not respond and she coaxed. "Do you have a fever, Kon?"

He shook his head vaguely.

"You must sit up," she told him repeatedly, and with persistent coaxing and prodding she got him propped against the head of the bed. He started coughing again. She loosened his shirt, put a wet towel on his head, and brought him tea, lecturing him all the while about how foolish he was to leave the hospital.

"I have to go, Geilla. I must face it . . . I must," he mumbled.

"I know. I know," she said softly. She tried to take his hand, but he pulled away. "You must take some medicine, Kon. Please."

"Leave me be. I don't want pills! I can't take pills!" he complained repeatedly, but in the end he submitted. He swallowed some capsules with the tea, and ate some bread and butter, but he would not permit her to remove his clothes to make him more comfortable. She felt he was resisting her, raising the wall he kept around himself. It grieved her for she wanted so to help him, to express her love for him in some tangible way. She thought she should sit with him, but she sensed that her fussing was making him uneasy.

He was silent, but his dark eyes followed her as she picked up the pieces of the broken glass and threw them away.

"I'll leave the cup for your whiskey, Kon. Try not to drink too much, O.K.?" she said and brushed the hair from his forehead. He felt so hot, she knew she would not sleep for worrying about him.

"Paul is more than . . . my friend, Geilla. He's the brother I never . . . I won't deny him . . . anything . . . anything," Kon mumbled and she feared he was delirious.

"Shh ... don't talk ... you must rest ... shhhh ... Paul is safe. Try to sleep," she consoled him.

She left his room and went to her own, but it was pointless to think of sleeping. She lay on her bed, and thought of where she would fit into Kon's life, now that Alyce had left him. I'm no further ahead, she concluded. He still won't open his heart to me. Paul is wrong about him. He'll never change. She checked on Kon in an hour. He still felt hot, but he was shivering. She found an extra blanket in the closet and spread it over him. She spoke softly to him, but he didn't seem to understand. He kept muttering about Paul.

If he's not better by morning I will have to call a doctor, she decided. I know he will howl, but I can't let him drag himself around in this condition. "Dear God, will he never be well!" she said in a half praying-half scolding whisper. She checked on him several more times, and towards dawn the fever passed and he slept. She arranged the blanket he had thrown off with his restless movements. Going to her own room, she undressed, slipped into bed, and fell into a deep, thankful sleep.

At mid-morning she was awakened by a soft knock on her door.

"Come back later," she called out, thinking it was the maid.

"I cannot wait!" a deep, but mellow voice answered. "I am the Angel Gabriel, come to raise the dead, and bid them partake of bread and tea! It is written that no one can rest in peace in this blasted hotel until they have had their tea!"

Geilla laughed aloud.

"Is Gabriel an Englishman then?" she asked, getting out of bed and throwing on her robe.

"No! He is a Greek who has been restored to life!" the voice resounded. "But you must open the door, for he has mistakenly materialized on the wrong side of it!"

"Ah! What a poor angel he is," Geilla answered opening the door.

Kon smiled shyly, and offered her a tray complete with tea, cups and bread. He looked pale and tired, but he was freshly shaven and dressed.

"I ... I do not mean to interrupt your sleep, but we must be going," he apologized.

"Not at all. I am glad to see you looking better."

He poured a cup of tea and handed it to her.

"I ... I hope I didn't keep you awake with my ... my rantings. If I said anything ... improper ... I am sorry. I was not myself."

She smiled. "You were quite proper, Kon — puritanical actually, and very stubborn."

"Stubborn, eh. Then I was my true self despite the fever."

Kon drank tea with her and then left. She hurried to shower and dress, for it was Saturday and she knew that Kon was anxious to get to the town hall in his village.

****

Geilla parked the car well away from the church on Sunday, for
Kon had insisted that they go on foot. It would cause a stir to arrive
in a car, he had told her, but she guessed that he wanted to retrace
the steps he had taken so often with his mother. The village had
changed, but the church had not. He did not recognize the faces of
any of the people they passed on the way to service, but then he had
never had many friends as a boy. Even as a young child he had gone
on the boat with his father.

Noticing how modestly the women, both young and old, were
dressed, Geilla was glad she had not worn her tight leather pants. She
imagined she was probably acting like a harlot by standing boldly in
the front of the church with Kon and a few of the men, instead of
huddling in the rear with the women and children. Well, if Kon was
that old fashioned, she would wait in the car, she reflected acidly. But
Kon did not suggest in any way that he wanted her to leave his side.
He was nervous, and she sensed that being in this village again, even
in the church he remembered so fondly, was not a pleasant
experience for him.

They had visited the church yesterday after a trip to the town
hall had proven fruitless. The priest had been very kind and helpful
and agreed to let Kon search through the church records. Kon had
poured over the carefully preserved collection of papers for several
hours, but had found little to satisfy him. He had been so
disappointed that the priest had suggested that if Kon came for
service in the morning, he would ask some of the older parishioners
if they knew anything of the Kononellos family.

Kon appeared engrossed in the ritual of the Mass when it
started, but about half way through, a large quantity of incense was
lit. A great fragrant cloud rose in the air and even as it ascended,
Kon began to cough. He tried valiantly to contain his cough, but the
incense overwhelmed him, and with tears rolling down his face, he
gasped and stumbled from the building. Though he panted and
struggled to draw in the cool morning air, he continued to cough.

Alarmed by the violence of Kon's coughing, Geilla scanned the
street hopefully for a cafe that might be open at this early hour. She
spotted one a block away and steered Kon toward it. As they arrived
she called out, "Whiskey! Hurry!" and a corpulent man with a scraggly
beard and a dirty apron scurried inside and reappeared with an open
bottle and a shot glass. Carelessly he poured some of the dark liquid
for Kon and grunted something in Greek. Kon grasped the glass and
gulped the whiskey, throwing back his head. He gasped several times
and held the glass for a refill. The waiter obliged without comment.

Kon downed the second glass more slowly and gradually his coughing subsided. The waiter muttered in Greek and Kon laughed and gave a brief answer. When the waiter moved to fill the glass again, Kon put his hand over it.

"What did he say?" Geilla asked after the waiter had turned and gone inside.

Kon grinned. "He said that whiskey was easier to swallow than religion."

"Despite his blasphemy, I'm glad his cafe was open," Geilla replied.

"There's no point in my going back to the church," Kon answered. "I forgot about the incense. I hope you enjoyed what little of the service you got to see."

"I did," she assured him. "It was very like those I used to attend, only more ornate."

So they sat and waited until they saw the people coming out of church. Then Kon disappeared inside the cafe to pay the bill and thank the waiter, who he learned was the proprietor, for his timely assistance. When they got back to the church, they saw the priest talking to a group of old women who were attired in the traditional black dresses and shawls. Geilla noted that they looked similar to all the old women in Italy. How dreadful to have to give up wearing bright colors, forever, she thought. She shuddered, wondering if the women ever got tired of dressing like inky mummies.

Geilla stood with Kon at a discreet distance from the women, but shortly the priest beckoned to them to join the group. Geilla smiled and nodded to the women, as did Kon, but she knew that he was being critically analyzed for any sign of familial resemblance, and she was being scrutinized for future gossip. How terrible for Kon to have to stand like a lost pup, hoping that someone would recognize him, she thought; but how much worse that no one did. After what seemed like ages, the women nodded stiffly and drifted away. The kindly priest was clearly discouraged, and seeing the sorrowful look on Kon's face, he spoke rapidly to him. As a parting gesture, the priest raised his arm and blessed Kon, who bowed his head, more from sadness than from piety.

"I am sorry I spoiled your sleep to bring me here on a fool's errand, Geilla," Kon muttered, taking her hand. "Perhaps we can find a pleasant spot to have . . . what will it be, breakfast or lunch?"

Her appetite was suddenly gone, but she could not hurt his battered feelings. "Breakfast would be fine," she answered. "Do you suppose they've ever heard of Irish coffee?"

"I doubt it, but it's time we taught them," Kon responded.

"What did the priest tell you after the women left?"

"He promised to ask about my family next week, if I would come back. I told him it was impossible."

"I'm sorry Kon, you . . ." she began, but before she could finish, she noticed a short stocky young man in a frequently mended, but well pressed suit, standing at Kon's elbow. He whispered furtively to Kon, and then dashed away as if he was afraid to be seen with him.

"What is it?" Geilla asked brightly seeing the dark cloud lift from Kon's face.

"We shall have to hurry our breakfast, Geilla. That fellow's Aunt Sophia knew my mother, and she has invited us to call."

"That's wonderful! I am so glad for you!"

Excitedly he took her hand, and looked eagerly at her. She thought he meant to say something and then the cloud returned.

"We'd better go," he muttered and let go of her hand. "I will show you the house I grew up in as we pass."

CHAPTER TWENTY-EIGHT

Sophia's house was small and sparsely furnished, and Sophia's greeting was formal and less than open-hearted. She closed the door behind them so quickly, Geilla sensed she was embarrassed to be seen with them. They sat in straight-backed chairs and Sophia served them each a glass of cold clear water and a dish of overly sweet apricot preserves. Geilla could not understand any of the conversation, and Kon discovered to his chagrin that his Greek was not as fluent as he had thought. He had been ashamed to speak it for so long that he was out of practice. Stamatis had commented that even though he swore like a fisherman, he pronounced his native tongue like a learned ecclesiastic.

"I see you have done well, Petros," Sophia began. "Fine clothes, big car, beautiful wife."

Kon started. "I have no wife, Sophia. Geilla is just a friend. She works with me."

"She is beautiful, nevertheless, and friendship can lead to marriage," Sophia said and laughed slyly.

"In this case it is not possible," Kon answered.

Geilla understood from Sophia's look that she was being discussed and she felt her cheeks flush. Good God! Why am I blushing? she thought. It's this damn dress! It's turning me into a hopeless provincial. I should have worn my pants and really given these women something to gossip about! When Sophia flashed her a motherly smile, however, Geilla was enchanted. After all, they were both trying to help Kon.

"Why have you returned after all these years, Petros?" Sophia asked, getting down to business.

"I have found the entry for my parents' marriage in the church records, Sophia, but there is no record of my birth in either the church, or the town hall."

Sophia hesitated. "You will not find it," she said slowly.

"Why? Surely it was recorded."

"Not in this village, Petros. Costa Kononellos was not your father."

"Not my father . . ." Kon gasped in shock. "Am I truly the bastard as I was called?"

"No! No! Not a bastard," she answered quickly. "Your mother was a widow. You were nearly a year old when she married Costa."

"A widow!" he answered in disbelief. "How did she dare to remarry?"

Sophia adjusted her shawl nervously and pondered how to answer him. "Your mother was very young when your father died. She grieved, but she did not want to spend her life alone. She was very . . . very lively," Sophia answered, or so Kon interpreted the word. He wondered just what the term "lively" encompassed, but Sophia seemed too embarrassed to elaborate.

"Did my mother ever speak of my real father?"

"Only once. She thought it would trouble you if you knew Costa was not your father. Your real father was an educated man, some kind of teacher, I think. His family disinherited him when he married your mother."

"But why? Was she so terrible? Was she really a . . . all those names she was called?"

"No! She was a very hard working woman, but an outcast nevertheless. She was a foreigner . . . an Albanian."

"Albanian? Merciful God, I can't bear to hear any more!" Kon groaned softly and put his head in his hands. The picture he had of his family was crumbling and he found it disconcerting. Even though he had hated what he thought were his origins, at least he knew what they were, until now.

Geilla saw that Kon was becoming more distraught as he talked with Sophia, but she could not begin to guess what he had learned. She took his hand to comfort him, and knew when he let her hold it, that he was deeply shaken. "What is it? What is wrong?" she asked in dismay.

"My mother . . ." he whispered hoarsely. "It is too much to believe . . . too much to explain."

Kon pulled absently at his hair and raised his head. "How . . . how did my father come to meet my mother?"

"Her family came to Greece after the war. They were extremely poor. I do not know the details. Your mother was beautiful, very beautiful. Your father was attracted despite her poverty. They were very happy until he was killed in an accident. He died shortly before you were born."

"You mean he never even saw me! I can't believe . . . Why did my mother ever agree to marry a fisherman?"

"A widow does not have a choice even if she is beautiful! Your father's people would not help her. She had a son to raise." Sophia paused. "And Costa could be very charming when he chose to be. I'm sure he told your mother a pack of lies about how rich he was."

"Do you think he cared for her at all?"

"I think, in the beginning, yes. He wanted sons by your mother. But all the little ones she had, died either before birth or shortly after. He tried to blame your mother, but you were living proof that she could produce a child."

Kon held his head in his hands and pulled at his hair.

"How did she die, Sophia? I know only that she was with me one, day and then the house was full of people, and someone told me she was gone. I remember I did not understand at first and Costa told me very harshly that she was dead. He acted as if it was my fault, but I never knew what I had done."

"It was cruel of him to say such a thing, Petros. Your mother died in childbirth, trying to force a large boy from her worn out body."

"Merciful God!" he moaned and put his face in his hands again. "I never knew."

"What is it that upsets you, Kon? What did she say?" Geilla asked, but Kon only shook his head.

"Your mother hardly told anyone," Sophia continued. "She had failed so many times, she became afraid to speak of an unborn child. She was so thin, no one guessed."

"I remember that Costa kept me on the boat that day . . . mending nets. I was always made to mend the nets. I could not go to school, I could not play games with the other boys. How he must have hated me!"

"Not all of him hated you, Petros. You must not think it. I'm sure you reminded him of your mother. You are very like her . . . tall and thin . . . and with her beautiful eyes. You always treated him with respect, thinking that he was your father. He didn't have anyone else."

"But why wouldn't he allow me to go to school? He made it very hard for me in life."

"I think that when he saw how much you wanted to go to school, he was afraid your desire for book knowledge was inherited from your real father. Your mother encouraged you, but Costa wanted to suppress any tendency towards education. Perhaps he feared he would lose his power over you if you learned how ignorant he was."

"He certainly thwarted my education. If it had not been for Father Demetrius I would not have learned to read or write. I think my mother hoped to make me a priest. She took me to church at every holy day and feast. Costa was always complaining about losing my help. I am ashamed to say it, but none of my mother's piety rubbed off on me."

Sophia smiled and patted Kon's hand as if he were a child.

"Evangelia was a good Christian woman, Petros, but she did not take you to church from piety. She took you so that Costa would not work you to death on his boat. It was the talk of the village how you could never stay awake during Mass. Evangelia would spread her shawl on the hard floor and you would be asleep before the first 'Kurie eleeson' rang out. And bless your heart, you could sleep through the most rousing sermons."

Kon looked at Sophia in amazement and then he began to laugh. His laughter grew into a deep riotous laugh that Geilla had never heard before. Suddenly he shouted in Greek and then he threw his head back and roared with laughter. Sophia looked startled at first, but then she too began to laugh.

"What is it? What's so funny?" Geilla demanded, thinking that Kon's grief had turned to hysteria.

"Oh, Geilla! I thank God that I came back!" Kon sputtered, but he could not stop laughing. He laughed so vigorously that he began to cough. He coughed until he clutched his side and doubled over.

Geilla was alarmed and shot a pleading look at Sophia who suddenly stopped laughing and scuttled from her chair.

"Kon! Are you all right?" Geilla asked excitedly.

"Yes," he gasped between coughs. "I've never felt better!"

Despite his declaration, Kon continued to cough helplessly. Sophia appeared in a moment with a glass of cognac and pressed it into Kon's hand. "Drink this!" she ordered.

Kon could only sip the liquid, but gradually his coughing subsided and he sat upright in his chair. Geilla was amazed to see him smile at her.

"Kon, are you all right? What were you shouting about? You looked so wild you frightened me!"

"I am sorry. I didn't mean to scare you. I was only declaring myself to the world."

Geilla looked at him questioningly. "What were you declaring?"

Kon looked at her hesitantly and Sophia refilled his glass.

"What were you declaring?" Geilla persisted.

He looked at her and grinned. "I've been a complete fool, Geilla. All my life I have carried this . . . this yoke, thinking that my father was a drunken brute and that my mother was some kind of saint. I hated to think I was like the one, for I knew I could never measure up to the other. Now I learn that my father wasn't my father, and my mother was no saint. She wasn't even Greek! You can't imagine how free I feel. After a lifetime of being ashamed of being the son of an ignorant fisherman, I was declaring myself at last. I am Petros Tsakapoulos, son of a scholar and a lusty mountain wench — good as any man alive!"

Geilla did not understand what he was trying to tell her, but she laughed at his enthusiasm. "Tsakapoulos?"

"Yes. Costa was only my step-father. I don't have to turn out like him, though God knows I drink too much!"

"Step-father?" Geilla responded in amazement.

"Yes! My real father was a teacher — a man of learning!"

"Are you going to try to trace him?"

"No. I have no idea where he was from. I don't even know his Christian name. It is enough to know that no part of me was inherited from Costa. Edgar and Carlin have each been a father to me. I don't need any other."

After they had bid farewell to Sophia, Geilla walked with Kon along the water. He seemed remote and lost in thought. She suddenly gave in to discouragement. Face the truth, she told herself; he is not going to forgive you. You are wasting your life waiting for him. You will never break down that wall he's built around himself. Taking a deep breath, she noticed that she had fallen several steps behind him as he walked on gazing into the sea. She hurried to catch up and took him by the arm to attract his attention.

"Kon," she announced firmly, "I've decided to quit the team."

He turned and stared at her, but was silent.

"I'm going away for . . ." she continued softly, but broke off. Save your breath, she told herself. He isn't interested. He's still fretting over Alyce.

"But . . . but you can't do that!" he stammered. "You can't just quit!"

"Why not?" she responded, shrugging her shoulders. "I'm not really needed on the team. Brad could find someone else in a minute."

"But I . . . but what about Paul? He would miss you. He's come to depend on you. You can't just abandon him."

She stepped in front of him and looked at him earnestly.

"Paul doesn't need me. Paul doesn't need anyone. We are only friends. He'll do just fine without me."

Kon looked astonished. "Only friends? But you sleep with him! Don't you love him?"

Geilla stared at him in shock. "Who told you that I . . . why that dirty little swine . . ."

"No! Paul would never . . . I found out by accident, the time you stayed at my apartment in Paris while I went to Cannes with Alyce. I got back a day early. I was so tired I just came in, put my stuff in the bedroom, and stretched out on the bed. I must have fallen asleep, because a while later I heard you and Paul come in. At first I thought to join you for a drink, but by the time I got my shoes on I could tell you two didn't want company. I waited until you went into the other bedroom and then I grabbed my bag and slipped out. When I showed up the next evening, you were alone. You never said anything, so I figured I wasn't supposed to know."

She drew in her breath sharply. "I didn't realize you knew!"

"I knew. There were other times too. Why? Why did you sleep with him if you didn't love him? Did you want to entice him and drive him crazy the way you did with me? Don't you know he has feelings? How could you use him?"

"Because you were never around!" she shouted and drew away from him in anger. "Every time I tried to approach you, you would shut me out. I have feelings and needs too, Kon! Was I supposed to play the virgin while you were off chasing Alyce? Paul was only a substitute, but he was always there when I needed him. I never pretended to him. He knows I love you."

"Me?" Kon said incredulously.

"Yes! Why do you think I joined the team in the first place? I can never make you believe it, Kon, but I love you. I've loved you since the day Alonzo died, and I came to know you as more than just his silent shadow."

He looked at her intently. "Don't tell me this, if it isn't true, Geilla. You have told me you loved me before, and then you left me for someone else. I can face it if you love Paul — just don't lie to me."

She took his face between her hands. "I have never lied to you, Kon. You just weren't ready to believe me. I never loved Paul. He knows I love you. He kept telling me you would wake up and turn to me, but you never did. He allowed me on the team for one purpose, and one purpose only. He kept other men away from me. You don't know how closely he guarded me."

Kon looked stunned. "I thought you . . . I don't know what to believe any more. My whole life has been turned upside down." He turned from her and walked on along the shore. She followed silently after him. Something has to be decided, she thought. I can't go on like this.

After a short time Kon quietly slipped his hand around Geilla's and pulled her to him. "I can't stop loving you, Geilla. God knows I've tried. Even when I told myself that I hated you, it tore me apart because in my heart I still loved you. I have never told you before, but I tell you now. My life is nothing without you, Geilla. If you love me as you say, will you consent to be my wife?"

"Kon, are you sure you are ready to marry? Are you sure you're not just upset over losing Alyce?"

"I am over Alyce! I've seen what a fool I was about her. How could I have been so blind?" He looked intently at her. "Marry me, Geilla. If you truly love me, declare your love once and for all, before the priest. I can't be happy with anything less!"

Geilla hesitated. She was almost frightened by his intensity. She was afraid it might be a product of his despair over Alyce. He had walled her out for so long, she was not prepared for this sudden reversal.

"I love you, Kon," she answered softly, "but perhaps we should wait a while before we marry."

"But why? I have wanted you my whole life?"

"Perhaps you only think you did. Perhaps . . ."

"No! I loved you then and I love you now. I can't go on if you leave again, Geilla."

"I'm not leaving. I just don't think you should make such an important decision when you are so upset."

"How in blazes can I be calm about you, Geilla? You torment me! There are times I cannot be in the same room with you, I ache so for you. Even a causal touch sends tidal waves of yearning ripping through me, threatening to drown my self-control. I've never felt that way about any other woman. I don't want to risk losing you again. Geilla, when you came into my room the other night with your damn pot of tea . . . it was like a revelation. I had been lying there feeling so sick and miserable and . . . and then you came. You were so kind to me. I expected you would be angry that I left you to take care of everything, but you weren't. You seemed truly concerned about me. You don't know hard it was for me to be with you and not lose control. How I envied Paul that he had you to love him. Alyce was never like that. There was no tenderness in her, no compassion. She took everything I gave. She tried to drag me into marriage, but she didn't really care about me, or my work, or my friends. I need you, Geilla. I can't bear the loneliness anymore. I swear I will throw myself into the sea if you turn me away again. Marry me! Say yes, please!"

She looked at him and shook her head. He was as tempestuous as ever. "Oh Kon, you are impossible! Absolutely impossible!"

"No! Never say 'impossible'! 'Impossible' is too cruel. I am difficult, I admit, and stubborn, and . . . and rash, and unworthy, and unholy, but not impossible! I can change! I promise. I will be better. I will be anything you want, only don't desert me."

She looked into his deep dark eyes and saw the longing. "I won't desert you and I won't ask you to change," she whispered and smiled. "I must be crazy, Petros Kononellos, but I love you just as you are. Life with you will never be dull."

"Then you will marry me? Say it! Say it aloud, please."

"Yes! Yes! I will marry you."

Suddenly he enfolded her in his arms. "Oh, Geilla, you have made me the happiest of men!"

She turned her face up and he kissed her gently, tenderly, as if testing if she would respond; and when she did, he pressed her to him and she felt the fire quivering through him. They clung to each other, oblivious to the wind, and the sea, and the passage of time.

At last when the cold wind, and the cries of the sea gulls brought them back to the present, Kon began to whisper excitedly to her. "I want to have a family, Geilla, sons and daughters, a house full of them. If it's too late, we can get them from the Children's Home. They have anything you want!" he said excitedly. "Boys, or girls, light-haired or dark . . . French, Italian, German. We can have our pick! They're not all perfect, but I don't care. I have no right to perfection."

"Kon! Kon!" she said, trying to interrupt him, but not succeeding. "Kon, calm down. I want to have your baby," she said, but he was so carried away with convincing her that he didn't seem to hear.

"A baby? If you want a baby, I will get a baby. Dio Mio, I am on the Board of Directors, they will have to give us a baby! I will withdraw my support if they won't!" he shouted. "I will ask Charlotte to withdraw her support! I will ask Carlin . . ."

"Kon! Kon! Calm down! It's not too late. We can try for our own baby."

"Our baby? Our baby?" he repeated, suddenly understanding the significance of her words. "Oh, Geilla, I have wanted . . . you will be so good as a mother. You are so patient . . . even with me."

Kon smiled at her, and she drank in the warmth of it. She could not deny him when he declared that they must return to the cafe to celebrate. She could not deny him anything when he smiled like that. They walked back slowly, hand in hand.

"Surely nothing is impossible, Geilla," Kon remarked as they went, "for here I am in my own village with you by my side!"

Kon was in an unusually outgoing mood when they arrived at the cafe, and asked the proprietor if he had any champagne on hand. The proprietor replied that he didn't cater to such expensive tastes, but that he did have some fine old wine that was begging to be sampled.

"Bring it then!" Kon exclaimed. "We wish to celebrate. We are to be married!"

The proprietor looked surprised. "Ah! I see you have had a successful day. This morning you came looking for a mother and tonight you find a bride. It is better. A man cannot win an argument with his mother!"

"And can a man ever win an argument with his wife?" Kon asked.

"Occasionally," the proprietor answered. "But it is better to lose, for then you can apologize and take her to bed to make up!"

Kon laughed heartily.

"What did he say?" Geilla demanded, guessing that their plans had been announced.

"He said he has some very good wine for us," Kon said and smiled.

"The hell he did," Geilla answered. "I think it's time I learned Greek."

"I will teach you if you wish, but all you really need to learn is 'ne'."

"Oh no," Geilla insisted. "I already know that word. If you wanted a 'yes' woman, you've picked the wrong one."

Kon laughed and kissed her hand.

"I think I have lost my first argument," Kon told the proprietor when he returned with the bottle of wine.

"But you have won her heart. That is a good beginning!" the proprietor assured him.

So they stayed to drink wine, and celebrate, and Geilla saw that for once Kon was eager to share his business with everyone. How he has missed the companionship that comes from being a part of a community, she thought as she watched him talk and joke with the men in the taverna. For her part, Geilla was anxious to depart, for she and Kon had planned to leave Mitikas and spend the night in Vonitsa. It was not a long trip, but she wished to avoid driving the local roads after dark. Despite her best intentions, however, it was dark by the time she and Kon bid the proprietor farewell and left the cafe.

At the last moment Kon expressed a desire to walk along the beach once more before he left his home village the final time. He took Geilla by the arm and led her away from the cafe. They had gone less than twenty yards, however, when she felt Kon jerk forward and let go of her arm. She heard Kon curse, and a moment later he was grappling with a dark figure on the ground. It was too dark to see who had the upper hand, but Geilla feared that it was not Kon. She ran for the cafe and throwing open the door she screamed, "Help! Bring a light! Kon is down!"

The proprietor knew enough English to understand that Kon was in trouble. He snatched up a lantern and followed her out. Two customers who had been talking with Kon earlier rushed after them. The group hurried down the street and the proprietor held the lantern aloft. The faint beam revealed two figures locked in a fierce struggle on the ground. Realizing that Kon was on the bottom, Geilla screamed, "Kon!" and flung herself at the unknown assailant. Her charge distracted him for a moment, and enabled the two men from the cafe to seize him and haul him away from Kon. Kon was panting and coughing violently when Geilla, and the proprietor helped him up. Even in the dim light from the lantern, Geilla saw that Kon's right hand was bleeding.

"Kon! You're hurt," she shrieked and tried to take hold of his hand.

"It's nothing," he insisted and concealed his hand behind his back. "Are you all right? Did he hurt you? I'll kill him if he . . ." he asked anxiously and put his left hand on her arm.

"No, Kon! I'm O.K.! Really!" she assured him quickly.

"Good! Good! Hold the light!" Kon ordered between coughs. "Let me see the face of the cur who tries to stab me from behind!"

The proprietor held the light higher and Kon approached his attacker. The man turned his face aside and tried to break away from the men who were holding him by the arms. As Kon grabbed the attacker by the hair, and forced his face toward the light, he could smell alcohol on the man's breath. He studied the man's weathered features and looked into the eyes that squinted back at him. Suddenly Kon drew in his breath sharply. "Christ Almighty! I know this man! Yianni! Why? We worked on the boat together! We shared the same loaf! You inherited my father's house after I left. I saw the deed at the town hall!"

"Yes, Petros!" the weathered old man shouted defiantly. "I claimed the house! In payment of money Costa owed me. He cheated me for years. I was his cousin and he treated me like scum. He treated you the same, but you were too weak to do anything about it! I thought you had crawled away to die, Petros! But no . . . now you come . . . you and your big car and your fancy clothes, sneaking around my house, and asking questions about Costa. He was not your father, Petros. It is I who have the right to that house. I will not let you take it away from me and my lawful son!"

Kon stared at Yianni in amazement. "How did you know . . .? My God, it was you who killed Costa!"

"Yes I killed him! I didn't plan to do it, but we had an argument and he struck me. We had both been drinking and I became enraged. For once I talked back to him, and defended myself. We fought, and in the heat of the moment, I pulled my knife and stabbed him. I was still in the house when you came back from the boat. I put out the light and hid behind the door, but in my excitement I dropped my knife. You heard the noise and I was sure you saw me. I panicked. I was covered with Costa's blood. I feared you would try to avenge him so I hit you. I didn't mean to kill you, but when I saw your blood I thought I had, and I fled."

When the old man had finished his grisly tale, Kon released his grip on Yianni's hair and put his hand to his own head. He coughed again and gasped, "My God! My God, Yianni! Why didn't you talk to me? I never knew you held such hatred for him. As God is my witness, I could never seek revenge on any man for Costa's sake. Had I stayed here I would probably have killed him myself one day. My sin would have been greater, because I believed he was my father. How I suffered, trying to love a father who was so brutal."

"Then you have not come to avenge him, and claim your property?" Yianni asked in bewilderment.

"No," Kon answered, shaking his head. "I thought his killer had been found years ago. Father Demetrius wrote to me that a man had been arrested shortly after I left. I came only to learn about my mother."

"Oh my God! Petros! That man was released after his shipmates returned to swear that he had been with them that evening. Alas, all is lost. My guilt has destroyed me. I see only evil everywhere. I will die in prison and bring everlasting shame on my family."

Kon hung his head and continued to cough, while the two men from the cafe began to haul Yianni away. Suddenly Kon called to them. "Wait!" Kon turned to the proprietor. "You told me you knew my father . . . Costa. Should any man mourn the death of such a one? He destroyed my mother. He made my life a hell. He drove Yianni to despair. I will not let him ruin another family. I will not give evidence against Yianni. In the name of justice I swear you all to silence!"

"But, Petros . . . the law," the proprietor objected.

"What purpose would it serve to send an old man to prison and shame his son? I have lived in shame my entire life because of Costa. I will not sentence another living soul to such a punishment."

Suddenly Kon held forth his right hand and they saw the blood dripping from it. "Put an end to this hatred. Yianni has spilt my blood and I forgive him. Swear on my blood you'll do the same!"

The proprietor drew back.

"In the hope of mercy . . . swear!" Kon gasped, and they were moved by his compassion.

There was a long silence, and then, one by one, the three men touched Kon's hand and swore an oath of silence.

"Return to your son, Yianni, and give him . . ." Kon began hoarsely, but before he could finish he was overcome by a fit of coughing. He staggered forward and sank to his knees.

Geilla sprang to Kon's side and tried to support him as he fell. She took his bloody hand between her own. "Kon! Kon, speak to me!" she implored.

Kon turned towards her, and gasped, "Bring the car, Geilla! I must leave this accursed village."

"No! You're hurt, Kon. I'll get a doctor."

"No! No doctor! Get the car. I must leave this village. The ghost of Costa haunts me. There is nothing for me here. Please . . . anywhere, but here . . ." he whispered and collapsed.

The men carried him back to the cafe and lay him on the floor, and Geilla bent over him.

"What's wrong with him?" one of the customers asked.

"It's his lungs," the proprietor declared. "Didn't you hear him coughing just now?"

"It's not his lungs," a third man argued. "He faints from loss of blood."

"Oh my God! Is there a doctor here?" Geilla suddenly shouted, breaking into their conjecture.

"No doctor. Only in Vonitsa," one man answered.

"Here, I will wrap his hand," the proprietor offered, taking a towel from behind the bar.

"It's more than his hand that bleeds," Geilla shouted. "He's been stabbed. Don't just stand there! Help me get his coat off!"

The proprietor was shamed to be ordered by a woman, but he hurried forward and began to help her. "Christ! That devil Yianni must have put his blade in his back. How could he forgive such a thing?" the proprietor called to the others in Greek, when he saw the blood on Kon's shirt. Geilla pulled Kon's shirt loose and the proprietor was surprised to see the bandage around Kon's ribs. "It's no wonder he faints – he is already wounded! Damn that drunken Yianni! He's done him serious damage!" he added seeing the gash on Kon's back. "Spiro! Bring me more of those towels!" he called again in Greek. "We should never have let Yianni go!"

Spiro brought the towels, and the proprietor began to tear them into strips. "Hold this," he said in English, handing Geilla a large piece of towel, and pointing to Kon's back. "Do you know Vonitsa?" he asked.

"I have seen it on the map. We were going there for the night."

"Good," he answered as he wrapped the strips of towel around Kon. "There is a doctor in Vonitsa. Take him there. You have a car?"

"Yes."

"Bring it. We will carry him."

Geilla started for the door.

"Wait! . . . not safe to go alone," the proprietor said in English. Then he called in Greek, "Spiro, go with her. Who knows where that idiot Yianni may be hiding."

One of the men who was sworn to silence came forward. "I go with," he said haultingly. Geilla nodded and he followed her out the door.

Geilla shivered as she hurried toward the car. She was thankful that she and Kon had checked out of their rooms and put their bags in the car. By the time she reached the cafe again, the proprietor had finished bandaging Kon, and the men carried him out to the car. Kon mumbled something in Italian and called, "Geilla," as they lay him on the back seat. Geilla touched his hand, then quickly put her hand to his forehead. God have mercy! That cursed fever is back. Don't get sick on me, Kon! Don't you dare get sick!"

"Be careful . . . many turns," she heard the proprietor warn. "I wish you luck. I hope it goes well for him. Tell us if he . . . We cannot hide more murder."

"I will send word," Geilla promised. "I am grateful for your help," she added hurriedly, and started the car. As she drove away, she realized how much she had always depended on Paul, and Jack, and Brad for strength and courage. When she had driven the truck from Bitola, she had known that Kon was in good hands. Now she was alone. She felt angry at the injustice of the situation. Was there no fairness, no clemency in the universe? She had done all this before. She had driven at top speed, over unfamiliar roads, peering into the dark for signs and watching for unannounced turns. She had taken Kon to a doctor before. Damn it! He was supposed to be well! Had it all been in vain? She could not bear the thought that she might lose Kon after he had at last opened his heart to her. "Don't you die on me, Petros Kononellos! Don't you dare! Do you hear me?" she muttered under her breath. She had feared he might die before, but then he had not really been hers to claim. He had belonged to Alyce, and to Charlotte, and to Paul.

Geilla drove like mad on that unknown road to Vonitsa, probing the darkness for markers, and spinning the wheels on turns. Fortunately, there was little traffic to avoid, but seeing no other lights heightened her sense of isolation. It seemed as if those twenty-two miles stretched before her without end. Don't you die on me, Kon! Don't you dare! Don't you dare die now, my love.

CHAPTER TWENTY-NINE

When Geilla realized that Kon was feverish, she knew the clinic in Vonitsa was not prepared to help him. He needed the new antibiotic immediately, but he was in no shape to swallow the capsules he had with him. While the young doctor at the clinic bandaged Kon, Geilla called Brad, who arranged for Major Allensworth to meet her at a small airport near Vonitsa. Over the doctor's shocked protests, Geilla bundled Kon up, put him back in the car, and raced to the airport.

Apparently Major Allensworth had not been impressed with the medical standards at the clinic in Florina, for he arrived in Vonitsa with a young American medic in tow. As soon as Kon was aboard the plane, he was started on blood plasma and oxygen. When the plane arrived in Athens, Brad, Mary, and Stamatis were waiting, and Kon was quickly transferred to the hospital. Geilla was encouraged to see the familiar figure of Stamatis, who despite his scraggly beard and rumpled clothes, looked commanding and competent, compared to the clean-shaven young doctor in Vonitsa. Geilla thought young Dr. Petralias had been more interested in patting her hand than in looking after Kon.

Kon suffered another severe bout of fever in Athens, but once again Stamatis pulled him through. He was standing over Kon when Kon awoke.

"Oh shit — not you again!" Kon muttered when he recognized Stamatis.

"Yes," Stamatis grumbled. "You return like the plague to disrupt my sleep, and ruin my digestion."

"I must not be as sick as before . . . you have not called the priest."

"I did not think you could sin so quickly. You have more stamina than I realize, if you need to confess again."

Kon grimaced. "That damned Yianni brought me down before I could manage a single trespass."

"Perhaps it was Father Léon's blessing that kept you safe then. If that blade had gone in only slightly higher it would have severed a spinal nerve. As it happened, it hit the bone and was deflected. You have some muscle damage, but it is superficial."

"I am glad the damage is superficial. The pain is profound."

"It pains you now?"

"Yes," Kon gasped. "I feel like a fish on a hook."

"The dose I gave was too little then. Will you accept what I prescribe?"

"Yes . . . must I beg to have more holes poked in me?"

"There is no need to beg. It is difficult to judge the dose for you. I will give more."

Stamatis stepped away from the bed and Geilla, who was sitting on Kon's left, called to him.

He turned his head stiffly, and forced a wan smile. "Geilla! So, I am not abandoned. Where am I?" He reached for her hand, and winced at the movement.

"We're in Athens. Major Allensworth flew you in."

"Major? Am I so important to rate a major?"

"You are to me, Kon."

Kon moved his right arm and noticed that his right hand was splinted and bandaged. "Dio mio, I am a sorry sight. Would you marry such a wreck?"

"Yes," Geilla answered eagerly. "I love you — even in pieces. Besides there is nothing wrong with your left hand, and I intend to slip a ring on it as soon as possible."

"Only on my hand? Not through my nose?"

Before Geilla could answer, Stamatis returned and gave Kon a shot of pain killer. "Be still and rest now."

Kon nodded weakly. "I will. Thank you. Stamatis? What of my hand?"

Stamatis looked solemn. "It is a good hand, Kon, large and strong. We must wait to see how it heals."

Kon bit his lip. "So be it. Thank you for the truth."

Stamatis hesitated, then put his hand on Kon's arm. "It does no good to worry. You must rest."

Kon nodded. "You were right to send me back to Mitikas. I put many questions to rest, and gained a bit of wisdom. As soon as I can stand, Geilla and I are to be married."

"Married!" Stamatis boomed. "Then you must be still and heal. A man must be able to do more than stand to enjoy being married."

"I will try," Kon said meekly, and Stamatis wondered if Kon had indeed gained wisdom, or if he was still in pain.

"Come for me if he does not sleep soon," he said to Geilla as he left.

****

Peter stormed into Francois' office in downtown Geneva, and threw his wet coat onto a chair. Francois judged Peter's mood to be as raw and blustery as the cold spring weather he had been out in. Seeing that Peter was alone, and angry, Francois guessed that Peter had recently had a quarrel with Geilla. Pre-nuptial jitters, Francois thought. It affects a lot of young men and women. Then they come to me, to draw up an iron-clad agreement to guarantee that their nuptial bliss will never fade. Damn! I'll have to tread carefully. If I dare ask Peter the reason for his mood, he'll explode.

Francois went to Peter, and offered his hand in greeting. "Come in, Peter. I didn't expect you until later. Where is Geilla? She should know about these things."

"I have not come about my will, or my property," Peter blurted excitedly. "I have come about the wedding. The Greeks have refused me, Francois! After all these years of being damned for being a Greek, I am not acceptable to my own people."

"Peter! What is this all about? Where is Geilla?"

"I took her home. They have humiliated me in front of her. I could not bear to face her questions. I have been walking in this blasted rain, trying to think of a plan. I need your advice, Francois. You are the only one who has not taken a stand against me."

"Peter, sit down, please. Calm yourself. I will get you a drink, and you can tell me what has happened." Francois went to a pull-down compartment in his bookcase and opened it to reveal a small liquor cabinet. He poured some brandy into two glasses, and handing one glass to Peter, he sat in front of his desk next to Peter. "Now, tell me what happened – from the beginning. Did you go to talk with the priest?"

"Yes, and he has refused to perform the ceremony!"

"On what grounds? Take your time. Try to remember exactly what he said."

Peter sipped his drink and struggled to control his anger. "At first he welcomed us, and we talked. And then he mentioned that I would have to produce a baptismal certificate. I said that was impossible, because I was not baptized in the village where I was raised. I have no records. He said that without written proof, or a living person to swear that I had been baptized in the church, he could not agree to perform the ceremony."

"Couldn't he just baptize you now, and carry on from there?"

"That's the terrible part. He can't do it now because I claimed I had already been baptized. I assume I was, but I can never prove it." Peter stood abruptly, and paced across the room and back, coming to rest facing Francois. "I had to wait ten long years for a piece of paper that says I am a bona fide Swiss citizen, Francois. I never thought that God would ask me for a piece of paper to prove I am a Christian! I thought a man's faith was in his heart."

"It is not God who asks, Peter. It is only one church. There are other churches."

"But I am a Greek! I thought the Greek church was my church."

"Sit down, Peter. How important is this to you? Do you intend to join the Greek community, and live by their rules? You have never felt the need before."

Peter sat, and held his head with his hands. "I don't know, Francois. I don't know what I believe. None of the people I have known and loved since I was a child are Greek. I don't even have a Greek friend to stand as a witness for me, and that's another stumbling block. I intended to ask Paul, but hell, Paul isn't even a Christian. He would give his life for me, and I for him, but he is not acceptable to the priest. Must I find a total stranger to stand by me on such an important day? I have had to fight Charlotte, and Edgar, and Carlin about this marriage. Must I fight God himself?"

"I cannot advise you about spiritual matters, Peter, but no one has the right to tell you what God to worship, or who you should marry. These things are for you to decide."

"I confess I don't know about these things, Francois. I thought it would be simple. I thought I would go to the priest, and he would arrange everything. When I tried to marry before, Claire's family wanted me to join their church, but they did not ask to see my credentials. They took me at my word."

Francois sighed. "You could always have a civil ceremony."

"I suppose so. What choice is left? I am ready to marry, but I did not expect to be forced to choose a new religion."

"Peter, I think you are too upset about this to decide right now. Let me investigate some options for you."

"Perhaps you are right, Francois. Ever since I went to Greece, my life has been sliced into little pieces. I don't know who Peter Kononellos is, or what he stands for any more. Is he Petros Tsakapoulos, or more like a Marneé?"

"You have changed over the years, Peter, but basically you are the same person."

Kon smiled wryly, "And I am still nothing but trouble for you, Francois."

Francois laughed. "Maybe so, Peter, but now it is you who pay me to help you out of it. You've come a long way. I'll admit, I never expected you to amount to anything, but under Charlotte's persistent tutelage you've turned out rather well. Unlike many people, you have been exposed to many different ideas and you don't think along narrow lines."

"You have helped me out of quite a few difficult situations, Francois. Edgar must have paid you well."

"In the beginning, I helped you to make Edgar happy, but later, I came to see that in your own impulsive way, you were taking a stand against injustice. That business over the Armenian boy at the university . . . you were right to defend him from those bigots. I did not appreciate it at the time, but you saw immediately that a person was being treated unfairly, and you took a stand. We have some ideas in common, Peter. What I try to do in a court of law with words and precedents, you do directly with fists and a knife. I cannot let church authority make you miserable in this matter. You deserve to be happy, and I know you will fight for it. I was too weak. I gave in without a struggle, and I have regretted it ever since."

"Of what do you speak, Francois?"

"My family was Catholic, Peter. I was raised under church rule, but when I went to university, I met and fell in love with a Jewish girl. I wanted to marry her, but my family would not allow it. They threatened me with damnation, and I believed them. I didn't fight for what I wanted, and I learned what damnation really is. Eventually I left the church, and broke with my family, but I never found a woman to match the one I lost. I have only the law to comfort me. State authority can be changed to fit the times. It can prevent people from hurting each other, and punish those who do. There is no argument against church laws, Peter. The only option is to find another church."

"I am glad to find an ally in this matter, Francois."

"Now you must go and talk this over with Geilla."

"No! This is my affair! I must settle it . . ."

"Don't be stubborn, Peter. Geilla will be your wife. You must learn that your business is now her business. You don't have to fight alone, Peter. She is a strong woman. Let her help you."

"I will consider it, Francois. At least I must go, and apologize for my bad temper. This cannot be easy for Geilla."

Several days later, Francois called Peter, and arranged to meet with him and Geilla in Peter's apartment. Geilla had been staying there ever since she and Kon flew back from Athens. For once Kon had taken Brad's advice, and not gone on another assignment after returning from Greece. He had been working closely with Edgar, and seemed content.

"I've been very busy, Peter," Francois said when Peter greeted him at the door.

"Welcome, Francois. I am eager to hear what you have learned. Let me take your coat."

"Good evening, Geilla. It's nice to see you again. I hope all this rain hasn't discouraged you about moving to Switzerland."

"Not yet, Francois, but it's a good excuse for coffee and a liqueur. Let me get you some."

"I have taken the liberty of putting together a wedding package, which can be quickly arranged if you both agree," Francois said, as he settled back on the couch and sipped his coffee. "Among my acquaintances is a superior court judge, by the name of Anthony Guichard. He is due to retire soon, but has never had the honor of officiating at a wedding. When I mentioned your case to him, he said he would be delighted to perform the ceremony. He said you would be free to write your own vows, as long as you let him know in advance what you intend to say. I did some research, and came up with these three examples of what young people are pledging these days," Francois continued, handing Peter and Geilla each some papers.

Peter glanced at the papers and smiled. "I appreciate your work, Francois."

"Now wait. There is more. I had my secretary ask around, and she located a small non-denominational chapel that is shared by several religious groups. I went to look at it, and it's not bad. There are no stained-glass windows, or gold-leaf icons, but there is a plain altar on which you may place any pictures you wish, and the seats are padded and comfortable. There is no organ, but they have a lovely old piano that would have a good tone if it was properly tuned. I think that with some potted palms, and some flowers, the place would serve very well. As for the reception, Charlotte insists on planning that, so you'll have to talk with her. Well . . . what do you think?"

Peter was silent for a moment, but Geilla spoke up immediately. "I think it would do wonderfully! I will have to think wisely about what I can get Kon to promise."

"I will promise anything, if it will make you happy, Geilla," Kon said, coming out of his reverie. "I think you have made a very good proposal, Francois. You seem to have thought of everything."

"I'm glad you approve, Peter. I think the wedding will have meaning because you planned it yourselves. And yes, did I mention that the chapel is fully carpeted?"

"No, but it sounds better and better as you talk," Geilla answered.

"I thank you for all your effort, Francois. We have been talking it over, and we have come to the conclusion that a civil ceremony is best for us," Kon said, reaching to take Geilla's hand in his. "We are not exactly go-to-church-every-Sunday people, and this way our children will be free to choose their own faith."

"Well said, Peter. Here is the number of the minister I spoke with at the chapel. He will be happy to arrange a time for you to see the chapel, and set a date."

"How can we ever thank you for all your help, Francois?" Geilla responded.

"By staying happily married. I hate divorce cases!"

"We will do our best to oblige," Kon commented.

****

The music started, and Geilla moved down the aisle on Brad's arm. Under Charlotte's supervision, the chapel had been beautifully decorated with ribbons and flowers. Although the chapel was small, it seemed to Geilla that it was a long walk to Kon's side. Paul was standing beside Kon in front of the altar, and she saw him wink at her, as if to say 'I told you so'. Paul had been in Chicago for the past two months, but had made a special trip to attend the service.

The three of them were a strange triangle. Paul was not the wedge who sought to drive them apart. He was the apex, the peak that drew them together. He knew that Kon needed Geilla, long before Kon realized it. Geilla suddenly felt jealous of Paul. Kon was always so open with Paul, and so guarded with her. She knew that even now, if Paul asked for her, Kon would give her up. Kon had given his trust to Paul, and Paul had never let him down, whereas she had disappointed him twice. She at last understood how strong the bond was between Kon and Paul, though they were so different.

Paul was like an evergreen, Geilla mused. When the snows of adversity came down on him, he was flexible, and would sway and bend. He let nothing damage him. He was the same in every season − presenting the same soothing fragrance to all, and welcoming them under the bower of his care. It was his nature to be strong and to heal, but like the evergreen of the north, he was cool, always cool.

Kon was the cactus. Spiny sharp and rigid on the outside, but soft with secret reservoirs of life on the inside. A blow to Kon left a permanent scar. Like the cactus he could endure the most rigorous environment, but would flower only rarely. And like the cactus flower, Kon's offerings were exquisitely beautiful and fragile. Each smile, or word, or handshake was sincerely meant, and bestowed with the warmth of the south. How she loved that warmth. How she loved the rare flower of his smile, for she was one of the few who were allowed to pass beyond his barrier of protecting thorns.

When everyone was in their proper place, and Judge Guichard seemed about to begin, a stranger suddenly appeared with two wreaths of flowers. Kon looked surprised for a moment, then leaned toward Geilla, and whispered, "The wedding crowns!" Kon smiled broadly as the stranger reached to place a crown on Kon's head. As the man turned to place a crown on her head, Geilla suddenly recognized him. It was Stamatis! A clean-shaven Stamatis, wearing a stylish black suit and a tie. Geilla knew that he had been invited to the wedding, along with his wife, whom Kon had met at the hospital in Athens, but she had not anticipated he would bring this bit of Greek tradition with him. Geilla saw from Kon's expression that he truly appreciated the gesture, although in the orthodox ceremony, the priest would have placed the crowns.

Stamatis must have enjoyed Geilla's shocked expression, for he winked at her, and placed the crown on her head. "I will not let him be married without ceremony, like a Calvinist," Stamatis whispered, nodding his head in Kon's direction. Geilla could only laugh.

At last the judge cleared his throat, and began the ceremony. There was no chanting, or lighting of incense, but as Geilla and Kon recited the vows they had written themselves, the chapel was filled with love and joy. If Kon was the slightest bit nervous, it didn't show, and he seemed to be having the time of his life. Geilla was more sedate and took the ceremony more seriously. Her first wedding day had been a sad, lonely, blur, and she wanted to etch every detail of today's joyous occasion into her mind.

As the brief ceremony ended, Kon bent to kiss his bride. It was a chaste kiss, an everyone-is-watching-us kiss, but as his lips gently brushed hers, she felt a promise of the fire that was in him. "I have loved you always, Geilla," he whispered. He hoped that at last he had proven Zoel wrong about not being good enough for Geilla. Geilla took Kon's right hand, which was badly scared, in hers. She was grateful that aside from some stiffness, his hand was functional. Carlin had declared that no cosmetic surgeon could have done a better job than Stamatis had in stitching Kon's hand back together. Perhaps now that Paul is back, I can coax Kon into letting him look at it, Geilla thought. After all, Kon hides less from Paul than he does from me. At that moment she discovered that she was no longer jealous of Paul. They would always be friends, the three of them.

****

After more kisses and handshakes, and calling of good wishes, the group drove to the reception. Charlotte had wanted to hold the reception in the garden at the Marneé residence, but Edgar convinced her that since the spring weather had been unusually wet, she should plan an indoor party. So Charlotte had reserved space at one of the finest Italian restaurants in Geneva, and personally went over the menu with the chef. She also obtained the chef's permission to bring in a huge assortment of Greek pastries, and a special Swiss chocolate wedding cake. There will be lots of children at the reception, and they will want sweets, she had told Edgar.

Charlotte had insisted on arranging everything for Peter, and his bride, and had spared no effort or expense to make the occasion festive and memorable. The guest list was short, but the guests were united in their pleasure of seeing the man they knew either as Peter, or as Kon, so happy. Naturally, Mario and Tina were there, with three of their five children. Unfortunately, Nona Louise had passed away the year before. Then there was the aging Giovanni and his wife Lucia, Giorgio and his wife, and their brood of seven. Peter had been obliged to beg Giorgio to accept the money he sent, so that the family could fly to Geneva and stay at a hotel. Giorgio had at last yielded to Peter's arguments that it would be an educational experience for the children, and hadn't Giorgio often said how much he wanted to dance at Peter's wedding? Rudy and Karina came, bringing their curly headed little boy, Jonathan Peter von Steiger, whose name was bigger than he was. Little J. P., as he was affectionately called, charmed everyone, but he was particularly intrigued by a very dignified lady by the name of Mademoiselle Antoinette Flambért, who was a veritable fountain of fascinating stories.

Dr. Stamatis and his wife Constantina came, bringing Vangeli, the young Greek boy from Florina with them. At Brad's suggestion, Stamatis planned to take Vangeli to a hospital in London after the wedding. Although Vangeli had recovered from the fire, he was still badly scarred, and Stamatis felt he would benefit from an innovative skin grafting operation which two British surgeons had developed. Through The Foundation, Brad had arranged for several private donors to cover the cost of the trip and the operation – all in the name of research, of course.

Mary and Brad were there. Brad came to give the bride away and Mary acted the dual role of matron-of-honor, and mother-of-the-bride. As usual, Mary was handling both jobs with complete aplomb. And of course there were Charlotte and Edgar, Carlin, Albert and Charles, who was still getting around on crutches, Jack, Francois, Judge Guichard, Paul, and a very interesting young woman named Nea Cortlin.

Nea was a gifted clothes designer, and the artistic soul of the small dress boutique that Mary had maintained a financial interest in, even after her marriage to Brad. Nea had created a street-length, brocade sheath for Geilla for the wedding, working from only Geilla's measurements and one hasty fitting. The dress was closely cut, yet strangely demure, and the particular shade of lilac that Nea selected looked absolutely stunning on Geilla.

Nea was a dazzling picture herself, with her deep green eyes, and long auburn hair, that shimmered with vibrant red highlights. Mary noticed that throughout dinner, Paul never took his eyes off Nea. He was too cynical to believe Nea's hair color was natural, but he was fascinated by how beautifully her lustrous, cascading mane set off her emerald eyes and her alabaster shoulders. He found her conversation much to his liking also, and as she talked with Carlin, Paul learned that in addition to designing dresses, Nea also painted, made pottery, and raised orchids. As the various courses were being served, Charlotte saw Paul staring across the table at Nea. She guessed that the artistry of her carefully chosen menu was totally wasted on Mr. Artier. Well, never mind, she thought, he was obviously enjoying a feast, if only with his eyes. I do wish he would give more attention to his plate. It's about to go over the edge.

Brad noticed that Dr. Stamatis was very attentive to his wife, Constantina, at dinner, and how quickly he escorted her to the dance floor when the music started. When Brad mentioned it, Stamatis only grunted, "We are talking." After further questioning, however, Stamatis muttered, "I see this obstinate young Kononellos, a countryman of mine, change his ways and show more sense than a goat, and I ask myself, 'Am I not older, and wiser than he? Should I remain a lonely old fool? But he is not a true Greek,' I say. 'He cannot hold a grudge until death. He dares to forgive a man who wronged him. Must I suffer because I am Greek?' Maybe these Swiss can teach me something, eh? Ah, here comes a wise man now," Stamatis concluded, seeing Carlin approach.

"Wise or not, I cannot say, since I don't know what you have been discussing," Carlin said, shaking Stamatis' hand, "but I am glad you could get away long enough to help us celebrate. I am very grateful for all you have done for Peter. He looks truly fit and happy."

"I have done my bit to keep him healthy, but it is this woman who has made him happy. She will be good for him. You doubt it?" Stamatis asked, seeing the cloud pass over Carlin's face.

"This marriage is not what I would have wished for Peter."

"But why not? He loves her. She loves him."

"Does she? She has treated him shabbily in the past. Am I to believe she has changed?"

"You either mistake her motives, or she has changed, but she loves him now. Believe me, she would die for him. I have seen it."

"She certainly does put on a good act. I only hope she can continue to fool Peter."

"It is no act, my friend, I will swear to that. She was with him when she thought he was breathing his last. She had no thought, but for him. When he called for another woman, she put herself aside, and sent for the woman, thinking it would save him. You cannot fake a love like that."

Carlin was surprised to hear such a tale from a crusty old surgeon like Stamatis. He smiled. "I will hope you are right about her. She did give in to Peter's every wish about the wedding arrangements. By the way, those crowns were a brilliant touch. Peter loved it."

"By God I will make a true Greek of him yet!" Stamatis boomed. "I will start with a dance. Albert promised to find a record player. I have brought some real wedding music."

When the Greek music started, Stamatis and his wife schooled Kon and Geilla, and led them through the steps. Geilla was relaxed, and delighted in seeing Kon abandon himself to the music and the gaiety. His laughter bubbled up from deep inside him, from that one secret part of him that had never been crushed. Perhaps only Albert and Charles had seen that side of Kon. If Geilla had not known Kon better, she might have thought that he was drunk; but he wasn't high on alcohol, for he tended to be exceptionally quiet when he drank too heavily. He was just responding to the abundance of love and friendship that surrounded him.

Later, when Geilla slipped away to freshen her make-up,

Charlotte followed her. "I have never seen Peter look so happy, Geilla. He's always wanted a family of his own."

"I know, and I appreciate how much stability you and Edgar have provided for him."

Charlotte hesitated, then began quietly, "Peter will not be easy to live with, Geilla. He's very secretive, and hard to know. He'll never tell you anything, and you must learn to ask questions. Peter calls it 'the inquisition,' but if you don't ask, you will never learn if he's coming home for dinner, or going on some mission for three months. You must also learn to tread carefully, or he will fly in your face about interfering in his private life."

"Yes, I know Kon is a very private person, but he knows he can be himself with me."

"Of my three sons, I have always worried about Peter the most. He came to me so late. I could not mold him. I could only polish him a little, and try to repair some of the damage. He's been a good son. I will miss him."

"Believe me, I'm not trying to steal him from you, Charlotte. Being married to me will not change the way Kon feels about you."

Charlotte looked suddenly tearful. "Oh, Geilla, please be good to him. He is so easily hurt."

Geilla suddenly realized how unhappy Charlotte was over Kon's marriage to her. She took both of Charlotte's hands in hers and spoke deliberately, "Whatever you may think of me, I do love your Peter with all my heart, and I want us to be friends, Charlotte."

Charlotte smiled bravely. "I hope it can be so, for we must pretend to be, for Peter's sake."

"Yes, for Peter's sake," Geilla repeated slowly, realizing that she would have to wait for acceptance from Kon's 'family', as she had once waited for forgiveness from him. She hoped they would not be as difficult to convince.

As the party was ending, and Kon and Geilla were saying their final good-byes to their guests, Kon saw Paul standing beside Nea. Despite his preoccupation with Geilla, Kon had noticed that Paul had been extremely interested in Nea. Indeed, after dinner the two had hardly stopped talking long enough to dance or drink. When Geilla began to talk with Nea, Kon pulled Paul aside.

"Could you possibly keep the Ferrari exercised while I am gone? It's not good to let the engine sit idle."

"What? You would trust me with your precious car?"

"Well . . . why not? If you are as good with machinery as you are with women, I have no worry. Perhaps you can persuade Nea to go for a drive with you."

Paul grinned. "Now there's an idea! Why didn't I think of that?"

"No imagination, I guess. She will be quite interesting for you to handle — the Ferrari, I mean."

"I bet she is."

Kon toyed with his silver key ring, before tossing it to Paul with a sly grin. "Don't let anything overheat, my friend."

"Thanks. I'll keep it cool."

When at last the final good-byes were said, Kon and Geilla were startled to see an indecently long, gleaming white limousine, complete with uniformed driver, arrive to take them to the airport. The limousine had been ordered by Jack and Paul, as a parting joke on Kon, who found it more embarrassing than the traditional tin cans and shoes.

Edgar laughed, and came forward to Peter when he saw the distressed look on Peter's face. "Now, now — no objections, Peter. This is your day to remember."

"Remember what? That I rode to the airport in a giant marshmallow like some pompous ass! Whose idea was this? It was yours, wasn't it?" Kon said, turning toward Jack, who could not contain his smirk. "Yep! And Paul's."

"Paul? I always thought you were sensible. I'll get you two for this, I swear. Just wait until . . ."

"Oh shut up, Kon," Paul laughed. "Your bride awaits!"

"All right! All right! There's no escaping my fate at this late hour. I should make you two come along to see that I don't get shot at by some God damn socialist!"

"Wear a vest, Kon," Jack called, knowing how reluctant Kon always was to put one on.

Everyone laughed, and Geilla pulled Kon into the back seat, pushing a small valise aside to make room for him. "Someone must have left this," she muttered absently, and continued to wave to the gathering.

Kon pulled the door closed and waved also, as the car slid down the street. "The valise is a little wedding present from Brad, Geilla. I'm afraid I won't be joining you in Majorca until later."

Geilla was momentarily shocked speechless, then found her voice with a vengeance. "What do you mean, you're not coming with me? This is our wedding trip!"

"I know," Kon said, taking her hand, "but an extremely urgent matter has come up, and Brad asked me to investigate."

"Why you? Why didn't he send Jack, or Paul? Wait until I get my hands on Brad!"

"Now be sensible, Geilla. The job is in Amsterdam, and I'm the only one on the team who reads Dutch. It has to be me."

"Why didn't you tell me? Did you think I wouldn't notice that I was on the plane without you? And what am I supposed to do in Majorca alone — sit in the room and stare at my matching luggage?"

"I'm sorry," Kon said contritely. "I thought you would find Majorca more pleasant than waiting in Amsterdam. I'll change the ticket at the airport, if you insist."

"How could you think I would enjoy myself without you? We're supposed to be together now. Dio Mio! Charlotte was right! You never tell anyone anything!"

"I'm sorry. I only just found out myself. I didn't want to spoil such a beautiful day . . . forgive me."

"You should have told me! I am your wife! We are supposed to share things!" Geilla ranted in her disappointment. "Oh, Kon, you are absolutely imposs . . ."

Geilla never got to finish, for Kon's lips were on hers, and his arms pressed her against him. Magically her anger faded, as she felt his yearning. How could she stay angry, when they had so little time, before his damn sense of duty took him away. Oh well, Majorca could wait, she thought. Perhaps I can find a way to help him get this job done faster, but he's going to have to change. I will not be an inquisitioner.

ORDER FORM

If you have enjoyed this book and would like to order one for a friend, please send $11.50 plus $2.00 for postage and handling for the first book and $.75 for each additional book. California residents add 7.75% sales tax ($0.89) for each book.

Make check or money order payable to:

ZENAR BOOKS
P.O. Box 686
Rancho Cordova, CA 95741-0860

Allow 4 to 6 weeks for delivery.

Name _____

Address _____

_____

City _____

State/Zip _____

Prices subject to change without notice.